I0666769

PROJECT XP38

BY: KATHERINE E. HETHER

Book 1 in the series is Project XP38.
Book 2 in the series is Project Wraith.
Book 3 in the series is Project Canaveral.

Printed in the United States of America

Raintree Press, LLC
12180 South 300 East
Suite 1238
Draper, Utah 84020

www.raintreepress.com

PROJECT XP38
By: Katherine E. Hether

This book is dedicated to Fr. M. J. Joachim J. Tierney,
Dr. James E. Hether, and the late
Captain Paul Graffeo.

A special thanks to Filmmaker, Stephen Brown and
Skip Cowell at Gabby Mobile Productions for the awesome
covers of each of the books in the trilogy.

I would like to give another special thanks to
Jean Tessier and Stephen Brown
for editing this book.

Project: XP38
© Library of Congress Control Number 2018941149
Copyright 2017: TXu 2-083-504

ISBN 978-0-9885980-6-5

www.katherinehether.com

Contents

Chapter 1

Corté de Azuré

Watching from an upstairs window at his father's mansion, on the coast of Corté de Azuré, Mario LaBasco Jr. spotted a limo just entering the long driveway. "Here they come, right on time," Mario Jr. remarked to his right-hand man, Giorgio Pulini, across the room. "I can smell the money already!"

"What makes you so sure the old man will take the deal?" Giorgio questioned.

Holding the curtain back, still peering out the window, Mario Jr. whispered under his breath, "Let's just say a LaBasco will take the deal!"

"What did you say?" Giorgio asked, reaching for the doorknob.

"I get my thirst for money from my Papa," Mario Jr. laughed. "Papa will take the deal. It's as good as in the bank!"

"Are you ready to go downstairs?" Giorgio asked as he opened the door.

"I'm always ready to make money!" Mario Jr. continued his obnoxious laugh and left the room as the doorbell rang.

Charles, his father's long-time butler, opened the front door. "Sen. Frank, Gen. Thompson, please come inside. Mr. LaBasco is waiting for you," he greeted as Mario Jr. and Giorgio joined them in the entryway.

"Sen. Frank," Mario Jr. greeted and extended his hand, "I hope you had a pleasant trip. This plans to be a great day for all of us."

"If your father is in agreement with you, I'm sure I'll have an even better trip home," Sen. Frank smiled as they shook hands.

"I'm sure we'll all have nicer trips with the profit this promises for all involved," Gen. Thompson added as he joined in the conversation, shaking Mario Jr.'s hand.

"Gentlemen, if you'll please follow me, Mr. LaBasco is waiting," Charles requested, leading the way to the conference room.

Mario Sr. was at the conference table with Alonzo DiMeglio, his enforcer sitting to his left side going over some papers. He shuffled them together and looked up. "Don't bother sitting. This won't take long," Mario Sr. stated as a very surprised Mario Jr. took his seat at his Papa's right side. "I'm not interested in your proposition."

"Mr. LaBasco," Sen. Frank started to say as he sat his briefcase on the table.

"Senator I'm not interested!" Mario Sr. exclaimed and looked him straight in the eyes. Mario Jr. glared over at Giorgio in astonishment. "I could have told you this over the phone, but I wanted to make sure you are clear on this matter. I want nothing to do with this bizarre scheme of yours; is that perfectly clear?"

"What do you mean?" Sen. Frank questioned. "This is no scheme I assure you. We already have everything lined up with all the parties involved. This is foolproof! It's easy money!"

"I don't call this easy money," Mario Sr. declared as he glanced over at the general. "I call this treason."

"You're no Boy Scout yourself!" Gen. Thompson boldly spoke up as Alonzo glared at him and pressed a button under the table. "That is why we brought this business deal to you. It is well known that the LaBasco Family does not back down from anything. Alonzo has the reputation of being the most ruthless in the business."

"In our line of work, we take care of business," Mario Sr. stated. "This so-called business deal is not in our line of work. This meeting is over!" the old man declared, further infuriating Mario Jr.

"This meeting is over!" Alonzo exclaimed as he got up from his chair as the door opened. "Charles will show you the way out."

"Gentlemen, if you will follow me, I'll show you to the door," Charles stated as several armed men joined him.

As the door closed behind them, Mario Jr. slowly rose from his chair, shaking his head in disbelief. He folded his arms as he walked around the table still not saying a word. He stopped directly in front of his father. He leaned over the table bracing himself with his arms. He looked straight into his father's eyes. "Papa what did you just do?"

"Mario, we want nothing to do with this deal or these men," his Papa stated, looking up at him. "They are nothing but trouble."

"But Papa this deal is foolproof!" Mario Jr. exclaimed. "I checked it out myself!"

"You want to do business with a dirty United States senator and an Air Force general, who is a traitor to his own country," Mario Sr. affirmed. "Do you realize why they wanted to involve us?"

"Well, yeah Papa," Mario Jr. began. "They can't do their own bidding. They need us to do the actual work and with a phenomenal profit for all of us. The general is right. It is easy money! Giorgio and I could have taken the project over for you; after all I am a pilot."

"You're right," Mario Sr. confirmed as he sat back in his chair. "They wanted us to do their dirty work. They also wanted us to take all the risk, so their hands stay clean. The feds are always watching our moves. We would take all the blame and they would reap all the benefits."

"Your Papa's right," Alonzo affirmed. "It seemed to be a set up. When you checked them out; did you find Frank is known for double-crossing his fellow senators to get his bills passed? He also has a history of people going to federal penitentiary for deals in which he was allegedly involved. Thompson is no choirboy. How do you think he got to the top? They need someone to go to jail, while they make a fortune."

"Son, what they also want is someone to commit treason," Mario Sr. stated. "Is that what you're willing to do for them?"

"It's not treason!" Mario Jr. exclaimed, raising his voice. "Russia is not the United States! It was good money! Thompson was right; we're not choirboys! How do we make our money?"

"We relocated our businesses from the United States because of the feds," Mario Sr. admitted. "What they wanted would endanger the entire world. Yes, we make good money, but not at that price. With what they wanted us to do, we would never be able to wash the stench from our hands," he said and returned to his paperwork. "You need to go somewhere to calm down. Rethink your assessment of their business deal. I will call you later. I have some other work for you to do."

"You called that wrong Boss," Giorgio said as they left the house.

"I can't believe what I just heard," Mario said, gritting his teeth, walking toward his limo. "Lately, I've noticed Papa and Alonzo getting a little soft."

"Alonzo may be getting older," Giorgio stated as he opened the limo door. "But he's still someone you don't want to tangle with," Giorgio said as Mario glanced up.

"Just the woman I need to talk to," Mario Jr. smiled as he pointed to the car coming down the long driveway. "I want to talk to Mama alone. Perhaps I can still salvage this deal. She has a lot of influence with Papa. Have my laptop ready when I get back. Now I know I need to begin the groundwork we talked about earlier. I also need to summon my bird-dog to do my bidding," Mario Jr. said as he walked toward his mother's car.

Chapter 2

Flight #1014 Newark Liberty Int'l. to Paris

Two Years Later:

"Well gentlemen, it seems that our two persons of interest are staying pretty quiet on this flight," Kathe Tierney stated to the two male security flight attendants, Jack Davies and Jay Towers. "It looks like we're going to make it into Charles de Gaulle without incident. Thank goodness the Ole Girl is wrong this time," Kathe noted as she glanced over the cabin watching most of the passengers sleeping.

"Copy that," Jay laughed as they conversed via ear buds. "Does Linda Ramsey, the Head of Alby Airlines Security, know that you girls call her the Ole Girl?"

"What the Ole Girl doesn't know won't hurt her," Kathe laughed.

"By the way, where did Ramsey get this information?" Jay asked.

"It was an anonymous tip," Kathe continued. "Ramsey did check with Interpol. They are both on the list of special interest people that Homeland Security is watching, so she wanted us aboard. The female is going to Munich later tonight. Ramsey wants me to stay on that flight with her," Kathe answered as she noticed Jack carrying a drink toward a passenger near the rear.

"Jack that drink is not for 40H is it?" Kathe asked.

"Yes," Jack answered.

"Turn around," Kathe ordered, watching from the middle galley through a two-way mirror. "He's had too much already. I've noticed him watching you and Jay for the past hour. He seems to be very interested in your whereabouts. And I don't like the way he stares at the female flight attendants, especially Carrie Anne."

"Okay," Jack answered as he turned back toward the rear galley. "I was thinking the same thing. I made him agree this is the last one for the night."

"Always stay with your gut feeling," Kathe affirmed as she started a fresh pot of coffee. "It is never wrong."

A few minutes later, the silence was broken as passenger 40H dropped some magazines on the floor and fumbled trying to pick them up. Kathe was checking the cart for supplies in the galley when she heard the noise and looked up. "Jay why don't you go over and help Mr. Wonderful pick up his magazines. Perhaps he needs a pillow and blanket. With any luck maybe he'll take a nap."

"I'm on my way," Jay agreed and headed straight to passenger 40H.

Kathe watched from the galley as Jay helped him. She got a bad feeling noticing the way he watched Jay walk away. Then she noticed passenger 40H checking for Jack again. He stumbled getting up from his seat. He tripped toward the rear lavatory and glanced over his shoulder for their whereabouts. Carrie Anne Mobley, Kathe's best friend was in front of passenger 40H entering the rear galley. He kept his eyes on her, watching her every movement. He re-checked the guys' positions. "Jack, keep an eye on..." was all Kathe had time to say.

Passenger 40H reached for Carrie Anne, grabbed her around the chest, and put something to her neck. Carrie Anne gasped as he pulled her tightly to him, pushing a small sharp object into her neck. "Jack

9

approach him slowly and try to talk him down," Kathe ordered. "He has something at Carrie Anne's neck. Jay, get ready to distract him from that side of the plane when I'm in place. I've got an idea." Instantly pushing the panic button on the top left side of her cell phone JAKE, she alerted Alby security headquarters of trouble.

"Tierney what's going on up there?" Ramsey questioned.

"We have a man holding what looks like a clear object to Carrie Anne's neck in coach by the rear galley," Kathe warned as she poured a cup of coffee.

"Is it one of our persons of interest?" Ramsey asked.

"Negative, it is the Middle Eastern man sitting in 40H," Kathe confirmed and cleared the line.

Linda Ramsey alerted the pilot of the aircraft, Capt. John Roberts of the trouble. Second Officer Munroe alerted Second Officer Michaels, who had been resting in the officer's bunk, just outside the cockpit door to the situation. Officer Michaels instructed the attendants in first class and in business to lock down their cabins as he zoomed the security camera to monitor the situation.

Jack glanced back toward Kathe for directions. "Block his view of me and keep him busy," Kathe stated. "I think he could use some fresh coffee," she whispered, moving into the aisle. Kathe lifted the cup to Jack and motioned for him to walk toward the man. Luckily, it had been a lengthy night flight and only a few passengers awakened from Carrie Anne's desperate gasp. Air marshal Ron Stone in the last row on the opposite side, sat up and began to assess the situation. Marshal Stone watched as Jack walked calmly toward the man, talking very quietly to him.

Kathe noted the deep raspy tone in passenger 40H's voice, which reminded her of another flight a few years earlier that changed her life forever.

"Don't come any closer! I'll do it!" Passenger 40H screamed as Carrie Anne cried out, waking all the passengers.

"Sir, put the object down and we'll talk about it," Jack stated softly, trying to block his view of Kathe edging closer. "You don't want to hurt her. I'm sure it's a matter we can easily clear up."

"Stop you stupid American!" Passenger 40H snapped. ""You don't know who I am!" he declared as the passengers began to stir, making him even more nervous.

"No," Jack calmly stated. "I don't know who you are, but you seem to be troubled. What can I do to help you? Perhaps you would like another drink. We can sit and talk about what's bothering you," Jack offered, edging closer as passenger 40H pressed the object to Carrie Anne's neck.

"No!" Carrie Anne cried out as she moved her throat away from him and a trickle of blood dripped down her neck.

"Okay, I'll stop," Jack agreed holding up his hands. "Why don't you let her go? She can get us both a drink. We'll sit in the galley and talk."

Marshal Stone noted Kathe slowly edging closer, motioning toward him and Jay to enter the galley from that side of the plane. Slowly unloosing his seatbelt Marshal Stone waited for the opportunity to help. Kathe signaled Jay to distract him.

"He's right!" Jay exclaimed as he moved toward passenger 40H from the other side of the plane. "I think we can all use a drink!"

Passenger 40H shifted his attention to Jay, "Don't take another step! I'll kill her!" He warned as he turned slightly toward Jay and pushed the object a little deeper into her neck.

"Nooo!" Carrie Anne screamed out in pain and struggled to wiggle away from him.

Kathe took advantage of that split second of confusion to shove Jack to the right, startling the assailant. Marshal Stone slipped out of his seat and hurried into the galley with Jay right behind him. Passenger 40H lost his grip on Carrie Anne, who dropped into the empty back middle row seat with Jack covering her. Kathe took one step forward and splashed the hot coffee on passenger 40H burning his left forearm and chest.

"Ahhhh!" Passenger 40H screamed out in pain, bent forward, grabbing Kathe's left wrist with his right hand.

Kathe twisted her wrist away from his grasp, kneed him in the face, knocking him backwards. Marshal Stone and Jay lunged for the passenger. They wrestled him to the floor and handcuffed him.

Using the galley phone Kathe alerted Capt. Roberts, "The situation has been cleared. Please alert the gendarmes. I'll clear the last few rows and we'll zip tie him to the seat."

"Good job, glad your team was aboard," Capt. Roberts replied. "I will also inform control that this situation is contained. Officer Munroe will make an announcement to the other passengers. We will be on the ground as quickly as possible. Control is clearing airspace for us to land," he explained, clearing the line as Kathe glanced at her broken watch.

"Jay can you and Marshal Stone handle him?" Kathe asked, while they were checking him for weapons.

"We've got him," Jay replied as Jack came back to help them.

"I have Carrie Anne sitting in the seat, holding my handkerchief on her wound," Jack reported. "She's shaken up, but she'll live."

"I've got to help calm the passengers and move the ones out of the last two rows," Kathe stated. "We'll zip tie him there. Jack, please find and secure the object he used. I'll seal this area off until we do," Kathe said as she reached for the intercom.

"Ladies and gentlemen due to this morning's incident I'm going to close the back two lavatories," Kathe announced. "You may use the ones in business. I'm sorry for any inconvenience."

Turning back to Jack, "I'll have someone from business take your station," Kathe finished as she listened to Officer Munroe assuring the passengers that the situation had been contained. As soon as Munroe finished, Kathe asked the other flight attendants to resume morning duties. In a matter of minutes, passengers were beginning to calm down and the smell of fresh coffee filled the air. She quickly checked the roster and found seats for the six passengers to relocate. After relocating the passengers, Kathe finally had time to check on Carrie Anne. "Are you alright?"

"How can you so calmly ask me if I'm alright?" Carrie Anne glared at her as she moved the bloodstained handkerchief away from her neck. "I just had a knife shoved in my neck! After this," Carrie Anne added, "next time I see the three of you get on a flight with me, I'm getting off!"

"Oh really," Kathe chuckled. "I was just thinking about putting you on my team. You seem to be a magnet for troublemaking men," Kathe smiled as Officer Michaels joined them.

"Are you two, okay?" Michaels asked as Marshal Stone and Jay brought the assailant out of the galley. They zip tied his arms and feet to the last seat near the window.

"I'm not okay!" Carrie Anne snapped, looking around Kathe, glaring at the man across from her.

"All in a day's work," Kathe replied, moving the handkerchief away from Carrie's neck checking her wound more closely. "It's just a flesh wound. I've had a lot worse. Officer Michaels, would you take Carrie Anne to first class and find her a seat?"

"Yes, I'll get the first aid kit and tend to her wound also," Michaels said as he helped Carrie Anne up from the seat. "I'll make a few butterfly stitches. That will suffice until we land," he said as Kathe's cell phone JAKE rang.

"Capt. Roberts reported that you had quite a problem up there," Ramsey said, scrolling down her computer screen. "Passenger 40H boarded as Mohammed Rhamíd. His passport photo is blurry. Capt. Roberts said he had sharp object. What kind of object was it?"

"It looked like a small clear knife," Kathe replied. "I'll send you a picture of him and the object in just a minute."

"How in the world did he get anything like that on board?" Ramsey wailed, pressing her intercom button. "Wanda, get me Randall with TSA and a cigarette!"

"You quit smoking Boss," Wanda Evans, Ramsey's private secretary answered, pulling up the work schedule on her computer. "Remember your blood pressure? And there is no smoking in public buildings or around me!"

"You're landing on French soil soon," Ramsey said as she rolled her eyes, getting back to Kathe. "When the plane docks a security team will board. Lt. Jaco from the gendarmes will relieve Marshal Stone of Rhamíd's custody after the passengers deplane first. Then Lt. Jaco's men will secure and take Rhamíd off the aircraft. Each member of your team will have to make a statement. Oh, and since lover girl is involved, it's your neck if she's not at the debriefing."

"She'll be there," Kathe affirmed. "Carrie Anne's only missed a few debriefings," Kathe reminded Ramsey with a sigh. "I don't know why you worry so much."

"I guess I've made it my job," replied Ramsey as she took the roster from Wanda. "How are our other two guests?"

"They stayed very observant and quiet during the situation," Kathe reported.

"Great, I already have someone in the terminal waiting to follow them when you land," Ramsey explained. "I'll keep you informed," Ramsey said and cleared the line.

"Kathe, can I have a word with you?" Jack asked as Kathe snapped a picture of Rhamíd. "After we get on the ground, I need your help."

"What's wrong?" Kathe asked, texting the picture to Ramsey.

"We can't find the weapon," Jack replied as he turned away from Rhamíd.

"What do you mean you can't find it?" Kathe whispered. "We all saw it."

"Jay and I've been searching for it," Jack admitted as Officer Michaels joined them.

"Who has the weapon?" Michaels asked.

"It hasn't been found yet," Kathe whispered so Rhamíd could not overhear.

"It couldn't have gone far," Michaels said as he glanced around the galley floor. "I'll go back and check the video. Maybe I can see where it went."

"That's a good idea," Kathe agreed as Carrie Anne came up behind her.

"I feel better after Officer Michaels bandaged me up," Carrie Anne reported. "Can I come back to work?"

"If you're sure you can handle it?" Kathe quizzed. "I think it will help settle the passengers down, if they know you're alright," Kathe admitted, watching Rhamíd making eye contact with Carrie Anne.

"I should have slit your throat when I had the chance," Rhamíd sneered with his deep raspy voice.

"That's enough out of you," Marshal Stone warned.

"Try to keep him quiet," Kathe cautioned, noticing an elderly woman fidgeting a few seats away. "Carrie Anne, work the other side of the plane. I'm going to have to move that lady," Kathe said as she pointed to an elderly woman two seats away.

"American dog!" Rhamíd jeered as other passengers began turning around to look at him. "You don't know who you're messing with."

Leaning over Marshal Stone pulled the zip ties on his wrist tighter, "I told you to be quiet! I'll gag you if I must," he warned as Rhamíd noticed Jay bending down to look under the seat across from them.

"What is the matter American dog?" Rhamíd jeered. "Lose something?"

"Where's duct tape when you need it?" Jay fumed as he stood up glaring at Rhamíd. "Perhaps Marshal Stone should gag you."

"What's wrong pretty American Boy?" Rhamíd boasted as Jack walked in between them. "Why don't you tell me what you are looking for and maybe I can help you find it," Rhamíd snickered as he tried to look around Jack.

"Jay I've been listening to him," Jack whispered. "You're wasting your time looking for the weapon. He knows we don't have it."

"That means he knows where it is," Jay concurred. "He is too calm and arrogant. I'll go tell Kathe," he said and walked to her. "Jack and I have been observing Rhamíd," Jay reported. "He was mocking me while I was looking under seats. He knows we don't have the weapon. That means he knows where it is."

"Michaels is checking the security video trying to see where it went," Kathe stated. "I was watching him the whole time through the galley window. I did not see him pull out a weapon. It just appeared. Why don't you check the seat pockets in that area? Maybe it fell inside one of them," Kathe offered and walked to the front of the plane.

"Officer Michaels, did you find anything?" Kathe asked as she joined him.

"I started the camera after he already had the knife at Carrie Anne's neck," Michaels admitted as he rewound the video for Kathe to view. "I couldn't see where the knife went after you kicked him."

"Stop right there," Kathe stated studying the film. "Rewind it to me throwing the coffee...right there...slow it down...he's bending forward...he's grabbing my wrist...I'm kicking him...he's flying backwards...no knife. I don't see it either," Kathe confirmed as she linked JAKE to the camera system. She copied the file and sent it to Ramsey. "Let's see if Ramsey or Dr. Sydney can check frame by frame. Dr. Sydney is the head technological adviser at Alby Control and runs all our computer systems. The way Rhamíd is acting he must have the weapon on him. I'll call Ramsey after I get the passengers ready to land," Kathe said as Capt. Roberts signaled final approach.

"Let me know what Ramsey says," Michaels stated as she walked away.

"Ramsey," Kathe greeted as she entered the middle galley, "Rhamíd acts as if he knows we can't find the weapon. He could very possibly have it on him. He also said, 'you don't know who I am.' Check his passport. I bet it's fake. I just sent you a copy of the security tape. Do you want us to search him?"

"I'm receiving the file now," Ramsey said as she opened the file on her computer. "Don't touch him. You're on foreign soil. The gendarmes will have to search him," Ramsey explained. "I'm more concerned how he got a sharp object through security on this end. I've checked the airport security tapes personally and they are clean. I am checking now for a possible accomplice. I will get back with you. Just make sure you document everything in your flight log."

Taxiing to the terminal, Capt. Roberts spoke, "Officer Munroe and Officer Michaels along with me would like to thank you for choosing Alby Airlines for your flight today to Paris, France. The local time is 7:00 am. We will have you at the terminal in just a few minutes where a team of specialists will be waiting. I am going to ask everyone to stay seated until the gendarmes, the French police, enter the plane. As soon as they are in place, our Chief Purser Kathe Tierney will begin your deplaning. We will have first class and business exit from R1, and cabin will use R5." With a sigh of relief, he looked at Munroe. "I'm glad Tierney's team was aboard. This could have had a different ending."

"You're right," Officer Munroe agreed. "I don't think Marshal Stone could have handled this alone."

"According to Barry, her team handled it perfectly," Capt. Roberts affirmed as the jetway connected to the craft.

"All except finding the weapon!" Munroe reminded him.

"They didn't find it yet?" Capt. Roberts questioned.

"No, Barry said they're still looking," replied Munroe.

"Well, this plane will be grounded for a few days until it is found," stated Capt. Roberts. "That's a job for security and the gendarmes now that we're on French soil."

Jay and Officer Michaels opened the coach door across from the galley, welcoming three gendarmes aboard. They escorted them to the prisoner. Kathe called Capt. Roberts from the back galley informing him they were in place. Capt. Roberts informed Paris Tower and they cleared the plane. "Flight attendants the cabin has been cleared to deplane," Capt. Roberts confirmed.

"On behalf of Alby Airlines, we again welcome you to Paris, France," Kathe stated. "Please be careful opening the overhead bins as luggage may have shifted during the flight. There are special agents located in the terminal to assist you to your next destination," Kathe finished and hung up the intercom. She alerted Ramsey that the persons of interest were ready to deplane.

"Lt. Jaco," Kathe greeted as she walked out of the galley. "I'm Kathe Tierney, the chief purser. I will have to leave you with Marshal Stone, Alby security agent Jay Towers and Officer Michaels for now. I must assist the attendants in clearing the plane. I do request that your team does not take pictures or move the prisoner until after the passengers have deplaned."

"Your request is granted," Lt. Jaco confirmed. "I will talk with you later," he replied, cautioning one of his staff to put his camera away.

As the last passenger in coach class left the plane, Carrie Anne came running up to Kathe. "Hey, did you see the gorgeous gendarmes that came aboard? How's your French?"

"Carrie Anne don't you ever think of anything except men?" Kathe asked, opening her flight log. "We need to have that cut on your neck looked at first. You may need a real stitch."

"My neck is fine," Carrie Anne declared. "You're the one that said it's just a flesh wound."

"Yes, it's a flesh wound," Kathe stated. "I don't want Ramsey upset that we didn't have it checked. Get your head back down to earth," Kathe warned, writing in her log without looking up. "We'll have to go to a debriefing with the gendarmes, either at their station or here at Alby security headquarters. It hasn't been determined yet."

"That's exactly what I had in mind; reporting to security only my way," Carrie Anne beamed as she went to get her stowed items.

"I don't mean like that," Kathe replied as she glanced up at her. "You're going to keep on until one day Ramsey fires your fanny."

"Oh, Kathe, you're funny," Carrie Anne laughed. "Think French," she chuckled as she glanced back over her shoulder.

Capt. Roberts and Officer Munroe found Kathe still charting the incident. "We will see you and Carrie Anne at the debriefing, won't we?" Capt. Roberts asked.

"Yes, captain of course," Kathe answered just as the security team brought Rhamíd to exit the plane.

"John this is Lt. Jaco," Officer Michaels introduced.

"I'm pleased to meet you," Capt. Roberts replied, shaking his hand.

"We've been searching for this man for a long time," Lt. Jaco admitted. "Your roster has his name as Mohammed Rhamíd. He uses many aliases. This is the first time with this name. I will contact Ramsey at Alby Control and speak with her. He must be having a bad day. I'm surprised to see him getting caught for something as sloppy as this," reflected Lt. Jaco. "Have your people on standby this afternoon. I want to be present at your debriefing. I want to personally book and interrogate him first. I lost a partner a year ago because of him," Lt. Jaco stated as he turned to deplane.

Rhamíd stopped in the doorway, turned and held his fingers up in the shape of a gun. He fanned the crew ending with a popping sound aimed directly at Kathe.

Capt. Roberts turned to Officer Michaels, "I take that as a threat, don't you?"

"Yes, that was a threat on all of us," Kathe interjected. "I will make a note on my report to Ramsey."

"Did you find the weapon?" Capt. Roberts asked as Lt. Jaco's men took Rhamíd off the plane.

"No, my team searched the area," Kathe admitted, putting her iPad in her bag. "I did send Ramsey a copy of the video. She'll be able to look frame by frame and find it."

"I don't know what could have happened to it," Jay remarked as he joined them. "Rhamíd sure thought it was funny when Lt. Jaco asked for it."

"He has to have it on him," Jack declared. "I told that to Lt. Jaco. He said they would do an extensive search at the station."

"Well, I'm ready to catch 40 winks before we're questioned," Capt. Roberts said as he yawned. "Munroe and I just flew this baby from New York to Paris in seven and a half hours. I have the feeling it's going to be one of those long debriefings."

As Kathe reached for the rest of her gear, Carrie Anne hurried up behind her waving a piece of paper. "Guess who we're having lunch with today?"

"I plan to sleep through lunch and as close to dinner as possible," Kathe replied, closing the closet. "I'm not having lunch with anybody."

"Wrong!" Carrie Anne protested. "We are having lunch with two French gendarmes at 11:00. They are picking us up as soon as their shift ends this morning at 10:00," gleamed Carrie Anne as she kissed the paper and put it in her purse.

"Wrong!" Kathe commented. "We're going to the hotel and rest before we go to the debriefing. Then I have a late flight to Munich. I promised Ramsey that I'd stay with you to make sure you show up,"

Kathe said as she reached for JAKE.

As the two walked to the terminal Kathe called Ramsey, "Did you find out anything else on Rhamíd?"

"I just got off the phone with Lt. Jaco," Ramsey explained. "He said Rhamíd has a long list of aliases. His real name is Rhasheéd Saíde. This was a new alias. That's why our own databanks did not match the name with his photo. I have already started profiling him. We're lucky he didn't slit Carrie Anne's throat from what I've read so far. I'll know more when Lt. Jaco calls me after his interrogation. Is Carrie Anne still upset or is she back to her old self?"

"She's got visions of us having lunch with two of the gendarmes that were with Lt. Jaco," Kathe smiled as she glanced at Carrie Anne. "Does that answer your question?"

"I figured as much," Ramsey scoffed. "I don't care if you must pull her bottom out of bed. She better be there!" Ramsey warned, hailing Wanda. "Get me my Winston's!" she yelled and cleared the line.

"What did the Ole Girl have to say?" Carrie Anne asked, waiting for Kathe to catch up.

"The usual threat," Kathe cautioned. "Just make sure your rear end is at that debriefing or my rear end will be at the Equator."

Walking past baggage claim entering customs, Kathe and Carrie Anne stopped abruptly facing a mad house. "I guess several flights came at the same time ours did," Carrie Anne whined as she searched for a quick way around them.

"Great," Kathe hissed, "this will probably take at least an hour for us to get through Customs. We'll get to the hotel just about the time we must leave for the debriefing. I have a late-night flight with my person of interest to Munich. Oh well, who needs sleep," Kathe sighed and checked JAKE for the time. "I broke my favorite watch wrestling with that idiot."

"This isn't happening!" Carrie Anne yelled as she pushed toward the front of the crew Customs line, dragging Kathe by the arm. "No way, I have a date. Come on. I do not intend to be late. Excuse me, pardon me, I have an emergency! I must go to police headquarters!"

"Police headquarters," Kathe laughed as Carrie Anne pulled her along in the crowd, causing Kathe to bump into someone. "Jordan Mills," Kathe sighed with relief, "what a small world? How's my former brother-in-law?"

"Kathe I'm glad you ran into me," Jordan chuckled giving her a hug.

"What's up?" Kathe questioned, giving him a kiss on the cheek.

"I found an apartment last time I was here, and the rent is reasonable," Jordan began. "I wanted to know if you and Carrie Anne wanted to co-rent it with me. We're usually not here at the same time."

"Carrie Anne is in a hurry as usual," Kathe replied, looking around for her. "I'll talk to her on the way to the hotel. Are you staying at the Gay Parí?"

"Yes, I am call me when you get settled," Jordan said as Kathe hurried to catch up with Carrie Anne.

"Thanks for waiting for me," Kathe said, showing her passport and ID to the customs agent.

"I don't know why you don't ever get with that good looking hunk of man," Carrie Anne demanded as she retrieved her passport and glanced back at Jordan.

"Get real Carrie Anne," Kathe argued as they left the terminal. "He is my ex-brother-in-law. Remember he is married to my ex-husband Peter's sister."

"So! You did say 'ex,'" Carrie Anne shrugged her shoulders as she hailed a cab.

"You're sick Carrie Anne," Kathe stated as the cab pulled up in front of them.

Chapter 3

The Gay Parí Hotel

"Welcome back Ms. Tierney and Ms. Mobley," Ramoné greeted at the front desk. "Your room is ready as usual."

"Ramoné, has anyone called for me?" Carrie Anne begged.

"Yes, an Inspector Miglior called about 15 minutes ago," Ramoné stated as he reached for a note on his desk. "He left a number for you to call," he said, handing her the paper and Kathe the room key.

"Thanks, Ramoné," Kathe called back as she walked to the elevator. "If he's single, I'm a Chinese cook," Kathe whispered to Carrie Anne.

"You're just jealous," Carrie Anne gleamed as she pushed the elevator button. "His left hand was bare."

"His ring finger had an indent of a wedding band," Kathe cautioned. "You might want to make sure, before you get too involved."

As they entered the room, Carrie Anne pushed past Kathe to get ready for her date. Kathe threw her suitcase on the bed, sat down in a chair, kicked off her shoes as JAKE rang, "Hey Jordan?"

"Kathe are you okay?" Jordan asked, opening his hotel room door.

"What are you talking about?" Kathe questioned as she flipped through the TV channels.

"I rode over to the hotel with Barry Michaels and John Roberts," Jordan said. "They were talking about the incident you had on your flight. They said you gave that idiot a cup of coffee that he won't soon forget."

"Let's just say, coffee has a new meaning for him after today," Kathe laughed.

"If only Peter could see you now," Jordan smiled as he sat down on the bed. "You're someone to be reckoned with."

"Thanks Jordan, I appreciate that," Kathe said as someone knocked on the door.

"I'll get it!" Carrie Anne giggled as she rushed past Kathe. "You're right on time," Carrie Anne stated as she opened the door. "Are you coming Kathe?" she asked as she glanced over her shoulder.

"No," Kathe answered as Carrie Anne closed the door. "I hope she's back in time," she said as she returned to Jordan. "If she's not at the debriefing on time Ramsey will have my head."

"Let's go over to the apartment and then have an early lunch," Jordan said as he checked the time. "I promise to have you back in time for a nap."

"Okay I'll meet you at the front desk in twenty minutes," Kathe agreed as her stomach growled. A quick shower and a change of clothes made her feel like a new woman. Noticing the time, she hurried out of the room.

As she rushed to the elevator, JAKE notified her that she was receiving a text. Glancing to see if the lobby button was illuminated, she checked the text from an unknown number. "You should have come with us for lunch. Mitch's friend was expecting you."

"Not interested," Kathe text back as she entered the elevator.

"Well, if it isn't the most beautiful flight attendant Alby has working for them," said a voice behind her.

"Capt. Garth McCollum," Kathe said, glancing at him.

"I have a layover this evening," Garth smiled. "Would you care to have dinner?"

"No thank you," Kathe replied. "I make it a policy to never date pilots or married men."

"My wife is on a different continent," Garth declared. "She doesn't have to know," he tried again as the elevator stopped and the door opened.

"That's exactly why I have the policy," Kathe smiled. "Have a good dinner. Perhaps you should call your wife if you're lonely," Kathe mentioned as she glanced over her shoulder and greeted Jordan with a hug.

"Excuse me, Jordan's a pilot and married," Garth argued as he held the door open. "What's wrong with me?"

"He's my brother-in-law," Kathe smiled. "I always stick to my policy," she stated as the door closed.

"What was that all about?" Jordan asked.

"He asked me out and I reminded him of my policy again," Kathe answered.

"He does have a reputation with the ladies," Jordan admitted as they left the building. "It's too bad. He's got a beautiful wife."

"Too bad he has no morals," Kathe confirmed. "Where is the apartment building you mentioned?" she asked as Jordan hailed a cab.

In a dark hotel room not far from the Charles de Gaulle Airport a phone rang. "Yes," Saíde answered with his deep raspy voice as he lit a cigarette.

"I just got off the phone with my attorney!" the angry voice on the other end exclaimed. "He said that he had to save you again! After you missed your last target, you were to lay low until I contacted you. But not you, you twisted imbecile! What is it with you and flight attendants? You pulled a knife on a plane full of witnesses! And of all the airlines in the world you did it on Alby! I have got too much at stake for you to screw up this deal! If I didn't need you, I would kill you myself! Lucky for your ass, Genero got you off on a technicality again!"

"I didn't do anything," Saíde defended. "I was headed to the bathroom. It was all the fault of that flight attendant," his sick twisted mind argued as he put his cigarette down and sprayed burn medication on his arm.

"That's not what I was told from two eyewitnesses!" he snapped. "Forget the flight attendant! Check your email. Try not to botch this job! Got that!" he screamed and slammed the phone down.

"That flight attendant gave me a look," Saíde groaned as he glared out the window. "I'll run into her again. And that broad who threw hot coffee on me," he snarled. "It's always on a technicality because of my ingenuity; not your fancy attorney," Saíde bragged and took another drag off his cigarette.

Pulling in front of the apartment building, Kathe noticed how similar it was to the Gay Parí Hotel. It was only ten minutes away. It was a modern, beautiful, new building. A "For Lease" banner hung over the front door. The building was made of sheer glass. The grandeur of the foyer enhanced the beauty of the building. Jordan did all the talking with the Realtor, Zoe Marlette. Before they knew it, they were on the 21st floor and entering the apartment.

The view of Paris was breathtaking from every room. It had four master bedroom suites. The kitchen was fully equipped. The price was just what Jordan and Zoe had discussed. "Kathe what do you think?" Jordan asked her.

"It sure beats staying in a hotel all the time," Kathe insisted. "I can leave things here and not have to pack so much."

"I agree," Jordan smiled. "It will make layovers more practical. I can have a set of golf clubs here; the course isn't far away," he said as he turned to Zoe. "We'll take it."

"I brought a lease with me," Zoe replied as she opened her briefcase and handed it to Jordan.

"I have the down payment with me," Jordan said as he reached in his coat pocket and handed Zoe a check.

"I have my checkbook for my share," Kathe stated as she sat down at the table.

"I'll run down and make a copy of the lease and get an extra set of keys," Zoe said as she left the apartment.

"This place will cost twice this much next year," Jordan said as he gazed out the living room window to the park. "I'm glad I got the lease for two years with another three-year option," he said looking over the bar.

"Why is it such a deal?" Kathe inquired. "They should have gotten twice this much," she noted, running her hand across the back of the leather couch.

"Because it's a new building and they're trying to fill it up quickly," Jordan replied as Zoe came back with the keys and lease.

"Here's your set of keys and copy of the lease," Zoe smiled as she handed Kathe the keys and Jordan the lease. "I want to be the first to welcome you officially to our building. Today is my lucky day. I also rented the apartment across the hall from you to some rock stars from London. They're moving in this weekend," she explained as JAKE rang.

"Excuse me, I have to take this call," Kathe said as she walked away.

"The debriefing is in one hour," Ramsey stated. "It's going to be at the airport security room by Internal Affairs instead of the police station. Don't forget to find Carrie Anne. Make sure you're both there on time!"

"That was a quick interrogation," Kathe noted as she glanced at the time.

"Wasn't it?" Ramsey said and cleared the line.

"Jordan the debriefing time is in one hour at the airport," Kathe said as Zoe left the apartment. "We need to head back now," Kathe said as she marveled at the view one last time.

Arriving back at the Gay Parí, Kathe and Jordan ran into Jay and Jack coming back from lunch. "Did Ramsey call you?" Kathe asked.

"She called us a few minutes ago," Jack answered. "We can meet you at the front desk at 1:15 and ride together. We just need to run upstairs for a minute."

"I hope I can find Carrie Anne by then," Kathe said as they walked toward the elevator.

"Just give her a call," Jack suggested.

"She lost her cell phone somewhere in New York," Kathe complained. "She was late to work and didn't have time to get a new one," Kathe stated as she pushed the button for the 12th floor.

"I'm Jay Towers," he introduced as he stretched his hand to Jordan.

"I'm glad to meet you," he said. "I'm Jordan Mills, a longtime friend of Kathe."

"Actually, Jordan's my former brother-in-law and the one who talked me into becoming a flight attendant," Kathe admitted.

"Then he knows you've got certain skills," Jay hinted.

"Yes, I'm one of the few people that know Kathe has skills," Jordan acknowledged.

"I'm Jack Davies," he shook Jordan's hand. "I have seen you talking to Kathe from time to time in different airports," he said as the elevator stopped on the 12th floor.

"I'm sorry I never introduced you," Kathe apologized getting off with Jordan as Jay held the door open. "Where are my manners? Jay and Jack are on my security team."

"By the looks of you two, I know she's in good company," Jordan remarked.

"Do not let her size fool you," Jack laughed, reaching for the button. "She can hold her own with anybody."

"See you downstairs in a few minutes," Kathe said as the door closed.

Upon reaching her room, Kathe noted the door was slightly ajar. Signaling Jordan to move to the left side she reached for her gun. Quickly pushing the door, Kathe crouched down to sweep the doorway, and found Carrie Anne sitting on the couch.

"Where have you been?" Carrie Anne asked as she turned off the TV. "I was just about to call you. You know Ramsey will have a fit if we're late."

Holstering her gun, Kathe signaled Jordan to come into the room. "What happened to your hot date with Mr. Body?"

"Carrie Anne you're not losing your touch, are you?" Jordan teased as he gave her a hug.

"Moi," Carrie Anne answered as she looked him straight in the eyes. "If I had the time, I'd let you see for yourself," she teased and turned to Kathe. "Mick got called back to the station. He said something about my assailant having an expensive attorney show up. And by the way, Kathe for dinner I want egg fu yung," she snickered. "He didn't have a wedding ring on his finger."

"So much for an early lunch," Jordan said as he noted the time. "I didn't think signing the lease would take that long. Sorry about lunch," he replied, leaning over and giving Kathe a kiss on the cheek. "Give me a call after the debriefing. I'm dying to know what's going on."

"I have to work a flight to Munich tonight," Kathe explained. "When I get time, I'll give you a call," she said and walked him to the door. "Are you here for the night?"

"Yes," Jordan stated. "I don't know too many people, who work long flights and takeoff again. See ya love."

"I'm only taking my overnight bag with me," Kathe said, picking up her small bag. "I'll be back tomorrow around noon."

"That's fine," Carrie Anne said as they left the room. "I'll be in and out. Mick is probably going to stay here since you're leaving."

"Carrie Anne," Jack welcomed as he leaned against the front desk. "It's nice of you to make it on time for a change."

"Thank you," Carrie Anne smiled, put her arm around his neck, and pulled him very close. "I didn't know you were keeping tabs on me."

"That's because you're never around when Ramsey starts screaming at us because you're not with us," Jack rebutted. "It's times like that we feel like gluing your fanny to our suitcases!"

"Strange, I never did it on a suitcase!" Carrie Anne beamed. "What an option!" she exclaimed heading for the door.

"Carrie Anne compared to you we look like choirboys," Jay joined in the conversation.

Carrie Anne shrugged her shoulders and threw him a kiss, "It's a talent!"

"Now that we've established your talent, may we go to our meeting?" Kathe asked as she led the way to the door.

Arriving at Charles de Gaulle Airport, Kathe quickly checked the status of her flight to Munich. "So far it's on time," Kathe sighed as JAKE rang.

"Kathe is everybody with you?" Ramsey asked as she searched for her notes on her desk.

"Everybody except our pilots," Kathe replied, allowing the others to walk ahead of her.

"I've been talking with Lt. Jaco," Ramsey replied. "Rhasheéd Saíde has an extensive criminal history. However, in each case he has been adjudicated due to a technicality. With all the new technology that Homeland Security has in place, it is hard to believe he got through the checkpoints. Dr. Sydney is checking into it. He also has one heck of an attorney, Damiano Genero. He has suspected Mafia ties in the U.S. and Europe. Saíde is already out on bond."

"You're kidding, aren't you?" Kathe asked as she looked around for her friends.

"No, make sure Carrie Anne stays with Jay and Jack at the debriefing," Ramsey cautioned. "They are to take her back to the hotel and stay with her. Saíde is somewhere in Paris. You are to report to Lt. Jaco. He said he lost a partner to Saíde a year ago. You may find something he has missed. After this incident, I realized that JAKE is due for an upgrade. Dr. Sydney and I are working on it."

"I understand," Kathe affirmed as she cleared the line and joined the others. "I just got off the phone with Ramsey," she told them. "Saíde is already out on bail. Carrie Anne is to stay with you two here at the debriefing. You are also to take her back to the hotel and stay there with her. I'm heading over to talk with Lt. Jaco. Ramsey wants me to search for something Jaco may have missed."

"But I have a date tonight with Mitch," Carrie Anne pouted. "I'm not staying with them."

"You can still keep your date with Mitch," Kathe advised. "It would be better for him to stay with you in the room, since I am leaving for Munich. Let the pilots know what is going on with Saíde. I'll see you at noon tomorrow."

Chapter 4

Saíde's Release

"Ms. Tierney," Lt. Jaco greeted in the entryway of the gendarmes municipal building. "I just got off the phone with Ramsey. She said you were a block away, so I came down to personally show you to my office."

"Why thank you," Kathe said as Lt. Jaco led the way to his office. "It seems the passenger on last night's flight, which you identified as Rhasheéd Saíde has an extensive criminal history. With all the new technology at the security checkpoints, I cannot believe Saíde was able to board the flight, much less already released from custody."

"I explained to Ramsey that Saíde is noted for being able to change his identity," Lt. Jaco began as they entered his office. "He's one slippery creature. This is the first time we had him on something I thought would stick. Then in walked his attorney, who already had the paperwork signed by a councilor and it was all over. All I could do was watch him walk out with his attorney."

"It appears you need to do some in-house cleaning," Kathe stated as she sat down across from his desk. "This man wasn't in custody more than a few hours. That is record time to have papers filed and signed by one of your councilors. He attacked a flight attendant mid-flight. He held her against her will. He cut her neck and made it bleed in a cabin full of witnesses. There is no bail for that crime?"

"You're right Ms. Tierney," Lt. Jaco confessed as he leaned back in his chair. "It is totally absurd. I've already talked with my directeur about it. He read the court order and couldn't believe it either. He's looking into it. Unless he finds a loophole, our hands are tied," Lt. Jaco admitted. "Ramsey said you wanted to ask me some questions. I just emailed her everything I have on Saíde."

"Ramsey mentioned you lost a partner to Saíde a year ago," Kathe began. "What happened?"

"Roberto Muar and I were investigating several local stabbings of young women," Lt. Jaco shared. "Roberto received an anonymous tip of a man who fit the description of Saíde by a local merchant. It was late in the evening, and I had an abscessed tooth and was able to see my dentist. Roberto said he'd check it out on his way home and see me in the morning. The next morning Roberto didn't show up to work. I found him and his wife at their home in bed stabbed to death. We also found the shop owner the same way in the alley behind his shop. Saíde seemed to vanish; this is the first time he has resurfaced. I cannot believe I had to let him go. Roberto and I were partners for twenty years. Our children are the same ages," he said as he buried his face in his hands.

"I'm sorry you lost a good friend," Kathe sympathized. "But we must stop Saíde now. I saw the crazed look in his eyes and the way he picks his victims. The flight attendant he pulled a knife on during Flight #1014 is my best friend. I remember the way he kept up with the two male flight attendants and the way he glared at Carrie Anne. I was just about to warn my team when he struck. May I have a copy of the court order?"

"I sent a copy to Ramsey a few minutes ago," Lt. Jaco, answered.

"If you don't mind, I would like a paper copy," Kathe requested. "I don't have time to check with Ramsey. I must catch a flight to Munich in less than an hour."

"Sure, if you would like one," Lt. Jaco agreed and picked up the court order as his phone rang.

"I'll make the copy," Kathe offered and reached for the papers as Lt. Jaco walked away to answer the call.

"Here's the original," Kathe stated as Lt. Jaco returned to his office and started looking through a pile of papers on his desk.

"I apologize," Lt. Jaco stated. "We have an emergency that I have to attend to now."

"This is all I need for now," Kathe stated as she set the order on the corner of his desk. "I'll see my way out," Kathe said as she left his office.

In the cab on the way back to the airport, Kathe looked over the original court order. She noticed the weight of the paper felt a little heavier than normal. She held JAKE over the paper to scan the seal. Just as she thought, it came back as a forgery. She called Ramsey. "Have you had a chance to read the court order Genero brought to Lt. Jaco?"

"Yes, I can't get over the fact a councilor would sign a release; especially on a man with his history," Ramsey scoffed. "We had Saíde dead to rights!"

"There are crooked judges everywhere," Kathe affirmed. "This document is a forgery."

"Why do you think it's a forgery?" Ramsey asked.

"Because I have the original in my hand," Kathe admitted. "JAKE scanned the seal and crosschecked it with the seal in Paris court records. It's close, but it's not a match."

"How did you get the original court order?" Ramsey inquired.

"You don't want to know," Kathe giggled, glancing through the document. "It is signed by Jacques dé Laurent. See what you can find on him," Kathe requested as the cab came to a halt at the airport. "I'm back at Charles de Gaulle."

"Okay, I'll look into it while you're on the flight," Ramsey agreed. "I've already arranged for someone on the ground in Munich to stay with our person of interest as soon as you land. I'll get back with you concerning dé Laurent," Ramsey cleared the line.

Kathe checked the time and hurried to Concourse B as JAKE rang. "Hello," a Russian voice said as her face lit up.

"Yorg," Kathe answered getting on the tram. "Where are you?"

"I'm about 35,000 feet above the Atlantic Ocean on my way to Paris," Yorg replied.

"I have a short flight tonight to Munich," Kathe explained. "Then the same route back in the morning. I should be in around noon. I'm staying at the Gay Parí with Carrie Anne."

"I'm staying there too," Yorg smiled. "I'm sure you will need a room free from Carrie Anne's tricks. I'll leave a key at the front desk," he said as he rolled his eyes.

"I might have to take you up on that offer," Kathe replied. "Carrie Anne has a new inspector friend. The tram is stopping; I must go. Bye," she said as the tram stopped, and she headed down the crowded hallway to Gate B9.

"Well, this is going to be an interesting flight," a familiar voice rushed up behind Kathe as she approached the gate.

"What is that supposed to mean?" Kathe asked as she greeted her friend, Kayla Martin.

"Did you hear what happened on Kathe's last flight?" Kayla asked her best friend Nina Norell. "It's only the talk of Alby."

"No, what happened?" Nina questioned. "I'm just getting to work."

"Now girls, this is a routine flight," Kathe insisted. "I'm just keeping my eye on one person. But I will say if any questionable Middle Eastern males are on board I may leave."

"Just don't ask Kathe for a cup of coffee," Kayla laughed. "I heard she has a new way to serve it," Kayla giggled as she filled Nina in on all the details as Kathe walked ahead of them down the jetway to the plane.

"Kathe," Nina called to her, "how is Carrie Anne?"

"The same," Kathe glanced back at her. "She is always looking for 'Mr. Right' one man at a time," she said as they all laughed.

After stowing her bags, Kathe found the roster and gave out assignments to her staff as passengers started filing into the cabin. 'This is a long day,' Kathe thought as Kayla made her way back up to the front.

"Did you see him?" Kayla asked whispering to Kathe.

"Did I see who?" Kathe asked, assisting an elderly woman to her seat.

"Don't you know who the man in 6B is?" Kayla drooled. "The one with the long blondish hair," she said, pointing to the middle of this section.

"Kayla if you're getting like Carrie Anne, I'm changing jobs," Kathe whispered.

"That's Rick Travis, bass guitarist for Light Crimson!" Kayla exclaimed. "I hope I get the chance to ask for his autograph."

"Alby's policy is to never bother the passengers," Kathe politely warned her co-worker as she noted her person of interest entering the plane. "We see lots of famous people on our flights."

"Okay, I'll get his napkin or cup or something," Kayla smiled and walked back toward her station.

"If you do give me a piece of it, I'll send it to my son Pete," Kathe laughed as Kayla turned around, giving the okay signal.

"Kathe," Nina approached her after the first duties of the flight were finished and the passengers were settling down for the short flight. "I'm meeting Tierra and her brother for dinner when we land. Would you like to join us?"

"Sure, I haven't seen Tierra in a couple of months," Kathe answered, reaching for some pillows in the overhead bin. "I'm starving after everything that's happened today. I haven't had time to eat."

"Okay, I'll call Tierra as soon as we land," Nina smiled. "I know she will be excited to see you," Nina said, walking back to her section.

"Excuse me," Kathe said as she accidently bumped into the man Kayla was drooling over as she turned around. He grinned at her and continued reading his magazine. As Kathe walked away, he looked up and watched her walk to the front of the plane. He shook his head, smiled, and returned to his article.

The flight was a quick one and went off without any hitches. Kathe noted that her person of interest watched her from time to time. She texted Ramsey letting her know what she observed. She was glad when the pilot signaled final approach into Munich. On the ground, as the passengers were deplaning, Kayla was up front talking to Kathe when the British star walked past them. He smiled at Kathe and handed her a magazine where the band was featured on the front cover, which he autographed.

"Thanks for the nice flight, Rick Travis." Kayla grabbed the magazine out of Kathe's hand. "You lucky gal! I must have this! I collect signatures of stars."

"I guess," Kathe laughed and relinquished it. "If I don't give it to you, I'm sure I'll never hear the end of it."

"Great!" Kayla giggled as she pulled a wadded-up a napkin and dirty cup out of her pocket. "I'll put it with the other souvenirs I got from him!"

As the last passenger left the plane, Nina hurried over to them. Reaching for her bag, "Kathe are you ready for dinner with Tierra?"

"Sure," Kathe affirmed as she reached for her overnight bag in one of the compartments.

"I'll call Tierra and tell her we are on our way and that you will be joining us," Nina said as they headed down the jetway.

Kathe, Kayla, and Nina headed for the escalator to the lower levels to leave the airport. Kayla was staring at the magazine article she acquired when the girls passed by the guitarist again. This time he was with two friends. Kayla stopped in her tracks, "There is Rick Travis again! Look who's with him! The guy on the left is Troy Rollins, the drummer. The one of the rights is lead guitarists, Collin Jones. Let's walk over closer, maybe I'll get lucky!"

"Right!" Kathe chuckled as they walked out of the terminal. "The way the girl is hanging on Travis, you would have to get more than lucky," Kathe said as she looked at the row of limos that lined the road. "How are we supposed to know which limo belongs to Tierra's brother?"

"Tierra told me the driver would hold up a sign with my name on it," Nina assured her as she glanced around. "There he is!" Nina exclaimed as she pointed to a chauffeur in front of a dark gray Rolls Royce.

"That man does not look like the average chauffeur," Kathe noted as she gazed at the 6-foot-two, 210-pound, blondish-brown hair, blue-eyed hunk with a five o'clock shadow. "What kind of business did Tierra say her brother was in?"

"Tierra didn't say," Nina answered as they approached the limo.

"I could forget Rick Travis for that man," Kayla grinned as she pointed at him.

"He's uncharted territory," Kathe cautioned. "I'd stay with Travis; you know what he does for a living, just to play it safe."

"Kathe," Kayla tapped her on the shoulder. "You worry too much!"

Chapter 5

Tierra's Brother Nicki LaBasco

"Ladies," the chauffeur greeted as he opened the door. "Which one of you is Nina Norell?"

"I am," Nina, answered. "This is Kayla Martin and Kathe Tierney," she introduced.

"Yes," he checked a paper in his pocket. "They are on my list to pick up. Please make yourselves comfortable," he said as he held the door open.

"Is the restaurant far away from the airport?" Nina asked as she got inside.

"No ma'am, it's about ten minutes away," he answered as he closed the door.

"Tierra's brother has some serious money!" Kayla whispered running her fingers across the dark-gray, leather interior. She pointed to the glass separation from the driver, bar, telephone, and television.

"Down girl," Kathe laughed. "It's all standard equipment. I swear you're getting more like Carrie Anne."

"Carrie Anne does know how to snag the rich ones," Nina added.

"Yes, but she doesn't know how to keep them," Kathe reminded her as the Rolls Royce pulled up in front of a beautiful old restaurant. The door attendant opened the door and the three women got out.

"Do you have a reservation?" The hostess asked as she informed them of a short wait.

"We are with the LaBasco party," Nina answered.

"Please follow me," the hostess smiled, reaching for three menus. "Your party is waiting for you." Following the hostess through the restaurant, Kathe noted they were headed to a private room with several men standing against the back wall.

"Wow, it's great to see the three of you!" Tierra greeted as she got up and hugged Nina. "I've really missed being on the circuit and seeing everybody."

"Nothing's changed," Kathe remarked as she gave Tierra a hug. "It's just the routine trip from the states to Europe."

"Don't listen to Kathe," Kayla blabbed as Tierra hugged her. "You know Kathe never tells it like it is."

"That's because she's a work-a-holic," Tierra said as they sat down. "This is my younger brother Nicki."

"I'm pleased to meet you," Nicki said and motioned to the waiter. "Would you ladies like a cocktail?"

"Kayla and I will have a margarita," Nina spoke up.

"I'll have a scotch and water," Kathe answered.

"I'll have another martini," Nicki ordered, and the waiter left the room. As the girls looked at the menu and chatted with Tierra, Nicki noticed Kathe's eyes scanning the room. "They work for me," he remarked, motioning to the men against the wall.

"Do you come here often?" Kathe asked as she changed the subject.

"You might say so," Nicki admitted as Kayla opened her oversized purse pulling out the magazine Rick Travis signed.

"Tierra, look what Kathe gave me," Kayla grinned as she held up the signed magazine.

"Rick Travis was on your flight?" Tierra's eyes widened as she gazed at his signature. "And you actually talked to him?"

"It wasn't a conversation," Kathe explained. "I accidently bumped into his arm and said excuse me. He just looked up and smiled. I was surprised he gave me the magazine when he left the plane."

"Then we saw him as we left the terminal with Collin Jones and Troy Rollins," Kayla bragged as she put the magazine back in her purse. "Travis is so good looking! I wanted to grab him on the plane."

"Kayla's getting more like Carrie Anne every time I fly with her," Kathe added.

"Oh, my gosh!" Tierra exclaimed. "I forgot to ask you about the one and only Carrie Anne Mobley?"

"She's the same," Kathe informed her. "She's presently stalking a French inspector."

"Where did Carrie Anne meet a French inspector?" Tierra inquired as she glanced over at Nicki.

"It's a long-complicated story," Kathe replied as she rolled her eyes.

"Long and complicated story is right!" Kayla exclaimed. "Their flight from New York to Paris yesterday ended up with an intoxicated male passenger pulling a knife on Carrie Anne.'"

"What happened?" Nicki asked as he took a sip of his drink.

"I'm not allowed to talk about it," Kathe answered. "But I will say one thing. They've already released the man who did it."

"Released him?" Nicki questioned. "How could that be?"

"It's under investigation," Kathe stated as she looked down at the table.

"I bet Ramsey's went ballistic," Kayla stated, taking a sip of her drink.

"Ramsey's always ballistic about something," Tierra complained also sipping her drink. "She and I tangled earlier this afternoon on my returning to work," she began as the waiter interrupted the conversation with the arrival of their food.

"Tierra why did you take a leave of absence the last few months?" Nina asked as the waiter and his helpers left the room.

"We had a little family problem," Nicki answered as Kathe noted Tierra getting nervous. "We brought Tierra home for her protection. Our father's a rather big businessman here in Europe."

"Is it safe for Tierra to return to work?" Kathe asked, noting the tone of his voice and his careful choice of words.

"The problem has been taken care of," Nicki answered as he looked Kathe straight in the eyes.

"When do you start back to work?" Kathe asked as she glanced at Tierra.

"Tomorrow finally," Tierra replied. "I'm leaving for Paris and then back toward the U.S. Ramsey may switch me to the South American circuit."

"Ramsey is a hard boss," Kathe confirmed. "But she's hardly ever wrong. She worries for the safety of every employee at Alby. If you've had a serious family problem, a change in scenery and co-workers might be the best answer for you."

"I assure you Kathe," Nicki affirmed as he looked right at her. "I'm staying in contact with Linda Ramsey concerning this problem. If I didn't think Tierra was safe; she wouldn't be leaving my sight."

"I apologize if you took what I said the wrong way," Kathe remarked as she glanced at his men around the room. "A man of your stature thinks the same way I do concerning the protection of our family and colleagues," she said as she glanced at her empty wrist. "I forgot my watch is broken," she said as she checked JAKE for the time. "It's getting late, and I've worked nonstop for over twenty-four hours."

"I'll have my chauffeur take you to your hotel," Nicki offered.

"I have an early morning flight tomorrow as well," Tierra confirmed. "I think I should call it a night also. I must get used to getting up early for work again."

"That you do big sister," Nicki said as he stood up. "It was nice meeting you ladies. I hope we meet again Kathe. It's been interesting chatting with you this evening."

"I never know what the skies have in store for me," Kathe smiled. "Having time off is a rarity for me."

In the hotel, Kathe got ready for bed quickly. Kayla was trying to unwind from the day. "Hey, what did you think about Tierra's brother Nicki?"

"He's nice, but nobody to get involved with, why?" Kathe asked.

"I think he's cute," Kayla confessed. "Did you notice a wedding ring?"

"He wasn't wearing one," Kathe assured her. "Now I know why Tierra doesn't talk too much about her family," she said as she spread the blanket on the couch and fluffed the pillow.

"Why?" Kayla questioned.

"I'd rather not say," Kathe answered lying down.

"There are two beds in the other room," Nina noticed Kathe on the couch.

"I know, but I prefer the couch," Kathe answered. "That way, I won't wake anybody up in the morning."

"Don't wake me early," Kayla begged, heading for her room. "My next flight leaves in the evening. I plan to sleep until then. See you later."

"Okay, I'll see you in the clouds," Kathe replied. "Goodnight, it's been fun."

In a hotel on the south side of Moscow, a phone rang. "Yeah Boss," he said lighting a cigarette. "I've been waiting for your call."

"I've been watching the Internet and haven't seen my news yet," questioned the voice on the other end.

"I don't know why," he answered nervously. "It went off without any problems. Just like you said, I found him in his office and took care of business," his raspy voice snickered. "He was busy with a woman when I got there, so she left with him."

"As soon as it's confirmed, your money will be delivered in the usual way," he affirmed. "Try not to bother anybody on your way home this time," he warned and hung up the phone. "Thank God, he didn't botch it up this time!"

JAKE's alarm went off at 5:30 am. Kathe woke up finally feeling like she had a good night's sleep. She got up and began to get ready for work. As she entered the bathroom, she turned on the water to let the shower heat up. Just before she stepped in JAKE rang. "Hello."

"Good morning," Ramsey said. "Jeannie Rafferty's on the other line wanting to talk to you. Is this a good time?"

"Sure, connect us," Kathe smiled. "Hi Jeannie, are the kids, okay?"

"They're great," her friend said. "The older two have been a little depressed lately. They've had it with the winter weather."

"Me too," Kathe replied. "How's my baby?"

"He misses his mommy," Jeannie answered. "When do you think you'll be back in the U.S.?"

"I have to ask Ramsey," Kathe answered. "I'm in Munich getting ready to go to Paris."

"The kids need to see you soon," Jeannie replied. "Christmas Day went too quickly. They miss you."

"I miss them too," Kathe admitted. "I work out of necessity, not enjoyment. Are they there now? Can I talk to them?"

"Yes, I'll put them on the phone," Jeannie conceded. "You know Peter has been quite unhappy lately."

"Jeannie I'll talk to the kids," Kathe stated. "I don't want to even hear Peter's name, much less what he's doing," she said, turning off the water.

"Sorry, but he asked about you when he brought the kids back yesterday," Jeannie added. "He almost looked like he was going to cry."

"Jeannie please, just put the kids on the phone," Kathe continued. "I'll let you know when I can visit again," she replied as she checked for lines around her eyes in the mirror. Jeannie put the kids on one at a time. Kathe filled the older ones in on where she had been and what stars she had seen on her flights. Heather could not believe she gave Rick Travis's autograph away. She begged her mom to get another one for her if she saw him again. Pete said he could have sold it on eBay for about $500 and cautioned her not to give any more away. Kathe never mentioned any of the problem flights to her kids or to Jeannie. As far as the kids knew, she was just another flight attendant. Ramsey had made sure the Rafferty's shielded her children from all knowledge of the disaster years earlier that changed her life. She remembered her flight and the hot shower waiting for her. She said her goodbyes and continued getting ready for work.

Walking into the airport, Kathe checked the screen for her departure gate for the flight and headed for the escalators. She looked around for Tierra but did not spot her. She decided to get a cup of coffee at the restaurant before heading to the gate.

"Kathe, I'm glad you're here," Tierra said with a sigh of relief, spotting her at the restaurant a few minutes later. "I'm a little nervous."

"Why?" Kathe asked, paying for her things.

"Ramsey didn't tell you why I had to take a few months off work?" Tierra asked as they walked to the gate.

"No, Ramsey's been too busy sending my team on special details," Kathe admitted. "I hardly remember Christmas," she remarked as she swiped her ID badge to open the jetway door.

"I started to get threatening notes and phone calls at work," Tierra began as they walked down the jetway.

"What kind of threats?" Kathe asked.

"I'm sure you realize what kind of business my family's in," Tierra whispered as two other attendants passed them.

"Well, I kind of got the picture last night," Kathe affirmed. "I noticed the bodyguards."

"I haven't talked to Papa in years, except when my mother died," Tierra explained. "I don't want anything to do with him or his business," she said with tears beginning to swell in her eyes. "Every once in a while, like a reoccurring nightmare, someone clashes with him, and I end up scared for my life."

"What about your brothers?" Kathe asked.

"My older brother is as bad as Papa," Tierra admitted. "Nicki and I have always been close, even more so after what happened to our mother. The brakes on her car mysteriously went out when she was leaving the house a little over a year ago."

"What did the police report say?" Kathe asked.

"My brother Mario handled the investigation along with the police," Tierra stated. "Alonzo took Papa to the hospital due to his heart condition. Alonzo also stayed at the hospital with Papa fearing someone was after him too. Strangely enough, the police and Mario deemed it an accident. However, that never sat right with Nicki or Alonzo," she replied, wiping a tear from her eye.

"I do remember you were on leave for a few months a year ago," Kathe stated.

"Yes, my family brought me in for protection until the investigation was finished," Tierra confirmed. "Now, a year later, the nightmare has begun all over again. At least, the person who threatened me has been taken care of or so says my older brother," she said as they reached the plane.

"Tierra there are bad people everywhere," Kathe comforted. "You can't help what your family does for a living. All you must answer for is yourself."

"Thanks for listening and being a great friend," Tierra smiled. "I feel safer flying with you."

"That's funny," Kathe chuckled and reached for her iPad. "Carrie Anne wants to get off a plane when she sees me boarding."

The day's work had begun. It was not a meal flight, so coffee and a light snack were all the passengers required. As Kathe was handing out magazines JAKE rang. "Kathe," Ramsey's familiar voice spoke. "I have some good news. Hold on a second," holding the phone away from her mouth. "Wanda, get me a pack of Winston's!"

"What is the good news?" Kathe asked. "I could use it."

"I'm sending your team with Yorg to Russia," Ramsey announced. "Alby signed the contract I have been working on for the past two years to land in Moscow. I want to make sure that there are no problems with the contract. You will stay there for a couple of days and then I am sending you back to the U.S. You could use a little R and R. Jeannie called and said that your kids would like to see you. You worked all through the Holidays and have not taken a real vacation in about six months. How's that for good news?"

"Congratulations on landing the contract with Russia," Kathe replied. "The flight to Russia sounds great, but you know how I hate to go to Colorado."

"You have a beautiful home in Florida," Ramsey offered. "Take the kids with you for a week or so; I'm not taking no for an answer."

"I'll go to Russia and then I'll talk to you again," Kathe retorted. "It's so hard for me to go back to Colorado, too many haunts. The kids do not have Spring Break for a while. I can't just take the older ones out of school."

"You're right about their school," Ramsey replied. "You know you can't stay up in the air all the time. You need a break, or this job will get to you. I'll talk to you later, bye," she cleared the line.

"Here you go, Boss," Wanda smiled as she tossed Ramsey a pack of Winston's.

"I told you never to give me these, even if I begged!" Ramsey screamed, ripping the pack apart and throwing it in the garbage can next to her desk.

"You're making me crazy!" Wanda shouted as she ran her hands through her hair and walked back to her desk. "Make up your mind!"

"I did!" Ramsey retorted. "You're supposed to keep them away from me! My blood pressure has its own altitude, and my doctor doesn't like it that high!"

As Kathe put JAKE back on her belt, she noticed a young mother traveling alone with twins. The mother was frantic as both began to cry. Taking one of them, Kathe walked the cabin rocking the child. She picked up empty snack papers. She remembered how many times she held babies while doing other tasks at home years earlier. Her old life haunted her from time to time. She missed her children, but after what happened, she couldn't live that kind of life again. The captain signaled they were fifty miles out just as Kathe got the baby back to sleep.

"She fell asleep just in time," Kathe told the mother placing her in the car seat and covering her with the blanket.

"Thank you for your help," the young mother smiled. "I don't know what I would have done without you."

"The pleasure was all mine," Kathe smiled as the captain signaled final approach. "That's my cue," she said as she hurried to the galley.

"Ladies and gentlemen," Kathe announced, "please make sure that your seats and tray tables are in their full upright and locked positions. We are on final approach into Charles de Gaulle Airport. We will be on the ground in just a few minutes. Please stay seated until the aircraft has docked at the gate and the captain turns the seatbelt sign off."

On the ground, Kathe again reached for the intercom. "On behalf of Alby Airlines, Capt. Richards, and the entire flight crew, welcome to Paris, France. We hope your trip was satisfactory and you will keep Alby Airlines in mind the next time you fly. Inside the building are agents who will be glad to help connect you with your next flight or assist you in any way," she finished.

The plane came to a halt at the docking bay, and she thanked the passengers for flying with them as they deplaned.

Tierra hurried up front as the last passengers were leaving the rear of the plane. "I'd like to talk with you," she told Kathe.

"Let me grab my bag," Kathe said, opening the closet door. "I'll walk you to your gate. Where are you heading now?"

"I'm changing flights and heading to Newark," Tierra stated as they walked down the jetway. "After that I don't know where I'm going. Ramsey wants to talk to me about my family. What should I say? Papa is not the average dad!"

"Ramsey isn't stupid," Kathe discussed. "She knows what he does for a living. Her job is to keep you and those around you safe," Kathe assured her friend as they stopped at her gate. "She'll probably assign someone to fly with you for a while. At least until you feel more comfortable."

"You always seem to know what to say to make me feel better," Tierra admitted. "Maybe, I'll see you in New York," Tierra added as she waved goodbye.

"I'll see you in the clouds," Kathe said and headed for the tram.

Chapter 6

Kathe's Self-Appointed Guardian Angel

The cab came to a halt in front of the Gay Parí. Kathe paid the cab driver and walked through the circular door to the front desk, where Ramoné was on duty. "Ms. Tierney, welcome back."

"Ramoné, it's always a pleasure to be here," Kathe smiled. "I almost feel like I'm home."

"Maybe that's because you're always here mademoiselle," Ramoné smiled, winking at her.

"Do you know if Carrie Anne is in our room?" Kathe asked.

"I'm not sure, but I do have a message and a key for you," Ramoné stated as he reached for an envelope.

"Thank you," Kathe answered as she headed for the elevator. "Wake me up as soon as you arrive. Room 808, Yorg."

The elevator came to a halt and Kathe went to her room first. She remembered her apartment a few minutes away. I need to check with Jordan to see when we can start using it, she thought. I can't wait to show it to Yorg. Putting the key in the door, Kathe quietly entered, knowing Carrie Anne was probably still sleeping. She opened the bedroom door noticing two lumps in the bed. I don't know why I share a room with her. I pay the bill and she sleep with some idiot. Then I must get a different room, Kathe thought to herself. She tiptoed across the room and took her suitcase.

She got back on the elevator and pushed eight. Getting off the elevator, she hurried to Yorg's room. She used the key and turned the doorknob slowly. Entering the dark room, she reached for the light switch. She could see the bedroom door was ajar. She put her things down, took her coat off and laid it on the couch. Walking over to the door, peering into the room, she could see daylight peeking through the shades. In the dim light, she smiled as she looked at her self-appointed "Guardian Angel." He stood 6 foot-4 inches, about 200 pounds. He joined the Russian military as soon as he was out of high school to pursue a career as a pilot. The military put him on the Olympic Weightlifting Team when he was in his twenties due to his incredible strength. After that, he was on special assignment on the Weapons Research Project, before being the first assigned to Alby on an International Anti-Terrorist Coalition.

Leaning her head on the doorframe folding her arms, Kathe remembered the first time she met Yorg. You never know when you meet someone, just what effect they will have on your life. Carrie Anne, Yorg, Jay, Jack, and I started working at Alby Airlines the same day. It was as if God placed us together for a special purpose. Ramsey had worked as the Assistant Controller for two years, yet the maiden flight, where she was solely in charge was Alby Flight #1237. Ramsey called it her baptism by fire. She handled everything professionally and was promoted to the Head of Alby Security. She immediately appointed Dr. David Sydney to spearhead and secure Alby's computer systems with a technology that she helped him design. It was Yorg's first assignment on an American-based airlines, and it was one he never forget. For the first time since the death of his wife, he learned to deeply care for another woman that day. Jay and Jack, both Marines who just finished two consecutive tours of duty in Afghanistan and Iraq. Carrie Anne and I were green, she chuckled. We were fresh from flight school. I thought it was going to be a new beginning after what I'd been through during the ugly divorce. Instead, I was thrown into hell, before my new life began. I'm now with people who I trust with my life.

Kathe flinched remembering the pain she experienced after the shooting. Yorg would not let me die. He stayed by my side, never doubting that I would recover. He helped me with the decision that changed my life. A decision that would not only affect my life, but the lives of my children. A decision that once I pulled that trigger, I would be unable to ever go back to a normal life again. Yet, I couldn't let this happen to anyone else. I remember the long grueling hours we spent training in martial arts and weaponry. A smile came over her, I remember the surprised look on Yorg's face, the first time he found himself looking up at me from the mat. He jumped up lunging straight at me and I nailed him again.

She unfolded her arms and quietly walked toward the bed. He was sound asleep. She sat down on the edge of the bed and turned on the lamp. Yorg opened one eye, then the other when she sat down. He smiled as he gently pulled her down to his level and hugged her. "Now, this is a perfect wake up call," he said with his charming Russian accent.

"You said if Carrie Anne was busy to come on up, so I took you up on it," Kathe kissed him on the cheek.

"I saw her coming in last night as I was coming back from dinner," Yorg admitted. "She was hanging all over some guy, so I left a note and a key at the front desk for you," he said still embracing her. "I don't know how you two survive as best friends."

"Yes, you do," Kathe smiled. "I guess after all we've been through together, I just overlook her problem."

"Problem!" Yorg exclaimed. "I've heard women like her called a lot of things in several different languages, but never a problem," Yorg laughed, pulling the pillow under his neck.

Kathe kissed him on the cheek and sat up. "Well, I'm ready for lunch and I want to show you an apartment. Jordan rented it yesterday and it's about ten minutes away. It has a common area, kitchen, living room, plus four master bedrooms. It has a magnificent view of the Seine River."

"You know my government will never allow me to do that," Yorg stated.

"It's better than a hotel," Kathe insisted. "We can leave some of our things in a large walk-in closet. We always stay together anyway. You can share my room," she said as she walked to the bathroom and reached for a towel. "Come on, get out of bed, get showered and let's go," she insisted and threw the towel at him.

"Hey!" he laughed as he caught the towel and she turned around. He got out of bed and draped the towel around his waist.

"I'll go down to the restaurant and rustle you up a cup of coffee while you shower," Kathe smiled. "I'll be back!"

"I'll have to start taking cold showers, if you keep this up," Yorg grinned. "I may be one of your best friends, but I am built a little differently than you," he snickered and walked toward the bathroom. "Make sure the coffee only has cream in it."

Kathe hurried down to the hotel restaurant. "Hey Kathe," Jordan called to her from his table.

"What are you doing still at the Gay Parí?" Kathe asked as she sat the coffees on his table. "I thought you would be at the new apartment."

"I can't this trip," Jordan replied. "I was over there some last night and earlier this morning. Yesterday's little surprise from McCollum got me thinking. Since this is going to be co-ed, we need some ground rules. We don't want any problems. The lease is in my name."

"Jordan, coming from you, I'm surprised!" Kathe laughed. "McCollum's not the only one with a reputation with the ladies. I've known you quite a while."

"That you have," Jordan smiled and sat back in his chair. "I've flown with McCollum for years. He can be quite persistent especially if he's been drinking. You need to be careful around him."

"I can take care of myself," Kathe reminded him. "I'd worry more about Carrie Anne, who's going to be living there. I don't know that rules will stop her from her games, but you can try."

"You've got a point," Jordan laughed. "Rules would be a waste of time."

Kathe reached over and gave him a kiss on the cheek. "Stop worrying so much. We are all adults and professionals. The apartment will work out fine."

"Will Yorg be going in with us?" Jordan asked.

"Oh, my gosh!" Kathe exclaimed. "I told him about it as he was getting in the shower," she said as she checked JAKE for the time. "I've got his coffee and it's getting cold. I want to take him to the apartment sometime this morning. How about in an hour or so?"

"That sounds fine with me," Jordan answered. "Call me when you're ready."

"You got it," Kathe smiled as she hurried to the elevator.

Yorg was dressed and waiting for Kathe when she arrived back at his room. "I just got off the phone with Ramsey," Yorg said as he reached for his coffee. "Why didn't you tell me you had a problem with your flight yesterday?"

"I haven't had time," Kathe replied. "A drunken guy pulled what looked like a clear knife on Carrie Anne."

"Are you sure it was a knife?" Yorg asked.

"It was a small clear object that broke the skin," Kathe explained. "I can't believe he's already back on the street," she said and reached for her coat. "No matter if the weapon was found or not, he had his arms around a flight attendant, midflight, threatening to kill her. Not to mention in a plane full of passengers."

"That's absurd," Yorg answered. "Ramsey said you have the original court order and JAKE proved it is a forgery."

"Yes, first I noticed the weight of the paper was wrong," Kathe continued. "JAKE scanned the seal and checked it with the Parisian court records. It is close, but not the same," she admitted. "I bet the councilor is a fake as well."

"Ramsey is still trying to track the councilor down," Yorg said.

"She's wasting her time," Kathe admitted. "He doesn't exist. Somebody's got pull in this area."

"Or with Saíde," Yorg added. "With everything Ramsey has found on this guy, it is not a question of if he'll come after you, but when," Yorg cautioned as he helped her with her coat.

"Saíde made a gesture threatening all of us as he was escorted off the plane," Kathe commented.

"You are the one who burned him with coffee," Yorg warned. "Didn't it cross your mind that he might come after you?"

"What difference does it make?" Kathe quizzed. "I'm always looking over my shoulder anyway," she stated as they headed toward the elevator.

"Was the knife ever found?" Yorg asked as the elevator came to a halt.

"Not to my knowledge," Kathe answered. "I have no idea where it could have gone. It was apparent he knew we didn't find it. That's why Jay, Jack, and I think he had it on him," she stated, walking toward the front door. "I better leave word at the front desk for Carrie Anne that I'm with you. She's with one of the gendarmes handling this case."

"No problem," Yorg stated as he watched her walk over to the front desk. He shook his head as several men took a second glance at her. She was very beautiful. Her shoulder length straight blonde hair was slightly curved. Her dresses were always above her knees showing her shapely legs. Time and age had not taken a toll on her. His thoughts drifted back to Flight #1237. Closing his eyes for a second, he remembered the terrorist shooting her.

"Hey guy, are you deep in thought?" Kathe asked, grabbing his hand.

"Maybe," Yorg bent down, kissing her cheek.

"What was that for?" Kathe asked, glancing strangely at him.

"Nothing, I just got caught in the clouds for a second," Yorg admitted as they headed out the door. "Ramsey told me yesterday that Alby was finally cleared to land in Russia. She wants your team to be on the first flight."

"This will be a feather in Ramsey's cap as she moves up the ladder," Kathe admitted, entering the revolving door. "I can't believe I am finally going to meet your sister Ylia. What's she like?"

"She is ten years older than me and raised me after our parents died," Yorg explained as they walked down the sidewalk. "She's a medical doctor at a hospital in Moscow. Ylia was responsible for my interest in weightlifting when I was in high school, and she never missed a match. I remember watching her study for exams in the bleachers glancing down at me with a smile," he said as they stopped at a crosswalk.

"I can't meet her empty handed!" Kathe exclaimed and pointed to a department store. "Let's go in for a minute. What does she like?"

"You don't have to get Ylia anything," Yorg protested as he held the door open.

"I'm not taking no for an answer," Kathe replied as they walked toward the Housewares Department. "Tell me more about her?" Kathe asked as she scanned the aisle looking for a gift.

"After Mikél died, she refused to let me hide in a bottle of vodka," Yorg sighed.

He looked into Kathe's eyes, "And she's not a bit like you. She works all the time and hates shopping."

"Well, I work a lot too," Kathe argued. "I pull double shifts all the time!"

"I guess in that case, you two do have something in common," Yorg smiled.

"And we both love you," Kathe answered, walking off, glancing over her shoulder. "I didn't know big guys like you blushed," she teased, stopping at a glass teapot. "Does she drink tea?"

"As a matter of fact, she does," Yorg remembered. "She has an old teapot with a cracked lid."

"Then a teapot is it!" Kathe exclaimed, picking up a clear glass teapot. "Do you think she'll like this one?"

"Yes, Ylia will like the plain one," Yorg admitted. "Her tastes are very simple, like mine."

"Great, I'll be right back," she said and paid for the gift. "Can you hold this for me?" Kathe handed the bag to Yorg as JAKE rang. "Hello, Jordan, yes...okay we will meet you in the hotel lobby in half an hour...Bye."

"We better hurry so we can drop the teapot off in the room," Yorg said, leading the way out of the store.

Forty-five minutes later, the three pulled up to the apartment building. "Au Summit L'Appartement," Yorg commented as he got out of the cab. "Nice building."

"It will be perfect for us to leave our personal things while we travel," Jordan stated as they got onto the elevator.

"I'm getting tired of living out of a suitcase, with just the bare necessities of life," Kathe quickly added.

"I've traveled with you," Yorg smirked. "You bring more than the bare necessities."

Searching for the key in his pocket as the elevator door opened, Jordan accidently bumped into two men hurrying inside. "Sorry," Jordan said. "I didn't see you."

"No harm done mate," replied the blonde man as the elevator door closed.

"Those must be the British Rock Stars that live across the hall," Jordan surmised as he walked over to the windows opposite the elevator. "Look at this view! You can see all of Paris!"

"It's beautiful," Kathe added, holding Yorg's arm. "Come on, I can't wait to show you the inside."

Entering the apartment Yorg was impressed. "This is very nice," he said, looking around.

"Look at this view from our own living room!" Jordan exclaimed. "This is breathtaking!"

"Just as I said, something a little more comfortable for us," Kathe remarked. "And it will be easier to unwind after long flights."

"That's exactly right," Jordan agreed. "Yorg, we can let you in on the apartment lease without having your name on it," he said as they shook hands. "I also forgot to tell you; there's a gym fully equipped downstairs, with a swimming pool and a sauna. We'll look at it on the way out."

They finished the tour of the apartment and headed out. Coming out of the elevator were some scantily clad women with full stage make-up. Jordan did a double take. "We're going to have interesting neighbors to say the least."

Arriving at the gym, Yorg was delighted, raising an eye as he scanned the gym. "I'm very impressed!"

"This is perfect for us," Kathe smiled. "I hate the thought of working out at the Gay Parí tonight. This gym makes theirs look like a retirement center," Kathe added as JAKE rang.

"Hey," Carrie Anne remarked. "Did you get my message I left at the front desk?"

"I sure did," Kathe replied. "I guess I better sleep in Yorg's room."

"Sorry," Carrie Anne giggled. "This guy is incredible. How would you like me to fix you up with a friend of his?"

"Not on your life!" Kathe stated firmly.

"You're all work," Carrie Anne snickered. "You need to learn how to relax, like me."

"That's not what I call relaxing," Kathe expressed. "I guess I'll see you sometime tomorrow," she cleared the line and looked at Yorg, "If we're going to work out before I hit the hay, we better get back to the Gay Parí."

"Okay, but next time we will really have a workout," Yorg replied as he scooped out the Nautilus equipment.

"I don't know why I didn't show you the gym first," Jordan joked. "I wouldn't have had to even show you the apartment," he said, opening the door, checking his watch. "I've got to get back. I'm meeting some friends soon."

"Yes, and we have to hit the gym," Yorg remarked. "I don't want our girl to get lazy."

After working out close to two hours, Kathe realized it was almost 10:00 pm. "Yorg, old buddy," she said, gasping for air. "I cannot do another thing. If we don't quit now, I won't have enough energy to walk to the elevator."

"You're right," Yorg agreed. "I'm bushed. I need to do this more often."

"You'll get to at the new apartment," Kathe added.

"Okay," Yorg said as he sat up on the weight bench. "Let's go upstairs," he said, grabbing his sweatshirt. "You're not too tired to give me a massage when we get upstairs, are you?"

"I think I can muster enough energy for that," Kathe said with a smile as she put on her cover up.

Back in the room, Yorg jumped in the shower first. "I'll hurry," he said. "I'm all sweaty." After five minutes, he came out of the bathroom with a towel draped around his waist.

"That was quick," Kathe said, watching the news. "I'm trying to see when this snow is going to stop. It's snowing heavily right now," she said, picking up her bathrobe on the way across the room. "I'll be right out. Get ready."

"No!" Yorg exclaimed. "I can't wait. You'll have to wash your hair and blow dry it, by that time I'll be sound asleep, and you'll get out of massaging me. I'm first then you can take your turn."

"But I'm sweaty," Kathe whined.

"Girl's glow," Yorg proclaimed. "Men sweat. I'm clean; now work your magic. I have not worked out like that in a while. I don't want to be sore," he said as he lay across the bed.

"Okay it's your call," Kathe said. She reached into her suitcase for her lotion and climbed up on the bed next to him. He turned over on his stomach and she began to rub his muscles.

"Hey, that's cold!" Yorg shouted as he rose from the bed.

"Get back down!" Kathe ordered. "You wanted the abridged version; you're getting it," she laughed, pushing him down with both hands. "It'll warm up quick!" She began with his shoulders continuing down his back and moving out to his aching arms. His triceps were bulging, she noticed as she formed her hands around them. "Gosh, your arms are bigger than any I've ever seen. Have you ever thought about competing again?"

"No," Yorg yawned. "I'm too old to compete."

"What does age have to do with it?" Kathe questioned. "You're in better condition than most people in their early twenties."

"Russia is very particular about athletes," Yorg stated. "They have to be young and strong."

"I'd put money on you against any young athlete," Kathe affirmed.

"I think you're just a little prejudiced," Yorg smiled. "Now this is the way to end a day. This makes the workout worth it," he yawned again.

"You don't feel as tight as you did," Kathe said ending with his neck. She heard a knock at the door. "That must be the extra blanket and pillow I asked for at the front desk."

After answering the door, Kathe grabbed her bathrobe, and headed for the bathroom. She didn't hear JAKE ring. But suddenly, she felt a very warm sensation under her right clavicle. "Ouch!" she cried as she snuck past Yorg, who was already snoring. She reached for JAKE on the nightstand. Why did I agree to put these gizmos in me? I'm not a guinea pig, she thought as she answered JAKE.

"There you are?" Keith answered.

"How may I help you after such a warm summons?" Kathe asked.

"I'm sorry I had to use your implant," Keith apologized. "You didn't answer JAKE. Your scheduled trip to Russia has just changed."

"What could be more important than the maiden flight to Russia?" Kathe asked.

"In between Ramsey's cussing and swearing, I gathered that someone over her head had ordered it," Keith explained. "She just told me to have you get over to Heathrow ASAP! You are on Flight #402 to London at Gate 16C. It looks like you are heading for the states. I'll call you with your assignment when you land. You better hurry it leaves in forty-five minutes."

"But I just got out of the gym," Kathe whined. "I haven't showered."

"Sounds like a personal problem to me," Keith laughed. "The clock is ticking," he said, clearing the line.

She rushed to change clothes.

Chapter 7

A Sudden Change of Schedule

Arriving back at Charles de Gaulle Airport, Kathe hurried into the terminal and found Gate 16C as JAKE rang. "Are you at the airport yet?" Ramsey inquired.

"Yes, I'm walking to the gate as we speak," Kathe answered. "I'm tired and need a shower," she whined.

"Don't worry!" Ramsey exclaimed. "You're not working this flight. You can take a short nap on the way to Heathrow. I need you rested and ready to go!"

"What do I do then?" Kathe asked.

"I need your talents and a special crew," Ramsey snapped. "Carrie Anne will meet you there. Jay and Jack will be flying with you also."

"Which special talent of mine are you talking about?" Kathe wondered.

"I'll tell you in London," Ramsey said, hanging up.

Entering the plane Kathe introduced herself to the senior flight attendant Terri Patterson, who was busy preparing for takeoff. Kathe stowed her luggage. She sat down and tried to get comfortable. "Here's a pillow and blanket," Terri said. "If there is anything I can do for you, let me know."

"I'm sure all I need is some sleep," Kathe replied. Terri reached into her apron and handed her a headset, "These are if you want to listen to the radio."

"Thank you, the music will drown out the engine noise," Kathe said, reaching for them.

"They're broadcasting a live Light Crimson concert tonight," Terri stated. "They are my favorite band. I had tickets, but due to a flu outbreak, I got called into work."

"I'll listen to the concert and keep you updated," Kathe said, putting on the headset, fixing the pillow and blanket.

"Thanks, that would be great!" Terri exclaimed as the engines of the plane began warming up. "I've got to go the passengers are starting to board."

The next thing Kathe knew, Terri was waking her. "We're landing in London in a half hour. You might want to wake up a bit before we get there. Can I get you coffee or hot tea?"

"Coffee would be nice," Kathe answered, sitting up.

"Here's a fresh cup for you," Terri said, handing her the cup.

"Thanks, that band was great," Kathe said, putting on the headsets. "I haven't had time to listen to music in a while. I'll see if it's still going on."

"Terri," Kathe called her over a few minutes later. "I just caught the end of a newscast saying that one of the members of Light Crimson fell off the stage during the last song."

"Who did they say it was?" Terry sighed.

"I don't know," Kathe apologized. "I'll keep listening. If I hear more, I'll let you know."

"Thanks," Terri answered as the pilot signaled for the flight attendants to get ready to land. "I've got to go."

"Don't worry, I have other ways to check," Kathe smiled. "I'm sure he'll be fine," Kathe said handing her the cup. Great, Kathe thought as the pilot cut off the radio station preparing for final descent.

Kathe thought I'll try the Internet, reaching for JAKE while the plane was taxiing to the gate.

"Any news?" Terri hurried back.

"No, I'm really sorry," Kathe said. "I'm sure it will be all over the Internet soon. Thanks for the flight."

"You're welcome," Terri smiled. "I hope we see each other again."

Just as the plane was docking, JAKE rang. "I landed about an hour ago and I've been waiting for you," Carrie Anne whined, looking toward the escalator. "Where are you?"

"I'm heading down the jetway," Kathe replied. "I need to find a place to shower before takeoff. Yorg and I just finished working out when Keith called and told me I had forty-five minutes to get to the airport. I changed clothes and left."

"That proves Ramsey's up to something!" Carrie Anne snapped, walking down the long hallway. "I'll meet you outside of the Alby Security Department."

"Where are you headed?" Terri asked, catching up to Kathe.

"I'm going to the Alby Security Department," Kathe answered.

"I'm going near there to catch my next flight," Terri admitted. "It's quiet a walk from here to the escalator upstairs."

"Just to let you know," Kathe declared. "I checked the Internet for any current information on Light Crimson and there's nothing there. It's usually there first. Sounds like their holding information from the public."

"I guess I'll find out tomorrow what happened when I read the paper," Terri sighed.

"They're supposed to be in America tomorrow to kick off their new tour," Terri remembered, rounding the last corner. "They may have to cancel a few days. Here you go. Take that escalator to the upper level. Alby Security Department is on your right. Hopefully, I'll see you again."

"Unlike you, I never know where I'm going," Kathe admitted. "I'm supposed to be on my way to Russia and got switched at the last minute. Nice meeting you. Bye."

Kathe entered the upper deck and headed for Alby Security Department down the long hallway. It was after midnight. She wanted to find Carrie Anne and a place to shower. Rounding the corner, she saw Carrie Anne looking a little blue.

"I thought you'd never get here," Carrie Anne sighed. "What took you so long?"

"This is a big airport and I landed about a mile from here," Kathe complained as her phone rang. "Hold this, please," she requests, handing her tote bag to Carrie Anne.

"I trust you had a restful flight to London?" Ramsey inquired.

"Yes, it was short, but effective," Kathe reported.

"I need you to find Carrie Anne," Ramsey began. "She should be..."

"I'm with her now," Kathe interrupted.

"I want the two of you to report to security and ask for Lt. Samuel Partridge," Ramsey ordered. "He will need to see your IDs and he will provide instructions. I'll call you on your flight and see how you're doing."

"What do you mean; how I'm doing?" Kathe inquired as Ramsey cleared the line. "That does it!" she looked at Carrie Anne. "Ramsey just skirted the reason why our schedules changed and hung up on me!"

"I know what you mean," Carrie Anne agreed. "I was supposed to go to Scotland this week and work my way back toward the states. It's not like Ramsey to switch flights like this."

"It must have something to do with Saíde," Kathe declared. "She wants us to report to security and ask for Lt. Samuel Partridge."

Entering security, they headed straight to the front desk. "Excuse me," Kathe interrupted. "I'm looking for Lt. Samuel Partridge."

"Lt. Partridge is in his office," Tyra answered. "May I give him your names?"

"I'm Kathe Tierney and this is Carrie Anne Mobley," she introduced.

"The lieutenant has been expecting you," Tyra sighed. "It will be a few minutes before he can see you. We've had a busy night and he's interrogating a suspect."

"I just flew in from Paris," Kathe stated. "I would like to freshen up before I takeoff again. We're going to run down to the employee's quarters for a few minutes."

"I guess that will be all right," Tyra commented. "I'll page you when he's ready for you."

"No problem," Kathe agreed, turning around. "Let's go."

"We've got to hurry!" Kathe exclaimed, checking JAKE for directions. "I've got only a few minutes to pull this off. It's to the left."

"There it is on the right," Carrie Anne stated. "There's a guard in the middle of the doorway. Excuse us."

"This facility is off limits!" he declared, crossing his arms.

"Off limits?" Kathe contested. "This is for employees of Alby."

"Yes, it is, but now it's not," he sneered. "It's off limits!" he sharply stated as Kathe read his badge. "You heard me, leave the area now!"

"Bad move buddy," Carrie Anne declared as she took a few steps back. "You don't know who she is."

"I don't give a care who she is," he took a step toward Carrie Anne.

Kathe reached for her badge and shoved it in his face, "Well now, Officer Tim Daily as you can see my Class 9A Security Clearance ranks way over your pay grade. Now, you move aside. I'm in a hurry!"

"Ms. Tierney," Officer Daily stammered, reading her badge, putting his hands down to his side. "I was ordered not to let anyone in here for another two hours."

"Well," Kathe sneered, "I'm ordering you to move out of my way!"

"Just a moment," Officer Daily pleaded as he knocked on the door. "Let me just check with their security."

"What seems to be the problem?" a man asked as the door slightly opened. "I told you no one is to come in here!"

"Yes sir, but this is Ms. Tierney," Officer Daily introduced. "She is a security agent who needs to use these facilities."

"I just flew in from Paris after a very busy day," Kathe added. "Without any notice, I was ordered to come here tonight with just a nap. I must work all night. I need to shower and change clothes."

"Just a minute, I have to clear this with Mr. Ross," he said, closing the door.

"I'm Payton Ross," he introduced, widening the door. "Our plane won't takeoff for another two hours and the boys are getting hungry. We'll take them down to get something to eat while you come in and freshen up. All but Joe, who is lying on the couch. He hurt his neck tonight on stage and took a pain pill. He doesn't feel like going anywhere."

"Thank you, I really appreciate it," Kathe said as they filed past her. "I'll keep an eye on him."

"She works here," Rick Travis grinned. "She worked a flight I was on a few days ago. I never forget a body like that."

"Mr. Travis, isn't it?" Kathe blushed as they walked off.

"Do you know who these guys are?" Carrie Anne screamed.

"Sh...," Kathe pointed to the one sleeping. "He's not feeling well. Don't disturb him."

"Do you know who he is?" Carrie Anne whispered.

"No, and I don't have time to find out," Kathe remarked, hurrying toward the showers, looking for a towel.

Following Kathe into the shower area, Carrie Anne hurried in front of her. "I can't believe you!" she said, pointing back toward the other room. "He's the lead singer for Light Crimson for goodness sakes!"

"I don't care," Kathe repeated. "I need a shower. I must go to work. I need a towel and there is no, read my lips N-O towel in here!" She said frantically continued looking under all the cabinets. "Carrie Anne, find me a towel. Go down to housekeeping and get one. I'm jumping in the shower, please hurry," she ordered, starting to strip.

"Can I keep him?" Carrie Anne requested, pointing toward the other room.

"No!" Kathe stopped. "Get out of here!" Kathe pointed her finger straight at Carrie Anne. "Don't you dare leave me here, see some good-looking guy, start talking to him, and forget all about me! Got it!"

"Kathe Tierney do you honestly think that I, your very best friend would leave you stranded?" Carrie Anne questioned.

"Yes, I do!" Kathe proclaimed. "I'm desperate! Please hurry back!" Kathe begged, finishing stripping, and got into the first shower by the door.

As Carrie Anne left the room, she bent over Joe and gave him a kiss on his forehead. Walking to the door, she blew another kiss at him, "If only you were awake, I'd show you Alby in a whole new way!"

Kathe had just finished washing her hair when she heard the first page. She quickly reached up and turned off the water. "Carrie Anne," she called. "Carrie Anne, where's my towel?"

Carrie Anne did not appear.

"Come on Carrie Anne, where is my towel?" Kathe demanded and turned the water back on to warm up. Turning it off again, she yelled, "Carrie Anne where are you?"

Silence filled the entire area. She started to get worried. "Carrie Anne, if this is a joke, I don't think it is funny!" Kathe exclaimed as she suddenly had a sinking feeling in the pit of her stomach. Again, security paged her. Carrie Anne got sidetracked, she thought. I'll kill her! "Carrie!" she desperately called again. Before she could finish a white towel appeared through the opaque glass door. She let out a sigh of relief, "Carrie Anne, I'm sorry for what I was thinking about you."

A strange British male voice answered her back. "I'm sorry, but your friend hasn't come back yet. All I have for you to use is my shirt. It's clean. I just put it on less than an hour ago when I left the hospital."

"I can't believe this is happening!" Kathe exclaimed. "Here I am soaking wet and embarrassed to open the door!"

"Please take my shirt and use it," he insisted. "I must lie back down on the couch. My neck is hurting so badly, I can't stand it."

"You're the man on the couch?" Kathe quizzed.

"Yes, I am," he answered. "Please lady, I can't stand up much longer. Your friend didn't come back, and I'm trying to help you."

"Thanks," Kathe sighed, reaching around the door, grabbing the shirt, and quickly closing the door as the man disappeared.

"I can't dry off on a silk shirt this expensive!" Kathe exclaimed without thinking. "It will ruin the shirt!"

"It's okay," he replied. "I don't mind," he said, trying to sit down on the couch. "It hurts to sit down," he whined. "Use the shirt. I'll have my manager get me another one out of my suitcase when he returns."

"Give me a minute and I'll help you," Kathe offered. "Let me get something on first." She fumbled for her short, silk, beige chemise in her suitcase as security paged her again. "That's me they keep paging. I'm supposed to be in the security department for a special assignment!" When things could not get worse for her, she whimpered, "Oh, no! I've ruined your shirt for good." She could not believe what had happened. What a time for Mother Nature to come, "No, not now!" She reached for her purse checking for European change but couldn't find any. "Oh, no! This stupid machine doesn't take quarters!" Kathe screamed as she hit the machine several times.

"Ahem," he cleared his voice with only his arm stretched around the corner. "Here's a quid that fits into the machine"

"I'm so embarrassed!" Kathe snapped. "I can't believe this is happening to me! At least, I will never see you again! I mean," she fumbled for words. "I'm so embarrassed! For years I have never depended on any man. Now you've rescued me twice in five minutes," she reached for her phone, complaining as security paged her again. "This is Tierney. I'll be in your office in fifteen minutes," she cleared the line.

"You wouldn't believe the day I've had," Kathe stated as she stood before him in only her chemise. "Let me help you sit down," Kathe said as she skillfully supported his head with her left hand. "Just relax your neck muscles and lean on me. I've got you," she said as she helped him sit down and then lie back down on the couch. She placed a pillow under his neck for support. "I can't believe how much you're suffering, and still got up to help me. I can't thank you enough."

"I couldn't leave a damsel in distress," he smiled. "I can't believe I fell off of that stage tonight!"

"You're the member of Light Crimson that fell off the stage?" Kathe questioned, rearranging the pillow to make him more comfortable. "I just left one of your biggest fans. She had tickets to the concert and got called into work. She'll never believe I ended up meeting you. Thank you for coming to my rescue. Are you feeling better now?"

"Yes, I do," he admitted as she walked to the other room to get dressed. "This is the best my neck has felt, since I left the hospital."

"You need to see a chiropractor and massage therapist when you get to your destination," Kathe advised as she finished getting dressed. "They can relieve your neck problem." Security called her again. "Give me five minutes," she said and hung JAKE on her belt. She quickly used her blow dryer and styled her hair. "I'll put my make-up on in the plane," she said, walking back into his room, and put on her red jacket. "How do I look?" she asked smoothing down her collar.

"You look like an angel," he sighed.

"Now let me pay you for that silk shirt and a quid," Kathe said and pulled out her checkbook.

"Put it away," he grinned. "The pleasure was all mine."

"That was an expensive shirt," Kathe insisted, sitting down, and opening her checkbook.

"Worth every pound," he smiled, remembering the way she looked in the shower.

"Well, if you won't take my money," Kathe smiled as she put it back in her bag. "I guess it's goodbye," she said as she gathered her things. She stood before him, "It was nice meeting you, even though it was awfully strange to say the least. Remember to see a chiropractor and a massage therapist; they'll help you recover quickly from your injury," she said, walking to the door. She turned back around one last time. "Maybe we will meet again in the clouds someday," she smiled as she opened the door and left.

"Wouldn't it be something, if I am her special assignment," he thought. "They were flying in a special flight attendant to assist me on the plane. She must be the one."

Chapter 8

A Special Assignment

Carrie Anne was standing next to the elevators talking to his band members when Kathe found her. "Thanks for the towel ex-best f-r-i-e-n-d!" she snapped as she grabbed Carrie Anne by the arm and dragged her away.

"Oh, no! I forgot all about you," Carrie Anne sighed looking back at the band members. "I hope to see you again," she called back to them.

"I can't believe you left me stranded!" Kathe sneered as they rounded the corner heading for the security department.

"I'm sorry," Carrie Anne apologized. "Did you see how dreamy Rick Travis is in person? And why didn't you tell me you met him?"

"I did not meet him," Kathe objected. "He was on a flight I worked a couple of days ago and gave me his autograph."

"Can I, have it?" Carrie Anne begged. "Please!"

"I gave it to Kayla Martin," Kathe stated. "Come on before we're both unemployed," she said, hurrying into security and stopping at the front desk.

"You gave it away?" Carrie Anne complained. "What's wrong with you?"

"I'm back to see Lt. Partridge," Kathe said to Tyra at the desk.

"I've been paging you for quite a while," Tyra stared over the top of her glasses.

"I got stranded, you might say," Kathe glared at Carrie Anne.

"Lt. Partridge cleared his schedule for you," Tyra stated. "I'll show you to his office," she stood up, motioning for them to follow her.

Stopping at his office door, Tyra knocked first and then opened it. She held it open for the two girls. "Here are Kathe Tierney and Carrie Anne Mobley," she introduced and closed the door behind them.

"I have a special assignment for the two of you," Lt. Partridge announced. "Actually, it's for Kathe."

Kathe held out her hand to shake his, "I'm Kathe Tierney."

"You are usually the chief purser," Lt. Partridge stated. "On this flight, Carrie Anne will take that role. The Rock Band Light Crimson is leaving for the United States. They usually travel by private jet. Their jet has engine problems, and they must be there tomorrow. I had to put them aboard one of ours. We need your team to make sure none of the passengers bother them. There is another problem. One of them," he stopped and looked through papers on his desk, "was injured tonight and needs you to take care of him."

"I'm not a nurse!" Kathe protested. "I'm a security agent!"

"I know who you are," Lt. Partridge declared. "I'm just as surprised by this as you are. Someone higher than Ramsey insisted on you taking care of him. Here are your papers. Head for Gate 112A, Flight #581. You leave in twenty-five minutes. I suggest you hurry."

"Now, I know why Ramsey wouldn't tell me about this assignment!" Kathe fumed as they walked to the gate. "This is a far cry from my job description!"

"Ramsey usually sends you into a situation with guns blazing," Carrie Anne giggled. "I think the Ole

Girl is losing her mind."

Stowing their bags, Jay and Jack greeted them, "Hey what's the big emergency? One minute we're told we're flying with Yorg to Russia," Jack complained. "The next minute, Ramsey's practically having a cow that we can't get to Newark fast enough."

"I know what you mean," Carrie Anne affirmed. "I was having dinner with my inspector friend and had to leave before my entrée arrived."

"I'm not buying the scenario that Ramsey needs a security team to babysit a rock band," Kathe stated as she checked the time. "We had better get ready for takeoff."

Kathe slowly walked upstairs shaking her head thinking, what am I going to do. I thought I would never see him again. This can't be happening to me. She prepared one of the couches for him to lie down on after takeoff. She located some towels to moisten and place in the microwave to lay across his neck to relax his muscles. "Well, I'm finally using something I learned from my time stuck with Peter," she thought. "He was a lousy husband, but a great orthopedic surgeon. I do know how to relax muscles. I thought I'd never do this kind of work again." She heard the elevator and held her breath as the door opened. The second most embarrassing moment of her career stood before her.

"Well, here we are again," Joe grinned. "Who would have thought I was your special assignment?"

"You two know each other?" Jack asked as he glanced at Kathe.

"We met earlier this evening," Joe smiled, "in the employee's quarters."

Noticing the gleam in his eyes, Kathe could feel her face getting redder by the second. "I thought I'd never see you again!"

"That sounds like my cue to clear this area," Jack chuckled as he helped Joe to his seat. "I'm going back downstairs, where it is safe," he said as the pilot signaled ready for takeoff. Payton, Joe's manager was just coming up the staircase to check on him. "Sir, you have to get back to your seat," Jack insisted. "The pilot just signaled we are clear to depart."

"Just one minute, I need to check on Joe," Payton insisted as he walked over to Joe. "How are you feeling?"

"I've had better nights but," Joe smiled as he glanced toward Kathe, "things are looking up." The plane jerked as it began to back up.

"Sir, you must get to your seat now," Jack demanded. "The tug is pushing the plane backwards."

"Are you sure you're going to be okay up here?" Payton asked. "Maybe I better sit with you?"

"Payton I'll be fine," Joe insisted. "I'm going to take another pain pill and rest. There's nothing you can do for me," he said trying to lay his head against the headrest.

"We have never been formally introduced," Payton said, turning to Kathe. "I'm Payton Ross, Joe's manager. If Joe needs anything, come, and get me."

"I'll take good care of him," Kathe assured him. "You must get to your seat now. The plane is preparing to taxi to the runway."

"I'm on my way," Payton answered as Jack escorted him to his seat.

Kathe felt so awkward. She knew her face was as red as a beet. She couldn't believe the way her luck was running. Her mind was racing with all kinds of embarrassing thoughts. After all, he had seen her in the shower.

Joe broke the ice, "I guess tonight has been a shocker for both of us."

47

"It has been a very embarrassing moment for me," Kathe replied.

"Don't worry, I won't tell anyone," Joe grinned. "The glass was opaque. I only saw your distorted shape. I've met a lot of women, but not too many shy ones. You left the lounge in such a hurry, and I was in such pain, I couldn't remember your name. I'm Joe Sherrod."

"I'm Kathe Tierney," she introduced, noticing the pain in his face. She reached for a pillow and placed it behind his neck. "Does this help take the tension off your neck?"

"Yes, thank you," Joe sighed. "You seem to be good at taking care of me. Are you a nurse?"

"No, I'm not," Kathe answered as the engines began to pick up speed. "I better sit down and buckle up," she said as she quickly sat next to him.

The plane roared down the runway and in seconds they were up in the air in the cold darkened January night.

"What happened at the hospital?" Kathe asked.

"They took x-rays," Joe explained. "The doctor said there were no broken bones. He said it is strained muscles and prescribed pain pills. He said it would last a few days. We had already planned to come to the United States to promote our new album. Our private jet is down, so here I am with you."

"It's strange," Kathe admitted as the pilot signaled that it was safe for the attendants to move about the cabin. "I was supposed to be on Alby's maiden flight to Russia and was rerouted," she stated as he tried to reposition his neck. "Would you be more comfortable lying down?"

"Yeah, I did feel better on the couch in the lounge," Joe admitted.

"I have a couch set up for you," Kathe smiled. "Do you think you can walk with just me helping you or should I get one of the male attendants?"

"I can walk okay, if you can help me get up," Joe said as he unbuckled his seatbelt.

"Go ahead and lean your weight on me," Kathe replied as she helped him stand up.

"I'm up," Joe said as he leaned against her. "Are you alright with this? I don't want to injure you."

"No, you're fine," Kathe confirmed as she skillfully helped him walk to the couch. She helped Joe lie down the way she did in the employee's quarters.

"Thank you, I feel much better," Joe grinned at her.

"May I get you something?" Kathe asked as she covered him up with the blanket.

"Not right now," Joe answered. "I just need to rest."

"If you need anything, just let me know," Kathe replied turning to leave.

"Don't go," Joe requested. "I like talking with you. How did you learn how to take care of injured people?"

"Let's just say in my previous life, I had different skills," Kathe admitted.

"What kind of previous life are you talking about?" Joe quizzed.

"I was married to a surgeon," Kathe stated.

"I didn't realize you were married," Joe said glancing at her left hand.

"I'm not anymore and never again!" Kathe exclaimed.

A sigh of relief came over the star. "Good. I mean...I'm sorry to hear that," Joe stuttered. "I mean...I'm glad you are not married. I mean...are you divorced?" He couldn't believe he asked that either.

"I guess I am," Kathe giggled as JAKE rang.

"How's the superstar doing?" Ramsey asked worried that she had an injured passenger on one of her planes.

"He's resting," Kathe assured her.

"Be careful with him," Ramsey warned. "I don't like hauling injured passengers around. If there is any change in his condition, call immediately and I'll have the pilot land near the nearest hospital. We don't want to get sued."

"He'll be fine," Kathe reassured her. "He just strained his neck muscles."

"That's good to hear," Ramsey sighed. "The reason that this trumped the maiden flight to Russia is Saíde. I have been working on his profile. I think he is about ready to strike out at our airlines again. Make sure the others are aware of this situation. I've got another call," Ramsey said, clearing the line.

"How can you use your cell phone during a flight?" Joe asked as she put JAKE back on her belt.

"It's a perk of my job," Kathe answered as she pondered what Ramsey said.

"What did you mean before your call by saying you guess you are?" Joe quizzed.

Wondering what Ramsey meant by 'ready to strike' Kathe suddenly realized Joe was talking to her, "What?"

"You said you guess you are divorced before the phone rang," he said. "What did you mean by guess?"

"Oh," Kathe looked away for a second. "I am divorced. I never like to use the D word. It is kind of depressing."

"I'm sorry," Joe apologized. "I didn't mean to make you feel bad."

"You didn't," Kathe smiled as Carrie Anne poked her head upstairs. "It was a long time ago."

"How's it going?" Carrie Anne asked as she joined them.

"Okay," Kathe replied. "My passenger is settled in for the flight."

Carrie Anne hurried over to her whispering, "Guess who I have a date with tomorrow night?"

"I have no idea," Kathe smiled. "I thought you were depressed about your Paris inspector?"

"Nothing mends a broken heart like a date with a superstar!" Carrie Anne whispered.

"Yorg is right about you," Kathe said as she shook her head. "You're one of a kind," she said with a smile. "You have the ability to bounce from man to man without blinking an eye."

Carrie Anne glanced over at Joe, "Want to make it a double?"

"No way, besides he hurt his neck," Kathe whispered.

"Maybe, he'll feel better by tomorrow night," Carrie Anne said, shrugging her shoulders.

"Carrie Anne, no way!" Kathe whispered back with force.

"One of these days you'll change your mind," Carrie Anne proclaimed and then walked over to Joe. "Payton asked me to check on you. How are you feeling?"

"You can tell him I feel the same," Joe shared. "I just need to rest."

"Where are you staying in New York?" Carrie Anne asked.

"I don't know," Joe maintained. "Payton makes all the arrangements. I just go where he says."

"I just wondered if by any chance, you were staying at the Hotel International," Carrie Anne continued. "That's where Kathe and I usually stay when we're in town. I'll ask Payton. I have to get back downstairs," Carrie Anne said as she walked toward the stairs.

"Wait!" Kathe hurried over to Carrie Anne and whispered, "Tell the guys that Ramsey is assembling us because she suspects we're going to have a problem with that passenger from the other night."

"What kind of problem?" Carrie Anne whispered.

"She has reason to believe that he will strike back at the airline," Kathe whispered.

"What does that mean?" Carrie Anne asked.

"She didn't say," Kathe answered. "Just tell them to be aware of their surroundings and that goes for you too."

"Great, this is what I get for flying with you!" Carrie Anne blurted out. "Just when I land a date with a rock star, you screw it up! I'll tell the guys," she whined and hurried off.

"May I get you something to drink?" Kathe asked as she walked back to Joe.

"I'll take a Coke," Joe replied as he tried to get more comfortable. "What did Carrie Anne mean by saying, that's what she gets for flying with you?"

"Don't worry about it," Kathe smiled. "I'll be right back with your drink," she said as JAKE rang.

Chapter 9

Getting Acquainted

"I have Jeannie Rafferty on the line for you," Ramsey said. "Do you have time to talk?"

"Sure, put her on," Kathe replied as she poured a Coke. "Jeannie how are the kids?"

"They're fine, but they miss their mother, especially Joey," Jeannie reported. "He had another bad dream."

"Oh, my poor baby," Kathe sighed. "Let me talk to him," she said, handing Joe his drink. "Joey," she said as she walked away from Joe. "Jeannie said you had a bad dream."

"Yes," Joey pitifully sniffled. "I was on the bottom of the pool at Daddy's house again and nobody was there."

"Pumpkin, you're okay," Kathe comforted. "That won't happen again. Bob and Jeannie take very good care of you. They won't take you over to Daddy's house again when he's not home. You don't need to worry about that, I promise."

"She scares me Mommy," Joey said, sniffling harder.

"Pumpkin, she won't hurt you," Kathe assured him. "Mommy will make sure of that. I need to talk to Jeannie. I'll see you as soon as I can. I love you, put Jeannie on the phone," she said as a tear ran down her cheek.

"Same old nightmare!" Jeannie exclaimed. "Same evil Stepmother!"

"Tell Peter that since Joey is still having nightmares, I'm contacting my attorney," Kathe proclaimed. "I'm asking the judge to amend his orders to make Peter's presence mandatory at all visitations. To further ensure Joey's safety, I'm also requesting that Pete and Heather be with him at every visit. That will alleviate Joey's fear of being alone with Helen. Also tell Peter, if this doesn't work, I will request court-monitored visitation."

"My pleasure!" Jeannie beamed. "I'll let you know what Peter says. Goodbye."

After calling her attorney, Kathe returned to Joe. "I'm sorry I had to take that call and that it took so long."

"I didn't mean to eavesdrop on your conversation," Joe apologized. "I never would have guessed you have three children," he said remembering how she looked in the shower. Three kids, no way with that body, he thought.

"I didn't realize I was talking so loud," Kathe stated. "You have good hearing. Are you finished with your drink?" She changed the subject as Joe reached to hand her the cup. As he did a sharp pain went down his arm. He pulled his arm back quickly. "Is it time for your pain medication?"

"Yes, but it makes me drowsy," Joe admitted. "I don't want to take it."

"We won't be in Newark for hours," Kathe advised. "Why don't you take it?"

"I'd rather talk with you," Joe managed a smile. "You seem to be helping me more than the pills do."

"Let me do something that will help relax your muscles," Kathe said and walked to the galley. She put a wet towel in the microwave for three minutes. She took it over to Joe. "Can you lay face down for a while?"

"I don't know," Joe answered. "I haven't tried."

"I need you to take your shirt off," Kathe suggested. "Is that okay with you?"

"That's fine with me," Joe snickered as he unbuttoned his shirt. "I think that's only fair."

"It's for medical purposes only," Kathe declared. "Let me help you," Kathe said and helped him turn over. She placed the pillow under his forehead, so he could lay face down and still breathe. Then, she placed a dry towel around his neck and the hot towel over it. "This is moist heat. It will help relieve the tight muscles in your neck."

"How do you know it will work?" Joe questioned.

"I just do, let me know if it gets too hot," Kathe warned.

"You're not leaving, are you?" Joe inquired.

"No, I'll be right here," Kathe assured him. "Maybe if you feel up to it before we land, you can sign an autograph for my friend that missed your concert. I'm afraid I left her worrying which member was hurt tonight."

"Deal," Joe said as the heat began taking effect. "This feels good."

"I knew it would," Kathe smiled.

"Have you ever been to one of my concerts?" Joe asked.

"No, to tell you the truth I work all the time," Kathe replied.

"Don't you ever go home?" Joe quizzed.

"Not too much," Kathe sighed. "Ramsey, my boss keeps me busy."

"Don't you live with your kids?" Joe questioned.

"Is the towel still warm?" Kathe questioned avoiding the subject.

"Yes, it feels good," Joe sighed. "You avoided answering my question?"

"You sure ask a ton of questions," Kathe replied as she took the towel off his neck. "What is your life like? I mean as a Rock Star."

"I'm like you," Joe confirmed. "I work a lot and I'm not home much."

"Are you married?" Kathe asked.

"No!" Joe declared. "I was once, but like you, I'm not interested in it anymore."

"I'm just going to massage the muscles in your neck," Kathe explained as JAKE rang.

Noting it was Yorg, she put JAKE on speaker and started working on Joe's neck, "Hey, you're on speaker I'm working."

"Where are you headed?" Yorg asked as Joe raised an eyebrow surprised to hear a Russian male voice.

"I'm en route to Newark," Kathe stated. "Where are you?"

"I'm heading to Russia," Yorg explained. "I'm taking the teapot to my sister. I didn't have anywhere to leave it. I couldn't find Jordan to put it in the apartment and I haven't had time to get a key."

"That's fine," Kathe replied. "Please tell Ylia that I'm sorry I can't meet her this trip."

"Why did Ramsey change your team's flight plan?" Yorg inquired.

"Currently, we're working on a special assignment for her," Kathe explained.

"What kind of a special assignment?" Yorg asked her.

"Whom are you talking to?" Joe asked.

"Who's that?" Yorg insisted. "I thought you were at work."

"I am," Kathe said. "I'm massaging a passenger."

"Like you massage me?" Yorg demanded.

"No, silly!" Kathe laughed. "I'm at work. I'm taking care of a passenger, who was injured and must be in New York in the morning."

"You're not a nursemaid!" Yorg declared.

"Since when did you start caring what I do at work?" Kathe laughed.

"Since you started massaging male passengers," Yorg muttered. "Ramsey asked me to do some checking for her when I get to Russia. Can you walk away from your special assignment for a minute?"

"Yes," Kathe replied. "I'll be right back," she told Joe as she walked away and took JAKE off speaker. "I can talk now."

"Ramsey believes Saíde was in Russia yesterday," Yorg explained. "It seems that a general and his secretary were murdered. Their throats slit. In addition, on the same day they found a flight attendant at the airport the same way. She thinks Saíde could be dealing with a questionable renegade general. That is why I was not rerouted with your team," he said as he picked up the Glide Slope. "I had better get back to work. I have to check my approach plates."

"Yorg, if Ramsey's suspicions are true, we need to be careful," Kathe cautioned. "She is never wrong."

"Watch your back," Yorg warned. "You're the main one he's after!"

"I always do," Kathe replied and cleared the line.

A long silence followed as Kathe returned to work on Joe's neck. "Are you okay?" she asked as she rubbed his neck and shoulders.

"Please don't stop," Joe sighed. "That really feels good...Who's the Russian?"

"He's a pilot," Kathe answered. "Let me help you turn over. I need to work on you face up."

"Okay," Joe said as she helped him slowly turn over.

"Do you live with him?" Joe inquired as she continued to work on him.

"Boy, you don't miss much, do you?" Kathe laughed. "Are you writing a book?"

"Maybe or I might be writing a song," Joe stated. "I do that for a living you know."

"Four of us just rented an apartment in Paris," Kathe stated. "We get tired of staying in hotels. We can't have any personal things with us."

"Steve just signed a lease on an apartment in Paris," Joe realized. "Wouldn't it be funny if it were the same building?"

"I have found in my many travels that the world is a small place," Kathe added as JAKE rang again. "Hi, you're on speaker phone," Kathe said. "I'm massaging your special assignment."

"I have a phone call from Colorado that you probably won't take," Ramsey stated.

"Who is it?" Kathe asked as she gently pulled up on Joe's neck.

"It's Peter," Ramsey sighed, "he says he needs to talk to you. He said it's very important. I told him it better be for real."

"You know I don't talk to him," Kathe insisted. "Tell him to go through my attorney."

"I already did," Ramsey admitted. "It's your call, what do I do with it? I'm off duty in a few minutes."

"Tell him you're transferring his call to me," Kathe smiled. "Put him on regular AT&T line and send the call to the usual phone booth in the Fiji Islands," Kathe said smiling at Joe. "I saw it on a commercial once."

"You got it," Ramsey laughed and cleared the line.

"Isn't Peter your ex?" Joe asked.

"Yep!" Kathe smiled. "And he is about to be a very aggravated ex," Kathe laughed as she finished working on Joe. "That should make you feel better," she concluded and placed the pillow back under his neck.

"I do feel much better now," Joe smiled as he moved his neck around.

"You probably should get some rest," Kathe offered. "I'll leave you alone for a while."

"I can't rest," Joe contested. "You didn't answer my question," he grinned as he glanced over at her.

"What question was that?" Kathe asked as she stood over him.

"How close are you to that Russian pilot?" Joe questioned.

"That's one question you'll just have to wonder about," Kathe smiled as she shrugged her shoulders.

Chapter 10

An Unthinkable Twist

The pilot signaled they were an hour from Newark. By this time, coffee had been brewing, and the smell carried throughout the plane. Kathe looked at her wrist, "Darn, I keep forgetting I broke my watch. What time is it?" she asked Joe.

"It's 11:00 am in London," Joe said. "How did you break your watch?"

"It's a long story," Kathe answered. "Are you ready for a cup of coffee and some breakfast?"

"I'd love it," Joe smiled, stretching a bit. "I didn't eat much last night."

"It's been quite a trip," Kathe added. "That would make it 5:00 am local time. We'll be landing at Newark in a little less than an hour."

"I like night flights to the United States," Joe shared. "I usually sleep all the way here and then I'm ready for a long day at the studio. I can't believe I stayed awake the whole time. I really enjoyed talking with you. Come to think of it, I'm not even a bit tired."

Jay came up with a tray for Joe. Payton was right behind him, "I see you're feeling a lot better."

"Yes, I do, thanks to Kathe," Joe declared as he sat up and reached for his shirt. "I don't know how she does it. She put some heat on my neck and massaged it. It hardly hurts now," he said as he easily moved his neck around.

"How much do I owe you for Joe's massage?" Payton asked as he reached for his wallet.

"It's included in the price of the ticket," Kathe shied back placing Joe's plate on the tray.

"We'll be landing in Newark soon," Payton said to Joe. "The press will be there, and you know the fans will be too. Think you can handle it?"

"Sure, I can," Joe said, glancing at his food.

"Great!" Payton replied. "Now I can have my coffee," he said as he paused for a second. "I worried all night for nothing," Payton turned to Kathe. "It seems you are a miracle worker. The doctor said it would take days for Joe to recover and I may have to cancel some of our engagements. You put him back together in a few hours. And to think that when he told me that we would have to wait for them to fly you to London, I almost put us on another flight. That would have been a huge mistake!" he snapped, walking to the steps. He stopped at the top of the steps and turned around, "a huge mistake!"

"Anyone could have done what I did," Kathe replied as he walked downstairs.

"Do you believe in fairy tales?" Joe asked eager for Kathe's response.

"I used to believe in fairy tales with knights in shining armor, but not anymore," Kathe stated.

"I wouldn't be too sure of that," Joe smiled. "From the way you talk, I think you still do," he said with his boyish charm.

"What's that supposed to mean?" Kathe said, glancing at him.

"I just think you still believe in happily ever after," Joe insisted. "It's okay, I'll keep this secret too," he smiled and winked at her. "No one else could have helped me the way you did. You have a natural healing talent. Maybe you should go back into the health field."

"You really don't know me," Kathe smiled, "looks can be deceiving."

"You have a way of never finishing a conversation," Joe declared. "Are you aware of that?"

"I've been told that before," Kathe replied.

"I suppose by the Russian pilot?" Joe questioned.

"What is it with you and the Russian?" Kathe laughed.

"You won't tell me what he is to you," Joe said as he tilted his head.

"No, and I'm not going to," Kathe insisted. "Be careful moving your neck around. You still need to see a chiropractor and a massage therapist."

"Do you know a good chiropractor in New York?" Joe asked.

"As a matter of fact, I do," Kathe said. "I'll give you one of his business cards. I have one in my purse," she said as she went to the galley to get it. "You should make an appointment with him today," she said, handing him a card. "Most of Alby goes to him. He's good."

"Thanks," Joe turned the card over and looked at the back. "There's nothing on the back of the card."

"So," Kathe looked at him.

"I at least expected your telephone number," Joe said, holding the card up to her.

"What for?" Kathe asked.

"Most girls usually give it to me without asking," Joe smirked still holding his hand out.

"I guess I'm not most girls," Kathe declared.

"What if I need to talk to you again?" Joe questioned.

"I think the odds of us ever seeing each other again are next to none," Kathe admitted.

"You're not going to give me your phone number, are you?" Joe quizzed.

"No, you are here in the states for a while," Kathe smiled. "I'll probably stay here one day and go back to Europe."

"You did say it's a small world," Joe reminded her.

"I did say that," Kathe agreed. "But it's a big airline," she insisted with a smile. The pilot signaled final approach into Newark.

"At least," Joe said as he handed her back the card, "Would you please write something for me to remember you by?"

Reluctantly, she reached for the card, "Only if you autograph this one," she hands him another card, "For my friend Terri Patterson." As he autographed the card, she thought for a second then wrote, 'I hope all your days are flight worthy, Kathe Tierney, Alby Airlines'.

They exchanged cards as Kathe sat down next to him. She quickly put her seatbelt on, and the plane touched ground. Jay poked his head up the staircase as the plane taxied to the gate. "Payton wanted me to tell you to sit tight until the other passengers are off the plane. He wants you to make a grand exit. The press will be here."

"Okay, thanks," Joe said as he reached over and kissed Kathe on the cheek. "I'm going to miss you. I haven't said that in over a year. Not since I told our first lead guitarist, Paul Leven, farewell when he died. I guess my falling off the stage had a purpose after all."

"What purpose?" Kathe asked as she glanced at him.

"Meeting you," Joe admitted.

"Joe, let's go," Payton interrupted as he poked his head up the stairs. "Come on the press and your fans are waiting!"

Looking back over his shoulder winking at her Joe said, "It is a small world. I'm sure I'll see you around."

"Don't hold your breath," Kathe insisted. "It's a big airline!"

Carrie Anne passed Joe coming up the stairs, "Come on, I've got a date...oh boy...Do I have a date!" She noticed Kathe's eyes were a little moist. "What happened to you?"

"Nothing, nothing at all," Kathe said as a tear ran down her cheek.

"That's not true, what happened?" Carrie Anne insisted. "You're almost crying."

"Joe really turned out to be a nice guy," Kathe admitted.

"I hope Travis isn't that mushy!" Carrie Anne exclaimed.

"You have a date with Travis?" Kathe asked, raising an eyebrow.

"I sure do!" Carrie Anne gasped. "Isn't he gorgeous? And he's not married, I already asked."

JAKE rang as Kathe and Carrie Anne joined Jay and Jack by the lower-level galley. "How long before you get here?" Ramsey asked.

"We're just leaving the jetway," Kathe explained. "It will be a few minutes."

"I can hardly hear you," Ramsey said. "What is that noise in the background?"

"Fans screaming for their favorite rock stars," Kathe answered as she stopped and watched Joe for a second.

"I forgot about them," Ramsey said, rolling her eyes. "How is the one who was hurt?"

"He's doing much better," Kathe shared as they went up the escalator to the terminal. "He's signing autographs as we speak."

"I knew you could handle it," Ramsey confirmed. "Hurry up and get to my office with your team," she said and cleared the line.

As Kathe hung JAKE back on her belt, she looked down the staircase hoping to catch a glimpse of Joe one more time. Security was tight around them. Screaming fans surrounded the band members as they signed autographs. As Kathe watched for a second, Joe seemed to sense her presence and looked up where she was. Both of their faces lit up as they waved to each other. She did the Sign of the Cross over her heart and walked away. Joe watched until Kathe was out of sight, then he turned back to signing autographs.

Chapter 11

An Unusual Layover

Entering the security department heading straight for Ramsey's office Wanda was the first to greet them. "Welcome back team," Wanda smiled. "The Ole Girl just asked me to locate you, you're late."

"How can we be late," Jack declared. "We came straight here."

"I know," Wanda gritted her teeth. "It's her; walk softly she's trying to quit smoking, again."

"Not again!" Carrie Anne rolled her eyes. "I'm staying out here with Wanda. Tierney hurry up and let's get out of here before she sees me."

"I got ya," Kathe snickered as she walked in the office with Jay and Jack.

Ramsey was at her desk engrossed in a conversation with Lt. Jaco. "Just a minute," she signaled holding the phone away from her face. "I don't have time to talk right now. Go get some rest and I'll see you tomorrow here at 0800. And bring Lover Girl with you."

"That does it for us," Jay said, opening the door. "We're exhausted."

"See you tomorrow," Kathe yawned.

Carrie Anne was busy telling Wanda all the details of her meeting Rick Travis. "That was quick," Carrie Anne said as she glanced up.

"Ramsey's on the phone," Kathe answered. "She told us to get some rest," Kathe said, turning to Wanda. "See you tomorrow at 0800. Good luck with the Ole Girl. Maybe she'll make it this time."

"I'm not holding my breath," Wanda complained. "This last time I had to give her a pack during Flight #1014. When I did, she ripped them up and yelled at me not to give them to her no matter what. The next thing I knew she threatened to fire me if I didn't give her another pack."

"Hang in there," Kathe smiled. "If anybody can do it, you can," Kathe picked up her luggage and they left the office.

The cab pulled up in front of the Hotel International. "I'll hurry in and check on our room," Carrie Anne said as she jumped out of the cab.

"I'll pay the cab as usual," Kathe sniped as she glared at Carrie Anne, reaching for her wallet. She paid the driver and found Carrie Anne at the front desk in a heated discussion with the clerk. "What's the matter?" Kathe snickered, joining her in a long line.

"I'll tell you what's the matter!" Carrie Anne snapped.

"What's wrong?" Kathe asked again as the clerk helping her left the room.

"I'll tell you what is wrong!" Carrie Anne sneered.

"Well?" Kathe prodded.

"Well, we have no, watch my lips, 'N-O', Room in this Hotel!" Carrie Anne exclaimed.

"Why?" Kathe asked.

"Why?" Carrie Anne screeched. "You want me to tell you why?"

"Yes, I do," Kathe laughed forgetting how tired she was. "I haven't seen you this riled in quite some time."

"What are you laughing at?" Carrie Anne demanded.

"Not what, who," Kathe smiled. "I'm laughing at you."

"And why, pray tell, are you laughing at me?" Carrie Anne shouted getting into her face.

"Because you sound like a Baptist minister when you get all worked up," Kathe laughed.

"Well, like one, I get my point across!" Carrie Anne exclaimed, pounding the bell on the counter.

"Yes! You sure do," Kathe continued laughing as the clerk came back with his supervisor.

"Miss Mobley, I'm afraid I need to apologize to you," the supervisor said. "For some unknown reason we have had a mistake in reservations. I have you down as coming in on Friday. Today is Wednesday and we are all booked up."

"I called from over the Atlantic Ocean about four hours ago confirming our reservations," Carrie Anne stated. "The person I talked with said we were confirmed for today and they would see us in a few hours, not Friday!"

"Like I said madam," he replied. "There has been a mistake in reservations. I am sorry, but your room won't be ready until Friday," the agitated supervisor strained his voice trying not to shout.

"Is the rock group Light Crimson staying here?" Carrie Anne asked.

"I'm sorry," he grinned. "That is privileged information. We cannot give out any information about other guests."

"Can you tell me if Jay Towers or Jack Davies checked in yet?" Carrie Anne asked.

"Again madam," he smiled. "I cannot give out any information about our guests. Perhaps, I can give you the name of another hotel?"

"I can find the guys," Kathe said, dialing Jay. "Have you checked into the hotel yet?" She listened and repeated for them to hear, "Hotel International, room 621. We're in the lobby. Carrie Anne and I will be right up," she cleared the line and glared at the supervisor. "They're in your hotel, room 621, if you want to know. Thank you for messing up our reservations and all the 'UN-help' you've given us. Carrie Anne let's go!"

"Do you believe that idiot?" Carrie Anne asked Kathe as she pressed the button for the elevator.

"What do you want to bet our Friday reservations will be messed up also?" Kathe declared. "Sixth floor, let's go."

Carrie Anne knocked as Jack opened the door, "What's up?"

"It's a long story," Carrie Anne whined. "Remind me never to tell you about it. We don't have reservations here until Friday."

"And we probably won't have reservations then, thanks to Carrie Anne performance," Kathe relayed.

"Do you two need to stay here?" Jack asked.

"Yes, do you guys' mind?" Kathe asked.

"No, you know that we don't mind," Jay answered. "We heard you were staying with Carrie Anne. Jack heard her making plans with her newest lover boy, so we got the suite with two rooms and four beds."

"Thanks, I knew I could count on you guys to look out for me," Kathe stated.

"I've got a date in a few minutes," Carrie Anne smiled. "I need to use the bathroom first. I probably won't be in till late," Carrie Anne said, grabbing her stuff and heading for the bathroom.

"Where are you meeting Travis?" Kathe inquired.

"I told him I'd meet him in the lobby," Carrie Anne called over her shoulder.

"You're lucky you did that," Kathe announced. "I doubt the front desk will give any messages to room 621."

"Why is that?" Jay asked as Kathe headed for her room. "Carrie Anne started a ruckus at the front desk a few minutes ago. We're lucky we weren't thrown out of the hotel."

"Thanks for getting the front desk mad at us Mobley!" Jay snapped.

"Don't mention it!" Carrie Anne yelled and began singing a Light Crimson song in the shower.

Kathe changed her clothes, took the blanket and a pillow off the bed. She threw it on the floor between the wall and the bed. She poked her head out the door, "Remember we have to be at Ramsey's office tomorrow at 0800, good night." She set the alarm for 6:00 pm. and closed her eyes.

Chapter 12

Trouble at Rizo's Jewelry Store

Right on schedule, JAKE's alarm went off. Kathe heard the guys stirring in the next room. "Want to go to dinner with us?" Jay asked as she poked her head out the door.

"Sure," Kathe agreed. "I need to look for a watch if I have time. That idiot broke mine the other night when he grabbed me."

"Is Carrie Anne back yet?" Jay asked.

"No, I don't expect her; she's in love again," Kathe chuckled using JAKE to Google the nearest jewelry store in Manhattan.

"I made dinner reservations at 7:00 pm at the Olive Garden in Times Square, is that okay?" Jack asked.

"Sure, I'll meet you there," Kathe agreed as she read the options. "I'm in luck. There's a jewelry store just down the street. Call me when they're ready to seat us and I'll hurry over," Kathe answered and rushed to the shower.

Forty-five minutes later, reaching to open the door at Rizo's Jewelry a clerk stopped Kathe. "Madam, I'm sorry it's 7:00 pm and our store is closing for the evening," he said with a rather shaky voice and perspiring profusely. "Perhaps, you can come back tomorrow?"

"I checked online," Kathe replied, glancing around the inside of the store. "It has your store hours listed to 9:00 pm," she declared quickly noting the other clerks were standing back against the walls, instead of close to the display cases.

"We've changed owners," he said, widening his eyes as he looked straight into hers. A bead of sweat was beginning to drip down his forehead. "I'll have to remind him to change the website."

"I see you still have a few patrons inside," Kathe winked at him and pushed past him. She pressed the top left panic button on JAKE alerting control as well as the top right button putting it on speaker.

Keith Gordon, second in command at Alby Security was on duty when the panic button on JAKE sounded. Dr. Sydney, Alby's computer specialist had just entered Keith's office to talk with him. Muting his phone, "Kathe's in trouble again," Keith told Dr. Sydney. "Listen."

"I only have a second," Kathe said. "My husband Jay is next door at the Olive Garden waiting for me. I saw online that you have the Motiva Watch that I have been looking for. I just need to check the price. I want it for my birthday next month," she said, glancing quickly through the cases and stopping at the Motiva display.

Dr. Sydney hurried over to Keith's computer. He began overriding some of JAKE's communication software. "Now, you can call Jay and we can talk without them hearing us," he stated as he typed more commands for the system. "I'm recording the phone call. This is exactly what I need to finish the upgrade on JAKE."

Keith quickly called Jay Towers, "I'm patching you through to JAKE. Kathe's in trouble."

"Jack and I are waiting for her," Jay said, motioning for Jack to come over to him.

Kathe carefully noted that one of the customers motioned for the old man to go behind the counter. "Oh, here it is! I want that one! May I try it on? I must check it out quickly, before my husband Jay misses me. I told him I was going to the restroom. The wait at the Olive Garden is long so I ran over here," she said as her team listened. "Can you tell me the price? Not that one...yes, that one, with the diamond in the middle...Are you alright sir? You seem to be sweating quite a bit. Jay does that when his sugar is low; he's a diabetic. I have a packet of his insulin paste in my purse. Do you need it?"

"She's in trouble alright," Jay explained. "She knows we're waiting on her at the Olive Garden."

"I'm showing her at Rizo's Jewelry by Olive Garden in Times Square," Dr. Sydney said, locating her with her GPS, and widening his range for the nearest Precinct. "I'm calling NYPD Precinct #20 and I'll conference them with you. Keith, you are connected to them," he said, typing on his computer.

"Jay and Jack go to ear buds," Keith commanded as he picked up his phone.

"We're leaving the Olive Garden," Jay reported as they hurried away putting their ear buds in place. "We're on it!"

"This is Keith Gordon, second in command at Alby Airlines in Newark Airport," he introduced. "We have a possible 459 going down at Rizo's Jewelry next to the Olive Garden Restaurant in Times Square. Alby Airlines Special Security Agent Kathe Tierney is on location. Two other agents were at the Olive Garden. They are en route to the scene. I am connecting you with live feed from Kathe's cell phone. You can only hear what we do."

"Alby Control, this is Sgt. Ron Stiletto," he said. "We're listening and sending Lt. Petrosky and Commander Rieker of Swat to meet with your people on scene. Keep us online. Can she handle the situation?"

"Affirmative," Keith replied. "One of my agents just informed me that they were going to do a walk-by to assess the situation."

"Sir, do you need some insulin paste?" Kathe asked again and reached into her purse.

"Stop right there!" shouted a man behind her as he shoved his gun in her back. "The old man told you the store was closed! You should not have pushed past him and come in here," he declared and turned to one of his companions. "Put the closed sign up and make sure he locked that door! We don't want anybody else walking in on us!"

"Oh, my God!" Kathe exclaimed. "You have a gun in my back! Oh! Please don't shoot! I just got back with my husband! We've been separated for four long months! I love my husband and our six beautiful children!" she began to cry hysterically holding up her hands.

"Put your hands down!" he ordered. "We don't want anyone passing by to get suspicious," he glanced at the front windows. He watched two men walk up to the left window showcase. "Turn around slowly and act like you're with me!"

"She's hysterical!" Stiletto retorted. "She can't handle it!"

"Sgt. Stiletto it's an act to buy time, she's single," Keith reported. "She's telling us there are four assailants inside and six hostages plus herself," Keith relayed as Kathe turned around slowly facing her assailant. She noted Jay and Jack standing at the window.

"Alby Command this is Lt. Petrosky with NYPD," he joined the conversation. "We are going to set up a command post in the building across the street on the second floor. Give us a few minutes."

"Affirmative," Keith replied. "Jay, why don't you keep looking at the showcases for a few minutes? NYPD needs time to set up."

"Copy that," Jay said pretending to show a watch to Jack. "We have Tierney in sight. There is a

Caucasian male in his early thirties, about 5-foot-ten with dark brown hair holding her right arm and keeping her close to him."

"She said he has a gun to her back," Keith relayed. "Do you have a visual?"

"Negative," Jay answered. "Wait a minute, his other hand is in his coat jacket and yes, now that he's moved sideways it appears he's holding a small revolver."

"They are amateurs," Jack added, looking away from the window. "Look at the other three men. They all have one hand in their coat pockets."

"How many other people do you see inside," Keith asked.

"Just like Tierney said," Jay answered. "It looks like six hostages and four assailants," he confirmed as Jack pointed to another item in the showcase.

"This is Lt. Petrosky, we're in place," he advised them. "I see a woman with short, blonde hair in her 30's facing a man in a dark suit holding her arm, is that your agent?"

"Affirmative, my other agents are the two men at the right window showcase watching the situation," Keith reported. "They have just confirmed that there are four assailants and six hostages. They also noted the man holding on to our agent is holding a small revolver in his coat pocket. They have no idea we're on to them. Request my agents help you with this matter. Kathe works with them, and they know each other's moves."

"Have them report to Swat Commander Rieker in our Swat Team's van located in the alley, just north of the building," Lt. Petrosky approved.

"Roger that," Rieker acknowledged, "they are to work with our team as per your orders."

"I'll send them over," Keith stated. "You two have my permission to join their Swat Team."

"Affirmative, we are on our way," Jay answered as they walked away from the window.

"I have the store," Lt. Petrosky assured them as they hurried into the alley.

"I'm Alby Airlines Special Agent Jay Towers," he introduced showing his badge to Commander Rieker, waiting for them outside the van.

"I'm Alby Agent Jack Davies," holding up his badge.

"I'm Commander Rieker, come in gentlemen," Rieker said as he opened the van door. "I know that you have just assessed the situation."

"Yes, Alby's Special Agent Kathe Tierney is inside the jewelry store," Jay confirmed. "She alerted Alby Control of the situation about 1845 this evening.

"How did she alert control?" Rieker questioned.

"We're not sure yet," Jay replied. "What we do know is that there are four perpetrators and six hostages. They appear to be amateurs. Do you have the layout of the store? We can show you where the people are positioned inside."

"Yes, I do," Rieker stated, leading them to a table with his men already studying the building plans.

"This first case in the front on the left is where Tierney is standing with one of the assailants," Jay pointed out. "He is holding onto her arm and has a gun in his coat pocket."

"Can she handle this kind of pressure?" Rieker's sergeant asked.

Jay glanced up to make eye contact with him, "I assure you, she's the best thing that ever happened to those hostages."

"It appears that they are mostly concerned with the front entrance," Jack added. "There are two men strategically placed as customers by the right front jewelry case."

"There is a young black male about 17 years old guarding the back door," Jack continued. "His eyes look glassy as if high on drugs."

"Are you suggesting we should enter from the rear?" Rieker asked.

"Yes, I am," Jack declared. "They positioned themselves out in the open. The hostages are the ones behind the cases. We enter from the back. The hostages simply fall to the floor to take cover."

"I agree with Jack," Jay affirmed. "We should have plainclothes officers walk by the store to keep down suspicions that we are on to them. We can signal them when we are ready, and they can enter from the front. The surprise at the back door will help keep down the casualties."

"Even though we cannot talk with her," Jack admitted. "Tierney is highly skilled in situations like this. She can hold her own with the man holding a gun on her."

Muting all of NYPD from Alby's team, Dr. Sydney stated, "Jay when you are ready, I will let Tierney know you are coming in via her implant."

"Good idea," Keith agreed.

"It's too bad Kathe can't converse with us via her implant," Dr. Sydney noted. "This is the second time in a week Ramsey, and I needed to talk with her and couldn't."

"Roger that," Jay agreed as Dr. Sydney unmuted the call.

Picking up his cell phone Rieker continued, "Petrosky, as you heard, the Alby agents explained the positions of the people inside. From what they say a surprise at the back door is the best option. They noted a young black male apparently on drugs watching that entrance. They stated that Tierney is highly skilled and can handle herself. When we enter from the back door, your people can enter from the front near the showcases," he said as Jack pointed to the diagram. "They suggest we should have some of our people walk by and window shop. That will distract them until we get into place."

"I'll send some of my people to pass by," Lt. Petrosky said, motioning for them to leave.

"I'm sending my men to check the status of the alarm on the back door and get it opened," Rieker stated, signaling them to leave.

"Keith, do you agree with us?" Lt. Petrosky asked.

"Affirmative, I trust my people's judgment," Keith answered.

"Roger that," Rieker agreed as they left the van. "We will let you know when we're ready," Rieker stated to Lt. Petrosky as they hurried to join his men.

When they arrived, the alarm was already off, and the back door was opened. One of Rieker's men was still trying to pick the lock to the showroom door. "I got this door," Jay whispered, pulling a wire out of his phone, and placing it into the lock. They watched as Jay's phone instantly opened the lock. Rieker signaled Jay thumbs up on the technology.

"We're ready," Rieker announced to Lt. Petrosky. "Are your men in place?"

"Copy that," Lt. Petrosky acknowledged peering through his binoculars at his men. "Alby Control my people are in place. We're ready to enter."

"Copy that," Keith said as Dr. Sydney used Kathe's implant to signal her.

"Ouch!" Kathe screamed grabbing her clavicle as everyone heard her on speaker.

"What's wrong with you?" her assailant asked as she began to panic, shaking her head and breathing very hard. Jay and Jack drew their guns.

"You're not going to kill me, are you?" Kathe wailed. "I've just got back with the man I love," she began to cry profusely, reaching out to him with both hands. "It's taken me so long to get him back!"

"Shut up!" he ordered pulling her closer to him, noticing people at the window. "Because of you I can't have my people behind the counters," he barked forcefully. He was getting more nervous. "You there," he said to the old man behind the counter as he reached in his pocket. Again, he glanced around making sure no one was watching. He handed a black cloth bag to him. "Start placing the jewelry in this bag and don't touch that silent alarm or you're dead!"

"What about our bags Michael?" the young black male asked, holding up his bag.

"Don't say my name and get back to the door!" Michael ordered, glancing at his accomplice, and then the people outside. "The plan was to have our people change places with the clerks and get the stuff. This stupid woman," glancing at the window he raised his gun and smashed Kathe in the face across her left cheek.

Falling backwards into the glass counter Kathe grabbed her cheek. Her facial expression changed from fear to anger. "Michael, that is going to cost you!" Kathe whispered.

"Kathe knows you are coming in," Keith confirmed.

"What did you say?" Michael asked in disbelief as she stood upright. Jay signaled to Rieker to get ready.

"I said," Kathe rubbed her cheek noting his finger was off the trigger, "Michael, that's going to cost you now!" She screamed as she kicked her surprised assailant between his legs.

The front and rear doors burst open simultaneously. The young male panicked and raised his gun at Rieker, who shot him. The two at the other counter raised their hands in surrender.

Kathe's assailant stunned by her actions, fell forward grabbed his crotch with his left hand and raised his gun at her. Quickly kicking the gun out of his hand, she reached behind her back and pulled her gun smashing him across his face. She bent over him and grabbed him by the front of his shirt. She looked him straight in the eyes and pointed her gun directly at his forehead. "Michael, the next time you hit an innocent woman, you better make sure you know who you're hitting. Looks can be deceiving!"

"Do you need any help?" Jay asked, hurrying over to her.

"Not with this amateur," Kathe chuckled. "Well Michael, what do you think about your first and last robbery?"

"He'll have lots of time to think about it," Jack laughed as he joined them. "Michael, do you know how long you're going up the river?"

"You and your buddies are facing," Jay sighed, "kidnapping, robbery, and assaulting an officer with a deadly weapon for starters."

"Your young friend is going to live," Jack laughed. "You are all going to jail together."

"I'll take it from here," Rieker stated as he joined them and pulled out his handcuffs. "Nice job lady. You had control of this situation the entire time. We could use an officer like you on my Swat Team."

"Thanks, but you couldn't afford me," Kathe said as Rieker handed Michael over to another officer.

"There's an ambulance outside," Jay said, looking at the cut on her cheek. "You need to put something on that cut."

"Is it bad?" Kathe questioned as she looked around for a mirror.

"If it makes you feel any better," Jack joined her. "Your new friend Michael has a worse one."

"Oh, I made sure of that!" Kathe beamed looking in a mirror on the opposite case as she reached for JAKE. "Keith thanks for your help."

"Anytime, Lady," Keith confirmed. "You guys get out of there before the press starts taking pictures. I had the Olive Garden hold your reservations. Have a nice dinner and be here at 0800," he reminded.

"You got it," Kathe said, clearing the line, and motioning for the guys to leave.

Lt. Petrosky was just entering the store with the press interviewing him. "Wait a minute, Ms. Tierney," Lt. Petrosky said walking up to her as Jack took off his jacket and held it in front of the camera.

"You can't do that!" screamed the camera operator trying to maneuver around him.

"No cameras!" Jay joined in by pushing another camera to the side. "Turn them off. She's off duty and wants nothing to do with this."

"No cameras they said!" Rieker ordered joining them. "Turn them off! This woman wants anonymity. She just saved the lives of all these people. That is the least we can do for her."

"I need you to give us a statement on what happened tonight," Lt. Petrosky said as the cameras clicked off. "I want to thank you for your brave assistance."

"Keith at Alby Control will handle anything you need from us," Kathe assured them. "It's your collar. I was just in the right place at the right time."

"Wait a minute!" Lt. Petrosky insisted. "I didn't say you could leave."

Kathe flashed her badge, "You have no jurisdiction over us. We're out of here," she proclaimed as they walked out the door.

"Please wait, Madam!" called a voice running up behind them as they hurried away. "Madam, I want to thank you!"

Kathe stopped as the old man hurried over to her. "I'm Victor Rizo. I want to thank you for saving my family and my store. You put yourself in danger. How did you know that we were being robbed?"

"Let's just say," Kathe smiled, "today was your lucky day. I just needed a watch."

"That's right, the Motiva with the diamond," his face lit up. "Come back to the store and pick out the one you want. It's a gift."

"No gift is necessary," Kathe said, glancing at Jay and Jack. "We're glad your family is safe," she smiled as they walked away.

Chapter 13

Looking for Carrie Anne

JAKE's alarm sounded early the next morning as Kathe sat up on the floor checking to see if Carrie Anne was back yet. Her cheek was still stinging as she remembered last night's events. As she got into the shower, the water began to revive her. She hurried washing her hair wondering if Carrie Anne remembered the meeting at 0800. She finished and wrapped a towel around herself. She walked out to the other room where the smell of coffee was getting stronger. "Thanks for the coffee," Kathe said as Jack held up the morning paper.

"You made the headlines," Jack read. "Mysterious woman stopped jewelry heist in Times Square."

"Thank God, they kept my name out," Kathe said reading the article.

"Thank God, and Ramsey," Jay chuckled. "She's got pull in this area. I've already talked with her this morning. If we hurry," he checked the time. "We'll have time to grab some breakfast at McDonald's on the way. I could use a breakfast burrito and hash browns," Jay said, walking toward the bedroom.

"If you're finished in your bathroom, may I use it?" Jack asked holding his clothes.

"Sure, go ahead that way we can hurry and have time to eat," Kathe said. "I'll dress in the room."

Kathe was admiring herself in the mirror as Jack came out of the bathroom, "Looks great to me."

"Why Jack," Kathe blushed, "how long have we worked together?"

"Oh, I'm not blind," Jack grinned. "I do know a beautiful woman when I see one."

"Thank you," Kathe finished tugging at her skirt. "Do you think this is too short?"

"No!" Jack exclaimed. "It looks great just the way it is on you!"

Coming out of his bedroom Jay said, "You guys ready? I'm starving for a burrito."

Kathe looked at her wrist out of habit, "I keep forgetting I don't have a watch. What time is it?"

"It's 7:00 am," Jay answered. "We have just enough time to eat and head for the airport. I'll get our coats."

"Has Carrie Anne called you?" Kathe asked, checking JAKE for missed calls as she reached for her coat.

"I haven't heard from the girl," Jay replied.

"And I'm not missing another meal looking for her," Jack declared calling her. "It went straight to her voice mail," he reported and left a message. "It's almost 0800. Do you know where your boss is?"

"You're wasting your time," Kathe remembered. "She lost her cell phone the other day. I don't think she's got another one yet. She was in too much of a hurry to meet Travis."

"Not good," Jay retorted. "Here we go again! If we show up without Golden Girl, Ramsey's going to have our heads!"

"I have an idea," Kathe said, reaching for JAKE, and calling control, "Ramsey."

"Tierney where are you?" Ramsey demanded.

"Do you happen to know in which New York hotel Light Crimson is staying?" Kathe asked.

"No, why do you want to know?" Ramsey questioned.

"I have a feeling Carrie Anne is with one of them," Kathe cringed.

"Do you mean to tell me Carrie Anne isn't with you?" Ramsey howled.

"Welllll," Kathe hesitated as the line instantly cleared.

"I guess we better go to a bar, instead of Mickey D's," Jack sighed. "It's going to be one of those mornings."

"This is not the way I wanted to start our day," Kathe stated A JAKE rang. "It's Ramsey!"

"They are staying in the same hotel as you," Ramsey confirmed. "They are in suite 2101. Get up there and see if she is with them. Look Tierney, I need her here now!"

"I'm on my way," Kathe sighed. "Wait a minute. How did you find out?"

"I called the front desk," Ramsey stated.

"I thought they weren't allowed to give out information about their guests!" Kathe snapped.

"You're not as persuasive as I am," Ramsey smirked. "I simply told them that I would declare that hotel off limits to Alby personnel! Believe me that statement gave me clout."

"I'm sure it did," Kathe laughed. "I'll be there at 0800 as requested with Golden Girl!" she said, putting JAKE back on her belt. "You two go ahead and eat. I'll go get Golden Girl and meet you at the airport."

"Do you want us to get you something?" Jay asked.

"I'm fine," Kathe answered. "After this, I'd probably get indigestion anyway," she said, grabbing her purse, and opening the door.

"Good luck on your search for our Golden Girl," Jay said. "I feel so sorry for you. You always must find that irresponsible girl! I'm sick of always having to make excuses for her. Ramsey's not the most pleasant person to be around when Carrie Anne doesn't show up on time."

"Will you guys do me a favor?" Kathe asked as she put her coat over her arm.

"Sure what?" Jack asked. "Have Wanda issue Carrie Anne another cell phone."

"Will do; she better not lose this one," Jay said, handing Kathe a key. "Here's an extra key to the room."

"Thanks," Kathe said, pressing the up button as they pressed the down.

Inside the elevator, Kathe pushed the button for the twenty-first floor, she thought of how many times she's done this. The door opened and out she went looking for suite 2101. She knocked on the door. There was no answer. She waited a moment and knocked again. Still there was no answer. I hate doing this, she thought. I never know in what condition I will find her. She crossed her fingers and knocked on the door again.

This time a very tired Collin Jones dressed only in his boxers answered. As he opened the door, he walked back to the couch and laid down by the girl. He did not say a word to her.

"Hey, is Carrie Anne Mobley here?" Kathe asked.

He did not say anything.

"Excuse me, is Carrie Anne Mobley here?" Kathe asked again.

Again, Collin ignored her closing his eyes.

Kathe walked over to the couch, bending over him, "Hello...Hello...is Carrie Anne Mobley here?"

"I think so, there's a woman with Travis," Collin sighed.

"That would be her," Kathe affirmed. "Where are they?"

"In one of the rooms down the hall," Collin answered. "Now please go away, I'm tired."

"I'm sorry for waking you," Kathe apologized. "Thanks for the info," she shuttered looking around the room in disbelief at the mess. There was a long hallway with several bedrooms off the living room. A large window from floor to ceiling was at the end of the hallway. Great, Kathe thought. Where do I start first? She could be anywhere. With my luck, she will be in the last room. How do I get myself into these situations, she thought as she walked down the hallway to the first door? Must have been one heck of a party. She pushed the first bedroom door open and peered inside. Never again, she thought to herself, I'll never do this again!

Kathe went to the next bedroom. Quietly turning the doorknob, she peered inside the room as a familiar voice said, "What are you doing here?"

Kathe was so embarrassed! She could not believe it was HIM! How in the world could she keep running into this man? "I...I... I'm looking for Carrie Anne," she stuttered as he turned on the light.

"I think she's in the next room," Joe said, pointing to the left and starting to get up.

"Oh, please," Kathe began. "Don't get up on my account...I mean some guy sleeping on the couch in the front room let me in...I must find Carrie Anne...we're late for a meeting. I didn't mean to interrupt you."

"Wait," Joe begged, reaching for his pants on the floor.

Kathe closed the door and hurried to the next room. She opened the next door, finding Carrie Anne sound asleep next to Travis. She shook Carrie Anne.

"Kathe, what are you doing here?" Carrie Anne whined, turning on the lamp.

"I'll tell you what I'm doing here!" Kathe whispered angrily. "I'm keeping your fanny out of trouble! And getting embarrassed, I might add!"

"What time is it?" Carrie Anne asked, holding her head.

"It's 0740 am," Kathe whispered as Travis woke up.

"What's the matter?" Travis asked shielding the light from his eyes.

"Carrie Anne is supposed to be at a meeting," Kathe explained. "I'm sorry for waking you," she said, turning her back to Carrie Anne. "Do you remember where we are supposed to be at 0800 this morning? And with whom?"

Carrie Anne's eyes widened with fear. "Oh, no! Ramsey's office!" she jumped up and started frantically looking for her clothes. She grabbed her head again. "Oh, my head is killing me!"

"That a girl," Kathe grinned. "I'm glad you're back among the living. At least, I have the satisfaction that you have a bad hangover."

"What's the big hurry?" Joe asked, standing in the doorway.

"We have a meeting at 0800 with our boss," Kathe answered not turning around to look at him.

"Some idiot pulls a knife on me on a flight," Carrie Anne blabbed as she quickly dressed.

"Carrie Anne, watch what you say!" Kathe warned her.

"What happened?" Joe asked, walking over to Kathe and facing her.

"We're not supposed to talk about it," Kathe answered as she avoided eye contact.

"Not with me, but with that Russian?" Joe questioned.

"That Russian as you put it," Kathe said, looking Joe straight in the eyes, "is a close friend of mine."

"How do I get to be in that category?" Joe asked, folding his arms across his chest.

Pointing at his room, "Not like that!" Kathe exclaimed as she pushed past him. "Travis I'm sorry I woke you up. Carrie Anne, are you coming?"

"Yes," Carrie Anne whined, glancing at Travis. "Travis, I'm sorry I have to leave; you are awesome!"

"You too," Travis sighed, reaching to turn off the lamp.

Leaving the room Kathe glanced back at Joe, "I'm glad your neck is better!" Quickly stepping over a mess on the floor, Kathe hurried to the front door. Carrie Anne was right behind her straightening her clothes. Joe just stood in the hallway and watched them leave.

In the hallway on the way to the elevator Kathe declared, "Carrie Anne, I will never pull your tail feathers out of any room again! I don't care if you are fired! That was the most embarrassing thing that has ever happened to me in my entire life!"

"Really?" Carrie Anne questioned, pointing her finger at Kathe. "If I didn't know better best friend, I'd swear you were falling for Joe Sherrod!"

"Don't you dare say that?" Kathe declared. "This time you've gone too far!" she looked at her wrist. "What time is it?"

"It's ten minutes after eight," Carrie Anne whined. "Oh, no, Ramsey is going to fire me this time for sure!"

They hurried outside and hailed a cab. In a half hour, they pulled up in front of the airport. Kathe knew Carrie Anne was scared this time; she actually paid for the cab. Arriving at Ramsey's office, Wanda warned them, "I'd tip-toe in; she's on day three, again."

"Great," Carrie Anne said under her breath walking into the office. "I've got one awful hangover and a boss having nicotine withdrawals!"

"Well, Ms. Mobley," Ramsey stopped the meeting. "I'm sure glad you could finally join us. I hope I didn't inconvenience you in any way," Ramsey sarcastically noted as she threw a cell phone on the table in front of her. "Don't lose this one! And always keep it on you! Do you understand?"

Taking their seats next to Jay and Jack, Captains Roberts, and Munroe, nodded a hello to them. Capt. Michaels looked at Carrie Anne giving her the good job signal. She looked back at the playboy pilot and wrinkled up her face at him.

"When you two are finished making faces at each other!" Ramsey sneered. "We will continue our meeting. Alby has a serious problem. Rhasheéd Saíde, the man who allegedly had a knife at Carrie Anne's neck is suing Alby for $10,000,000.00. It is imperative that we find the knife. When I talked with our attorney, Mr. Ellis said that when he spoke with each of you separately, you all described the exact same knife. Sometime during the coffee incident and Jay grabbing him, the knife was lost. Kathe, tell me what happened."

As Kathe went over the details of the flight Yorg called.

"Yorg, what have you got?" Ramsey answered. "You're on speakerphone. I'm in the meeting with the crew from Flight #1014. I believe this concerns all of them."

"Your hunch was right," Yorg admitted. "It seems that Saíde was in Moscow. One source told me that a man fitting Saíde's description was seen in the area moments after Gen. Lundidivocof, and his secretary were found stabbed to death in his private office. The general was working in conjunction with Gen. Yetsun, overseeing a project that I worked on years ago concerning a revolutionary prototype weapons system. At the airport, just after a man fitting the description of Saíde was spotted, a flight attendant was found dead in the men's bathroom with her throat slit. I'm on my way back to Newark. I will see you soon," the line cleared.

"During my profiling of Saíde," Ramsey continued. "I discovered that this man appears to have Mafia ties in the U.S. and Europe. I don't believe he is just a serial killer. He must be working for someone. I just haven't figured out for whom yet. However, I do believe the killing of young women is his MO." Picking up a photo from her desk and throwing it down on the table, "This is Rhasheéd Saíde, remember his face. He uses many aliases and disguises. He is easily lost in a crowd. I'm circulating his picture to all airlines. His profile shows him to be a very arrogant assassin. I believe that is why he blatantly told you as he left the plane that we haven't seen the last of him."

While Kathe was at the meeting, Joe was sitting alone at the end of the hallway, staring out the window at New York City. His mind kept drifting back to the flight to Newark. He thought about how Kathe took care of him. He smiled as he remembered how they had first met at the airport, never imagining he would ever see her again. Then, he remembered this morning when she pointed toward the room where the girl, he was with still slept. The words, not like that, played repeatedly in his head. He started shaking his head no, as he thought to himself, I could never be interested in anybody ever again, not after... He stopped himself. He could not stand to think of her name.

"Did some girl in a short dress come in here this morning or was I dreaming?" Collin interrupted as he sat down next to him.

"What do you mean?" Joe questioned.

"Man, early this morning," Collin explained. "I was sleeping on the couch in the front room, and someone kept knocking on the door. I think she was looking for the girl Travis was with last night or did I dream the whole thing?"

"She was no dream," Joe confirmed. "She was the flight attendant who took care of me on the flight over here. She came for Carrie Anne. They had a meeting this morning."

"You are a lucky stiff!" Collin smiled. "I would have fallen off stage too, if I knew someone who looked like that would be taking care of me."

"I can't forget the way she looked at me this morning when she saw me sleeping over there." Joe pointed toward the bedroom.

"Is her name Kathe?" Collin asked.

"Yeah, why?" Joe quizzed.

"Travis and Carrie Anne were talking about a Kathe who works with her," Collin stated. "Carrie Anne said she was staying with two guys she knew. So, I don't think she could have been too disgusted with you."

"Maybe you're right," Joe sighed.

"Let's go down and get something to eat. I'm starving," Collin said as he stood up and stretched. "I'll see if Troy and Babs want to grab something to eat with us."

Getting a little hungry, Kathe looked down at her wrist. Darn, she thought. I can't keep checking my phone every time I need to know the time. I must get a new watch somehow today, as Ramsey finally concluded the meeting.

"I don't have to remind you not to talk to anyone outside this room, except Mr. Ellis, Lt. Jaco or myself," Ramsey cautioned. "I don't want to start a panic. Is that clear?" Ramsey asked, glancing around the table. "I want all of you to be especially mindful of your surroundings. If you so much as think that someone is watching or following you, you are to call 911 immediately. I cannot emphasize this enough.

This man WILL come after us! You are dismissed, all except Tierney. I need to talk to you."

"I'm going back to the room and get some sleep," Carrie Anne said to Kathe.

"Which room?" Kathe asked.

"Jay and Jack's room, where else would I go?" Carrie Anne said rolling her eyes. "After your wakeup call this morning, I doubt Travis will want me back."

"You just make sure you keep that cell phone on you at all times," Ramsey interrupted. "One more time being late, and you are on report. Do you understand me, Lover Girl?"

"I understand," Carrie Anne said leaving the room as Kathe called to her. "I need to go shopping later for a watch. Do you want to go?"

"It all depends on what time," Carrie Anne whined. "I'm tired and I've got a hangover. I need to sleep it off."

"It probably won't be any time soon," Kathe replied. "I'll call you when I'm done here."

"Okay," Carrie Anne affirmed and left the room.

"Kathe, I'm sending you over to Sydney," Ramsey stated. "He has some new updates to install in JAKE and a little something for you," she said picking up her things.

"What do you mean, something to install in me?" Kathe questioned. "I'm a person, not a robot."

"After Flight #1014," Ramsey declared. "I realized that JAKE could do much more than it is now. Sydney and I were already working on it. We got lucky last night when he just happened to walk into Keith's office when you were in Rizo's. He was able to override some of JAKE's software while you were on speakerphone. How do you think the thieves could not hear what everyone else was saying and still hear you? He has been working on it all night. Now hurry down to his office. I've got to get back to work," she said as they left the room.

"I wonder what Dr. Sydney's got in store for me this time," Kathe thought. "I feel like a bionic Barbie doll." She thought walking toward his office as she continued reminiscing, "look at how my life has changed. It's so strange how God pulls people together from all lifestyles when He has a purpose for us. Ramsey left her job at the Pentagon when they tabled her JAKE Project. Dr. Sydney saw the corruption in the establishment at the same time walking out on his job with the government. God knew that Dr. Sydney was just the right person to get Ramsey's JAKE Project working to save lives. How quickly he perfected JAKE's technology interfacing it with Alby's computer system. Then God had a different plan for me. I blossomed from a wimpy stay home mom to a flight attendant. Almost killed, God made me stronger to lead Alby's Security Team protecting others. They have so much money invested in this body that Dr. Sydney bought the house next door in Florida to ensure my safety. I can't believe the incredible special features he designed in both our houses. How does he think of all these things?"

Upon reaching his office, Amy his assistant buzzed her inside. "Kathe, how are you?"

"It's been a while, hasn't it?" Kathe said.

"Too long, you look great," Amy smiled.

"Thank you," Kathe replied. "Ramsey said Dr. Sydney has something for me?"

"He sure does," Amy grinned. "He has been working on it since last night after your confrontation at Rizo's Jewelry. He has a fantastic new toy for you to try out!"

"This isn't going to hurt, is it?" Kathe asked.

"Come on," Amy motioned for Kathe to follow her into the lab. "He is waiting for you."

"Kathe!" Sydney gave her a hug. "Have I got some new toys for you and JAKE!"

"Your toys are quite something," Kathe admitted. "I can't believe what you've done with both of our houses."

"I wanted to make sure you're safe at home as well as work," Sydney proclaimed.

"I think you've been watching too many James Bond movies," Kathe laughed.

"James Bond has nothing on me," Sydney boasted. "Besides, in your line of work, we don't want any problems following you home. You don't have backup at your house like here. In addition, your children need to be able to visit you there safely. That's why I bought the house next door and modified them. Now, I have a few more toys for you and JAKE."

"Doc are these new toys going to hurt?" Kathe inquired.

"JAKE, no it's a machine," Sydney stated. "It doesn't feel pain."

"Not JAKE," Kathe insisted. "Is this going to hurt me?"

"What's a little pain?" Sydney asked. "A little pain never hurt anybody. Where is JAKE? Can I see it?"

She reached on her belt and relinquished JAKE to him. Holding it in his hand, he walked off talking to it. "Have I got some new gadgets to put on you." He took JAKE over to his work area, picked up some tools and began working.

"Should I prepare Kathe for surgery?" Amy asked.

"Surgery!" Kathe exclaimed. "Nobody said anything about surgery!"

"Relax," Amy assured Kathe as she reached in a cabinet and handed her a gown. "It's not like you think. It's another implant. Just go in the dressing room, take off your top and bra, put this gown on with the opening in the front."

"Implant what for?" Kathe asked from the dressing room.

"You know Dr. Sydney," Amy smiled. "He likes to go over things himself. He will be here in a minute or two. He's almost finished with JAKE. You can just sit down on the examination table when you're ready."

After Kathe sat down, Amy took her blood pressure and checked her other vitals.

"Why do I get the feeling I'm a guinea pig?" Kathe inquired as Amy finished.

"You are as a matter of fact," Amy laughed as she placed the stethoscope around her neck.

"Thanks a lot!" Kathe snapped, glaring at Amy.

"I didn't mean to be so cold about it," Amy apologized. "But you are the prototype for his work," Amy said, putting on her gloves. "Lay down, this won't take long," she said bringing the surgical tray over and turning on the surgical lamp.

"It's nice to know I'm so valuable," Kathe said lying down on her back. Amy covered her up with a sheet and positioned the lamp directly above her.

Dr. Sydney entered the room with JAKE in his hand. "It's ready for you now," he said putting it on the table. "And I'm ready for you," he washed his hands. He put on his surgical gloves. Amy handed him a needle. He held the needle up and squeezed some of the fluid out of it. Amy pulled the sheet down and moved the front of the gown out of the way.

"Now Kathe," Sydney explained. "I know you don't like needles. But this is going to be just a little prick to numb the area," he said as he stuck the needle just under her left clavicle. "Ramsey told me about your problem with Flight #1014. Ever since then, she and I have been working on ideas to upgrade JAKE. Last night I witnessed the lack of communication we still faced. I realized that with all the technology JAKE has, it is still lacking in its original purpose, communication. This device I'm installing in you will enable JAKE to pick up your voice and anyone near you. We will be able to hear what is going on around you, as well as communicate with you. I've already installed JAKE's counterpart."

"Wait a minute," Kathe protested. "Are you telling me this is a transmitter and a receiver so you can hear me and the person with whom I'm conversing?"

"You understand perfectly," Sydney said making a small incision as Amy blotted the area.

"Don't you think this is a little personal?" Kathe insisted looking away.

"It's mostly only activated by you when you're in distress," Sydney explained. "It works off your heart rate or the panic button on JAKE," he said as he used a probe to pick up a small device.

"I don't like the sound of that," Kathe objected. "Who else can activate it?"

"Mostly you," he reassured her and reached for a small plastic strip.

"Mostly is not a yes or no answer; ouch!" Kathe whined as he placed it inside her. "If Control has good reason, they can activate it from here," he said as he reached for the sutures.

"Isn't that an invasion of privacy?" Kathe questioned. "My privacy!" she asked as he closed the opening.

"It is only for your security," Sydney insisted. "If anyone tries to harm you, it is a way we can actually hear what is going on. Say, for instance, the incident with Saíde. Ramsey would know while it was happening, what was happening. The best part about it, is she can talk you through the situation. I can't wait to test it today!" He exclaimed as Amy wiped the wound with betadine solution. He stood back from the table. "You can get up now. I'm finished. Now that didn't hurt too much, did it?"

"You're done?" Kathe realized.

"Of course, I'm done," Sydney confirmed. "I told you it wouldn't take long. Now I want you to get dressed and go back to Ramsey's office. I want to see my new toy at work."

Minutes later, Kathe grabbed her purse, waved goodbye to Amy and left. She hurried back to Ramsey's office.

"How do you feel?" Ramsey asked as Kathe entered the office.

"I feel okay," Kathe said standing in front of her desk.

"Well, did it hurt?" Ramsey asked.

"I didn't realize Sydney was finished," Kathe said as she pulled her blouse down and showed her implant.

"It looks normal to me," Ramsey replied. "He said it was small. But I never thought it would be this small," she said closely examining the area. The phone rang. Sydney repeated word for word everything they said. "Well, I'm impressed! You did it Doc!" Ramsey hung up the phone. "It works! He heard everything we said to each other. Now I'm more in control of situations you encounter. JAKE far supersedes anything the military uses. And the Pentagon said it would never work!"

"I would like to say one thing," Kathe said looking straight at Ramsey. "I don't want you turning this thing on listening to my private life."

"Kathe Tierney, I'm shocked!" Ramsey exclaimed. "Sydney, Keith, and I are the only ones who even know about this. Do you have any more questions?" she said turning back to her computer.

"Will I have any problems going through security?" Kathe asked.

"Not at all," Ramsey confirmed. "Neither of your implants are detectable. You are a flight attendant like all the others."

"Well, I feel like a bionic Barbie doll," Kathe laughed.

"Get out of here!" Ramsey laughed and pointed to the door.

Chapter 14

Not You Again!

Stepping out of the cab at the Hotel International reaching for her wallet, Kathe paid the cabby. She turned in a hurry bumping clumsily into some people scurrying for the empty cab. She dropped her purse and some of the contents fell out. She began reaching for her things scattered on the sidewalk.

"Kathe?" a now familiar voice called to her.

She slowly glanced up. There stood Joe with some of his band members and their dates. "Not you again!" Kathe exclaimed.

"I can't believe the way we keep running into each other," Joe smiled as he handed her a lipstick.

"Thanks," Kathe said, putting it in her purse.

"I'm surprised you're alone," Joe asked.

"Why?" Kathe asked.

"I thought you would be with one of the two men I heard you were staying with?" Joe inquired.

"What are you talking about?" Kathe asked as she took a step back.

"I heard you are staying with two men," Joe said looking straight into her eyes.

"I don't know where you get your 411, but I would change sources," Kathe retorted as she hurried off.

"Wait!" Joe begged watching her storm off.

Kathe threw her hands in the air and kept walking to the revolving hotel door when Joe grabbed her left shoulder.

"Kathe, wait!" Joe pleaded turning her around.

"Ouch!" Kathe wailed.

"What's wrong?" Joe asked. "Are you alright?"

"No, I mean, yes," Kathe stated. "I'm okay," she rolled her eyes still annoyed with him.

"I'm sorry for what I said," Joe apologized.

"I want you to get one thing straight," Kathe insisted as she poked him in the chest. "I do not sleep around with men! Not one man, not two men, not any men! I am staying in a suite with two male flight attendants that work with me. Carrie Anne screwed up our reservations, so we had no place to stay yesterday when we arrived. They said we could stay in their room. Only she stayed in your suite with Travis. Now, does that answer your question?"

"Yes!" Joe beamed. "That's all I wanted to know," he said as his friends called to him. "I guess I have to go now," Joe grinned and hurried back to the cab.

"Unbelievable!" Kathe exclaimed.

"Carrie Anne was looking for you," Jay said when Kathe finally got back to the room.

"Where is she?" Kathe asked as she placed her purse on the table.

"She left a few minutes ago with the same guy she was with last night," Jay replied. "She said not to wait up for her."

"Great, I wanted to go shopping with her," Kathe whined. "I still need to buy a watch. Do you two want to go shopping?"

"Nope, we finally have some time off," Jay declined. "We're heading for the bar downstairs. Want to join us?"

"No thanks," Kathe said, walking toward her room as JAKE rang. "Tierra are you still in New York?" Silence for a second. "Great, I need to go shopping myself. That's okay... I would love to meet her...I will be in the lobby in ten minutes. Bye."

"Who was that?" Jay questioned as Jack came out of his room.

"Tierra LaBasco," Kathe replied. "She wants to introduce me to someone Ramsey assigned to fly with her for a while."

"We're off for a few days, so we'll be out late tonight," Jack warned. "Make sure you take your key."

"We may end up in Carrie Anne's boyfriend's room," Jay said. "They are at another party to kick off their tour. After that party, there is a private party here at the hotel. Her friend invited us."

"Okay, I'll probably be in bed early," Kathe said. "I need to catch up on my sleep. Don't drink too much. Remember what you said the last time the two of you had hangovers."

"We'll be careful Mommy," Jack chuckled.

In the lobby Tierra and a friend were waiting for Kathe. "Tierra I'm so glad you're still in New York," Kathe greeted them. "Carrie Anne was supposed to go shopping with me this afternoon and like usual, stiffed me for a date."

"So, what else is new with Lover Girl?" Tierra laughed. "Kathe, I want to introduce you to CC Sims. She will be flying with me for a while. Ramsey has us working the South American Circuit hoping the threats on my life will stop."

"Glad to meet you CC," Kathe shook her hand. "Have you been working for Alby long?"

"I came aboard a couple of months ago," CC stated. "I really like the job and travel. I was hoping to fly the European Circuit. However, since I'm fluent in Spanish and Tierra's not, I'm heading for Mexico and points south."

"Ramsey's worried about my family's business compromising my safety as a flight attendant," Tierra continued. "I never get involved in it. I have no contact with the business or my family unless they contact me."

"Has this ever happened to you before?" Kathe questioned.

"All my life!" Tierra snapped. "It iş common in my papa's line of work. He seems to be good at one thing: making enemies. Something happened on one of your flights a few days ago that triggered Ramsey to be more vigilant concerning me. She wants CC and I to stay together and to tell you the truth, I feel better about it. I know my papa and older brother are very thorough. They are positive that man will never bother me again. However, something about it does not sit right with my younger brother Nicki. Speaking of Nicki, his birthday is coming up. I'm heading for Mexico, so I will not get to be with him. I saw Ramsey today. She said you were here. I was wondering if I bought Nicki a present, do you think you could take it to him?"

"I'd be glad to take it for you," Kathe stated. "Let's get going," Kathe started through the revolving door. "Where do you want to shop?"

"I don't know New York very well," Tierra said. "CC is from here." she turned to her. "Where do you suggest?"

"It depends on what you want," CC replied.

"I need a watch," Kathe told her.

"Rizo's Jewelry is near here," CC answered.

"I already looked there!" Kathe blurted. "I didn't see anything I liked."

"Okay," CC said, surprised by her response. "Not Rizo's then, which has a great selection. Let's try Macy's Department Store. It's a few blocks away."

"What do you have in mind for your brother Tierra?" Kathe asked. "Maybe we can find him something there."

"I got Nicki a watch last year," Tierra admitted. "Maybe I can just browse the store for some ideas," she said as CC hailed a cab.

The three girls got into the cab. "Macy's on 5th Ave. please," CC told the driver.

"How long have you known Tierra?" Kathe asked.

"We met at Ramsey's office a few days ago when she arrived back from Europe," CC stated.

"What did you do before joining Alby?" Kathe inquired.

"I taught high school Spanish in the Bronx," CC replied. "I got bored teaching and became a flight attendant."

"I took Spanish in high school and haven't spoken a word since," Tierra confessed. "Ramsey assured me that it's like riding a bicycle, I'll pick it up again quickly."

"Ramsey's right," CC said. "The best way to learn a language is to have to speak it. You'll be speaking the language fluently in less than a month."

"I hope you're right, but I'm going to miss seeing Nicki," Tierra said, reaching into her purse and pulling out a picture from her wallet. "I took this picture after my mother died," she showed them. "It is the only one I have of my two brothers and Papa. One thing is for sure, I won't miss my papa and older brother or the pressure of the family business," she said as she put it back.

After an hour browsing Macy's, not finding anything they liked it was CC who decided she was hungry. "Let's grab something to eat. I'm starved, aren't you?"

"Yes," Tierra agreed.

"Me too, I didn't have time to eat today," Kathe said. "I spent most of my day at control."

"I have the perfect place for us to eat," CC said as she hailed another cab. "It's on the way to the hotel and it's a hot spot for superstars. Maybe we'll get lucky and see someone famous. It's my favorite restaurant in the city. All the locals hang out there and watch for the stars," CC said waiting for the hostess to take their names.

"Wow!" Tierra exclaimed as a very sexy man walked past them. "I wonder if he's on the menu?"

"That's Michael Bolton!" CC gasped. "I told you this is a perfect place to eat and drool at the same time," CC giggled as the hostess asked how many in their party. "Three," she answered.

"You're in luck," the hostess smiled. "I have a table in the back corner by the private dining room," she said reaching for three menus.

After the girls sat down, they noticed how noisy the private dining room was. Waiters kept passing them by with trays of booze and food. "Someone's having a great time," Tierra said as she scanned the menu.

"Look who's sitting three tables from us," CC pointed.

"That's Laura Brannigan!" Tierra exclaimed.

"I told you this is a fun place to be," CC said looking over the menu.

"It's good to see someone having fun that I don't have to serve," Kathe laughed.

"You are right about that," CC agreed as Carrie Anne rushed past their table.

"Carrie Anne!" Tierra called to her.

"Tierra!" Carrie Anne exclaimed hurrying over to them. "I haven't seen you in forever. You're looking great," she said as she turned to Kathe. "Did Jay and Jack give you, my message?"

"Yes, they said I just missed you," Kathe stated. "Thanks for ditching me again."

"I was waiting for you, and you'll never guess what happened," Carrie Anne beamed. "Travis stopped by the room and asked me to this bash. They're kicking off their tour with a concert tomorrow night here in New York. Travis gave me passes to get in too. How do I look beside a Rock Star?"

"Great, but be careful," Kathe cautioned. "By the way, this is CC Sims. She's new to Alby."

"Great to meet you," Carrie Anne shook her hand. "Welcome aboard. Tierra how long are you going to be in New York. I want to spend some time with you if I have some free time. Know what I mean?"

"Yes, I do know what you mean," Tierra giggled. "I'll be here for two more days, then I'm off to Mexico."

"Mexico!" Carrie Anne exclaimed. "Why there?"

"It's a long story," Tierra said. "I'll tell you sometime when you're not in a big hurry," she glanced toward the private room.

"You're right, I've got to get back," Carrie Anne giggled and then jogged up the steps.

Just as the girls were finishing their meal, the party in the private dining room started to break up. The guests began trickling out of the room. Kathe could not believe the luck she was having as she noticed a familiar face walking down the stairs, complete with a girl holding his arm! She slumped down in her seat. She grabbed a menu that the overworked waiter had left on the table to hide her face.

"Oh, Kathe!" Carrie Anne called to her. "I'll be upstairs again tonight."

Kathe tried to ignore her by holding the menu closer to her face and acting as if she did not hear her.

"Kathe," Tierra nudged her arm. "Carrie Anne is talking to you."

"Kathe...Kathe...Kathe Tierney!" Carrie Anne exclaimed as Kathe slowly dropped the menu, wishing she could strangle Carrie Anne. "Tierney, I'll be upstairs at a party."

"No, way!" Joe exclaimed walking right behind Carrie Anne. He shook his head in disbelief that Kathe was in the same restaurant. He pulled his arm away from the girl who was holding on to him and rushed out the door. The girl he was with scurried to catch up to him.

"Have a nice time Carrie Anne," Kathe glared as she shook her head in disbelief. "I'll see you tomorrow."

"That was Joe Sherrod behind Carrie Anne?" Tierra stated. "He looked like he had seen a ghost when he saw Kathe."

"Did you see how he dropped that girl's arm and bolted for the door?" CC chuckled.

"Kathe why did you act like you didn't want to be seen?" Tierra asked.

"It's a long story," Kathe sighed reaching for the check the waiter had laid on the table. "I'll get the check," she said as she walked to the register thinking, I hope I can make it back to the hotel without running into Joe and his lady friend again.

The girls left the restaurant and went outside to look for a cab. The winter weather seemed to have more of a chill. Just as CC was ready to hail a cab, Tierra noticed a hobby shop next to the restaurant. "Wait! Don't grab a cab. I know what to get Nicki and it's in that shop over there." Tierra said as they entered the store and headed straight for the trains. "Ever since Nicki was little, he has collected trains. He mentioned in Munich that he hadn't bought anything new for his train collection in years. He also said that he wanted to get interested in them again." She scanned the different train selections. "Great!" she exclaimed as she picked up a replica of a 1940 German engine. "This is a replica of the one Nicki and I saw in Munich the other day. I'll take it."

In the cab, Tierra told the girls about Nicki's train collection. "He mentioned that he didn't have this one. "Sure, you will have room in your suitcase?"

"Sure, I will," Kathe confirmed. "It will fit in my overnight bag."

"How soon will you be in Munich?" Tierra asked.

"I have no idea," Kathe said. "I'll call Ramsey tomorrow and ask her. Oh, we're back at the hotel."

"Want to come up to our room and have a night cap?" Tierra asked as they entered the lobby.

"No, I'm tired," Kathe conceded. "I need to get up early tomorrow to find a watch. Do you want me to take the train now?"

"No," Tierra stated. "I'll give it to you tomorrow, along with Nicki's telephone number. I want to wrap it," she said holding up the bag.

"It was nice meeting you CC," Kathe said as she gave her a hug. "I'm sure we will cross paths again. With the luck I've had for the past week or so, I'll probably end up going to Mexico with you."

"Somehow I get the feeling you're talking about the luck you've had with Joe Sherrod," CC teased.

"You're right," Kathe grinned and headed to the room.

The guys were not back yet, so Kathe took the opportunity to take a hot shower. Then she grabbed her blanket and pillow off the bed, set JAKE's alarm and fell fast asleep.

Chapter 15

Light Crimson's Party

Up on the twenty-first floor, the party was already in full swing. Payton had made sure of that. Camera crews from local TV stations were filming the first hour to air after the evening news. The hotel had beefed up its security for the group's safety. Now, the United States would know that Light Crimson was back on tour with their latest album. The concert sold out months in advance.

Jay and Jack were at the party. Carrie Anne was all over Travis and thrilled to death to be on television. Payton thought a flight attendant was good for Travis' image of being a hard rock swinger. Several hours had gone by and the party stayed strong. The television crews had left. The high energy that seems to radiate from these parties was in the air. The group was ready to get back into touring mode.

"I thought we had a life of fun," Jay said to Jack. "Look at all these people. I have never seen so much booze in my life. Look at some of the skirts these girls are wearing. Any shorter and you could call them underwear!"

"You're right," Jack answered as Carrie Anne passed by him. "Hey Carrie Anne. Have you seen Kathe this evening?"

"Yes, as a matter of fact I did," Carrie Anne stopped with them for a minute. "She was at the same restaurant we were for dinner."

"Was she with Tierra?" Jack asked.

"She was with Tierra and some new flight attendant," Carrie Anne said. "I forgot her name. Why?" she asked as Joe and his date walked up and joined in the conversation. "Are you worried about her?"

"Worried about who?" Joe asked.

"About Kathe Tierney," Carrie Anne answered.

"I just hate to see her always alone," Jack said. "You're always with some guy. She's always alone."

"Doesn't she ever date?" Joe asked.

"No, she never dates," Jack answered. "She knows a lot of people. She's never alone."

"She has Yorg!" Carrie Anne chimed in. "I'd die for a chance at that Russian machine."

"Yorg," Joe's curiosity peeked. "Who is he?"

"He's a Russian pilot working for Alby," Jay answered.

"What's he like?" Joe asked.

"He's about 6-foot-four," Carrie Anne drooled. "He was on the Russian Olympic Wrestling Team. He has muscles all over that gorgeous body of his. I've been trying for years to get Kathe to get me a date with that machine, but she says I'm not his type."

"Maybe she likes him herself," Joe hinted.

"Likes him, she loves him," Carrie Anne blurted. "But not the way you think."

Jack butted in, "They're like brother and sister. Kathe doesn't get physical with anybody and hasn't as long as I have known her."

Travis joined the conversation, "If she's such a virgin, how in the world did you two get to be best friends?"

"It's a long story," Carrie Anne began. "Kathe doesn't like me to talk about it. But I will say that Yorg, Jay, Jack and I met her the same day."

"Why can't you tell us?" Joe's curiosity was even more aroused.

"I'd get fired!" Carrie Anne stated. "Kathe has that much pull with our boss. Let's change the subject."

Collin was looking around for a free spot to get a little romantic with a girl. He walked over to the group. "Hey Carrie Anne, can I use your room for an hour?"

"I don't have a room of my own," Carrie Anne informed him. "I'm staying with these guys," she pointed to Jay and Jack.

"What do you say mates?" Collin asked them.

"Someone might be in there asleep." Jay answered.

"That's okay," Collin laughed.

"We won't take much room," the girl he was with added.

Carrie Anne turned to Travis, "I'll go down to the room and check if she's there. I forgot to bring something with me."

"Do you want me to go with you?" Joe asked.

"No, I can go by myself," Carrie Anne insisted as she turned to Jay. "Give me your room key."

"What did you forget?" Jay asked handing her his key.

"My cell phone," Carrie Anne smiled.

"You like to live dangerously, don't you?" Jay cautioned. "Just this morning, Ramsey warned you to always keep it on you! If I, were you, I wouldn't push her buttons? She was on the verge of firing you!"

"I forgot it," Carrie Anne giggled. "I'll be right back," she said as she reached up, Alby Airlines nuzzled Travis' cheek and started for the door.

"Hey, Carrie Anne, mind if I go with you?" Joe asked as he hurried after her.

"I figured you would come," Carrie Anne smiled as he opened the door for her.

Alone in the elevator Joe asked her again, "Why can't you tell me about the relationship between Kathe and Yorg?"

"I already told you," Carrie Anne took a sip of her drink. "They're just friends. There's nothing else to tell."

The elevator stopped on the sixth floor. Carrie Anne reached for the lights as they entered. "I guess she's still out," Joe sighed, looking around the empty sitting room.

"Let me check in our room," Carrie Anne pointed to the one on the right. Quietly slipping into the room, picking up her purse off the bed, she saw Kathe asleep on the floor next to the window. Slipping back out to Joe she whispered, "She's asleep. I need to use the bathroom. I will use the one in the Jay's room. Wait here quietly. I will be right back."

Joe peeked into her room. He didn't see Kathe on the bed. He slipped into the room and walked toward the window. There he saw Kathe asleep on a blanket between the bed and the wall. She was lying on her side hugging the pillow. She's like no other woman I've ever met, he thought. She turned over and the blanket slipped showing her low-cut pink silk nightgown. He remembered how she looked in the shower. How embarrassed she was when he gave her his silk shirt to use as a towel. That was only two days ago, he thought. Yet I keep running into her in the strangest places. I feel like I've known her forever.

Or am I beginning to want to know her forever? Turning to leave the room, he saw Carrie Anne standing in the doorway signaling him.

"You're lucky Kathe didn't wake up and see you staring at her," Carrie Anne whispered. "She would have killed us both! You have no clue what she can do," Carrie Anne told him as they left the suite. "She's a light sleeper usually. Thank God, she was exhausted from working a lot of doubles lately."

"There are two beds in that room," Joe mentioned. "Why is she sleeping on the floor?" he asked as they walked to the elevator.

"Maybe someday you'll get to know her well enough, and she will tell you," Carrie Anne said.

"Why all the secrecy about her?" Joe demanded.

"You better keep your mind on the girl you're with at the party," Carrie Anne stated. "I noticed she looked a little sad when we were talking about Kathe."

"That girl means nothing to me," Joe declared. "I just met her here in the hotel," he said stepping into the elevator.

Getting off the elevator on the 21st floor, Joe gently pushed Carrie Anne against a wall and held her. "Carrie Anne why all the secrecy about Kathe?"

"Travis is waiting for me," Carrie Anne begged, taking another sip of her drink. "I can't tell you."

"I'm not moving until you tell me about her!" Joe demanded. "We can stay here all night," he folded his arms in front of him.

"Okay," Carrie Anne agreed, taking the last gulp of her drink. "But remember if you tell her, I told you, I'll be unemployed. Kathe is the highest paid flight attendant in the history of Alby. She is not a regular flight attendant. Don't ask me to expound on it. I can't tell you. She is a workaholic. She is divorced. Her husband left her for another woman. She has three kids but does not live with them. She has a beach house in Florida compliments of. She doesn't date anyone. She is a size 4. She likes roses and daisies. Does that satisfy your curiosity?" She started to walk away and then stopped, "She never got over the reason for her divorce. You're wasting your time. She'll never trust another man like that again!"

"Thanks Carrie Anne," Joe smiled. "There is something special about her. I won't tell her you told me."

"I guess I finally broke down and told you because I'd like to see her happy someday," Carrie Anne admitted. "If she won't get that close to Yorg, she won't ever get close to another man. Don't waste your time."

"I said the same thing once, only in reverse," Joe told Carrie Anne as they walked to his room. He went straight over to the bar. He poured a stiff drink as Carrie Anne walked up behind Travis and put her arms around him. Joe walked over to Collin while Babs and Troy were talking to him.

"Can we use their room?" Collin asked.

"No," Joe quickly replied. "Someone is sleeping in there."

The phone rang in a sleazy hotel in Harlem. "Hello," his deep raspy voice answered.

"I just got word that Tierra LaBasco is in New York for a few days," the man on the other end declared. "Don't botch it this time!" he hung up. "Let me see about dear old Papa now," he said as he turned on his laptop.

The warmth of the sun fell through the window of the hotel room as Kathe opened her eyes. For a second it felt like she was home in Florida. Wow, she thought, I'm ready for winter to be over. I'm sick of the cold and snow. Maybe I ought to tell Ramsey that she is right, I need to go home on an R & R. I haven't been to Florida since before Christmas.   She sat up on her makeshift bed and looked out of the low-framed window at New York. The city was just beginning to wake up. The sun was bright on the snow. She raised one arm, stretched, and yawned as she heard the door open. She jumped up to check. "Well, good morning boys! Are you just getting in?"

"Do you have to be so cheery," Jack moaned as he opened his bedroom door.

"It's a beautiful day," Kathe gleamed. "The sun is out. New York is waking up. We don't have to work. Yes, I do have to be cheery. I haven't had a complete day off in a long time," she said as she followed them to their doorway.

"Go shopping or something," Jack whined as he pulled the covers over his head. "Just don't make any noise. My head feels like it's under the engine of a 747."

"What was I thinking?" Jay snapped. "I hate hangovers...Oh, it hurts to talk...It hurts to think. Kathe, get dressed and go down to the lobby, find us something for our heads, please hurry. Take some money out of my wallet...Take my wallet...I don't care."

"Okay, I'll hurry just for you two," Kathe agreed. "I'll pay for the pain pills, I owe you."

"For what?" Jack asked, pulling the covers off his head.

"For a great night's sleep!" She laughed and leaned against the doorway.

"Oh, that is mean Tierney!" Jack exclaimed. "Really mean! Next time you don't have a room to stay in you can sleep on a park bench!" he replied pulling the covers back over his head.

"I take it back," Kathe chuckled as she headed for the bathroom.

She got dressed quickly. She put on a pair of tight-fitting jeans, a long red pullover sweater with a big neckline that fell off one shoulder. She grabbed her Reebok's from her suitcase. She reached for a brush in her sling purse. She made sure she had her room key and left.

Downstairs Kathe went to the lounge and ordered coffee. She went by the gift shop and picked up some Tylenol, and then hurried back to their room. Quietly opening their door, she noted both men asleep, so she tiptoed into the room and left the Tylenol next to Jay's wallet. Carefully closing the door, she decided to shop for a watch as someone knocked on the door. Maybe it's Carrie Anne, she thought as she hurried to answer it. "You, again!" she gasped as Joe stood there with both hands in his jean pockets.

"Hi," Joe smiled. "I...I couldn't sleep. I...I thought maybe you would like to go for some coffee. But... I see you already have some."

Kathe had her coffee in her hand and coat across her arm. "The guys," she pointed to the other room, "came in a few minutes ago from your party and needed some Tylenol. I ran down to get them some, so I grabbed a cup, but I could use another."

"Are you going somewhere?" Joe asked.

"I seem to have my first full day off in months," Kathe smiled. "I thought I would go shopping. I still haven't gotten a watch."

"I'm free until about 4:00 pm," Joe offered. "Would you like some company or are you meeting someone?"

"No," Kathe scrunched her nose. "I mean yes, I would like some company and no, I'm not meeting anyone. Most of the people I know were at your party last night. I think they're all hungover." She looked at him closer, "Why aren't you?"

"I didn't drink as much as them," Joe admitted. "I have to be in good shape for tonight's concert."

"That's right it's all over the news," Kathe smiled. "How's your neck holding out?"

"I think you cured me on the plane the other night," Joe grinned.

"I hope the stage has a fence around it tonight," Kathe said with a wink.

"I'm not usually so clumsy," Joe admitted. "I think I can handle it tonight," he said helping her with the door.

"Maybe I'll say a prayer for you," Kathe said closing the door. "Are you ready?"

"Sure, let's grab some coffee first," Joe replied as he pushed the button for the elevator. "I need some caffeine."

"Where's your girlfriend?" Kathe asked as she glanced at him.

"The girl I was with last night at the restaurant?" Joe said as he looked away.

"Last night and the night before, yes that one?" Kathe inquired.

"She's not my girlfriend," Joe declared. "I just met her here in New York," he said avoiding her eyes as the elevator stopped.

"Do you usually sleep with girls you just met?" Kathe questioned as they entered the coffee shop.

"Sometimes I do," Joe answered honestly. "Do you want something to eat?"

"I never eat breakfast," Kathe admitted. "I'll wait if you want something," she said reaching for her wallet ordering two coffees.

"I'm not much for breakfast either," Joe admitted. "I'll get it," he grinned, pulled out some cash from his pocket and paid for the coffees.

"Thanks," Kathe smiled as she put her wallet away.

"You're welcome," Joe said reaching for some napkins. "Where do you want to shop?" He asked zipping up his jacket.

"I don't know," Kathe said. "Do you have any ideas?"

"You're the one from the states, not me," Joe said taking a sip of his coffee. "This hits the spot."

"I may be from the states, but not from New York," Kathe stated. "I'm usually in and out of here before I can sightsee. This is a long way from where I'm from."

"I think I saw a jewelry store next to the Olive Garden on Times Square," Joe suggested. "We can walk in that direction."

"No!" Kathe replied quickly. "I...I looked there the day we arrived."

"I read in the paper someone tried to rob them a few nights ago," Joe remembered.

"I was there in the early part of the day," Kathe declared. "I read the article. The robbery was in the evening. I think I remember a department store on the next block. Let's walk. The sidewalks are pretty clear, and the sun feels great."

"Okay with me," Joe agreed.

"I'm so ready for some sunshine and warm rays on my face," Kathe confessed.

"Maybe you're getting homesick for Florida?" Joe mentioned as she stopped and turned in front of him.

"How did you know about Florida?" Kathe quizzed.

"I think you mentioned it on the flight the other night," Joe tried to play it off.

"I did not mention it the other night," Kathe refuted. "I said I lived on the East Coast. Who told you?"

"Must have been someone at the party last night," Joe took another sip of coffee and walked to the crosswalk.

Kathe stood there for a second, wondering if Carrie Anne drank too much and started talking about her. She caught up to him. "It had to be Carrie Anne. The guys wouldn't have said anything. What else did she say about me?"

"Not much," Joe said staring at her. "As a matter of fact, she refused to say much about you or Yorg!"

"Why does his name always creep up in our conversations?" Kathe asked.

"When you were massaging my neck, he asked you if you were massaging me, like you do him," Joe wondered. "I have been wondering just how you massage him?" he asked and walked around her.

"Why do you want to know?" Kathe questioned as she caught up to him again.

Joe didn't answer as the 'walk' signal appeared and they started across the street.

"Not like you think," Kathe answered. "I'm not as free spirited as you or Carrie Anne."

The department store was the second building from the crosswalk. As they stopped in front of it, Kathe noticed a boutique next door. "Hey," Kathe grabbed his arm, "Can we go in there first. Look at that dress!" She hurried inside and headed straight to the dress rack. She pulled out a light pink A-line dress with large, black buttons on the top, and a wide, black belt. "Look it has a matching jacket. What do you think?"

"Pink does look great on you," Joe stated. "Why don't you try it on," he said and took a sip of his coffee.

"I've never worn anything pink around you," Kathe declared. "How do you know what I look like in pink?"

Not wanting her to know he had seen her last night in her nightgown, he said shrugging his shoulders, "With your coloring, pink must look good on you."

She glared at him as she passed him on the way to the dressing rooms.

The shop owner noticed his coffee cup was empty. "Would you like some more coffee while your wife is trying on the dress?"

"Yes, thank you, but she's not my wife," Joe replied.

"I'm sorry," she said and took his cup. "I'll be back with your coffee in a second."

"What do you think?" Kathe asked as she modeled the outfit for him.

"It looks like you all right," Joe smiled. "But I like the tight jeans and the sweater better personally."

"You don't like it, do you?" Kathe quizzed looking in the full-length mirror.

"Yes, I like it on you," Joe agreed. "I just like your tight jeans better," he toyed with her.

"I'll take it," Kathe said to the clerk.

She came out of the dressing area with the dress over her arm, "How much do I owe you?"

"The gentleman has already paid," the clerk stated as Kathe turned to Joe.

"Why did you pay?" Kathe asked. "I do have money."

"I know," Joe smiled. "You're the highest paid flight attendant at Alby Airlines."

"Did Carrie Anne tell you that?" Kathe demanded as they left the shop.

"This type of boutique isn't my style," Joe evaded the question. "Let's grab a cab and go somewhere else."

"I thought you didn't know New York," Kathe said as he waved to a cab. "You don't like my new dress, do you?"

"It looks nice on you," Joe smiled at her. "Of course, I think anything you wear would look great, especially with that butt."

"Okay, but I have to buy a watch sometime today," Kathe agreed. "I think I want a dressy one this time."

"Come on," Joe said as the cab stopped at the curb, and he opened the door. "5th Avenue and 10th Street please."

"Looking for anything in particular sir?" the cabby asked.

"Yes, there was a leather shop somewhere near Channel 10's TV Station," Joe said. "Do you know where it is?"

"Sure, it's just up ahead," he said pulling up in front of it. "Is this where you had in mind?"

"Yes, thanks," Joe handed the cab driver a hundred-dollar bill, "keep the change."

"Thank you," the cab driver said. "Do you want me to wait?"

"No, we'll be here for a while," Joe stated. "Thanks," he said as they got out.

"You made his day," Kathe said impressed with his generosity again.

"Can I buy an outfit I'd like you to wear tonight at the concert?" Joe asked glancing at her.

"I didn't know I was going," Kathe stopped and looked at him.

"I'm inviting you," Joe smiled. "I've seen you at work, now I'd like you to see me at work," he grinned and held the door open.

"Maybe I'll go," Kathe smiled. "However, my job is not like yours. I don't know months at a time where I will be. I get called in on a moment's notice all the time," she told him as they entered the leather shop. "Only," Kathe added, "I'll pay for my own outfit."

Inside the small, crowded shop, Kathe realized it was not her usual style. Joe laughed when he saw the look on her face. The patrons ranged from tough biker to punk boys with their girlfriends hanging on them. She noticed some of the tattoos looked X-rated or should have been. "You, okay?"

"Sure, I'm okay, but are they?" Kathe questioned as she touched his shoulder pointing out a man with a purple Mohawk.

"Well at least, I finally got you to touch me," Joe grinned. "I've been trying to use my British charm all morning on you, with no luck."

"I didn't realize I was such an iceberg," Kathe replied as she glanced sideways at him.

"I'm used to girls throwing themselves at me," Joe stated as he glanced at her.

"I don't throw myself at any man," Kathe answered as JAKE rang.

"Hello," Tierra greeted. "I want to meet up with you to give you Nicki's present."

"Sure, I'll be back at the hotel in a couple of hours," Kathe said watching Joe search for a pair of pants.

"That may be too late," Tierra sighed. "I'm going out to lunch with CC and some friends we met last night, after we left you. CC and I want to stay in a crowd since we both feel like someone has been watching us all day. I think I'm overreacting from all that stuff with my papa."

"Do you need me to come and get you?" Kathe asked.

"No, I'm sure we are both just overreacting," Tierra said. "I will feel better once we leave New York."

"Why don't you leave the present with Jay or Jack?" Kathe offered. "I'm staying in their room. They are probably still in bed. I left them with some bad hangovers this morning," she said watching Joe eying a leather jacket.

"I already tried there," Tierra said. "I knocked on the door and no one answered."

"They are probably still passed out," Kathe stated. "Are you sure you don't want me to come and get you?"

"I'm positive," Tierra insisted. "The more I think about it, I know it's just my nerves."

Kathe caught Joe's attention, "I need to meet a friend and pick up a package to take to Munich. Where can we meet her?"

"We're going to be here for a while," Joe admitted. "It's not too far from the hotel."

"I'm not too far from the hotel," Kathe said as she walked over to the counter and read the address from their business card.

"Okay, we'll meet you there in a few," Tierra said and cleared the line.

"My friends will be here in a few minutes," Kathe said as she walked back to Joe.

"What do you think of these?" Joe asked holding up a pair of black, leather pants with a matching jacket.

"It looks like you," Kathe grinned coining a phrase from him.

"Would you feel safe in here if I try these on?" Joe wondered as he noticed her staring at the people in the store.

"Of course," Kathe shrugged her shoulders. Walking toward the dressing area, Joe picked out a short, black, leather, mini skirt and matching jacket. He called to her, "This is what I'd like for you to wear tonight." He reached for her size. "Do you think this will fit? It's a size 4."

"How do you know my size?" Kathe questioned.

"Carrie Anne told me," Joe grinned as he held them up to show her. Kathe pushed his hand down and looked right at him.

"What else did my ex-best friend tell you about me?" Kathe demanded.

He smiled with that boyish charm of his, "Nothing, nothing at all."

Kathe grabbed the outfit from him, "Where's the shirt?"

"You wear the jacket without a shirt," Joe grinned. "Let's try these on before your friends get here."

Entering the co-ed dressing area, Joe pointed to the only empty room. "You can try the clothes on first. I'll wait out here if you promise you'll model it for me?"

A stringy, haired girl with one of those X-rated tattoos leaned toward Kathe, "I wouldn't leave a good-looking British piece like that by himself, sister."

Grabbing Joe by the arm, Kathe pulled him inside of the dressing room with her.

"I'll wait outside," a very surprised Joe said and started to back out.

"No," Kathe approved. "I trust you're a British gentleman. Turn around and I'll change."

He did as she requested. However, she did not notice the door had a very, narrow, full- length mirror. He could not believe Kathe did not see it. He almost closed his eyes and then a smile came over his face as he watched her change. "Okay, you can turn around. How do you like it on me?"

He turned around blocking the mirror. "Turn around so I can see the back," Joe requested. "Wow! You look hot in that outfit. Tonight's performance will soar because I'll be singing just for you," he turned back around.

"Me and a stadium full of fans, most of them female," Kathe said as she changed into her clothes. "I'm glad you're such a British gentleman."

"I come from a long line of them," Joe stated with a perfect straight face. "Are you ready, it's your turn to turn around?" He said still blocking the mirror as he tried on his clothes. "How do you like this?"

"It looks great on you," Kathe said as she turned around. "It will drive all the girls crazy, especially me." JAKE rang interrupting them. "Hello," she answered, "Are you okay? I'll be right there, I'm in the dressing area in the back of the store," she said pushing past Joe. "I've got to go!"

"Tierra, here I am," Kathe called as she hurried out of the dressing room area and saw her. She noticed that CC was staying by the front door watching the street as Tierra hurried to her. Joe hurried out to Kathe.

"Him?" Tierra pointed. "That's Joe Sherrod again!"

"Yes, it is," Kathe said noting Tierra looking over her shoulder as CC joined them.

"Oh, my gosh!" CC exclaimed positioning herself between Tierra and the door. "You're Joe Sherrod!"

"Shhh..." Joe said as he reached to shake her hand. "I'm glad to meet you, but don't say my name too loudly."

"I'm sorry," CC apologized. "You look much better with Kathe than that girl you were with last night."

"I think so too," Joe smiled.

"Kathe here is Nicki's cell number," Tierra said as she glanced back to the door and handed Kathe a piece of paper. "I called him this morning. I told him you were coming to Munich with something for him. Do you know when you'll be there?"

"Not yet," Kathe said. "Why are you two looking over your shoulders? Do you still feel like you're being followed?" Kathe asked as she put the paper in her purse.

"Yes, we do!" Tierra finally admitted. "There, I finally said it!"

"It seems that a tall, lanky Middle Eastern man keeps showing up wherever we go," CC reported as she watched the front door. "It could just be coincidence," she said as the man walked into the store, spotted them and quickly turned down another aisle. "That's him!" CC exclaimed, pulling Tierra behind a rack of clothes. Kathe pulled Joe behind the rack also.

"Why are we hiding?" Joe asked.

"Stay here!" Kathe commanded. "I'm going to get a better look at him," Kathe said as she followed the clothes rack to the back of the room and peered around it. She rounded the end of the rack where Joe could not see her. She pulled out her gun as she headed toward the next rack carefully searching for him. She peered around it and slowly walked toward the first rack near the cash register counter.

"She's got a gun!" yelled a customer as he walked between the two racks and dropped to the floor.

Saíde glanced around recognizing Kathe. He pushed the first rack of clothes toward her, shoved people out of his way and fled the store. "Alby Security!" Kathe yelled as she dodged the rack, rounded the counter and ran out the door. She holstered her gun as she took off after him down the city street.

"Whose got a gun?" Joe questioned. "Where's Kathe?"

"Kathe said to wait here," CC insisted as she reached to stop Joe and missed. "You are too famous to go outside alone," she said as she followed him to the door. "You're safer with us."

"Is Kathe chasing the man you thought was following you?" Joe questioned as he looked outside the door in all directions.

"I'm not sure," CC stated as she pulled Joe back inside the boutique.

"Where did she go?" Joe confronted CC.

"When you've known Kathe long enough," Tierra answered. "You'll know what we mean."

"Carrie Anne told me the exact same thing!" Joe snapped. "What does that mean?"

"Why don't you go ahead and pay for the clothes," CC suggested. "I'm sure Kathe will reimburse you for hers. That way we'll be ready to leave when she returns."

"Someone needs to tell me what is going on," Joe insisted as they walked to the register.

Ramsey immediately picked up the rise in heart rate and began monitoring the situation locating Kathe on GPS, "Tierney I can hear you running. What's going on?"

"Saíde is here!" Kathe reported. "I'm on Canal, two streets over from 5th Avenue near Channel 10's TV Station chasing him. He is two blocks ahead turning west on...hold on...Walker Street...he's turning down an alley between two buildings," Kathe reported as she rounded the corner and pulled out her gun. She entered the alley. "I lost him! It's empty. There's a solid brick wall about 10' high at the end. There is no way he could have scaled it."

"Are you sure it was Saíde?" Ramey demanded.

"I'm positive," Kathe confirmed. "He followed Tierra and CC into a boutique. We made eye contact and he pushed a clothes rack over and bolted," she said breathing heavily as she caught her breath. "There are several doorways," Kathe reported as she walked toward the first one and turned the doorknob. "I'm checking one now to see if it's open."

"Don't go in there!" Ramsey ordered as she listened to Kathe kick the door in. "Stand down Lady! You have no backup!" She ordered, calling NYPD. "Police are en route!"

"I'm sweeping the doorway," Kathe said as she kicked open the door. "Your hunch has to be right. You said yourself; he's going to come after us! He was following Tierra and CC. I've got to get him now while we can still find him!" Kathe attested, slowly approaching the next doorway.

"I'm ordering you to stand down!" Ramsey screamed. "Stand down! I am putting you on report! It could be a trap! He could be after you! You were in the boutique too! Get out of there now, is that clear?" Ramsey bellowed, pounding her fist on the desk. "Get out of there, now!"

"You're right," Kathe agreed, backing out of the doorway and down the alley. "He could be after me. They weren't on the flight that night," she said as she stopped. "Wait a minute. When Tierra called a few minutes ago, she stated that she and CC both felt that someone was following them. She blew it off thinking it was just nerves. Then, when they got to the boutique, they admitted a tall, lanky Middle Eastern man kept showing up where they were. As they were describing him, he walked in. Saíde had to have been following Tierra!"

"You could be right!" Ramsey confirmed. "She has had threats on her life recently, which were supposedly solved by her family. As soon as the police get there, go back to the boutique, and bring the girls to my office! This means that Saíde is in New York. I hate it when I'm always right," Ramsey declared as two squad cars came to a screeching halt. Kathe alerted them to the situation, and they took over the manhunt.

The police were already at the boutique when Kathe returned. "There she is! That's her!" shouted the owner behind the counter. "That's the lady with the gun!"

"Officer," Kathe stated, holding up her ID as they approached her. "I was in pursuit of a suspect that pulled a knife on a flight attendant."

"Ms. Tierney," Officer O'Hare replied. "Linda Ramsey alerted us of your pursuit and asked us to watch the two flight attendants in the boutique. Unfortunately, the other officers still have not located your suspect."

"He entered the alley and I lost him," Kathe stated as the shop owner joined them.

"Aren't you going to arrest her?" the owner demanded. "She scared my customers!"

"She's a security agent for a major airline," Officer O'Hare stated. "You're lucky she was in here when the male suspect entered your establishment. He's a known terrorist. Ms. Tierney, we had your friends wait for you in the first dressing room with an officer standing guard."

"Thanks officer," Kathe said as she hurried to the back of the boutique.

"Where did you go?" Joe demanded as Kathe showed her ID to the officer and opened the door.

"What just happened?" Tierra interrupted.

"You might still be in danger," Kathe stated, closing the door.

"How can I still be in danger?" Tierra began to sob.

"Ramsey said Tierra's family took care of that matter," CC stated.

"I recognized the man that was following you," Kathe stated.

"Is he the same man that was on Flight #1014?" CC questioned, remembering the file she read before taking the assignment.

"It was the same man," Kathe stated. "We need to get you out of here," she said, opening the door.

"Why was he following us?" CC asked as they walked out of the building with Officer O'Hare and his men surrounding them. "Tierra wasn't on that flight."

"I'm not sure yet," Kathe added. "But he was definitely following you."

"Will somebody tell me what is going on?" Joe requested. "Why are the police escorting us out of the building?"

"I can't say right now Joe," Kathe looked at him. "You're going to have to understand," Kathe said noticing people staring at them. "Ramsey wants me to escort Tierra and CC back to control."

"Here I go again," Tierra whimpered with tears streaming down her cheeks.

"Joe, I hate to say this," Kathe glanced at him. "You have to come too. He may have seen you with us," Kathe cautioned as an officer hailed a cab.

"You need to explain to me why you took off after a man suspected of following them," Joe said as he squared off in front of her and held her by her shoulders.

"We just met," Kathe declared. "If you get to know me long enough, you'll understand," she answered as the cab stopped.

"That's what Tierra and Carrie Anne told me," Joe said, glancing at CC.

"Don't look at me," CC contested. "I just met her myself."

"Thank you, Officer O'Hare," Kathe said as they got into the cab.

Chapter 16

A First Date Against Orders

Stopping first to pick up a Guest ID badge for Joe, they entered control. Kathe greeted Wanda, "This is Joe Sherrod. Could you please keep an eye on him, while we talk with Ramsey?"

"Only if I can keep him!" Wanda beamed. "Be careful she was on day two until you disobeyed her this morning. Now I must start with her all over again."

As the girls entered Ramsey's office, Kathe noticed her watching Wanda and Joe through the open blinds. "Who is that guy and why did you bring him to my office?" Ramsey bellowed as she watched Wanda's flirting.

"That guy, as you put it, was with me when Saíde entered the boutique," Kathe answered.

Ramsey peered through the blinds, "I've had it with you this morning! Now whom is Wanda drooling over?"

"Let's try this again," Kathe stated. "He is the guy that was with me in the boutique when Saíde recognized me. I'm off duty and was with a friend shopping when Tierra and CC called me and asked if they could meet me. Shortly after they got to the boutique, Saíde entered. He recognized me, knocked over a rack of clothes and took off. As you well know, I took off chasing Saíde, leaving him in the boutique with Tierra and CC. So, when you ordered me to bring them back to control, I had to bring him with me because Saíde is still in the area and might have seen us together!"

"How do you know that Saíde saw him with you?" Ramsey snapped.

"We were all standing together talking and Saíde got a clear view of all four of us," Kathe admitted. "It was you who said Saíde is very thorough, so I couldn't take a chance and leave him at the boutique."

"You still didn't answer me!" Ramsey snapped, turning toward Kathe. "Who is he? I know all your friends and I don't know who he is?"

"Evidently, you don't know all my friends," Kathe smiled. "But you ought to know who he is. He was your special assignment for me on the flight to the states two nights ago."

"That's not that rock star!" Ramsey screamed as she glared at him.

"In the flesh," Kathe smiled. "We are staying at the same hotel, and we keep running into each other. So, we decided to go shopping and talk. You know, there is an herb called Holy Basil that you might want to start taking. It helps calm your nerves."

"Don't get smart with me!" Ramsey declared, walking to her desk.

"I was just worried about your blood pressure," Kathe offered. "It seems to be sky-high today."

"Tierra," Ramsey changed the subject. "I thought this business with your father's family was all behind us. But it may not be. Kathe said that you felt like someone was following you today. When did this start?"

"After we left Kathe at the hotel last night," Tierra began. "CC and I went off with friends for a nightcap and we just had a weird feeling."

Interrupting, CC added, "Last night it was just a feeling. However, today was different. We noticed that every store we entered this morning, he was there."

"Was he with someone?" Ramsey asked.

"No, he was always alone," CC reported.

"This doesn't make sense," Ramsey stated. "Why would Saíde be following you? I will arrange for you to leave later today on the South American circuit. I will have Ralph, my bodyguard, go with you to the hotel to retrieve your belongings. Please wait in my outer office with Wanda until I finish with Kathe."

Closing the door behind them, Ramsey turned her attention to Kathe. "We have a little unfinished business about you not listening to me. First, Sydney's transmitter works perfectly. I felt like I was right there with you. Especially, when I told you to stand down and get out of the alley, since you had no backup! Next, I heard you kick in a door as I am still telling you to stand down and then you stepped inside! You could have been shot or worse yet, killed! I would have heard that too! I had to give you a direct order," pointing at her, "to get out of that alley or put you on report! Would you like to explain why you disobeyed a direct order?"

"I saw Saíde!" Kathe reiterated. "I identified a man who pulled a knife on one of my flight attendants during a flight. The gendarmes let him go due to falsified documents, which I discovered. I had him four feet in front of me. I have a gun and a license to kill! Did you really want me to let him go?"

"No," Ramsey agreed, calming down. "I do want you to get him. However, you can't kill someone for pushing a rack over. We must get something more on him or find out what he did with the knife. One thing is for sure, I'm adding Yorg to your team, because you seem to listen more to him than to me. After today, all heck is going to break loose. Get rid of Glitter Boy. He's too visible and a sure target for Saíde," Ramsey warned, pointing to him through the two-way window.

"My private life is my business," Kathe smiled and opened the door. "Try the Holy Basil," she said and left Ramsey's office. "Girls, you can stop drooling now," Kathe smiled, putting her arm around Joe. "We're leaving," she grinned as she glanced at the two-way window and waved to Ramsey.

As the door closed behind them, Joe and Kathe heard the girls screaming with excitement. "I have that effect on women," Joe smiled. "You'll get used to it. Let's go get something to eat, I'm starving."

"May I take your order, madam?" the French waiter asked.

"I'll order for the lady, if I may?" Joe asked looking over at Kathe. "Le dame aura la picante de poulet avec la salade de noix de pécan épinards avec vinaigrette à part. Je vais avoir le même, avec un verre de vin blanc. Je vous laisse choisir votre favori."

"For someone who doesn't know his way around New York," Kathe complimented Joe. "You know your way around."

"I had to film a segment for one of our new videos near here yesterday around lunchtime," Joe explained. "We ate here," he said changing his facial expression to serious. "Now, have I known you long enough for you to tell me what happened this morning?"

"No," Kathe answered. "And if you want to get to know me more, you won't ask me again." He started to say something as JAKE rang interrupting them. "Sorry," she said as she answered. "Hello," Kathe answered. "Yes, put Jeannie on."

"Kathe the kids are fine," Jeannie admitted. "Joey has a boo-boo and he wanted to tell his real mommy."

"Put Joey on the phone," Kathe insisted. "Hi Joey.... Yes, its Mommy." Silence... "Okay, let me kiss it on the phone, mmmmm.... (kiss). I will come and see you soon. Mommy loves and misses her baby. Bye."

"Kathe," Jeannie continued. "Ben Tierney had a heart attack yesterday. I took Pete and Heather to see him early this morning. He keeps asking for you. It doesn't look good. He made me promise to ask you to come and see him."

"This is not a good time for a visit," Kathe sighed. "Plus, I don't want to run into Peter," she complained, fiddling with her silverware.

Pete begged Jeannie for the phone, "Hey, Mom, how are you doing?"

"Pete," Kathe smiled. "I'm doing fine."

"What are you up to?" Pete asked.

"I'm having lunch with a friend," Kathe answered.

"Who are you having lunch with?" Pete inquired.

"You'll never believe who I'm having lunch with," Kathe teased.

"Carrie Anne?" Pete guessed.

"No, it's a man," Kathe offered. "I know you watch him on TMV," she said winking at Joe.

"Mom, who is it?" Pete asked as Joe reached for JAKE.

"Hello Pete," Joe said. "Your mother tells me you're a big fan of mine." Silence filled the other end of the line. "Pete...Pete...are you there?" Joe winked at Kathe. "Pete this is Joe Sherrod. Your mother says you like my music."

"No, way!" Pete exclaimed. "No Way! No Way!" was all he could say.

Joe handed JAKE back to Kathe. Pete was still screaming with excitement. "Hey guy, it's Mom. Pete...Pete....would you please put Jeannie back on."

It took a minute, but Jeannie finally had the phone, "What happened to Pete?"

"It's a long story," Kathe smiled. "I must go. I will call you later today. Bye." She hung up JAKE. "I think you made Pete's day."

"Thank you," Joe smiled.

"For what?" Kathe asked, shrugging her shoulders.

"For making my day," Joe replied, reaching for her hand just as the food arrived. Slowly releasing her hand, "We get interrupted no matter where we go, don't we?"

Lunch was eaten without any further interruptions. They talked about his concert. "We're leaving for California in two days to work on more videos and a special for TMV. Then we will fly to Atlanta, Miami, Denver, and New York for shows. We will go back to Europe for a short break before we begin our regular tour of all fifty states."

"It sounds exciting," Kathe smiled. "I know I better get a few autographs to give Pete and a few friends of mine," she said toying with her food.

"How about one for you to keep?" Joe questioned.

"I have a special memento already," Kathe grinned. "I still have a silk shirt of yours."

"I'm the one who should keep that shirt," Joe insisted. "After all, it is my shirt. I want the memory of it," he said with that boyish grin of his.

Embarrassed Kathe looked down, "I don't know what it is about you. Until I met you, nothing out of the ordinary ever happened to me. I've had some of the most embarrassing moments of my life these past few days."

"I have to admit, I can say the same thing," Joe raised a glass of wine. "A toast to the most wonderful, embarrassing moments of both of our lives." The glasses clanged and each took a sip as JAKE rang again, "I wish you would turn that off."

"If I turned it off, I'd get fired," Kathe admitted, noticing it was Carrie Anne.

"I'll double your salary," Joe grinned.

"Now, that's an offer I might not refuse," Kathe answered. "Hello."

"Kathe, have you seen Joe today?" Carrie Anne began. "Payton is going crazy looking for him and hotel security can't find him either."

"He's right here," Kathe handed JAKE to Joe. "This time it's for you. It seems as if you were a naughty little star and left the hotel without telling your manager."

"What are you talking about?" Joe stated reaching for JAKE. "Hello."

"Where are you?" Payton hollered. "Do you realize that I've had half of New York out looking for you?"

"Payton, I'm a big boy," Joe proclaimed. "I'm over 21 and I know how to take care of myself."

"Where are you?" Payton insisted. "I'll send Brock and RJ to get you!"

"No, I'm on a date," Joe advised. "I'll be there in about an hour," he said putting JAKE on mute. "Sorry, Payton always gets cranky before a performance."

"I'm responsible for your safety!" Payton affirmed. "I'm sending them over to escort you back!" Payton argued as Joe took the phone off mute.

"I'll be all right," Joe insisted. "I'm with Kathe at the same restaurant that we ate at yesterday, end of discussion."

"You know," Kathe said reaching for JAKE. "It seems that both of our bosses don't like us together."

"Payton's not my boss," Joe declared. "He's, my manager. I pay his salary. He doesn't own my personal life."

"Fancy that," Kathe smiled. "I just told Ramsey the same thing about you."

"Waiter," Joe got his attention, "The check please."

Kathe reached for the check from the waiter.

"Not today, it's my treat," Joe said taking the check. "I haven't done this in a long time."

"You haven't done what in a long time?" Kathe asked as she relinquished it.

"Had a nice lunch with a beautiful lady," Joe smiled. He took cash out of his pocket and placed it in the holder.

"Let's go," Kathe said. "We need to get you back to the hotel."

Twenty minutes later, Kathe and Joe arrived back at the hotel heading straight for his room. "You know, I feel like I'm going to get in trouble with my parents for coming in late," she smiled.

"Me too," Joe laughed opening the door for her.

Payton was inside pacing the floor, "Joe!" He stopped, "Don't you ever pull this stunt on me again? You scared the heck out of me!"

All the party guests had left the suite except for Carrie Anne. Babs whispered to Troy, "Do you notice something different about Joe?"

Troy looked over at his friend, "No what?"

"Don't you notice Joe is smiling again?" Babs whispered.

"You're right," Troy noticed. "He is. I haven't seen Joe look like that since long before the split with you-know-who."

Collin was sitting on the couch on the other side of Babs. He overheard them and nodded too.

Payton was still yelling at Joe as he ignored him. He was still holding the packages from their shopping trip. "Do you want me to take these down to your room?" Joe asked Kathe.

"I will take them myself," Kathe whispered. "I don't want Payton to get any angrier with you."

"Payton," Joe interrupted, "if you're finished yelling at me, I'm going to help Kathe take these packages down to her room."

"No, you're not leaving this suite," Payton insisted. "We need to get ready to go to the concert tonight!"

"Yes, I am," Joe declared. "I'll be back in a few minutes," Joe looked at his friends grinning on the couch. "What are you guys looking at?"

"Nothing, nothing at all," Troy answered. "Are you taking the limo with us to the concert or are you riding with Kathe?"

"Let's go Kathe," Joe said turning to leave the room.

"Brock, go with him!" Payton commanded.

"No Brock, I'm going by myself," Joe insisted.

"We have to leave for the concert in a few hours," Payton argued. "I need you well rested and ready to go!"

"Payton is right," Joe realized. "I have been up all night."

Brock went with them despite Joe's disapproval. In the elevator down to her room Joe asked, "What are you wearing to the concert tonight?"

"I thought I'd wear my new pink dress you bought me," Kathe answered.

Brock snickered as Joe's raised an eyebrow.

"Just kidding," Kathe laughed. "I'll wear the leather skirt and jacket," she smiled as she found her key and opened the door, "Shhh...I don't want to wake the guys in the other room. I left them this morning with bad hangovers."

"I'm sorry for what I thought about you and them the other day," Joe apologized closing the door leaving Brock in the hallway.

"It's okay," Kathe accepted. "I guess it would seem likely for you to assume that considering your lifestyle," she said wrinkling up her nose at him. "Apology accepted." She placed the packages on the couch.

As she turned to face him, Joe gently grabbed Kathe around her waist and pulled her to him. "We have to leave by six o'clock. I'll call you as we're leaving our suite," he said as he cupped her face and gently kissed her. To her surprise, instead of pushing him away, she put her arms around his neck and enjoyed every moment of it.

"We got to go Joe," Brock warned opening the door, startling them.

"I guess it's time for you to leave," Kathe said stepping back from his embrace.

"I'll see you in a few hours," he said and kissed her again.

As the door closed, Kathe leaned against it and thought, what did I just do?

The phone rang in a hotel in Harlem. This time his raspy voice was hesitant, "Hello."

"Explain to me, how you missed her again!" his angry voice screamed. "I handed her to you. Are you on crack?"

"Boss, it's not my fault," he stammered. "I had her and her new little friend right in my sights in a leather boutique in the Bronx. I was waiting for her to go into a dressing room and was going to do away with her there. It was perfect. Then...that flight attendant from the airport saw me."

"What happened?" the voice of the other end insisted.

"That same flight attendant on that Paris flight was in there," he stated. "She recognized me. I had to leave. I'm going to slash her throat!"

"I'm running out of patience with you!" his secret boss exclaimed. "Change your appearance. I will call you," he barked as he clicked an icon on his desktop.

Chapter 17

Pulled Away from the Concert

Kathe kicked off her shoes, laid down on her makeshift bed, still not believing how wonderful it felt to be kissed like that again. She couldn't believe how fate kept crossing their paths and how embarrassing moments turned into excitement. The mere thought of Joe made her feel alive again. Composing herself, she reached for JAKE and dialed Jeannie. "I have a second and thought I'd call you back."

"Who is this?" Jeannie questioned.

"It's Kathe," she stated. "Who do you think it is?"

"I'm sorry," Jeannie realized. "But for the first time, I honestly didn't recognize your voice. I'm glad you called. Peter just called me. His father's condition is worsening. He begged me to call you. Ben desperately wants to see you."

"You know I can't stand going out there," Kathe complained. "It's hard enough when I visit the kids. I wish you wouldn't have been so stubborn and moved to Florida."

"Bob and I have talked about it," Jeannie admitted. "Our families live out here. Our parents are getting older. We need to help take care of them. Otherwise, I see your point and we'd probably move," Jeannie said putting vegetables in a crockpot.

"I know you would Jeannie," Kathe sighed, rolling over to look out the window at the busy streets below.

"Ben was always close to you," Jeannie reminded her. "You need to come out here and see him. It's not his fault what Peter did to you and the kids," she said as she shushed the kids coming in from play.

"I know it isn't," Kathe admitted. "Today is the first day I had off in months."

"Kathe Tierney, you and I both know that if you want to come here Ramsey will let you," Jeannie stated. "The only person Ben is asking for is you. One of the nurses asked where you were this morning. Peter said that he would stay away from the hospital while you visit Ben. He's been put on the critical list."

"I'm sorry," Kathe whined. "I just can't," she said pulling the curtain back to widen the view of New York. "My conscience tells me that I should go. But my heart cannot stand the chance of running into Peter or his lovely wife."

"You're the one that will have to live with the consequences," Jeannie declared.

"You're right," Kathe sighed. "I will talk to Ramsey when I get back this evening. I've been invited to Light Crimson's Concert tonight."

"Light Crimson Concert!" Jeannie exclaimed. "Pete was saying something about a rock star this morning when he finely calmed down. He said something about he talked to Joe Sherrod. Then, he ran off telling Heather and Christy. He's been on the phone all day telling everyone he knows."

"I went shopping and had lunch with Joe Sherrod," Kathe admitted. "I met him on a flight this week."

"It's not like you to have a date," Jeannie replied, adding stewed tomatoes to the pot.

"Don't get any ideas," Kathe cautioned. "It was just shopping and lunch. He was just grateful, I think. He hurt his neck in London. I took care of him on the flight over here. That's all."

"Except you're going to the concert tonight with him," Jeannie hinted.

"Me and 20,000 other people," Kathe added.

"I don't know if I should tell Pete that you are going to the concert," Jeannie smiled. "He can't take another shock. He'll be calling you, wanting to know if you saved him a napkin or cup to sell," she whispered as Pete walked into the kitchen.

"You're right," Kathe advised. "Don't tell him tonight. Well, I need to get ready for the concert. Give the kids a kiss for me. Talk to you soon."

A few minutes later, Kathe got out of the shower and looked in the mirror. As she dried her shoulder length hair, she thought about scrunching it with mousse and spraying it. That would give her a wild look. She put on her makeup thinking of Joe. He was not her type at all, and she wasn't his type either. There was something about him...She shook her head no. There was no way...any man... would ever be in her life like that again. Putting her skirt on she noticed it was about three inches above the knee. Standing in front of a mirror she noticed how perfectly it fit the shape of her hips. Remembering how she had not worn jewelry in a long time, she thought how wonderful her bracelets would look with this jacket. She reached in her purse to a secret compartment. She decided on a diamond tennis bracelet, ring and slider necklace with a teardrop diamond. She quickly found the matching earrings. Sitting on the edge of bed, she put on black lace nylons and boots. Walking back to the mirror she thought how strange these clothes felt. They were totally out of character. As she looked at herself in the mirror, she began thinking of what Joe does for a living. Ramsey's words rang through her head, Get Rid of Him! But not tonight. She was going to enjoy the evening with someone special for the first time in a long time. Tonight, she was not carrying a gun, protecting anyone, looking for a terrorist or serving anyone on a plane. Tonight, she was a beautiful woman again. A knock at the door broke her concentration. She hurried to the door only to find Carrie Anne and Babs, Troy's wife.

"The band had to leave for the concert hall early," Carrie Anne said as she peeked into the guy's room. "They had to recheck the sound system one last time. The guys are still asleep. Are they alive?"

"Yes," Kathe admitted. "I heard them stirring a few minutes ago. In all the years, I have known them; I have never seen them this wasted. How much did they drink?"

"I have no idea," Carrie Anne remembered. "They started before they got to the party and left heading for a night cap about 3:00 am."

"No wonder they're still sleeping!" Babs added. "I'm the drummer, Troy Rollins' wife, Babs. I'm very glad to meet you."

"I thought you had met Kathe," Carrie Anne apologized.

"No," Babs admitted. "Today was the first time I saw Kathe with Joe when they came back to the hotel suite."

"I'm glad to meet you," Kathe replied.

"The pleasure is all mine!" Babs insisted. "Any girl that can put the sparkle back in Joe's eyes, Troy and I want to know."

"What do you mean by that?" Kathe asked.

"Let's just say Joe hasn't been happy in quite a long time," Babs declared. "I know all of us in the band can say Joe has a war story to tell about love. I thought I'd never see an honest smile back on his face again."

Carrie Anne headed for the door, "Speaking of honest love, mine is waiting. Let's go."

On their way to the concert, Carrie Anne was telling Kathe how wonderful Travis is. She poured herself a drink. "Want one?" Carrie Anne offered the girls.

"Sure," they said as Carrie Anne bartended.

"Boy, do I need this!" Kathe said, taking a sip. She looked at Carrie Anne, "Jeannie called me earlier and said Peter's father had a heart attack. He is asking for me. She wants me to go to Colorado."

Carrie Anne reached for the scotch, "Hold on, I didn't make your drink strong enough! There's no way you're going!"

"My conscience tells me I should," Kathe admitted. "But my heart tells me to stay away!"

"Go with your heart!" Carrie Anne warned. "It's bad enough having to go there to see the kids. Knowing Peter, he'll make sure you're in the hospital room and walk in with his wife."

"I see Kathe has a war story of her own to tell," Babs said, toasting them.

"Kathe's story makes war look like a walk in the park!" Carrie Anne blurted. "Especially, the way Peter acted when . . ."

"Carrie Anne ease up on the sauce!" Kathe interrupted.

"The gall of him!" Carrie Anne snapped. "He brought her to the hospital in London. I thought Ramsey was going to shoot him herself. Believe me, she thought of it!" Carrie Anne laughed and sipped her drink.

"Carrie Anne, that's enough!" Kathe advised.

"I'm sorry," Carrie Anne apologized. "It slipped. Don't go to Colorado. I'm sorry Kathe, but every time I hear Peter's name, I see red."

"We're here!" Kathe changed the subject as the limo arrived at the arena. She was amazed that there was already a large crowd filing into the building. "Babs, is it always like this at their concerts?"

"Oh, this is just the beginning," Babs explained. "It's still two hours till show time."

The limo passed several broadcasting vans and came to a halt at a back entrance. Security ushered them inside the arena where the band was warming up. When Kathe walked in Joe was singing. He saw her and waved. She was mesmerized as she walked down to the stage. When the song finished, Joe jumped off the stage to her.

"I'm glad you came," Joe smiled as he helped her take her coat off and laid it across a chair. "Turn around let me see the outfit," he said as she modeled it for him. "You look great in that outfit!" he exclaimed pulling her to him, "I have to ask your forgiveness."

"For what?" Kathe insisted.

"I was afraid that you wouldn't wear it," Joe kissed her on the cheek.

"Well, I have to admit I really had to debate between this and the new pink one," Kathe laughed and turned around to modeling it for him again.

"You do look great in pink," Joe winked. "However, tonight you are in my world and now you look like you belong with me," holding her hands he stepped back and gazed at her. "I see you've added your own personal touch. The black lace stockings and boots complete the outfit."

Looking around at the stage Kathe said, "I've never been to a rock concert. I'm impressed."

"This is what I do for a living," Joe grinned. "I kind of sing for my supper."

Carrie Anne and Babs had joined Collin's girlfriend, Suzanne Grant, who had just arrived from London. "Hey Joe," Troy called to him. "We're going to the dressing room."

"Okay, we'll be there in a few minutes," Joe stated. "I want to show Kathe around the stage," he said as they left the arena. He turned to Kathe, "Do me a favor, please?"

"What?" Kathe asked.

"For tonight," Joe smiled. "Do you think you could pull the zipper of your jacket down just a little? I do have the big and bad image to maintain, you know," he pulled the zipper down to show her cleavage.

Pulling it up a tad, Kathe smiled, "We'll compromise. Is this, okay?"

"I think you ought to wear it down a couple of inches more," Joe beamed. "But that's a start," he said as he walked her up on stage and showed her around.

"I never knew such thought went into your work," Kathe said as he gave her a funny look. "I mean, I never really thought of the actual planning that goes into your stage."

"It has to be designed so people can see us from all of the seats," Joe shared. "The lighting has to be exciting and mood setting. We have to be able to freely move around," he said jumping off a platform to the one below.

"Safely, I hope," Kathe wrinkled up her nose at him.

"Hey, if it wasn't for my falling, we may never have met in the employee's quarters," Joe winked.

"You're never going to let me live that down?" Kathe quizzed.

"Not on your life," Joe teased. "After all, you do owe me a shirt."

"I'll buy you one," Kathe insisted.

"Oh, no," Joe demanded. "I want my original shirt back. It has special memories for me," raising his eyebrow at her.

"No, way!" Kathe exclaimed. "That's my souvenir!"

"Yes, way!" Joe lied. "My mother gave me that shirt. I want it back," he leaned closer and kissed her again.

"Hey, Lover Boy," Payton interrupted. "You must go to the dressing room. Security is opening the doors to the public any minute."

"One of these days we won't be interrupted," Joe promised as he reached for her coat, and they left.

Joining the others in the dressing room, Joe noticed everyone had changed except him. "Hurry up mate," Collin urged. "It's getting to be time. RJ just reminded us. We go on in an hour."

Carrie Anne's cell phone rang. "Oh, no, not now!" she whimpered. A look of relief came over her face as she looked at Travis, "I'm clear for two more days." She walked over to him putting her arms around him, "I thought I'd have to leave now. Ramsey is good at giving us no warning." She looked over at Kathe, "Right Kath?"

"Ramsey is known for that," Kathe agreed.

"Why don't you quit?" Babs asked her.

"I couldn't find another job that pays this well," Kathe told her as Joe walked in on the end of the conversation.

"I told you I'd double your salary, if you quit," Joe added.

"You'll double her salary," Carrie Anne laughed. "Let's see, she makes six figures a year."

"Mobley, cut it out!" Kathe demanded.

Joe looked at Kathe with astonishment, "You must be the highest paid flight attendant at any airlines."

"What makes you so important?" Payton asked.

"Nothing," Kathe looked down at the floor embarrassed. "I just work a lot of extra shifts, that's all."

"For six figures you must work continually," Payton smirked.

"Sort of," Kathe glared over at Carrie Anne.

"I'll lay off the sauce," Carrie Anne agreed.

"Twenty minutes till show time," RJ blurted out opening the door. Joe pulled Kathe away from the others.

"Do you want to go for dinner after the show?" Joe asked. "I'm usually starved."

"I never eat that late," Kathe said. "But I'll go," she glanced away.

"Why the sad look?" Joe asked.

"Nothing, I just hope someday Carrie Anne finds someone to tame her down," Kathe admitted. "She's too wild. That's not good."

"She just likes to have fun," Joe replied. "Life should be fun. Some people go all the way through life not knowing what fun is. You know it always seems like Carrie Anne stops a conversation short, especially when she is saying something about you."

"Carrie Anne shouldn't talk about people," Kathe replied, looking straight in his eyes.

"In other words, I still haven't known you long enough?" Joe raised an eyebrow.

"That's right," Kathe assured him.

RJ opened the door again, "Ten minutes till show time!"

"Okay, guys get ready," Payton began getting them pumped up. "Do what you have to do." He opened the door, "Listen to that crowd! They want you! You are whom they paid to see! Let's get ready for them!"

Joe stood up, "No questions for now." He pulled Kathe up to him, "Someday, maybe?"

"Someday, maybe," Kathe confirmed.

RJ opened the door, "Let's go your fans are ready!"

Joe walked over toward the door, "Wish me luck."

"Break a leg," Kathe winked.

Security escorted the girls to their reserved seats. The crowds were electrifying. They were stomping their feet, clapping their hands in unison with a song on the PA system. Suddenly the lights dimmed, and the crowd quieted. Collin struck a chord on his electric guitar, and it began. The British Flag, used as a curtain, fell to the floor. Joe belted the first note, and the crowd was on their feet screaming. Girls started throwing flowers on the stage. Babs leaned around Carrie Anne to Kathe. "It's the old Joe we used to know!"

Carrie Anne leaned over and said, "Look at Travis, whoa!" They were well into their fourth song before the crowd started to settle down. Kathe found herself standing and screaming with the crowd. Carrie Anne looked at her in shock, "I never thought I'd see you like this."

"Me either!" Kathe exclaimed.

When the concert was half over Joe introduced a new song, "We have a new song we'd like to sing for you. It's on our new album." The crowd wailed, "I'd like to do something a little different." He jumped off the steps near Troy's drums and the crowd went crazy again. "I made a bet with Collin," he pointed over to Collin, who raised his guitar. "I told Collin that this is the top song on our new album. I'm going to sing it and we'll..." he took a breath, "We'll... let you be the judge." His sense of humor was at its height. Collin hit the first guitar note. Just as the crowd went crazy, JAKE rang. It was on vibrating mode. She could not feel it due to the vibrations from the speakers. Ramsey used the new implant. She tried to talk to Kathe, but she only heard the loud noise. She used the original implant, which shocked Kathe.

"Ouch!" Kathe screamed, reaching for her clavicle. "Oh, no," she thought as she reached for JAKE. "Ramsey, I must leave this arena. I can't hear you in here."

Kathe looked at Carrie Anne and pointed to JAKE. "It's Ramsey; I can't hear." she said, stepping into the isle, and hurrying into the foyer. "Ramsey, are you there?"

"Where are you?" Ramsey snapped.

"I'm at a rock concert," Kathe replied. "Can't you hear the excitement?"

"I could hear that noise in Russia, which isn't where you're headed," Ramsey discussed. "I want you immediately to come to control. After what happened today, I am sending Yorg with you to Colorado. I must be getting soft in my old age. Peter called me and sounded overwhelmed with his father's failing health. He begged me to let you see his father because he might not make it through the night. Peter said his father threw him out of his room and told him not to ever come back, if you don't come to see him."

"Ramsey . . .," Kathe started to say.

"Don't say anything to me," Ramsey interrupted. "I'm sending you there and then you are heading to Russia. See your kids while you're there. You won't be back in the states for a while."

"Ramsey, do I have to leave now," Kathe complained. "I'm having fun for the first time in a long time," she leaned her head against the wall.

"Ben might not make it till morning," Ramsey warned. "I dislike Peter just as much as you do, but Ben isn't Peter. I don't have to remind you that when you were in the Intensive Care Unit in London, Ben never left your side. You will go and that's an order!"

"I know Ben was always more than a father-in-law to me," Kathe attested. "You're right. I don't belong here anyway," Kathe sadly hung-up JAKE and started to walk back into the arena. Opening the door, she watched Joe cross the stage one last time, before leaving the building.

In the cab, she called Ramsey, "I'm on my way to the hotel to get my things and I'll be there in a few minutes."

"You're leaving on Flight #604 to Denver which leaves at 11:00 pm," Ramsey advised. "Saíde is still in New York; use caution coming into the airport. Yorg will be waiting for you in my office. We just finished a nice discussion about your disobeying direct orders."

"When did Yorg get back from Russia?" Kathe asked.

"About an hour ago," Ramsey stated. "He's just as worried about you as I am. This business with Saíde is serious. Somehow, it looks like he could be involved in the LaBasco's business. Neither of us thinks it's a coincidence that Saíde showed up where both you and Tierra were this afternoon."

"I don't think it's necessary for Yorg to go with me to Colorado," Kathe stated. "I don't need a bodyguard. Have you forgotten; I am one?"

"After your bout with Glitter Boy today, I'm beginning to think that you're not thinking very clearly," Ramsey commented. "Did you ditch him at the concert as I instructed?"

"I just left, didn't I?" Kathe confirmed as she peered out the window.

Back at the hotel Kathe stopped at the gift shop and bought some colorful wrapping paper, wired ribbon, scotch tape and a card. She hurried to her room. The guys were gone. She put the bag with the things she had just bought on the bed. She found the freshly laundered shirt in her overnight bag and wrapped it in paper. Using red ribbon, she made a large bow. Then she took the card and wrote, 'Thanks for the Best Embarrassing Moments of my Life, the Lunch, the Shopping, the Concert, the Entire Day! I'll see you in the clouds! Oh, and definitely maybe, someday, Kathe.' Opening her suitcase as she glanced in the mirror, she decided not to change. Since it was so out of character, Saíde wouldn't recognize her. She used her hands to fluff up her hair to give it a wilder look and sprayed it. She grabbed a piece of paper off the table and wrote, 'Thanks for letting me stay with you. I'm off to Colorado. See ya...Don't party so hardy next time.' Then Kathe hurried out of the room.

The same clerk that had seen her leave earlier was still on duty. "Madam, I'm surprised to see you back so soon. Is everything okay?"

"I'm fine," Kathe smiled. "I just got called into work," she reached into her purse for some money. "Would you please see that Mr. Sherrod gets this package? He's in room 2101." She handed him the package with a nice tip.

Taking the package, "I will make sure he gets it. Thank you, madam." He slipped the money into his pocket and put the package on his desk.

She picked up her suitcases and headed out the door.

Chapter 18

Double Trouble in Denver

Entering Newark Airport, heading straight for control, Kathe hurried to Ramsey's office. Opening the door, she greeted Yorg with a hug, "I'm so glad to see you."

"Wow!" Yorg exclaimed as he stood back. "Where did you get that outfit?"

"What happened to your hair?" Ramsey snarled.

"After you warned me to check my surroundings because of Saíde," Kathe explained. "I decided he would never recognize me like this. Even if I walked past him," Kathe laughed modeling the outfit.

"You got that right!" Ramsey exclaimed. "I have to admit you must be getting over Glitter Boy and thinking the way you should."

"Who is Glitter Boy?" Yorg asked.

"The passenger I was massaging on the flight the other night when you called," Kathe answered.

"Some blame rock star!" Ramsey interrupted. "That Kathe seems to have taken a fancy to like a PET! She knows that she cannot get involved with someone, who is on the cover of every magazine and all over TV! The one she better have ditched for HIS and HER safety tonight!" Looking at her watch, "Now get out of here. Your plane leaves in 20 minutes from Gate 34C, Flight #604. Unfortunately, you are going to have to go dressed like that to Colorado, since you do not have time to change. Yorg keep your eyes peeled. Saíde could be anywhere. We don't want to lead him straight to Kathe's children."

"And Ramsey sure doesn't want me to have a life and be human again!" Kathe snapped leaving the room. "I must stop at the employee's quarters and get another coat. I didn't have time to go back into the dressing room and get mine," she said as Yorg pushed the elevator button.

Kathe leaned her head against the window of the 747 Whisper Jet. She watched out the window as they left Newark and headed off into the night. Ramsey arranged for them to sit in first class. The seats were bigger so they could stretch out and get some rest. Yorg had just flown in from Russia. He was exhausted. He knew Kathe well enough to know that she needed to be alone with her thoughts.

Four and a half hours later the flight attendant woke them. "Good morning, we will be arriving in Denver in about 30 minutes. You might want to wake up a bit. Would you like a cup of coffee?"

"Thank you, I can't believe I slept the whole way," Kathe said, stretching away from Yorg.

"I have to admit that's the most sleep I've had in weeks," Yorg admitted. "I flew straight from Russia to New York. I was told that you disobeyed a direct order. We still must talk about that," he said as she reached for her purse.

"There's nothing to talk about," Kathe glanced at him. "I made that perfectly clear to Ramsey yesterday," she stated as she fixed her makeup.

"Don't pull that on me," Yorg stated. "I know you too well. You were told to stand down; you had no backup! You still kicked a door in and swept the area. Ramsey's right, you could have been killed!"

As the pilot signaled final approach, Kathe continued, "I'm sorry. I thought our job was protecting passengers and crew. I saw Saíde, I went to take him out, end of discussion."

"There you go again using the word 'I' instead of the word team," Yorg cautioned. "You were alone in an alley looking for a man who is a known killer," he glared at her.

"Excuse me," Kathe whispered. "And just who do you think we are?"

As the flight attendant was giving instructions to the passengers for landing in Denver, Kathe looked down at her empty wrist. She forgot her coat and didn't get to buy a watch. It was not like her at all to be so forgetful. Looking at Yorg, "What time is it?"

"It's only 1:30 am," Yorg said.

"Jeannie and Bob will be sound asleep," Kathe realized. "We'll just take a cab."

"Ramsey has a car waiting for us," Yorg instructed. "We are going straight to the hospital for two reasons. First, I don't want anyone to see you here just yet. We are doing this to protect your children. Secondly, we don't want to run into your ex -husband."

"Just once, I would really love to see my children wake up in the morning," Kathe admitted. "In addition, I need to change my clothes. This outfit is totally wrong for this part of the country. But you're probably right."

"Ramsey wants us in and out of here as quick as possible," Yorg stated. "This is just a favor out of respect to your father-in-law and the timing is all wrong."

Entering the hospital, Kathe and Yorg went straight to the Intensive Care Unit and asked for Ben Tierney. The charge nurse was busy charting and acted quite annoyed as she peered over her glasses at Kathe. "Exactly, who are you and what is your relationship with Mr. Tierney?"

"I'm Kathe Tierney," she introduced.

"So, you're the missing daughter!" the nurse scoffed. "I'm glad to see that you finally took time to visit your father. You're all that he's been asking for!"

Kathe saw the name on her badge. "Mabel, let me explain something to you. I'm his ex-daughter-in-law, not his daughter! His son divorced me and remarried someone else. Get the picture!"

"I...I'm...I'm sorry," Mabel stuttered. "The way he talks about you, we all thought you were his daughter."

"I was married to his son for 10 years," Kathe advised as they followed Mabel to his room. "Ben and I have stayed close, and we see each other every time I come to Denver."

"Please forgive me," Mabel apologized. "I didn't know. I've been a nurse for twenty years. You would be shocked at some of the family situations I've seen," she said as they entered his room.

Ben opened his eyes as they entered. "Kathe," his weakened voice called to her. "I knew you'd come."

"Ben what are you doing worrying me," Kathe smiled as she bent down and gave him a kiss on the cheek. "You know I'm the one with the dangerous occupation. You are retired. This is supposed to be the fun part of your life."

"I knew you'd come back to us," Ben smiled as Kathe picked up his weak hand.

"When you're better," Kathe smiled and squeezed his hand. "We can go to my house on the beach in Florida."

"I'd like that," Ben whispered breathing very shallow and labored.

"I'll take the kids with us," Kathe continued. "Pete and you can do some serious fishing."

"Just like old times," Ben managed a smile.

"That's right," Kathe acknowledged. "You guys catch all the fish and I get sunburned." Motioning toward Yorg, "Do you remember Yorg when you came to see me in London?"

"It's good to see you again Ben," Yorg replied as he touched Ben's shoulder. "I remember sitting up with you one very long night waiting to see if Kathe was ever going to wake up again."

"I might be old," Ben managed a smile. "But my mind is sharp as a tack. I'm glad to see that you are still protecting our girl. I read in the paper last week about the man with a knife on an Alby Jet was disarmed. I figured it was Kathe," Ben said as he struggled to catch his breath.

Mabel came back in the room, "I hate to interrupt your visit, but Mr. Tierney is still very weak. We don't want to tire him out."

"I understand," Kathe agreed. "I'll be back with the children once school is out. I want you to rest and think of that fishing trip."

"Promise?" Ben quizzed as she kissed his cheek.

"Promise," Kathe said. "I love you Dad," she said and left the room.

Leaving the hospital, passing the family waiting room, they caught a glimpse of Breaking News on the TV. There was an ongoing threat at the Salt Lake City Airport. Stopping to watch the broadcast, JAKE rang. "Tierney, is Yorg standing by you?" Ramsey solemnly asked.

"We're just leaving Ben's room," Kathe confirmed.

"If no one is around, put JAKE on speaker" Ramsey requested.

"Yes, we're alone in the ICU Family Waiting Room," Kathe said. "We're watching a Breaking News report about the airport at Salt Lake City."

"That situation has been ongoing for three hours," Ramsey explained. "It's not an Alby Jet, thank God. However, what I'm withholding from the press is that Alby Flight #247 in Denver was shut down on the tarmac, just before it was due to takeoff. Dispatch put me through to Denver police. You're never going to believe this, but their Captain of Anti-Terrorism with his entire Swat Team was deployed one hour ago to help Salt Lake City. I've got a bad feeling about this one. Our plane is just sitting there dead with 403 passengers and crew aboard."

"What about Homeland Security in this area?" Yorg asked.

"Their field agents were also deployed to Salt Lake," Ramsey admitted. "The media in Denver is being kept at bay, as much as possible. We have locked down all terminals in every airport across the country. We don't know if any other city has been targeted. I know I was trying to keep your visit to Denver low key; however, you are the only two in the area who are trained to handle my aircraft. I want you in there before Homeland Security and the FBI get involved. I need Kathe's expertise with JAKE to get her onboard to give me inside information. Just like Salt Lake, there are no demands yet. They are just sitting at the gate with the engines off. We have no communication between the pilots and dispatch. Get to the airport. I'll alert security there that you are coming in to help. I'll fill you in on the details as I get them."

At the car Yorg popped the trunk. They moved their bags to the backseat, taking out their guns, extra bullets, and ID badges. Kathe also took out a pair of black pants, a long black sleeve shirt and her black running shoes.

"Well, that's it for low key," Yorg stated as they got into the car.

"I know," Kathe said pulling the visor down and looking in the mirror. "I can change my clothes to go to work, but I have too much hair spray to brush out the wild look. I look ridiculous."

"I like your wild look," Yorg smiled, glancing over at Kathe. "We're here to save lives, not be at a beauty pageant. Let's try to stay away from the media as much as possible. I told Ramsey that this was a bad idea! I didn't want you to come here! It's bad enough with Saíde following you and Tierra! Now, we're flung right into the middle of an airport crisis in a town where your children live!"

"If worse comes to worse," Kathe said, glancing at Yorg. "The kids won't even know that I was here. We'll finish this job and hop on the next jet home," she said as he pulled in front of the terminal and parked in the emergency lane.

"Alby Security," Yorg declared as he got out of the car and held up his ID badge to the police officer approaching them.

"I did my part," Kathe said as they hurried into the terminal. "I'm glad I got to see Ben and tell him I love him," she said as JAKE rang.

"Are you at the airport yet?" Ramsey asked.

"We just entered the terminal and are heading for security," Kathe said as she put her ID badge around her neck.

"Take the first elevator just past the main security checkpoint," Ramsey advised. "Lt. Dan Armstrong is waiting for you. I will contact dispatch and tell them you just arrived. When it's time to monitor the situation, Sydney will use your new implant and have dispatch patch us all together. We have one ray of hope. Flight #247 is from Denver to Mexico City. Among the crew on board are Capt. John Roberts, First Officer Richard Munroe, CC, and Tierra. They know how to handle themselves aboard a flight with trouble like this. When the time comes, they'll know what to do."

"Ramsey there's something about CC that you are not telling me, but I know when I get onboard that aircraft she will help us," Kathe attested.

"I was wondering how long it would take you to figure that out," Ramsey sighed. "She is very capable to handle this kind of situation. That is all I'm allowed to say about her. Get upstairs, find out what's going on, and let me know what your assessment is."

Coming out of the elevator, a Denver police officer met them and took them straight to Lt. Armstrong. "I'm Lt. Dan Armstrong. I'm the Officer in Charge, since Captain Harris and our Swat Team were deployed to Salt Lake City," he glared at Kathe. "You're not what I expected?" The lieutenant blurted as he stared at the thin, wild hair, 5-foot-four, well-endowed woman. "According to Linda Ramsey, you are both members of an Elite Anti-Terrorism Team."

"Don't let my hair style fool you," Kathe declared. "I was at a rock concert when I was ordered to come here."

"What have you got for us?" Yorg snapped very annoyed at his crudeness.

"It's the first flight of the morning, Alby Flight #247 from Denver to Mexico City," Lt. Armstrong explained. "All we know is that when the engines were warming up, the pilot was in normal communication with dispatch. Just before they disconnected the auxiliary air, the engines suddenly shut down. Since then, there has been no movement inside the plane. It's just sitting there. Strangely enough, it is mirroring the incident that is happening in Salt Lake City that started three hours earlier."

"Do you have any sharpshooters?" Yorg asked. "And if so, what are they equipped with?"

"I have six officers with M40 SWS chambered in 7.62 NATO and 10x42 Leopold M3A Sniper Optic," Armstrong replied.

"That will help," Yorg stated. "We cannot let that plane takeoff. I also need to see the schematics of that plane."

"It will take me a minute to get the schematics," Armstrong replied as he reached to answer his cell phone.

"Ramsey can send them to us on JAKE," Kathe said as they looked out the smoked glass window at the perimeter of the plane.

Hanging up his phone Lt. Armstrong joined them, "We have another problem on the main level. A custodian just found a male body stuffed in the janitorial closet. He has been stripped of his clothes and ID. My men are checking on his identity now."

"We need to see the body," Kathe requested. "If my guess is right, it has to be a crew member."

Moving around the officers on the scene, Kathe put on a pair of gloves. She reached down and pulled the sheet carefully off the victim's face. "It's Richard Munroe," she identified as she uncovered the rest of his body. "He was the First Officer on this flight. He was also one of the officers on Flight #1014 with the Saíde incident. There are no stab wounds. The discoloration around his neck suggests his neck was broken."

"We can now safely assume that the First Officer is a terrorist," Yorg declared as he turned to Lt. Armstrong. "Have your officers check with the outside crews to see if they observed the First Officer doing anything unusual when he did his walk around the outside of the plane. Kathe, have Ramsey check Salt Lake City to see if they can find any dead bodies."

"Since this started three hours after Salt Lake City, Ramsey also needs to alert the other airports to be on guard three hours from when this started," Kathe added reaching for JAKE.

"Let's get back upstairs and finish our assessment of the perimeter," Yorg said as they hurried off.

As Kathe finished filling Ramsey and Dr. Sydney in on their findings, they passed the media as they were heading back to the elevator. Kathe stopped and pulled Yorg aside and whispered, "I just got an idea. It's so crazy it just might work. We can use the media to distract the terrorist long enough for me to get onboard."

"Kat," Yorg cautioned. "We need to stay out of the media. We don't want the media airing this causing more nationwide panic!"

"No, no, no, you don't understand," Kathe explained. "We are going to use the media to distract the terrorist inside the plane, long enough for me and perhaps someone else to get onboard. We are not going to let them air the footage just yet, but they can tape it. We will tell them they can have exclusive rights to air it when this is done. They are just a local TV station. We will make a deal with them and think about it Yorg. It will work. What do terrorists want? To cause panic; they're probably wondering where the media is now. We both get what we want. In exchange for the exclusive rights, they can have no footage of you and me."

"Right now, it is our only option," Yorg agreed. "Let's get upstairs and see what the schematic of the plane looks like. We don't know how much time we've got."

Lt. Armstrong watched in amazement as they studied the schematics. He listened as they consulted with Ramsey and Dr. Sydney. Sydney spoke first, "The news media should be interviewing Lt. Armstrong at the end of the jetbridge at an angle as close as possible facing the cockpit. That should keep their eyes away from the tarmac."

"I agree," Yorg confirmed. "There is a luggage truck and catering truck to the right of the cockpit.

This will provide cover for Kathe to wait for my signal to make her move. I will be watching through my scope for the terrorist's focus to change to the newscaster. This should buy Kathe a few seconds to get safely under the plane and enter the electrical equipment access hatch."

"That should work," Ramsey agreed. "Except Armstrong's men are regular police officers and not Swat trained in this kind of tactics. Does he have someone he trusts to go aboard with Kathe?"

"Yes, I do," Lt. Armstrong affirmed as one of his officers brought in a ground crew. "I'll send McNamara with her. He has military experience. According to this aircraft's fueler, the first officer was under the mid-section of the aircraft for quite some time."

"What do you mean, for quite some time?" Kathe asked the man.

"The first officer was doing the walk around," he explained. "He went under the plane as I was standing on my ladder, under the right forward wing ready to attach the fueling nozzle. I even said, 'good morning,' and he did not turn around and look at me or say anything. I realized that I needed something from my truck and went to get it. He did not come out from under the craft until I got back and completed the hook-up. I even asked him if everything was okay. Again, he ignored me."

"Check under the craft for any wireless cameras before you start," Sydney requested.

"Make sure Kathe and McNamara are heavily armed and each of them has a drill and periscope," Ramsey added. "Once inside, Kathe can try to locate CC or Tierra. I hope that they will be able to help or distract the terrorist. Yorg, you and another officer will target the terrorist in the cockpit from the roof of the terminal. It is early morning there. The sun coming over the mountain will be very bright behind you, which will give you cover. I just sent a picture of Capt. John Roberts so you will know which pilot not to shoot," she said as she checked her computer screen. "Remember the terrorist may have changed seats with Roberts hoping to confuse us," Ramsey changed screens. "The air marshal is on the right side of the plane, seated in row 42G, which is an aisle seat. Armstrong, station your men around the perimeter of the plane to keep it from leaving. Have your people use caution, there may be more terrorists disguised as ground crew. I want you all to understand that under NO circumstance is that plane to leave the ground! I don't want another 9/11!"

"Yorg," Sydney instructed, "for you to successfully break the glass in the windshield, one of you will have to shoot the windshield. A second bullet will have to go in the same point of impact to penetrate through the glass and kill the terrorist."

"Understood," Yorg confirmed. "An officer and I will target the terrorist in the cockpit from the roof. I have my 338 magnums with a Shepherd Scope that has a kill flash. It will not reflect the sun. The officer with me will make sure no one is on the ground watching us. I will be able to assist Kathe and McNamara from that angle to get safely under the plane. When Kathe is ready, the officer will shoot the windshield first and I will use the same point of impact to break the glass and take out the terrorist."

"Dispatch," Ramsey continued, "that is when the cockpit will be clear and communications with the pilot should be reestablished."

"Copy that," dispatch answered.

"If something goes wrong," Yorg declared. "I will make sure the plane never leaves the ground. Have you heard from Homeland Security yet?"

"No, and we don't have time to wait for Homeland Security," Ramsey informed them. "Armstrong this has to be your best performance in front of the camera. Everything depends on you keeping the focus away from that tarmac."

"There is another potential problem," Sydney cautioned. "Kathe, when you open the electrical equipment access hatch, you must quickly get inside and immediately close the hatch. A warning light will show on the pilot's EICAS display panel. Hopefully, the terrorist in the cockpit will be focused on the interview and not the panel."

"Sydney is right," Ramsey confirmed. "Kathe that door must be closed quickly. I have already spoken with the TV station manager. The reporter has agreed with our terms and conditions. Armstrong only answer his questions; do not offer any other information. It will not be aired now, but be careful what you say, it will be aired when this is over. Do not mention Yorg, Kathe or my name. This is your collar. You are taking all the glory. Remember, everyone must hold his or her position to wait for Kathe's signal. Let's get this show on the road."

As the television reporter interviewed Lt. Armstrong at the end of the jetbridge, Yorg watched through his scope. He could see the plan was working, "Kat, go! Move now, both men have just turned their heads and are watching Armstrong."

"Copy that," Kathe said as Yorg watched her and McNamara inch their way from the terminal to the catering truck.

"Stop!" Yorg warned as they froze. "The first officer is looking around," he peered through his scope. "Go hurry, he's looking away again."

"Moving," Kathe replied as they hurried over to the front wheel of the plane and stopped.

"Stop and hold your positions!" exclaimed an officer looking through his scope from the right side of the plane. "It looks like there is something small and round under the plane in the center."

"Kat, do you copy?" Yorg asked.

"Copy that," Kathe answered, crouching down, and peering around the tire. "I see it. It is a wireless, wide-angle, PTZ camera."

"That explains why the first officer was under the plane so long," Sydney affirmed. "He has a monitor in the cockpit. Kathe use JAKE to override its frequency with your own feed. Tape about thirty seconds. That should be ample time for you to get inside and close the hatch."

"Copy that," Kathe confirmed as she recorded the footage under the plane with JAKE. "I've got the film ready to feed it back to the monitor. Are we clear to continue?"

"You're clear from my angle," Yorg affirmed.

"They're clear from the back of the plane," replied an officer.

"Right side clear," another reported.

"Left side clear," the last officer confirmed.

"Copy that," Kathe replied as she pressed enter. JAKE instantly overrode their cameras frequency and motioned for McNamara to follow her.

Crouching down and hurrying over to the left side of the plane, Kathe quickly located the hatch. "I'm ready to open the hatch now," she alerted. "I'm turning the handle. We're entering the electronic equipment access hatch," Kathe whispered and made their way inside. Capt. Roberts noticed the warning light on the EICAS display panel and slowly moved his hand to cover it. "I'm closing the hatch now," Kathe reported as Roberts closed his eyes for a second of relief.

"You're okay," Yorg relayed. "The terrorist didn't see the red light. He was looking at Armstrong

112

keep going."

"We see the door in the bulkhead leading to the cargo bay," Kathe stated. "We are in the cargo bay and making our way to the hatch, which leads underneath the main cabin. McNamara is drilling next to the hatch now."

As McNamara inserted the flexible periscope, he gave Kathe the all-clear signal. "There is no movement," McNamara whispered. "Everyone is just sitting and looking forward. I can see a flight attendant sitting in the jumpseat," he said as he moved away for Kathe to look.

Bending the flexible periscope for a better view Kathe looked inside, "CC is the one sitting in the jumpseat. I'm going to open the hatch and see if I can get her attention." Kathe motioned for McNamara to resume position with the periscope. "I'm turning the hatch lock now."

Holding his finger up to Kathe, McNamara whispered, "I think the flight attendant sees the periscope, hold on… yes, she does, she is holding up a finger."

Kathe opened the hatch using the drill bit to pry apart the Velcro. CC coughed to cover the noise. When Kathe heard CC coughing, she opened the corner of the carpet, just enough for CC to see her. CC folded her hands in her lap as she looked away from the carpet. She held up two fingers and then put her hands back down. As she moved her hands, straightening her dress, she used sign language to say 27A and 27J. By putting her one hand down toward the floor, she signed, laptops handcuffed to bombs. First officer brought aboard. Video displays changed to monitor passengers. With her hand reaching backwards, she motioned to the cockpit, one terrorist. Lastly, moving her hand back up to her watch, she signed 45 minutes to detonation. Kathe put the carpet down and backed away.

As McNamara kept an eye on the cabin, Kathe consulted with Yorg, Sydney and Ramsey. "Kathe," Ramsey said. "I just got word that Homeland Security and the FBI are on scene. Give me a few minutes to bring them current with the situation, then I will patch them through to you."

"Make it quick, we are running out of time," Kathe warned as she checked the time. "We only have less than 42 minutes."

"Kathe, Sydney is patching them through to you," Ramsey stated as she answered her office phone.

"I'm FBI Agent Walter Jones," he introduced. "I'm impressed with your assessment of the situation and plan to end this siege as well as Salt Lake City."

"I'm Capt. Holter of Homeland Security," he introduced. "We have two bomb squads waiting. As soon as you secure the targets, we will storm the exit doors on the wings using catering trucks. Bomb squads will cut the handcuffs and remove the laptops. Dispatch will have the captain make an announcement, telling the passengers in the cabin to remain seated until we remove the laptops. Then we'll open all the doors and use the emergency chutes to evacuate with my men helping the passengers."

"Kathe and McNamara will have to drill a hole under the seats where the two terrorists are sitting in the 27th row," Sydney declared as he checked a computer model. "After you confirm the targets and are ready, signal Yorg. Simultaneously, all three of you will shoot through the seats and cockpit. We're waiting for your signal."

"And Kathe," Ramsey confirmed as she got off her office phone. "Homeland Security did find a dead pilot in Salt Lake City. Our hunch was right; these two situations were meant to blow up together. Salt Lake City is working on the same plan. Security at Atlanta's Hartsfield-Jackson Airport just arrested two men carrying laptops with explosive devices hidden inside."

McNamara gave the all-clear signal that nothing had changed in the cabin, as Kathe lifted the carpet again, giving a five-minute signal to CC. Quietly, McNamara and Kathe crawled to the middle of the cargo bay and located the seats where the targets were seated. They held up small drills and put holes under each seat. Using their flexible periscopes, they both confirmed the targets. Pulling the periscopes down, while attaching silencers to their weapons, Kathe gave McNamara the signal. "We're ready; we're putting our guns in place."

"Copy that," Yorg replied as he and the officer with him zeroed in on the target in the cockpit. Yorg then took over the count looking through his scope, "We're ready on three, two, one! "Pfftt, Pfftt, Pfftt."

"The target is down in the cockpit," Yorg declared. "I repeat. The target is down in the cockpit."

Placing the periscopes in the holes located under the seats to check, Kathe and McNamara both confirmed targets down. "Targets are down over the wings," Kathe confirmed signaling McNamara to follow her. "The targets are both down. We're hurrying to tell CC to stay seated. There may be others aboard."

"Dispatch, you are clear to contact Capt. Roberts," Yorg declared.

"Copy that," dispatch answered, reestablishing communications.

"Captain Roberts," Sydney asked. "Is the countdown still going on?"

"Affirmative," Captain Roberts declared. "The bombs are still live. The countdown continues."

"I'm going to kill the cameras watching the passengers for six seconds," Sydney stated. "Kathe, are you back at the EEA Hatch?"

"Affirmative," Kathe answered.

"Signal CC as soon as the cockpit's door slightly opens to grab the briefcase with the bombs and hand it to you," Sydney ordered. "I'll restore the cameras while you hand it to the Bomb Squad from under the EEA Hatch. Then, sweep the plane for more hostiles."

"Copy that," Kathe said, slightly lifting the hatch signaling CC. "She's ready when you are. She's telling the passengers in first class to stay still."

"Bomb Squad, meet Kathe under the plane, take the laptop, and then destroy it in your truck," Sydney advised. "It is still counting down. This should stop the bomb in the cabin from detonating."

"Copy that," Capt. Holter agreed. "We are ready."

"I'm en route to help clear the plane when you're ready," Yorg said, leaving the rooftop.

The silence in the cabin continued as the cockpit door slightly opened. Roberts pushed the briefcase to CC, who handed it to Kathe. Kathe handed the briefcase to the Bomb Squad and rejoined McNamara at the hatch. Kathe then slightly lifted the hatch door and signaled CC they were coming inside.

Lifting the carpet from the hatch, CC whispered to the passengers in first class, "It's okay, they are Alby Security. Stay seated and be quiet."

Kathe and McNamara entered the plane. They split up on each side of the fuselage and began their sweep of first class. CC followed them to business telling the crew that they were security.

"We're entering the third compartment," Kathe said, locating the two terrorists slumped over in their seats. She checked the one on the right side, secured the laptop and noted the timer as McNamara checked the one on the left and signaled it stopped. "Sydney, you were right. The countdown on the two laptops have stopped."

Entering the last section, they each swept the opening at the same time. The startled sky marshal jumped to his feet and drew his gun. Tierra jumped out of her seat and held up her hands, "She's Alby security! I know her! She's okay!"

"All three targets are down," Kathe reported to the sky marshal. She noticed a man sitting on the last row in the middle aisle grin as he reached in his coat pocket.

He stood up pulling out his cell phone and raised it in the air shouting, "Praise to A . . ." as Kathe shot him between the eyes. He fell forward as the passengers around him scurried out of their seats screaming. McNamara dove around them grabbing the cell phone out of his hand.

"Thank God!" McNamara exclaimed, holding up the cell phone. "This phone has its own bomb!"

"What just happened?" Yorg yelled, entering the plane through the EEA Hatch. "Dispatch, we have another gunshot!"

"Yorg, dispatch!" Kathe reported. "We found a fourth terrorist with a cell phone that has its own bomb. I repeat we found another bomb. He was sitting on the last row in the middle aisle. He's down. I repeat all four targets are down. Dispatch, send in the Bomb Squad to collect these three remaining bombs."

"Copy that," dispatch answered.

"I'll alert Salt Lake City and Atlanta that there is a sleeper onboard with his own cell phone bomb," Ramsey exclaimed.

"McNamara, you and the sky marshal secure the laptops," Kathe requested as Yorg joined them. "Yorg help me open the wing exits!"

At the same time, entering from right and left third doors of the fuselage from the catering trucks, the bomb squads entered through the wings. They detached the laptops from the terrorists' wrists and placed them in disposable containers. They quickly left the plane and drove away from the gate.

"Dispatch, tell Capt. Roberts to open all the doors and release the chutes!" Yorg exclaimed as he and Kathe opened the second window exit rows.

"All flight attendants, we are emergency evacuating this plane!" Capt. Roberts announced.

"People, we need to empty this compartment," Yorg ordered as he and the sky marshal helped the passengers deplane from the left window. Kathe and McNamara helped passengers on the right-side windows.

"First two compartments are empty," CC declared as she came back to them.

"Aft compartment is empty," Tierra reported.

"Let's clear this bird!" Yorg ordered as he reached for CC's hand and helped her onto the chute, then Tierra, while Kathe and McNamara left from the right chute.

On the ground, hurrying under the plane to Kathe, CC hugged her, "I was so glad to see you!"

"I can't believe you saw that last terrorist," Tierra cried. "He was going to blow up the plane right in front of our eyes!"

Capt. Roberts hurried over to them, "I'm glad you were in this area of the country. I knew something was up when I noticed the EEA Hatch light up," he said, hugging Kathe. "That is two flights in two weeks that could have had different endings. Richard Munroe was supposed to fly with me today. What happened to him?"

"I hate to tell you," Yorg said, reaching for the captain. "Munroe was found murdered, evidently by the terrorist in the cockpit."

"Oh, my, God," Capt. Roberts sighed, collapsing to the ground. "He has a wife and two small children."

"Captain," Kathe said, reaching for his hand, "we need to get away from the plane. Homeland Security's bomb squad is checking for more devices."

"Kathe's right," Yorg reiterated, helping Capt. Roberts to his feet. "Let's get inside the terminal."

Entering the terminal, the passengers were waiting for them. Everyone stood up and applauded them for saving their lives. Lt. Armstrong's men formed a line to hold the passengers back. Reaching out to shake Yorg's hand, "I'm Capt. Holter of Homeland Security and this is Agent Walter Jones of the FBI," he introduced. "We wanted to meet the two Alby Security Agents that are responsible for saving the lives of hundreds of innocent people across the United States."

Kathe stepped closer to Capt. Holter and whispered, "You have this all wrong. We're not here. We do not want any credit for this situation. I'm sure Ramsey has already explained it to you. This was all masterminded by Lt. Armstrong of the Denver Police Department."

Yorg pulled Kathe closer to him, "tell Armstrong, thanks for a job well done. His team was exemplary," Yorg said, and they hurried out of the terminal.

Leaving the airport heading to Jeannie and Bob's house, JAKE rang, and Kathe put it on speaker. Ramsey said, "Thanks to your quick-thinking Salt Lake City and Atlanta have a happy ending too! I must admit, Homeland Security asked me if they could borrow you two. I assured them that you only work for me! I also had to sidestep the fact of telling them how we could talk to Kathe, without her holding a phone or wearing an earpiece. We have McNamara to thank for that. He asked Armstrong to find out. He meant to ask Kathe before she left but had to secure the cell phone bomb. Sydney and I are not ready to debut the technology of JAKE yet. The TV station is keeping its word, with no mention of anybody other than the local PD. Enjoy your kids while you can. I'm getting you out of there later tonight," Ramsey cleared the line.

Arriving at the house a surprised Jeannie opened the door. "Kathe, how did you get here? I'm watching TV and the airport has been shut down for hours. Something about an Alby Jet, four terrorist, two laptop bombs, and a cell phone bomb!" Jeannie exclaimed giving her friend a hug. Taking a step back she stared at Yorg, "I'm Jeannie Rafferty," reaching for his hand.

"I'm Yorg Vuslick," he introduced.

"So, you're Kathe's Russian!" Jeannie blurted.

"Jeannie, you're beginning to sound like Carrie Anne," Kathe laughed.

"I'm so sorry," Jeannie blushed, "but that's what Carrie Anne calls him."

"No offense taken," Yorg replied with a smile. "I'm well aware of how Carrie Anne thinks about me."

"Wait a minute, why aren't you at the airport?" Jeannie questioned.

"The situation has been resolved," Kathe answered as they entered the foyer. "The airport is reopened."

"I don't want to hear about it!" Jeannie requested. "I don't want to know what happened but thank God you're safe. Are you going to be in the news? What am I going to tell the kids?"

"There's nothing to tell, we had nothing to do with it," Kathe calmly replied. "Have the older kids gone to school yet?"

"Yes, the bus just left a few minutes ago and Joey is sleeping," Jeannie answered. "Why don't I believe you had nothing to do with the airport? Just look at you, you're a mess."

"Just watch the news and see for yourself," Kathe offered.

"I just came with Kathe to see Ben, which we did first thing this morning," Yorg added.

"I didn't know you knew Ben," Jeannie stated.

"Yes, we met when Kathe was in the hospital in London," Yorg admitted. "Is there somewhere I can shower and change?"

"Sure, I'll show you the children's bathroom," Jeannie replied as she ran ahead of him to check if it was clean. "It's probably a mess."

"I don't care," Yorg insisted as he followed her. "I just need to clean up."

While Kathe was in the master bathroom showering, the doorbell rang. Jeannie went to the door halfway expecting it to be Peter. It was a UPS delivery for Kathe. Jeannie signed for the box. Kathe came out of the bedroom. She tiptoed into Joey's room to see him. There was her baby sound asleep. She gently moved the covers away from his face as a tear fell down her cheek. Look what I miss, she thought as he smiled in his sleep. Gently rubbing the side of his cheek, whispering his name, "Joey...Joey." Suddenly his sleepy eyes opened. He rubbed them as if he were dreaming. "Hey baby," she whispered. "It's really me."

"Mommy!" Joey exclaimed and jumped into her arms. He wrapped his arms around her neck, "Mommy, you came home!"

"Yes, I'm home," Kathe smiled and rocked him in her arms.

"Are you going to stay with me?" Joey begged.

"I'm here now," Kathe said, changing the subject. "Are you as hungry as me?"

"Yes, Mommy," Joey said, "But I have to go potty."

"You go ahead," Kathe smiled. "I'll meet you in the kitchen with Aunt Jeannie and make your breakfast."

"Look what just came for you about 15 minutes ago by UPS," Jeannie pointed to a large box on the table. Kathe looked at the box. The return address was from New York.

"It must be my coat I left in New York," Kathe said as she opened it. "Carrie Anne must have sent it to me on a later flight."

"Mommy, you're still here," Joey exclaimed and jumped into her arms.

"I told you I'd meet you in here," Kathe smiled and kissed him. "I want to make your breakfast." She sat Joey down at the table and made him a scrambled egg, a piece of toast and a banana. "Look how big you're getting."

"Did you bring me a big present?" Joey asked as Yorg entered the room. "Who's that?" Joey asked as he reached for his mother.

Walking Joey over to Yorg, Kathe introduced, "Joey this is a very good friend of mine. He's a pilot that I work with, his name is Capt. Yorg Vuslick. Yorg this is my youngest son, Joey."

"Are you going to marry my mommy?" Joey innocently asked.

"Joey, what did you just say?" Kathe snickered.

"Let's just say your mommy and I are very good friends," Yorg replied.

"My mommy brought me a big present," Joey smiled and pointed to the box.

"No, Joey," Kathe said. "I just came to see Grandpa in the hospital. This big box is a coat I forgot in New York," she said as she looked inside and pulled out her coat. "I can't believe Carrie Anne remembered to send it to me." Then she noticed, under the coat was a box covered in the same wrapping paper she used to wrap Joe's shirt. She picked it up as Joey reached for it. "No, Joey, let Mommy open it. I don't know what this could be."

"Joey, why don't we take your breakfast into the other room," Yorg suggested. "You can show me your Star Wars toys, while Mommy opens her present," Yorg suggested as he reached for Joey's plate. "I think your mommy needs a few minutes alone," he said, and they left the room.

"It's from a jewelry store on 5th Avenue," Jeannie gasped as she walked closer.

Kathe opened the box slowly, "Oh, look at this watch!" She held it up for Jeannie to see. It was a beautiful gold and diamond Rolex. Jeannie peeked in the box to see if there was anything else. She handed Kathe an envelope. Kathe read, Thanks for the few days I got to spend with you. I hope that 'Maybe Someday' will be soon, Joe. Another note was under that one. 'Here are some autographed pictures of me for your son Pete. One of the pictures has all our signatures. Tell Pete I hope it brings him at least $500. LOL!"

"Kathe, look at the diamonds in this watch!" Jeannie exclaimed. "Who gave this to you?"

"Joe Sherrod!" Kathe replied as she looked in the box and found a bag. She opened it and concert shirts fell out. Another note was in the bag. Here are some shirts for your kids. There is a shirt for you to sleep in with just me on the front. Next time you must sleep in a man's room wear this instead of your low-cut pink nightgown. "He did see me in pink!"

"What are you talking about?" Jeannie eagerly inquired.

"Yesterday we were shopping, I picked up a pink dress and asked him what he thought," Kathe explained. "He told me I looked good in pink. Only I never wore pink around him. I asked him how he knew I looked good in pink, and he said, he guessed it would look good with my coloring. That son of . . . He must have seen me the night before in Jay's room sleeping in my pink nightgown."

"Wow, that's over my head!" Jeannie laughed as she picked up the wrapping paper. "That's the doorbell again," she said, hurrying to answer it. She returned with a bouquet of Peace Roses in her hands. "Look what you just got!" Jeannie set them down on the table next to the box.

Kathe took the note, which read, "By now you know my secret about the pink nightgown. I figured I better send roses. Carrie Anne said these are your favorite. I told you yesterday morning that I could not sleep; now you know why, Joe."

"You hit the Jackpot!" Jeannie exclaimed as JAKE rang.

"Hello," Kathe answered.

"Well, do you forgive me?" Joe asked.

"Joe how did you get JAKE's number?" Kathe asked.

"I told Carrie Anne I'd torture her if she didn't give it to me," Joe replied. "She arranged for someone at control to patch me through to you...Well, you didn't answer my question. Do you forgive me?"

"You are something else," Kathe beamed. "Yes . . . I forgive you. But when did you see me in my pink nightgown?"

"Carrie Anne forgot her cell phone the night of the party," Joe confessed. "I went downstairs with her to see if I could see you. And I did!"

"Why didn't you wake me?" Kathe asked.

"You looked so peaceful, and I was with someone else at the party, remember?" Joe admitted.

"Yes, I do remember," Kathe addressed.

"Carrie Anne helped me find you," Joe explained. "I felt so bad when the concert was over, and Babs told me you left. I couldn't believe my luck. I went back into the dressing room and the first thing I saw was your coat. I went back to my hotel and as soon as we walked inside, the clerk at the front desk handed me your package. You totally messed with my head!"

"I'm sorry," Kathe sighed. "I didn't mean to do that. Maybe I'll see you when I get back to New York."

"When are you coming back?" Joe asked.

"Late tonight, I'm not sure what time," Kathe shared. "By the way, thank you for the watch, but I can't accept it."

"Why not?" Joe quizzed.

"This is a diamond Rolex," Kathe said as she admired it. "You just can't go around buying strangers expensive presents."

"You're not a stranger," Joe admitted. "You haven't been a stranger, since the first time I laid eyes on you. I remembered you wanted a dressy watch. Is it dressy enough?"

"It is definitely dressy enough," Kathe confirmed. "When are you leaving New York?"

"Early tomorrow morning we head for California," Joe replied.

"Maybe sometime our paths will cross again in the sky," Kathe wished out loud.

"Since I have to leave you with some 'Russian Hunk,' as Carrie Anne puts it," Joe sighed, "with a body she's been eying for years. Will you promise me something?"

"What's that?" Kathe asked with a smile.

"If you massage him again," Joe continued, "this time massage him like you did me. Maybe next time I see you, you'll massage me like you did him."

"I can't believe you're still thinking about that," Kathe smiled.

"I've got to go," Joe said. "Payton is summoning me."

"Thanks again for your friendship and the gifts," Kathe said as she heard Payton called Joe again.

Jeannie was surprised to hear her friend laughing with another man. "It's good to see an honest smile on your face again."

"Funny you said that," Kathe confessed. "One of his friends, last night at the concert, told me the same thing about him," she said as she peered outside the window at the mountains. "Let's go get the kids from school."

Chapter 19

Her Two Worlds Collide

Joey was entertaining Yorg by showing him all his new Star War toys when Kathe found them. "Jeannie and I are going to pick up the kids from school. I only have a short time to see them. Do you want to come?"

"I do Mommy," Joey said, running to her.

"We're supposed to stay together, or did you forget?" Yorg raised an eyebrow.

"No, I didn't forget I don't have a normal life," Kathe said and led the way to the kitchen. "Let's go."

"I called the school," Jeannie said, hanging up the phone. "They'll have the kids waiting for us. I even pulled Christy out. I know she'll want to be with all of us. I didn't tell them you were here. I wanted it to be a surprise. I called Bob and he is going to meet us at the McDonald's by our house."

A few minutes later, the van pulled up in front of D'Evelyn Jr./Sr. High School. The kids were waiting outside as the van stopped in front of them. "Mom's here!" Heather shouted as Kathe opened the door and hugged her. "I've missed you so much!"

"I've missed you, too!" Kathe declared.

"Did you bring me any autographs?" Pete asked as he reached around Heather to hug her too.

"Pete, is that all you think about?" Jeannie asked swatting at him from the driver's seat.

"Sorry Mom, I'm glad you're here," Pete answered as he ducked away from Jeannie. "Well, did you?"

"Yes, I did," Kathe explained. "I just received a box with T-shirts from last night's concert for everybody. Joe also autographed some just for you to sell."

"Mom," Heather whispered. "Who's that man sitting next to Joey?"

"Yes, Ms. Kathe, who's that man?" Christy asked.

"That's a pilot friend of mine that I work with," Kathe introduced. "His name is Capt. Yorg Vuslick."

"That's your Russian!" Christy burst out with a big smile.

"Not you too!" Kathe exclaimed, glancing at Yorg. Yorg smiled as Christy's face turned bright red.

"I'm going to kill Carrie Anne," Kathe muttered under her breath. "Don't be embarrassed, your mother said the same thing!"

Leaning toward Kathe, Jeannie whispered, "But he looks just like Carrie Anne described him!"

"If all the pilots look like him," Christy whispered. "Maybe I'll become a flight attendant when I graduate!"

"No!" Kathe and Jeannie shouted at the same time.

"It's not that glamorous of a job," Kathe continued. "I spend a lot of time sitting at an airport waiting to catch a flight with no pay. I only get paid in the air. You know Carrie Anne; she adds her own twist to the job. Get in the van; let's go get some lunch."

After the kids piled into the van, Kathe introduced Yorg, and the van pulled out of the parking lot. Bob met them at McDonald's near their house and had lunch. They stayed there about an hour catching up on the routine of each child. Then Bob took Christy home while Jeannie took them to the hospital.

Entering the hospital, Jeannie pushed ahead of Kathe to make sure Peter was not there. She motioned the all-clear and Kathe walked past the nurses' station. "I don't know what you did this morning," the charge nurse admitted. "The morning shift noticed a marked improvement in Mr. Tierney, right after you left."

"That's great!" Kathe smiled. "I'm glad I came."

As they walked in the room, good old Peter was just coming out of his father's bathroom. Kathe couldn't believe her luck. She started to leave the room. However, Ben opened his eyes. "Kathe," he exclaimed. "You're back. Look who's here."

Peter looked flabbergasted when he spotted Yorg with Kathe. "We'll come back later when you're alone," Kathe said, reaching for Yorg's hand, and stepping backwards.

"No!" Ben snapped. "Peter can leave! I want to see you again." Peter did not budge for a second. Without looking at his son, Ben ordered, "Peter, I told you to leave now!" Peter did not say a word as he left the room.

Kathe went to Ben's bedside and kissed him on the cheek, "I hear you're feeling much better."

"Much better, since I saw you early this morning," Ben's voice sounded a little cheerier.

"Must be the fishing trip to Florida, I promised you," Kathe smiled as she took his hand and noticed it was not as cold. "I see that the fire is coming back in you. You just threw your son out of the room in front of his own children," she gave him another kiss on the cheek.

"I should have thrown him out five years ago and you would have never left," Ben stated with a smile. "Kathe, I want you to know that I still think of you as my daughter-in-law, not Helen," he turned toward grandchildren. "Your children agree with me."

"Yes, grandpa, we do," Pete answered.

Standing by Yorg, Kathe watched her children with their grandpa. For a few seconds, she missed a part of her old life. Looking at her new watch, "Ben, it's getting close to dinner time and the kids have homework. We need to go and let you rest," she said. "Yorg and I will be back to see you before we leave tonight."

Peter was standing with Jeannie and Joey as Kathe and Yorg walked past them. "Jeannie, we'll meet you in the van," Kathe declared.

"Wait a minute," Peter ran up to her.

Yorg put his arm around Kathe's waist and pointed his finger at Peter, "You made your choice five years ago, she is with me now!"

Jeannie passed Peter saying, "She's not the little wimpy, crying wife, she used to be Peter. You had better leave her alone. She came here out of respect and love for your father, not because of you."

"I know that Jeannie," Peter stated. "I just want to thank her for coming and tell her how great she looks."

"I think you better save that kind of talk for Helen," Jeannie grinned and hurried to catch up to them. "I'm sorry," Jeannie apologized to Kathe walking outside in the parking lot.

"He's still the same jerk," Kathe admitted as she reached for Joey's hand. "I can't believe I was so stupid for so many years."

"I can't believe how he ran after you," Jeannie said in disbelief. "He wanted to thank you for coming and tell you how nice you look. The gall of him after what he did to you!"

"Believe me after seeing the look on his face, when Yorg told him that he made his choice five years ago, that I'm with him now was priceless," Kathe gleamed.

"Yorg said that to Peter!" Jeannie began to dance all the way to the van. "Yes . . . Oh, yes . . . He deserved that!"

Yorg and Kathe spent the rest of the evening with her family. Pete had an offer for $500 for the autographed picture of the band. But to everyone's surprise, he turned it down and decided to keep the photo. They ordered pizza and just had fun together. After dinner Yorg showed the children a model of a Boeing 777 that to Kathe's surprise, he brought for them. They immediately began asking Yorg questions about what it was like to be a pilot as the doorbell rang. Jeannie glanced over at Kathe saying, "Watch this be Peter."

Kathe whispered, "After what Yorg said to him earlier today, he'd have to be an imbecile to show up here." As Jeannie answered the door, Kathe saw a different side of Yorg that she had never seen before.

"The 777 is one of the most sophisticated planes ever built," Yorg showed them. "It has a wingspan equal to two-thirds of the length of a football field. It can weigh over 300 tons," Yorg said as he took the roof off and showed the inside. "It carries a maximum of 419 passengers, 14 flight attendants, with two pilots in the cockpit. It also has one additional pilot for those long-duty periods flying overseas," he said pointing to the officers' bunk. "This is where the extra pilot rests during flights."

"Mom and Ms. Kathe don't want me to be a flight attendant," Christy replied. "They say it's boring," Christy said as Jeannie rejoined Kathe on the couch. Peter stood in the doorway of the room and listened.

"You were wrong!" Jeannie whispered.

"I can't believe him," Kathe snickered as Yorg winked at her.

"Ms. Kathe's job is much more boring than mine," Yorg continued.

"Well, how long does it take you to fly to Europe?" Pete asked.

"It takes about 8 hours to fly from Newark," Yorg glanced over at Peter, "where your mom and I are based to Charles de Gaulle Airport just outside of Paris."

"It must get really boring with nothing to look at but clouds," Heather stated.

"Much of a typical flight can be quite routine," Yorg admitted. "We usually fly overseas at night. Can you imagine what it's like to fly for five or six hours with nothing but the occasional flashing lights of a passing airplane and the stars to keep you company. The only people we must talk to are the various Oceanic Control Centers when we make our position reports over the ocean. "But boring...no way! Let's see just how boring you think a Category III or Cat III landing is."

"What is a Category III landing?" Bob asked as Joey sat on his lap.

"It's a landing performed in near zero visibility, where the airplane actually lands by itself with minimal pilot input," Yorg explained. "Picture this...it is now 8:30 am, Paris time and we are about 15 minutes from landing. It's the foggiest day that you have ever seen, and the visibility is barely 400 feet. We are going to have to perform a Cat III approach and landing...also known as an Autoland. It's up to the autopilot to land the plane," he said as he demonstrated with the model.

"You mean a computer is going to land your plane?" Pete questioned and sat up in his seat.

"The 777 is so sophisticated that as long as all three autopilots agree, yes, it can land by itself," Yorg confirmed. "The approach usually begins somewhere around 3000 feet and 10 miles from the runway, where the aircraft intercepts the extended runway centerline. The plane is now flying directly to the runway. At about 1,500 feet and five miles out, the aircraft will intercept the glide slope. This is when it descends on a precise path to the touchdown zone of the runway. My job, at this point is to closely monitor the aircraft's instruments and ensure that the autopilot is doing its job. I keep my hands barely resting on the yoke and throttles, my feet on the rudder pedals, just in case something goes wrong."

"Does that feel like cruise control on our cars?" Bob questioned.

"Yes, it does," Yorg affirmed. "It's just like when the car accelerates going up a hill. You feel it happen, but you do nothing. We are prepared to take control if we encounter any problems."

"What kind of problems?" Pete asked.

"Like we lose the localizer or glide slope signal, or the three autopilots don't agree with each other, or an aircraft taxies onto an active runway, or one of a dozen other things go wrong," Yorg shared. "I would have to abort the landing. Now depending on the problem, I have either to disengage the autopilot and hand fly a missed approach, or command the autopilot to do it," he said as he showed the model rising. "Then again, depending upon the particular problem, I must decide to try another approach or land at another airport."

"What about the landing gear?" Pete interrupted as his father cleared his throat.

"The landing gear flaps," Yorg explained as he glanced over at Peter, "and engine reverse levers are the only controls that the autopilot can't activate. The first officer lowers the landing gear at my command about 5 to 6 miles from the airport. Now back to the approach...if all is going well, at 100 feet above the ground the first officer will announce, alert height. This just reminds me that we are about to land...Remember I still cannot see a thing out the windshield. At about 50 feet I feel the yoke coming back...the aircraft is beginning to flare. Moments later at about 25 feet, I feel the throttles being retarded to idle. Still, I cannot see anything outside the window. Let me tell you...that's eerie! Moments later, we can feel the main gear touchdown. As the nose is gently lowered to the runway we can, only now, begin to see the runway centerline lights flashing beneath us. We are still traveling at approximately 150 miles per hour. Just as the nose gear touches the ground, we can feel the brakes automatically being applied. It's now that I get to contribute to this miraculous feat by raising the reverse levers; thus, causing the engines to slow the aircraft more efficiently."

"Wow! I want to be a pilot!" Pete exclaimed, jumping to his feet, "That's so cool!"

"And I know now that I really want to be a flight attendant," Christy declared, glancing at her mom.

Kathe checked her watch and noticed the sad look on Peter's face as he watched the excitement of their children. She turned to the children, "Well, now that you children don't think our jobs are so boring, it's time for you to get to bed. You have school tomorrow. Pete if you really want to be a pilot, take lots of math courses; it's all math," she advised. "Now off to bed."

"I want Yorg to put me to bed," Joey said as he jumped off Bob's lap and reached for Yorg to pick him up. "Oh, hi Daddy," Joey said in Yorg's arms. "I want to be a pilot like Yorg. He and Mommy are going to put me to bed."

"Good night, Daddy," each of the kids said as they passed by Peter.

"Peter is there anything else I can do for you tonight?" Bob asked as Jeannie joined him. "Don't you have an early morning surgery? It is getting late."

"I came to talk with Kathe," Peter insisted. "Would you please ask her to come and talk with me?"

"I think Kathe and Yorg made their point pretty clear this afternoon, don't you?" Jeannie said as

Bob opened the front door.

"Good night, Peter," Bob grinned, motioning for him to leave.

Kathe enjoyed helping Joey get ready for bed. She tucked him in, gave him a kiss, turned out the light, and then slowly closed the door.

"I didn't want to spoil your time with the kids," Yorg said as they left the room. "Ramsey called me earlier, while we were having pizza. She wants us away from the kids. We must leave now, if you want to see Ben one last time. Our flight leaves at 10:30."

Kathe and Yorg said their "Goodbyes" to Jeannie and Bob and left for the hospital. At the hospital, they heard that Ben was feeling much better from his doctor. He was amazed at how Ben's heart was rejuvenating. His prognosis was great. "Hey, dad, I don't think you should pay this doctor," Kathe teased. "I think you ought to send me his fee. I think some good old-fashioned love fixed you up just fine." She bent over and kissed him.

"At the rate you're healing," his doctor shared. "I may just send you home tomorrow. I have never seen anything like this. I think I will have to change my diagnosis to missed daughter, instead of cardiac infarction. Next time you miss this girl, try giving her a call," he excused himself and left the room.

"Peter came by again to see me," Ben relayed. "He said you wouldn't talk to him this afternoon."

"I don't have anything to say to him," Kathe confessed. "Let's talk about you. Where are you going to stay when you spring this place?"

"I have to stay with Peter and Helen," Ben sighed.

"Good, I'm sure they can take good care of you," Kathe stated. "I had the visitation orders changed so Helen is never alone with any of the children. I'll make sure Jeannie brings them over to see you on a regular basis."

"I'm glad you did that after what happened to Joey," Ben admitted. "The kids don't like to go over there anymore."

"We've got to go," Yorg reminded Kathe checking his watch. "We can't miss our plane."

"You're leaving already?" Ben questioned.

"Yes, we have to work for a living," Kathe said, giving him a hug and kiss. "I'll call and check on you in a few days."

"Yorg, she's stubborn," Ben cautioned, shaking Yorg's hand. "I know you'll take good care of her."

"I'll always take care of our special girl," Yorg assured him.

As they left Ben's room in ICU, Peter was talking to a nurse. He glared at Yorg, and Kathe as JAKE rang, "Hey, lovely lady!"

"Joe!" Kathe beamed, glancing at Yorg. "Give me a sec," she stated as she walked away. "I can barely hear you. Where are you?"

"I'm in the middle of a concert under the stage," Joe stated. "Collin is doing a solo right now. I just wanted to call you," he said trying to get away from the loud music.

"You know you're not supposed to be calling me on JAKE," Kathe warned. "This is a secure line and it's monitored."

"I told you that Carrie Anne arranged it for me," Joe confessed.

"I'm leaving for New York in about 35 minutes," Kathe told him.

"Great!" Joe perked up. "What time are you arriving? I'll meet you," he said as she glanced over at

Peter. He was still staring at them. The look on his face was noteworthy. "I'm not quite sure. I'll text the time to you when I find out."

"Do you want me to get us a room?" Joe asked.

"No," Kathe declined. "I'm not sure where I'm being sent next. Ramsey wants to talk to us."

"That's my cue!" Joe exclaimed. "I've got to go. Call me when you land, promise?"

"Promise," Kathe cleared the line, and they left the hospital.

"Kathe," Peter called outside the building to her. "I just want to tell you…" he said as she slammed the car door and drove off.

The flight to Newark wasn't full. First class was practically empty. Kathe hurried to her seat and texted Joe regarding their six o'clock arrival. "Plane looks pretty empty," Yorg said to the flight attendant.

"Haven't you seen the news?" she asked him. "People have been cancelling flights all afternoon, since the incidents in Salt Lake City and this airport," she replied as she walked past them. "We're already ready to push back."

"Kat, I saw you texting someone just before we took off," Yorg stated. "Was it Joe?"

"Yes, he wants to meet me when we land," Kathe said putting her purse under the seat.

"You know Kathe," Yorg began. "I've never interfered in your private life. However, Ramsey is right on this one. Joe's too high profile for you to be involved. Look what we did this morning. Just being seen with you, you're putting him in danger. You have a known murderer following you. You heard Ramsey. You're not safe with Saíde on the loose. It's not maybe, but when is he coming for you."

"Yorg, for the first time in a very long time," Kathe confessed. "I feel like a normal woman. It's just not fair that I can't have that type of life again. I know Ramsey's right, but I'm just not ready to let him go. We have so much fun together. He makes me laugh. He helps me forget the humiliation of what Peter put me through," she said staring out the window.

"Life's not fair," Yorg reminded her. "You and I both know that. You made that life changing decision the first time you pulled that trigger. We both know that we can never go back to a normal life. Get your head back in this game! Your life and those around you depend on it!" Yorg warned as he leaned back in his seat and closed his eyes.

JAKE woke Kathe up right on time. She sat up feeling well rested and excited. She quickly called Joe at the hotel. "Kathe?" a sleepy voice answered.

"I'll be on the ground by 6:00 am," Kathe smiled.

"What gate?" Joe sat up in his bed.

"At Gate D703," Kathe answered.

"I'm on my way!" Joe said as his feet touched the floor. He hurried in the shower and was ready to leave in 15 minutes.

Kathe and Yorg deplaned and walked down the large corridor around security, taking the escalator down to the main floor. "Cover for me please," Kathe requested. "I want to see Joe for a minute."

"Remember our talk," Yorg cautioned. "I'll cover for you to say goodbye, but you can't be with him, and you know it." His eyes saddened as he watched her run to Joe.

Standing at the end of the escalator wearing sunglasses, hands in his leather jacket pockets was Joe. Kathe noted his face lit up when he saw her. He picked her up and swung her around. He sat her down on the floor as Yorg sadly walked past them.

"I can't believe how much I missed you!" Joe exclaimed as he picked her up again and spun her around.

"I forgot how wonderful this feels!" Kathe exclaimed as she looked into his hazel eyes. His blonde hair was almost twice as hers. He was totally the opposite of Yorg, and the other pilots she flew with daily, right down to the dangling gold earring. Noticing that people were beginning to stare at them Kathe whispered, "I think we need to get out of here."

Joe looked up, "You're right. Let's go." He picked up her overnight bag and they started for the exit. They barely made the auto train. "Let's go back to the hotel. Payton will have a fit, if he notices I'm gone."

"He's one person that will be glad when I leave," Kathe mentioned.

"Not really," Joe admitted. "He made some comments about how my personality has improved."

"Why?" Kathe questioned as she held on to the pole. "Are you an old grump?" She asked as she looked into his eyes.

"No! Just had an, I don't give a care attitude," Joe smiled as he bent around the pole and kissed her.

"I know that attitude well," Kathe confessed. "I've been accused of that myself," she said as the auto train came to a halt. They made their way up the escalator to the street exit. There they took a cab to the hotel.

The traffic was horrible. "What time do you need to be back at the airport?" Joe asked.

"I wasn't supposed to leave," Kathe admitted. "I asked Yorg to cover for me."

"Is he here?" Joe asked.

"Yes, he flew in with me," Kathe said. "He went ahead to Ramsey's office."

"Maybe I'll get to meet him," Joe said as the cab arrived at the Hotel International. Just as it pulled in front of the hotel and stopped, JAKE rang.

"Tierney!" Ramsey hollered. "Ditch Glitter Boy and get back here immediately! I'm assembling your team. We've got a situation at Gate A20!"

"I'll be right there," Kathe answered, turning to Joe. "I have to get back to the airport. There's an emergency. I'm needed now."

"What's wrong?" Joe asked, reaching for her.

"I don't know," Kathe answered. "I have to hurry. You are leaving for California in about an hour. Maybe I'll still be there and get to say goodbye."

"I'll go with you," Joe insisted, reaching for her hand.

"I have to go to work," Kathe declared and kissed him. "You will not be able to see me. I must hurry. Get out of the cab!" she ordered, reached around him, opening the door. Joe got out of the cab stunned at the change in her attitude. "Driver, back to Newark Airport, and step on it," Kathe stated showing her ID. Kathe was already talking to control as Joe watched the cab speed away.

Joe hurried up to his room to find Carrie Anne. She could find out what the emergency was. Opening the door Payton greeted him screaming, "Where have you been?"

Pushing right past Payton, Joe asked, "Where's Carrie Anne?"

"I asked you a question Joe," Payton screamed. "Where have you been?"

"I went to the airport to meet Kathe," Joe explained as he took a deep breath to calm down. "She got a phone call in front of the hotel and had to head right back. Now, where is Carrie Anne? Maybe she can find out what's going on?"

"Carrie Anne is getting ready to leave," Payton replied as he calmed down. "She's going to work the flight to California, which by the way, we are leaving for the airport in 10 minutes. Get ready to go."

Joe headed for Travis' room. He knocked loudly, "Carrie Anne, Carrie Anne, open up!"

Travis opened the door, "Hey, what's up?"

Joe passed Travis and walked straight to Carrie Anne, "Something is wrong at the airport. Kathe got a call and had to head right back. What's going on?"

Carrie Anne looked at Joe, "What are you talking about?"

"I met Kathe this morning at the airport," Joe explained. "We took a cab to the hotel. Before we got out of the cab, she got a call. She kicked me out of the cab and sped away. Can you find out what is going on?"

"There's probably nothing to worry about," Carrie Anne said, reaching for the phone. "I'll see if I can find out for you."

Payton came in the room giving them a five-minute notice. Joe hurried to his room and got his bags ready to go. Everybody was waiting in the front room except Carrie Anne. When she came out of the room, she looked worried. "What's happening?" Joe asked her.

"Tell him on the way to the airport," Payton ordered as he opened the door and gave Brock and RJ the ready sign.

On the way to the limo, Carrie Anne filled Joe in on what details she knew. "There is a hostage situation and Ramsey has it hushed up," she reported. "That's all I could find out."

"What does that have to do with Kathe?" Joe demanded as they left the hotel.

"I can't tell you," Carrie Anne said as they got into the limo. "Maybe we'll find out before we takeoff."

At the airport, a security team met the limo at Alby's Curbside Check-in. Screaming fans were waiting for a last glimpse of Light Crimson surrounded the limo. One of the guards knocked on the driver's window. "All flights on this terminal have been cancelled until further notice. Linda Ramsey has arranged for your entourage to wait in the private lounge near her office for your security. Give us a minute to clear the road and then follow my car to a secure door."

Carrie Anne pointed out Ramsey's corner office with the open blinds as they entered the lounge. Joe watched Ramsey through the glass wall intently hoping to find out what was happening. Carrie Anne saw Wanda walking back to her desk. "I'll ask Wanda; she'll know," Carrie Anne said to Joe and hurried to Wanda.

"Wanda what's going on?" Carrie Anne asked.

"We have a hostage situation," Wanda whispered.

"Where's Kathe?" Carrie Anne asked.

"She'll be here in a few minutes," Wanda said as she sat down at her desk. "She's with Yorg and her team getting suited up."

"What do you mean suited up?" Carrie Anne looked worried as she glanced over toward Joe.

"I think Ramsey is having them put on bulletproof vests," Wanda assumed.

"Bulletproof vests!" Carrie Anne loudly exclaimed in shock.

"Sh, sh, sh..." Wanda cautioned her as her phone rang. She stood up, "I've got to go," she said and hurried into Ramsey's office.

Kathe and Yorg were walking back to Ramsey's office. Yorg was holstering his pistol. Carrie Anne noticed them first. Then Collin noticed, "Joe, look," he said pointing at them.

"Who's that with Kathe?" Travis asked Carrie Anne.

"I've got a bad feeling about this one," Carrie Anne gasped as she shook her head watching as Jay and Jack joined them. "Something is definitely wrong."

Joe stared at them coming up the corridor, "Is that Yorg with Kathe?"

"Yes, it is," Carrie Anne answered.

"Those are the two guys from our party the other night," Collin said.

"They are part of Kathe's team," Carrie Anne reported.

Yorg's face was serious as they entered the front area. Ramsey came out of her office irate, "Look Tierney, I have enough to worry about without you showing your fanny!"

"I'm not showing anything," Kathe calmly replied.

"You get down that hall and put your vest on now!" Ramsey ordered. "I already have one dead lady! I don't need another one!"

"I'm not wearing it," Kathe protested. "I am supposed to pull a child away from this man. He might see it. Besides, it will be in my way."

"You're safer with the vest," Yorg cautioned as he put his arm around Kathe.

"No, no vest," Kathe insisted. "I can't handle it. It is too heavy. I can't stand it."

"Let's take this to my office," Ramsey said as Sydney joined them. Kathe didn't notice Joe and the others a few feet away. In Ramsey's office, Yorg helped Sydney put a button camera on Kathe's shirt.

"Make sure you pan the room so I can see where the child and mother are," Sydney requested. "Yorg will have a monitor set up by Lt. Tanner so they can watch you inside."

"I can also tell you what to do if you get into a situation and can't control him," Yorg added.

"He's right," Sydney agreed. "Ramsey and I will be watching from here. Make sure you follow our orders. We will have a different perception of the situation than you will."

As Ramsey answered another phone call, Yorg whispered something to Kathe. He pulled her closer to him and kissed her forehead. Joe watched not taking his eyes off them. He saw Kathe lower her head, close her eyes for a second and make the Sign of the Cross. Then, they all left the office. Kathe still did not see Joe or the others in the room. Instead of leaving via the front door, they went down the long corridor.

Another monitor was delivered to Ramsey's office. Sydney reassembled his computer equipment and attached the monitor. "They are setting up a command station in Ramsey's office," Carrie Anne told them as they watched through the glass.

"Can we go inside and watch?" Joe asked.

"Ramsey doesn't want you near Kathe," Carrie Anne cautioned, putting her hand on his shoulder. "I don't think it would be wise to ask her. I try to stay away from Ramsey as much as possible."

Joe glanced over at Carrie Anne and left the lounge. He walked over to Wanda's desk, "Would you ask Ramsey if I can watch what is happening on that monitor?"

"This is not the time for you to bother Ramsey," Wanda warned.

"I know Ramsey doesn't want me around Kathe," Joe pleaded, reaching for Wanda's hand. "Please, just ask her for me," he looked into her eyes. "I'm really worried."

"I could get fired for this," Wanda whispered as she slowly walked to Ramsey's office.

"Mr. Sherrod would like to know if he can come in and watch Kathe on the monitor?" Wanda asked. "He is worried for her safety."

Ramsey glared at Wanda a second and then a big smile came over her face, "Yes, he can watch this, if he stays out of the way."

"Are you sure about this, Boss?" Wanda questioned, noticing the grin on Ramsey face as she looked over at Joe.

"Positive," Ramsey acknowledged.

"You've got something up your sleeve!" Wanda snapped, crossing her arms in front of her chest. "I can smell it from here!"

"Always," Ramsey grinned, glancing back at her. "Go get him."

"I don't have time to talk," Ramsey said as Joe entered her office. "Stand over there," she pointed to a corner. "And keep quiet."

Dr. Sydney finished setting up the command post. He began typing on the computer with several windows popping up on various display screens. The small button camera enabled the computer to show everything Kathe saw as she headed for the tram to the difference concourses. With a few more keystrokes, he expanded the view of the hallway. He also linked it with a camera that was outside of the men's bathroom on Concourse A showing the doorway.

Sitting at a cell phone-charging station near the tram station, a blonde, olive-skinned man disguised as an executive made a call. "My plane has been delayed at Newark," he reported. "I'm going to be late."

"What's wrong?" A deep Italian voice questioned.

Glancing at the airport monitor he said, "I'm not sure, but all flights are being delayed."

"This better not be any of your doing!" The Italian bellowed.

"No! I swear!" He exclaimed. "I changed my looks and I'm heading to Munich like you said."

"Make sure you leave the flight attendants alone!" He cleared the line and turned on his laptop.

Dr. Sydney switched back to monitoring Kathe. He typed a few more commands and pressed enter. At the top of the screen Kathe's vitals: heart rate, blood pressure, and respiration appeared. As he followed her movements down the corridor toward the tram Kathe suddenly stopped. Her heart rate jumped off the monitor.

"What's going on?" Ramsey asked as she stood behind Sydney watching the monitor.

"I'm not sure," Sydney replied. "I think something scared her," he said contacting her.

"Sydney, scan the area to my left," Kathe requested. "See the man sitting at the third cell phone-charging station from the left; it is Saíde with blonde hair. Tell Ramsey to look at him. He's noted for changing his appearance. Take away the business clothes and picture him with blonde hair."

Ramsey got closer to the monitor, "I can't be sure?" She admitted and hurried over to the door, "Carrie Anne, get in here!"

"Jay, Jack, is that Saíde?" Sydney asked.

"It looks like his face, but the hair color," Jay said as he tried to get a better look at him. "The face could be his, I can't be sure."

"I'm with Jay," Jack concurred as Carrie Anne joined Ramsey. "I can't be sure either."

"Look at the man at the third cell phone-charging station from the left," Ramsey requested. "Is that

Saíde?"

"He needs to get a hairdresser," Carrie Anne replied. "That's cheap, hair color from a dollar store. But yes, that's him!" She answered, rubbing the cut on her neck.

"Are you sure?" Ramsey asked as Sydney snapped a picture of him.

"Yes!" Carrie Anne exclaimed. "When a man has a knife to your throat, you don't tend to forget his face."

As they identified him, Saíde glanced in their direction, spotted Kathe, cautiously picked up his briefcase and started walking toward the arriving tram.

"He spotted us!" Kathe exclaimed as they started to follow him. The tram stopped and people flooded the area getting off.

"Where is he?" Jack asked dodging passengers trying to find him.

"We lost him in the crowd!" Kathe confirmed, looking around at Jay. "I didn't see which way he went, did you?"

"No," Jay answered, trying to look inside the tram. "He's not inside."

"There he is!" Yorg exclaimed, pointing to the escalators. "He's heading down the escalator toward C and D concourses."

"Jay, Jack, go after him," Ramsey ordered.

"Roger that, Boss!" Jay confirmed as he and Jack headed for the escalators. "We're on it!"

"I'll have TSA join you," Ramsey said as Sydney alerted TSA and circulated a picture of Saíde to every security checkpoint, ticket counter and officer in the airport.

Kathe and Yorg hurried to Gate A20 where they met with Lt. John Tanner of the New Jersey Police Department. He was still taking statements from the witnesses and the parents of the victim. "You've got to help my Becky!" cried an older woman. "I heard a gunshot, and I heard her scream! He killed my Becky!" wailed the woman as her husband held her. "He killed my Becky!"

"I couldn't stop my daughter," the elderly man cried. "She broke away from me and went in after our granddaughter," he said with tears streaming down his face. "We heard her scream, and the gun went off. She didn't come out."

"Lt. Tanner," Yorg interrupted. "Ramsey sent us to help with this situation."

"Yorg, Kathe, thanks for coming," Lt. Tanner greeted. "Ramsey assures me you two have a better way to get inside than my men do," he said as he briefed them from his notes. "Believe it or not, this is a family disaster from what we can gather from the couple over there." He pointed to an older couple surrounded by paramedics trying to calm them down. "That is Frank and Dorothy Saunders. They are the parents of the woman we believe was shot in the bathroom. Their daughter, Rebecca Anne Saunders Maulder was taking her daughter Tonya to California to get away from her husband, Ted Maulder. Ted recently lost his job and started drinking heavily, as well as verbally abusing them. The grandparents stepped in when their daughter caught Ted violently shaking the four-year-old two days ago. Ted found them here at about 0645 (6:45 am) this morning. He grabbed the child and headed for the men's room. Rebecca ran after them screaming for help. There were two men in the restroom at the time. They saw that Ted Maulder had a gun in one hand and the child in the other. He ordered the men to leave. As the last one was leaving, he heard Mrs. Maulder pleading with her husband to give her the child. She screamed, and he heard a shot behind him. He turned just in time to see her fall to the floor."

"Are you sure there were no other men in there?" Yorg asked.

"The two men didn't think so," Lt. Tanner answered. "We heard him kicking in the stall doors checking."

Suddenly Ted, who was in his late twenties, stuck his head around the doorway. He was jittery. The child was crying in his arms trying to get down. Yorg and Kathe quickly hid behind a wall out of his sight. "I want a plane ready for Mexico! I want this hall cleared! I'm going to lose it! I'll kill us all!" He demanded stepping back inside.

"This is the first time we've heard a peep out of him," Lt. Tanner stated, shaking his head.

"His eyes were glazed," Kathe noted. "It looked like he was on more than just alcohol. We've got to work fast."

Mr. Saunders ran over to Lt. Tanner crying, "He's crazy, my Rebecca thought he was on drugs. That's why he lost his job. You must get Tonya out of there! My daughter might still be alive! Do something!"

"Mr. Saunders we're doing everything we can," Lt. Tanner replied, motioning to one of his men. "Tom, take Mr. Saunders over to his wife and stay with them."

Sydney was checking the layout of the bathroom on his computer with Ramsey. "Yorg I'm sending you and Kathe a copy of the layout of the bathroom on JAKE," he said lowering a screen and opening another. "Ask the man who saw Mrs. Maulder fall, where she is on the floor."

"Lt. Tanner we need to speak with the man that was in the bathroom and witnessed Mrs. Maulder falling to the floor," Yorg requested as he glanced at Kathe. "Did you get the file yet?"

"Yes, here it is," Kathe showed him.

"Here is John Wright," Lt. Tanner introduced. "He saw Mrs. Maulder fall."

"Can you show us where Mrs. Maulder fell?" Kathe asked, holding JAKE for him to view.

"She fell right there," Mr. Wright said, pointing to the diagram. "Right in front of the middle two sinks. I saw blood trickling on the floor toward the wall."

"Thank you, that will be all," Lt. Tanner stated.

"Sydney did you see?" Kathe asked.

"Yes," Sydney answered, continuing to study the layout.

"Why is Kathe there?" Joe asked Ramsey from behind.

"I'm not sure why I let you in here," Ramsey cautioned. "Maybe it is so you will see something you don't like and leave my top agent alone! Just keep quiet or get out!" Joe immediately stepped back and listened as they conferred among themselves. He noticed that Carrie Anne looked scared to death.

Ramsey made her decision, "Yorg we're going to have to send Kathe into the bathroom. She will have to act like she is getting away from an abusive boyfriend," she said glancing over toward Joe. "She will have to run into the men's room crying and upset. She will need to act bewildered and confused that she is in the wrong bathroom. Once inside she can determine what to do. She could try to trade herself for the child or she could offer to negotiate for them to leave for Mexico together. I trust her judgment. She'll know what to do. Once Kathe gets Ted outside the bathroom Yorg and Lt. Tanner's men will take it from there," Ramsey stated. "What do you think?"

Lt. Tanner was the first to speak, "I think it might work. He's desperate now. He's looking for a way out of this mess."

"He has finally realized that he is cornered," Yorg agreed. "He will more than likely make the trade. I think Kathe can persuade him of that."

"Kathe, what's your feeling?" Ramsey asked, stepping away from the desk to watch Joe's reaction.

"He's probably beginning to come down off of what he was on," Kathe stated. "His rationale is compromised. I think I can be persuasive enough."

"I note a bit of hesitation in your voice," Ramsey declared. "This man is desperate; his back is against a wall. You must know for sure, LADY! Can you pull this off?" She asked as Joe held his breath, listening to Kathe' answer.

"Like I just said," Kathe confirmed. "It's obvious he is mentally unstable. There's no talking him down. There is no other way to get the child safely out and not to mention, Mrs. Maulder could still be alive."

"You're right," Ramsey agreed as Kathe checked her weapon and holstered it behind her back. "There's no talking Ted out of there. Get in there and do what you must do. John, get your men in place and let's get this done."

"Copy that," John said, signaling his men to take their positions.

Joe was petrified as he listened and watched. "Kat look at me," Yorg instructed. "Let's do this quickly, the faster the better. We must take him by surprise. After Denver yesterday, this is just a walk in the park for you. I can hear and see everything that goes on in there. Any sign of Mr. Maulder freaking out, drop to the ground and roll under a stall. I'll come right in and blow him away."

Kathe took a deep breath, "Give me a second." She tried to cry.

"Look upset!" Yorg exclaimed, pulling half her shirttail out. "Get into the role, cry Kat!" He ordered as he messed up her hair and slapped her across the cheek.

"You just slapped me!" Kathe snapped as tears streamed down her face, grabbing her cheek. Joe clinched his fist as he watched, and Carrie Anne ran out of the room.

"You're crying real tears, aren't you?" Yorg stated. "Now get going," he ordered as Kathe ran down the hallway crying straight into the men's room. As she turned toward the sink, they were able to see Rebecca Maulder lying on the floor. A pool of blood was trickling toward the wall. Kathe ran over to the first sink looking in the mirror. Holding her hands up to her face, wiping the tears away, she cried harder. Joe watched both monitors intensely. On one was Kathe inside the bathroom. The other monitor viewed Yorg with Lt. Tanner watching their monitor. Silence filled the air.

Kathe sighed deeply, looked into the mirror, trying to compose herself. She straightened up, stepped back leaning against the wall. The camera showed Ted Maulder sitting on the floor against the back wall between the stalls. He had a blank stare on his face, a gun in one hand and clutching the child to his chest. The child was no longer crying; just staring at her mother.

"That's odd," Ramsey noted. "Ted isn't aware you're in there."

"He appears to be in a trance of some kind," Sydney noted. "It depends on what drugs he's on and how long he's been using. Kathe, use extreme caution; he can snap out of the trance, go berserk, and start shooting.

"He's starting to move around," Ramsey noted. "Don't look at him or Mrs. Maulder. Look in the mirror and cry; maybe that will bring him out slowly."

Kathe slowly turned back toward the mirror and began to cry, "Not again . . . he hit . . . me again . . ."

Ted glanced up at her, dropped the child, jumped to his feet, and pointed his gun at Kathe. "Don't move! I'll shoot!"

"Oh, I'm sorry," Kathe said, turning to face him. "I must be in the wrong bathroom. This must be the men's bathroom! I'll leave," she said stepping backwards.

"Don't move!" Ted ordered. "Shut up! Let me think!" He yelled and waived the gun at her.

Joe heard Yorg tell Kathe to put her hands up in the air slowly. He felt secure knowing Kathe could hear Yorg telling her what to do. "Act like you don't see the woman on the floor," Yorg cautioned. "Tell him your boyfriend hit you. Show him your cheek."

"My boyfriend hit me while we were in the elevator," Kathe said, turning her cheek toward him. "As soon as the door opened, I ran as fast as I could to get away from him. I heard him trip, so I ran into the women's bathroom. I knew I would be safe in here. But this is the men's bathroom. I must get out of here, before he comes. Please let me go," she pleaded holding her hands toward him.

"Don't pretend you don't see my dead wife on the floor!" Ted screamed, holding the gun directly at her.

"Please, Mister," Kathe begged. "I have enough problems; I won't tell anybody. Please let me go. I must get away from my boyfriend. Please let me go," she started to cry. "I'll take the little girl with me."

"No!" Ted screamed. "Tonya is my daughter! Do you hear me! She's mine!"

"Okay, she's your little girl," Kathe said very softly. "I understand. Can I please go?"

Then Ted started ranting, "Becky was going to take Tonya away from me, but I couldn't let her do that! She wanted to take my baby away from me! I stopped her! I stopped her!" Then he looked straight at Kathe and raised his gun to her head. "Did you come to take my little girl? Did her father send you to get my daughter?"

"No, way," Kathe pleaded. "I told you my boyfriend and I had a fight. I'm sorry. I ran into the wrong bathroom. I'll leave," she backed up a little more.

"Don't you dare!" Ted walked closer to Kathe still pointing the gun at her head.

"Try to get on his side," Yorg advised. "Offer to help him."

"I know what it's like having something taken away from you," Kathe shared. "My boyfriend beats on me and takes my tips every day. I've got to get away from him," she said, glancing at his daughter. "Hey, maybe we can leave together. I heard some men outside say they are getting a plane ready to go to Mexico. Maybe we can get on that plane. I can help you with the little girl."

"You're doing great Kat," Yorg encouraged. "Keep him talking."

"That plane is for me," Ted said lowering his gun. "I told them I'd kill us all if I don't get a plane to Mexico." He thought for a second, held his gun back to Kathe's head taking another step closer to her. "Wait! How did you hear that if you were running from your boyfriend? I think you're lying to me." Flicking his gun toward his wife, "Her father sent you in here, didn't he? You're trying to trick me and take my little girl!"

"No, I'm not lying to you," Kathe stated as Yorg rushed to the entrance of the bathroom. "Look at my cheek, see my boyfriend hit me. I just want to get away from him. I can go with you. I can help you with your little girl. I like kids, but my boyfriend hates them," she tried to calm him down.

"He's not buying this!" Ramsey pointed at the screen as Ted began ranting about his wife again. "I can see it in his eyes! We need to get Kathe out of there! He's going to shoot her! Do something now!"

Sydney began thinking out loud, "Yorg, the child is far enough behind Ted for you to enter. Kathe should drop to the floor, roll toward the child, and shield her from a stray bullet."

"You're right Sydney," Yorg agreed. "I'm going to try to sneak into the bathroom now. My only worry is my reflection in the mirror. He might see me and grab Kathe. He's very close to her."

"I see that," Sydney affirmed. "However, you have the advantage of telling Kathe to move and block his view."

"Go, Yorg! Get in there!" Ramsey interrupted as Yorg rounded the long entrance wall to the bathroom. Yorg drew his gun and listened. Joe couldn't believe what was happening. It was like watching a movie; only it was Kathe's life on the line with no retakes.

"Kat, I'm coming in," Yorg whispered. "I need you to move sideways to the right to obscure me from the mirror. When I yell, drop to the floor. Do you understand?"

"Yes," Kathe whispered, still listening to Ted rambling like a mad man about his dead wife. She slowly stepped to the right as Yorg had said. Ted didn't notice. He was still babbling.

"I'm entering the doorway and coming toward the opening now," Yorg said, slowly making his way down the entrance, not making a sound. He could hear Ted rambling. Using a small mirror, Yorg peeked around the corner. He saw Kathe with Ted about a foot from her with his gun aimed right at her forehead. He saw the child in the back sitting against the wall. His gun cocked ready to fire. Yorg whispered, "Ready, three, two, one, drop!"

Kathe instantly dropped to the floor and rolled under the first stall. Yorg rounded the corner pointing his Walther PPK straight at Ted's head. "Put the gun down now!" Yorg ordered. "Put it down! It's over!"

Crazed Ted yelled, "No!" Ted turned toward Kathe, who was shielding the child, and raised his gun at her head. Yorg fired one shot, striking Ted in his right temple, dropping him to the floor. Blood spewed everywhere. The child screamed as soon as the shot fired.

Joe almost threw up watching Kathe pick up the child, hugging her tightly. "It's okay," Kathe comforted. "I have you. It is okay. I'm going to take you to your grandmother," she said as she turned the child's head and hurried out of the room.

Yorg checked Mrs. Maulder, "Send in the paramedics; Mrs. Maulder is still alive!"

Lt. Tanner rushed into the bathroom with the paramedic's right behind him.

The Saunders rushed to their granddaughter. "Tonya!" Mrs. Saunders cried. "I've got you! Grandma has you! Grandpa and I are going to take care of you," she said holding her tightly.

"You risked your life to save my Tonya," Mr. Saunders cried looking at the doorway, "Is my . . . is my Becky gone?"

Before Kathe could answer, paramedics rushed Mrs. Maulder out of the bathroom. "We've found a weak pulse," a paramedic stated putting an IV in her arm. "We're on our way to Jersey General Hospital," he said hurrying off.

"My Becky's alive! My Becky's alive!" Mr. Saunders exclaimed, looking toward the sky, "Thank you, Jesus! My Becky's alive!"

"Mr. and Mrs. Saunders come with us," another paramedic requested. "We'll follow your daughter's ambulance to the hospital. The doctors want to check the child and you need to be with your daughter."

"Thank you," Mrs. Saunders sobbed, hugging Kathe. "You saved my family!"

Yorg walked over to Kathe and put his arms around her. Everyone in Ramsey's office listened, "Kat, I can't believe how I felt when I saw another man with a gun held point blank at you."

"When the gun went off," Kathe admitted, "I didn't know who fired it. I closed my eyes tightly. It reminded me of being shot all over again."

Yorg tightened his grip around Kathe holding her in his arms, "I'll never let anyone harm you again; I promise."

Joe turned to Ramsey, "What are they talking about?"

"I think it's time for Kathe to tell you goodbye," Ramsey advised. "You two don't mix," Ramsey declared, shaking her finger at him. "Now, you know what she does for a living. You must understand that by being together, it's just endangering both of your lives."

"She's right," Sydney agreed, glancing at Joe. "You have no business with Kathe. A relationship would not only endanger your lives, but her team, and your friends as well. You heard Yorg refer to the two terrorist attacks yesterday and the third one stopped. Where do you think she went after we pulled her away from your concert? Their names were kept out of the papers. She's the best in this business. Go on with your fame and leave her in the shadows. That's where she belongs with her team."

Still staring at Joe's face, Ramsey said, "Yorg, bring Kathe back to my office, another job well done by both of you! You saved a lot of lives yesterday, and I think Mrs. Maulder is going to live."

"We'll be there in a minute," Yorg said still holding Kathe in his arms. "She's trembling from the adrenalin. Let her calm down."

"I'll see you as soon as she's ready," Ramsey concurred.

Sydney turned to Ramsey as he packed up his equipment, "I taped this whole ordeal. I'm going to study it to see if we need any more improvements. I'll let you know my findings."

"Your new additions to JAKE worked great," Ramsey complimented. "Let me know what you find," she said as Sydney left the room.

Chapter 20

Lost and Found Saíde Again

As Kathe and Yorg left the area, Lt. Tanner was outside the terminal being interviewed on FNN News. Wanda was the first to congratulate Kathe and Yorg on a job well done as they passed her desk. Kathe entered Ramsey's office with one thing on her mind.

"Did you get Saíde?" Kathe asked as she spotted Joe in the room. "Did you allow Joe to watch the monitors?"

"Yes, I did," Ramsey answered. "I told you to get rid of him. You disobeyed me, so I let him see your job description. He just saw for himself why you two can't be together."

"I'm in shock!" Joe exclaimed, staring at Kathe.

"Thanks, Ramsey!" Kathe snapped, turning, and running out of the room.

Joe, mentally exhausted from the tension rushed out after her. "Kathe, wait!" he called catching up to her, grabbing her by the arm, and turning her around to face him. "What did you just do?"

"I can't believe Ramsey let you in her office," Kathe stated. "Did you watch the entire thing?"

"Yes, I've never prayed so hard in my life," Joe answered, holding her in his arms. "I couldn't believe Ramsey and Yorg would put you in that dangerous situation." He stepped back and looked at her. His face still showed the strain of the frightening ordeal. "Since I met you, I felt so happy. I even went against my own vow, never to want to get too close to any one woman again. Are you a flight attendant or a cop?"

Payton rushed down the hall, "Joe, the airport is resuming departures and our flight to California is ready to board. Say your goodbyes." Joe was still holding Kathe. Payton repeated as they announced the boarding of their flight, "Joe come on now. They're boarding our flight. We can't miss it; we have contracts to fulfill!"

Kathe was looking down at the floor. She slowly raised her head and looked Joe straight in the eyes, "You better not miss your flight."

"Is that all you can say?" Joe questioned, pulling her closer to him.

"This is who I am," Kathe confessed. "This is what I do for a living. I rescue people in trouble. You will never understand what it's like, when in a split second, your whole world can change! You can never go back!" Pointing to Ramsey's office, "They did not put me in danger!" Pointing to her chest, "I put myself in danger! I too put my guard down wanting to be with you. I enjoy being with you. I don't want to let you go, but Ramsey is right. You are in the news all the time. I'm a ghost. Just by being seen with me, I am putting you in danger. Please go, you will miss your flight. You have contracts to fulfill and so do I."

Payton called out to the superstar again as they started walking back toward Ramsey's office. Babs hurried over to Kathe and hugged her, "I'm so glad you're safe." Travis and Carrie Anne joined them.

Carrie Anne embraced her friend, "Kathe, all you have to worry about with me, is my shenanigans." She smiled a little, then her faced saddened again, "And I have to worry about you being killed." She started to cry again as they hugged.

Kathe pulled away, "Carrie Anne, remember your promise. Don't tell Travis or any of the others, please."

"That's what best friends do best," Carrie Anne said fighting back tears. "We keep our secrets."

Ramsey and Yorg stepped out of her office. "Carrie Anne, your job as a flight attendant started ten minutes ago," Ramsey bellowed as her cell phone rang. "You better get these people onboard," she said as she answered the call.

Joe was the last to leave. He just stood there sadly watching Kathe for a moment. "Yorg," Joe finally said, shaking Yorg's hand. "Please take good care of Kathe."

"I always will," Yorg answered putting his arm around Kathe. "I will never let anyone hurt her again. You have a plane to catch, and we have work to do," he said as Joe slowly walked away.

"That was Jack," Ramsey hung up her cell. "They lost Saíde. It's as if he vanished into thin air."

"Are you checking all the planes before they leave, especially the ones to Europe?" Yorg warned studying a picture of Saíde. "And don't forget private planes. Wait a minute. I believe I saw this man in France at the hotel one night," he said, pulling out a black pen and scribbling over his blonde hair.

"Are you sure?" Ramsey inquired.

"I'm almost positive," Yorg affirmed looking around for Kathe. She was standing along the back glass wall, staring out at the jets getting ready to leave from the security runway. She watched a tug push Joe's plane back from the gate. She closed her eyes, leaned forward resting her head against the glass. Yorg walked over to her and said as he turned her toward him, "Are you okay, Kat?"

She leaned into his chest, "I just wanted something I can't have."

He wrapped his arms around her resting his head on hers and murmured, "So, do I."

Ramsey cleared her throat, "If you two can get your heads back to the problem we are working on, I would appreciate it. I have a call into Jaco. It's strange that suddenly Saíde would show up here in New Jersey and New York, especially when Yorg thinks he saw him at the hotel in Paris. Tierra and Kathe were both staying there. He needs to check the security cameras. I don't know how he seems to flip-flop between Europe and the U.S. so easily."

Lt. John Tanner entered Ramsey's office, "I want to thank you two for helping me with the hostage situation. I must fill out reports on this for the NJPD," John reported. "Sgt. Russell filled me in on the Saíde situation. Unfortunately, two private planes got off the ground before we realized they weren't searched yet."

"You're kidding me!" Ramsey snapped. "I was afraid of that with all the confusion." She reached for the button on the side of her phone summoning Wanda, who hurried into the room. "I want you to find out what two private planes left this area in the past hour and where they were going."

"You got it!" Wanda replied, hurrying back to her desk.

"Kathe did you see Saíde in Paris after he was released from jail?" Yorg asked her.

"No, I didn't," Kathe answered. "I only saw him at a boutique in New York and this morning at the cell phone-charging station."

John walked toward the doorway, "One thing I can tell you about this guy, he is after something or someone. He's taking way too many chances."

"You're right, lieutenant," Yorg confirmed. "He is taking too many chances."

"We better keep Kathe in sight at all times," Ramsey expressed. "He seems to turn up around her more than anybody."

"Kat, before Flight #1014, did you ever see Saíde?" Yorg asked her as Lt. Tanner excused himself.

"No, Yorg, never," Kathe assured him.

"Think Kat, maybe in Colorado or Florida?" Yorg inquired.

"No, I have never seen him before the flight to Paris," Kathe assured him. "I'm positive without a doubt."

"Who was with you when you saw him at the boutique?" Yorg asked.

"Joe, Tierra and CC," Kathe stated. "Wait a minute. Joe was here at the airport today. Tierra and CC are not."

"When you saw Saíde at the boutique was Joe staying at the same hotel?" Yorg quizzed.

"Yes, his room was on the twenty-first floor," Kathe answered. "Tierra and CC were staying there also."

Ramsey looked disturbed as Jay and Jack joined them, "I still don't think this guy is after Joe. Tierra was already in Europe when Saíde was on the plane to Paris. CC was here in Newark. Kathe, you are the only one of the four that was on the flight to Paris that night. He must be after you."

"Impossible, I was just working," Kathe stated. "I haven't made any new enemies. Besides, why would he pull the knife on Carrie Anne, instead of me? He had plenty of chances."

"That is a good point and the only thing that doesn't make sense," Ramsey replied. "Yorg, you stay with Kathe. I don't want her alone at all until we find Saíde. Remember Richard Munroe was the first officer on Flight #1014. He was killed on the flight in Denver with Tierra and CC aboard."

"We have no evidence that Saíde was in Denver," Kathe reminded them.

"This guy worries me!" Ramsey admitted. "This isn't as cut and dried like the problem we had earlier."

Wanda came in the room with her report, "The private planes were owned by two companies. One company, based here in the U.S. with headquarters in Manhattan, left at Gate E-3. The company is Gemstones International. It is a jewelry chain and has flown out of here for 12 years. The second company, Reminiscent Art Collections also flies out of Newark Security regularly. It is based out of Paris and left at Gate E-2."

"Thank you, Wanda," Ramsey said, reaching for the report. "Jay," she said, handing him the report. "I want you and Jack to check the two flights that got away. I want background checks on everyone aboard."

"You got it," Jay said as they left the room.

"By the way," Wanda added, "Yorg is scheduled to leave about 10:30 this evening. He is still the pilot of Flight #4320 to London."

"Of all the wrong times Yorg has to leave," Ramsey growled. "You two better get cleaned up and rested. I suggest you stay in the security lounge. Kathe doesn't need to be visible. We don't know where Saíde is." She pointed at Yorg, "Don't let her out of your sight!"

"Would Kathe be safer going home to Florida or Colorado?" Wanda asked. "I can arrange a flight for her."

"No," Yorg answered, "she's safer with me and in public. If he is after her, it would be easier for him to pick her off in Florida."

"Thank you," Kathe sarcastically replied. "Nicely put, I feel very secure that I'm not going to Florida. I've had enough of the negatives for the day," she said, reaching under Wanda's desk, taking up her purse and overnight bag. "Bye, Wanda," she called as she left the office.

"What's wrong with Kathe now?" Yorg asked, watching Kathe leave.

"That's easy, her heart is breaking," Wanda answered as she sat down. "As long as I have known her, I never saw her fall for any man. And what a catch he was," Wanda said, resting her head on her hands all dreamy eyed.

Yorg hurried to catch up with Kathe, "What is it with you?" He said, facing her, "What's wrong with the woman I...?"

"As you and Ramsey already pointed out, it doesn't matter," Kathe stated. "I'll be fine as soon as we get in the air," she replied and pushed past him.

A light went on inside Yorg's head, "So, that is what Joe meant by me taking care of you."

Kathe turned around, managed a smile, and clapped her hands, "Congratulations, you caught on!"

After a well-deserved rest, followed by a hot meal, they headed for work. As Yorg came aboard, Captains Rick Slater, and Rob Richardson congratulated him on a job well done with the hostage situation.

Kathe took her position as chief purser going over the pre-flight checklist with speed and accuracy. After ten minutes of organizing, the passengers began to board. She was back in business overseeing the full load. She had 13 attendants under her command.

The flight was routine. It would be landing in London about 7:30 am. Kathe was trying to stay busy. She didn't want to think about Joe. However, toward the end of the flight, she received a call on JAKE from Carrie Anne. "Hi, Carrie Anne what's up?" She curiously asked, knowing Carrie Anne was with Joe in California.

"We're just getting back from a late-night snack after the concert tonight," Carrie Anne said. "Joe didn't say a word on the flight to Los Angeles and stayed to himself before the concert. All the band members are excited about the success of tonight's concert, except for Joe. He hasn't really spoken to anyone the entire ride back to the hotel. I wish I could do something to help him," she said, handing the phone to Joe.

"I didn't mean to hurt Joe," Kathe replied. "I knew better than to get involved. But there was just something about him, I couldn't let go."

"I'm glad you didn't let go," Joe told her as Kathe's eyes widened. "I'm sorry for the way I acted this morning. I was shocked to see you in danger. Although thinking back, you handled yourself very professionally. You have nothing to blame yourself for; I'm the one who went after you. I truly believe that God put us together for a reason. Think about all the crazy ways we kept running into each other. I don't know how, but we will be together again. It's a small world."

"But it's a big airline," Kathe affirmed. "At least, now you understand why I can't be with you and the reason I get paid so well," she said as she heard the cue from the cockpit. "I must go. I must prepare the cabin for landing. Promise me you'll put a smile on your face and be grateful for the time we had together. Some people go through life and don't have half that time to share with anyone. Maybe, someday I'll see you in the clouds again. Break a leg on your tour."

The line cleared and Joe handed the phone back to Carrie Anne. "Do you feel better, now?" Carrie Anne asked.

"I feel like I lost a big part of me," Joe admitted, closing his eyes.

"I've learned one thing in this job," Carrie Anne affirmed. "It's a small world. I'm sure you'll see her again."

"Thanks, Carrie Anne," Joe managed half a smile. "I just told Kathe the same thing."

Collin was sitting on the other side of Joe and joined in the conversation, "The world could get even smaller if you wanted it to."

"What do you mean by that?" Joe asked, glancing at him.

"I mean," Collin smiled, "if you love her, you'll find a way to be with her again."

"It wouldn't work out," Joe sighed as the limo pulled into the hotel entrance.

After landing at Heathrow Airport, the crew headed for the hotel and went straight to their rooms. Kathe woke up about 8:00 pm. She had been sleeping on the floor of Yorg's room. She quietly got up, took a shower and got dressed. Yorg was still sound asleep. She decided to go down to the restaurant and get something to eat.

As she entered the restaurant, she saw an old friend, Shelley Nobles sitting at the bar. "Shelley," Kathe greeted as she walked over to her friend.

"Heyyy Katheee whattt yaaa doin?" Shelley asked.

"Shelley, it's been a long time since I saw you," Kathe admitted, sitting next to her. "I think you've had a little too much to drink, don't you?"

"Nooooope, not yettttt," Shelley said, reaching to put her arm around Kathe. She missed and almost fell off her bar stool. "I'm just startinnn to drink, I'm gonna gooo to Munich tonight. That's in Germany, you knoe…. I gatta hour to dry out."

"No, way," Kathe gasped. "Do you really have a flight tonight?"

"Yepppp!" Shelley announced. "III can make itttt. IIII got it allll figured outtt. I'm goinnn to Germany on a biggggg birddd," she said, ordering another drink as the bartender approached.

Kathe signaled no to the bartender. He acknowledged and kept walking. "Shelley, why don't I help you to your room? You look a little tired."

Shelley hesitated for a moment, "Noooope, I have a nnnother hour to drinkkkkk, and I ain't budginnn."

"I don't think it works quite like that," Kathe stated. "I think you better come with me, while you can still remember your room number."

"Oneee hourrrr," Shelley insisted.

"When you report to work drunk tonight," Kathe began. "The captain will report to Ramsey, and you'll be fired. Now is that what you want?"

"Nooooo!" Shelley insisted, trying to stand. "I can'tttt loseeeee myyyyyyy jobbbb?"

"Good choice, what's your room number?" Kathe asked helping Shelley, stand up.

"2…something…2…It'sss upstairs…214, IIII thinkkkkk," Shelley said as she almost fell.

"I think I better hold on to you," Kathe admitted as she reached for her.

"Wowwww!" Shelley exclaimed. "Why issss the room beginning to spinnnnn?"

"Not the room girlfriend, you are," Kathe confirmed. "Let's go. We can make the elevator," she said trying to help her stumbling friend. Once inside the elevator, Kathe leaned Shelley up against the wall and pushed the second-floor button.

Fumbling in her purse for the key, Shelley began to laugh. "Where are you wittle key? Wittle key, wittle key, IIII can't find you. IIII think the wittle key is hiding from meeee. It's allllll goneeeeee," she said, almost falling over as the elevator stopped, and the door opened.

"We'll find the wittle key in a minute," Kathe said. "Let's find your wittle room first," she said as she found the sign showing the room numbers. "Great! Your room would have to be all the way at the end of the hall. Let's go happy girl."

Helping her friend to her room, Kathe held her against the hall wall with one hand and found the key. Getting her inside, Shelley fell face first on the bed. As Kathe took her shoes off and put the blanket across her, Shelley began to cry. "IIII can't go throughhhh with itttt. T.J. Whiteeee excuseee meeee," she said as turned over and raised her hand to salute. "Captainnnn T.J. Whiteee told meeee I have toooo, because heee loves his wifeee, and not meeee. I'm just a funnnn timeeee," she began to cry harder and turned over mumbling, "I'mmm just a funn timeeee." She cried herself to sleep.

Remembering Shelley had to work a 10:30 flight to Munich, Kathe reached for JAKE. Holding her breath and crossing her fingers she called control.

"Kathe," Keith answered. "I heard about the great way you and Yorg handled this morning's incident. I was hoping to congratulate you both."

"Keith," Kathe sighed, "am I glad to hear your voice. Yorg is still asleep. I need you to check on something for me. Could you check to see where Shelley Nobles is now?"

"Just a minute," Keith answered putting her on hold. "You should be able to find her at Heathrow getting ready for a 10:30 flight tonight to Munich. Do you want her cell phone number?"

"No," Kathe looked over at Shelley passed out on the bed. "Keith does this flight continue on somewhere else or does it come back to London?"

"It has a layover for the night in Munich and goes back to London in the morning; then several other destinations, why?" Keith questioned.

"Shelley can't make the flight tonight," Kathe confided. "I will take it for her. Will I be back at Heathrow in time for my departure?"

"Hold on, let me check your schedule," Keith replied. "Yes, you could make it. I show her flight getting back to London tomorrow morning around 8:00 and your flight to Moscow departs at noon. You have enough time to make your flight."

"Okay, show me taking her flight," Kathe declared. "I need to see someone in Munich anyway," she said with a sigh of relief.

"Wait a minute," Keith cautioned. "No, can do! I show a note on your schedule that reads 'Keep Tierney and Vuslick together!' It's written in big bold red letters. You better let Shelley take her own flight."

"No, can do," Kathe shared. "Shelley has a little problem. She can't make the flight. I will take it for her. I'll be fine."

"I'm not going against Ramsey," Keith declared holding firm.

"Keith, I'm not one for blackmail," Kathe smiled, "but we both know I know..."

Before she could finish her sentence, Keith changed his tune. "Okay, but if I get in trouble with Ramsey, I'm taking you down with me."

"Deal," Kathe smiled, getting her way. Before she left the room, she found a paper and pen and left Shelley a note, which read, "Shelley, you probably will not remember seeing me last night in the bar here at the hotel. You were smashed. I am taking your flight to Munich tonight. I will work it back here tomorrow at 8:00 am. You must meet me at Heathrow and take over your own schedule. That's all I can do. No one else knows you were drinking. Kathe Tierney." She left and headed for her room.

Slipping quietly inside her room, Kathe found Yorg still asleep. She changed quickly into a uniform. She took Nicki's present that Tierra had given her out of her large suitcase and put it in her overnight bag. Then she wrote a note for Yorg, "I found Shelley Nobles smashed downstairs in the bar. I helped her to room #214 and put her to bed. Please wake her up about 6:00 am. I will arrive back at Heathrow at 8:00 am. She needs to meet me at the gate and finish her own day's schedule."

At the airport, Kathe called Keith at control again, "What flight am I taking to Munich?"

"Flight #409 at Gate D24," Keith sighed. "Remember Ms. Blackmail, if Ramsey finds out we're both finished at Alby! Ramsey doesn't know the word mercy!"

"You worry too much," Kathe laughed. "I left Yorg a note telling him where I am and for him to make sure Shelley meets me to finish her schedule. Yorg was tired after this morning; you better make sure he is up before 6:00 am."

"You like to live dangerously, don't you?" Keith asked. "That big Russian isn't going to like this. He might have me fired for helping you."

"I can handle the Russian," Kathe stated. "Stop worrying, this is a walk in the park for me after this morning. Besides, technically I'll only be gone a few hours," she said and cleared the line.

Ten minutes later, Kathe was boarding her flight. She did not know the other crewmembers, so she didn't worry about Ramsey finding out. Once up in the air, she remembered to call Nicki LaBasco. He was sending a car to pick her up at the airport. He said he would send the same driver as before. Once she landed, Kathe retrieved her things and headed for the street exit. She recognized the limo driver and hurried to him. To her surprise, Nicki and another man were in the limo.

"Ms. Tierney, this is a friend of mine, Dider," Nicki introduced. "I hope you don't mind, I decided to get a midnight snack at my favorite restaurant."

"Pleased to meet you Dider," Kathe answered. "No, I don't mind. As a matter of fact, I haven't eaten since yesterday, so a midnight snack will be great."

"Would you care for a drink?" Dider offered.

"I'll have a scotch and coke," Kathe decided.

"Tierra told me that she's not flying to Europe," Nicki began. "I haven't had time to talk with Ramsey yet concerning the switch. Do you know anything about it?"

"Tierra is still apprehensive about the threats on her life," Kathe said. "Ramsey assigned CC Sims to fly with her until she's more comfortable working alone. CC is a native of New York and new to the field. She was a High School Spanish Teacher. So, Tierra is showing CC the ropes and CC is helping Tierra brush up on her Spanish."

"I'm glad to hear that," Nicki admitted. "Tierra isn't the only one still concerned about what happened in our family."

"Somehow the less I know about that subject, the better I feel," Kathe wrinkled up her nose.

"You sound just like Tierra," Nicki chuckled as they pulled in front of the same restaurant from a couple of weeks ago.

"Do you eat here often?" Kathe asked.

"Yes," Nicki answered. "I own it."

"The food is fantastic," Kathe grinned as they got out of the limo.

Inside they were escorted to a private dining room. There Nicki ordered a hearty meal for a midnight snack. Kathe ordered a small steak and salad with a sparkling water. "Dider could one of your men bring me the large blue bag from the limo?"

"Sure, Vinnie will go," Dider signaled him.

When Vinnie returned to the dining area, "Here's your bag, ma'am."

"Happy Birthday!" Kathe exclaimed, handing Nicki the present. "Tierra wanted me to give this to you. I was with her when she picked it out. She was so pleased. She said it was just what you have been looking for. Oh, wait a minute," she said, reaching for JAKE and videotaping it. "Smile I want to send a video of you opening it to her."

"Yes!" Nicki exclaimed, ripping the paper off. "I have been looking everywhere for this one. I told Tierra I was starting my train collection again." As he examined the engine, his face lit up like a little boy. "Thanks Sis, this is perfect. I love you," he said holding it up."

"I'm sending it right now," Kathe pushed send as the food arrived. "This is a happy ending to the rough day I had."

"What happened at work today?" Nicki asked.

"I wouldn't want to bore you with the details," Kathe changed the subject.

"Vinnie, go get the car," Dider requested after dinner. "Ms. Tierney has an early flight tomorrow."

"We'll wait outside if it's all right," Nicki said to Dider as he opened the door for them. "It's a beautiful crisp night."

"That's fine with me," Kathe answered, putting on her coat. "I love the view of the old streets."

"That's odd," Dider replied, opening the restaurant door for them. "Vinnie's not back yet. He parked around the corner."

"Maybe he went to get some petrol," Nicki replied. "He said it was low on the way to the airport."

"I'm going to check," Dider replied and walked away reaching for his cell phone. Returning, Dider interrupted their conversation, "Excuse me, Vinnie didn't answer his phone. I don't like this! I'd feel better if we waited inside."

"Here comes Vinnie," Roberto noted, pointing down the street.

"Vinnie is driving awfully slow," Dider noted, reaching for his cell phone. "That's not like him."

Kathe reached in her purse, grabbed her gun and holstered it behind her back while their attention was on the limo. "The person after Tierra could also be after Nicki," she thought.

"Vinnie, are you alright?" Dider asked as he turned to Nicki. "Something is wrong! Let's get inside!"

Suddenly the limo sped up and veered toward them. Dider pushed Nicki down to the ground and covered him. "Kathe, get down!"

The limo skidded sideways and came to a screeching halt. The back door swung open as a man opened fire on them. Kathe screamed as she fell to the ground and rolled behind a bench. Her heart rate soared, and JAKE alerted control. Dider took a bullet in the arm. Nicki reached for his gun to help. Roberto shot at the man and killed him. The front door of the limo swung open, another man jumped out and headed straight for Nicki. Jumping to her feet, Kathe used JAKE's Taser on him. He fell to the ground trembling uncontrollably. Two more men got out of the other side of the car and fired at them as Nicki's men took them out. The limo did a U-turn and the driver rolled down the darken window.

"Saíde!" Kathe screamed, reaching for her gun. Saíde threw the limo in reverse and rolled up the window. He sped away zigzagging down the street. Kathe joined with Nicki's men firing at the limo. She shot out one of the back tires causing Saíde to lose control of the limo slamming into a sign, before speeding off.

Nicki's bodyguards helped him up as Kathe hurried over to help Dider. "If your limo wasn't bulletproof, we would have had him!"

"I should have expected something like this would happen," Dider sighed, reaching for his handkerchief, and holding it over his wound.

"It's just a flesh wound," Kathe noted after she moved the cloth away and looked at it. "This was a direct assault on Nicki. Do you know who they are?"

"I thought you were a flight attendant?" Dider questioned. "You seem pretty well equipped with a Taser as well as a Walther PPK 380. Not to mention, you handled yourself very well under fire, and you know this is a flesh wound."

"Let's just say, I'm not your average flight attendant," Kathe smiled. "I recognized the driver. He is a known killer and usually uses a knife on his victims."

"Roberto is dead," reported another bodyguard interrupting their conversation.

"I can't believe this happened," Dider said as they walked over to examine the body. He turned around and walked to the man under the influence of the Taser. "At least we have this one alive," Dider stated leaning over him. "Nicki and I are beginning to think we know what is going on," he glanced up at Kathe. "However, we aren't ready to say just yet. I'm glad you Tasered him, instead of shooting him. Maybe we can get some answers."

"I was trying not to use my weapon," Kathe admitted. "I'm not supposed to be here. My boss is going to have my head," she said as the sound of sirens approached them.

Control was calling Kathe. However, she wasn't ready to talk to anyone and ignored the calls. One of Nicki's bodyguards led them back into the restaurant. She pulled herself together enough to answer the second time JAKE rang. It was Keith. While Nicki and his bodyguards were answering questions from the police, she had a few questions of her own to answer.

"Are you alright?" Keith asked frantically.

"Yes," Kathe's voice was still shaking.

"Your heart rate is still way too high," Keith stated. "It's going off the monitor."

"I just witnessed Saíde trying to kill Nicki LaBasco," Kathe admitted. "That's enough to do it!"

"What happened?" Keith asked.

"I had dinner with Tierra LaBasco's brother, Nicki," Kathe said. "We were leaving the restaurant when Saíde and a handful of men commandeered Nicki's limo and came after him."

"Oh, my, God!" Keith exclaimed. "Are you sure?"

"Yes, I'm sure," Kathe confirmed. "It was Saíde with his blonde hair that we saw this morning at Newark. He saw me here and was just as shocked as I was. He must have gotten on one of two private jets that took off this morning, right under our noses!"

"We're dead!" Keith exclaimed. "Ramsey is going to have our heads! I might as well start looking for a new job! No, I might as well book myself to Madagascar! I think that's the only country Ramsey doesn't have control over!"

"Keith let's look at this more calmly," Kathe realized. "We found out Saíde is in Munich."

"Great, all we have to do is tell Ramsey he shot at you tonight!" Keith snapped. "She said all along she thinks he's after you. You were supposed to stay with Yorg, and I let you go."

"Actually, he didn't shoot at me," Kathe replied. "Technically, he was driving the limo; the people with him were shooting at Nicki LaBasco, not me."

"Your heart rate is calming down," Keith sighed.

"Thanks for the 411," Kathe smiled, "I would have never guessed."

"Hold on," Keith requested, "I have another phone call." He put Kathe on hold for a while. She glanced over at Nicki and noticed the police seemed to be giving him a hard time. They found Vinnie with his throat slashed.

"Tierney!" Ramsey, not Keith was now on the line. "What are you doing in Munich?"

"I was having dinner," Kathe cringed.

"Don't you get smart with me!" Ramsey snapped. "Put Yorg on the phone, now!"

"Wellllll...he's not actually here," Kathe crossed her fingers.

"What! Just where, is he?" Ramsey demanded.

"He's in London," Kathe cringed again.

"London!" Ramsey yelled, opening her office door, "Wanda! Get me a pack of cigarettes. I picked the wrong day to quit smoking again!" She took a deep breath, "Now, pray tell Kathe, why you are in Munich and Yorg is in London?"

"I promised Tierra I would deliver a present to her brother, and I did," Kathe stated.

"I made it perfectly clear to you to stay with Yorg, didn't I?" Ramsey demanded as she flickered her lighter.

"I forgot?" Kathe gritted her teeth. "You know how it is?"

"No, I don't know how it is," Ramsey bellowed. "Perhaps, you would like to explain how it is. I seemed to have missed that memo!"

"Well, Ramsey," Kathe offered. "You know I'm so used to flying all the time, I just forgot and came here."

"Who is there with you?" Ramsey demanded, tapping her unlit cigarette on her desk.

"Nicki LaBasco and several of his bodyguards," Kathe said. "There are also several dozen of the Munich police. I'm safe now. Did you hear that I recognized the driver of the limo tonight?"

"Yes, I overheard you talking to Keith," Ramsey shared. "And by the way, it wouldn't do Keith any good to go to Madagascar. I do have connections there too! Now, let me talk to the officer in charge."

"Yes, ma 'am," Kathe replied, walking over to the officer talking to Nicki. "My boss would like to have a word with you on my phone," Kathe said handing him JAKE.

The officer talked to Ramsey for a few moments. Ramsey filled him in on Saíde. "Miss," he said to Kathe, "you are to come with me to the police station. You are to remain there until a certain Alby pilot comes for you in the morning. His name is Capt. Vuslick," he handed JAKE back to her.

"Do you understand this time?" Ramsey tested her. "Or should I have them place you under arrest?"

"Ramsey that is so unfair," Kathe whined.

"Unfair, Lady?" Ramsey snapped. "I don't want to go to your funeral! You stay at the station until I can fly Yorg over there and that's an order! Do I make myself clear this time?"

"Yes, ma 'am, perfectly clear," Kathe concurred.

Chapter 21

Unwelcomed Visitors for Light Crimson

Kicking the door open, guns at their sides, Saíde and the last hired thug stormed into the rundown hotel room. Saíde picked up the phone, dialed the same number he always reported to after a job. Lighting a cigarette, he slammed the lighter down as he began to talk. "Not yet, that same flight attendant was with him."

"Did she see you?" he asked.

"Yes," he listened to orders, and slammed the phone down. Smashing his cigarette out on the table, he turned toward the man in the room. "We'll go again with a bonus when I contact you. This time it will be more difficult. Now that LaBasco is on to us. And the woman he was with tonight was that Alby flight attendant that poured coffee on me. This time she's mine!"

"Mario!" Mr. LaBasco screamed. "I just got off the phone with Nicki! We got trouble! Someone just tried to kill him at his restaurant!"

"Papa is he alright?" Mario Jr. asked.

"Yes, you and your boys get over here now!" Mario Sr. requested. "We've got some talking to do!"

"Yes, Papa, we'll be right over," Mario Jr. replied as Giorgio Pulini entered his office.

"You look troubled," Giorgio noticed as he sat down on the couch. "Did everything go all right?"

"That idiot screwed up again," Mario Jr. admitted. "That's the third mark he's missed, my sister twice, and now my brother."

"Alonzo's not stupid," Giorgio cautioned. "We've gotta work fast before he figures this out."

"You're right," Mario Jr. agreed. "Our unfinished business just got delayed. First things first, Papa wants to see us now. Get the boys and meet me at the taxiway. I have to tell Jada my papa has summoned me again."

"Nothing ever worries you, does it?" Giorgio asked.

"Sure, but I truly believe in what Mama told me before she died," Mario Jr. smiled. "Mario, she said, there is always another day," he laughed as he walked off. His obnoxious laugh got louder all the way upstairs.

Entering his bedroom, Mario Jr. walked over to a glamorous brunette sitting at the vanity combing her long hair. She was wearing a black negligee. He put his hands around her shoulders and rubbed her neck. "Baby, you're not going to like this, but I have to go out," Mario Jr. said as her face saddened.

"Mario," Jada pitifully whined, turning toward him. "What could be more important than me?"

He glanced into her eyes, ran his fingers through her hair, "Nothing my pet."

She fumbled with his belt buckle, "Then, why did you tease me?"

He backed away from her, "No tease, my precious pet. Papa beckoned and I must jump, at least for now." He walked to the door to leave, "Don't wait up for me. I'll return as soon as I can," he left the room as blew her a kiss.

She stomped her feet, picked up her brush, screamed, and threw it at the door. Mario was walking down the stairs, "Oh," he smiled as he heard something hit the door. "I do like the rough ones," he laughed all the way downstairs.

Forty-five minutes later, Mario landed his Leer Jet at his papa's private airstrip, near his fortress on Corté de Azuré. Arriving at his papa's security-tight mansion on the coast, he jokingly reminded Giorgio not to forget to look worried. Giorgio immediately complied.

"Mr. Mario," Charles greeted, opening the door, "welcome home. Your papa is expecting you." He led the way to the large study off his papa's private office.

"Mr. Mario and Giorgio," Charles announced, opening the door to the study.

Mr. LaBasco was sitting at the head of the conference table with Alonzo and twenty other members of the family. "Mario," his papa reached up to hug him. "You got here in record time."

"Well, you did say Nicki was in trouble," Mario said as he glanced out of the corner of his eye at Giorgio.

"Yes, I'm afraid we must have someone trying to muscle their way into our territory," Mario Sr. reported as the other men started talking amongst themselves.

"I don't understand," Mario Jr. stated. "We've been at peace with the other families for quite some time."

"Rumor has it that the Falcini's are trying to gather territory," Alonzo reported. "Although, I haven't been able to prove it."

"I heard the same rumor just the other day," Mario concurred. "I forget whom I was talking to when the subject came up," he said, looking around at the other members of the family, remembering how he started the rumor himself.

"Take your seat next to me son," Mario Sr. pointed to the chair on the right side of him.

The meeting began with Mario Sr. speculating about the recent incidents regarding his children. He started with how someone had tried to harm Tierra and how Mario's men had settled that family problem. Then, he began talking about the attempt on Nicki's life earlier that evening. Each man at the table speculated on what they thought was happening.

When he got to Giorgio, he looked right at the old man. "Mr. LaBasco, we took care of the Bozo that bothered Miss Tierra. I personally believe that you should let us handle this problem."

"Yes, Papa," Mario Jr. added. "Let us handle this matter for you. After all, you still have the FBI and NYPD looking at you."

"It was a strange coincidence that we were in New York when the Senator was murdered," Alonzo glared at him. "It's as if someone seems to be leaking information to the papers."

The men at the table started agreeing with Giorgio and Mario Jr. Mr. LaBasco listened to the others as they agreed it would be better to keep the heat off Mario Sr. However, Mario Sr. also knew that his two sons did not get along. It had escalated since the death of their mother.

"I disagree," Mario Sr. stated. "I think Nicki should come here. No one would ever dare to strike at him here."

"I stand with Mr. LaBasco," Alonzo concurred. "It is well known within the family that the brothers do not get along. Nicki will be more comfortable here."

"Papa, the polizia are still trying to implicate you in the death of the man we iced while you were protecting Tierra recently," Mario Jr. quickly added knowing he had only one more chance at his sibling.

The men at the table began to agree with Mario Jr. again. Mr. LaBasco listened as they each expressed their reasoning.

"Alonzo has his hands full," Mario Jr. stood up, "keeping up with your lawyers and the accusations from the polizia. It would not be good if another problem appeared in this house," he said as everyone at the table agreed.

"It seems to be the favor of this committee to let Mario and his boys see to this problem," Mr. LaBasco announced as every man at the table stood up and applauded except for Alonzo.

Clearing his throat as the men sat back down Alonzo spoke, "I want this understood," he declared standing and looking at each man. "Mr. LaBasco, my gut feeling is Nicki should come here. I've never had a problem handling the polizia or working with our attorneys. If anything happens to Nicki," he glared straight at Mario Jr. and then Giorgio, "they will answer to me!"

"Alonzo," Mario Jr. said, standing and turning to face him. "I will prove to you that I harbor no ill will toward my brother. I will handle Nicki's problem with speed and precision," Mario stated and glanced at Giorgio. "If you will all excuse us, we have work to do," he said hugging his papa. "I'll call you in the morning, when I have decided how to handle this problem."

In the Leer Jet heading home, Mario answered his phone. "We'll be there tomorrow late afternoon," he smiled turning to Giorgio. "The unfinished business is ready for us in Russia."

"What about your brother?" Giorgio asked.

"This takes priority over killing my brother," Mario smiled. "Remember, first things first Giorgio. You need to learn patience," he said switching coordinates for Russia. "I think I'll have my brother and some of his men brought to my house while we're gone. Then, we'll arrange for our Iranian friend to deal with him."

"Boss, that man is an idiot," Giorgio confirmed. "Why do you use him?"

"To throw the great Alonzo DiMeglio off, my friend," Mario chuckled.

In Los Angeles, the crowds were going crazy caught up in the passion of the love song Joe was singing from one of their previous albums. Carrie Anne, sitting next to Babs, turned to her, "I could never get tired of this," she said, watching Travis on stage. It even crossed her mind that maybe he could be the one! Everyone who ever knew Carrie Anne, knows that sentence was not in her jargon. Suzanne had been checking her watch all evening. Even Babs had asked Suzanne if she had somewhere to go. She glanced at her watch one more time and left the arena. Two more songs had finished as she returned to her seat with unwelcomed guests. Carrie Anne noticed Babs looked worried as they talked amongst themselves.

"Who are the girls with Suzanne?" Carrie Anne asked Babs.

"One of them is Shaunda Smythe," Babs explained. "She dates Travis. The other one is Joe's ex-wife, Cara Carrington."

Carrie Anne instantly felt sick to her stomach, "What do you mean, one of them dates Travis?"

"They are always together when Travis is in London," Babs replied. "She never comes on tour with him."

"Why did they come here?" Carrie Anne requested.

"I don't know, but I noticed Suzanne kept looking at her watch," Babs stated, leaning closer to Carrie Anne. "She knew they were coming. Joe's not going to like this."

Carrie Anne was worried for the rest of the concert. She was glad when it was over, and the band left the stage. She wanted to know what was going on with those two girls.

Babs motioned for Carrie Anne to hurry backstage, "Let's go Carrie Anne."

"What are you going to do?" Carrie Anne asked hurrying to keep up with her. Babs showed her pass and they rushed into the room. Babs ran straight for Joe telling him that Suzanne kept checking her watch during the early part of the concert. She left for a short time and came back with Cara and Shaunda. Joe stormed into the shower.

Suzanne and the girls walked into the room. Travis was coming out of the shower with a towel draped around his waist. Shaunda shouted Travis's name, ran over to him, and threw her arms around his neck. They both acted glad to see each other. Watching them, Carrie Anne felt a lump swell in her throat. Then surprisingly, the two of them walked off arm in arm right past her. Babs hurried over to Carrie Anne and tried to cheer her up. Joe walked out of the shower and Cara headed for him. Joe pushed by her and stormed into the dressing room. Shaunda came out rejoining Suzanne with a gleam in her eyes. Cara tried to go into the dressing room but was stopped.

"What's going on?" Carrie Anne asked Babs as she tried to hold back tears.

"I'm not sure yet," Babs whispered, "but whatever it is, it's not good. No one knows what happened between Cara and Joe. He won't talk about it. That's unusual because all the guys are very close. All I do know is that Joe hates her with a passion and doesn't ever want to see her again."

Joe stuck his head out the door and yelled for Payton. Troy came out of the dressing room and asked Brock to find Payton. "Where did they come from?" Troy asked his wife as he joined her.

"I don't know," Babs answered. "Suzanne seemed very preoccupied at the concert, constantly looking at her watch and then she left and came back with them."

Collin came out of the shower shocked to see Cara and Shaunda with Suzanne. He pulled Suzanne away from them, whispered to her and left for the dressing room.

Payton hurried past them and headed straight to the dressing room with Brock. Carrie Anne noticed that Cara had turned her back on Payton when he passed her. He stayed in the dressing room a good ten minutes. He came out annoyed, glanced at the unwanted girls as he approached Carrie Anne. "Carrie Anne, can I see you alone for a moment?"

Carrie Anne walked apprehensively with him toward the door. "Would you mind going ahead to the hotel?" Payton asked her as he opened the door. "Travis wants to talk to a friend of his for a while."

Carrie Anne glanced at Babs and Troy and fought back tears. "Okay," was all she could say. She turned and left the room. Babs and Troy started to follow her, but Payton told them to stay and wait for the others.

As the cab pulled in front of the hotel, her cell rang. "Carrie Anne," a very familiar voice said to her as tears started to trickle down her cheeks. "Payton has asked me to replace you with another flight attendant. Collect your things and report to the airport. I need you to go to Europe. While you've had your head in the clouds, Kathe was with Nicki LaBasco in Munich and witnessed Saíde trying to kill him."

"Is she alright?" Carrie Anne questioned.

"By the grace of God," Ramsey concurred. "Yorg is on his way to retrieve her. I had the Munich police place her in protective custody."

"I thought Kathe was supposed to stay with Yorg and go to Russia," Carrie Anne remembered.

"She was, but she left while he was asleep," Ramsey explained. "She ran into Shelley Nobles and ended up working a shift for her to Munich. She met up with Nicki LaBasco."

"What was she doing with him?" Carrie Anne inquired.

"Delivering a birthday present from Tierra," Ramsey answered.

"Was that Saíde at the Newark Airport with the blonde hair?" Carrie Anne quizzed.

"Yes, you were right," Ramsey complimented. "He changed his hair color and evidently managed to leave on a private plane before we could stop him. Kathe identified Saíde as the driver of LaBasco's stolen limo. The one that was used to get close enough for a Mafia-style hit, enough questions. Your plane leaves for Newark in less than an hour. Get moving lady, you need to hurry," the line cleared.

Carrie Anne felt horrible after speaking with Ramsey. Now she knew Travis had Payton get rid of her. She turned the television on while she packed to see if she could hear anything more about Kathe or Nicki LaBasco but left before she did.

About an hour later, the group came back to the hotel. RJ entered the room first to make sure Carrie Anne was gone. He gave the all-clear and everyone went inside. Cara was still with them despite the way Joe felt about it. As they settled down in the room, Collin went over to turn off the TV that Carrie Anne had left on. Reaching for the remote, he heard the newscaster reporting on the attempted murder of Nicki LaBasco. It showed the police talking to Nicki with Kathe sitting next to him at the restaurant. "Joe, come here quick!" Collin called.

Joe hurried over to the television. "Look," Collin pointed to the screen. "Isn't that Kathe Tierney sitting next to the man the police are talking to?"

Joe couldn't believe his eyes, he got closer to the television for a better look, just as the camera switched to a different angle. Now, it only showed the back of her head, with a close upside profile of LaBasco. The camera moved to the outside of the restaurant as the newscaster gave the details of the alleged shooting. The report continued, showing the slain bodyguard on the sidewalk covered with a sheet. The camera then switched to a view of the limo driver, who was found with his throat slit a few blocks away. The newscaster ended the report by saying, "An Alby Airlines flight attendant, whose name was withheld due to security reasons, was with LaBasco at the time of the shooting."

Babs and Troy ran over to Joe's side. "Maybe it wasn't Kathe," Babs tried to console Joe.

"Yeah, there are lots of flight attendants working in Europe," Troy added.

"Besides, wasn't Kathe supposed to be going to Russia with Yorg?" Collin added, trying to downplay it.

"It looked like her!" Joe snapped as Cara tried to get close to him. "Carrie Anne isn't here!" Joe shouted shoving Cara away. "Payton, get her out of here or I'm leaving!".

"Joe please," Cara begged. "I've traveled all this way to be with you."

"Payton!" Joe yelled for him again as Payton walked into the room looking quite distressed.

"Look Joe, she's your ex-wife, not mine, you talk to her," Payton began. "I'm not a messenger. I'm your manager."

"You are my manager!" Joe snapped. "I pay your salary! Get her out of here!" He yelled, stormed past her and left the room. Payton signaled for Brock to go with Joe.

Travis and Shaunda were happily reunited. They were leaving for their own room that RJ had arranged.

Collin was still upset with Suzanne for bringing Cara to LA. He realized that she had planned it behind his back. He knew Joe hated Cara and didn't like seeing his friend tortured by her. "I'm going to find Joe," Collin said walking to the door.

"You're not leaving here!" Payton snapped. "Brock and RJ are both gone. You know you can't go anywhere without one of them with you."

Collin glared at Suzanne. "Thanks a lot!" he snapped as he went over to the couch and laid down. Suzanne hurried over to Collin to try to smooth things out.

Babs was still busy trying to switch channels to see the news about the LaBasco shooting. "I can't find that newscast again," she whined to Troy. "I like Kathe. She's good for Joe. I can't find it on any channel. I wish I could put his mind at ease. Joe is so worried about her."

"You are not going to put his mind at ease," Collin interrupted, pulling it up on the Internet. "It was Kathe on the news," he said as he walked over and showed her. "I saw a different shot of them with her sitting next to Nicki LaBasco. That's why I called him over."

"He's in love with her, can't you see!" Babs admitted. "He's miserable without her."

"There's nothing we can do," Collin commented. "It's up to them to decide what to do about her job."

"Collin is right Babs," Troy agreed. "Her job stands in the way of their happiness."

Chapter 22

An Unforgettable Trip to Moscow

Yorg entered the police station in Munich and asked to speak to the commanding officer. "Capt. Hiers is out on another call," the overstuffed man glared over his glasses at Yorg. "I'm in charge, may I help you?"

"Linda Ramsey from Alby Airlines sent me here to pick up Kathe Tierney," Yorg said. "I'm Capt. Yorg Vuslick," he told the disgusting man in front of him.

The officer sat up and took notice of Yorg, "You got some ID with you?"

Yorg reached inside of his coat pocket and took out his ID badge. "This should be sufficient," Yorg said, handing him his ID. "I'm in a hurry. We have a flight to catch."

The officer handed Yorg back his ID, "Come with me. I'll take you to her." He led Yorg down a corridor leading to the cells. The door was ajar on the first cell. Kathe was sleeping on the lower bunk. "Here she is," he whispered. "She was exhausted after the upsetting evening she had, and this is the only place I could find for her to rest."

Yorg entered the cell and stood there for a second watching Kathe sleep. He bent down, "Kat," he whispered.

She opened her eyes slowly. "Yorg!" She exclaimed, sitting up, and throwing her arms around his neck. "Boy, am I glad to see you?"

"Heavens Kat," Yorg declared. "You scared the heck out of me! After Ramsey called, I was privileged to catch you on the newscast! You could have been killed! Thanks to you, Ramsey is steamed at both of us! You weren't supposed to go anywhere without me! Remember Saíde?"

"Saíde!" Kathe's eyes widened. "I saw him! He was driving the LaBasco limo for the hit men that shot at Nicki."

"Are you sure?" Yorg asked.

"Complete with his blonde hair," Kathe declared. "He recognized me and sped away. If the limo wasn't bulletproof, I would have gotten him! He had to have gotten away from Newark on one of the two private jets. We have to find out which one."

"You're right," Yorg agreed. "Since they were private jets, someone let him on board. That someone could possibly be his boss."

"I'll check with Ramsey," Kathe said. "At least, I got a few rounds off as he sped away."

"You're lucky to be alive!" Yorg exclaimed. "That's the second time you've been in his way!"

"If he wanted to kill me," Kathe expressed. "He would have done it. He had a gun in his hand. To him I'm just a flight attendant. He was after Nicki LaBasco. They found Vinnie, the real limo driver dead. His throat was slashed."

"Why didn't he shoot you?" Yorg questioned. "You are not just a flight attendant to him. He knows that you can identify him. Remember his threat to you when he was taken off the plane in Paris."

"Well, thanks a lot," Kathe looked sideways at him, "I guess I'm lucky he doesn't think like you. I would be dead!"

Standing and pulling Kathe up to him, "Let's quit giving Saíde the chance and opportunity to do it."

He pointed a finger at her, "You're staying with me. Do you understand?"

"You're beginning to sound like Ramsey," Kathe retorted, fixed her skirt, and ran her fingers through her hair.

"Good!" Yorg declared, "We're only thinking of your safety." He turned to walk out of the jail cell. "Come on, we have a plane to catch."

"Where are we going now?" Kathe asked.

"Russia," he answered. "Let's see if you can stay out of trouble there."

She licked her index finger, drew an imaginary line straight down, and grinned back at him. Then she grabbed her overnight bag, her purse and followed him. "Did you bring my other suitcase?" She asked as he signed her out at the front desk.

"Yes," Yorg answered, putting a copy of the receipt in his front pocket.

"Well at least, now I can say I've spent the night in jail," Kathe snickered as Yorg glared at her. "It was just a joke," she laughed.

"A thought just came to me," Yorg confessed. "I could be signing for your body in a morgue. I guess I'm not in a joking mood." He turned and motioned for her to follow him.

As they boarded the 777 Whisper Jet, JAKE rang, "I'm just checking to see if you and Yorg are heading for Russia?" Ramsey questioned.

"Yes, and don't worry, I'm fine," Kathe replied.

"That I already know," Ramsey declared. "But the people on the other line are still worried about you. Bob and Jeannie are holding for you," she snapped still riled at Kathe.

"Kathe, you're on speaker," Jeannie stated. "We saw the newscast and have been trying to reach you all night. Are you alright?"

"I'm fine," Kathe proclaimed. "I'm boarding a flight to Russia right now," she said stowing her things.

"Gosh Kathe, whatever happened to the little housewife that lived next door?" Jeannie questioned.

"Your job is hard on our nerves," Bob admitted as he rewound the DVR watching the newscast over again.

"I didn't see the newscast," Kathe admitted. "You know how they doctor them up to look worse than they really are. I'm fine. It's over and I must get to work. Where are the kids?" She asked as she reached for her roster.

"I sent them to bed," Jeannie stated. "Ramsey assured us you were all right. Bob and I just wanted to hear it from you. I promised Ben, I would call you and then call him back."

"Well, I'm fine," Kathe said. "You can pass the word along. I must go now. Bye," she said as JAKE rang again. "Hello."

"Hello," his voice sounded distraught.

"Joe, is that you?" Kathe asked stepping into the galley for privacy.

"Yes, I thought I recognized you on the newscast tonight," Joe sighed. "It said you were involved in a shooting in Munich. I've watched it on the Internet a dozen times. I just wanted to hear you say that you're okay," he said sitting on the edge of his bed.

Tears welled up in her eyes at the sound of his voice. Fighting them back, she tried to lighten her voice, "It must have been some newscast. You are the third person this morning that has called about it.

You know how reporters are. And the Internet splices clips together. They always seem to change the news to make it sound gloomier than it really is. I'm surprised you are even the least bit worried. Don't tell me you are going to start believing all the news you hear. Don't subscribe to the pulp magazines just yet."

Her rambling seemed to cheer Joe up, "I guess you're right. I'll hold off on my subscriptions for now."

"How's your tour going?" Kathe asked leaning on the counter.

"A little empty, I miss you," Joe admitted as he leaned back and looked up at the ceiling.

"I'm sure you'll find a way to fill your time," Kathe smiled. "I've seen how you rock stars operate."

She chuckled as Yorg poked his head out of the cockpit, "Are you going to be ready for passengers to start boarding this bird sometime this morning?"

"I've got to go to work," Kathe declared. "I am getting nasty remarks from the pilot. If I get fired, I'd have to take you up on that job offer. And I don't work for a song," she laughed.

"Just say the word and I'll hire you in an instant," Joe paused for a second. "I'm glad I talked to you."

"Me too!" Kathe beamed. "Happy flights!" she cleared the line.

Yorg looked at her, "Who was that?"

"Just an old friend," Kathe said, putting JAKE away.

"Joe?" Yorg quizzed.

"Yes," Kathe admitted. "He saw the news and wanted to hear that I was all right. I think he's finally accepting my job."

It was a long flight, and the plane was half-empty. Her mind kept racing back to conversations with Joe as JAKE rang, "Kathe, I'm at your house in Florida. How can I get inside?"

"Carrie Anne?" Kathe questioned. "I'll call Ramsey and have her call the Martins next door. They will let you inside. Wait a minute, why aren't you in California?"

Carrie Anne started to cry, "Because Travis' girlfriend from London came to visit him. He decided I was in his way and had Payton tell Ramsey to ship me off." She sobbed harder, "You don't know how embarrassed I felt being told to leave. He didn't even have the guts to do it himself."

Kathe was shocked. Joe didn't mention anything about it to her. "Gosh, I can't believe it. Travis seemed to enjoy being with you. I don't know what to say."

"There is nothing for you to say," Carrie Anne cried. "I can't believe I was beginning to like him. I mean like him, as in maybe he was The One," she sobbed even harder.

"I bet by tomorrow you'll have someone else lined up to make you forget about him," Kathe said as the passengers filed past her.

"No, I've had it with men this time," Carrie Anne declared. "I can't talk about it I've got to go," the line cleared.

Kathe called Ramsey immediately to find out what happened. "I got a phone call from Payton," Ramsey relayed. "He told me to get Carrie Anne out of Travis' hair immediately. He was cold about it. I was going to send her to Europe, but she was so upset, I sent her on leave to your house in Florida."

"That's fine," Kathe said. "Just call the Martins and have them let her in the house and have them check on her tomorrow. She sounded pretty torn up about being dumped this time."

"Okay, I'll call the Martins," Ramsey agreed as Wanda rushed in her office. "I have to go . . . Wanda insists on talking to me."

"Shelley Nobles was just admitted at a London hospital as a possible suicide," Wanda stated. "They're holding on line two."

"I'm not getting paid enough for this job!" Ramsey snapped answering the line.

Yorg turned on the fasten seatbelt sign signaling the crew of approaching turbulent weather. They were about an hour from Moscow. Kathe picked up the intercom, "Ladies and gentlemen, the captain has just turned on the fasten seatbelt sign. We have a little turbulent weather ahead. Please stay in your seats with them fastened securely. Thank you." She hurried and stowed her cart and took her seat.

Twenty minutes of extreme weather bouncing the plane around as Kathe's intercom rang...it was Yorg. "Kathe, we are about thirty minutes from Moscow. We will be coming out of the turbulence soon; however, it is snowing hard at the airport. The latest reports indicate fair to poor braking action, due to snow on the runway, so I would like you to prepare the cabin for landing a little earlier than normal. I want you and your crew down early...they'll be closing the airport as soon as we are on the ground."

"Understood," Kathe replied and then she announced, "Ladies and gentlemen, in preparation for landing in Moscow, the crew will be coming through the cabin one last time to collect anything you would like to discard. Please make sure that all your personal items are properly stowed under the seat in front of you, all tray tables are locked, and seat backs are in their full and upright position. We will be on the ground shortly."

As Kathe put the intercom back, JAKE rang, "What do you know about Shelley Nobles?" Ramsey demanded. "I know that you covered her shift last night."

"I saw Shelley in the hotel in London," Kathe admitted. "She wasn't feeling well so I took her shift," she said, covering for Shelley.

"I have a situation with her in the ER at a London hospital," Ramsey declared. "I need to know why it appears that she tried to commit suicide. Now, what do you know about her?"

"I found her about 8:15 last night in the bar at the hotel," Kathe answered. "She had been drinking. I don't know how long, but she was very tipsy when I found her. She said she had a flight to Munich at 10:30. I took her to her room and put her to bed. She was depressed, mumbling something about T.J. White and his wife. She cried herself to sleep. I called Keith and covered her flight. I left Yorg a note, asking him to make sure she was at the airport this morning at 8:00 to work her shift."

"That's what I needed to know," Ramsey sighed and cleared the line. "Wanda," Ramsey yelled. "Find Capt. T.J. White. I need to talk to him. Call the hospital in London and tell them to check Nobles for possible pregnancy."

As the aircraft headed toward runway 32R at Domodedovo Airport, Yorg bellowed, "Gear down final descent check!" Just as the glide slope came alive, the first officer simultaneously threw the landing gear lever into the down position and began reading the final descent checklist.

Moments later approach control interrupted with, "Alby 263, contact Domodedovo Tower on 119.7"

"Roger, 119.7...Alby 263," Jonathan replied as he switched frequencies. "Domodedovo Tower, Alby 263...Alby 263... marker."

"Alby 263, Domodedovo Tower...clear to land on runway 32R," Control advised. "Wind 280 degrees at 15 knots. The runway has just been plowed and braking action is poor but tricky."

"Roger, Alby 263, clear to land on 32R," Jonathan repeated. "Gear is down and locked...understand braking action poor."

"Just great!" Yorg complained, "Since they just plowed the runway, no other aircraft has landed to give an accurate braking action report. So, our destiny is in the hands of some clown in a truck, who had trouble stopping on the runway. It's the best information we have so we'll go with it. Winds 40 degrees off the runway heading at 15 knots...it's doable."

The aircraft broke through the overcast sky at 300 feet and revealed an awesome sight. The snow was still falling at the airport at 150 knots, it appeared to be going sideways. The onrushing snow illuminated by the landing lights produced a hypnotic effect.

"This reminds me of a scene from a movie where the observer is in the helm of a spaceship, hurling through the cosmos at warp speed," Jonathan observed.

"Kill the nose light!" Yorg yelled.

"Nose light off," Jonathan confirmed as he immediately turned off the nose gear light. The glare from the snow diminished enough for Yorg to see the approach lights and runway threshold.

As Flight #263 crossed the end of the runway, Yorg lowered the left wing while applying right rudder to keep the aircraft pointing straight down the runway. He then closed the throttles and applied just enough backpressure to the yoke to initiate the flare. Just as Yorg completed this maneuver, the left main gear contacted the runway. He smoothly lowered the right wing until the right gear was also grounded.

As Yorg lowered the nose gear, a gust of wind forced the front of the aircraft sharply to the left. Undeterred, Yorg applied just enough right rudders to re-center the nose down the runway and completed the landing. With all three gears firmly in contact with the ground, Yorg simultaneously threw both engines into reverse and applied full braking. "Not too much reverse," Yorg said to himself, "We don't want to initiate a skid now, do we?"

While standing on the brakes, Yorg could feel the antiskid working overtime, applying and releasing hydraulic pressure to the brakes many times a second. "Thank God for antiskid," Yorg reflected.

As the aircraft decelerated, Jonathan called, "Eighty knots," as Yorg slowly took the engines out of reverse. Jonathan continued calling..." Sixty knots, forty, twenty, ten," as Yorg carefully exited the runway via the high-speed taxiway on the left and headed for the terminal.

"Man am I glad I'm flying with you," Jonathan admitted. "A landing like this one, that we walk away from has got to be good!"

"All in a day's work," Yorg smiled. "I can tell I'm home, this is typical weather for my country," Yorg laughed taxiing to the terminal.

Kathe let out a sigh of relief as she reached for the intercom, "On behalf of Alby Airlines, we would like to be the first to welcome you to Moscow, Russia where the local time is now 5:30 pm." As the plane taxied to the terminal, she could hear the wind howling. Great, she thought. Carrie Anne is at my house in beautiful warm sunny Florida, and I am here in the land that time forgot.

As the last passenger deplaned, Yorg came out of the cockpit. "What did you think about the landing?"

"Do you mean when we were dancing on the ice?" Kathe smiled. "I wasn't worried at all knowing you were in control of this plane. After all, you're home in Mother Russia."

"Do you think your kids would have been impressed?" Yorg asked.

"I know Pete and Heather would love it," Kathe replied. "However, Christy would totally freak out. She's more like her mother. Her feet need to be firmly on the ground."

"Oh, by the way," Yorg sighed. "I called my sister, and she is fixing dinner for us at her apartment. We need to hurry," he said as he retrieved his stowed bags.

"I finally get to meet her," Kathe said putting her iPad away. "I can't wait to see the malls here. After that landing, I need a good shopping trip to settle my nerves," she said reaching for her stowed bags.

"I know how you like to shop," Yorg winked. "But we might not have time for your shopping spree."

The two left the airport and took a cab to his sister's apartment. "So, this is what Russia looks like," Kathe said as they drove to a very humble looking apartment building. She noticed Yorg shaking his head. "What's wrong?"

"I get very depressed every time I come home," Yorg confessed. "I am always glad to leave. I wish someday I could take Ylia out of this country for good."

As they approached the front door, Kathe grabbed hold of Yorg's arm. "I hope your sister likes me."

"I'm sure she will as much as I do," Yorg replied as they heard footsteps coming quickly to the door.

"Yorg, Yorg," the door opened. A tall, thin woman about forty-five years old, threw her arms around her brother's neck.

Kathe's first impression of Ylia was that she favored Yorg. She was dressed very plainly with no make-up. Her hair was pulled back in a bun and she wore thick black glasses.

"Yorg, eto dejstvitelno tu!" Ylia said, giving him a kiss on the cheek.

"Ylia, moya Ylia, ya doma!" Yorg exclaimed hugging her. Yorg sat her down and she noticed Kathe. "Come," she hugged Kathe. "Where are my manners you must be freezing out here," she said, holding the door open and reaching to help Yorg with the bags. "You must be Kathe. I've heard so much about you."

"I hope it has all been good," Kathe smiled, glancing over at Yorg.

"Of course, it was all good," Yorg smiled. "But that was before yesterday."

Ylia looked surprised, "What happened yesterday?"

"She was supposed to be with me, and she slipped out of our hotel," Yorg began. "Then, she left the country we were in and got shot at, that's all."

"I was not shot at," Kathe refuted with attitude. "The people I was with were shot at. Let's get that straight!"

"It won't be long before they start shooting at you!" Yorg snapped, raising his finger at her.

"I just happened to be at the wrong place at the wrong time!" Kathe defended, poking him in the chest.

"You're safe and that is what matters," Ylia joined in the conversation. "You are also with my Yorg, and he will always keep you safe. I have great trust in my brother. Please make yourself at home. I have dinner almost ready."

Yorg headed for the kitchen. "Ah, I thought I smelled my favorite," he said, picking up a spoon, reaching in the pot, and tasting the food.

"Yorg stop that!" Ylia exclaimed, swatting at him. "We have company. Where are your manners?"

"I left them in New York, besides Kathe doesn't mind," Yorg smiled. "We share food all the time," he looked at Kathe. "What are you laughing at?"

"A little brother in a man's body," Kathe giggled, and they all laughed. Next to the pot on the stove was the teapot Kathe gave to Ylia. "I see you are using the teapot we bought for you."

"Thank you, I use it every day," Ylia said, glancing over at her brother. "I see a change in you which I never thought I'd see again. It is good to have you back."

"Let's give thanks," Yorg said as they sat down at the table and bowed their heads.

Dinner was great. Yorg finished eating his weight with his sister's cooking just as Ylia's phone rang. "I feel like a bad hostess, but I must leave for the hospital. I have a patient with an emergency."

"We understand," Yorg replied. "Kathe and I will do the dishes. She owes me one from this morning."

After Ylia left to go to the hospital Kathe began to clear the table. "I'll wash and you can dry," Yorg said looking under the sink for the soap.

"You're kidding," Kathe smiled. "Alby's numeral uno pilot actually washes dishes?"

"Yes, I do," Yorg sighed, watching Kathe clear the table not saying a word.

"Why the sad face?" Kathe asked, glancing at him.

"Memories," Yorg confessed. "Sometimes when I'm with you, old memories begin to haunt me. For a second, I saw Mikél walk to the sink," he confessed, gazing out the window.

"I'm sorry," Kathe said, putting the butter in the refrigerator.

"It isn't your fault," Yorg stated. "Ylia quickly noticed how much I have changed since I have been flying with you. She thought we were dating. I told her we were best friends. She doesn't understand how a man and woman can be just best friends." He walked over to her, put his arms around her waist, and pulled her against him. "Thank you for making my life bearable these last few years. If I had not met you, I don't think I would have ever climbed out of my shell, after my Mikél died. I guess that's why I got so mad when I picked you up in Munich this morning. I don't want to lose you. I couldn't go through that again."

Kathe hugged him tightly, "We have such a strange relationship. Carrie Anne says I will not get her a date with you because I keep you to myself. It's hard to define the love we have for each other. I feel so safe and at peace with you."

"I know my Mikél is gone," Yorg admitted. "I never would have thought that I would be able to match the love . . ." He paused, released her, stepped back, and changed the subject. "Let's finish straightening up before Ylia gets home."

It was late when Ylia arrived back at her apartment. Yorg had fallen asleep on the couch and Kathe was asleep on the floor next to him. They woke up the next morning to a telephone call. It was for Yorg. Oddly enough, it was his commander. Kathe couldn't believe how they knew he was back in Moscow already. Yorg finished his conversation saying he would be ready in an hour.

"Where do you have to go?" Ylia asked him from her bedroom doorway.

"I have to go to the base," Yorg replied. "I'm sorry the phone woke you up. They want to talk to me."

"It's okay," Ylia smiled. "You shower while I make your breakfast."

While Yorg ate breakfast, Kathe showered and dressed. "You didn't have to get up so early," he said to her as she walked in the kitchen.

"I'm going with you," Kathe announced as she poured a cup of coffee.

"You can't go on base with me," Yorg said, pushing back his chair.

"Oh, yes, I can," Kathe stated. "I've been ordered to stay with you no matter what," she contested taking a bite of toast.

"You can stay with Ylia," Yorg retorted, checking his watch.

"I have to be at the hospital at 10:00 am for my shift," Ylia stated. "I tried to get off work, but I couldn't. She can stay here."

"I'm not supposed to be alone," Kathe contested. "I guess I'll have to go with Yorg," Kathe said as a knock at the door stopped the bickering.

It was a military escort sent to pick up Yorg. He was also a very old and dear friend of Yorg's. They greeted each other. Turning toward Kathe, "Ivan, I want you to meet my other best friend. This is Kathe Tierney."

"She's a woman!" Ivan declared.

"Good eye," Ylia teased, hugging her brother's longtime friend. "Yorg is getting more Americanized each time I see him."

"Maybe I should try for a transfer too," Ivan smiled. "Mne nuzena novaya podruzka s taki me ze formami kak I ona." (I need a new best friend with a body like hers.)

"I'm sorry, I'm at a disadvantage," Kathe refuted. "I don't understand Russian," she said, shaking his hand. "I know that you speak English and would appreciate you doing so."

"Ah, an American woman with spunk," Ivan slugged Yorg in the arm. "I'm very sorry," he said glancing at her. "I said that I should maybe apply for a transfer. I'm in need of a new best friend like you. Most of the women in our country aren't as soft looking like American women."

"I'm afraid you would be out of luck," Yorg smiled at Kathe. "There's only one Kathe Tierney."

"It figures you would get the best," Ivan admitted. "We better get you to headquarter; you have a busy morning planned. I promise to have him back before dinner."

"I'm going with you," Kathe said, reaching for her purse.

"You're not allowed, my spunky new American friend," Ivan laughed. "This is Russia, and we are going to Red Square. You could be shot as a spy."

"She has to go with me," Yorg admitted. "I'm under orders from my American boss not to let her out of my sight. She has a way of getting into trouble when she's not with me."

"Don't say I didn't warn you old friend," Ivan contested. "This is not America, I too, would get shot if she's caught with us."

On the drive into Red Square, Kathe noticed armed guards patrolling as they stopped. "This is the general's personal car," Ivan told Kathe. "You must stay in the car for your safety. The windows are tinted so no one can see inside. Yorg and I have a meeting. It shouldn't take too long."

"Can't I walk around the square and look at some of the buildings?" "Kathe asked.

"Please, just stay in the car," Yorg begged. "It will be better for all of us. Remember you are not supposed to be here."

"Great, I'm stuck in a car in freezing cold weather," Kathe whispered, watching them walk off. "I better check on Carrie Anne," Kathe thought and reached for JAKE. "That's odd, she's not answering.

Maybe I should call Ramsey. She almost sounded suicidal about the way Travis dumped her. Let me try one more time," she called again.

"Hello," Carrie Anne sleepily answered.

"I was just about to hang up," Kathe admitted. "What took you so long?"

"Kathe, how nice to hear from you," Carrie Anne whispered. "I'm busy right now. Can I call you back later?" she said, shushing someone next to her.

"Wait a minute!" Kathe demanded. "What's going on? Who's that? Are you still at my house?"

"I'll be right back," Carrie Anne whispered, slipping out of the room. "You were right about me finding someone to replace Travis."

"You're with someone in my house!" Kathe exclaimed as she made sure no one was near the car. "Carrie Anne are you crazy? Here I am freezing my tail feathers off in the coldest place on earth and my best friend is in my warm bedroom in sunny Florida with someone she just met! How dare you bring a stranger into my house and my bed!"

"As if you have ever slept in this room or in this bed!" Carrie Anne snapped. "You always sleep on the couch downstairs; would you chill out! He's not a stranger. He's one of the eight college boys who rented a house a couple of doors down."

"What neighbors?" Kathe demanded, lowering her voice as a soldier walked past the car. "What eight college boys? I haven't been home in months! I don't even know my neighbors and you're sleeping with one of them! You have done some idiotic things before, but this takes the cake! Get him out of my house now!"

"Calm down, we're going to a party at his house later tonight," Carrie Anne explained. "You don't have to get so upset. He's not going to steal you blind," she said, peeking into the room at him.

"I'll see your fanny in Europe!" Kathe exclaimed, hanging up JAKE and calling control. "Ramsey, I need your help! Carrie Anne is sleeping in my bed with a college kid, who is renting the house a couple of doors from me, get the picture? Send her anywhere, PDQ!"

"And this is the same person you were worried about yesterday?" Ramsey laughed.

"Yep!" Kathe whispered as two armed guards walked past the car. "It sure is. I told her she would find someone to replace Travis, but I didn't mean in my house!"

"I was just about to call you anyway," Ramsey changed the subject. "We found a dead flight attendant in Paris. Her throat was slashed, and a note was pinned to her saying, "This is your fault."

"I was afraid of this happening," Kathe affirmed. "After all, I was responsible for stopping his hit on Nicki LaBasco last night. I'll tell Yorg."

"Don't feel too bad," Ramsey stated. "It was just a matter of time until he came after the airlines. I'll bring Carrie Anne back to control. You can consider her gone; your house is safe."

Kathe looked up as Yorg and Ivan got back into the car. "You look like someone ruffled your feathers," Yorg noted. "What's wrong?"

"Carrie Anne, need I say more?" Kathe scoffed, glaring at him.

"What did she do this time?" Yorg asked, reaching for her hand.

"As we speak, she is with a college kid in my house and in my bed!" Kathe complained.

"It doesn't sound abnormal for Carrie Anne," Yorg smiled as Ivan looked at him in the rear-view mirror. "I don't see why you're upset."

"Why can't you understand why I'm upset?" Kathe asked. "Did you not hear me say that she is in my house, my room, and my bed! Yes, I'm mad!"

"Yorg, if I get transferred, that's the kind of best friend I want," Ivan laughed, glancing back at them.

"No! you don't!" Kathe and Yorg both exclaimed.

"She must be something!" Ivan laughed. "I can't wait to meet her!"

"Trust me old friend, you don't want her," Yorg laughed as they passed the airport.

"Where are we going?" Kathe wondered, noticing the surroundings.

"To another airport that is close by," Ivan explained. "Besides a few spies, you'll be one of the few outsiders ever to be at this airport," Ivan admitted with a worried look on his face.

"I'm not going to get shot, am I?" Kathe inquired. "I seemed to be having one of those days . . . No! I take it back. I seem to be having one of those weeks!"

"Just stay in the car and be quiet," Yorg warned. "I'm dead serious," he said, changing into a flight suit.

"Great, Moscow is a great place to be this time of year," Kathe complained. "I'll just sit in the car and freeze to death while I'm waiting for you," she said as the car slowed and turned down a long narrow road. There were armed guards everywhere. "I get an awful feeling seeing all these armed guards," she said, staring out the window.

"You should," Ivan informed her. "They have orders to shoot to kill and ask questions later," Ivan relayed as he slowed down and turned down another road.

"Kathe, get down on the floor," Yorg said, reaching for a blanket. "I have to cover you up for a few minutes."

Ivan stopped at a security gate and handed the guard a large, sealed envelope. The gate opened and the car passed through pulling inside of a large hangar.

"Stay in the car and don't let anyone see you," Yorg told her.

Kathe watched as Yorg, and Ivan inspected a most impressive fighter jet. Yorg climbed up the ladder to look inside. He whistled as he glanced at the instrument panel.

Several men entered the hangar with a general and more guards. Strangely enough, she noted the men looked Italian and European. Yorg and Ivan saluted the general. He saluted them back and Yorg climbed into the jet and put on his helmet. He lowered the canopy as the jet was towed out of the hangar. She heard Yorg start the engines. Ivan accompanied the men out of the hangar. Yorg taxied to a runway. She quickly checked to make sure JAKE was on silent because she noticed a guard checking around the car. As she was putting it on silent, it rang. She ignored it. There was no way she could answer it with the guard still walking around the car. She did not relish the idea of being tortured or shot. Then she started to feel the electrical implant beckoning her to answer. The pain was almost unbearable when she was finally able to answer, "Ramsey, not now. I'll call you as soon as I can. I'm with Yorg. Trust me," she reported as she heard the jet returning to the runway and stopping near the hangar. As Yorg climbed out of the jet, Kathe watched the men question him. She watched the interpreter translate. "One of the Italians looks so familiar," she thought. "Where have I seen him recently? She wondered as Yorg, and Ivan saluted the general and hurried back to the car.

Once inside, Yorg took a deep breath whispering, "Get us out of here before they see Kathe. I've got a bad feeling that our good friend, Gen. Yetsun is up to something again!"

"I agree!" Ivan exclaimed as he slowly drove out of the hangar, while the men were still talking to the general.

"Yetsun is allowing one of the Italians to take pictures of the cockpit!" Yorg exclaimed.

"This is what we've feared!" Ivan admitted. "I need to make some calls after I drop you off."

"I left my cell phone at Ylia's," Yorg said, reaching for JAKE. "Ramsey, I need to leave Russia ASAP. It must appear that I am being called into work for an emergency."

"Consider it done," Ramsey agreed. "It just so happens that I do need you and Kathe in London. I'll call you with your itinerary as soon as Wanda reschedules you."

"What was that all about?" Kathe asked, glancing at Yorg.

"Don't ask," Yorg cautioned as Ivan glanced at him in the rear-view mirror. "You don't want to know!"

Arriving back at Ylia's apartment, Ivan and Yorg talked privately for quite some time before Ivan left them. Yorg called Ylia at the hospital apologizing for them having to leave. Within another ten minutes, Wanda called with their immediate departure.

"You're on Flight #621 departing at 12:30 pm local time," Ramsey stated. "I need Kathe to check on someone at the hospital for me. Call me when you are on your way and I will tell you what to do," she said and cleared the line.

Chapter 23

A Father's Fatal Decision

Joe had gotten his own room at the hotel. He couldn't stand looking at Cara much less stay in the same suite. The band was scheduled to appear in an interview at TMV. While Brock was getting coffee, Joe was getting ready in the bathroom. He heard voices in the other room thinking Brock was back and opened the door. As he saw the housekeeper making the bed, Cara appeared in the doorway. She caught him off guard, pushed him back into the bathroom, "I want to talk to you!" She yelled slamming the door behind her.

"I'm listening," Joe folded his arms across his chest and leaned against the counter.

"Joe," Cara smiled, trying to put her arms around him.

"Just talk!" Joe insisted, pushing her away.

"I'm honestly sorry for what I did," Cara apologized as tears welled up in her eyes. "Let's put it in the past and start again."

"Is that all you want to say?" Joe coldly asked.

"Joe," she whined, reaching for him again as he deflected her arms. "I came all this way because I love you and I can't stand living without you."

"You don't know the meaning of love!" Joe declared. "I told you a year and a half ago to get away from me! We made a deal! I even paid for your deeds! The bargain was that you would stay away from me, and I would not tell our parents the reason for our divorce! I don't want anyone to know the pain of why we split!" he pointed his finger at her. "I've kept my end of the bargain! Now, get away from me!"

He opened the bathroom door and hurried into the next room as Brock returned to the room, "You," he ordered, pointing to the bathroom. "Get her out of here and keep her way from me!" Joe demanded, grabbing his coffee, reaching for his jacket, and slamming the door behind him.

Cara stood in the doorway of the bathroom with tears streaming down her cheeks. She looked at Brock and softly said, "You just wait, he'll change his mind. He'll take me back."

In Paris things were already beginning to happen with a new employee working in the kitchen at Mario's house. While on the way to Russia, Mario called Nicki from the cockpit. "Nicki, Papa, and I decided that my men will escort you to my house until we find the person responsible for the contract on you. They landed at the airport and are outside your gate waiting for your guards to open it. I apologize for not being there, but something came up with work. I'll see you hopefully tomorrow morning."

"I'm sorry for their wasted trip!" Nicki snapped. "I already told you that I'm not going anywhere! I also told my guards at the gate not to let them inside!" he hung up and called his father. "Papa, Mario's men are here to take me to Paris. I already told Mario that I am not going to his house! Dider can keep me safe right here!"

"Like he kept you safe the other night?" Papa asked. "I was opposed to your going to Mario's to begin with, but I am still under investigation for the death of Sen. Frank and Tierra's last incident. Your brother assures me that he will keep you safe at all costs. I know you two don't get along, but he is loyal to the family and me. I'm ordering you to go with your brother's men-end of discussion."

"Papa, Dider and I suspect Mario's up to something," Nicki admitted. "If Mario and his men are so good, why are you under suspicion for what he did? Maybe we should send for Tierra again. I'm still concerned for her safety."

"Let me and Alonzo worry about my problems," Papa insisted. "Your sister is fine. Ramsey personally assured me that she had assigned a bodyguard to her. Tierra doesn't know it."

"I'll go, but only because you are ordering me," Nicki sighed. "I do not trust my brother! And I'm going to prove to you why!" he stated hanging up and opening the door to his office. "Dider, tell Mario's men we're getting ready to leave. We'll meet them at the gate."

"Nicki, you can't mean that?" Dider questioned. "We have proof that Mario is up to something behind your papa's back!"

"We intercepted something written in code meant for Mario," Nicki admitted. "We still don't know what it says. Maybe this is our opportunity to find out what Mario's doing. Since he's away we'll have the run of his house. I plan on looking for more evidence to take to Papa."

"I still don't like this," Dider replied, shaking his head. "I think you should go to your Papa and show him what we intercepted. Alonzo might be able to break the code."

"Mario is Papa's favorite child," Nicki admitted. "I have to be sure of what we have before I expose him to Papa."

"Then, go to Alonzo," Dider suggested. "He doesn't trust Mario either. If he can't break the code, he'll find someone that can."

"Not without full knowledge of it first," Nicki declared. "Get us ready to leave."

Arriving back at his house in Paris they next day, Mario greeted Jada, squeezing her rump and giving her a kiss. "Nicki," Mario greeted his brother as he joined them. "I'm sorry I couldn't be here when you arrived yesterday. I trust you had a safe flight."

"Yes," Nicki replied. "Jada has been a very gracious hostess."

"I'm sure she took very good care of you," Mario smiled glancing at her. "I'll have to make up for the other night later."

"Oh, I'm sure of that," Jada grinned hugging him. "You've been gone a few days."

Turning back to his brother, "Nicki let's talk. Jada, go paint your nails or something. Nicki and I have some business to discuss."

"Mario!" Jada screamed and stormed out of the room.

"I do like the rough ones," Mario gleamed.

Andre, the butler, was instructing the new employee on how to carry a serving tray with food and drinks. It was nearing lunchtime and Mario and Nicki were finishing their meeting.

"By the way," Nicki confronted, "we need to talk about some troubling news that I've been hearing bits and pieces concerning you and some Iranians."

"You don't have to worry little brother," Mario smiled. "There's nothing to talk about. I don't know any Iranians. Just relax and enjoy your stay here. Whoever is responsible for putting a contract out on you will be dealt with severely. You can trust your big brother," Mario stood up to leave the room. "Now, I must make Jada happy, if you know what I mean. I had to leave her a couple of nights ago in a very unsatisfied way. You know how Italian women are," Mario began his obnoxious laugh.

"I understand the type of women you like," Nicki replied. "I think I'll change clothes and relax in your swimming pool before lunch. I'm getting tired of the cold weather."

"Ah!" Mario grinned. "What a wonderful idea. Jada and I will join you in a few minutes. I'll have Andre bring in a bottle of my best vino for you to enjoy," he said starting upstairs.

Jumping in the pool Nicki swam several laps before Andre brought out the wine. Nicki got out of the pool, dried off, and sat down on a lounge chair.

"Mr. LaBasco asked me to bring you some vino," Andre said, bowing graciously and pouring the wine.

"Thank you," Nicki stated, taking a sip of wine, and leaning his head back.

"Anything else I may get for you?" Andre asked.

"Yes, would you send in Dider?" Nicki asked. "Giorgio wanted to show him the security measures in his office."

"Yes, they have stepped up our security for your stay," Andre affirmed. "I'll send for Dider," Andre smiled and walked away as Nicki turned up the music on his iPhone.

Just as Andre reached the doorway, he checked to make sure Nicki wasn't looking. He nodded his head, and the new employee came into the room. He quietly pulled a small knife out of his belt buckle as he quietly approached Nicki from behind. "This is from your brother!" he whispered as he slit Nicki's throat from ear to ear. He dropped the knife by the body as ordered and hurried back to Andre.

"Mr. LaBasco will be pleased," Andre grinned, opening a secret passage for the assassin to exit. Then, Andre hurried back to the kitchen.

"It's so nice having your brother visiting with us," Jada smiled as Mario held the door open for her.

"Yes, it is," Mario grinned. "I see he's enjoying some vino."

"Nicki, how do you like our pool?" Jada called to him.

"He can't hear you," Mario smiled. "He's wearing headphones."

"He's probably listening to music relaxing with his wine," Jada smiled, walking toward him. "Nicki, how do you like our pool? Nicki?" Jada asked, touching his shoulder as his head fell forward. "There's blood everywhere!" Jada screamed and fainted.

"Finally, that idiot did something right," Mario grinned as he examined the body. "You were right little brother about not trusting me. He reached for his phone, "Giorgio, seal off the house!"

"What's wrong?" Giorgio asked.

"Nicki . . ." Mario pretended to sob. "Someone killed Nicki by the pool."

"We're on our way!" Giorgio exclaimed as he told Dider.

"Nicki's what?" Dider sighed. "How could this happen? Where is he?"

"At the swimming pool," Giorgio stated, opening the door. "It's this way."

Dider hurried ahead to the south side of the house. He found Mario helping Jada out of the room. "Dider, I found him," she cried as Andre walked out of the kitchen.

"Andre, take Jada to her room and stay with her" Giorgio ordered. "Mario, you need to sit down," Giorgio said, helping him into the room to a chair away from the body.

"This can't be happening," Mario sighed.

"I'll handle this," Giorgio picked up his phone and gave orders to seal off all exits. "I guess I better call the gendarmes," he said as the sound of men running through the house filled the hallways. Several men entered the pool area with guns drawn.

"I can't believe this," Mario cried. "What am I going to tell Papa?"

"I'm in just as much shock as you!" Giorgio snapped. "All our men are loyal. Who would dare to put contracts on this family? Much less come into your residence?"

"No intruder could get inside this fortress!" Dider exclaimed. "You and I were just going over your security. This is an inside job, and you know it! That's why you called me away from Nicki's side!"

"Dider, you need to calm down," Giorgio cautioned. "You're in shock. Don't say something you'll be sorry for later. I'll handle this."

"I'm sure you will!" Dider scoffed. "Like you've handled everything else!" he snapped, glancing under the lounge chair. "Well, look what I found. Here's the bloody weapon conveniently left at the scene!"

"Let me remind you again that you are a guest in this house!" Giorgio cautioned as the doorbell rang. "That's the gendarmes," he checked his phone. "They might be able to lift a fingerprint."

"Who are you kidding?" Dider screamed. "There won't be a fingerprint!"

"I should call Papa," Mario sighed. "Giorgio, bring them to me."

A short time later, every news media worldwide released the story of Nicki LaBasco's murder.

Arriving in London, Kathe and Yorg had not yet heard the news. In the cab on the way to the hospital Yorg called Ramsey. "We're on our way to the hospital as you requested."

"Good," Ramsey sighed. "Shelley Nobles tried to commit suicide. She's been asking for Kathe."

"Isn't that the flight attendant Kathe covered for a few days ago?" Yorg asked.

"Yes, she is," Ramsey confirmed. "I think Kathe can comfort her and give her some encouragement to want to live. She's been down a few bad roads herself and recovered. There's another major problem. I guess you haven't heard the news yet?"

"No, we've been traveling," Yorg admitted.

"Nicki LaBasco was murdered about an hour ago at his brother's house," Ramsey affirmed. "It seems that Saíde has struck again!"

"What do you mean again?" Yorg quizzed.

"Didn't Kathe tell you about the flight attendant found dead in Paris?" Ramsey quizzed. "She had a note attached to her clothes saying, 'This is your fault.'"

"No, when did you tell Kathe?" Yorg asked, taking Kathe by the hand.

"When you were in Russia," Ramsey answered. "Kathe probably forgot to tell you. She was so mad about Carrie Anne at her house with some man. This proves Saíde was in Munich at the first attempt on Nicki, and then in Paris at the time of Nicki's death. The details of Nicki's murder have not been released. However, I talked with Alonzo, and he said Nicki's throat had been slashed and the knife was left behind."

"It's inconceivable that Saíde could penetrate Mario's fortress," Yorg cautioned.

"Isn't it?" Ramsey agreed. "Alonzo is furious! He told me to send Tierra home until he gets to the bottom of this. I already have her and CC en route to Corté de Azuré."

"Why is Saíde after the LaBasco family and our airlines?" Yorg questioned.

"That's what we must figure out, and quick," Ramsey confirmed. "Don't let Kathe out of your sight!"

"I won't," Yorg agreed as they arrived at the hospital. "We just got to the hospital."

"I'll keep in touch," Ramsey said and cleared the line.

Yorg paid for the cab and looked around the front of the hospital. "There's a bench over there," he pointed. "Let's sit down for a second."

"Isn't this the hospital Shelley Nobles was taken," Kathe questioned as she sat next to him.

"Yes," Yorg sighed. "She tried to commit suicide a few days ago."

"I'm not surprised," Kathe admitted. "She babbled something about T.J. White and his wife."

"Ramsey thinks you can help Shelley over her depression," Yorg relayed. "You've conquered some hurtles in your life and came out a stronger woman," he smiled at her.

"I'll do what I can," Kathe stood up.

"Something else happened today," Yorg sighed, standing up. "Nicki LaBasco was murdered at his brother's house a little more than an hour ago."

"What is happening?" Kathe cried, throwing her arms around him sobbing. "I've got to call Tierra!"

"Ramsey has Tierra and CC already en route to Corté de Azuré," Yorg conveyed. "Alonzo is furious. He wants Tierra home until he gets to the bottom of this. There's something else," he sighed. "It looks like Saíde did the hit inside Mario's residence. Nicki's throat was slashed, and the weapon was left behind."

"This proves Saíde was sent to murder Nicki," Kathe declared. "One doesn't just walk into a LaBasco home. Someone on the inside got him close to Nicki."

"It would appear so," Yorg agreed as Kathe reached for JAKE.

"Poor Tierra," Kathe sighed, "she and Nicki were very close. I need to call her. Maybe I'll catch her before she boards a plane."

Tierra was in shock when Kathe called and handed the phone to CC. "Tierra was told that Nicki was murdered while staying at his brother's house," CC stated. "Alonzo doesn't trust Mario and sent for us to stay at her papa's house."

"Is there anything I can do?" Kathe asked.

"Not now," CC replied. "When Tierra calms down I'll have her call you. We're almost to the airport now."

"I'll see if Ramsey will let me go to the funeral," Kathe replied.

"Tierra would like that," CC confided. "She's nervous about being around Mario and her papa has a bad heart."

"I'll get back with you," Kathe said, clearing the line. "I need to call Ramsey and see if I can go to Tierra," Kathe said, glancing at Yorg.

"No, that is the last place you need to be," Yorg declared. "I need to keep you away from the LaBasco family until we see what Saíde's next move is and who is helping him. I think you're right about this reeking of an inside job."

"What if Saíde's next move is Tierra?" Kathe snapped. "I need to protect her! CC just said that Tierra is scared to be around Mario."

"Alonzo is a very wise man," Yorg stated, walking into the hospital. "After this, I'm sure Alonzo will watch every move Mario makes. He will protect Tierra. Let's go see Shelley and get this over with."

"I would like to visit Shelley Nobles," Kathe said to the lady at the information desk. "I'm not sure about her room number."

"She's in room 5404," the lady stated, checking the computer. "You must take the D Elevator to that wing."

"Thank you," Kathe answered as they headed down the hallway. "I don't know what I'm going to say to Shelley," Kathe admitted as they got into the elevator.

"You have a lot of faith and compassion," Yorg smiled. "I'm sure you'll say the right thing," he said, getting off on the Psychiatric Wing.

Kathe picked up the phone by the locked entrance, "I'm Kathe Tierney. I'm here to see Shelley Nobles in room 5404."

"Let me check the roster," the nurse stated. "Yes, you are cleared to visit her. The gentleman with you must wait in the visitor's area around the corner," she said, buzzing Kathe inside.

An aide took Kathe to Shelley's room. As Kathe walked into the room, she noted Shelley didn't look any better than the last time they met. "Shelley," Kathe said, walking over to her and giving her a hug.

"I was hoping that you would come," Shelley said, avoiding eye contact.

Kathe pulled a chair closer to the bed and sat down, "Do you remember me taking your flight to Munich the other night?"

"No, I don't," Shelley admitted. "I'm glad you helped me to my room and left me a note. I'm sorry I was so drunk. I also need to thank you for working my shift," she looked away.

"That's what friends are for," Kathe smiled. "You mentioned something about T.J. White and his wife that night."

"I was always so sure of myself," Shelley began to sob. "Until I met T.J. White."

"I've flown with him before," Kathe admitted. "He's married with children."

"Yes," Shelley sighed. "I know. I'm pregnant with his baby," she looked away as tears streamed down her cheeks. "I tried to kill myself, but it didn't work. Ramsey talked to the doctors, and he said the child could have birth defects because of what I used," she began sobbing again. "I couldn't even do that right," she buried her head in her hands. "Ramsey told me she'd help me when I get back to New York and to be more careful next time."

"I'm sorry," Kathe sighed as silence filled the room for a couple of seconds. "Have you seen or talked to T.J.?"

"No . . ., and I don't ever want too!" Shelley snapped, looking at Kathe. "He...he told me to get rid of it. He told me...I couldn't have the baby because it would kill his wife and he loves her."

"I'm so sorry," Kathe reached for her hand.

"He said he hated me for getting pregnant," Shelley sobbed. "It was all my fault. He said he was just lonely and that I meant nothing to him."

"What a horrible thing to say to you," Kathe stated as she sat down next to Shelley on the bed. "It was just as much his fault. You know sometimes when life seems to take a bad turn, we must hang in there. Somehow, God turns things around. Do you know what I'm trying to say?"

"I don't want a lecture about God!" Shelley blurted, pulling the covers over her head.

"I'm not trying to lecture you," Kathe continued. "Everybody goes through problems. You're not alone. I can't speak for T.J., but I'm sure this has affected him deeply. Call it a wakeup call for cheating on his wife. All I'm trying to say is your time for happiness will come when you least expect it. Please don't give up on God. He'll never give up on you," Kathe said, lifting the covers from Shelley's face. "I felt the same way that you do at one time in my life in this very hospital."

"You did?" Shelley looked at her. "You have everything."

"You really don't know me," Kathe confided. "I was married once and have three children. They live with friends, while I work to support them. I went from a happy mommy-type to a person who felt like you do. I hung in there. Now you see how much God blessed me." She moved Shelley's bangs out of her face, "Guess who gave me a similar talk when I was where you are?"

"I don't know," Shelley sighed.

"My friend Yorg," Kathe admitted. "Carrie Anne refers to him as my Russian. His wife was murdered before he came to work for Alby. He had to reinstate his life with God the same way I did."

Shelley reached her arms around Kathe crying on her shoulder, "I would have never guessed. You always seem so happy."

Kathe checked the time, "I must go now. I hope the next time I see you; a smile will be back on your beautiful face." She left the room after they exchanged goodbyes.

"Ramsey wants us to go to Paris," Yorg said as Kathe returned. "It seems that the man who killed Nicki has been found dead."

"That was quick?" Kathe questioned.

"Lt. Jaco wants you to identify the weapon and see if it's the same one Saíde used on Flight #1014," Yorg relayed.

"So, they are reporting Saíde is dead?" Kathe grinned.

"Lt. Jaco seems to think so," Yorg shared. "Ramsey has a plane waiting for us to leave for Paris," he said as they entered the elevator.

"After the week I've had," Kathe said, pushing the button. "Maybe there is a silver lining to this dark cloud after all."

Chapter 24

Nicki LaBasco's Funeral

Arriving at Charles de Gaulle Airport, Yorg and Kathe took a cab immediately to the police station. She was very anxious to make sure Saíde was in fact dead. Then she could get on with her life. They arrived at the station and went straight to Lt. Jaco's office.

"Ms. Tierney," Lt. Jaco greeted, shaking her hand.

"Lt. Jaco this is a friend of mine, Capt. Yorg Vuslick," Kathe introduced.

"Captain Vuslick, I'm glad to meet you," Lt. Jaco shook his hand. "Ramsey said you would be traveling with Ms. Tierney. I want to get right to the reason I have sent for you." He walked over to his desk. "On my desk, I have lined up five different knives. Can you pick out the knife you saw Rhasheéd Saíde holding to Carrie Anne Mobley's neck on Flight #1014 to Paris?"

Without any hesitation Kathe pointed to the one in the middle, "This one with the sliver handle and clear blade."

"J'ai lue!" Lt. Jaco exclaimed. "That's the knife that was found near Nicki LaBasco's body."

Kathe's expression immediately changed from happy to sad as she looked over at Yorg. "That is the actual weapon that killed Nicki?"

"Yes," Lt. Jaco declared. "I have some other questions to ask you."

"What would you like to know?" Kathe asked. "I was just with Nicki a couple of days ago."

"I would like Yorg to wait outside," Lt. Jaco mentioned. "I hope you don't mind."

"I would prefer to stay with Kathe," Yorg refuted.

"It won't take long," Lt. Jaco insisted and then Yorg left the room.

"I understand that you were with Nicki LaBasco when the first attempt on his life was made," Lt. Jaco stated as he reached for his note pad.

"That is correct," Kathe answered.

"What were you doing with an alleged Mafia leader?" He asked peering over his glasses at her.

"I work with his sister Tierra," Kathe answered. "She bought Nicki a birthday present in New York. She asked me to give it to him the next time I was in Munich. It just so happened a friend of mine was sick, and I took her flight to Munich."

"Go on, what happened?" Lt. Jaco urged.

"I arrived on a late-night flight," Kathe continued. "Nicki picked me up at the airport and we went to dinner at a restaurant he owned. It was a beautiful crisp night. After dinner, Nicki wanted to wait in front of the restaurant while his car was brought around. It seemed to take forever. Dider, his bodyguard wanted to take us back inside, but I remember Nicki suggested that the driver may have gone to get some petrol. Then one of the men noticed the limo approaching us very slowly from a distance. I also remember having a very bad feeling as the car approached; something was wrong," she said, finishing the details. "I told all of this to the Bundesgrenzschutz (German authorities)."

"I know you did," Lt. Jaco affirmed. "I read the report and talked with the lieutenant there today. What happened next?"

"When Saíde recognized me," Kathe continued. "He threw the car in reverse and sped off. I returned fire along with LaBasco's men. We went back inside the restaurant and gave statements to the Bundesgrenzschutz. Ramsey had me put into custody for safety, until Yorg picked me up the next morning. I've been with Yorg ever since the incident."

"And you're positive Saíde was driving the limo?" Lt. Jaco questioned.

"Yes," Kathe confirmed. "He changed his hair color to blonde. I identified him at Newark Airport at a cell phone-charging station the day before. I couldn't pursue him at the time. I was working on a hostage situation, so Ramsey sent two of my team members after him. They lost him. Two private planes slipped out, before the airport was sealed. He must have been on one."

"I'll check with Ramsey about the two planes," Lt. Jaco stated referring to his notes. "A body was found by Mario Jr.'s goons about an hour after Nicki's murder. We think the man is Saíde, although it is hard to identify him, since the body was badly charred. Another one of these knives along with Saíde's wallet was found near the body. I'll know more when the lab boys give me their report."

"So, you think Saíde is dead?" Kathe asked.

"I'm waiting on the forensic report before I make any conclusion," Lt. Jaco stated. "However, you are an eyewitness, linking Saíde with the first attempt and he does use these knives as his calling card. I think the lab will confirm the charred body as his. He stood up, "You are free to go. I will report to Ramsey as soon as I hear from the lab."

Kathe left the room and joined Yorg. "Lt. Jaco is waiting for the lab to confirm the body is Saíde's."

"Good, let's go over to the apartment and wait for the findings," Yorg stood up stretching. "I'd love to go down to the gym and work out. Do you know if Jordan's in town?"

"I don't know," Kathe, answered. "I haven't heard from him since we were here in Paris last week," she said as they left the building and hailed a cab.

As they entered the elevator, some Brits joined them and reminded her of Joe. She wondered how he was doing on tour in the states. Yorg noticed them eying Kathe as they walked to their apartment. She put the key in the door and noticed that they were entering the apartment across the hall. A couple of whistles were heard as she closed the door behind her.

"Looks like you're a hit here," Yorg teased, putting his bags down.

"Just what I need," Kathe smirked as she walked over to the window. "Look at this beautiful view."

Yorg stood next to her for a moment admiring the view. Looking at his watch, "It's 4:30. I want to work out in the gym before dinner. What about you?"

"I want to just kick my shoes off and lie down," Kathe admitted. "I need to call Tierra and talk with her. I also want to call my kids before dinner," she said, taking her things to their room. Yorg changed and went to the gym in the basement. Kathe sat down on the couch and called Tierra.

"Hello, Kathe," Tierra sighed.

"I'm so sorry about Nicki," Kathe said.

"I apologize for not talking to you this morning," Tierra began to cry.

"I understand," Kathe replied. "It seems so surreal. I was just with him a few days ago."

"I know," Tierra sighed, "all day I've watched the video you sent me with him opening his train. Were you hurt that night?"

"No," Kathe stated. "I just got back from Lt. Jaco's. He said Mario's men found Saíde already."

"Mario said he is the one who killed my Nicki," Tierra began to cry again. "I can't believe Nicki's dead. We've always been close. Europe will never be the same for me . . . Are you coming tomorrow?"

"What time?" Kathe could hear someone calling Tierra in the background.

"Eleven o'clock," Tierra stated. "I've got to go. Papa's heart is bothering him. Alonzo had to call the doctor and I believe he just arrived. Bye, see you tomorrow."

"Bye," Kathe cleared the line and called Jeannie.

"Peter had just brought Ben over to visit the children," Jeannie said. "Let me put them on one at a time and then you can talk to Ben."

Kathe talked with each of the children and then Ben. "Kathe," Peter said, grabbing the phone. "Hello . . . hello . . . Kathe . . . Kathe are you there?" He listened for a moment and handed Jeannie back the phone. "She hung up."

"That shouldn't surprise you," Jeannie grinned.

Lastly, Kathe called Ramsey, "I would like to attend Nicki LaBasco's funeral tomorrow."

"I'm glad you called," Ramsey stated. "I was about to call Yorg. Lt. Jaco just confirmed through dental records that Saíde was the man killed today. You can go to the funeral. Then, I think you should go home for a while. You have been in too many stressful situations lately."

"I don't need to go home," Kathe insisted. "I'll be okay."

"Sydney told me you need an R & R," Ramsey insisted. "I will let you work your way back to Florida. Then you will have a couple of weeks off in the sunshine to rest."

"Where is Carrie Anne?" Kathe asked.

"She's here in Newark," Ramsey replied. "She'll be heading for Europe at the same time you're coming back to the states."

"I'll call her later," Kathe said. "Is she still feeling bad about Rick Travis?"

"We are talking about Carrie Anne Mobley, aren't we?" Ramsey chuckled. "I heard she was with some man yesterday at the hotel. You know Carrie Anne doesn't stay down long."

Yorg was tired and sweaty when he opened the door to the apartment. Kathe finished her conversation with Ramsey. "I'm going to take a shower, then let's go to dinner, I'm starved. Somehow, when I travel with you, I never eat much."

At dinner about an hour later, "I talked with Ramsey while you were at the gym," Kathe stated. "Ramsey said Lt. Jaco confirmed that Saíde is dead. I told her that I would like to attend Nicki's funeral. It's tomorrow at 11:00."

"I'd feel better if I go with you," Yorg declared, reaching for her hand. "I don't trust the lab report."

"It will be better if I go by myself," Kathe admitted. "I'm afraid a stranger would make everybody nervous, especially now."

"I suppose you're right," Yorg agreed. "I find it hard to believe that Mario's men could find Saíde that fast. The way the body was found makes it too sketchy. I'm not sold on the fact that Saíde is dead."

"Ramsey said Lt. Jaco confirmed his death with dental records," Kathe stated. "Tierra is expecting me. Her father has a heart condition. I need to be with her. We have been friends for a long time. I must go. I'll be fine."

"But I do want you to still be careful," Yorg conveyed. "Your face was plastered all over the news, during the first attempt on his life and that was just a few days ago."

"You're right," Kathe agreed. "After we eat let's stop at a store. I'm going to wear my navy suit. I'll buy a wide brimmed hat and a pair of large sunglasses. That should conceal my identity."

"That will work," Yorg concurred. "I'm going to talk with Lt. Jaco. I can't believe he so readily confirmed his death."

"I will be interested in what Jaco has to say," Kathe shared. "Call me after you talk with him. After the funeral, Ramsey is sending me to Florida for R & R. So, I guess you will be rid of me for a while," she said, reaching for her glass of wine.

"Miss you, is more like it," Yorg grinned, clinking their glasses together.

"Right!" Kathe grinned. "You'll miss me like a bad hangover," she laughed, tipping her glass to him.

Pulling away from the funeral home, where Nicki's wake just ended, Mario picked up his phone, "Make sure you lay low until I'm ready for you. Whatever you do, stay away from the airport and that flight attendant!"

"Okay, Boss, I'll stay in this hotel until you call me," Saíde agreed, reaching for his cigarettes.

"Nicki might have intercepted something I need," Mario admitted. "I must wait until I seal up his house for my papa. Then, I can get inside and look for it. If I can't find it, my sister might know where it is."

"I'm an expert in getting information out of people," Saíde bragged. "Let me know if I can help you," he pulled his blade out of his belt buckle and ran it across his cheek. "It will be my pleasure."

"Now that you're dead, make sure you stay out of sight," Mario warned. "You'll get your fun and revenge later," he laughed as Giorgio opened the door for him.

After dinner and a quick shopping trip, Kathe and Yorg went back to the hotel. While Kathe was getting ready for bed, Yorg called Ramsey. "I can't believe you're letting Kathe go to the funeral alone," he declared. "I don't believe that Saíde is dead."

"Calm down," Ramsey stated. "I've been on the phone with Jaco most of the day. I too doubted at first, but they have dental records. We are talking about the Italian Mafia. From everything I have seen about Mario and Alonzo DiMeglio, they are extremely thorough. Saíde killed Nicki in Mario's own house. You better believe, they had that town sealed off in a matter of minutes. I even had Jaco email me a copy of the dental records and photos of the corpse. Sydney said it was a match," she concluded. "I'm glad the ordeal is over. We got off lucky when Saíde went after the LaBasco family. Let Kathe go, she needs to be with her friend. Then I'm sending her home to get some much-needed rest," Ramsey insisted still looking at the dental records on her screen.

"I want to talk to Jaco," Yorg declared. "Can you give me a few days off?"

"You've got it, but you're wasting your time," Ramsey said and cleared the line.

The next morning Kathe was up early and ready to leave for the airport. Yorg was up to see her off. "I have to admit," Kathe said, pulling her suitcases to the door, "having this apartment is nice. I don't have to worry about leaving something behind. It will be here when I get back."

"It does feel like we actually have a place to call home," Yorg agreed. "I'll see you when you get back from Florida," he said, giving her a big hug. He pulled her closer to him and gave her a very affectionate kiss. He stepped back, "I dreamt I kissed you like that before I woke up this morning. I wanted to see if it felt the same," he said, holding her tight.

To her surprise, Kathe put her arms around his neck, and returned the kiss just as affectionately. Stepping back, she said, "Well, did it?"

"Truth?" Yorg implored.

"Truth," Kathe responded.

"It felt better than the dream!" Yorg smiled, pulling her back into his arms.

"I'm certainly glad to hear that a real kiss is better than a dream," Kathe beamed and stepped away. "I've got to get to the airport," she said, glancing at her watch.

Within an hour, Kathe arrived at the airport in Corté de Azuré. She sent her luggage ahead to the states, except for her overnight bag. She took a cab to the house. Security was so tight there that she couldn't get through to Tierra. She finally got through to CC.

"I forgot to call you," CC explained. "There is a lot of tension between Alonzo and Mario Jr. It's like we're in a thick fog. Due to security reasons, Alonzo moved the time up an hour. We're just leaving the church."

"I'll meet you at the cemetery," Kathe stated.

"I'll tell Tierra," CC affirmed. "I'll save a seat for you."

"I'll see you there," Kathe confirmed as she glanced at the cab driver. "Azuré Cimetero per favore (Azuré Cemetery please)."

Security was even tighter at the cemetery. "Aspettare qui per me, (Wait for me)," Kathe told the cab driver as she got out. She walked to the entrance and showed her Alby ID badge and got through the security checkpoints. She worked her way through the crowd toward the gravesite. As soon as she saw the family sitting by the casket, she stopped ducking behind a tree.

"Oh, my, God!" Kathe whispered under her breath. "The man sitting next to Tierra is the man, I saw in Russia a few days ago," she thought. "He is the one that took the picture of the cockpit on that fighter jet," she looked behind the last row of people sitting. "There is the other man that was with him and General Yetsun. Now I know why they looked familiar that day. It was from the picture that Tierra showed me of her with her two brothers, Nicki, and Mario," she thought as someone bumped into her.

"Scusami, (excuse me)," the man said, glancing at her.

"Va bene (It is okay)," Kathe replied, tipping the brim of her hat to hide her face. That funny feeling in her stomach came back as the priest began the last prayer. Kathe hurried back to the taxi. "All 'Aeroporto (the airport)," she told the cab driver as she got back in the cab. She quickly called Ramsey, "Is there a flight leaving here soon. I'm ready for my R & R now. This was very depressing."

"You're in luck," Ramsey answered. "I have a flight leaving soon for London and then Newark. One of the flight attendants just called in sick. Wanda has been frantically searching for a replacement. How quick can you be there?"

"I'm ten minutes away," Kathe noted as the cab entered the freeway.

"I'll tell Wanda that you are taking the flight," Ramsey approved and cleared the line.

"Mario is up to something with General Yetsun," Kathe thought as the cab entered the airport. "I've got to change clothes quickly and get aboard," Kathe thought as she hurried into the bathroom. "This tiny airport will be filling up soon with people leaving after Nicki's funeral. I don't want anyone to recognize me." As the plane left the ground, Kathe looked at her schedule Wanda texted her, said a quick prayer and did the Sign of the Cross. "I have a short layover in London and off to Newark," she read as she glanced out the window. "I hope this whole mess with Saíde, and Mario LaBasco is over by the time I come back to Europe," she thought as the plane soared through the clouds.

The flight from London to Newark was a full and a busy one. Kathe finished serving dinner and had the passengers settled in for the evening. She lowered the big screen as the news was highlighting the day's events. It mentioned Nicki LaBasco and showed pictures of the cemetery. Then it switched over to the news from the states, where it showed clips of Joe and the group on a TMV special. They announced the new member of the band, who took Paul's vacant position. It felt good to hear Joe's voice, especially after the day she had. Terri Patterson was working the flight with her. They talked most of the way about how Kathe met Joe after their last flight.

"I can't believe you left me and met him!" Terri exclaimed. "What's Joe like? Does he look great in person?"

"Slow down," Kathe laughed. "Your mind is going 100 miles an hour. I have an autograph for you. It's in my bag. I will get it," she said, walking to the closet.

"Oh, my gosh!" Terri grabbed the card. "I cannot believe you got him to autograph it just to me! Thanks, Kathe!" she exclaimed as she gazed at his signature. "I never dreamed that I would get his autograph."

"I seem to have made your day," Kathe smiled.

"You made my life!" Terri grinned, starring at it. "Do you think you'll ever run into him again?"

"Who knows?" Kathe chuckled. "It's a small world," she said as the pilot signaled final approach into Newark. "I guess it's back to work. I must make the announcement."

The plane had not finished taxiing to the gate when JAKE rang. "Hello," Kathe said, noticing the snow had melted in Newark.

"Kathe," Ramsey said, "I have a flight to Atlanta for you leaving in two hours. Carrie Anne is at the Hotel International in room 634 and wants to see you before you head south."

"Thanks, I'll call and have Carrie Anne meet me at the airport," Kathe replied. "Anything else I need to know?"

"I want you to know the new implant works perfect," Ramsey declared. "When you fell to the pavement the other night during the LaBasco shooting, control was able to hear everything that went on around you. I was the one, who called the police."

"I wondered how they got there so fast," Kathe expressed.

"Sydney is a genius," Ramsey admitted. "I'm sure glad he is on our side."

"Me too!" Kathe confirmed. "Just remember not to listen in to my personal conversations."

"Your personal life is safe," Ramsey chuckled. "See you in a couple of weeks. Have a great R & R," the line cleared.

"Are you ready for some breakfast?" Kathe greeted Carrie Anne at the tram on Concourse A. "Are you okay? It's awfully early for you to be up and wide awake."

"I'm leaving this morning," Carrie Anne shared as they entered a coffee shop. "I haven't been feeling well. I think partying all the time is catching up with me. So, I decided to get a good night's sleep for work this morning . . . And Ramsey threatened my job if I am late to work again."

"I figured something was up," Kathe said, looking around the shop for a seat. "Hey, Wanda is sitting by herself. Let's sit with her," she said, walking to the table. "Wanda, can we sit with you?"

"Kathe, welcome back," Wanda smiled, moving her purse off the table. "Of course, you can," she glanced up at Carrie Anne. "Thanks, Carrie Anne," she smiled as Carrie Anne sat down.

"For what?" Carrie Anne asked.

"I just won a bet with the Ole Girl," Wanda grinned. "I bet her $20.00 that you would be on time for work this morning."

"I'm not that bad of an employee," Carrie Anne smirked.

"Let me put it this way," Wanda smiled. "Between Ramsey screaming about you and her new health kick, I'm surprised I'm still sane."

"Kathe did you go to Nicki's funeral?" Carrie Anne asked, changing the subject.

"I'm shocked you asked me," Kathe glanced over at her. "Now, I know something is bothering you. The only things you ever talk about are men, fun times, and love in that order."

"She's got a point Carrie Anne," Wanda agreed. "This is a first for you."

"I do think of other people," Carrie Anne protested. "Tierra is also one of my friends."

"Then, I apologize," Kathe confessed. "They changed the time at the last moment for security reasons and I missed it. What happened between you and Travis?"

"Nothing," Carrie Anne sighed, looking away.

"Carrie Anne Mobley!" Kathe stared at her. "I've known you for years and I know when something is bothering you. What's up?"

"You know my motto on men," Carrie Anne confided. "Love them and leave them. I've lived by that motto since my divorce from weirdo with his want-to-be live-in and mother."

"You mean your husband that took his mother on your honeymoon," Wanda giggled.

"Yeah, that one," Carrie Anne confirmed. "The husband that also moved his mother in with us the day we got home from our honeymoon."

"So, don't tell me you're changing your motto?" Kathe quizzed. "All kidding aside; what happened?"

"I'm not changing my motto," Carrie Anne sighed. "Especially, after Suzanne arranged for Rick's girlfriend and Joe's ex-wife to join the band in Los Angeles. Payton conveniently sent me to the hotel to wait for them. The next thing I knew Payton asked Ramsey to replace me."

"It's called being dumped," Wanda giggled, taking a bite of her donut.

"Thanks," Carrie Anne frowned, "I would have never guessed."

"That didn't slow down your hormones," Wanda chuckled. "Ramsey sent you to Kathe's house and I had to ship you out of there at Kathe's request."

"Wanda's right," Kathe confessed. "You had some strange college man at my house."

"Not to mention the passenger Carrie Anne met on the flight to Atlantic City after she left your house," Wanda grinned.

"How did you hear about that?" Carrie Anne glanced at her. "I met a Karate instructor on the way to a tournament in Atlantic City. I stayed with him on a layover and watched him compete. I figure I can learn enough from him to join Kathe's team."

"I don't think my team is ready for a steady diet of you," Kathe insisted.

"And I'd have to listen," Wanda added, "to them constantly complaining about your extracurricular activities. That, along with Ramsey trying to quit smoking, I'd have to look for a new job," she checked the time. "I've got to get back to work," she said as she stood up. "Thanks again for the $20.00 Carrie Anne, and Kathe have a nice R & R," Wanda said as she left.

"What do people really think of me?" Carrie Anne asked after Wanda left.

"What people?" Kathe asked.

"You know, the people we fly with," Carrie Anne requested.

"I'm afraid I don't know what you mean," Kathe said as she noted the change in her demeanor.

"I was really beginning to like Travis," Carrie Anne confided. "I thought we had fun together . . . Then, some girl comes to the concert, and he acts like he doesn't know me . . . Worse yet, he had Payton get rid of me . . ." she looked confused. "He didn't even say goodbye or get lost . . . I couldn't believe he did it. I really thought he and I had something . . . For the first time, I really thought maybe my ship had come in."

"I've never seen this side of you," Kathe shared. "You always love them and leave them. You never even look back. Have you tried contacting Travis?"

"I'm afraid to," Carrie Anne's eyes teared-up. "I think for the first time in my life I feel cheap. Is that what people really think of me, cheap? I mean you never sleep around. Not even with Yorg and you always stay in his room," she looked baffled. "How do you do that? People really respect you. I... I feel like they look down on me."

"Carrie Anne, you're one of a kind," Kathe confessed. "I worry about your safety sometimes, but I never condemn you. I guess it's because I know what happened to you in your marriage. I hope someday, you will settle down, and find Mr. Right."

"So, you think I'm sleazy too?" Carrie Anne surmised.

"I didn't say that," Kathe reflected. "I said, you are one of a kind. No one's perfect; some people just handle pain in different ways than others. You're my best friend and you always will be, along with Yorg and my team."

"What do you think I should do about Travis?" Carrie Anne asked.

"I don't know," Kathe declared. "You are asking the wrong woman about men."

"I asked Ramsey if I should try to see Travis," Carrie Anne admitted. "You want to know what she said."

Kathe looked straight at her, "Knowing Ramsey, she probably said keep away from him on her airlines."

Carrie Anne burst out laughing, "That's exactly what she said!"

Kathe looked at her watch, "Wow, I must get going. I'm going to miss my R & R." She said her goodbyes to her friend, "Hang in there, you'll find Mr. Right someday. Just be patient," Kathe said and walked away. "Travis really made Carrie Anne begin to question herself," she thought as she found Gate A21. Maybe there's hope after all.

Chapter 25

An Unexpected Guest on R & R

Kathe called control and got her flight schedule to Florida. She was glad she was going to be just a passenger. Ramsey had left work and told Keith to tell her to enjoy her rest. For a moment she thought of calling Jeannie and the kids as the 747 was loading passengers. After thinking about what she'd been through lately she decided not to call. She knew they would want her to go to Colorado to see them. She needed some alone time to sort out the events of the past few weeks. The fact that Mario was in Russia viewing an experimental jet started haunting her. "What was he doing with it?" she thought. "Now I know that this is not over yet." She slept all the way to Hartsfield-Jackson Airport in Atlanta. She woke up as the plane landed and was taxiing to the gate. She gave Keith a call, "I just landed at Hartsfield-Jackson Airport. What's my next flight?"

"You're in luck," Keith reported. "You were slated for a long layover; however, Ramsey pulled some strings to keep you on your present flight. Its next stop is MCO Airport in Orlando. It takes off in forty-five minutes."

"Perfect!" Kathe exclaimed. "My car is parked there. Would you call and have the valet get it ready for me?" she looked outside. "It's odd to see trees in bloom down here. My favorite dogwoods are beautiful."

"I'm showing it's warm and rainy down there," Keith stated, checking the weather. "The sun should be out most of your R & R; enjoy it. You deserve it. I'll have your car ready for you," he cleared the line.

The flight to Orlando was quite bumpy as the weather worsened. She chuckled as she thought of the past few weeks. She disarmed a passenger with a knife, stopped a terrorist attack with laptop bombs, ran into a bathroom with a maniac holding a gun on her, and was involved in an ambush in Munich. How ironic would it be, that she survived all that to be killed in a crash, going home on R & R? As they neared Orlando, she noticed that the thunder and lightning was easing up. The captain signaled final approach. She knew the rain was not letting up as they flew over I-4 getting ready to land. Suddenly, the engines accelerated as the plane began to climb. Something was wrong on the ground and the traffic controller was not going to let them land. She watched the rain from the window. The clouds were thick, and visibility was poor. They circled the airport for thirty minutes and the passengers began to complain. The flight attendants were running out of excuses. At last, the pilot signaled for the attendants to prepare for landing.

"This is First Officer Johnson," he introduced. "We apologize for the delay, but due to the storm we were unable to land. We have just received permission. We will have you on the ground in just a few minutes. Flight attendants prepare for landing."

On the ground, Kathe took her time getting off the plane. She hated going home to an empty house. She found her keys and the alarm code in the zipper compartment of her purse. The storm intensified and was raging furiously. The lights in the terminal began flickering as JAKE rang. "Hello," Kathe slowly answered, wondering if Ramsey had changed her mind about her R & R.

"Kathe, my friend," Ramsey began. "I hope you are still inside the terminal. I see you're having a terrible storm down there."

"Yes, Ramsey," Kathe said, rolling her eyes. "I'm still in the terminal. If you remember, I am on a doctor-prescribed R & R. I'm not going up on any plane in this storm for any reason."

"I wouldn't send you up in that terrible storm again," Ramsey gritted her teeth. "Besides all flights are on hold until after the lightning stops," she smirked while nervously tapping her pencil on the desk. "What kind of a boss do you think I am?"

"The kind that wouldn't think twice about sending me back to work as soon as the flights resume," Kathe admitted.

"I'm hurt," Ramsey stated. "I can't believe you think I'm that kind of a boss."

"Right, and whales don't live in the ocean!" Kathe exclaimed.

"Let's get serious for a minute," Ramsey cleared her throat. "The reason for the delay in landing was two of Alby's jets had a little mishap on the ground. One of our jets tapped the wing of another. We will reroute most of the passengers when the storm is over. However, we seem to have a problem with one of the passengers."

"I can hear the wheels beginning to turn in your head," Kathe confessed. "So, just have Alby put the passenger up in one of the many hotels. There are quite a few here in Orlando and one at this very airport."

"It's not that easy," Ramsey complained. "When the passengers were getting off the plane, some fans recognized him. Security had to pull them away from him. He's upset. I have already talked to his manager and told him it was his lucky day; you just landed there. I told him that you would be happy to have a guest at your private home on the beach in Daytona until he can get there."

"You mean, I'm on R & R and I have to work, not as a flight attendant, but as a babysitter?" Kathe demanded.

"Not a babysitter," Ramsey declared. "He is old enough to take care of himself. He's potty trained, I think!" she exclaimed, snapping her pencil in half. "I can't believe I'm doing this, but I have my back against a wall! You know him!"

"Who is it?" Kathe asked.

"It doesn't matter," Ramsey confessed. "I was ordered by my boss to have you do this. On the record, it is against my better judgment. Just report to the security department and remember your promise. Keep you distance from him! I've already told them you are on your way . . .Oh, and by the way, he doesn't know you are coming to get him!"

"Ramsey's never been ordered to do anything by her boss," Kathe noted. "She is not making sense," Kathe thought as she walked toward the security department. It was as busy as Newark's Security Department, especially with the ground incident that just happened. Sighing, she reluctantly walked to the front desk.

"Excuse me, Sir," Kathe said, showing her ID to the officer. "I'm Kathe Tierney. Linda Ramsey sent me here to pick up someone."

"Greg Lilly," he introduced, checking her ID. "I'm glad you're here. Our special guest seems very agitated about something. I don't think it has anything to do with what happened with our jets or the fans."

"Great," Kathe sighed. "I come home on R & R from Europe, only to have an irate person staying at my house. Where is this wonderful person?"

"I'll take you to him," Officer Lilly offered as they walked down a hallway toward a private lounge. "I'll never understand these people. All they want is to become famous. Then, once they're famous, they want their privacy," he said, opening the door.

Sitting with his back to the door, watching the rain was a familiar form. Officer Lilly cleared his voice and caught his attention. As he slowly sat up and turned around, Kathe couldn't believe her eyes, "Joe! Are you okay?" She hurried over to him.

"What are you doing here?" Joe asked, standing up.

"I was going to ask you the same question," Kathe admitted. "I live here. I just flew in from Newark on R & R. Why aren't the others with you?"

"They're still in California," Joe replied. "I came ahead of them," he said and turned to look outside at a bolt of lightning. "It's a beautiful storm!"

"Not when you're circling the airport because you can't land in it," Kathe admitted. "I'm supposed to take you to my house. Payton and the others will pick you up tomorrow afternoon," she said as Officer Lilly held the door open for them.

As they left the lounge, she retrieved her luggage, which she had sent ahead. Next, they headed toward the Alby Employee's Parking Garage. They entered the garage, and she showed her ID to the attendant in the booth. As they waited, Joe tried to imagine what kind of car she would drive. To his surprise, it was a flame, red Chevy Corvette with a Targa top.

"Wow! I'm impressed," Joe confessed. "I like the color. It's you!"

"Thank you," Kathe smiled, looking at it. "Isn't it beautiful?"

"To say the least, but I'm surprised you drive a Corvette," Joe chuckled as she pressed the trunk release on her FOB.

"Why?" she looked over at him.

"I don't know," Joe confided. "I was just trying to imagine what kind of a car you would be driving. This wasn't what I had in mind," he smiled as he got into the passenger seat. As she pulled out of the garage and onto I-4 East, the rain began to slacken. "How far is it to your house?"

"About forty-five minutes," Kathe replied. "But in this rain, it might take longer," she paused for a moment. "You never did answer me about why you are separated from the others?"

"You're right, I didn't tell you," Joe stated as Kathe started weaving in and out of the traffic until it cleared.

"Hang on," Kathe said, speeding up.

"Your car handles like a dream," Joe complimented as she passed several semi-trucks and pulled in front of them.

"Thanks, she's a beauty," Kathe smiled. "It's my one joy to come home to," she said as they slowed down a bit. "Can I ask you a question?"

"I might not answer, but go ahead," Joe said, glancing at her.

"I had breakfast with Carrie Anne this morning in Newark," Kathe stated. "She said Travis had Payton get rid of her. I felt sorry for her. For the first time since I've known her, she was worried about what people thought of her."

"I don't know," Joe answered. "A friend of Travis' came to visit him from London. I guess he felt awkward and asked Payton to help him out. Don't ask me if he likes Carrie Anne. I never get involved in my friend's business."

"I don't blame you," Kathe replied as she veered to the right to continue I-4 toward Daytona Beach.

"You are very different from Carrie Anne," Joe said as he glanced at her.

"Yes, I am," Kathe affirmed. "She's one of a kind. Hey, see that sign. That's our exit."

"Boy, that trip didn't seem to take long at all," Joe said as she changed from I-4 to I-95 South toward Miami. Taking the next exit, she got off the freeway at Port Orange, and turned left on Dunlawton heading east.

"I thought this was a beach town?" Joe questioned as he looked around.

"It's about four miles ahead to the bridge, and then it will seem like a beach town," Kathe said as she cleared all the lights.

"Now, this is a nice view of the ocean?" Joe gleamed as she drove over the bridge.

"Yes," Kathe agreed and turned right at the second light. A huge bolt of lightning flashed directly in front of them as another round of torrential rain began.

"Are we almost there?" Joe asked. "The lightning is very close."

"The road narrows," Kathe explained as the wind picked up. "It's about another two miles to my house. I live at the last house at the end of this road."

Kathe passed a restaurant and came to a four-way stop sign. She drove straight through the stop sign, pulled into the last house on the left stopping in front of the wrought iron gate. "Thank goodness I programmed the code into the 'vette before I left last time," she smiled, pushing the button and the gate opened.

As she pulled into the garage, the storm was raging. "We made it just in time," Kathe sighed. Unlocking the door, she turned off the alarm, just as the house phone rang. "Kathe Tierney, and the phrase is 'to be or not to be.' I will be home for two weeks. Thank you," she cleared the line.

"It's raining so hard I can barely see the ocean," Joe said, looking out the kitchen window.

"It is violent," Kathe admitted. "I better find a flashlight. The electricity might go out any minute," she said as she began frantically looking through several drawers. "Finally," she said as she tested it. "Thank God, it still works. Now would you like a drink?"

"What do you have?" Joe asked as he followed her into the family room.

"I don't know, Carrie Anne was here earlier this week," Kathe said, turning on the lights. She reached for some glasses under the bar, and then went back into the kitchen to get ice.

"The lightning strikes are gorgeous over the ocean," Joe admitted, watching through the glass walls near the bar. The wind was howling, and the rain came down harder.

"I'm glad we're home," Kathe replied, standing beside him. "I would hate to be driving in this. What would you like to drink?"

"Scotch on the rocks," Joe answered, glancing around the room. "You have a beautiful home. But, like your car, it's not what I expected."

"Do I look like an apartment dweller who drives a clunker?" Kathe grinned.

"No, I'm sorry," Joe apologized. "I didn't mean to insult you," he took a sip of his drink. "I guess I pictured you living in an apartment and maybe driving a mid-sized car."

Kathe laughed, walking over to the couch, kicking off her shoes and sat down. "Believe it or not, I used to be that way," she said, tipping her glass toward him. "I was the perfect little mommy-type driving a van full of kids."

He walked over to her, "Why the big change?"

She looked down at her glass and picked at an ice cube. "My life changed. I'll never again be that kind of person," she said as JAKE rang. "Yorg," Silence for a second. "No, it's okay. No, I didn't think anything of it. Honest it's alright. I didn't think you were being that way." She listened again, "I didn't talk to Tierra. Did you talk with Lt. Jaco?" Silence again. "Okay, call me when you talk to him. Take care. I love you back. Bye."

She sat JAKE on the bar and poured herself another drink, "Would you like another one?"

"Yes, please," Joe answered as she reached for his glass and poured him another one.

"What did I do with that flashlight?" Kathe asked as the lights began to flicker.

"It's in the kitchen," Joe remembered as he hurried to get it. He came out of the kitchen just as the lights flickered and went out. To his surprise a backup generator kicked on and the lights resumed. "Your lights came back on? What happened? They are very dim."

"The electricity isn't back on," Kathe declared. "It seems that Dr. Sydney installed backup generators to run my house. I've got to thank him."

"Where was Yorg when he called?" Joe wondered, turning the flashlight off and setting it on the table.

"He's at our apartment in Paris," Kathe answered.

"Is that the one across from the Seine River?" Joe inquired.

"Yes, and it also has a beautiful view of the city," Kathe described.

"I know that has to be the same building where Steve just rented an apartment," Joe said, walking over to the couch. "I can't remember the name."

"You know the realtor said she rented the apartment across the hall to some Britts," Kathe affirmed. "You could be right. I don't know who Steve is."

Joe sat down on the couch next to her, "Do you always end your conversations with Yorg, saying you love him?"

"Yorg and I are just friends," Kathe reiterated. "I thought I already told you that."

"I never tell anyone I love them, unless I mean it," Joe pried.

"I do love Yorg," Kathe admitted. "However, it's not what you think. We are held together by a special bond."

"A child?" Joe questioned.

"Nothing like that," Kathe insisted. "It has something to do with the airlines. That's all I will say about it, so let's change the subject."

"Finally, the electricity is back on," Joe said as the generator turned off and the lights brightened. "I can't wait to see the rest of your house. The downstairs is beautiful."

"Come on, I'll show you around," Kathe offered. "It's a very open floor plan. That way I have a perfect view of the beach from each room. It has a two-sided black marble fireplace dividing the living room from the family room. There is a circular stairway in the family room leading to the second floor. The loft at the top of the stairs houses a regulation sized pool table," she said as they walked down the hallway to the guest bedrooms, and then over to the master bedroom. "I love this master bedroom. As you can see three sides are constructed of heat resistant smoked glass. The waterbed is round on a black, marble pedestal," she said as they walked toward the bathroom.

"A round waterbed?" Joe laughed as he reached to touch it. "It is a waterbed."

"The builder had a bad back," Kathe laughed as she walked toward the bathroom. "He said it was the only thing that saved him from back surgery."

"This is my kind of bathroom," Joe admired. "That is a quite large, marble Jacuzzi."

"The builder said it's modeled after his," Kathe admitted. "He said it's his wife's favorite get away from their children. The shower is slate like the floor and has multiple showerheads; it's like taking a shower in a waterfall."

"I noticed the ceiling over the bed and Jacuzzi is also smoked glass," Joe admired. "I bet you can look up at the stars."

"You can lay in bed and look at the stars," Kathe beamed. "Unfortunately, tonight, it's cloudy."

"Which room do you want me to sleep in tonight?" Joe asked.

"You can sleep in here," Kathe answered. "I always sleep on the couch downstairs," she shied away from him.

"You mean you never sleep in here?" Joe questioned.

"I always sleep on the couch," Kathe confessed, looking away.

"Why?" Joe asked, gently pulling her face toward him.

"I never sleep on a bed," Kathe said. "I have nightmares," finishing her drink. "I need a refill. Are you ready for another?"

"Sure, just one more," Joe smiled. "Anymore and I might want to make good use of this room; except I've witnessed you at work."

"You're right," Kathe smiled, "you learned first-hand that looks can be deceiving."

"I promise to be on my best behavior," Joe replied as they walked downstairs. This time Joe fixed the drinks while Kathe found the television remote and flipped on TMV.

"This is Talbot McAllister for TMV News," she introduced. "All of Hollywood is talking about Light Crimson today. Steve Day joined the band, as the guitarist taking the place of the late Paul Leven. Payton Ross, manager for the group was doing some fancy footwork trying not to say why lead singer, Joe Sherrod was not at the interview. According to our sources, the lead singer was under contract to appear this afternoon. 'No comment' was all Ross would say. Rumor has it that Sherrod's ex-wife was seen hanging around the group all week. Could they possibly be getting back together? That's it for tonight."

The regular house phone rang, and Kathe answered it, "It's for you Joe," Kathe said, handing him the phone. He took the phone and handed her a drink.

"Payton, I'm not answering my cell phone because I don't want to talk to anybody!" Joe exclaimed. "I'm at Kathe's house in Ponce . . . Yes, she's here with me . . . I don't give a flip about contracts. I won't stay around if she doesn't leave," Joe explained, and then listened. "No, Payton," Joe ordered. "You Get Rid of Her Now! Don't Come Here with Her!" Joe objected, slammed down the phone, gulped his drink and poured a double.

"Do you want to talk about it?" Kathe asked very surprised at his actions.

"No, I don't!" Joe snapped. "I'm sorry. I didn't mean to snap at you." He walked over and sat down on the couch next to her. "I just can't believe how far some people will go to destroy you."

"But, according to TMV," Kathe replied. "You were under contract to attend this afternoon's interview and you didn't. I am sure you have Payton upset. He's responsible for making sure you uphold your contracts," she said, glancing at him. "Have you heard a word I said?"

"I just told Payton that I don't give a flip about contracts," Joe declared. "I will continue to not show up if he can't keep her away from me," he said, looking down at his glass. "I thought I had it all again. I even found myself enjoying just being with you. Everyone noticed that in New York. Then, just as I started to let my guard down, you go into that bathroom in Newark, and could have been shot by a madman."

"I helped save the mother and her child," Kathe stated. "That's what I do for a living."

"But you have three children of your own," Joe continued. "What would have happened to them if you had been killed?"

"They would have missed me for a while," Kathe affirmed. "I don't live with them anymore. Not because I don't want to, but because my job is too dangerous. That is why Ramsey and Yorg didn't want me to stay with you. I'm shocked Ramsey had me pick you up at the airport and let us be together again. You are glitz and glitter, and I must stay in the shadows. I make deadly enemies. Once upon a time, I lived a very happy life. But as you just said, some people go out of their way to destroy you."

"What about you with that Mafia leader?" Joe quizzed. "I thought I saw you on TV. I went on the Internet and watched the newscast several times. What were you doing with him? You could have been shot in a Mafia-style hit. Look at you. You are a very beautiful woman. Do you have a death wish?"

"No, I don't," Kathe insisted. "However, if you don't slow down on the scotch, you may have one in the morning. I was delivering a present to Nicki LaBasco for his sister, whom I work with. I was just in the wrong place at the wrong time."

He stood up and made another drink. Kathe turned up the volume on the TV as she watched his video. Joe was singing a love song, "That's a beautiful song. It seems so warm."

"It's from our old album," Joe stated. "I wrote it when I was in love."

"I never really heard of you until a few weeks ago," Kathe confessed. "I guess I'll have to buy some of your CDs. You're very good."

The house phone rang again. Joe quickly answered it thinking it was Payton. He closes his eyes, clenches his fist, yelling, "Get this straight! I don't ever want you to call or come around me again!" He slammed the phone down. Then he grabbed it again listened for a dial tone. "You don't mind if I leave it off the hook, do you?"

"No," Kathe noted his reaction.

"Where is your bathroom?" Joe asked as he sat his drink on the bar.

"Through the living room on the other side of the entryway," Kathe said, pointing the way.

While Joe was in the bathroom, she went upstairs and changed for bed. She hoped he would see that she was tired and go to bed. When she came back downstairs, she was wearing black silk pajamas. She turned on the alarm system and wiped up some of the mess that he made when he poured his last drink. He looked at her, "Kathe what makes some women loving mothers and some not?"

"I don't know," Kathe stated. "Why do you ask?" She sat back down on the couch for a moment.

"You," he began. "You put yourself in danger to support your children. I have heard you on the phone with them. You really love them." He thought of the girl who called him a few minutes earlier. "I was in love once. Once upon a nightmare. Oh, I was head over heels in love with her." Leaning against the bar, he slid down to the floor as Kathe hurried to him. She sat down on the floor next to him. "When we got married, she knew I wanted a family. She said she was afraid she couldn't get pregnant. She liked to party and use recreational drugs occasionally. But I loved her anyway." He took another sip of his drink. "She said after two years of trying, that she couldn't get pregnant. I suggested we adopt, but she did not want someone else's child. So, we kept trying." Kathe got up and got him a napkin. He took another sip of his drink. "During our last tour Cara, the number 1 model in all of London, wife of the famous rock star Joe Sherrod, didn't want to go with us. She wanted to pursue her career while I was pursuing mine. She . . . she said she wanted to give her body a rest. Maybe when I got back, we could try again," he satirically laughed. "She gave her body a rest alright. I came back early. I watched her agent help her get out of the car. She walked very sluggishly with her agent aiding her," he took another sip. "Before they came in the door, the phone rang. I answered it. It was the nurse from the hospital. She had forgotten to take her post-surgical instructions home with her," tears streamed down his face as he held his glass up to the light.

"No wonder, you're upset," Kathe said, sitting next to him. "I don't know what to say."

He reached for her, "She lied to me. She finally admitted that she didn't want to lose her perfect figure or have children. She enjoyed her career and lifestyle. I thought we had everything together-happiness, fame, and money. It never occurred to me that I couldn't trust my own wife. And then," he looked at Kathe and smiled, "when I least expected it, you accidently appeared in my life. I couldn't believe how you took care of me, a perfect stranger. You took the time to stop getting dressed, after a very embarrassing moment, I might add, just to help me because I was hurt. You didn't know who I am. Then he began rambling about Paul dying, and some of the other disasters that had happened to the band.

Wiping the tears from his face, Kathe confided, "I have been in a similar situation. The pain eventually dulls. However, it never goes away. I guess that's why I now live a very different lifestyle. I could never go back to that kind of life. I could never take the pain of failure again."

"That's the way I feel," Joe said, looking up at the ceiling. "I thought I had my head on straight until she showed up in LA. I never wanted to see her again. When I did, I felt just as angry as before. She kept showing up with Suzanne wherever we went. Finally, after the last concert I couldn't stand seeing her anymore. I hopped a plane to Orlando. I was going to Miami, which is where the band is heading in a few days." He sat his glass down on the floor. "I've never walked away from the group or a contract before. They don't even know why Cara and I broke up. I didn't want anyone to know. I'm an only child; it would kill my parents."

"Life is really something, isn't it?" Kathe shared. "Take you for example. I would have never guessed you felt like that. Look at Yorg. Everybody at the airlines thinks he's invincible; that is everyone except me. Yorg was married several years ago. His pregnant wife was murdered. One of the generals wanted him to commit high treason. When Yorg refused to do it, the general had her killed. Ever since then, he has blamed himself for her death."

"I know I'm not the only person horrible things happen to, but after a while, you need a little help," Joe said, leaning his head on his knees.

"One thing I've found is when you least expect it, help is sent," Kathe smiled. "I wasn't scheduled to come to Florida. Weird things just keep happening. What were the odds I'd be landing from Newark the same time you came in from California and couldn't takeoff for Miami?"

"The plane I was on didn't takeoff due to a mishap, with another plane on the taxiway," Joe remembered. "Maybe you're right. You were sent to help me."

Kathe looked up at the clock above the mantel, "It's 3:00 am. I guess we need to get some sleep. The storm has let up. I hope it's sunny tomorrow. I'd love to lie on the beach and feel the warm sun on my face." She stood up, opened a closet door, and took out her pillow and blanket. "You can sleep upstairs. We'll talk more tomorrow."

He put his arms around her waist and pulled her close to him. "Thanks for listening," he said and gave her a goodnight kiss on the cheek.

The raging storm woke Kathe up about 11:30 am. She sat up on the couch, hoping it was not going to rain for next two weeks. Watching the storm out of the room's glass walls, she saw it was high tide. The water was all the way to her retaining wall. She heard Joe coming downstairs, "I'm surprised you're up so early."

"The storm woke me," Joe admitted. "The thunder sounds so close."

"It always sounds closer at the beach," Kathe declared. "Look at the ocean. The waves are enormous. It looks almost like it does during a hurricane. Are you hungry?"

"I'm starved," Joe admitted.

"I'll take a quick shower and hurry to the store," Kathe said, rushing up the stairs. "It won't take me long."

"Do you mind if I go with you?" Joe called upstairs.

"No, I just need to get some summer things out of my closet," Kathe said as Joe followed her to the master bedroom. He watched her as she looked through all the clothes for shorts. She held up several before finally deciding to put on tight, jean shorts with a pink cami.

Joe folded his arms and leaned against the wall, "You mean to tell me you looked through all these clothes and you ended up with jean shorts and a cami?"

"I decided I'm in uniform all the time," Kathe reflected. "So, I figured I might as well be comfortable for a change," she said, heading for the shower. "I'll be out in a few minutes."

He lay across the bed waiting for her. A few minutes later, she came out wearing nothing but a towel. She sat at her vanity and put on her make-up. The electricity began to flicker again. "Do you feel better about things today?"

"Yes, I do," Joe confessed, watching her. "Please don't tell anyone. I'm not sure why I told you. I guess it was the scotch. Why do I feel so comfortable being with you?"

"I'll be ready to leave in a minute," Kathe said, changing the subject. She walked to the closet to get dressed.

Exiting her long driveway and turning on A1A, they headed straight for the nearest grocery store. The rain was steady, but not as heavy as before. She showed Joe the beach and a few sights along the way. The market was very busy for a rainy Saturday. Joe watched as she decided on some fruit. She picked up some fresh papayas, "Do you like these?"

"Yes," Joe said. "I also like bananas and apples." He pushed the cart as they walked over to the meat section.

"Tell me, do you want to go out for dinner or are you brave enough to try my cooking?" Kathe smiled.

"I don't know," he quizzed. "Can you cook?"

She bit her bottom lip and thought for a moment. "I don't know. It's been a long time. As a matter of fact, other than making simple eggs and toast. I can't remember the last time I did." People walking by them smiled overhearing their conversation. It seemed likely that they were newlyweds. "Do you like chicken?"

"It depends," Joe smiled, glancing at her.

"Depends on what?" She questioned as her face seemed to glow.

"On how you cook it," Joe smiled.

"How do you like it?" Kathe grinned.

"Anyway, but fried," Joe answered.

"Great!" Kathe exclaimed. "We'll grill it," she said on her way to dairy section. There she picked up eggs, cheese, coffee creamer and a few other items. JAKE buzzed and she answered.

"Kathe, is Joe still with you?" Ramsey asked.

"Yes, he is," Kathe replied, glancing around for him. "Payton called me a few minutes ago. They can't get out of LA until tomorrow, so they won't arrive until Monday morning. Put him on the phone."

"Ramsey wants to talk to you," Kathe said, handing JAKE to Joe.

"Payton wanted me to tell you that Cara is leaving for London," Ramsey affirmed. "He will personally put her on a plane this afternoon. The band will not be able to join you until they finish with TMV. They will join you in Daytona on Monday morning."

"Tell Payton to call me when Cara is in the air," Joe stated. "Is there any way you can make sure she goes to London?"

"Payton already asked me to let him know when she arrives there," Ramsey confirmed. "I told him I will notify him the minute she is on British soil."

"I appreciate your help," Joe said, handing JAKE back to Kathe.

As Joe found the shortest line Kathe remembered, "I forgot sweet potatoes. I'll be right back."

"Okay," Joe said, picking up a magazine with his picture on the front cover. As he read the article, he realized Kathe had been gone for quite a few minutes. Looking around for her, he started unloading the groceries. The older man behind him said, "Your wife is over there," he pointed to the soda section.

"She's not my wife, but thank you," Joe said, putting the magazine on the counter to buy it. He noticed the man looked at the picture, and then at him.

"Amazing resemblance, isn't it?" Joe said, reaching to help Kathe with the cokes, pretzels, and popcorn. "Where are the potatoes?"

"Unbelievable, I forgot them," Kathe said, hurried off and returned with them as Joe was placing the last item on the counter. "Good, I made it back in time," she said, reaching in her purse for her debit card.

Joe pulled out his credit card, "This is on me."

"No, this is on Alby Airlines," Kathe smiled as she paid. Leaving the store, "Can you put the groceries in the trunk? I'd like to get a newspaper."

"I'll be glad to," Joe stated as she tossed him the keys and hurried off. He closed the trunk and looked around for her again. The same older man, accompanied by his wife was putting groceries in their car next to him. Joe held his umbrella over the man's wife. He noticed the man bought the heavy, metal magazine with his picture on the front. Joe reached for it.

"I told my wife you had an uncanny resemblance to the lead singer of Light Crimson," he said, pointing to the picture.

His wife looked at Joe, and then at the magazine, "He does look exactly like the man on the cover."

Joe took the pen out of Harry's shirt pocket and wrote, "Thanks for helping me find my friend at the market today, Joe Sherrod."

As Joe handed it back to Harry, he showed his wife, "I bought this magazine. I knew it was him!"

"I'm Mabel," she introduced. "Gosh, we've never met a famous person before."

"Come to think of it, you were on the news last night for skipping out on an interview," Harry remembered.

"Guilty, I'm not supposed to be here, let's keep this our secret," Joe said, walking back to the Corvette to wait for Kathe.

"Thank you, Mr. Sherrod," Harry said, getting into his car as Kathe hurried back to the 'Vette with the newspaper.

"I got the last one," Kathe held it up. "I wanted to catch up on the local news to see if there is anything special happening this weekend."

Harry backed out of his parking spot, stopped behind them, rolled his car window down, "If she's not your wife, you ought to marry her. You look great together."

"I'll keep that in mind," Joe chuckled as he opened the car door for Kathe.

"What was that all about?" Kathe asked, getting into the driver seat.

"Harry, and Mabel were standing behind me in line and recognized me from the magazine," Joe showed her. "I was surprised he bought the magazine, so I autographed it for him. They were excited to meet a famous person. I couldn't let them down."

"You're not supposed to be in Daytona," Kathe reminded him leaving the parking lot. "I hope they don't call the press. I'm sure Payton is still trying to appease TMV about your breach of contract."

"That is Payton's fault," Joe declared. "I told him to get rid of her and he refused. He told me that she was my ex-wife, not his."

"That's interesting," Kathe glanced at him stopping at the stop sign. "He had no problem getting rid of Carrie Anne for Travis. Why not her?"

"I didn't know Payton got rid of Carrie Anne," Joe admitted. "She was gone when I came out of the dressing room."

"Payton called Ramsey and had her switch Carrie Anne's schedule," Kathe informed him, pulling into the driveway.

While they were putting the groceries away, the sun finally came out. "The sun really does shine in Florida," Joe told her.

"Yes, it does," Kathe smiled. "After breakfast, let's go outside and enjoy it."

"I can't wait," Joe smiled. "I'm tired of freezing weather and snow."

After breakfast, Joe changed to his bathing suit and put on some music. Kathe came out in a bathing suit with a couple of beers. She transferred the house phone to JAKE. "That is so aggravating," she admitted, sitting beside him. "That's about the third phone call I've had in ten minutes, with no one on the other end."

"Maybe, it's just a wrong number," Joe replied as he peered over the seawall at the water. "Let's walk down to the beach and look at the ocean. It's low tide and there are lots of shells near the water."

"There is something about the ocean that makes me feel grounded," Kathe admitted, walking down to see the shells.

"Your home is beautifully surrounded by three sides of water," Joe pointed to the inlet. "It is so peaceful and inspiring," he said, picking up a colorful shell.

"Let's walk down to the jetty," Kathe said, pointing to a manmade pier to the south. I will show you where the boats come into the river from the ocean. It's a nice place to go fishing."

"Tell me," Joe wondered, glancing at her. "How do you afford this house? It has to cost a fortune and the taxes must be astronomical."

"I got it as part of a settlement," Kathe answered.

"Is it part of your divorce settlement?" Joe asked as they walked.

"No, from something else," Kathe said, glancing away.

"What?" Joe begged as he stood in front of her.

"Boy, you are one for questions," Kathe chuckled.

"Nicki LaBasco?" Joe guessed.

"I just met Nicki a few weeks ago," Kathe shared. "I told you that his sister works with me," she said, walking up the steps to the jetty.

"Does Yorg co-own this house with you?" Joe asked as he climbed up the rocks.

"No," Kathe stated as they walked to the end of the jetty. "Why would Yorg own a house with me?"

"You said he co-rents an apartment in Paris with you," Joe quickly answered.

"Me and four other people, as a matter of fact, I probably should call one of them," she offered as they sat on the bench at the end of the pier. "Jordan lives here in Daytona, and I think he's home on leave too," she said as something caught her eye in the water. "Look," she pointed. "There is a pair of dolphins swimming to the right of us."

"And there is a baby dolphin with them," Joe pointed as he reached for his cell phone. "Where did the baby go?"

"There it is," Kathe smiled, snapping a picture of the family. "They are amazing."

"Who lives here that you co-rent an apartment with?" Joe quizzed, returning to the conversation.

"My ex-brother-in-law," Kathe explained. "Capt. Jordan Mills is a good friend. He helped me get my job with Alby after my divorce," she said as she stood up to leave. "Maybe we should see if he and his wife, Patti, would like to go out to dinner with us tonight."

"That is fine with me," Joe agreed. "After all, I'm the one that crashed your vacation."

"I'll give them a call," Kathe smiled as they walked back toward her house. "Last night on TMV, it said that you have a new band member."

"Steve Day is our new guitarist," Joe explained. "He joined us in California. He had to miss New York due to another contract. However, now he is officially a member of the band. He replaced Paul Leven, who died a few months ago. You might say, we've had a few problems that we've had to overcome. Troy Rollins was in a bad car accident. While he was recuperating the rest of us worked on a new album," he said as JAKE rang.

"Hello," Kathe answered, noting it was from her house phone.

"I'd like to speak to Joe," a British woman declared.

"Just a moment," Kathe said, muting the call. She looked at Joe, "There is a British woman on the house phone line."

"Does it sound like Babs?" Joe asked.

"I don't think so," Kathe answered as Joe reached for JAKE.

"Hello," Joe answered as his face turned red and he handed JAKE back to Kathe.

Kathe quickly put the phone on mute and forwarded the call. "I'm transferring her call to the same phone booth in the Fiji Islands that I do with Peter. It really upsets him, especially when he gets the bill."

"I wish I could see the look on Cara's face when she figures out what you did," Joe chuckled. "Can you find out where the call came from?"

"Sure, give a minute," Kathe replied and called control. "Keith will call me back in a few minutes with the answer," she said as they walked up the steps to her deck.

Inside the house, Joe went into the bathroom, while Kathe tried to call Jordan and Patti. "I'll try again later," she thought as JAKE rang.

"Your friend is not going to like this, Tierney," Keith reported. "The phone call came from a cell phone located at Hartsfield-Jackson Airport in Atlanta. His ex-wife has changed her flight schedule. She's headed for Daytona."

"Can you stop her?" Kathe requested.

"No," Keith stated. "There's no law about changing your mind and going to Daytona Beach."

"Call Ramsey," Kathe urged. "She might be able to pull some strings."

"I'll get back to you soon," Keith said and cleared the line.

"Whom were you talking to?" Joe asked as he joined her.

"It was Keith at control," Kathe answered. "Ramsey will call me back in a few minutes. You know, being with you makes me feel special. I would like to take you to one of my favorite restaurants tonight. I even feel like dressing up, is that okay?"

"You're on," Joe smiled as they hurried upstairs to get dressed.

A few minutes later, Kathe walked down the spiral staircase wearing a one-piece navy-blue pantsuit. The low-cut, V-neck and flowing palazzo pants was stunning on her. She added a two-carat single blue topaz, teardrop necklace that fell just above her cleavage, a bracelet, and matching earrings. Joe looked at this amazingly beautiful woman walking toward him. "I hope you like what I'm wearing," she smiled. "I haven't dressed like this in a long time."

"You are radiant!" Joe smiled, putting his arms around her waist, pulling her closer, and kissing her. "There is something about you," he said, gazing into her eyes. "I feel like I've known you forever," he admitted and kissed her again.

"Well," Kathe took a step back. "We better leave for the restaurant before we change our minds, and you have to eat my cooking."

"Let me think which bridge I should take to Panama Jim's," Kathe said as they drove down A1A toward Daytona Beach.

"I saw the headlines today about filmmaker, Stephen Brown shooting a documentary on three eaglets hatched in Centennial Park in Holly Hill," Joe said. "Is that close to where we are going?"

"It's very close to the restaurant," Kathe answered. "Why?"

"My father is a member of the Audubon Society in London," Joe stated. "I called him and read the article to him. It is very rare for bald eagles to have three chicks. He asked me if I could go by and take a picture. I brought my camera, just in case."

"Holly Hill is just over the Mason Avenue Bridge," Kathe answered as she turned left to go over the bridge. "The restaurant is just over the bridge to the left," Kathe said, showing him as they passed it. "All we have to do is turn right on Ridgewood Avenue, which is right here," she said as she made the turn. "There is the Chamber of Commerce," she said, turning into the left turning lane. "I think the park is just over the railroad tracks."

"There it is," Joe pointed as Kathe turned right into the parking lot. "There is the truck for Gabby Mobile Productions. That's Stephen Brown's Company," he pointed out and looked around. "There are several men and a tripod set up over by the last pavilion by the lake," Joe saw as they got out of the car.

"Let's go meet them," Kathe suggested as they walked toward the pavilion.

"Well, if this isn't a first for me," filmmaker, Stephen Brown chuckled taking their picture. "A beautiful woman in a stunning evening dress out in the middle of a park. I'm Stephen Brown, what can I do for you?"

"Kathe Tierney," she introduced shaking his hand. "This is a friend of mine, Joe Sherrod."

"This is my general manager, Will Russell, my editor, Skip Cowell, and East Volusia Conservation Chairman for the Audubon Society, Dave Hartgroves," Steve further introduced as he pointed to three more gentlemen joining them. "And here comes two of my camera men, Tony and Bruce; and my model set designer, Joey."

"Your company is very impressive," Joe replied. "I can see why you made the headlines with that award winning photo. My father in London is a member of the Audubon Society. I read him the article this morning about the three eaglets hatched by bald eagles," he said as the birds flew over them. "They are magnificent," Joe said as he and Stephen snapped several shots of them.

"They are beautiful birds," Stephen agreed as Joe shot several pictures of one of the eagles flying over the lake and grabbing a fish. "Did you read the interesting story behind the City of Holly Hill moving the nest?"

"Yes, my father was amazed that the adults stayed with the eggs," Joe admitted. "I brought my camera and was interested in the type of lens you used to capture that picture?" he asked as he held up his camera.

"I used a 1200 f2.8 with a doubler, which changed the speed to 2400 f5.6," Stephen admitted. "I have to admit I took the advice of a friend of mine that works in Newark. He is the one who told me about the doubler, which is the fastest long-range, experimental government lens."

"That's odd," Kathe mentioned. "I work with someone in Newark that thinks out of the box, like you do."

"I'll tell you something else that is odd," Stephen admitted. "A few days ago, a weird fellow came to the park asking me questions about long range camera lens. What did he say his name was Will?"

"I believe he said his name was Tagert," Will replied. "I remember we talked about not trusting why he needed a lens of that magnitude."

"He was the type of person, you didn't want to meet on a dark street," Skip confided.

"There was something else about him," Stephen admitted. "He was very adamant about me not taking his picture," he said, glancing at Joe. "I know who you are now! You're the lead singer for Light

Crimson. You're supposed to be in California."

"Guilty," Joe smiled, putting his arm around Kathe. "As you can see, I'd rather be in Daytona with an Alby Airlines flight attendant."

"The friend from Newark I told you about works for Alby Airlines," Stephen declared.

"If your friends name is Dr. David Sydney," Kathe smiled, "I work with him. He's a genius in technology."

"I guess the old saying that you can't judge a book by its cover is right," Stephen declared. "Sydney is a good friend of mine. I don't know exactly what he does for a living, but I do know he works with high technology, and security for the airlines. If you work with him, you must be more than a flight attendant."

"You are very observant," Kathe smiled, squeezing Joe's hand. "Looks can be deceiving."

"We better get going," Joe added, glancing at his watch. "We're going to miss our dinner reservations. It was nice to meet you. I look forward to the publication of your documentary. Thanks for taking the time to talk with us."

"Anytime," Stephen smiled as they walked away. He shot several pictures of them getting into her Corvette with the eagles flying above them. "Skip these pictures are just for me," Stephen explained. "I know Sydney wouldn't want a picture of one of his agents on the cover of a magazine."

"You're right about that," Will agreed as she drove off. "Sydney is very reserved when he talks about his work. It has to be highly classified."

"I understand," Skip replied. "I'll put them in a special file, labeled Stephen only."

"Now, all we have to do is back track to the restaurant," Kathe said as she turned right on Ridgewood Avenue. "Stephen is a very interesting man."

"His work is amazing," Joe said as Kathe pulled into Panama Jim's parking lot. "I noticed you gave me the high sign to leave when he talked about your work."

"He is a very observant man," Kathe replied as she parked the car. "His camera is not the only eye he has for detail."

"It is odd that Stephen would know Dr. Sydney," Joe replied. "I watched him in Ramsey's office that morning with the bathroom incident. He methodically thought out every instruction you and Yorg were given. He knew the man was on drugs and how to control him," he said as he got out of the car.

"He is a genius," Kathe said as Joe held the 'vette door open for her. "What a day this has been? I met a famous filmmaker and I'm having dinner with a famous rock star," Kathe said, getting out of the Corvette.

"Your home is so inspiring," Joe confided as they walked to the front door of the restaurant. "Or maybe you're so inspiring; while you were upstairs, I jotted down the lyrics of a song."

"What's the song about?" Kathe asked as they walked up to the young hostess.

"May I help you?" the hostess asked, starring at Joe.

"Table for two," Kathe replied. "If possible, we'd like to sit outside on one of the gliders. Oh, by the way," turning her attention back to Joe. "If Jordan is in town, he'll probably be here tonight. This is his favorite restaurant too."

As the hostess walked away checking on a table for them, Joe leaned over and whispered, "the title is 'Pieces of Love'. It's a song about our lives together."

"Is it about both of our lives or both of our professions?" Kathe smiled. "I'd like to see it when we get back home tonight?"

"I usually don't like my work to be seen before it is done," Joe replied as the hostess came back. "But I might make an exception for you."

"I found a glider table," the hostess said as they followed her through the restaurant out to the back deck.

"Wow, you never cease to amaze me," Joe grinned. "These tables are gliders."

"Do you want one for two or are you expecting friends?" The hostess asked, hardly containing herself.

"Just for two, thank you," Joe replied.

"Shennelle will be your server tonight," the hostess stated. "She'll be right with you," she said, quickly turning around, reaching for her cell phone.

As they ordered drinks, the sunset began to reflect brilliant colors on the buildings across the river. "It appears that the lights twinkle like the stars on the various condominiums as well as on the bridge," Kathe noted.

"As do the lights shimmering on your blonde hair and jewelry," Joe smiled, reaching for her hand. "It's nights like this, I wish we were on a houseboat. The waves gently rocking the boat are so soothing."

"I think it would be very romantic going from marina to marina," Kathe agreed. "There's a place that rents houseboats somewhere here in town. I know Jordan and Patti have done that before. Someday when we have more time, we can do that."

Watching from the outside bar, an off-duty Alby pilot, Capt. Garth McCollum was ordering another drink, "Well, I'll be! What a small world this is after all!"

"What are you talking about?" His friend, Capt. Tom Bernard asked.

"I didn't know she came here," Garth said, starring at her. "This is quite a distance from Newark," he smiled, taking a sip of his drink. "Tom isn't that Kathe Tierney?"

"Where is she?" Tom asked, searching for her.

"On the second glider from the end on the right," Garth said, pointing to her.

"Oh, my, God!" Tom confirmed. "Yes, it is and look at what she's wearing!"

"Look who she's with!" Garth sneered. "She won't date pilots. Apparently, she prefers men with long hair and an earring," he protested, watching Joe led Kathe to the dance floor.

Joe held Kathe's hand as they walked up to the lead singer, while the band was taking their break. He whispered something to the lead singer. The singer handed Joe his microphone and battery pack and instructed the band members. The lead guitarist started the song. As they began to dance, Joe sang the love song that Kathe liked on TMV the night before.

Cameras and cell phones began to flash as people on the deck recognized the famous singer, while the two were lost in each other. When the song ended, Joe dipped Kathe and kissed her. As the applause began Kathe looked around and cautioned, "I think we better leave."

"I think you're right," Joe smiled, waving to the crowd. "Thanks for the song," Joe told the lead singer handing him the microphone and backpack. The crowd continued to applaud Joe, as he and Kathe hurried back into the restaurant toward the front door.

Jordan, Patti, her brother, Peter, and his wife, Helen, were at the hostess booth waiting to be seated. Jordan spotted Kathe and Joe, hand in hand, as they entered the main dining room. He saw Garth following closely behind them. "Kathe, look out!" Jordan warned noting that Garth had too much to drink.

"Well, if it isn't Alby's most beautiful flight attendant, right here in Daytona!" Garth said, grabbing her shoulder.

"Garth, grow up!" Kathe ordered. "Let go of me!" she demanded, breaking out of his hold, and stepping back.

"I know why you don't date pilots," Garth insisted, pointing at Joe. "You're turned on by guys like that!"

"Garth, leave her alone!" Tom begged, catching up to them and pulling Garth back. "You've had too much to drink," Tom declared as cameras started flashing.

"Where's your big Russian now?" Garth questioned. "I wonder what he would think of this guy!" he exclaimed, pulling away from Tom. He grabbed Kathe by her wrist.

Twisting out of his hold, Kathe warned, "Capt. McCollum, public intoxication is against company policy. I think you need to leave with Capt. Bernard."

Jordan hurried over to help as the press entered the restaurant. "Garth, she's right, you've had too much drink," Jordan warned. "The press just arrived. You don't want any trouble. I know Ramsey's already had several complaints against you from other flight attendants. She'll fire you for this behavior."

"I don't care," Garth snapped. "I'm off duty for a few days and not in uniform," he said, shoving Jordan aside, and lunging for Kathe.

"What's your problem?" Joe yelled hitting Garth in the nose.

"What the . . ." Garth yelled, falling against the wall.

"The lady asked you to leave her alone!" Joe stated as Garth came at Joe swinging.

Kathe blocked Garth's punch knocking him to the ground. "Capt. Garth McCollum you're on report!" Kathe snapped as Tom and Jordan subdued Garth while police officers entered the restaurant.

"I hear you're in a tiff with our self-proclaimed playboy pilot," Ramsey stated as Kathe answered JAKE.

"He's drunk," Kathe reported. "He is here with Tom Bernard."

"Just what Alby needed," Ramsey gritted her teeth. "You're with someone I don't want you to be with and one of our pilots just got the cops and press involved."

"The press is here," Kathe admitted, glancing around the room.

"Let me speak to one of the officers," Ramsey sighed.

"Officer, my boss from Alby Airlines would like a word with you," Kathe said as she showed him her ID and handed JAKE to him.

Garth was holding his nose, wiping the trickle of blood with his handkerchief. "He broke my nose!" Garth yelled to the officer. "That's assault," he smirked and turned toward Tom.

"Garth McCollum," the officer stated as he handed JAKE back to Kathe. "I am placing you under arrest for interfering with the protective custody of an Alby passenger by Alby Security Agent, Kathe Tierney."

"He broke my nose!" Garth loudly protested. "That's assault with battery!"

"It seems like you're the one doing the assaulting," the officer stated as he looked at Joe. "Linda Ramsey would like to know, if you would like to press charges against Capt. McCollum?"

"Absolutely!" Joe agreed as two officers removed Garth from the restaurant.

Jordan introduced himself to Joe, "I haven't met you yet. I'm a close friend of Kathe's, Jordan Mills."

"Kathe told me about you today," Joe said as they shook hands. "She wanted us to meet you here for dinner."

"Not like this," Kathe answered, noticing who was standing next to Patti. "It seems that you have some special company visiting you," she said, looking around at the reporters. "And I need to get Joe out of here. We'll catch up with you later."

"Later," Jordan said, giving her a kiss on the cheek.

"Thanks for helping us," Kathe smiled. "Call me later," she said as the press immediately shoved a microphone in Joe's face.

"Mr. Sherrod, why did you leave California without the band?" Reporter Cindi Lane asked. "What about your contracts with TMV?"

"No Comment!" Joe replied.

"Mr. Sherrod, rumor has it you're getting back with your ex-wife, who's this woman?" Cindi Lane asked, glancing at Kathe.

"No Comment!" Joe said, reaching for Kathe's hand while Peter glared at them. Police officers held the crowd back as Joe led Kathe out of the restaurant. They hurried to the Corvette. Peter pulled away from Helen and hurried outside, just in time to watch them drive away.

Minutes later, as they pulled into the driveway JAKE rang. "Well, it's been an interesting couple of weeks!" Ramsey exclaimed. "Is Joe, okay?"

"Yes, he's alright," Kathe said as she pressed the button to open the gate.

"Are you okay?" Ramsey asked.

"Yes," Kathe answered, looking down at her bare wrist. "Except, I must have lost my bracelet when Garth grabbed my wrist."

"How's your wrist?" Ramsey quizzed. "Do you have any bruises?"

"No, no bruises; just lost my bracelet," Kathe sighed as she opened the garage door. "I guess it was worth losing to see Garth's nose broken and him being hauled off to jail in handcuffs."

"Put Joe on the phone," Ramsey requested. "I need to make sure he's not further agitated because of another problem with the airlines."

"Mr. Sherrod, I'm recording this conversation," Ramsey cautioned. "Since you are in protective custody of Alby Airlines, I need to make sure you are not injured."

"I'm fine," Joe agreed as he got out of the car.

"Security Agent Kathe Tierney states you are not injured," Ramsey stated. "Is that true?"

"I'm not injured," Joe concurred.

"Am I correct in stating that you are going to press charges against Capt. Garth McCollum for hitting you?" Ramsey questioned.

"Yes," Joe concurred. "I've already told the police I will press charges against Capt. McCollum."

"Since you are in Alby's protective custody, you do not have to make a court appearance," Ramsey explained. "The lawyers for Alby will handle everything for you. I appreciate you keeping this out of the press as much as possible."

"You don't have to worry about that," Joe confirmed. "I'm not supposed to be here."

"What Tierney is keeping from you, is that your ex-wife was trying to go to Daytona," Ramsey reported. "Ms. Carrington is currently being held at Atlanta's airport, due to no openings on any of the airlines into Daytona, Orlando, or Jacksonville. I arranged that for you. Payton and the others are leaving for the airport in a couple of hours. However, I have no grounds to keep holding her in Atlanta. I need a trump card to send her back to London. Do you have something on her?"

"Yes, I do," Joe confided. "Tell her if she doesn't leave for London, I am calling her parents and mine. How soon can you get her in the air?"

"The next flight leaves in thirty minutes," Ramsey said, typing on her computer. "I'm reserving a seat as we speak. I'll get right back to you as soon as she is airborne," Ramsey said and cleared the line.

"Why didn't you tell me Cara was on her way to Daytona?" Joe.

"I didn't want to upset you," Kathe smiled. "I had Ramsey working on it. If anyone can turn Cara around, she can."

Chapter 26

Kathe's Past Discovered

Yorg was still not convinced that Saíde was dead. Even with dental records, something didn't add up, "Level with me Lt. Jaco. Do you really think the body they found was Rhasheéd Saíde?"

"It's funny you called," Lt. Jaco admitted, checking his computer. "I just received a missing person report on a male about the same build as Saíde. Two things still bother me. One, it's no secret that there has always been bad blood between the two LaBasco brothers. Why would Nicki go to his brother's house? I've been checking since the attempted hit on Nicki the other day with Kathe Tierney. Word on the street is that the Falcini's are trying to muscle in on Nicki's territory. Secondly, how could Saíde, who was seen at the first attempt on Nicki's life, get through the security of Mario's own home a few days later?"

"That's exactly what I was wondering," Yorg concurred as he walked over to the window and peered outside. "I've already called Kathe and warned her. It's also funny that the body was charred beyond recognition. I've been doing some checking myself. I talked with some of the businesspeople in the area. There was no high-speed chase that morning. The storeowner across the street said, suddenly, I heard a car crash and saw the flames."

"I'm going back there and do some more checking," Lt. Jaco concluded. "The dental records came out of nowhere very quick. I have been trying to catch Saíde for some time. I could never find an address for him, much less his dentist. Do you want to meet me there?"

"Yes, I have a phone call to make first," Yorg agreed as he checked the time. "I can be at the scene in twenty minutes," Yorg said, cleared the line to call his sister.

Walking in the house Joe was pleased, "Well, today had a strange twist. I never would have thought your boss would thank me for anything concerning you."

"I have to admit Ramsey surprised me too," Kathe admitted. "Just when I think I know her, she throws me this curve."

"I don't know about you," Joe said, putting his arms around her waist, "but I'm starved. We didn't eat and I know we didn't pay for the drinks."

"I'll call Panama Jim's and pay over the phone," Kathe offered. "They are probably still busy with the police. Chicken on the barbie or do you think you're ready for my cooking?"

"I think we better go for the barbie," Joe smiled. "I know how to do that, especially since you can't remember the last time you cooked."

"I don't blame you," Kathe laughed. "I don't think I would trust my cooking either. Overall, it was a perfect evening. We met filmmaker, Stephen Brown, and his crew on location for his new documentary for the Audubon Society. I can't believe how wonderful I felt when you sang to me. And we did get rid of Garth. You still don't have a clue, who the couple was with Jordan, do you?"

"You mean the man with the heavy-set woman?" Joe questioned.

"That was my ex-husband Peter," Kathe giggled, "and his beautiful new wife, Helen. Wait a minute; I wonder why they're in Florida? Peter is supposed to be taking care of his father, who just got out of the hospital. Oh, well, I guess I'll call Jeannie tomorrow," she said as JAKE rang.

"I need to talk with Joe!" Ramsey exclaimed.

"It's Ramsey," Kathe said, handing him the phone.

"Let me talk to Cara," Joe's mood changed to anger as he walked away from Kathe. "Can you connect us?" He waited for a moment, "I'm not bluffing! I've had enough of you to last me a lifetime! I'm calling both of our parents and telling them why we divorced, if you're not on that flight back to London." He paused for a moment, "It almost killed them when we broke up, especially when we didn't give them a reason. I sheltered that pain all these months by myself. I won't take this from you again. Get on that flight! Ramsey, can you hear me?"

"I'm listening," Ramsey answered.

"Ramsey call me with her verdict." Then Joe repeated some telephone numbers and hung up. "I think we both have had a day of exes," Joe said, walking over to Kathe. "Now, where were we?" He pulled her back into his arms.

"We were enjoying a perfect evening, just the two of us," Kathe kissed him.

"I have an idea," Joe offered, kissing her. "You call Panama Jim's. I'm curious as to what happened after we left, and I'll get the grill started," he said, kissing her again.

"Sounds like a well-planned evening," Kathe smiled, playfully touching his nose.

While Kathe called Panama Jim's, Joe set the mood by turning off a few house lights. He turned on the grill and lit some candles outside on the table, and then turned on some music.

"The manager, Robin at Panama Jim's just thanked us for the publicity," Kathe laughed as she set a tray on the table and handing Joe a drink. "She said the restaurant is packed with people talking about you being there and singing a song on the deck. She said our drinks are on the house. It was her hostess, who recognized you and called the reporters. Next time, she promises that her employees will be discrete about our privacy. She also apologized for the rudeness of her customer and hoped we would come back. Oh, by the way, she called me your wife!"

Taking Kathe in his arms, Joe whispered softly in her ear as they began to slow dance, "That's the second time today you've been mistaken for my wife," he admitted as JAKE rang.

"It's Jordan, I better take it," Kathe said, stepping back.

"Kathe sorry to call you so late, but I have your bracelet," Jordan announced. "The manager found it tonight after the police left. I'm pulling into your driveway."

"Jordan's in the driveway with my bracelet," Kathe grinned. "Let's go get it."

"Jordan," Helen snarled, "This can't be Kathe's house. Look at the size of this place. She's only a cheap, flight attendant."

"Of course, this is her house," Jordan smiled, glancing in his rear-view mirror. "You should see the inside."

Jordan got out of the car as Kathe and Joe came out to greet him. Patti hurried out of the car wanting to meet Joe. Peter reached for the door handle. Helen grabbed his arm, fuming in the backseat, "Where are you going?"

"I was getting out to talk to them," Peter answered.

"No! You are not!" Helen refuted. "You don't have anything to say to her!"

"Joe, I'd like to introduce my wife, Patti," Jordan said, shaking Joe's hand. "I can't believe Garth behaved so badly tonight. Sometimes when he's got several days off, he tends to drink too much. He has a reputation of thinking, he's God's gift to women."

"Glad to meet you Patti," Joe said, shaking her hand.

"Don't worry about Garth," Kathe added. "Ramsey's going to fire him."

"Here's your bracelet," Jordan smiled as he handed it to her.

"Thanks, I'm glad you brought it," Kathe beamed and handed it to Joe to put it on her wrist. "I'd invite you in for a drink, but I see you have my two, least, favorite people in your car."

"Don't worry, we don't want to intrude on your evening," Patti answered, pulling Jordan by the arm.

"I don't blame you," Jordan acknowledged. "Helen's getting nastier every time we see them. It's a wonder she lets Peter out of her sight."

"She has put on a few pounds, serves him right," Kathe smiled, glancing at the car.

"Yeah," Jordan laughed. "Peter's eyes almost popped out of his head when he saw you tonight in that outfit."

"We'll have you over when your company leaves," Kathe waved.

Walking back to the patio JAKE rang again. Glancing at it, "It's Ramsey," Kathe said, handing Joe the phone.

"I want you to know it took some doing," Ramsey admitted. "But Ms. Carrington finally is on a plane to Newark. I'll have security pick her up and escort her to the London flight. I must admit, the only reason she changed her mind was the telephone numbers you repeated. Just to let you know, Payton and the others will be there in the morning about 9:00."

"Thanks, Ramsey, I owe you," Joe admitted and cleared the line. He glanced over at Kathe, "Ramsey called you tonight during the fight, didn't she?" Joe asked as he handed JAKE back to her. "It was as if she knew you were in trouble," Joe said as they walked to the patio.

"You're right," Kathe admitted. "She did know. We better change the subject."

"Why did you and Peter break up?" Joe asked as he put the chicken on the barbie.

"I guess that's a fair question, since you confided in me," Kathe answered as she filled him in on the gory details.

"I wondered what happened to your marriage," Joe said as he took a sip of his drink. "How did you feel on your first flight?" He asked now that she was finally talking about herself.

"Horror!" Kathe grinned as they sat down to eat.

"That's exactly how I felt on my first gig," Joe laughed.

"How do you like your job?" Kathe asked and took a sip of her drink.

"It's harder than most people think," he said, sitting back in his chair. "There is no such thing as instant success. We've had our share of hard knocks," Joe said as they cleared the table and went inside the house. "But in the end, it was worth it. The money, the travel," he looked at her, "and the people you meet makes it fun."

"Why you turn off the things outside," Kathe suggested. "I'll do the dishes, and then we'll listen to some music."

"Deal," Joe approved and left the room.

After they both finished, they sat down on the couch. Joe turned on TMV and they watched a few videos. His arms were around Kathe now and her head was leaning on his shoulder. "This feels so good," she smiled up at him. "Finish your story about your job," Kathe insisted, kissing his cheek.

"There are no words," Joe continued, "that can explain how great it feels to be on stage with thousands of people cheering for you. It's the greatest feeling in the world. However, as with all things, it's not without problems. With Troy's accident and Paul's death, we all paid the price. I guess after everything we'd been through, when I realized, what Cara had done to me, I couldn't stand the unfaithfulness and lies."

"I know what you mean," Kathe agreed. "One lesson I've learned in this life, is there's more than one way to die," she said as he looked into her eyes. He kissed her with such tenderness. He stood up and pulled her up to him.

"It's time you started sleeping in a bed again," Joe declared as he picked her up and carried her up the stairs. The full moon shining on the glass ceiling made the bed gently glow. As Joe laid her on the satin bedspread, he lay down beside her as they gazed at the moon and stars. She still had not said a word. Her emotions were churning throughout her body. Joe felt such peacefulness as the moon glowed over them. "Kathe please don't say," he stopped in the middle of his sentence. He leaned over slowly pulling her zipper down, kissing her as he undressed her.

"I am," Kathe started to say as Joe put his finger to her lips.

"It's okay," Joe whispered and kissed her. Before she knew it, she was unbuttoning his shirt as he continued to kiss her. He gently rolled her over on top of him. She fell into his eyes as she bent down kissing him. He gently rolled over on top of her . . .

The warm morning sun woke Kathe up. She was still in Joe's arms as she had been all night. For the first time, in a long time, she slept in her bed without remembering Peter's betrayal. How great that felt. Suddenly, without warning her implant shocked her. She looked around the room for JAKE. Then, she remembered she must have left JAKE downstairs by the couch. She jumped up, hurried downstairs as Joe woke up. "Thank you, Ramsey, we'll be there," Kathe said as Joe joined her at the bottom of the stairs. He put his arms around her waist and kissed her.

"I forgot how wonderful it felt to be glad it's morning," Joe kissed her repeatedly around her neck.

She gently pulled away from him, "Don't you want to know who was on the phone?"

Teasingly, kissing, and nudging her shoulders, "Tell them we gave at the office," Joe insisted.

"It was Ramsey reminding us of your friends landing in Daytona in thirty minutes," Kathe warned.

"I forgot all about them!" Joe exclaimed as they rushed upstairs.

They made it to the airport as the plane was docking. They saw Payton and the others coming inside the terminal from the jetway. Joe held his breath for a minute. He hoped Suzanne and Shaunda had gone back to London with Cara. His face reflected his feelings.

"What's wrong?" Kathe asked as she noted the concern look on his face.

"Travis' girlfriend, Shaunda is with him," Joe stated. "She's Cara's best friend."

"It doesn't matter to me," Kathe said, watching them.

"I just don't want her talking to Cara about us," Joe shared, hugging her. "One thing in my life that I have learned, is not to trust either of them."

Babs ran over to them and gave them hugs. "I'm so glad to see you together again! You look great!"

"Thanks, Babs," Kathe smiled. "It's good to see you again."

"Well, if it isn't Mr. MIA," Payton stated as he joined them. "Kathe, I'm glad Ramsey said you were here. It took a lot of worry off me."

"Thanks, welcome to Florida," Kathe replied. "Ramsey has a limo waiting to take you to my house. Let's get the guys out of here before they're recognized."

The limo driver handled the luggage while they got into the car. "Follow me," Joe said, reaching for Kathe's car keys, "I'm driving the red Corvette over there."

"Whose car?" Collin asked.

"Kathe's," Joe answered. "Wait until Babs sees her house. Troy may have to take on another job."

They followed the ZR1 over the bridge. The tide was high as they turned on A1A south toward the house. "We couldn't ask for a better beach day," Joe said as he shifted the last gear and took Kathe's hand. He lifted it to his lips, "Kathe."

"Yes," Kathe looked at him.

"Nothing," Joe didn't finish the sentence as he stopped at the gate. "I bet Payton is getting one of his migraines from assessing the price of your car and property," Joe chuckled as he parked in the garage. "I hope you have lots of Tylenol. He's going to need it after he sees the inside."

"I'll open the front door for them," Kathe said as she hurried inside. "Welcome to my home," Kathe said, opening the front door. They entered the house and Joe started laughing when he saw the look on Payton's face.

"You look like you have egg on your face Payton," Joe chuckled. "What's the matter?"

"I guess I owe Kathe an apology," Payton admitted, gazing up at the chandelier.

"I believe you do," Joe smiled.

"I was only looking out for you," Payton declared. "I guess she's not a gold digger after all."

"Would everyone like to come into the family room," Kathe said as they followed her. "I want you to make yourselves at home," she said as she explained the layout of the house.

It didn't take long for everyone to settle in. Brock and RJ were glad they were staying at a private secluded house. Payton couldn't stand it anymore. He found Kathe and Joe outside sitting on the steps of the pool talking with Troy and Babs about the house.

"I think you should let us sleep in the master bedroom tonight, don't you?" Troy asked. "I bet we can stargaze from there."

"You're right, the view at night is beautiful," Joe said as he got in the pool. "And after the neighbors turn off their lights, the stars are amazing."

Payton joined the conversation, "Speaking of this house Kathe, how can you afford a house like this?"

"Gee, I don't know Payton," Kathe smiled. "I didn't pay for it."

"I knew it," Payton beamed. "Your boyfriend or somebody pays for it," he said, looking straight at her.

"No mortgage, it's paid for," Kathe winked. "No man owns me. I'm not a kept woman."

"I didn't mean it like that," Payton apologized.

"Yes, you did," Kathe grinned. "But I don't blame you for thinking that; after all, I'm just a cheap flight attendant." She laughed and looked over at Joe in the deep end of the pool.

"That was before I found out your job description," Payton disclosed as Travis came out of the house and dove into the pool beside Joe.

"This sure beats the snow and ice in Europe," Travis declared, glancing at Kathe. "Thanks for having us."

Collin and Steve joined them in the pool. "Right Kathe," Steve admitted. "It feels good to be able to move around freely. I'm already getting tired of hotels and security. I'm Steve Day. I'm sorry I didn't get to meet you when the others did."

Joe swam over to them, "Finder's keepers' mate."

"I thought you weren't interested in a relationship ever again," Steve reminded his friend.

"It's good to see the smile back on Joe's face," Babs said to Collin as he sat down beside her.

"She's definitely the one," Collin agreed, checking around to make sure Shaunda and Suzanne were not listening. "Cara sure didn't do it! I've never seen Joe so upset as I did the other night in LA."

"Me either," Travis affirmed. "I almost wish Shaunda, and Suzanne had left when Cara did. I've already talked with Shaunda about not mentioning Cara to Joe anymore."

"I did the same thing with Suzanne," Collin agreed. "I don't like seeing Joe hurt like that. Did Shaunda ever tell you why Joe and Cara broke up?"

"All Shaunda said was that Joe was being immature about something Cara did," Travis said, looking around for them. "Where are Shaunda and Suzanne?"

"I don't know," Collin said. "I'll go see what's keeping them."

Collin found them coming out of the master bedroom, "Are you ready to join us?"

"Yes," Suzanne smiled, hurrying down the steps.

"We were just looking around," Shaunda said as she grabbed a beer off the table and hurried over to Travis.

"There you are," Travis said as she kissed him.

"I was just looking at the house with Suzanne," Shaunda stated, glancing at Kathe. "Your home is beautiful."

"Thank you," Kathe said, handing Joe a towel as JAKE began to ring.

"Kathe, have you seen this morning's paper?" Jordan asked.

"No, why?" Kathe urged.

"You and Joe made the front page," Jordan informed her.

"Please tell me you're kidding," Kathe sighed as Jordan read some of it to her. "No way! The officer promised Ramsey he would keep it out of the paper! Thanks for letting me know. I'll go out and get a paper. I know Ramsey will kill me for this. I'll see you in Paris in a week. Okay, bye."

"How is Jordan?" Joe asked.

"He's fine," Kathe smiled. "He wanted to know how we were after the publicity we got in this morning's paper."

"What publicity?" Payton asked and sat up in his chair.

"Some reporters took pictures of Joe at the restaurant last night as he punched Garth McCollum in the nose," Kathe informed him. "The paper says, Joe broke Garth's nose and gave him a black eye. The officer in charge promised Ramsey he'd keep it out of the papers."

Payton stood up, "What are you talking about?"

Joe moved his chair closer to Kathe and put his arm around her. "Well, last night we went out to eat and a pilot that also works for Alby tried to bother Kathe, as we were leaving. He was drunk, loud, and obnoxious. He kept grabbing at her even when his friend, and Kathe's brother-in-law tried to stop him. So,

I grabbed him and broke his nose."

"Who is he?" Babs asked.

"He's a pilot for Alby," Kathe explained. "He has the reputation of being a ladies' man. He asked me out to dinner a couple of times. I told him that I do not date pilots, especially married ones. Then, he saw me with Joe, and having a few too many drinks, he wouldn't leave us alone. He grabbed me by the wrist, and Joe ended up hitting him in the nose. The police showed up."

"I need to see that article!" Payton exclaimed. "What's the name of the paper?"

"The News Journal of Daytona," Kathe stated.

"I'll pull it up online!" Payton exclaimed, hurrying off.

"You made the headlines!" Payton exclaimed as he hurried back to them with a printed copy of the article.

"Well at least, it's a good picture of us," Joe laughed as Payton ignored him.

Payton sat down and read the article to them. "This by the grace of God, can be turned into great publicity for Light Crimson, not to mention solving our problems with TMV. British chivalry is not dead. British rock star decks would-be attacker of an American flight attendant. I like the sound of that, don't you?" He immediately got busy making phone calls.

Joe kissed Kathe, "I believe we made his day. I know you've made mine."

Shaunda cleared her throat rudely trying to interrupt them. She glared at her best friend's ex. She stood there waiting for them to stop. Joe glanced over at her, "Do you need something?"

"No, she doesn't," Travis snapped, glaring at Shaunda. "Do you remember what we talked about?"

"I remember," Shaunda groaned and went back in the house.

"What's her problem?" Kathe asked. "You divorced Cara almost two years ago."

"I don't know, but don't let her get to you," Joe cautioned.

"I won't," Kathe said and gave him a peck on the cheek.

A few hours later, Brock was busy putting steaks on the grill. Joe came outside with a piece of paper and handed it to Travis. "I wrote this song yesterday. What do you think?"

Travis looked it over, "I like it! It needs to have a scorching melody!" He handed the paper to Steve.

"Travis is right," Steve agreed. "It looks like something Metallica would sing."

Collin looked at the lyrics, "I'm surprised at you mate. I thought you'd be writing more of a tender love song."

Kathe came out with the condiments from the kitchen. She was setting the table for them when JAKE rang. "Hello, Kathe," Tierra said as Kathe walked toward the beach for privacy. "I missed you at Nicki's funeral. I'm sorry Alonzo had to change the time for security reasons. I forgot to let you know. I wasn't thinking clearly. I don't know what I am going to do without my Nicki. He always called me several times a day."

"I understand," Kathe consoled. "When I found out about the time change, I tried to make it. But I couldn't get there in time, so I went back to work," she said as she heard CC in the background.

"Tell her!" CC insisted.

"What is CC saying?" Kathe asked. "Tell me, what?"

"Since Nicki's death," Tierra tearfully sighed, "CC and I both are worried about being here. The way Nicki died at Mario's house worries me that I'll be next. When we got here, the tension was so strong between Alonzo and Mario, you could feel it in the air. We overheard them having heated discussions on the phone several times. One was about how the killer got into Mario's house with his security. And why did Giorgio pull Dider away from Nicki to show him the extra security measures they put into place. The last one was concerning them finding the murderer so quickly, and the way he died."

"Did you talk with your father about it?" Kathe asked.

"No, he's not well and had to be taken to the hospital," Tierra stated. "Pauli is in charge while Alonzo is at the hospital with Papa. Mario insisted that he should stay here, but Alonzo refused to let him come near the house while he is away."

"Then, report this to Ramsey," Kathe suggested. "She can bring you back to work."

"No," Tierra whined. "If I tell her, she will call us into control and keep us there. I can't stand being caged up anymore. I just want to get my life back as normal as I can."

"Give me the phone," CC insisted, reaching for it. "Kathe, it's CC. I agree with Tierra; we're not safe here. I don't trust Mario. He didn't shed a tear at Nicki's funeral. Mario seemed devious, whenever he was around his father and Alonzo when we first arrived. He and Giorgio seem to whisper quite a bit to each other."

"I'm beginning to believe Yorg is right," Kathe confided, sitting down on the seawall steps. "He doesn't think Saíde is dead. Pauli is Alonzo's right-hand man. He will take good care of you. Stay inside the safety of the house until I can talk with Yorg and Ramsey. I suspect Mario is mixed up in something that their father would not approve. I'll get back to you as soon as I can."

"Okay, we'll stay inside until I hear from you," CC confirmed.

"Hang in there, I'll call Ramsey," Kathe cleared the line.

"Dinner is ready," Joe called from the top of the stairs. "Are you still on the phone?"

"I just got off, but I do need to make one more call," Kathe smiled.

"Anyone I know?" Joe inquired.

"I need to call Ramsey concerning Tierra and CC," Kathe said as JAKE rang again. She looked at Joe, "I'm sorry," she said as she answered her call. "Hello, I can barely hear you from the static on the line. Who is this please?"

"This is Ivan Tulski," he said, stopping in the woods to catch his breath.

"Ivan is that you?" Kathe questioned, trying to move JAKE away from the wind.

"I must talk to Yorg," Ivan insisted, hiding behind some bushes. "He isn't answering his phone. You must tell him; I believe that we are all in danger!"

"Ivan, I can't understand you," Kathe whined. "What did you say?"

"I have to go now," Ivan declared as he heard leaves crackling behind him. "You must tell Yorg that we are all...", the line went dead.

"I see you're still on the phone," Joe stated as he joined her on the steps. "Dinner is getting cold."

"I'm sorry," Kathe apologized. "That was an old friend of Yorg's. He sounded desperate to talk to Yorg. There was so much static on the line, not to mention this wind, I couldn't understand him. Then, it sounded like he was running, and said he was in danger."

"Danger, why?" Joe asked.

"I don't know," Kathe replied, standing up. "I need to go in the house and make two phone calls, and then I will join you for dinner. Don't make the others wait."

Inside her living room, away from her guests Kathe tried to call Yorg, but his phone went straight to voicemail. She called control. Keith was on duty. "I just received a call from Tierra and CC. They don't feel safe around her brother. See what you can do to call them back to work early and alert Ramsey."

"They are at her father's house," Keith said. "They should feel safe there."

Kathe noticed in the mirror that Shaunda was trying to eavesdrop from the family room. "Just have Ramsey call CC immediately. I've got to go," she said, cleared the line and hurried around the fireplace. "Can I help you?"

"No," Shaunda stammered and walked to the staircase. "I . . . I'm just going upstairs to lie down. I have a headache."

"I hope you'll feel better in the morning," Kathe said and headed for the patio.

"I made you a plate," Joe smiled when Kathe sat down next to him. "Everyone's almost finished eating."

"I'm sorry that my phone calls took so long," Kathe apologized, placing her napkin in her lap.

"Is everything alright?" Joe asked.

"Yes, I have one of those jobs that I'm on call 24/7," Kathe admitted, reaching for the steak sauce.

"About your job," Payton started to say.

"Excuse me," Kathe interrupted him. "I'm off duty now and I would like to enjoy my steak. Let's talk about something else."

After dinner, all the women except for Shaunda finished the dishes while the men sat down in the family room and watched TMV.

"I'll be right back," Joe got up, thinking he heard a thud from the room above them. He heard it again as he walked up the steps. He noticed the master bedroom door was closed and the light was on. He listened at the door for a moment and heard someone inside. He slowly opened the door and surprised Shaunda. "I didn't realize you couldn't be trusted around other people's property!" Joe exclaimed as Shaunda tried to push a box under the dresser.

"Why Joe, I don't know what you mean," Shaunda whined, leaning against the dresser, still trying to push a box under the dresser with her foot.

"It's pretty clear that you have been snooping through Kathe's dresser drawers," Joe snapped.

"I was just curious as to what you see in that phony American," Shaunda stated. "You could be with Cara Carrington, the hottest model in London. You're like a little schoolboy making a fool of yourself over a flight attendant."

"Get out of this room!" Joe demanded, pointing to the door. "I don't have to justify my relationship with Kathe to you!"

"Cara really loves you," Shaunda confided. "She hasn't been the same since you split. She wants you back and she's not going to take no for an answer. You two belong together. I don't know why you are so upset with her. The reason stinks," she sneered at him.

"I don't want to upset Travis," Joe explained. "I don't really know what he sees in you; you are just as deceitful as Cara. However, you are his girlfriend. I don't want to make him uncomfortable. Now get out of here and stay out of this room!" he shouted as Travis walked up the hallway.

"What's going on?" Travis asked.

"I'm sorry, Travis," Joe explained. "I caught Shaunda going through Kathe's dresser."

"I told you to leave Kathe alone!" Travis snapped. "What's wrong with you?"

"It is your funeral!" Shaunda chuckled, motioning slitting his throat as she turned to Travis. "Joe and Cara belong together! They were getting back together until this stupid flight attendant got her nails into him!"

"That's not true!" Joe exclaimed. "I haven't talked to Cara since the divorce, until she showed up with you at the concert. I don't ever want to see or talk to her again! It has nothing to do with Kathe!" Joe shouted as she reached for Travis' arm.

Travis shoved Shaunda's hands away, "I think it's time Brock and RJ take you to the airport. Get your things ready. I'll have Payton call the airport and book you a flight back to London," he demanded, pulling her down the hallway.

Joe was furious. Shaunda was just like Cara, deceitful and malicious. He was halfway out the door when something caught his eye sticking out from under the dresser. He walked over, bent down, and picked up a piece of paper. It was a newspaper clipping of the flight attendant that was shot by a terrorist. He started to put the paper on the dresser when he saw Kathe's name in the article. He couldn't believe it was from a London newspaper, around the time of Troy's car accident. As Joe read the article a lump rose in his throat. An Alby flight attendant was shot at close range trying to save a 2-month-old baby. The terrorist threw her out of the plane onto the runway after it landed. Joe's mind raced to the time. He remembered donating blood at the hospital while visiting Troy one night. He had rare AB-blood, the same type as the flight attendant. He closed his eyes and sat down on the bed. He remembered talking with Collin in the hallway by the emergency room as the ambulance crew raced past them. He could still see the blood-soaked body on the gurney as they ran past him. "My God," he thought, "that was Kathe!"

He finished the article and bent under the dresser to see if there was anything else. There he found a box and pulled it out. Inside was a scrapbook filled with articles of the terrorist attack on the Alby Jet. As he sat the box down on the floor, he saw something shiny. He reached under some papers to the bottom of the box. He pulled out a clear crystal Rosary. He held it in his hand as he looked through the book. He saw pictures of Kathe lying on the ground. One picture was of her lifeless body dangled out of the airliner by the shooter. As he read on, he saw a picture of Carrie Anne, splattered with Kathe's blood holding the baby. The next picture was of Yorg also splattered with blood. The last picture was of Kathe on the ground with the dead terrorist next to her. The article told how Yorg snapped the neck of the assassin with his bare hands. It also stated that Jack, Jay and some passengers subdued the other terrorists.

As Joe turned the next page, he looked up. Kathe was standing in the doorway watching him. She had tears in her eyes as she sat down on the bed next to him. "It was my maiden voyage," she began. "Oddly enough, it was also the first flight for Carrie Anne, Jay, and Jack. It was Ramsey's first time working as an Alby Controller. Yorg was on his first assignment to Alby on an America/Russian government sponsored anti-terrorism pilot program. That's our bond."

Joe put his arms around her and hugged her tightly. "I am so sorry. I was in the hospital when they brought you in that night. I saw them wheel you past me doing a heart massage. I even donated blood that night." He lifted her face up to his, "I also have AB- blood. I can't believe that was you." He kissed her and pulled her even closer to him.

"The only people who knew I survived were Dr. Sydney, Ramsey, Carrie Anne, Jay, Jack, Ben, and

Yorg," Kathe continued. "Yorg came to visit me the most. He . . . he pulled me through some really hard times, times I didn't want to live." Joe wiped her tears from her cheeks. "He made me live. He wouldn't let me die or give up-that is the bond we have. How did you find this stuff?" She took her Rosary from his hand, "I thought I had this put away, where no one would ever find it. I don't even know why I kept this stuff."

"I didn't find it," Joe confided. "Shaunda was up here going through your room," he pointed to the half open dresser drawers. "I heard something fall upstairs and remembered Shaunda had gone to bed early. I came upstairs to check on her. When I came in, it looked like she was trying to push something under the dresser. After I got her out of here, I noticed something sticking out from underneath the dresser. It was the article of the shooting. I glanced through it and saw your name."

"I'm sorry you found out," Kathe admitted. "I don't like to talk about it."

"Now, I know why you put up with Carrie Anne's shenanigans," Joe said. "I know these hurts, but I want to know everything about you. I looked at these pictures and I can't believe that this lifeless body was you."

With a deep sigh, Kathe closed her eyes for a moment and then handed him the Rosary. "Here, I would like you to have my Rosary. I had it on me at the time." He took the Rosary from her. He returned the scrapbook to the box and pushed the box under the dresser. He closed the door, turned off the light, and pulled her on the bed beside him.

Chapter 27

A New Song Unveiled

Very early the next morning as they were sleeping JAKE began to ring. Again, Kathe had left JAKE downstairs and couldn't hear it ring. Since it was not Alby control, the implant didn't activate. A loud knock at the bedroom door woke them as Joe reached for his pants and opened the door. Steve came into the room with JAKE, "How do I turn this thing off?"

Kathe reached for JAKE, "I'm sorry. I usually keep it near me." She sat up in bed and covered herself with the sheet. "Hello," Kathe yawned.

"I'm sorry for calling you so early in the morning," Yorg apologized as he looked at the pictures of Saíde's deadly car crash on his computer. "The more Jaco and I dig for information concerning the so-called car crash that killed Saíde, the more it's looking like a fake. And that's not all that is not adding up."

"I was afraid of that," Kathe sighed. "What else is wrong?"

"Ivan tried to leave a message on my phone," Yorg continued. "I didn't answer the call because I was with Jaco. Ivan sounded frantic. The message was garbled. I've tried to reach him at his home and at the base. No one has seen him."

"Gosh, Yorg," Kathe shared. "Ivan called me last night. I could barely understand him, due to static on the line and the wind outside."

"Did Ivan say what he wanted?" Yorg asked.

"I could hardly understand him," Kathe stated. "He sounded like he was running and out of breath. I thought he said the word danger, but I'm not sure, and then the line went dead."

"What time did he call you?" Yorg quizzed.

"Hold on," Kathe said, checking her call log. "He called at 8:07 pm. His wasn't the only weird call I received last night."

"What do you mean?" Yorg asked, glancing out the window.

"Tierra and CC called me just before Ivan," Kathe replied. "They said there was a lot of tension between Alonzo and Mario. They overheard several heated arguments between the two. One was about how the killer got in Mario's house with his security. And why did Giorgio take Dider to his office to show him how they stepped up security for them at the same time. The last one was concerning the finding of the murderer so quickly and the way he died."

"Jaco and I are going over all the evidence again," Yorg reported. "We haven't interviewed the dentist since he's on vacation for another week. None of the shop owners we spoke with were aware of a high-speed chase that day."

"According to Tierra, Nicki didn't trust or like his brother," Kathe admitted. "Why would Nicki go to Mario's house for safety? CC stated that she doesn't trust Mario either. She said he didn't cry at the funeral or act upset. She's noticed Mario and Giorgio acting strange and whispering around his father and Alonzo."

"Did you call Ramsey?" Yorg inquired.

"I left a message with Keith for him to call Ramsey," Kathe stated.

"Have you noticed anything else out of the ordinary, say around you," Yorg quizzed.

"No, I'm just enjoying the beach," Kathe answered, glancing at Joe.

"Are you sure you're not enjoying the beach with an old friend?" Yorg inquired. "Or you ran into someone from work?"

"What do you mean?" Kathe insisted.

"Oh, I was just reading the newspaper I bought this morning," Yorg declared. "The headlines read, 'Missing rock star found in Daytona Beach with mystery woman.' It further states that Joe Sherrod, lead singer for Light Crimson broke the nose of an Alby pilot, who was bothering his mystery woman. The name of the woman is being withheld at this time. It is a perfect picture of you, standing next to Joe as he is punching Garth. Jordan is also in the picture. Now would you like to explain why you're with Joe Sherrod after our little talk the other night?"

"Why don't you ask Ramsey?" Kathe quizzed. "I was minding my own business landing in Orlando, when one of our jets kissed the wing of another jet, taxiing in a thunderstorm. Joe was onboard the one heading for Miami. Some fans recognized him and stormed him for souvenirs. Ramsey ordered me to pick him up and keep him at my house until the band got here yesterday."

"Ramsey must have been ordered by someone higher up to put the two of you together," Yorg shook his head. "She's been trying to put nothing but distance between you. Why did Joe hit McCollum?"

"Garth and his friend Tom Bernard were at Panama Jim's," Kathe explained. "He's asked me to dinner a couple of times. He is obnoxious and never takes no for an answer. Even after, I told him about my policy on never dating pilots or married men. He had a little too much to drink and came after me. I told him to leave me alone and when he didn't, Joe hit him," she laughed. "Ramsey's firing Garth for assaulting an Alby passenger under my protection."

"That worked out well," Yorg stated. "I heard from other pilots, that McCollum has been bothering several flight attendants. Just remember who Joe is, what he does for a living, and who you are, and what you do for a living. It's for both of your sakes! They're plenty of other agents, who could have handled this situation. This wasn't Ramsey's best decision!"

"Got ya," Kathe agreed as she held her finger up to her mouth warning Joe to stay quiet.

"Getting back to Saíde," Yorg said, reading his computer. "If Tierra and CC are sensing Alonzo doesn't trust Mario, Ramsey needs to bring them back. It smells of an inside job."

"I'm beginning to feel that way too," Kathe said not wanting to tell him about the cemetery yet.

"I've got to find Ivan, even if I have to go to Russia," Yorg admitted. "You need to check in with Ramsey about the situation with the girls. Tell her that I'm checking on a lead I got from Jaco. I'll call her later after I figure out what to do," he said and cleared the line.

Holding a finger up for Joe to continue waiting, she dialed control, "Keith, did you get hold of Ramsey last night?"

"I left Ramsey a message to call Tierra and CC," Keith stated. "I know she had dinner plans with an old friend. We had a rough night here at the airport and I didn't get back to her."

"Yorg feels that we should get Tierra and CC out of Europe PDQ!" Kathe exclaimed. "He and Jaco feel that Saíde is still alive. Too many things are not adding up with Nicki's death. There's a lot of tension between Mario and Alonzo concerning it. Have Ramsey give me a call," Kathe said and cleared the line.

Joe laughed, "Did I hear you right? Our picture was on the front page in Paris."

"Yes, unfortunately we made the front page complete with a picture of you, hitting Garth," Kathe answered, shaking her head.

"I'll tell Payton," Joe smiled. "He loves good publicity."

"Joe, that may be good publicity for you," Kathe cautioned, "especially since you walked out on a contract with TMV. I understand that Payton is trying to smooth it over. But I was in the picture with you. The airlines may still have an issue with a man presumed dead. That could be dangerous for both of us."

"Stop worrying," Joe tried to play it down. "The odds of a maniac reading about us are slim to none. Now, that I know exactly how you are bonded to Yorg, I can't to get to know him."

"You weren't jealous of Yorg, were you?" Kathe asked, coyly touched the end of his nose.

"Me, jealous of a man you fly around the world with, whose room you sleep in, whom you massage?" Joe smiled. "Not to mention the way Carrie Anne describes him."

"Oh, my, goodness!" Kathe chuckled, leaning over and toying with his hair. "You poor little thing; no wonder you kept asking questions about Yorg. I know how Carrie Anne thinks about him."

Joe rolled playfully over on her and came up on top. "Of course, I was. What do you think?"

"Welllllllll . . . "Kathe exclaimed as she kissed him and . . .

Payton was the next to knock on the door a few hours later. "Joe, I just got a call from New York," he said through the door. "It seems there's a benefit in Orlando for the recent flood victims in Miami. I thought it would be great publicity if Light Crimson performs. I have already checked with the others. They'll do it."

Joe hopped out of bed and put his pants on before opening the door. "Payton today is a great day for publicity," Joe smiled. "You are not going to believe it, but Kathe talked with a friend in Paris this morning. It seems that the picture at the restaurant made front-page news, and yes, I will do the show. I want to talk to the guys about a new song I wrote. I'll meet you downstairs for coffee."

"I'll get online and look for the article," Payton gleamed and hurried downstairs as JAKE rang again.

"Tierney, Keith told me what you said," Ramsey affirmed, scrolling down her computer screen. "My mind wouldn't shut down last night. After tossing and turning half the night I got up. I have been checking these pictures of Saíde's car crash. I even woke Sydney to help me with some research. Sydney found a missing person's report of a man in Paris that fits the description of the charred remains. His name is Roberto Fonseca. I have a phone call into Jaco to check this man's dental records."

"Where did the original report come from?" Kathe asked.

"Jaco said it originated online," Ramsey reported. "Sydney's still trying to find the IP address. He said someone's good at covering their tracks and told me to bring the girls back now. I'm going to call Alonzo next. I can't tell Mr. LaBasco that the killer of his son may still be alive. Especially, since Nicki was killed under the protection of his other son."

"You've got that right!" Kathe warned. "Tierra warned that Jr. is Papa's favorite, and the muscle of the family. However, according to Tierra and CC, there is a lot of tension between Mario and Alonzo," she said as she filled Ramsey in on her conversation with the girls. "Yorg said it's beginning to smell like an inside job," she said, walking into the bathroom.

"It sounds like Alonzo also suspects foul play," Ramsey sighed. "We may have an ally to help us with Mr. LaBasco. I'm sure Alonzo needs to have hard evidence to take to him or he would have already done so. Jay found out that one of the private planes that got off the other day when Saíde was here was a legitimate jeweler. It's strange that he and Wanda can't find out anything on Reminiscent Art. I'm going to ask Alonzo if he knows the dealer. On top of this mess, I can't believe, I was forced to use you to pick up Glitter Boy. I saw the pictures of the fight at the restaurant online. This is what I warned you about. Keep your distance from him. They will be on their way to Miami tomorrow," she ordered and cleared the line. She quickly dialed Alonzo.

On the trip to the convention center, Payton was in a great mood after reading online the article from Paris. Kathe enjoyed being with the band members, especially since Shaunda was gone. When they arrived at the center, the band had a lot of work to do checking the sound systems and lights shows. They also needed to rehearse their new song. Kathe took the girls to Disney World to shop and have lunch. She even bought Joe a 'Grumpy Shirt' for the next time he was in a bad mood.

Babs loved the small shops and bought several souvenirs to take back to her nieces and nephews abroad.

Suzanne was caught up in the whole Magic of Disney animated park. Just as lunch was finished and they were getting ready to leave for the concert, JAKE rang.

"This situation is escalating," Keith updated Kathe. "It seems the more Ramsey checks into the LaBasco Family, the more she sees a pattern with Mario Jr. Alonzo was very receptive to help her find out about Reminiscent Art of Paris. She said to enjoy R & R while you can. She's bringing you in shortly."

At Heathrow Airport in London, Alby Flight #1670 was one of the last planes to land for the night. The itinerary was to layover and head back to the states the next evening. The flight crew rode to the hotel together, except for one of the attendants. She wanted to wait for her best friend traveling on the last Alby flight arriving an hour behind them. As Kayla Martin headed for the restroom, she noticed a man watching her. She felt a little uneasy as she entered the women's restroom. Kayla waited until two other women entered the room and left with them, checking for the man. She was relieved, not finding him. She headed for the nearest monitor to make sure Nina's flight was on time. The only people in this part of the terminal were Kayla and an older couple. She suddenly felt something sharp being stuck into her back.

"Don't scream and I won't hurt you," whispered a man from behind. He poked the object deeper into her side. "Act like you've been waiting for me and leave with me. Don't make a scene or I'll kill them!" He turned Kayla around to face him. With a smirk on his face, "Here I am dear; I trust you had a nice flight?" As he reached for her overnight case, "Let me carry this for you, you look tired." In horror, she walked with the man toward the employee's quarters. "That's right, do as you're told, and no one will get hurt," he nibbled at her ear.

In the lobby of the Hotel Rochester, about 1:00 am, Carrie Anne and Nina Norell were headed back to their rooms from the bar. "It's so strange," Nina admitted. "I still can't get hold of Kayla. Maybe her schedule changed, and she forgot to call me. I waited at the airport for over an hour and couldn't reach her by phone. She was supposed to land an hour before me and wait. We were going to get something to eat before coming to the hotel. This is not like her."

"Why don't you call control?" Carrie Anne asked. "If her schedule changed, they'll tell you. She might have gotten lucky and found a rock star," Carrie Anne laughed.

"She's not like you," Nina chuckled. "She collects souvenirs, not them."

"That's true," Carrie Anne giggled as they reached her room. "I am one of a kind as Tierney puts it. I'll see you in the morning. Good luck finding Kayla."

In Orlando, the girls rejoined the band at the convention center. The crowds were already streaming through the doors. Security escorted them to the dressing rooms. As Kathe watched Joe get ready, she started laughing at his attire.

"What are you laughing at?" Joe asked, looking at her.

"You don't spend too much on your wardrobe, do you?" Kathe laughed as she pointed to the holes in his jeans.

"These are my best jeans," Joe smiled, pulling her over to him. "Don't laugh they make me money."

"Well at least, you have low overhead," Kathe smiled as she put her arms around his neck. "I'm going to miss you when I go back to work,"

"I've been thinking about that," Joe caressed her face.

"I'd rather not," Kathe whispered, kissing him.

"Ten minutes," Brock yelled as he knocked on the door.

"I don't want you to leave," Joe admitted.

"Joe, for the first time in a long time," Kathe confided as she put her head on his shoulder, "I don't want to ever leave your side." Stepping back, she looked him directly in the eyes, "Thank you."

"For what?" Joe asked.

"For making me feel alive," Kathe declared. "I mean really alive again." Joe pulled her into his arms, held her tightly and kissed her.

Payton knocked, and then opened the door, "Show time! Let's go!"

Kathe took her seat next to Babs. Joe immediately took command of the crowd. They sang for about an hour when Joe calmed the crowd. "I would like to ask something of you Orlando, Florida."

The crowd roared.

"Here in Orlando," Joe said as he looked around the audience. "I'd like to try something we've never tried before."

The crowd went nuts again.

Joe looked over at Collin and gave the thumbs up sign. "Okay, Orlando," he continued. "I wrote a song about a woman I met."

The crowd went wild.

"She's a flight attendant, an American flight attendant," Joe encouraged the excitement of the crowd. "It's a song about our jobs always pulling us apart. It's titled 'Pieces of Love,' and it goes like thissss . . ."

Kathe watched Joe sing with deep emotion hanging on each word. The crowd loved every second of it. When the song was finished, the crowd was on their feet, cheering, as Joe took a second to catch his breath. Then Joe asked, "Well, Orlandooooo..." He walked around the stage to another side, "Well, Orlando, Floridaaaaaaaa..." The crowd cheered even louder, flickering their cell phones in the air. "Orlando, Florida, what do you think?" Joe asked, raising his arms and the crowd roared. He looked over to where Kathe and the others were sitting, touched his index finger to his tongue, and drew an imaginary line down.

When their segment of the concert was over, Kathe met Joe backstage. As she entered the dressing area she jumped into his arms, "The song was dynamite! It's going to be your biggest hit!"

"Did you see the standing ovation we got!" Travis gleamed. "And for a song we wrote the melody for today?"

"That's the quickest song, we've ever written!" Troy joined in the excitement.

"I'm awestruck!" Steve continued. "I've never seen anybody write a song in three hours!"

"Did you hear that crowd?" Collin high-fived Joe, "You're back to your old self."

Joe looked over at Kathe, "Yes mate, I'm back and glad to be here!"

The trip back to Daytona went by quickly as they were still on an adrenalin high from the concert. Inside the house, some headed for the bar, and some headed for their rooms. As Joe poured a drink, "Hey, let's go for a late-night swim."

"We're one up on you mate," Collin said as he and Suzanne came down in their swimsuits.

"It's a wonderful night to be outside," Kathe added. "I'll be right down," she hurried upstairs to change. Joe was right behind her. Scooping her in his arms, closing the bedroom door with one foot, he passionately kissed her as he gently laid her on the bed. "I keep dreaming that you'll stay with me and never . . . I swear, I'd stop breathing, if I never saw you again."

"Joe," Kathe whispered and passionately kissed him as Joe began to slowly undress her.

A little later, as Kathe was putting on her bikini JAKE rang. Joe took her hand and kissed it. He held his breath and listened. "Yes, Ramsey," Kathe answered.

"Kathe, you were right," Ramsey reported. "After talking with Jaco, Yorg and I started profiling Mario again trying to find something I might have missed. He has been seen with some Iranians, and Russians lately. I talked with Alonzo about some concerns I have about the safety of Tierra. I also told him about one of the private planes that got off the other day when Saíde was spotted. I even hinted to the fact that I don't trust Mario. Alonzo didn't agree with me, but he didn't disagree with me either. He said he can't escort Tierra over to the U.S. right now. He was relieved when I offered to send my personal pilot, Ralph Stevens, to bring them here on my private jet. This situation is rapidly escalating. Yorg said that someone he recently visited in Russia is missing. The caller tried to leave a message for him, but it was garbled. Yorg believes we have stumbled in Mario Jr.'s business with a renegade Russian general. I know you have houseguests and that they just finished a concert tonight, but I need to put some distance between you and them. I fervently hope that Saíde or Mario didn't see you in the papers with Sherrod. Enjoy what time you have left."

"Yes, Ramsey," Kathe answered, glancing at Joe. "It's okay; I don't have to leave just yet!"

As they were leaving the bedroom, JAKE rang again. Kathe breathed a sigh of relief, "Jeannie, how are you?" She put JAKE on speaker.

"I have a sad little boy who wants his mommy tonight," Jeannie began, holding Joey in her arms. "He had another bad dream."

"Put Joey on the phone," Kathe sighed. "Hi baby. I love you."

"Mommy," Joey whined.

"Jeannie says you miss Mommy," Kathe said looking at Joe.

A tearful little boy cried, "Mommy I had . . . another . . . bad dream."

"Do you want to tell Mommy about it?" Kathe asked.

"I'm afraid . . . I don't want it to be true," Joey whispered and buried his head in Jeannie's shoulder.

"Sweetheart," Kathe explained, "dreams are just dreaming, they don't come true. They're not real."

"Are you sure, Mommy?" His little voice seemed to lift.

"Yes, Joey, I am sure," Kathe replied, watching Joe's reaction.

"I dreamed you were going away and not ever coming back!" Joey exclaimed and buried his head in Jeannie's shoulder again.

"Joey, I have to leave you to go to work," Kathe explained. "I always come back. All you have to do is have Jeannie call me, just like now."

"Will you always love me?" Joey asked.

"Yes, you'll always be my baby," Kathe assured him. "I will always love you. Do you feel better now?"

"Yes, Mommy," Joey smiled and sat up.

"Okay, please put Jeannie back on the phone and go back to bed," Kathe said. "I love you, Joey."

"I appreciate it," Jeannie said as Joey hopped down and skipped to his room. "I think I know what caused this dream. Peter was over tonight. In front of the kids, he said that he saw you with some big rock star in Florida. He also brought a newspaper with a picture of the two of you. He said that I might as well start watching my pennies. You would probably be quitting the airlines, going off with him, and leaving us high and dry. The older kids were elated when they saw you with Joe Sherrod. I didn't realize Joey would believe his father."

"I can't believe Peter would stoop so low in front of his own children!" Kathe snapped.

"Yeah, Peter hasn't changed a bit," Jeannie agreed. "Well, are you coming out here to see us after you leave Florida or joining his tour?"

"I'm heading back to work," Kathe admitted. "I'm waiting for Ramsey to call me with my schedule. I'll give you a call when I find out. Give the kids my love. Bye."

Kathe swatted at Joe, "Beat ya in the water," and ran downstairs.

Joe ran after her, grabbed her on the staircase landing, "You could stay with me on the tour and not ever have to go back to work."

"You wish," Kathe said as they walked out on the deck. "It's not that easy."

"Now, I know where I have seen you," Steve pointed at Kathe. "Have you ever been to the Au Summit Apartments in Paris?"

"I share an apartment there on the 21st floor," Kathe stated.

"I live across the hall from you," Steve said, holding up his beer. "I thought you looked familiar. It is a small world."

Joe looked shocked, "I think it was inevitable for us to meet."

"I think you're right," Steve agreed. "You two were meant to be together."

Yorg arrived back in Newark and went straight to control. "Welcome home," Wanda greeted as she picked up the phone. "Yorg just arrived."

"Great," Ramsey sighed, "send him in my office."

"She's expecting you," Wanda smiled.

"Is she doing better with her nicotine withdrawals?" Yorg questioned as he stopped before the doorway.

"It's safe to go in there," Wanda chuckled. "She's learning to chew on them instead of lighting them."

"That's a start," Yorg smiled. "Thanks for dealing with her. If anybody can control her, you can."

"Why Capt. Vuslick," Wanda smiled. "I do appreciate your support," she said as he opened the door.

"Yorg come in and sit down," Ramsey greeted. "I've been going over some links that Sydney sent me concerning some activities he found on Mario. It shows underworld activity between the Iranians, and Russians. It looks like Mario is trying to purchase something big and it doesn't look like his father is aware of it."

"I truly believe you're right," Yorg confirmed. "Nicki must have uncovered something to that effect. However, before he had the proof, he needed to show his father, he was murdered. Somehow Saíde must be involved with Mario," Yorg continued as Wanda opened the door interrupting them.

"Sorry, Ramsey we have a problem," Wanda reported. "Officials at the Atlantic City Airport just found another flight attendant murdered, in the same manner as the others."

"That's it!" Ramsey bellowed. "I've had enough of that man!" she turned to Yorg as Wanda closed the door. "I brought you back to put you with Kathe's team. We must find out what Mario is after. We also must prove how Mario relates to Saíde before we can go to Alonzo. Tierra must know more than she is telling us. She can gain you access to the LaBasco secrets."

"If Tierra can get me inside Nicki's house," Yorg stated. "We'll start there."

"Boss, he struck again," Wanda reported as she rushed back in the office. "Kayla Martin was just found in Heathrow Employee's Quarters with her throat slashed also."

"That does it!" Ramsey snapped. "Put Tierney on the fastest flight here tonight and locate Jay and Jack."

"I'm on it!" Wanda exclaimed, hurrying to her desk.

At Kathe's house, everyone was winding down for the evening. "I feel bad about what I did to Carrie Anne when Shaunda showed up in LA," Travis admitted. "I really miss her. She was a lot of fun."

"She's too high maintenance!" Troy teased as JAKE rang.

"Carrie Anne, we were just talking about you," Kathe smiled. "You're on speaker."

"I hope it was all good," Carrie Anne teased. "I was worried that you were alone on your R & R, who are you with?"

"I'm with Joe and his friends," Kathe replied.

"Does the Ole Girl know about this?" Carrie Anne wondered.

"Long story, but she actually put us together," Kathe answered. "I'll tell you about it next time I see you."

"Carrie Anne, when can I see you again?" Travis asked.

"I thought your girlfriend, Shaunda was with you," Carrie Anne quizzed.

"I sent her away," Travis confessed. "We're finished this time for good. What would you think about Payton getting you reassigned to our flight crew?"

"I love it!" Carrie Anne exclaimed, patting her heart.

"I can't wait to see you," Travis admitted. "I'll have Payton call now."

"That's perfect, I'm in Newark," Carrie Anne stated. "I'm off duty. I can take the next flight to Daytona."

Kathe noticed Ramsey was calling on the other line, "Carrie Anne, you'll have to talk to us later, Ramsey is on the other line," Kathe clicked over.

"Tierney report to Alby Flight #971 in Orlando at 7:00 am," Ramsey ordered. "You can sleep all the way to Newark. When you land come straight to control."

Travis whispered to Kathe, "Ask her about Carrie Anne?"

"Travis wants Carrie Anne back on their flight crew," Kathe asked with reservation.

"What am I, a dating service?" Ramsey bellowed.

"Well, can she?" Kathe asked, crossing her heart.

"Consider it done!" Ramsey snapped. "She'll be there in the morning. Is there any other request from the Glitter Boys?"

"Actually, there is," Kathe took Joe's hand and he kissed hers.

"Don't even think about it!" Ramsey snapped and cleared the line.

"I don't want you to leave," Joe declared. "Call her back and quit your job. You don't need it anymore. I can take care of you and your family!"

"I wish it was that simple," Kathe whispered and kissed him. "It's 3:00 am," Kathe said, checking the time. "I have to leave in an hour for the airport." She looked over at Payton, "Don't worry about the house. Ramsey will call the security company to close it up when you leave. I've got to go and pack."

A few minutes later, Kathe was coming out of her closet with some uniforms, when Joe walked in the room. He sat down next to her suitcase. "I keep hoping you won't leave," he looked up at her. "I don't want to say goodbye to you again."

Kathe knelt on the marble pedestal in front of him, "If I could stay, you wouldn't be here much longer. You still have three more weeks of traveling to promote your new Album. I don't want to leave sad. I had such fun this past week with you. I don't think I've ever laughed so much in my life, nor felt such passion!"

"Promise not to get into any trouble," Joe requested as he looked sideways at her.

"I can't promise you that," Kathe chuckled. "You know what I do for a living," she said as she put on a pair of jeans and an over the shoulder, short-sleeved blouse. She handed him a bag off the dresser. "I found this at Disney and totally thought of you," she laughed as he opened it.

"Grumpy, a Grumpy T-shirt!" Joe exclaimed, holding it up. "You saw this and thought of me!"

"Sure, everyone said you were a grump, before you met me," Kathe insisted. "Every time you feel grumpy, I want to you put on this T-shirt and think of me. Then wipe that grump off your face and put that gorgeous smile back where it belongs."

"Miss you already," Joe confessed, cupping her face and kissing her.

As Kathe finished packing, Joe carried her suitcase downstairs, where the others were waiting to say goodbye. Babs gave her a hug, "I'm really going to miss you almost as much as Joe. I've really enjoyed your friendship."

"Thanks for putting the smile back on our tough guy," Troy added.

Even Suzanne gave her a hug, "I'm sorry again for all the trouble that I caused for you and Joe. I hope we can continue being friends."

"Thank you, I feel the same way," Kathe said and gave Collin a hug. "You have a very special lady."

"Sorry I called you a cheap flight attendant," Payton stated. "I was just trying to protect my superstar."

"Sorry again, that Shaunda gave you a bad time," Travis said, hugging her. "It's okay. I understand that her loyalty lies with her best friend."

Steve surprised everyone; he leaned Kathe backwards and gave her a kiss. As she pulled away from him, he laughed, looked at Joe and said, "Just wanted to say goodbye to my new neighbor."

"I guess I'll see you in Paris sometimes," Kathe winked at Steve.

Walking Kathe out to the car, Joe put her suitcase in the trunk. She threw her purse on the seat and leaned against the car. Putting his hands on the car enclosing her with his body, "I can't believe you're really leaving." He pressed his lips against hers. Minutes went by as they embraced. Then, Joe slowly pulled away from her.

She put her fingers to his lips fighting back tears, "I'll see you in three weeks." She got into the ZR1, started up the engine, backed out of the garage, and drove down the long driveway to the gate. He watched her as she drove away.

Chapter 28

Killing from the Grave

Landing at Newark, Kathe went straight to Ramsey's office. Wanda greeted her, "Kathe, you look rested."

"Thank you, Wanda," Kathe smiled. "Is Ramsey in this early?"

"She's been here all night," Wanda replied.

"What's going on?" Kathe quizzed.

"We've had a busy night," Wanda declared. "She's waiting for you," she said as Tierra and CC entered the office.

"Kathe," Tierra greeted her friends as Wanda answered her phone.

"Ladies, would you like to join us sometime today?" Ramsey scoffed, opening her door. As they entered her office, Yorg, Jay, and Jack were waiting. "I've got some bad news. This morning at Heathrow, Kayla Martin was found dead in the employee's quarters. Her throat was slashed."

"Oh, my, God!" Kathe exclaimed. "I just worked with Kayla before my leave."

"Another attendant was found dead in Atlantic City," Ramsey reported. "The estimated time of death was twelve hours after Kayla," Ramsey continued as Wanda rushed into her office.

"Boss, you need to get downstairs right now!" Wanda exclaimed.

"What's wrong?" Ramsey snapped.

"Lt. Tanner just called and said that a female body has been found!" Wanda exclaimed.

"Where?" Ramsey yelled, looking in her desk drawer for a cigarette.

"Employee's quarters just like the others," Wanda declared. "I've got a pack hidden in my desk," Wanda said, heading to get them.

"Tell him that I'm on my way!" Ramsey exclaimed. "What a stupid day to quit smoking. Kathe come with me! Yorg don't let these girls out of your sight! Jay, Jack, check the surroundings around our office."

Hurrying toward the door, Wanda threw Ramsey a pack of cigarettes as she passed her desk.

Entering the employee's quarters, Ramsey twirled an unlit cigarette between her fingers. "John, what have you got for me?"

"One of your flight attendants," John said, reading his notes. "Here it is. Her name is Paula Cates. Cause of death looks like the same as the others, her throat slashed. Her body is still warm, so whoever did this can't be far. We've sealed off this area until forensics arrives."

"John from everything I've learned about this guy," Ramsey reported, "he's long gone. You handle this end and let me know what you find. I must get back upstairs. I have a gut feeling; he is a puppet for a rich man who is pulling his strings. I'm beginning to believe that this is covering the real reason for his boss' actions."

"Will do," John answered as Ramsey left with Kathe.

"This is getting out of hand," Ramsey declared as they got into the elevator. "While you were on R & R, I did some extensive research on Mario Jr. He's got to be in the middle of all this mess. I suspect that Saíde is working for him. After this, there is no way that Saíde is dead! This is his work! I think it's time I had a little talk with Ms. LaBasco. She is going to level with me! She's not stupid. She knows more than she's telling me."

Returning to her office, Ramsey sat down in her chair and said, "I have assembled all of you today to talk about two different problems we have with the same common denominator. In case you have not heard, we have three dead flight attendants, within the last 36 hours. All three of the slain girls were found in the employee's quarters with their throats slashed. Kayla Martin was in Heathrow, 12 hours later Jane Smith in Atlantic City, and Paula Cates was just found here."

"Shouldn't we be helping Lt. Tanner?" Jay asked.

"The killer is long gone from the airport," Ramsey stated.

"It sounds like a dead man is coming for Kathe," Yorg declared.

"Does, doesn't it?" Ramsey continued. "This fits the MO of Saíde 100 percent. A man supposedly killed last week in Paris," she said as she strutted around her desk and leaned on it. "This all began with Flight #1014 when Alby had a run in with a now known hitman. He seems to be tied into Mario LaBasco Jr.'s business," she continued, looking straight at Tierra. "This whole thing started with your brother, Nicki calling me one day saying your life could be in danger. We pulled you from work and sent you home as he requested. Your family supposedly solved the problem. Nicki called personally assuring that the perpetrator was eradicated. You came back to work. Then, Nicki called a few weeks later asking me to keep an eye on you that you could still be in danger. Although this time, he did not want me to send you back to your father's house. Next, there was an attempt on Nicki's life, and then he was found dead at your brother's house!" Ramsey stopped for a second as tears filled Tierra's eyes and she began sobbing. "I'm sorry that sounded so cold. I didn't mean it like that, but I've got five dead flight attendants."

"It's okay," Tierra grimly stated. "I know how you meant it. I too believe Mario knows why my Nicki was killed."

"Okay, tell me why," Ramsey insisted.

"I can't say," Tierra looked away.

"What do you mean, you can't?" Ramsey demanded with Tierra refraining from eye contact. "Did you tell your father that you didn't feel safe around Mario?"

"No, Ramsey and I don't want to tell him!" Tierra glared at Ramsey. "And I don't want you to tell him either!"

"Why?" Ramsey demanded.

"I can't say," Tierra sighed. "I just don't want you to tell him either!"

CC interjected, "Nicki was killed at Mario's house under his protection. Mr. LaBasco is still in the hospital. We know Alonzo doesn't trust Mario either. Until one of us figures this out, I think Tierra is safer flying with Kathe's team."

"Alonzo is noted for having a loyal army at your father's house," Yorg stated. "Why would they send Nicki to Mario's?"

"Because Papa is under investigation for the death of Sen. Bernard Frank and the man that went after me," Tierra stated.

"You never said why you think Mario Jr. knows why Nicki was killed?" Ramsey demanded. "I'm waiting!'

Tierra broke down, "Nicki . . . sob . . . sob . . . Nicki called me . . . sob . . . after his life was threatened."

"The night he was with Kathe?" Ramsey asked.

"Yes," Tierra continued, "he said . . . he said that he and Dider intercepted a document that was meant for Mario, something about an Iranian. He said he couldn't go to Papa without more proof . . . sob . . . and he said, he was very close to getting it, something about the document was in code. He warned me not to go around Mario, that I wasn't safe either," she broke down and cried harder as CC consoled her.

"Kathe, do you have any input on this subject?" Ramsey asked.

"One thing is for sure," Kathe began. "Alonzo was relieved to send Tierra back to work. The girls overheard him arguing with Mario about Nicki's murder at his house with all his security and while he was home. And why did Giorgio take Dider away from Nicki to show him the added security measures as he was murdered. They also overheard them arguing about finding the killer so quickly and the way they disposed of him. It's too sketchy. Alonzo knows it's a cover-up. But he's cautious; he must prove it."

Ramsey sat on the edge of her desk, "You're exactly right. Now, after his supposed death we have three more attendants killed in the same manner. There's no way Rhasheéd Saíde is dead. He's very much alive or he's killing from the grave!"

"It's strange," Yorg interrupted, "Less than twenty-four hours after Saíde was supposedly killed and identified by dental records, Jaco checked a missing person report of another man. He didn't fit Saíde's description. This man turned out to be a German on vacation."

"Around the same time, I had Sydney do some checking for missing persons also," Ramsey stated. "Sydney found a missing person's report from a town not too far away from there of a man that fit Saíde's description. Sydney matched the dental records used to identify Saíde with those of missing person, Roberto Fonseca and it was a match."

"It's an old trick in my family," Tierra confessed, pointing her finger at Ramsey. "A family member wanted by the police suddenly is found dead. But they are relocated to another region."

"Do you think you would recognize the man following you two in New York the other day, if you saw him?" Ramsey asked.

"We sure would!" CC answered for her. "The man that followed us, scared us to death."

Ramsey pulled up the files on her computer, "That's strange; I can't find his mug shot." She pressed the intercom for Wanda, "Bring me a mug shot of Saíde?" After several minutes of waiting Ramsey called, "Wanda, where's the picture?"

"I'm searching for it," Wanda yelled back.

"Get me the paper file!" Ramsey yelled.

"I'll be right there," Wanda hollered, looking in the cabinet for it. She found the file on top of the cabinet under another file. "You are making me crazy, Boss," she said, handing Ramsey the file and hurried out of the room.

"That's odd," Ramsey remarked as she flipped through the folder looking for his pictures. "All the pictures are missing!" She called for Wanda again.

"Yes, Boss?" Wanda asked, rolling her eyes.

Going through the file, Ramsey screeched, "Where is the rest of this file?"

Wanda hurried into the office and looked over Ramsey's shoulder, "It all seems to be here."

"No, it isn't," Ramsey protested. "Where are all the mug shots we got from the gendarmes?"

"You know," Wanda looked puzzled. "When I went to get the hard copy of the file, I found it on the top of my cabinet under another file."

"What?" Ramsey screamed. "I couldn't find it in my computer. I know I saved the email of the mug shots." Turning to her computer, "What happened to the file? Wanda who's been in my office? Using my computer?"

"Wanda, see if you can pull it up on your computer!" Yorg requested as he hurried over to Ramsey's desk to help.

"I can't find it either?" Wanda shouted still searching on her computer. "Get John Tanner on the phone," Ramsey screamed, "Now!"

"He's on line 1 for you," Wanda shared a few seconds later.

"Ramsey, what can I do for you?" John asked.

"Someone has hacked into our computers," Ramsey explained. "All the mug shots of Saíde are missing, and all hard copies have been removed from the filing cabinet in Wanda's office."

"Why would anyone take the pictures out of his file?" John questioned, turning on his computer. "His death was confirmed with dental records."

"Apparently not!" Ramsey exclaimed.

"I'll be right up!" John stated as he checked his file. "I can't find them in my computer either!"

"Sydney," Ramsey called. "We have a major breech," Ramsey declared as she explained the situation to him.

"I'll get back with you," Sydney stated and cleared the line.

Lt. Tanner hurried into Ramsey's office, "Why wasn't I told that you don't believe Saíde is dead?"

"It never really set right with me," Ramsey confessed. "Jaco, and Yorg did some investigating after the fact. Think about it John, a man who no one can find and suddenly we have his dental records? It doesn't make any sense!"

"You're right, I've read his profile," John stated. "This is his MO and it's questionable about the LaBasco Family's integrity. We all know their reputation. Now, what have you got?"

"Come with me, John," glancing over at Tierra, Ramsey led him out of her office to talk privately about Mario Jr.

As they left the room, Yorg leaned over to Kathe, "I'm glad you're back. I missed you! I need to call Ivan and Ylia. I'll be right back."

"You haven't talked to either one of them yet?" Kathe inquired.

"No, and it worries me," Yorg said as he left the room.

Hanging up his cell phone, a frustrated Yorg waited for Ramsey to finish with Tanner. "I need to go to Russia, something's not right," he explained as Tanner left the office. "I can't get hold of my sister, Ylia, or my friend, Ivan."

"I was afraid of that," Ramsey said, reaching in her pocket. "Wanda handed me this note as our meeting started. Your clearance to land in Moscow has been revoked by your government until further notice."

"By whose orders?" Yorg demanded.

"Wanda, get me that general's name," Ramsey said, walking over to her desk.

"It's here somewhere," Wanda said as she shuffled through a stack of papers on her desk. "Here it is," she handed her the phone log.

"A Gen. Yetsun, do you know him?" Ramsey questioned.

"Yes, he's not to be trusted!" Yorg declared. "Now, I'm sure I need to go to Russia. I know something is wrong if he doesn't want me there."

"Absolutely not," Ramsey objected, glaring at him. "You are not going to Russia. I'll arrange for you and Kathe's team to fly to Europe to do some checking on Mario. Your cover must be your Alby jobs. I don't have jurisdiction to send you into a country otherwise. You are all going to stay together until we can figure out what to do," she said as they walked into her office.

"Did you get hold of Ylia or Ivan yet?" Kathe whispered to Yorg as he sat down beside her.

"No," Yorg whispered. "I need to go look for them. Yetsun called Wanda just as our meeting was starting and ordered me to stay out of Russia."

"That proves something is wrong!" Kathe whispered. "We'll figure a way to get there," she said as Ramsey began to talk again.

"You are all to stay together," Ramsey ordered. "I'm sending you to Europe tonight and I'll make sure you have enough time to do some investigating. Now, we know Nicki was killed because he found out that Mario is up to something. We must find that coded document. Tierra, can you get them inside Nicki's house?"

"It will be dangerous, but I can," Tierra responded.

"I've discovered Mario is trying to buy something big," Ramsey admitted. "I need you to find out what it is? I'll work on finding Saíde. Get some rest you're leaving tonight."

Eight hours later, over the Atlantic Ocean, Yorg walked up behind Kathe, "We've got to find Ylia and Ivan. I think, I know what Mario is after," Yorg stated. "As I was taking off this evening, it all came to me. What did I do in Russia?"

"That experimental jet!" Kathe interjected. "Saíde and Mario are planning to steal the jet and sell it to the Iranians! That's the connection between them."

"That is what I think," Yorg agreed. "Mario's profile shows that he is a pilot. Remember we saw someone taking pictures of the cockpit with a cell phone. Yetsun allowed him to take those pictures."

"Guess who it was?" Kathe confessed. "It was Mario Jr."

"How can, you be sure?" Yorg quizzed.

"Remember the funeral I didn't go to?" Kathe quizzed.

"You went!" Yorg glared at her.

"I didn't make the funeral," Kathe confessed. "Alonzo bumped the time up an hour for security reasons. But I did make the cemetery. I owe you a big thanks for making me go incognito. I got as close as I could without being recognized. I saw Mario sitting next to his father with the other man from Russia standing behind him."

"Dead men tell no tales," Yorg sighed. "Ivan was with me when I flew the jet. Yetsun is holding Ylia as an insurance policy to control me if he needs me. I know how to use the technology onboard. Ivan and I developed part of it and programmed it into that YAK U38. Ivan said Yetsun was calling the experimental jet, XP38. Ivan still could be alive, but the clock is ticking. We've got to find a way to get to Russia."

"It's not like we can borrow a plane, go there and look for them," Kathe thought out loud.

"Kathe that's it!" Yorg exclaimed. "I'll rent a plane!"

"You can't just charter a plane and fly to Russia," Kathe cautioned. "You would have to get clearance to land. You've been ordered to stay away."

"Not if I fly under the radar and land in a field," Yorg stated. "I know that area like the back of my hand."

"Yorg," Kathe said, grabbing him by his shoulders. "You can't do that. You would be shot on sight."

"I'll take that chance," Yorg admitted.

"No, you won't!" Kathe poked her finger in his chest. "There has to be another way," she thought for a second and then her face lit up. "Wait a minute, Carrie Anne can help us."

"I want to get to Russia, not get laid," Yorg chuckled.

"Carrie Anne knows pilots with their own small planes all over Europe," Kathe assured him.

"Let's ask her if she knows one that is crazy enough to fly me into Russia," Yorg argued.

"Don't laugh," Kathe confirmed. "She does know one that crazy. He's Australian and lives in London. He's as shady as they come from the way Carrie Anne described him."

"Perfect," Yorg grinned. "Call her and get his number. I've got to get back to the cockpit."

"Carrie Anne, do you remember that Australian, who lives in London?" Kathe asked quickly calling her.

"You mean Sean Redmond?" Carrie Anne frowned. "What would you want with him?"

"It's better if you don't know," Kathe replied. "All I can say is that Yorg and I need to slip in and out of somewhere without being seen. Why don't you give Sean a call and see if he's interested in helping us?"

"You can't trust him!" Carrie Anne warned. "He's a smuggler! There's no way you want to mess with him! He's a real cutthroat! Why do you think I got away from him?"

"Yorg and I can take care of us," Kathe stated. "I want you to find Sean and ask."

"Give me a minute," Carrie Anne said. "I'll try to find him."

"It took some doing, but Carrie Anne found Redmond," Kathe whispered to Yorg, after the plane landed and the crew headed for the hotel. "She left Redmond a message asking him to call her back."

"Hopefully, Redmond will remember what a good time she was and call," Yorg stated. "I still can't get in touch with Ylia. I'm worried that Yetsun has her. I know Ivan will not help him steal the jet. He is loyal to our country," he said as JAKE rang.

"It's Carrie Anne," Kathe whispered. "Let me have JAKE give Redman an alternate temporary number."

After talking to Redmond for quite some time, Yorg told Kathe, "he said he'll help me. He said he has flown in and out of there several times unnoticed."

"Do you think we can trust him?" Kathe inquired.

"Not we," Yorg objected. "I have no choice, but to trust him. I'm going alone."

"No, you're not," Kathe refuted. "I'm not letting you look for them alone. If something goes wrong JAKE can patch me through to Ramsey," she declared as JAKE rang again. "It's Redmond. He wants to talk with you again," she said, handing JAKE to Yorg.

"Redmond said he has friends in Moscow," Yorg said as he handed her back JAKE. "I gave him Ivan's name and some information. He's going to check with his sources and try to find out what happened. He said he'll call me back when he hears something, so I gave him my number."

"Great, maybe we won't have to go to Moscow," Kathe hoped.

"Kat, forget this 'we' business," Yorg insisted. "If I must go you aren't going with me. It will be too dangerous. If I'm caught, I will be executed. Yetsun is a murderer," he said, hugging her. "I've already lost Mikél to him. I'm not going to lose you too!"

"I'm not . . .," Kathe started to say as he put his finger up to her mouth.

"Not another word, Lady," Yorg declared. "You are not going! I've got to look at our flight schedule and determine the best location to slip away. But first, we need to get some rest and call Ramey for our flight information to Munich later tonight."

"After we rest," Kathe said as they checked into the hotel. "We'll plan the trip with Tierra and the team."

After resting during the day, everyone met to finalize plans to search Nicki's house. Kathe remembered the picture of Mario in Tierra's wallet. "We need to see the picture you have of your brothers. And is anyone still staying at Nicki's house?"

"No, Papa had Mario seal it up," Tierra confirmed. "He's not ready to deal with it yet," she said, reaching in her wallet.

"Is there anyway, we can get inside the house?" Yorg asked.

"I have a key and I know the alarm code," Tierra stated. "Just what are you looking for?" Tierra handed him the picture. "The one next to me is Nicki and the one on the other side of Papa is Mario."

"Thanks," Yorg said, passing the picture around to the others. "We need to find the coded document Nicki intercepted from Mario. This would prove that Mario is behind Nicki's murder."

"Kathe," Tierra confessed, "remember the night you, Kayla, and Nina had dinner with me and Nicki. Nicki had a big fight with Mario on the phone earlier that evening."

"Did you hear what it was about?" Kathe asked.

"Nicki was in his office," Tierra reflected. "I was walking by and heard Nicki yelling into the phone. It's not like Nicki to yell at anyone. They were fighting about Nicki going to Papa, if he didn't stop the deal, and then I heard the phone slam."

"What deal?" Jay asked. "Nicki came out of his office so upset he almost ran into me in the hallway. I asked him what was wrong," she said, wiping tears from her eyes. "He just said it was nothing for me to worry about. Once he had the rest of his proof he was going to Papa."

"It sounds like Nicki had some proof already," Yorg stated. "All the more reason for us to go to his house and see if we can find it," Yorg finished as the girls went to the lady's room.

Whispering to Jay and Jack, "I need to bring you two up to speed, without telling Tierra and CC. When Kathe and I were in Russia we saw Mario and his right-hand man with Gen. Yetsun. We didn't know who they were until Kathe saw them at Nicki's funeral. Yetsun ordered me to test fly a YAK U38 with a new stealth weapon technology for them. Yetsun called the experimental jet XP38 to Mario. We witnessed Yetsun allowing Mario to take several pictures of the cockpit. That means the deal is finalized."

"So, that places Mario in Russia, just like Ramsey thought," Jack concluded. "Ramsey also uncovered that Mario is trying to buy something big. It must be that jet."

"We need to ask Tierra who Mario's right-hand man is," Jay added. "That way I can check him out."

"Nicki must have intercepted something meant for Mario about the sale of XP38," Jack added.

"There is the motive for Nicki's murder," Yorg declared as the girls joined them. They went to work.

Chapter 29

Searching Nicki's House

After landing in Munich on the way to the hotel, the team passed by Nicki's house. Tearfully Tierra pointed, "There's my Nicki's house. I can't believe that he'll never be there again."

After checking into their hotel suite everyone sat down to discuss the final plans. Jay asked Tierra, "What is the name of Mario's right-hand man? I need to see what I can find on him."

"His name is Giorgio Pulini," Tierra replied. "I don't know too much about him."

"Thanks," Jay answered, opening his laptop, "that's all I need."

"Where in the house would Nicki keep important papers," Yorg asked.

"In his office behind his desk there is a wall safe," Tierra shared. "That's where Nicki keeps all his important papers. I don't know the combination. I walked in on him once and caught him closing it."

"Don't worry about the combination," Kathe added. "JAKE can handle that."

"Now, let's go over the layout of the guardhouse and house one more time," Yorg stated. "Tierra, do you have the keys?"

"I'm going with you," Tierra informed him dangling the keys in front of him.

"I have already been through this with you," Yorg objected. "It could be very dangerous. You must stay here. We can go faster without you."

"I'm not relinquishing these keys if I can't go with you," Tierra insisted. "I need to go to my Nicki's house one last time!" She tearfully insisted.

"No, Tierra," Kathe rubbed her back. "I agree with Yorg. Nicki's not there anymore. It won't do you any good going under these circumstances. You are safer here with CC and the guys. If we run into trouble and must fight our way out, you will only be in our way. You're not trained for this kind of work."

"They're right," CC agreed. "Every time you even mention Nicki's name you tear up. If there's trouble, you'll be too emotional, therefore placing all of us in more danger."

"You're right," Tierra burst into tears handing Yorg the keys.

Outside Yorg had Kathe use JAKE to borrow a car from the parking lot. "In the old days before chips were placed inside the key, we simply sparked two wires together to start an engine."

"Who taught you how to do that?" Kathe chuckled.

"My sister," Yorg winked.

"Your sister is a doctor," Kathe said as JAKE read the chip and started the car.

"Yes, but our father was a mechanic," Yorg chuckled. "He taught her how to do it and she passed it down to me."

"And I thought Tierra had the only family that passed things down," Kathe laughed, putting on her seatbelt. Slowly coming up to the estate Kathe noted, "It's just like Tierra said. There is the stone wall, the guardhouse on the left, black, wrought, iron gate and long driveway lined with trees."

"I see a transformer on each end of the estate," Yorg viewed. "But I can't tell which one goes to which house. We're in luck! The neighbors are entertaining, so we'll park behind that last car," he said pulling in. Making sure no one saw them; they reached for their duffle bags, took out their weapons, and positioned themselves on the opposite side of the car. "Tierra warned us that there are cameras on top of the guardhouse, pointing in each direction. Kathe use JAKE to see if they're activated."

"Just as I thought, this estate comes complete with microwave/infrared, motion detectors and security cameras," Kathe said, scanning with JAKE. "Affirmative, they are hot. They seem to be pointed straight down toward the sidewalk in front of the guardhouse, not the road."

"We're going to have to blow the transformer," Yorg decided. "That should buy us enough time to get inside the guardhouse and look for the alarm panel."

"But which transformer should I blow?" Kathe asked.

"Try the one on the right," Yorg suggested.

Lifting her gun Kathe attached her silencer, shot the one on the right side, which made the east side of the street go dark. "Oops! I guess we're the party poopers," she chuckled as Yorg took out the left side.

Hurrying across the street, Yorg opened the guardhouse using the master key Tierra gave him. "Aha! The computer does have a backup system like Tierra said," Yorg noted as he sat down. Hacking into the security system, Kathe watched Yorg set the cameras to show a still frame, while the link was down so anyone monitoring the system would be deceived. "It's set, let's go," Yorg said, and they hurried out.

Climbing over the wall using the wrought, iron gate, they dropped down and rolled behind the holly bushes. "I hate these bushes," Kathe whispered.

"Are you alright?" Yorg asked, glancing at her.

"Just a few minor scratches," Kathe whined, glancing at a cut on her hand.

"Put your night vision goggles on," Yorg requested. "Use JAKE to scan the perimeter of the driveway for microwaves."

Sweeping the driveway, Kathe stated, "We're clear to the last tree on the right. Let's go." Crouching down using the trees lining the driveway as cover, they inched their way to the last tree before the circular driveway began. Holding up JAKE, she checked the perimeter of the front door, "All-clear, let's move."

Reaching around to stop her as they reached the covered area Yorg cautioned, "Check the front door for motion detectors."

"All-clear," Kathe stated. "No motion detectors or infrared beams. The power is still down. Let's hurry inside," she said as Yorg used the key. "Remember Tierra said that the alarm panel is to the left."

Inside Yorg found the alarm and quickly disarmed it before the generator kicked on. "Mario and his men have been here," Yorg whispered, turning around to see the mess. "We need to make sure they didn't leave anyone here," he said as they began sweeping the open foyer and dining room.

"Do you smell something?" Kathe asked as they entered the living room from the dining room.

"No, must be your nose," Yorg replied as he looked around the large room. "This house has been ransacked. They know Nicki intercepted the proof," he surmised. "Let's clear the library next," he said as they stood on each side of the doorway. "Ready, on three, two, and one!" Opening the door, he dropped down and panned the room with his gun. Kathe stayed outside to watch his back. "Another mess," he commented, clearing the known panic room. "The panic room has been searched as well. Let's continue."

Panning the open family room, they went across to the kitchen and cleared it. Pointing to the pantry door, Kathe signaled Yorg that she was going to open it. She put her hand on the doorknob as Yorg signaled on his fingers, three, two, one. She opened the door as Yorg panned the inside with his gun. "That is an awfully small pantry for this size kitchen," Kathe whispered. "With a house and kitchen this size, it should go all the way back to the end of the wall."

"Maybe there is another pantry somewhere else," Yorg surmised. "We'll find it."

Coming back out of the kitchen, Kathe mentioned again, holding her jacket up against her nose, "Can't you smell it? It's getting stronger and it really stinks!"

"You know," Yorg stopped for a second taking a few breaths, "You are right and it's coming from Nicki's private office," he said as they stood on each side of the doorway. "On three, two, one," Yorg opened the door. They dropped down to pan the room when the stench hit them in the face.

"Oh, my, God!" Kathe screamed and fainted.

After closing the door, Yorg scooped Kathe up in his arms. He carried her to a couch in the family room and gently laid her down. He removed her goggles. He stroked the hair out of her face, "Kat, Kat, are you alright? Wake up Kat!" JAKE rang, "Yes," Yorg answered.

"Yorg?" Keith replied, watching the monitor, "Why are you answering JAKE? Is Kathe alright? Her heart rate and blood pressure suddenly took a dive."

"She has a little touch of the flu and fainted," Yorg lied. "She's okay, I'm with her," he reported and cleared the line.

Coming to, Kathe threw her arms around Yorg's neck, "Oh, my, God that was Dider! I'm so glad Tierra didn't come with us. He was tortured!"

"Will you be alright here?" Yorg quizzed. "I need to go inside and check the room? Tierra insisted that the proof is in the safe," he said, moving her bangs out of her eyes.

"I'm really nauseated," Kathe confided. "Give me a few minutes and I'll be okay. The smell is still getting to me," she answered as Yorg used his shirt to cover his nose.

A few short minutes went by and Yorg returned, "The place is totaled. Someone has gone through all the desk drawers and the safe is wide open. This was not a burglary; the valuables are flung all over the floor. They are looking for something specific. We need to talk to Tierra again. There must be somewhere else Nicki would have kept it."

"I'll call Jay," Kathe said, reaching for JAKE. "Jay, we're okay, but the proof isn't in the safe," she put JAKE on speaker. "Mario's men trashed the house, tortured, and hung Dider in Nicki's office. The safe is open and the proof is not there. Ask Tierra where else would Nicki hide an important document?"

Turning to Tierra, Jay reported, "They found the safe already opened. The house has been trashed. Where else would Nicki hide an important document?"

"I don't know," Tierra said, avoiding eye contact.

Knowing Tierra was lying, Jay got into her face. "Look Tierra, they are risking their lives trying to find out who killed your brother. Not to mention, other flight attendants that are being murdered, and it has something to do with your family! Look me straight in the eyes and tell me where your brother would hide it! Hurry up! They don't need your tears, they need help!"

Trying to compose herself, Tierra sobbed, "Upstairs, Nicki's train room. A secret room that only he, Dider and I know about in case of trouble. We could go inside until it was safe. Nicki built it after he and Mario had a huge fight about a year ago, when Mario threatened to kill him. It would be there."

"How do they get inside?" Jay demanded. "Come on!"

"If they enter," Tierra began as she took a deep breath, "from the main hallway, it's in the corner by the window. The train track runs across the windowsill. Where the train track turns the corner count two pieces of the track toward the windowsill and from underneath push up in the center. A door opens into a secret panic room. It would be in there."

"Do you copy that?" Jay asked them.

"We're already upstairs and entering the train room," Yorg said, pushing under the track, and the door opened. "We're in, thanks," Yorg cleared the line and closed the door. "Here's the light switch, let's remove our goggles," he said as they both took them off. He turned on the light.

"This room is meant to leave in a hurry," Kathe surmised as she rummaged through several suitcases filled with money. "I mean clear the building without any traces! I thought only Dr. Sydney built hidden rooms like this."

"You're right," Yorg looked around. "There must be an escape in here without going back into the house. Sydney would love to see this room," he said, opening drawers along one of the walls. "Nothing here," he said, reaching for the last drawer. Frustrated, he leaned against the wall, "Wait a minute. Let's think this out. What do we know about this guy?"

"In the short time I've been with Nicki," Kathe noted. "He appeared more passive-aggressive. Mario is the muscle behind his father's businesses. However, Nicki is not to be taken lightly."

Raising a finger Yorg added, "What have we learned, since we've been in this house?"

"That Nicki likes the element of surprise," Kathe answered. "Look at this room! It is the ultimate panic room. It has everything he needed at a moment's notice to clear the area. There must be an escape door leading outside," she said, looking around.

"This wall has drawers filled with different IDs, passports, currencies, etc.," Yorg pointed to the ones he had opened. "Look at this wall. It has every kind of gun he would need to take with him. However, look at the way these four guns have spaces under them. There must be hidden compartments," he said as he poked at the empty spots on the wall. To their surprise a compartment opened. He quickly opened each of the remaining corresponding compartments that lined up with each gun. Looking in the top one he said, "This has nothing but bearer bonds."

"This one has gold bullion," Kathe stated.

"Jewels," Yorg said.

"A Bible?" Kathe questioned opening it. "It's their mother's Bible. I need to give this to Tierra," she said, flipping through the pages, "It's not here!" she exclaimed and put it into one of the pockets in her cargo pants.

"It has to be in here!" Yorg exclaimed. "This is where he would have left it when he went to his brother's house. Nicki, where did you hide it!" Yorg shouted in anger turning around and shoving both his hands in the middle of the outside wall behind the door.

"Oh, my, God!" Kathe exclaimed as a hidden door slid sideways and a compartment extended out of the wall six inches wide by six inches long in front of their eyes. She reached inside and handed Yorg a single document folded in half.

"Bingo!" Yorg exclaimed as he read, "This letter is on Gen. Yetsun's letterhead. The rest is written in code," he said, putting it into his inside shirt pocket. "Let's get out of here."

"We need to get this to Sydney as soon as possible," Kathe stated. "He can crack the code for us. Then, we'll go from there," she said as they put on their goggles.

"Are your eyes adjusted to the dark?" Yorg asked, waiting a second.

"Yes, let's get out of here," Kathe suggested as they hurried into the train room. "Wait a second," she said as she took her goggles off and repositioned them. "My goggles were not right."

In Paris, the display panels monitoring Nicki's house blinked two times and came back online. To the guard's surprise, the still shot that was being fed to his monitor changed to show the back of Yorg's head and a side profile of Kathe. "Oh, no!" Roscoe exclaimed, picking up the phone and calling the servant quarters in Munich. "Vinnie, someone is in the train room in the main house! Let the dogs loose and get in there!"

Reaching for his glasses on the nightstand, "What do you mean, someone's in the house," Vinnie said, half asleep. "I told you earlier that the electricity was off in the entire neighborhood."

"Then explain to me, why I'm watching two people in there now!" Roscoe exclaimed.

"We're on our way!" Vinnie shouted, running down the hallway and knocking on Duke's door. "Get up! We have intruders in the main house! I'll get the dogs and meet you in the kitchen!"

"Boss, someone's in Nicki's house," Roscoe warned on his next phone call.

"I'll be right down!" Mario shouted and dialed his cell phone. "Giorgio meet me in the security room."

Kathe led the way as they headed quickly down the stairs to return to the car. Halfway down the stairs, "Dogs! I hear Dogs!" Yorg exclaimed.

Stopping in her tracks, Kathe listened, "They're heading this way from the kitchen."

"Go back to the panic room," Yorg ordered as they rushed back inside. "Check for a camera," he ordered, closing the door behind them.

"There's the camera," Kathe said, quickly using JAKE to knock it out.

Inside the panic room, they took a second to catch their breath, "We've got to find the escape door," Yorg gasped as he began feeling the outside wall for the control. "It's not here."

"I'll try over here," Kathe said as she felt the wall where the compartments were found. "We've got to hurry."

"Come on Nicki, where is it!" Yorg screamed as he kicked the baseboard in front of him.

"Thank you, Heavenly Father," Kathe sighed as she did the Sign of the Cross. A secret doorway opened to a stairwell leading down. "Where do you think these leads?" She asked as Yorg closed and locked the door behind them.

"It's got to lead to the outside behind that small pantry in the kitchen," Yorg stated. "He must have shortened the pantry to mask an escape tunnel," he said as she slowly led the way. "It's a dead end!"

"Now, what do we do Nicki?" Kathe questioned, stomping her foot.

"Did you hear that?" Yorg laughed. "I'm beginning to like this guy!"

"Hear what?" Kathe questioned.

"Stomp your foot again," Yorg suggested as she complied.

"Oh, yes!" Kathe noted. "The floor is hollow. It is a trap door. But how do we open it?"

"There's got to be a hidden latch," Yorg insisted. "Stand on the first step."

As she stood on the first step Yorg felt the floor with his hands, "Nothing, there's nothing here!"

"So far, each time we've had to push something inward to unlock each mechanism," Kathe declared. "Look for something invisible that we can push in," she looked around.

"There's nothing here, except three blank walls, stairs, a light and this handrail," Yorg shared.

"Wouldn't it be funny if it's at the end of this rail," Kathe giggled, pushing it."

"Oh, my, God!" Yorg declared as the floor began to descend. "Hop on, we're going down! It's an elevator platform."

"Who would have thought," Kathe smiled as they reached the bottom. Getting off the floor, "We're in a tunnel."

Yorg noticed a large lever, "Nicki thought of everything," Yorg said, pulling the lever. "This sends the floor back up," he said, watching it rise. "It comes complete with a lock down here so no one can follow," locking the lever into place.

"I don't know what Nicki has in store for us," Kathe grinned as they looked down the hallway. "But I bet it has four wheels and built for speed."

"After today, nothing surprises me," Yorg stated as they hurried down to the end.

"Just like I thought," Kathe giggled, "an underground garage. What a car!"

Back in Paris, "Did you download the security feeds from Nicki's yet?" Mario asked.

"Yeah, Boss, I just finished," Roscoe said, pulling up the file. "Here's what we got."

Standing in front of the monitor, Mario yelled, "That flight attendant! How does that broad keep showing up in my business? She's with some guy. Get a better angle of his face."

"I can't," Roscoe apologized. "That's all we got. He has goggles on the entire time."

"Did you let the dogs loose?" Mario asked still watching the video.

"Yeah, Boss, Vinnie and Duke are in the house looking for them," Roscoe replied. "They can't find them."

"What do you mean they can't find them?" Giorgio questioned.

"It's like they disappeared in the train room," Roscoe explained as he tried different angles. "They ain't nowhere to be found."

"Bring up the last section of the video!" Mario demanded. "They're leaving the room. Bring up the stairway camera. STOP! They are turning around and heading back to the train room. Pick up that camera again! Stop! What has she got in her hand? What just happened?"

"The camera went dead," Roscoe answered. "She held up something and shot at it!"

"Rewind it," Mario suggested. "What's in her hand?"

"It ain't no gun," Roscoe stated.

"Rewind it again and enhance the picture," Giorgio ordered. "It looks like a cell phone."

"Cell phones can't jam or shoot out signals!" Mario exclaimed. "The guy must have shot it. Get Vinnie on the phone."

"Okay," Roscoe replied.

"What do you mean the dogs can't find them?" Mario shouted.

"The scent stops in the train room in the corner to the right of the window," Vinnie explained.

"I'll be there in a couple of hours!" Mario screamed and hung up the phone. He motioned for Giorgio to leave with him. "Well, I'll be. It seems that my little brother has himself a secret room that no one knew about. No one except my baby sister. Since we didn't find Yetsun's document on Nicki or Dider's bodies, it would be in that room. Evidently, Tierra sent that flight attendant and her companion to find it. This changes everything. We have gotta make sure they don't give it to Papa."

"Maybe, they didn't find it," Giorgio stated.

"We can't take a chance," Mario confirmed. "Papa thinks I'm loyal to him. Alonzo suspects I'm up to something. This would be all Alonzo needs to take to Papa. If they found it and crack the code; I don't think Papa or Alonzo would be too happy with us."

"If they have the document, what are you going to tell Gen. Yetsun?" Giorgio asked. "We need it to finalize the sale."

"First things first, you worry too much," Mario smiled. "I will handle Yetsun after I take care of that flight attendant and Tierra. I'm sure Nicki told Tierra what I was planning. She needs that proof to go to Papa. Otherwise, she would have already," he said as they entered his office.

"Without that proof, we're safe," Giorgio stated as he sat down. "But when are we going to get Tierra?"

"Soon Giorgio, soon," Mario smiled. "We must use caution taking out dear sis. Alonzo is breathing down my neck since Nicki was killed at my house. He is monitoring Tierra very closely along with her Alby boss," he said, leaning back in his chair. "Speaking of killing people, I need to make a call. Get my Leer ready to leave for Munich."

"I'll have it ready in a half hour," Giorgio said and left. Mario picked up his cell and turned on his laptop.

"Yeah," Saíde's familiar raspy voice answered.

"I've got a special job for you," Mario laughed. "One that I know you'll like. You know that flight attendant that you've been itching to slash. She is in Munich with my sister. Use your source and check their flight schedules. Make sure whatever plane they're on doesn't land! I think she has intercepted something of mine. Make sure you don't screw up this time!"

"My pleasure," Saíde grinned, pulling up the Internet.

"Or it's your funeral," Mario muttered and cleared the line.

Returning to the hotel, Kathe was so nauseous she could hardly wait for the elevator to reach the seventeenth floor. She hurried to their suite to the nearest bathroom and threw up. Yorg was already telling the others what they found when she joined them in the sitting room. Kathe sat down on the couch by Tierra still feeling queasy.

"Are you okay," Tierra asked.

"I can't' seem to get the stench out of my noise," Kathe admitted. "I can't believe the viciousness of what we witnessed. Mario is one sick man!"

"Kathe's right," Yorg agreed. "From now on we must watch our backs. Dider had been severely tortured and hung above Nicki's desk. It was evident that he didn't tell them where the document was," he said, pulling the document out of his pocket.

Tierra burst into tears, "I've known Dider since we were kids. He was always my Nicki's best friend. What is happening to my family?"

"It's evident that your brother Mario is getting power hungry and trying to take over the business," Yorg surmised, glancing at Tierra. "That is why I believe Nicki was worried about you several months ago. I think Mario put a contract on both of you."

"Everything we seem to be uncovering," Kathe added, "points in that direction."

"Where did you find the document?" Tierra asked.

"In the secret panic room," Kathe answered. "By the way, your brother Nicki was a genius. He thought of everything right down to the secret exits."

"This document," Yorg continued, "is written in code for a Russian general who I know is a traitor to my own country. I believe that Mario is also connected to the disappearance of my sister and Ivan."

"Nicki and Dider," Kathe reflected, "must have overheard bits and pieces of Mario's negotiations to buy an experimental jet, XP38 which has stealth weapon technology from the general. Everything points to him trying to sell it to the Iranians. Remember Saíde is Iranian. This ties him to Mario. Saíde was the driver of the limo on the attempt on Nicki's life at the restaurant. Somehow, Nicki intercepted this document and figured out that Mario was going behind your father's back. Your father is no saint, but he's not a traitor. With the Middle Eastern problems in the world today, this jet would be lethal in the wrong hands."

"What's our next step?" Jay asked.

"I need to tell Ramsey we found the document and get it to Sydney," Yorg stated. "He can crack the code."

"How are we going to get it to Ramsey?" Jay asked. "Remember someone hacked into Alby control and deleted pictures of Saíde."

"Why can't we send it to the FBI?" Jack asked.

"Someone good enough to hack into Alby's computers could easily hack into the FBI's," CC quickly added.

"Just as we were leaving tonight," Kathe shared. "The electricity came back on, and we were picked up on a security camera. We were wearing goggles. I don't think they know who we are, but they know someone was there. Mario is very thorough. He can't take the chance that this document could get back to his father or Alonzo."

"Mario didn't know about the secret room," Tierra admitted.

"They sent dogs into the house when we were picked up by a hot camera," Yorg explained. "The dogs would have picked up our scent and led them to where it stopped. Mario is probably on his way to Munich now to find the room himself."

"Here Tierra," Kathe said, reaching in her pocket. "We found this in a hidden compartment."

"Mama's Bible!" Tierra exclaimed, glancing through the pages. "Nicki's most treasured possession! After Mama passed, Mario threw it in the garbage. Nicki found it and kept it. Thank you!"

"I'm glad I found it for you," Kathe smiled.

"Kat, the faster we get this document to Ramsey the better," Yorg reminded.

"You're right," Kathe said as she got up. "I'll call her now," she said, walking over to the glass French Doors leading to the balcony.

"Ramsey, we found the document," Kathe reported as she peered through the glass doors at the flowers on the balcony. "It was at Nicki's house in a secret room that only Tierra and Dider knew existed. Mario's men had already ripped the rest of the house apart. It is written on Gen. Yetsun's letterhead and is in code. We need Sydney to break the code before Tierra can go to her father. You were right about Mario trying to buy something big. It appears Mario is trying to overthrow his father and buy a Russian experimental jet, XP38 with stealth weapon technology to sell to the Iranians. That's the connection with Saíde. Should I scan it with JAKE and send it to you?"

"Negative, my computer was compromised," Ramsey warned. "Let me ask Sydney what the safest means is. He is still working on who hacked into our computers."

While Kathe waited, she turned to Yorg, "Ramsey is asking Sydney how we can safely send it," she stated as Ramsey connected the conference call to Sydney.

"Kathe," Sydney joined the conversation, "scan the document with JAKE and send it to my personal laptop. It is secure and not connected to Alby. I'm still working on our hacker."

"Copy that," Kathe replied, scanning the document, and then pressed send.

Instantly, the glass behind Kathe shattered followed by a faint gunshot. The bullet hit the vase just inches from Tierra's head.

"Ahhh!" Tierra screamed, grabbing her head. "Ahhh!" she screamed again as a second bullet hit the arm of the couch.

"Scramble!" Kathe ordered, rolling to the wall by the French Doors. She spotted the flash from the next bullet coming from the rooftop across from them. The bullet hit the table in front of the couch as Kathe drew her gun. "Rooftop!" she exclaimed, firing multiple shots randomly across that rooftop. The bullets stopped for a second.

Yorg pushed CC and Tierra to the floor and flipped the couch over them for cover. "Stay here!" he ordered.

Jay ran to a room on the left to look from that window. Jack ran to the opposite bedroom to do the same as several more shots hit the couch causing CC and Tierra to cry out.

"What is going on?" Ramsey screamed.

"We're under fire!" Kathe reported. "We've got a shooter on the roof across the street."

"I'll alert the police," Ramsey said, clearing the line.

"There are two of them on the rooftop across from us behind the gargoyle in the middle," Jay reported, taking several shots.

"I've got them in my sights," Kathe said, firing multiple times.

Yorg joined Kathe on the opposite side of the doorway and took multiple shots at the gunmen.

"Everybody down!" Kathe ordered as the spotter held up a machine gun. "Machine gun!" She exclaimed as the spotter sprayed the suite. Everyone took evasive actions as the bullets sprayed the entire suite from end to end. Jay, and Jack, dove under the beds in the rooms they were in facing the rooftop. Kathe got behind a vanity in the dining area as Yorg pulled the refrigerator forward, opened the door, and got under it. All windows and doors were shot out, the chandelier fell on top of the couch causing CC and Tierra to panic and scream louder. All the furniture in each room was destroyed as well as the TVs. Paintings on the walls flew apart and fell to the ground as did the lamps and light fixtures. Then, a surreal calm filled the air.

"They're on the move!" Jack reported. "They're heading for the rooftop access door!"

"Don't let them get away!" Yorg yelled, kicked the debris from the doorframe out of his way, stepped onto the balcony, and unloaded his clip at the fleeing assailants. "I've got the shooter," Yorg replied as he steadied his hand one more time and fired.

"The shooter is down," Jay confirmed as he reloaded his gun.

"The police helicopter is circling the roof," Jack stated. "The spotter is crouching behind the large, metal, exhaust pipe! The pilot can't see him! He's leaving this side of the roof!"

"The spotter is making a break for the doorway!" Kathe exclaimed as she fired, nicking him in the hand as he reached for the doorknob.

"The helicopter is circling back," Jack stated. "He got the door open and closed it before the pilot saw him. He got away!"

Everyone took a second to catch their breath and reunited in the main room. Jay helped Yorg lift what was left of the couch off CC and Tierra. "Oh, my, God!" CC cried, glancing around what was left of the suite. "What have we gotten into?"

"We're all going to die!" Tierra screamed and fell against the wall. Jack reached for her and held her up. "Mario is going to kill us all-just like Nicki!"

"Hold on to me," Jack offered. "There's no place to sit that doesn't have broken slivers of glass."

"This proves Mario knows we found the document," Yorg declared.

"He also knows Nicki told Tierra about the document," Kathe confirmed.

"He's desperate to shut Tierra up before she goes to her father," Jack stated.

"Not just Tierra," Jay sighed as the police broke the door down, "all of us!"

"Oh, my, God!" Lt. Herr exclaimed, entering with his men. "Is everyone alright?"

Chapter 30

Slipping Into Russia

Watching the noon news, Mario picked up his cell phone, "I can't believe I'm watching two idiots with ski mask caught on a security camera on the roof. Here's my favorite part," he said as he rewound the newscast. "You dropped your rifle and left behind a dead man, who can be linked to you and possibly me! You're supposed to be dead and now they have your prints!"

"No, Boss, I wore gloves, and the sniper I just met," Saíde reasoned, wrapping the wound on his hand.

"Where did you get this half-crazy scheme of shooting them at a hotel?" Mario demanded. "I told you to check their next flight and make sure the plane didn't land!"

"I checked their schedule like you said," Saíde appeased. "They weren't slated to leave anytime soon, so I located them at a hotel in Munich that the secretary set up for them."

"Lay low until I get back to you!" Mario snapped. "I hope you can do that right!" he hung up.

News traveled quickly; Joe sat in a hotel in Miami watching the breaking news from Munich. Reaching for his phone, "Kathe, where are you?"

"I'm in Munich," Kathe answered. "How's the tour going?" Kathe said, eagerly hurrying away from the others in the new hotel suite.

"I overheard you talking to Carrie Anne, something about a phone number," Joe mentioned. "Were you staying at the Leonardo Hilton?" he asked, watching the news show the inside of the destroyed hotel suite again.

"Why yes, we were," Kathe cautiously, answered.

"I'm watching breaking news in Munich," Joe took a deep breath, "and just put two and two together. You were involved in the sniper shooting, weren't you?"

"Guilty," Kathe sighed, "how did your fans in Miami like 'Pieces of Love?'"

"How can you so calmly ask me how the new song is doing?" Joe quizzed. "I'm not the one that just got shot at by a sniper! I can't believe you are still alive! Your hotel room was destroyed! I can't believe Yorg let this happen!"

"He was with me and my team on an assignment," Kathe admitted. "He didn't cause this."

"What kind of assignment are you on, Ms. Flight Attendant!" Joe exploded.

"I'm not at liberty to talk about it," Kathe replied. "I know that trust to both of us is important in our relationship. I didn't want to lie to you when you asked me where I am. You know what I do for a living."

"I thought we had something special in Florida!" Joe blurted. "I thought we both decided that we wanted the same thing!" his voice strained.

"We do!" Kathe insisted, sitting on the bed.

"How do we, when you do the most dangerous things, I have ever seen a woman do?" Joe demanded. "I'm on TV with fans cheering me and you are on TV either being shot at or blown up! Didn't you think about me as the shots ravaged your hotel room?"

"I didn't have time to think about anything except dodging bullets," Kathe stated.

"Why do you always take dangerous assignments with Yorg?" Joe demanded. "He's not invincible! Quit that dangerous job and come with me!"

"You know it's not that easy," Kathe reiterated. "I can't just walk away from my job!"

"Do you want Yorg and your job or me?" Joe shouted, pacing the floor.

"You can't ask me to choose between my job and you!" Kathe protested.

"So, for the rest of our lives you're going to put Yorg and your job before me?" Joe questioned as he stopped pacing and listened.

"Let's just say, right now I have to," Kathe declared.

"So, you're choosing Yorg over me?" Joe snapped.

"No, I'm choosing my job over you right now," Kathe insisted.

Glaring out his window, "Maybe having fun together for a while made us rush into something that we both need to think about!"

"Fun!" Kathe exclaimed as her eyes widened. "Is that what you think we had in Florida? I'm not one of your groupies and I'm not Carrie Anne. You're the first man I've been with since my divorce. I see now that I've made a horrible mistake!" Kathe admitted and hung up the phone. She ran to the bathroom and threw up.

Coming out of the bathroom, Kathe called control, "Ramsey can you hold my calls for a while?"

"Tierney what's wrong?" Ramsey noted her voice.

"You don't want to know!" Kathe exclaimed, clearing the line. She locked the door, fell across the bed and cried.

"Kat, room service brought dinner," Yorg said as he knocked on the door.

Kathe raised up and wiped her tears, "No thanks. I'm not hungry. I'm tired and want to go to bed."

"What's wrong?" Yorg asked, turning the doorknob. "You've locked the door."

"Nothing, everything is perfectly normal!" Kathe declared as she pulled the pillow and blanket off the bed. She laid on the floor and cried herself to sleep.

The next morning, Kathe awoke with Yorg in her room still trying to get through to his sister. Getting off the floor and putting her arms around him, she gave him a hug. "What time did you go to bed?"

"Late last night," Yorg stated. "After Joe called and I overheard you fighting, I knew something was wrong. I asked you if everything was alright, since you didn't want to eat dinner. When you answered 'nothing, everything is perfectly normal,' I knew you were upset. I stood outside the door listening to you cry yourself to sleep. Want to talk?"

"Apparently, there's nothing to talk about," Kathe confided. "My job will always be a problem to Joe," she sat down. "You still can't get through to Ylia?"

"No, I thought by now she would be off the special duty and be able to talk to me," Yorg leaned back on the bed.

"Did you get through to Ivan?" Kathe inquired as she laid down beside him.

"No luck either," Yorg shook his head.

"We need to talk to Ramsey," Kathe stated. "Do you want me to call her?"

"No," Yorg replied. "I do not want you to call about Ivan. Last night when you went to bed early, Ramsey called and gave us four days off. Now is the time for me to slip into Russia."

Tierra knocked on the door, "I heard you two talking. Can you join the rest of us for breakfast?"

Joining the others around the breakfast table, Yorg spoke, "I need to take a side trip to Russia. I know the answers to all our questions are there. Kathe, do you still have Sean's number? In the skirmish yesterday my phone got messed up."

"No," Kathe replied. "After I gave it to you, I had JAKE erase it before Ramsey found it."

"Call Carrie Anne and get it for me again," Yorg requested.

"Carrie Anne cautioned you about trusting Sean," Kathe reminded.

"I'm not a choir boy," Yorg glanced at her. "I can handle myself."

"While I'm in Russia," Yorg ordered. "I want everyone to use your personal Tablets or Laptops to find some information. Don't use Alby Computer Databanks. Someone seems to find us too easily. Jay, find out what you can about Giorgio Pulini. Tierra at some point, we'll need to bring Alonzo DiMeglio on board with us. Are you comfortable with that?"

"Yes, I trust Alonzo explicitly," Tierra replied.

"Jack, check with Ramsey and see if there's any more dead crew members," Yorg asked. "Maybe you can help her figure out a pattern to the women Saíde's chooses on his killing sprees."

CC interrupted, "Can I help Jack work on that?"

"That's fine," Yorg continued, "you all have to stay together anyway." Noticing Kathe fidgeting, "Are you okay?"

"Sure," Kathe answered as Jay poured another cup of fresh coffee. "After you call Carrie Anne, check with Wanda and get us a flight over to Vienna and hotel suite," he said as Kathe bolted out of the room.

Coming out of the bathroom, Kathe called Carrie Anne, "Hi, Carrie Anne."

"Kathe I'm glad you called," Carrie Anne said, standing across from Joe, "We're on our way to Memphis and guess who's sitting next to me?"

"I'm not interested," Kathe replied. "I'm in a hurry. I need Sean Redmond's number again. I had JAKE scramble my number and erase it after he called me. I gave it to Yorg, but his phone is messed up."

"I'll give you Sean's number, but he's nothing but trouble," Carrie Anne warned as Joe listened to her repeat the number.

"What is Kathe up to this time?" Joe asked, glancing at Carrie Anne.

"She needs a pilot, stupid enough to sneak her and Yorg into Russia," Carrie Anne blurted. "Forget I said that. It looks like she's going against orders, again."

Returning to the others, Kathe reported, "Wanda has us staying in room #334 at the Stadtpark Marriott Hotel in Vienna. Our flight leaves in an hour, so we need to hurry. Here is Redmond's number," she said, handing Yorg a piece of paper. He quickly left the room.

Four hours later, the crew checked into the Stadtpark Marriott in Vienna. The suite was beautiful, overlooking the entrance to the Vienna Zoo. About 4:30 that afternoon, Yorg was getting ready when Kathe knocked on his door. "Come in," he said, placing his gun in the holster in the small of his back.

"I need to talk to you," Kathe said.

"I'll talk with you about anything, except you going with me," Yorg insisted. "You're wasting your time."

"I'm not a little girl," Kathe stated.

"I don't want to hear it!" Yorg declared. "I can travel much faster without you. I don't have to worry about you," he said as he put his rifle in the bag.

"When did you start worrying about me being in danger?" Kathe questioned, starring at him.

"When I realized . . ." Yorg started to say and changed the subject. "When I get back, we'll talk."

"Look," Kathe pulling her navy sweater down showing her shoulders. She pointed to an implant, "After the incident with Saíde on the flight to Paris, Ramsey had Sydney insert this new implant. Now control not only can always locate me, but they can talk to me and," she released her sweater and pointed at him. "They can hear me also. It's activated by the sudden change in my heart rate, or it's activated by control, if it is ultra-important. I've used it already. A week ago, you saw the newspaper article when Joe hit McCollum in a restaurant. My heart rate alerted control. Ramsey heard what was going on and summoned the police. You need me if anything goes wrong. I can help you in more ways than one."

Thinking for a second, Yorg said, "It's too dangerous for you. I guess finally meeting your children made me realize that they need you."

"I love my children," Kathe reiterated. "They barely know me anymore. You know I stay away from them as much as possible for their own safety. The first time I pulled the trigger, I knew I could never live with them again. They live a normal and happy life with Jeannie and Bob."

"You can always marry Glitter Boy," Yorg smirked.

"After our fight last night, that's not an option," Kathe admitted. "Am I going with you, or do I call Ramsey and tell her what you're up to?"

Pointing his finger at her, "That is blackmail, and you know it!"

"You bet it is," Kathe grinned. "I'm not taking no for an answer. You seem to have forgotten that I'm the main person Saíde is after. I won't be safe until we get him."

CC knocked on the door, "Sean Redmond is here."

"I'll be right there," Yorg said, glaring at Kathe. "Okay, you can go, but only because I know you're right."

"Glad to meet you," Yorg said, shaking Sean's hand.

"Glad to meet you mate," Sean answered.

"This is Kathe Tierney," Yorg introduced. "She will be traveling with us."

"This isn't a trip to the mall," Sean cautioned, shaking her hand.

"I'm well aware of that," Kathe replied. "I will be fine," she answered, looking him straight in the eyes.

"I don't like taking a woman on a mission like this," Sean stated, glancing at Yorg. "You didn't mention taking a lady, especially a pretty one."

"She can hold her own," Yorg told him and opened the door. "Let's go."

It was just getting dusk as they entered the cab. They were taken to an obscure empty field outside of town. As the cab drove away, Sean asked for his money. "I'll give you half now and half when we return safely."

"Not good enough," Sean responded. "I want all my money up front just in case you get yourself killed."

"I only have half the money with me," Yorg stated. "The rest is back at the hotel. I gave it to the clerk to put in the safe with your name on it. You can't pick it up until one of my colleagues tells him it is okay. Here is your claim check." Yorg handed it to him, "Call the hotel and ask the front desk to check the claim number."

"I will," Sean replied and called the hotel.

"Yes, Sir," the hotel manager stated. "A Mr. Vuslick did in fact, leave a large envelope for a Mr. Redmond. It is here for him to bring the claim check for pick up upon approval of a third party."

"Thank you," Sean answered as he cautiously looked at Yorg. "Okay, let's go."

"Where's the plane?" Kathe asked, looking around the empty field.

"I flew in late last night and hid it at the edge of the trees across the road," Sean stated, lighting up a cigarette and leading them to the plane. "Help me uncover it and push it to the road. We'll use the road for a runway. We will fly low and follow the terrain. I do this several times a month."

The men talked about the mission all the way. Kathe sat in the backseat behind Yorg half listening to them, and half thinking about Joe. She kept thinking about the good and bad times they had and the last thing he said to her. Tears filled her eyes several times during the flight. As they approached the Russian border, Yorg reached around and squeezed her hand. Sean turned the lights off and dropped the plane even lower. With the moonlight, she could tell they were following a riverbed. After what seemed to be an eternity, Sean turned the lights back on and landed the plane in a field. They quickly covered up the plane again. Just as they finished, a car came down the road toward the field. They hurried away from the plane and hid among the rocks of the riverbed. The car stopped and turned its lights off and on two times. Sean smiled, "It's okay, my new friends. It is two of my comrades, Kiev, and Pushkin."

"Kat, stay here and cover me," Yorg whispered as he and Sean walked toward the car.

Kathe stayed low and unholstered her gun. She watched as the men seemed to know Sean and were very friendly.

"Kathe, it is okay," Yorg called to her. "This is my girlfriend, Kathe Tierney," he introduced as she joined them.

In the car on the way to their headquarters, Yorg talked with the men about Ivan and his sister. Kiev had already sent a scout to find Ylia. "I checked on your sister's location. She is being held under the pretense of taking care of a general's dying mother. She will be kept there for another couple of months at least," Kiev reported.

"How did you find out?" Yorg asked.

"I can't tell you comrade," Kiev replied. "If something goes wrong and you are captured, you could endanger the lives of many people. But I did know you would question our reliability, so I had my contact take this," he handed Yorg a photo of his sister at the hospital with an elderly woman.

"I have seen this woman," Yorg admitted, putting the photo inside his coat. "She's Gen. Broshniv's mother."

The car came to a halt in front of an old farmhouse in the middle of a large field. They entered the barn near the house and went to the horse stalls. The middle of the third stall had several bales of hay in the corner. The men opened a trap door from beneath the hay and went down the steps. Inside was a large group of civilians that made up the Freedom Fighters, operating old computers and radars.

"This is our underground headquarters," Pushkin said. "We brought you here, because I believe from the story Sean relayed that we are working on the same problem."

"I don't understand," Yorg stated.

"We have a contact in the Russian Army that none of us have ever seen," Kiev explained. "He too, is a Freedom Fighter like us. He was trying to help us protect our country's newest experimental fighter jet, XP38. Word has it that Gen. Yetsun is planning to steal it. He wants to sell it to the Italians, who are going to sell it to the Iranians. This technology would be fatal to the entire world in their hands. He says the same general tried years ago to steal one and failed. The only pilot who could fly that kind of technology refused."

"I think we are on the same team," Yorg smiled, glancing at Kathe. "It sounds like my friend Ivan is the Freedom Fighter you are speaking about. I'm still in the Russian Army. About a month ago, Russia finally cleared the use of the Moscow's Airport to Alby Airlines with me as the captain. Within twelve hours after landing, Ivan was sent to bring me to Headquarters for a debriefing concerning the International Anti-Terrorism Program that I am spearheading. After the debriefing, Ivan received a phone call and took me to a hidden airfield to test fly XP38 for Gen. Yetsun and his guest. Ivan and I worked on the stealth weapon technology aboard that craft. Now he is missing."

Pushkin interjected, "It sounds like your friend could be him. We lost contact with him just a little over a week ago. We only know him by his code name."

Yorg interrupted, "Is his code name Popeye?"

"Yes," Pushkin stated. "Popeye is our contact's code name. We are looking for the same man. About a month ago, Popeye was supposed to get us information on the best time to move the jet. We found a perfect place to hide it until we could figure out a way to stop Yetsun. He contacted us and said the people from Italy were back earlier than expected. He would have to lay low for a while. We've been trying to contact him ever since with no luck."

"Ivan called Kathe about a week ago looking for me," Yorg stated. "She said she could hardly hear him. It sounded like he was running and out of breath. She told him to call me in Paris. When he called, I was with the gendarmes investigating a crime scene and his message was cut off."

"Popeye told us Mario LaBasco Jr. is negotiating a deal to buy XP38 without his father's knowledge," Pushkin confided.

"I went through Nicki LaBasco's house after his murder," Yorg admitted, reaching in his jacket. "I found this document. I don't know what it means."

Kiev looked over the document, "Popeye mentioned something about a coded document. He was trying to intercept it. It is supposed to contain the date and time the XP38 is to be stolen and the names of the people to contact in the Middle East." He looked up at Yorg, "It is written in code. I will make a copy and try to have it decoded with your permission."

"I thought that would be the information it contained," Yorg said, nodding approval. "The day I test flew the XP38, one of the men at the airstrip with some Europeans was Mario LaBasco Jr. Neither one of us recognized Mario until sometime later when Kathe saw him sitting beside his father at his brother's funeral."

"Mario needs this document to complete the deal," Kiev surmised. "It wouldn't be due for Gen. Yetsun to learn that he doesn't have it. This could be the trump card we have been looking for to stop Yetsun."

"I work with Tierra LaBasco," Kathe explained. "She needs us to decode this document so she can take proof to her father about her brother. It looks like not only did Mario kill his brother, but he's trying to take over the business."

"Ilomrn ham (Help us)!" Dimetre yelled as he helped Jonas down the steps causing a loud commotion at the entrance.

"Ham hykeh meAnk (we need a medic)," warned a comrade. "Jonas óbin pacctpenrh (Jonas has been shot)."

The two men were brought into the room. Kiev ran to his comrades, "Dimetre, what happened to Jonas?"

"We found where Yetsun is holding some hostages," Dimetre began. "We located two of our men before a car pulled up and another man was dragged inside. He was blindfolded and badly beaten. We were going for a closer look when we were fired upon. We barely got away."

"Did you recognize the man?" Kiev asked.

"It was hard to tell," Dimetre replied as a woman ran over embracing him. "He was wearing a blindfold."

"Can you describe what little of him you did see?" Yorg asked.

"He looked to be about six-foot, big build, wearing a Russian uniform," Dimetre answered.

"That could be Ivan," Yorg stated. "At least, now I have hope that he is still alive. Can you take me to this place?"

"Yes, as soon as I get something warm to eat," Dimetre said and hurried off with his wife.

"Do you have a place where Kathe and I can change?" Yorg asked.

"Yes, Pushkin will show you to a room," Kiev answered. "He will show you where we keep extra snowsuits. Make sure you have plenty of ammo. If this is Popeye, we can't leave him behind."

Chapter 31

The Betrayal

Within a half hour, Kiev and a handful of his best men were ready to leave. "Where is Redmond?" Yorg asked.

"Sean is not coming with us," Kiev replied as they left the compound in an old Hummer. "He is just a smuggler. He doesn't get involved with our politics."

They headed for the farmhouse where Dimetre and Jonas witnessed the hostages. It was just before midnight and the weather was extremely cold with light snow just beginning to fall. Finally, the Hummer turned off-road and headed up a hillside. Kathe realized it looked familiar, "Yorg we have been here or near here recently, haven't we?"

"Yes," Yorg answered as he looked around. "This is the road to the secret airstrip outside of Moscow where XP38 is kept. We're entering from the back," he confirmed as the Hummer came to a halt.

"We must go by foot from here," Kiev said, turning to one of his men. "Pavel, go to the hospital and check on the doctor. We'll join you as soon as we are done here."

Dimetre pointed ahead of them, "They have Ivan in that farmhouse over the next hill. Your sister is just beyond the farmhouse about two kilometers in a private hospital. We will be able to rescue her after Ivan."

The bitter cold seemed to grip Kathe more than usual as she kept up with the men. They hurried through the deep snow. Finally, they stopped just on the top of the hill overlooking the farmhouse.

"I see about four or five guards around the perimeter," Yorg reported, looking through his binoculars. "I'm going down for a closer look."

"After my men were spotted tonight," Kiev cautioned, "it doesn't make any sense that they would only leave a handful of guards, especially if they have Popeye. We'll cover you," he said, motioning his men into position.

"Watch yourself," Yorg whispered to Kathe glancing around at the men, "and me."

"I don't trust anybody here," Kathe whispered. "I've got your back," she promised, watching Yorg leave. "There's a good spot," she thought as she laid across a rock behind some bushes. "It sure is cold," she thought as she began to shiver watching Yorg through her scope. She held her breath and steadied her aim watching Yorg just miss being seen by a guard as he peered inside a window. "That was too close," she thought as she followed Yorg around the back of the building losing him. She held her breath until she found him on the other side peering inside another window. Finally, he worked his way back to the hill. She noted Kiev's men making sure Yorg wasn't followed.

"Ivan is inside," Yorg reported. "He's barely alive. He doesn't look like he can make it very much longer. There are two other people also badly beaten in another room. One of them has his right hand wrapped up in a blood-soaked cloth. There are two guards in the room with Ivan, a guard in the kitchen, and five or six playing cards in the living room." Yorg bent down and began drawing in the snow with his knife showing Kiev and his men where the guards were outside of the building. "I need your men to secure the perimeter."

"I agree," Kiev said. "With this many guards inside, even when we secure the perimeter and enter the building, Ivan will be shot, before we can get to him."

"Not if we have someone on the inside protecting him," Yorg replied. "I have a plan," Yorg looked over at Kathe. "I need you to get inside his room."

"What do you want me to do?" Kathe asked.

"Kiev is right," Yorg discussed. "Securing the perimeter is easy. However, I'm sure as we enter the building the guards in his room have orders to kill Ivan."

"How do you expect me to get inside the house, much less Ivan's room?" Kathe question. "I can't just ring the doorbell and say, 'honey I'm home!'"

"You're going to do just that," Yorg grinned. "You're going to drive the Hummer up the driveway and pretend to have car trouble. Pop the clutch a few times; I will loosen a few sparks plug wires. If Ramsey patches you through to my earpiece, I can help you with the language. You can use your good looks to get the guards to help you. Then, you can ask to use the bathroom," he smiled. "Inside work your way to his room and tell me when we can join you."

"She won't be able to pull this off, comrade," Kiev said bluntly.

"Do this just like you did at Newark," Yorg said, looking into her eyes.

"I need to call Ramsey and have her patch JAKE to your earpiece," Kathe reminded him.

"We have no choice, make the call," Yorg ordered, shaking his head.

Reaching for JAKE, Kathe dialed Alby Control. With a deep breath and her thumb held up to Yorg, "Ramsey, I need your help. Patch JAKE through to Yorg's earpiece."

"Why?" Ramsey questioned.

"Because I need Yorg to be able to hear someone talking to me, translate it, and tell me what to say," Kathe admitted.

"What for?" Ramsey asked as Yorg reached for JAKE.

"Because Ramsey," Yorg explained. "We are outside a farmhouse near Moscow where our friend Ivan has been severely beaten and held prisoner. I need to send Kathe into the building so I can rescue him, and she doesn't speak Russian."

Ramsey sat straight up in her chair, "What are you two doing in Russia?"

"I take full responsibility," Yorg admitted. "Will you help us?"

"Do I have a choice?" Ramsey snapped, tapping her ink pen on the desk.

"It would be safer if you would just help us," Yorg affirmed.

"Don't you dare pull that Russian innocence on me!" Ramsey warned. "Hold on for a moment while I reach Sydney."

While they were waiting Kathe took her duffle bag out of the trunk, changed from her snowsuit to a regular jacket, scarf and gloves. She also strapped a small derringer to the inside of her right thigh. Ten long minutes went by until Ramsey rejoined them on the phone.

"Yorg, I have Sydney at your disposal," Ramsey stated. "Tell him what you need."

Yorg filled Ramsey and Sydney in on the situation and the plan at the same time. "This is doable, dangerous, but doable," Ramsey stated.

"Kathe doesn't need to take JAKE with her," Sydney informed them. "Yorg hang on to it. I haven't told even Ramsey, but Kathe's new implants are sufficient to globally communicate with her."

"When were you going to tell me?" a very surprised Ramsey demanded.

"When I had tested it out," Sydney beamed. "This is a perfect time."

"I will ride with Kathe as far as I can down the road, and loosen the spark plugs wires for her," Kiev stated. "Then, I will wait for Yorg and the others to get into position and join them."

"Tierney, your performance is critical to your staying alive," Ramsey warned. "Make sure you strap a gun to the inside of your thigh, high enough that they can't find it when they search you."

"It's already there," Kathe said as she got into the driver's seat. "I'm ready."

"Here she comes," Yorg relayed, watching through his binoculars. "She's stalling out in front of the house, right on time. The guards are surrounding the Hummer; they're getting her out of the car," he said as he listened and began telling Kathe exactly what to do and say as Ramsey and Sydney monitored the situation. "What looks like a lieutenant is joining them from inside; he's taking Kathe into the house. She's asking to use the bathroom. He's showing her the bathroom. Her accent is pretty good."

"Thank God," Ramsey sighed with relief as they heard the bathroom door close behind Kathe.

A few seconds later, Kathe flushed the toilet, turned on the water in the sink and whispered, "I saw the door to the room where Yorg said Ivan is located. I know a guard is waiting for me. It is dim in here and something stinks. I can't see how I can get away from the guard to get in Ivan's room," she said, reaching for a towel to dry her hands. Instantly, she got nauseated and ran to the toilet heaving.

"What's wrong?" Yorg asked.

"There is blood in the garbage can and a man's finger," she gagged. "Oh, my, God!" she continued, looking around the room. "The shower has blood all over it." She hurried back to the toilet, throwing up again as a guard began banging on the door ordering her to come out.

"I saw one of the other hostages with his hand wrapped in a bloody cloth that must be his finger," Yorg remembered. "Выйд ванной!" (Knocking on the door.) "He wants you to come out of the bathroom," Yorg translated. "Выйд ванной!" Knocking louder on the door.

"I have an idea," Ramsey offered. "Kathe, you're throwing up; that's good thinking. Slowly open the door, hold your mouth with one hand, rub your stomach as if you are pregnant, and then throw up again. The guard will probably leave you alone for a while."

"When the guard leaves the doorway," Yorg continued, "it might buy you enough time to slip into Ivan's room. Open the door slowly and do what Ramsey said. Kiev's men have already cleared the perimeter and are waiting to enter. I'm outside Ivan's window."

Kathe slowly opened the door, acted as if she was going to throw up again and pointed to her stomach. The guard rolled his eyes and went to the other room as she closed the door and threw up again.

After a few minutes spent composing herself, Kathe put her gun behind her back and peeked out the door. "It's clear," she whispered as she slowly turned the doorknob. "I'm leaving the bathroom."

"Wait, Kathe!" Sydney urged, typing on his laptop. "I'm opening the parameter of your implants. I hear two different voices in the room. They seem to be playing cards and they are to the right of the door. I am picking up three heartbeats inside the room. One is very weak. You may go to the door now."

"That should be Ivan," Yorg whispered, signaling Kiev's men to enter simultaneously with him. "We are all ready . . . Okay . . . On my count, three, two, one, now!"

Kathe kicked the door open, dropped low, shot two guards as shots rang through the entire house.

"Someone's behind you drop to the floor!" Sydney ordered as Yorg shot through the window and killed the guard behind her.

Kathe hurried over to Ivan while Yorg entered, swept the hallway, and then joined Kiev's men clearing the building. "Ivan, it's Kathe," she said, taking off his blindfold. "You're going to be alright," she said as Yorg joined her. He untied Ivan's hands and tried to make him comfortable.

"Yorg," Ivan barely whispered. "Old friend . . . I knew . . . you would come," he was gasping for air. "Underground . . . find Kiev . . . tell him . . . Popeye said . . . Yetsun . . . must not . . . steal . . . the jet . . . you must . . . promise . . ." Yorg held him closer. "Karl Raini perfected . . . our work . . . Yetsun killed him . . . He must not sell to . . .," he coughed, taking his last breath, and died in Yorg's arms.

"I promise my old friend," Yorg said, closing Ivan's eyes. "I will stop Yetsun this time!" Kathe took the blanket off the bed and handed it to Yorg as Kiev joined them. "I don't have time to bury you, old friend," he said, covering him after Kiev saw him.

"We found our friends in the next room," Kiev reported. "They are pretty beaten, but they will live. Was that Popeye?"

"Yes, he told me to go underground, find you and tell you that Popeye said not to let Yetsun steal the jet," Yorg stated.

"Farewell, Popeye," Kiev declared. "We're going to miss your help. I promise this time we will stop Yetsun!" He exclaimed as he glanced at Yorg. "We must leave. Someone will check on them soon. You surprised me," Kiev said, glancing at Kathe. "For a frail looking American woman, you know your stuff."

Leaving the room, seeing all the bodies lying everywhere Kathe ran to the bathroom heaving. Yorg came to the door and opened it. He went over to her and put his arm around her waist. He lifted her up, "Are you, okay?"

"I'll be alright," Kathe insisted. "The smell of blood is really getting to me."

"Something must be wrong with your nose, it's really sensitive lately?" Yorg questioned.

"You two get out of there before someone comes," Ramsey interrupted.

"We're leaving right now," Kathe said. "We're getting Ylia and leaving the country."

"What do you mean?" Ramsey screamed.

"You know exactly what I mean," Kathe explained. "We can't leave without Yorg's sister. Yetsun will kill her as soon as he finds out we tried to rescue Ivan, just as he did Mikél. They're holding her near here," Kathe said, getting into the Hummer.

"My people can't crack the code," Kiev declared, leaving the farmhouse as he hung up his cell. "My men will have Sean ready to leave as soon as we rescue your sister. Did Popeye say when Yetsun is going to steal the jet?"

"No," Yorg answered. "We have someone who will crack the code."

"How do you plan to get out of Russia, once you have your sister?" Ramsey inquired.

"The same way we got here," Yorg stated. "A smuggler friend of Carrie Anne's, by the name of Sean Redmond," he answered as Ramsey pulled up the Internet and typed in his name.

"We need to talk when the two of you get back," Ramsey affirmed. "We do not keep secrets from each other. Go ahead with your plans and call me when you are ready."

"We may be unemployed when we get back," Yorg cautioned, handing JAKE back to Kathe.

"Not on your life," Kathe grinned as the Hummer stopped down an icy road in the woods. "Who else would she get to do what we do?"

"Just beyond the bend is the private hospital," Kiev informed them. "Pavel works there as a janitor.

That's how we found your sister," he said, leaving the road and bringing the Hummer to a stop. "Follow me."

As they hurried through the woods and approached a building behind the small hospital, Pavel greeted them.

"What have you found out?" Kiev asked.

"The doctor was just finishing her work with the general's mother," Pavel reported. "I watched the guards escort her back to her room. It doesn't seem like any alert has been made from your earlier skirmish. We better move swiftly before they find out."

"Is there an outside entrance to the doctor's room?" Kiev asked.

"No, the only way in the hospital is through the front or back door," Pavel cautioned. "The doctor's room is in the middle of the building. There is a guard posted outside her door."

Yorg looked at Kiev, "Again, if we can get Kathe inside, she can help us get Ylia out."

"I'm not sure how the American woman can tell you exactly what is happening, but you're right," Kiev answered, glancing at Pavel. "How many soldiers are in the hospital?"

"More than usual and it has nothing to do with the general's mother," Pavel stated. "She's been here before."

Yorg glanced over at Kathe standing next to Pavel. He was short, just a little taller than she was. He also had very blonde hair, just like her. He looked toward Kiev, "What if we dressed Kathe up in Pavel's clothes? She can wear the hat down on her face more. If she doesn't make eye contact, she might pull this off."

"It won't work," Pavel disagreed. "I know the people inside. I always talk and joke with them. They don't let anyone inside without clearance."

"How can we get her inside?" Kiev wondered.

"I know," Kathe interrupted. "I can hold something to my mouth, like I'm injured and need a doctor. I won't have to talk."

"Perfect," Kiev agreed. "Pavel, do you have an extra jacket and hat?"

"Yes, in this building," Pavel said, reaching for his keys.

"Bring me a clean cloth, if you can find one," Yorg suggested.

"Why do you need a clean cloth?" Kathe questioned.

"For your injury," Yorg replied. "You need to look like you were hit in the mouth," he said, reaching for the cloth. Taking his knife out of his pocket, he made a cut on his forearm. "You know my blood is safe. I surely don't want to have to hit that pretty face of yours again," he smiled, wiping his blood on the cloth. "It will be light soon; we need to hurry. Call Ramsey and have her patch me through to JAKE again."

Pavel handed Kathe his jacket and hat. Yorg pulled the hat down over most of her face and handed her the cloth. "Ramsey," Kathe called and explained the plan.

"Sydney and I will be online with you," Ramsey confirmed and cleared the line. Kathe put JAKE inside her jacket.

"Hold this up to your face and walk bent over like you're in pain," Yorg suggested. "Pavel should be able to do the rest."

Yorg and Kiev watched from a distance as Pavel put his arm around her. She bent over, as they walked into the entrance of the hospital, just as the sun's rays began peeking over the mountain. Yorg noted the smell of blood was bothering her again. Inside he translated as Pavel explained to the guards and a nurse that his cousin was accidentally hurt. She held the bloody cloth closely to her face. She could hardly stand it. A guard escorted them down the hallway to a small examining room. Kathe bent over the table fighting back nausea. She did not want to lie down fearing they might notice she was a woman. The guard left the room to get the doctor. The door opened and Ylia walked into the room with the guard standing at the door. Ylia began asking questions about the accident. "Chto sluchilos," Ylia asked her as Yorg interpreted. "Ya vrach," Ylia continued.

"I'm a doctor," Yorg stated.

"Otkroj svoj rot," Ylia asked.

"What happened?" Yorg interpreted as Ylia tried to move the cloth away from her face. Kathe's eyes raced to Pavel. He answered for Kathe while Yorg interpreted so Kathe understood. "My cousin was working on a machine; something broke loose and hit him in the mouth. He hasn't talked since the accident," Pavel stated, carefully positioning himself between the doctor and the guard.

"Ylia it's me, Kathe Tierney," she whispered as Ylia's eyes widened in disbelief.

Ylia continued to direct all her questions to Pavel as she reached in the drawer for a pair of gloves. Pavel answered her as he continued to block the guard's view of Kathe's face. Ylia pretended not to find her otoscope and asked the guard to bring one from the room across the hall.

As the guard left the room, Kathe quickly moved the cloth from her face. "Ylia, we have to get you out of here! You are in grave danger!"

"What are you doing here?" Ylia asked astounded. "Why am I in danger?"

"We have no time to talk," Pavel answered. "Which exit has the fewest guards?"

"The front door," Ylia stated. "There are two rooms next to the back door that they are using as barracks."

"Yorg," Kathe said quietly, "there are more guards at the back door."

The party's over!" Kiev interrupted, rushing over to Yorg. "They found the farmhouse!" he exclaimed, signaling his men into position.

"Tell Pavel to lock the door to the room and find something to barricade it!" Yorg ordered. "Reinforcements just arrived! I'm going to set a small nitro-charge against the outside wall!"

Pavel instantly locked the door and dragged the exam table against it. Kathe turned a desk over for cover as guards pounded the door. "Yorg, blow it now!" Kathe ordered. Yorg ignited the nitro. Ylia screamed as the rubble flew into the room.

Yorg poked his body in the large hole, "Ylia, come on!" he exclaimed, reaching for her hand. "Stay low and keep up with me," he ordered as they ran toward the small building, dodging bullets, while Kiev and his men covered them.

"We can't stay here!" Kathe warned, reaching the building, and returning fire. "We've got to get to the Hummer!"

"No good! Soldiers are there," Kiev answered as Yorg looked around for a way out. "I've sent for help. But they are thirty minutes away!"

"We need a diversion, anymore nitro?" Kathe asked, glancing at Yorg.

"No more nitro!" Yorg exclaimed, looking around. "Pavel, what's inside this building?"

"Nothing that would help us, just my work supplies," Pavel answered.

"Look inside," Ramsey suggested as she analyzed the situation from control. "There should be something flammable. Stick a piece of rag in it, light it and throw it; you have got a bomb."

"Stay here!" Yorg ordered Ylia. He broke a window and climbed into the building.

"Look out Pavel!" Kathe exclaimed, reaching in her boot, and throwing a knife; killing a soldier that was sneaking up behind him.

"Thanks, my new friend," Pavel sighed as Yorg rejoined them holding two cans with rags poked inside.

"We've got one shot at this!" Yorg exclaimed. "We must make a breakthrough the woods when I throw this. Pavel which way do we go?"

"Toward the river!" Pavel exclaimed. "It doesn't freeze! I have a boat hidden there," he advised as Kiev signaled his men.

"Pavel, lead the way!" Kiev ordered.

"Kathe take Ylia with you!" Yorg ordered as he lit the rag in the first can. "Kiev and I will bring up the rear with my last can," Yorg declared, throwing the first can toward the soldiers.

As soon as it exploded, Kathe and Ylia raced toward the river dodging bullets as Pavel's men covered them.

"I can't leave Yorg!" Ylia cried, stopping when they heard the second explosion.

"Tierney, grab her hand and take her with you!" Ramsey ordered.

"Yorg can take care of himself!" Kathe replied, reaching for Ylia's arm. "We've got to make it to the river! He'll join us!"

Reaching the river, Pavel found the boat. Kathe and Ylia helped him uncover it as the shots got closer. "We've got to hurry!" Kathe exclaimed as she helped Pavel drag the boat through the thick reeds and launch it in the water. Pavel jumped in first and checked the motor.

"Yorg!" Ylia exclaimed as he cleared the forest with a few Freedom Fighters.

"Come on!" Pavel exclaimed as he tried to get the engine to turn over. "Come on!" he tried again. "Come onnnn . . ." he demanded as it finally turned on. "I got it working! Get in!"

"Ylia, get in the boat!" Kathe ordered as she knelt behind the reeds and covered Yorg and the few men joining them. Yorg slid beside Kathe as a few more Freedom Fighters made it to the clearing.

"No!" Ylia screamed as the last one fell to the ground. Kiev was seconds behind him and scooped him up in his arms. Yorg, Kathe, and the men covered them from the riverbank.

Ylia reached to help the injured man as they laid him in the boat. "I hear something coming!" Kathe exclaimed, looking around. "It sounds like a motor," she said as they cleared the bend. "We've got three PT boats with more soldiers coming toward us! What do we do now?"

"Can't make a run for it in the boat!" Kiev exclaimed. "They're cutting us off!" he admitted as more Freedom Fighters finally arrived from the trees to the right of them. "Thank God! They finally made it!"

"Well, I'll be!" Yorg exclaimed as Sean joined them in the reeds.

"Looks like you could use a little help," Sean said as he returned fire.

"I thought you wanted to stay neutral?" Yorg asked.

"The general and I go way back," Sean admitted as he took a few more shots. "The last dealings I had with him. He left me holding the bag with some Italians! So, I figured I better help the man who is putting a wrench in his latest scheme!"

"We have worn out our welcome!" Yorg pointed to the PT Boats. "Which way out of here?"

"My plane is just beyond those trees," Sean stated, pointing to the way he came.

"Take the women and leave, while we cover you!" Kiev ordered as he handed Yorg the copy of the coded document back. "Pavel will go with you as far as the plane. We couldn't break the code. Call me when you break it!"

"Thanks, for all your help," Yorg called as he slid backwards along the ground. "I'll be in touch," Yorg agreed and then made his way to the boat. "Sean's plane is close by," he told Kathe and Ylia as Sean called to them.

"Follow me!" Sean ordered, fanning his automatic weapon from left to right.

Kiev's men covered them as Yorg pulled Ylia through the deep woods. Yorg stopped about a kilometer away from the fighting for Ylia and Kathe to catch their breath.

"Don't stop yet," Sean warned as he kept going. "They can rest when we're airborne!"

"He's right, we've got to keep moving," Pavel agreed, reaching for Kathe's hand.

Up ahead on the top of the hill, Sean motioned for them to stop as they came up behind him. "Wait here," Yorg ordered Kathe, as he and Pavel joined Sean.

"Soldiers," Sean whispered, pointing to the open field. They went for a closer peek down the hill. "At least, they haven't disabled my plane."

"I only count six of them," Pavel noted, holding up his rifle, peering through his scope.

"Yes, my comrade," Sean agreed, pushing Pavel's rifle down. "However, we can't take the chance of a stray bullet hitting my plane."

"Sean's right," Yorg agreed. "We need a plan to lure them away from the plane."

"I have an idea," Sean suggested. "They are looking for you. I will pretend to have captured you. You can put your hands behind your necks and walk in front of me. I will hold my gun on you. When we get close enough, you can pull your pistols and we'll open fire."

"Sounds good to me," Pavel quickly agreed.

"What will we do with our rifles?" Yorg cautiously asked.

"I'll carry your rifles to make it look more realistic," Sean replied as the sound of gunshots behind them got closer. "You can keep your pistols behind your back. I know it will work."

"We have no other choice," Yorg agreed as they walked back to the others. "Kiev can only hold the soldiers off so long," he told them. Yorg explained the plan to Kathe as Ramsey and Sydney listened.

"This doesn't feel right," Kathe whispered to Yorg. "I don't trust Sean."

"So far, Sean has been on your side," Ramey confided. "However, I did run a profile on him and it's very sketchy. He seems to be very allusive in his travels and dealings. However, we do have an edge in that country; you're just a frail American woman. The soldiers would not suspect your talents."

"Make sure you position yourself to the left flank of Sean," Sydney added. "That will give you the advantage if he turns on you. You'll have enough time to get to your weapons at that angle."

"I don't see any other way out," Yorg agreed. "We'll have to go with this plan."

Kathe still did not feel comfortable with the plan as Sean collected their rifles. "Your rifle too, Lady," he said, extending his hand. "And your cell phone," he insisted as he reached for it.

"Why my cell phone?" Kathe questioned, reaching in her cargo pants pocket and handing it to him.

"I lost mine," Sean replied as he took Kathe's cell phone. "I'll pretend that I'm talking to someone as we're walking down there. They'll think I'm talking to their commander."

Ramsey slammed her hand down on her desk, "Tierney's right! How would the soldiers think Sean is talking to their commander if they didn't know him? Tierney be ready! He has sold you out! Yorg, do you copy? You've been sold out!"

"Yes," Yorg coughed, nodding an acknowledgement to Kathe. Kathe grinned and winked at Yorg as they started walking toward the plane. Yorg and Pavel walked in front of Sean as he held his gun on them and pretended to talk on her cell phone. Kathe with Ylia walked slower staying on his left flank.

As they neared the plane, the renegade soldiers instantly raised their rifles. "Kak raz vo vremya, Redmond!" Tovarich Letenant exclaimed as Sean handed him their rifles. "I told you I'd get them to come with me," Sean grinned as he walked up and took Yorg's pistol, as well as Pavel's. "Sorry mates," he smugly said, reaching toward Kathe. "Your pistol as well," he said as Kathe handed him her Walther PPK. "Gen. Yetsun pays me more money than you. No hard feelings, I hope. These blanks fooled you," he said as he emptied the blanks out of his rifle and pistol, and then reloaded his pistol in front of them.

He waved his loaded pistol at the women. "You two ladies move over with them," he ordered as Kathe and Ylia slowly moved toward Yorg and Pavel. Kathe stayed to Sean's left. "You know Pavel, I pretended to stay neutral for years to gain the trust of the Freedom Fighters, after Capt. Vuslick refused to help Gen. Yetsun steal the first Fighter Jet. My hard work paid off a couple of weeks ago when I was delivering supplies to you. I overheard Pushkin talking to his spy about moving XP38. I must admit Ivan was good. We never suspected he was a traitor to Gen. Yetsun until I recognized his distinct laugh. I got a bonus for turning Ivan in and telling Yetsun the plan. Yetsun was able to move the sale of XP38 up, so the Italians came early. We let Ivan see just enough to catch him off guard to signal you to come to Russia. You know the secret to success with Gen. Yetsun is to always deliver what he wants. There is a nice reward on Capt. Vuslick's head, just like Ivan's. I might be able to retire with the reward for Pavel, a high-ranking Freedom Fighter. Kathe Tierney will be another bonus, I'm sure."

"Tierney, it's show time!" Ramsey proclaimed. "You've got another pistol! Get it out! Take control! He doesn't know what you can do!"

Kathe began to breathe harder, acting as if she were afraid as she walked toward Yorg. "Yorg! Oh, no! What are they going to do with us?" Kathe cried, grabbing both sides of her face. Ylia reached to help her. "No!" Kathe pulled away from her. "They're going to kill us!" Kathe exclaimed and stopped in her tracks. "Yorg, what are we going to do?" She asked suddenly acting dizzy. "I'm going to faint," she gasped. "I can't take this," Kathe cried and stumbled. She fell face down in the snow as Yorg reached for her.

"Stop!" Sean ordered. "Don't touch her," he said as he walked closer, keeping his eye on the big Russian. "Keep an eye on them!" He ordered the soldiers as he bent down with the Letenant to check Kathe.

"Ya vrach," Ylia said as she reached for Kathe.

"She doesn't need a doctor," Sean smirked. "She's just a frail American like I thought," he laughed and turned toward Yorg. "I told you not to bring her."

"Kathe!" Yorg shouted as he started for her.

"Don't take another step!" Sean ordered as Kathe turned over, shot JAKE's Taser at Sean's throat with her left hand and shot the Letenant in his right temple with her pistol.

At the same time, Yorg snatched the rifle from the soldier next to him as Pavel lunged for Sean's rifle.

"Brosit pistolet!" Kathe ordered as the other soldiers raised theirs. "Drop them!"

"I'd do as the lady said," Yorg concluded. "Your commander is dead." He pushed Ylia behind him and backed away from Sean. Two of the soldiers glanced at each other, dropped to the ground and raised their rifles. Yorg shielded Ylia's eyes, while Kathe and Pavel shot them.

"Brosit pistolet, sejchas ze!" Pavel screamed, raising his gun at the last two alive. "Back away from your guns!"

Yorg walked over to Sean, stepped on his stomach, and placed his gun on Sean's forehead, "I do have hard feelings. I know you'll understand." He reached in Sean's pocket for the keys to the plane and the cell phone. "Whose cell phone is this?"

"An extra I picked up at the farmhouse," Kathe replied. "I thought it might come in handy. You noticed that I didn't hand Sean mine, didn't you? What are we going to do with them?"

"You can't shoot them!" Ylia protested. "That is murder! I can't be part of that!

"No, Dr. Vuslick," Pavel promised. "I will tie them up and take them back to headquarters. I'm sure they have information we can use against Gen. Yetsun. We never saw this coming from Sean. He has helped us numerous times," he said, glancing at the truck. "There should be some rope in the truck to tie them."

"Ylia, get in the plane," Yorg ordered as he helped Pavel tie the soldiers. "Kathe, start the engine for me. I'll be there as soon as I help Pavel. We need to get out of here."

"We need to hurry," Pavel warned as the sound of gunshots got closer. "They are almost to the edge of the clearing."

Yorg helped Pavel tie the remaining two soldiers up and load them in the back of the truck. "Thank you," Yorg said as they jumped down from the back of the truck, "for watching over my sister and helping us get out of here."

"It has been my pleasure serving with you," Pavel replied. "We still have to work together to stop Yetsun from selling XP38."

"I'll call Kiev when we break the code," Yorg stated as they walked toward Sean. "We'll know more then. Let me help you with Sean and we'll take off."

As Kathe started the engines of the plane, JAKE suddenly warned that the effects of the Taser had worn off on Sean.

"Stay here and keep the engines running!" Kathe warned Ylia as she changed places with Kathe in the co-pilot seat. Kathe hurried to the side door in time to see Yorg and Pavel reach to turn Sean over.

"Not so fast!" Sean screamed, raising a hidden Russian PSS2 at Yorg's head. "Now, who's going where?" Sean declared as he stood up. "Put your hands up! I can't have my retirement taking off on me. Yetsun wants you two alive or I'd drop you right now," he declared as the first of the soldiers came out of the woods. "Ah, my help is right on time. I see your buddies didn't make it out."

Kathe jumped down from the plane. She raised her rifle, took aim and shot Sean directly in the back of his head. "Yorg! Pavel!" Kathe shouted as Sean fell to the ground. "Come on! The soldiers are in the clearing!" Kathe screamed, covering them as soldiers rushed toward them from the forest.

Yorg and Pavel hurried to the plane and got inside. Pavel helped Kathe inside as Yorg hurried to the cockpit.

"That was too close!" Yorg exclaimed as Pavel closed the door. "You two sit down! We're going up!" Yorg exclaimed as he taxied to the road. He turned the plane around into the wind, accelerated, pulled the throttle back, and the plane lifted off the ground. "Thank God, you warmed the engines up for me," Yorg sighed, turning his head to see the soldiers still firing at them. "Another minute and we wouldn't have made it."

"Job well done! Ramsey congratulated as they took to the sky. "Make your way back to Vienna and leave no fingerprints when you ditch the plane. While you were preoccupied, I had the rest of the crew head back to Newark. They have your bags."

"What about Pavel and Ylia?" Kathe wondered.

"You will have to drop Pavel off in Vienna," Ramsey stated. "As for Ylia, she has to come to the states with you. Yetsun will have shoot to kill orders on all of you. I have a private Leer waiting to bring you here, so go straight to security and they will board you. You both disobeyed a direct order, and we are going to talk about it. You're offline unless you need me. I've got to check on the arrival of the others," she said and cleared the line.

"Pavel," Yorg said, turning his head, "I'll have to drop you off in Vienna. Yetsun will have everyone out looking for this plane when he hears what happened."

"No problem," Pavel stated. "I have relatives there that will help me get back to headquarters."

"Ylia," Yorg turned to her, "it seems you're relocating to the United States."

"I guess, I am," Ylia smiled. "I don't think either of us will be back to Russia as long as Gen. Yetsun is alive."

"We're not finished with the dear general yet?" Yorg proclaimed as he noticed Kathe yawning and fighting to keep her eyes open . . .

Chapter 32

Confronted with Kathe's New Secret

Hundreds of miles away another order is given, "Against my better judgment," Mario began, "I'm going to give you one last chance to ice my sister. Go into Alby's Computer Database and find out where she is now. I just talked with Papa, and he said she is on her way back to the states, or I would do it myself. Make sure you don't botch it up or else!" Mario shouted as he continued to type on his computer.

Hanging up his cell, Saíde turned on his computer and poured a drink in his Bronx hotel room. "This broad has nine lives," he murmured, hacking into Alby's computers. "Ah, she's arriving in Newark in about half an hour," he said as he stroked a few more keys. "I see your boss has you set up in the Hilton near the airport. This time I've got you!" He said, chugging his drink.

The next morning about 7:00 am Yorg, Ylia, and Kathe finally landed in Newark. Yorg called Jay from the airport and had him order breakfast, so it was waiting for them at the hotel. Room service just finished leaving the suite as they arrived. As soon as Kathe smelled the coffee, she excused herself for a moment as Yorg introduced his sister to the team.

"Come on, Kathe, we're waiting," Yorg called to her as she hurried into the room and sat down.

"I would like to say grace," Yorg offered as they bowed their heads and he thanked God for rescuing Ylia and their safe return.

"We've got a lot to be thankful for this morning," Jay added, passing the toast around the table. "Ramsey filled us in on the details."

"Yes, we do," Jack said, passing the toast to the other side of the table. "Everyone made it home alive."

"Everyone except my friend, Ivan," Yorg reported. "Tierra," he glanced over at her. "Ivan did find out that your brother is trying to buy the experimental fighter jet XP38."

"Do you have concrete evidence I can take to Papa?" Tierra asked.

"Not yet, but Ramsey and Sydney are now onboard with us," Yorg said, reaching for the butter.

"Sydney is already trying to break the code," Kathe added. "If anyone can do it, he can."

"Would you like some coffee?" CC asked Kathe passing a fresh cup to her.

"Excuse me!" Kathe quickly jumped up and hurried to her room.

"That's funny, Kathe doesn't look too good," CC noted, watching Kathe hurrying out of the room.

"And Kathe loves her coffee," Tierra remarked.

"Yes, she does," Yorg replied very concerned.

"Should I go check on her?" Ylia asked.

"No," Yorg sighed. "That won't be necessary. I think I know what's wrong with her," Yorg said as Kathe came back and sat down. "You need to hurry and eat. Your food is getting cold. We burned up a lot of calories this week and barely ate."

"I guess the stress got to me," Kathe sighed, picking at her food. "I'm really not hungry," she said, leaving the table, picking up a magazine, and sitting on the couch.

"That's strange," Yorg looked at her. "It's not like you at all," he stated as JAKE rang.

"Hello," Kathe answered, flipping through the magazine.

"Kathe, you'll never believe what's happening," Carrie Anne beamed. "Travis and I are a couple. I don't even get excited when I see other men."

"I'm glad you found someone to settle down with," Kathe said, curling up on the couch.

"Not just me, but you too," Carrie Anne added. "From what Babs tells me, you and Joe are a hot item! I promised Joe, I would tell him when you got back from Russia."

"You told Joe I went to Russia with Yorg?" Kathe murmured. "I guess Joe didn't tell anyone yet. The last time we talked we ended everything," she stood up. "I'm going to lie down for a while. I'll talk to you later," she said and cleared the line.

Yorg watched Kathe walk to her room again. He waited a few minutes then followed. He found her lying across the bed with tears streaming down her face as he sat down next to her.

"Yorg I'm tired and want to lie down," Kathe turned toward him.

"I notice you keep running to this room and you didn't eat," Yorg surmised. "Not to mention that suddenly the smell of coffee seems to bother you, just like the smell of blood. What's up?" He asked, gently moved her bangs away from her face.

"The food didn't look that great," Kathe complained, turning away from him.

"How are you going to explain running to the bathroom every time you smell coffee lately?" He questioned, leaning over her.

"I don't know what you're talking about," Kathe sighed.

"Don't you think it's time that we have a little talk?" Yorg asked as he turned her head toward him.

"About what?" Kathe replied, turning away from him again.

"Kat, something is wrong with you lately," Yorg said as he gently turned her face back to him.

"Nothing is wrong with me," Kathe insisted. "I've been through quite a bit, don't you think?"

"I know you have," Yorg gently stroked the hair out of her face. "Did I tell you, how proud I am of you?"

"No," Kathe tried to manage a smile.

"Well, I am," Yorg admitted. "You bravely helped me save Ylia's life, not to mention you saved me and Pavel." He pulled her into him, "Somehow it's like you are part of me." He suddenly began to struggle for words, "It's hard for me to put this into words."

She closed her eyes and held him tightly, "I know how you feel about me."

"I know something is wrong with you," Yorg admitted. "You haven't been yourself lately. You have been sick, tired, and dizzy. I'm not stupid." He rubbed her back, "I just want you to know that I'll marry you in a heartbeat."

She leaned back and looked directly into his eyes, "What are you talking about? I just have a touch of the flu, probably complicated by fatigue, from all we've been through. Thanks though," she reached up and kissed him on the cheek. "That's the sweetest proposal I've ever had."

"Kat, I did the math," he smiled at her. "The flu does not last this long. I want Ylia to have a look at you," he put his arms around her.

"Ylia doesn't need to have a look at me," Kathe insisted pulling away from him. "I'm fine. Go back to the others. I haven't caught up on my sleep yet."

Yorg stood up to leave and then he knelt beside her. "I meant what I said," he kissed her gently on the forehead. "In a heartbeat!"

She lay back down, "Go on, I don't need it." As he left the room, she closed her eyes knowing from experience that he wasn't wrong.

It was about 1:00 pm when Kathe finally woke up. She was surprised she had slept that long. She went out into the living room and noticed everyone was getting ready to go to the airport. "I was just about to wake you," Yorg said. "We've got a meeting with Ramsey at 1400 hours. Want me to order you something to eat, while you get ready?"

"No thanks, I'm not hungry yet," Kathe answered. "I'll get ready to go," she said, closing the door. She hurried to the shower. She looked through her suitcase and picked up the Light Crimson T-shirt Joe had given her. For a second, her mind raced to the moment Joe gave it to her. She closed her eyes thinking about their first meeting. Then a little bit of nausea made her suddenly remember the last angry words she said to him as JAKE rang.

"Hello," a familiar voice greeted. "Are you up yet?"

"Very funny Ramsey," Kathe laughed. "I'll be on time."

"I was talking to Yorg," Ramsey began. "He said you were not feeling good and had fallen back to sleep this morning. Are you okay?"

"I feel great," Kathe said, glancing in the full-length mirror.

"Yorg wants Ylia to give you a physical," Ramsey commented. "He said you have lingering flu symptoms. It's funny Yorg brought this subject up, because Sydney mentioned he wants to talk to you in person this afternoon after the meeting."

"I feel fine," Kathe insisted. "I just had a complete physical not too long ago. I think its fatigue complicated by jet lag," she assured Ramsey, cleared the line, and joined the others.

"You look like your old self again," Yorg smiled, watching her.

"Thank you, I finally feel rested," Kathe admitted. "Sorry I slept so long," she said, clipping JAKE on her belt.

"I expected it," Yorg smiled as they left for the meeting.

"Wanda," CC was the first to greet her, "we're finally home!"

"I hope you're all still smiling and still working at Alby when you leave," Wanda laughed. "You really infuriated the Ole Girl this time. I can't believe you disobeyed a direct order not to go to Russia."

"I didn't go to Russia," CC laughed.

"Me either," Jay smirked.

"I haven't been to Russia yet," Jack added. "You're the one who changed our schedule."

"I didn't disobey anyone," Tierra laughed.

"Well, that narrows it down to only two of you," Wanda grinned, glancing at Yorg and Kathe. "Just a word of friendly advice; if by chance, the two of you ever decide to disobey her again, Whatever You Do! Do Not Call Her and Ask for Help!"

"We'll keep that in mind," Yorg gleamed. "Ylia this is Wanda. She's the real boss around here."

"Ramsey won't fire us," Kathe laughed, "we've got job security."

"You're right about that!" Wanda smiled, walking toward Ramsey's office. "Who else is stupid enough to let her send them into a dangerous situation, plan on coming out alive, and doing it again," she stated, opening Ramsey's door for them.

"Ladies and gentlemen, if you'll please take your seats, we'll get started," Ramsey said as she greeted them. "And you must be Ylia," she said, reaching to shake her hand. "Dr. Sydney is waiting for you in his office. I've arranged for you to work with him while applying for a work visa in the United States. You can start as soon as you are settled. Wanda, please take Dr. Ylia down and introduce them. Perhaps, she can help Sydney crack the code he's been feverishly working on."

Sitting down at her desk and waiting for Wanda to close the door Ramsey continued, "Well, it's awful nice to have you all back in one piece. First, I want to know why you disobeyed a direct order and went to Russia? Let me start with you Yorg, what were you thinking?"

"The same thing you are," Yorg reminded her. "Until we solve this problem, no one in the airlines is safe."

"You're right, and that's why I haven't fired the two of you yet," Ramsey replied, looking over her glasses at them. "The way it now looks, we would have been involved in this mess anyway. When Tierney stopped Saíde on Flight #1014, we didn't realize that we were already sucked into this whole nightmare."

Yorg interrupted, "One of the Freedom Fighters spotted a Middle Eastern man, fitting the description of Saíde right down to disappearing knives, in Moscow about a year ago with Gen. Yetsun. That shows a direct connection with Mario, Saíde, and Yetsun."

"Then, why can't the police help us?" Jay asked.

"I'm working with them, the gendarmes, and Scotland Yard on an international level," Ramsey confirmed. "However, due to Tierra's family business, I don't want the press to get wind of this and plaster Alby all over every headline any more than they already have," she glanced at Tierra. "As far as they're reporting, we only have one flight attendant found murdered. We have convinced them it may relate to an old boyfriend. God forbid them printing we're involved in espionage, Mafia murders, and a serial killer!"

"But why does my brother want to buy that jet?" Tierra asked.

"Big money," Yorg responded. "It's not just a jet. It is an experimental fighter jet, codename XP38, which has stealth weapon technology. Ivan and I designed most of the internal weapon system. There was another engineer by the name of Karl Raini working with us. Ivan said Raini finished the project and then Yetsun killed him. Ivan's dying words warned me not to let Yetsun steal that jet."

"Mario doesn't want the jet," CC continued. "We suspect he wants to sell it to Iran; a country harboring terrorist that will turn on every country. If Yorg is right about the technology being stealth, we must stop it. Again, all we have is just speculation. We must have hard evidence."

"Ivan was killed because he wouldn't help Yetsun," Yorg affirmed. "He was working with the Freedom Fighters trying to hide the jet when Sean Redmond overheard them and told Yetsun. Yetsun called Mario Jr. and had him come to Russia earlier and finalize the deal. Evidently, Mario hasn't told Yetsun his coded document was intercepted."

"Why do you say that?" Jack asked.

"The jet hasn't been stolen yet, and Mario's still alive," Yorg retorted. "No one crosses Yetsun, and lives!"

"With Ivan dead, wouldn't that put you in great demand?" Ramsey questioned.

"It's a YAK U38," Yorg explained. "Any pilot can fly it. Ivan and I programmed the internal weapons system. I've worked with Raini before and can figure out how it works. Ylia was being held in case they needed me."

"That doesn't make any sense," Ramsey reminded him. "I was ordered to keep you away from Russia."

"Ivan's commander was Gen. Broshniv, who is very loyal to the government," Yorg stated.

"But the order came from Gen. Yetsun himself," Ramsey clarified.

"Ivan used Yetsun's name to warn me when he couldn't get through to me a couple of weeks ago," Yorg realized. "He knew that by using Yetsun's name, I would know something was wrong and come to Russia, which I did."

"That could mean that Raini could have trained someone else and that's why Yetsun killed him," Kathe assumed. "He could have been holding Ylia just in case something happened to the new pilot."

"That makes sense," CC added. "Again, it's still speculation and not proof."

Wanda knocked on the door as she entered, "Lt. Tanner is on line 1 for you."

Reaching for her phone, "What do you need John?" She listened and said, "I'll take care of it." She glanced at Kathe's team, "We've got a red flag on Flight #1517 tonight from Newark to Frankfurt/Paris. It departs at midnight. I'm putting every one of you onboard except Tierra and CC. I'm changing their hotel. I want to keep them in hiding for a while. Until Sydney breaks the code, it's business as usual. Now get out of here and get some rest before you leave. Wanda will have your schedule on the way out."

"What about Ylia?" Yorg asked.

"It's almost 5:00 o'clock," Ramsey said, noting the time. "I'll arrange for Ylia to stay with Wanda until you get back. Kathe, you need to meet with Sydney before you take off."

"Are you sure you're up to this assignment?" Yorg asked Kathe.

"Yes, are you?" Kathe lashed back glaring at him.

"What's this all about?" Ramsey inquired.

"Nothing," Kathe answered, heading for the door.

"I'm warning you two!" Ramsey snapped. "No more secrets, and don't even think about going behind my back again! I shouldn't have to remind you that in our business, Trust is Everything! Now get out of here and get some rest before you go to work."

Later that evening, while everyone was getting ready room service delivered fresh coffee. Yorg knocked on the bathroom door, "Are you decent? I have your favorite coffee. Open the door its hazelnut."

Putting on her mascara, Kathe held her breath as she opened the door and reached for the cup. "Thanks, I'll be out in a minute," she said, trying to close it quickly.

"Leave the door open," Yorg insisted, sticking his foot in the doorway. "I've seen you put your makeup on lots of times. What we must do is . . ."

At that moment, Kathe couldn't stand it any longer. She closed the door, gagged, and rushed to the toilet. When she turned around Yorg was leaning in the doorway, sipping his coffee. "Does the smell of my coffee bother you also?" He questioned looking sternly at her.

"Yorg, I . . ." Kathe started to say.

"Don't you dare say that you're okay," Yorg interrupted. "You and I both know what is wrong with you."

She threw her arms around him bursting into tears, "Yorg . . ."

Placing his coffee on the counter, Yorg picked her up and laid her on the bed. He bent down holding her tightly. "Yorg," she sobbed, "please don't tell anyone my shame."

"You know me better than that," Yorg said as tears filled his eyes. "You have no shame; you have me."

"It's not your problem," Kathe sighed, burying her head in his shoulder.

"It's not a problem," Yorg assured her. "I would never leave you. I'm in love with you, can't you tell? No one will ever have to know it's not my child. We're always staying in the same room," he looked into her eyes.

"It's ironic that you said that," Kathe confided, looking away.

"Why?" Yorg asked, gently pulling her face back toward his.

"Because here I am in your arms," Kathe admitted, "he said I couldn't decide on whom I had more allegiance to, you or him. He said maybe we made hasty decisions."

"He doesn't know?" Yorg inquired, gritting his teeth.

"No, and he never will," Kathe tearfully said. "I have enough problems now. I don't need anymore."

Yorg reached for a tissue on the table, "Dry your eyes, before someone sees you. I'll have Ylia check you when we get back."

"No, Yorg," Kathe declined as she sat up. "Promise me you won't tell anybody."

"Kathe no one is going to stone you," Yorg said, standing up.

"Yorg promise me," Kathe insisted. "I have children who know I'm not married. You know how Peter will talk about me to them."

"Don't worry about Peter," Yorg assured her. "He won't have anything to tell them," he said as JAKE rang on the nightstand next to him. "It's Carrie Anne. I'll get the phone while you finish your makeup; we've got a plane to catch," he said as Kathe went back into the bathroom. "Hello . . . yes, it's Yorg. Kathe is busy getting ready for work. Do I need to get her?"

"No," Carrie Anne giggled, "just tell her I'm working in the Frankfurt/Paris flight with you this evening. Light Crimson finished their tour, and they are already in Europe. Travis and Collin will join me in Frankfurt."

"I'll tell Kathe," Yorg stated and thought for a second. "Carrie Anne, can you get hold of Joe?"

"Yes, Joe's in London working in the studio," Carrie Anne reported. "I can call him."

"Give him a message for me," Yorg insisted. "Tell Glitter Boy that he has done enough damage to Kathe! Stay away from her! I'll take full responsibility for his carelessness! Make sure you give him my entire message!" Yorg declared and hung-up JAKE. He threw JAKE on the bed and stormed out of the room.

As soon as Carrie Anne hung up, she quickly called Joe in London. "I just had the strangest conversation with Yorg," she reported. "He told me to tell you, that you've done enough damage to Kathe and to stay away from her. He also said that he will take full responsibility for your carelessness. He also said make sure you tell him the entire message."

"What is he talking about?" Joe asked.

"I have no clue, but Yorg was furious!" Carrie Anne reported. "And one thing you don't want to do is make him mad!"

"I have no idea what he's talking about," Joe laughed. "Kathe and I ended it last time we talked. It sounds like he's flying on something more than Alby Jets."

Entering Newark Airport, Kathe went with Yorg to operations to get the flight schedule and to find out why two passengers had been red flagged. Captains John Roberts and Paul Wade were waiting for them.

"Well now, we feel better about this flight," John said, shaking Yorg's hand.

"What's that supposed to mean?" Yorg asked as he shook Paul's hand.

"We have two people of interest aboard," John discussed. "With you and Kathe working, I feel better about being up in the air with a plane full of passengers, and them."

"Gee, John," Kathe chuckled, "after the last few flights I've had with you, I thought as soon as you saw me board, you'd run."

"Just the opposite, Lady," John said as Yorg left them to sign for the flight. "The two of you put our minds at ease."

"It seems we have people of interest boarding my flight this evening," Yorg said to the controller, Arnold Brundage. "Do you know anything about them? I have a full flight. I do have the right to refuse their passage," Yorg reminded him glancing at the roster.

"Let me check," Arnold said, picking up the telephone. "This is operations. I have the pilot of Flight #1517 asking about the status of the persons of interest . . . I'll send them right up . . . thank you. He turned back to Yorg, "Keith is on duty tonight. He needs to talk with all four of you before takeoff."

"Thanks," Yorg answered, signing for the flight, and taking the roster with him. "We're heading straight up there."

"Have a safe flight," Arnold called to him.

"Keith is on duty," Yorg relayed as he joined the others. "We need to see him before takeoff."

"Let's find out what we're up against," Kathe said as she led the way.

Keith was waiting for them when they got off the elevator. "Good to finally see you again, Kathe," Keith said. "Captain's glad to see you as well. I know you're in a hurry so let's get down to business," he said, opening a file. "This is Sabrina Aline Macaby," Keith shared. "She will be sitting in row 24, seat J, next to the window. She is believed linked with this man," he said, showing the second picture. "This is Timothy Paul Patrick O'Brien. He was just a small-town thug until recently. He will be joining Sabrina on the connecting flight to Paris. He has been seen lately in the Middle East, and Russia. So far, Homeland Security can't pinpoint exactly what he was doing there. They have no concrete reason not to let either one of them board our aircraft. Just as a precaution, they are putting one of their own agents on this flight along with our air marshals. That is why Lt. Tanner insists on Kathe's team being aboard this flight."

Staring at O'Brien's picture Yorg said, "There is something about him. He looks very familiar to me, but I can't place him."

"They were both on a flight with me not too long ago," Kathe admitted. "Ramsey had me keep my eye on them; nothing happened. Where are the air marshals sitting?"

"Ours will be sitting in Row 27 seat J," Keith reported. "Homeland Security's' will sit in Row 26 seat G. Make sure you work that section."

"Does Homeland think there could be anyone else aboard this flight that could possibly be linked with them?" Yorg asked.

"Negative, I've already asked that question," Keith replied. "I made sure they double-checked. Ramsey has asked Dr. Sydney to try to monitor their conversation through Kathe's implant. She wants you to stay as close to them as much as possible." He glanced at his watch, "You better hurry. Have a safe flight."

"After this news, it's easy for you to say," Roberts chuckled as they headed for the door. "You're not the one up in the air with them."

"It's a changing world," Keith added. "Any problems give me a call. Oh, and Tierney, Sydney is in his office waiting to see you. He said it's a must before you get on the plane."

"Well, if it's a must, I guess I better go," Kathe said, glancing at Yorg. "I'll meet you on the plane."

Hurrying to Dr. Sydney's office, Kathe wondered what could be so urgent that it was a must to see him. "I hope he isn't going to put another implant in me. I'm not up to it," she thought as she knocked on his door.

"Come in," Sydney said, straightening some vials in a box on his desk. "Kathe it's always a pleasure."

"The same here unless you're going to put another implant in me," Kathe commented.

"No new implants from me," Sydney chuckled and sat down on the edge of his desk. "But we do need to talk face to face on this subject. It is great to see the implants in you working so well. Actually, they are working better than I ever imagined."

"What do you mean by that statement?" Kathe asked.

"I mean," Sydney got very serious, "Alby has quite a bit invested in your health and well-being. I can check your heart rate and blood pressure in the field. I know where you are always. I can help you figure out ways to get out of situations. I am also able to hear and sense other people around you," he crossed his arms, "or should I say, inside you. You are pregnant."

Kathe took a deep breath and looked away from him.

"You are human and a very beautiful, talented woman," Sydney began, rambling. "I remember a Spanish woman. I met her on vacation a couple of years ago, just before I started working with Ramsey on security issues at Alby. I had to make a choice, the woman, or my job. And what a woman she was; she had big . . ."

"Dr. Sydney!" Kathe interjected. "I think that's more information than I need to know!"

"Not really, I shaped your body after hers," Sydney smiled as he remembered.

"I really don't want to hear this!" Kathe insisted, placing her hands on her hips.

"What I'm trying to say is that everyone makes mistakes," Sydney admitted. "We need you in the field fully operational with all that is going on now. I've noticed that you have been sick quite a lot lately, and the smell of coffee is really nauseating you."

"Wait a minute," Kathe argued. "I know my body belongs to Alby, but my private life is still mine," she snapped, getting defensive.

"You're getting me all wrong," Sydney confessed. "You are like the sister I never had. I would never have you do anything against your religion or beliefs or mine, for that matter. I would never give you something to harm you or the child inside you."

"You are sure, aren't you?" Kathe questioned, leaning against the wall.

"Yes," Sydney confirmed. "A baby's heartbeat begins 18 days after conception. The heartbeat is very strong," he said as he picked up one of the vials. "We need you fully functional; not throwing up. I also have a degree in immunology and made this serum to help you with your morning sickness."

"Doctor, you know I can't take anything at this stage," Kathe refuted.

"Kathe, you're alive because of me," Sydney declared. "I held your heart in my own hand and massaged it until it could beat on its own. I'm surprised you don't trust me. The American Indians still use this old remedy today. It's mostly made of honey with a few other ingredients. You are strong and can take care of yourself even pregnant. Just use your weapons more instead of your fighting skills. Yorg already suspects and he will help you. Because you are one of the main targets, you must finish this job," he said, handing her the box. "Drink one every time you feel morning sickness coming on. It will not harm you or the child. Now give me a hug and go to work."

"Doctor, I don't want anyone to know yet," Kathe confided. "Please keep this our secret-promise?" She implored him. "I don't know what I'm going to do yet. Ramsey will have a fit!"

"When the time comes, you'll make the right decision," Sydney shared and handed her a small button with Velcro on the back. "If you have a chance, put this under Macaby's seat. It is a microphone like your implants. With this, you won't have to stay so close to her and arouse her suspicions. Ramsey has been profiling these two people. She is hoping she can tie them to Yetsun. Make sure you bring it back to me. Have a safe flight."

"Funny you said that," Kathe stated, opening the door. "Yorg had the feeling he'd seen the man before but can't place him."

Chapter 33

Joe Finds Out Kathe's Secret

Yorg left the cockpit door open so he could watch for Kathe. As soon as she entered the plane, he hurried over to her and whispered, "Are you feeling alright?"

"Yes, and very capable of working," Kathe answered as she reached for her flight log.

"If you need me, you know where I'll be," Yorg said, touching her nose.

"I'll be fine," Kathe smiled, putting one of the vials in her pocket and the rest in her overnight bag. She hurried over to Macaby's seat and placed the Velcro button-shaped microphone under it. She called Sydney to let him know it was in place.

As chief purser, Kathe prepped Carrie Anne and the other attendants. The flight would take about six hours airtime with a stop in Frankfurt. Since the flight was leaving so late most of the passengers would sleep. She wouldn't have to serve coffee until an hour and a half before landing. Welcoming the passengers aboard, she glanced over at Carrie Anne and noticed her give a cute man a double-take. She laughed as she remembered that Carrie Anne said just yesterday, I'll never look at another man. She shook her head and thought, "that will be the day the Earth stands still." "I'm going to work in the third section tonight," Kathe told her. "You can work first class, since you seem to have an interest here."

"I don't know what you are talking about," Carrie Anne smirked.

"I saw you do a double-take on the man in 2A," Kathe smiled and walked to her station.

After the jet was in the air, Yorg came over the intercom welcoming the passengers. Kathe noticed Macaby trying to get comfortable. She handed her a pillow and blanket. Macaby thanked her and snuggled in for the night. During most of the flight, Macaby just slept. She only got up once to use the lavatory, returned to her seat and fell back to sleep. "Glad the red flag is as tired as I am," Kathe thought as Jay noticed her fighting to stay awake.

"Long day," Jay said as Kathe entered the galley.

"I guess I still haven't recovered from my trip to Russia," Kathe said.

"Everything is quiet," Jay offered. "I'll cover for you, if you want to rest your eyes."

"Thanks, I'll be alright," Kathe smiled. "We will be landing in Frankfurt in about an hour. The flight into Paris will be an easy one," she assured him as JAKE rang. She reached for it as Jay went to help one of the passengers. "Hello," she said. There was no answer. "Hello," she said again with no answer. Not recognizing the number, "Peter, if this is you, I'm not in the mood for your jokes." Silence and then the line cleared. She put JAKE back on her belt. The same thing happened ten minutes later. This time she was annoyed and called control. "Keith someone is calling me on JAKE and not saying anything. I don't recognize the number. Would you check and see where the calls are coming from?"

"Are you trying to tell me you're getting prank calls on a secure line?" Keith asked, putting change into the soda machine.

"Yes, I guess I am," Kathe admitted. "Only a few close friends and family have this number. Peter hasn't annoyed me in a while. He's not supposed to have this number. He usually tries to get through via you. Has he called?"

"I haven't heard from him," Keith shared. "I will check and get back to you. How's our person of interest?" He asked, returning to his computer.

"Sleeping the entire flight like I wish I was," Kathe answered as he cleared the line.

A few minutes later, Kathe was trying to avoid the galley, where Jay was starting the coffee. Keith called her back, "Tierney, the calls are coming from a private home in London," he said, scrolling the information. "It is the residence of Joseph Sherrod Sr. Do you want the address?"

"No, I don't need the address," Kathe sighed, looking out the window.

"Do you want me to block the number?" Keith asked.

"Not yet," Kathe sighed.

"Okay, it's your call," Keith stated. "By the way, Ramsey is spending most of her time searching Saíde. She's determined that he can hide a knife somewhere on his person."

"That's what we've suspected all along," Kathe answered.

"Sydney reminded her that knives are not always made out of metals," Keith relayed. "It could be made to fit in something his is wearing. He also thinks he's very close to cracking the code."

"I have to go," Kathe stated. "Yorg is signaling to get ready for landing. Keep me informed," she said, trying to avoid people drinking coffee.

"Okay, just let me know if you need me to help you with your prank caller," Keith remarked and cleared the line.

The smell of coffee filled the plane. "I can't take this anymore," she thought and hurried to the laboratory. "I think it's time to try Sydney's remedy," she thought as she opened one of the vials.

A few minutes later, Kathe was composed enough to announce the landing in Frankfurt, thanking the passengers for choosing Alby Airlines. Within minutes, they were on the ground taxiing to the terminal. As the last passenger deplaned, Yorg and Roberts came out of the cabin to stretch their legs and talk with Wade.

Yorg noticed how tired Kathe looked, "How are you holding up?"

"I'm okay except for the wake-up coffee," Kathe whispered.

"Are you going to be able to handle the next flight?" Yorg asked. "You'll be serving more coffee."

"I've arranged for Stacey to help Jay," Kathe shared. "I'm sticking close to Macaby and O'Brien," she reminded him as Carrie Anne tried to leave the plane.

"Carrie Anne, you can't leave the plane," Kathe cautioned, checking her watch. "The next passengers will be boarding in five minutes."

"I can't get through to Travis," Carrie Anne stated, holding up her cell phone. "He's on this flight."

"What do you mean, Travis is on this flight?" Kathe exclaimed.

"Didn't Yorg tell you?" Carrie Anne quizzed. "Travis is meeting me on this flight. We're staying together in Paris. I'll be right back. I just want to see him."

"You'll see him in a minute lover girl," Kathe reprimanded. "You need to prepare this section for takeoff. I have to check the passenger list and talk with the other attendants."

Within in a few minutes passengers were boarding. As Kathe checked the passenger list to make sure O'Brien was sitting next to Macaby, she recognized two other names. "Oh, no!" she thought noticing Collin Jones and Steve Day on the list. She quickly scrolled down checking for Joe's name. "Thank God!" she thought looking up toward the heavens, "at least you still like me."

As soon as Collin saw Kathe, his face lit up. "Kathe, how are you?" Collin asked, hugging her, "You look radiant."

"Collin, thank you, and welcome aboard," Kathe greeted.

"Well, if it isn't my lovely neighbor," Steve smiled and kissed her hand.

"Doing well," Kathe winked.

"Great to see you again," Travis gave Kathe a hug.

"You too," Kathe smiled. "I'm going to leave you in good hands with Carrie Anne. I'm working in another area," she replied, noticing O'Brien passing her on the way to his seat. "Carrie Anne, get me a final head count in this area. I must check on the other compartments," Kathe said, following O'Brien. She watched where he placed his overnight bag. She noticed Macaby greeting him with a kiss as he sat down. She tried to stay as close to them as possible for Sydney to pick up their conversations.

After the plane was in the air, Capt. Vuslick welcomed the passengers on behalf of the crew and the smell of coffee began to circulate throughout the plane. She reached in her pocket, took out the vial and drank it. "Hope the doctor is right," Kathe thought. "Sorry baby, your mommy's job beats to a different drum than your father's."

"The cart is ready when you are," Jay reported, locating Kathe who was trying to avoid the galley. "Are you okay; you don't look so hot?"

"I can't seem to shake the flu," Kathe answered. "I've arranged for Stacey to help you with the cart. I've got to help a mother traveling with several small children on row 25." As she helped the young mother, Kathe noticed the smell of coffee no longer bothered her. She was staying close to the passengers of interest when Carrie Anne called for her.

"I need you to come to first class for a minute," Carrie Anne requested.

"You know I'm busy," Kathe replied. "I'm sure you can handle your job just fine," she answered, noting O'Brien pointing toward her whispering to Macaby. "Okay, I'll be there in a minute." Kathe said, turning away, "Sydney, I think O'Brien is getting nervous with me staying so close to them. I'm going to first class for a minute."

"Roger that," Sydney acknowledged. "The button is working, except for the loud toddler in the row behind them. I'm trying to filter the noise out. I will monitor them," he agreed as Kathe slowly made it up to the first-class section.

"There you are," Carrie Anne greeted as Kathe entered the section. "Collin wants to talk to you."

"Carrie Anne I'm working," Kathe protested. "This is your section; you talk with him."

"He wants to talk with you," Carrie Anne pleaded.

Kathe rolled her eyes as she walked to his seat, "Collin, you wanted to see me?"

"Yes, it's been a while since we talked," Collin stated. "How are you doing?" He asked as he dropped his snack on the floor. Reaching to pick it up for him, Kathe stood up too quickly and the room began to spin. She fainted, hitting her head on the armrest of the seat. Collin jumped up trying to bring Kathe around as JAKE rang.

"Jay, get an ice pack!" Carrie Anne ordered.

"Kathe," Collin whispered, holding her head in his arms. "Kathe, open your eyes," he requested as he gently patted her cheek. "She's not coming to," Collin said to Carrie Anne, who answered JAKE.

"Keith," Carrie Anne stated. "Kathe just fainted and hit her head on a seat. I've got to go," she said, reaching for the ice from Jay.

"I'll get the captain," Jay said, hurrying to the cockpit.

"She's really out," Collin whispered to Yorg as soon as he got there.

"Jay get the smelling salts," Yorg ordered, looking up at Collin. "This will wake her up," Yorg said, putting the smelling salts under her nose. "Kat, can you hear me?"

Kathe immediately opened her eyes and shoved the salts away, "Oh, help me to the bathroom."

Yorg helped Kathe up slowly and walked her to the bathroom. Collin watched very closely as he got back in his seat. Kathe came out a few minutes later feeling relieved. Yorg helped her to the only empty seat, which was directly in front of Collin. He handed her an ice pack and knelt beside her, "You, okay?"

"Yes, a passenger dropped something," Kathe recalled. "I bent down to pick it up. I must have come up too fast, that's all. Sydney gave me something for my nausea, and it seemed to be working, until you stuck the smelling salts under my noise. I'm embarrassed, but I can go back to work now?" she said, getting up.

"No, way," Yorg argued. "As your captain, I order you to stay in this seat until we get to Paris. You've got a small knot on your head," looking closely into her eyes. "Your eyes look okay. I don't see any signs of a concussion. Keep the ice on about ten more minutes and no falling asleep." He looked at Carrie Anne, "Don't let our patient fall asleep; she has a small bump. Hope I don't catch your flu." He touched her nose playfully, then looked at Collin, "Thanks again for your help."

"No problem," Collin answered, watching Yorg walk back to the cockpit.

Carrie Anne rushed to Kathe, "What happened?"

"I just can't shake this flu," Kathe complained as she held the ice on her forehead.

"It must be a long-lasting flu, since you've been sick for over a month," Carrie stated. Kathe prayed that Collin did not hear her. "If I didn't know better," Carrie smirked, "I'd say you were PG, but everybody knows it wouldn't happen to you."

"Carrie Anne Mobley, be quiet!" Kathe ordered. "Someone might hear you," she whispered, slouching in her seat.

Carrie Anne tried to be funny and leaned toward Collin behind Kathe. "Collin, what would you think if some girl was throwing up and fainting for about a month?"

Kathe couldn't believe this was happening as she listened to his answer. "Where I come from, the girl is usually in a family way," Collins's tone sharpened.

"In most cases I'd say yes, but not with Kathe," Carrie Anne giggled. "Everybody knows she's way too proper."

Kathe could feel Collins eyes on her. She couldn't stand being in that seat one more second. She stood up and hurried to the rear of the plane. "Where are you going?" Carrie Anne called to her.

"Back to work!" Kathe snapped.

Just before Kathe entered the third section, Yorg caught up with her. "I came to check on you and Carrie Anne told me you just left," Yorg whispered, sternly at her. "I thought I gave you a direct order to stay in that seat!"

"I couldn't," Kathe explained. "Didn't you see who Carrie Anne was talking to about my situation?"

"No, who?" Yorg asked, looking back toward first class.

"Three of someone's best friends and band members," Kathe informed him.

"Leave it to Carrie Anne to run her mouth," Yorg confessed. "You can go back to work if you are sure, you are alright. Ramsey called and wanted you to stay close to our special guest as they are deplaning if you can. It seems that Sydney might have heard them talking about a general and a jet. A baby started crying in the seat behind them and he couldn't be sure. She wants me to talk with Jaco on what we found in Munich and Russia, in case she missed something. I'm to go there as soon as we land," Yorg said, glancing around the corner toward the two people of interest. "He looks so familiar. I just can't place him. I don't want him to see me, in case he recognizes me. Do you feel like going with me to see Jaco?"

"I want to go to our apartment and get some rest," Kathe confessed. "There's enough room for the guys to stay there. I will ride over with them," she told him.

The rest of the flight was quiet. Kathe announced the landing of the aircraft. As soon as the jetbridge connected to the craft, Sydney spoke to her via implant. "Kathe, follow our two guests if possible. I heard them talking about meeting a general. They are being very cautious. I want to see if they mention his name once they clear the plane."

"Roger that," Kathe whispered, unlocking the door. Carrie Anne joined her by the front door as the passengers deplaned. She noticed Collin and Travis stayed seated as the next cabin came forward. "Why aren't they leaving?" Kathe asked, leaning closer to Carrie Anne.

"They're waiting for me," Carrie Anne said as O'Brien and Macaby approached the door.

"I'll be right back," Kathe whispered. She followed them down the jetway to the terminal. She noted Macaby getting suspicious, ducked into a shop, and whispered to Sydney, "They're on to me."

"Okay, Ramsey has someone in place that will take over," Sydney said, alerting the other agent.

Entering the aircraft, Kathe couldn't believe Carrie Anne was still talking with Travis, Collin, and Steve while Jack and Jay finished their duties. She rushed past them to retrieve her stowed baggage hoping to avoid Collin. She could still hear him say, where I come from the girl is usually in a family way, leaning against the closet, she waited for them to leave.

"Are you coming?" Jay asked, walking to her compartment. "Yorg wants you to stay with us while he's with the gendarmes."

"I know he told me," Kathe affirmed as she reached for the Velcro button under the seat. "Our new apartment has enough room for all of us to stay. Are all the passengers off?"

"What's up with you?" Jay quizzed. "You act as if you are hiding from someone. We're all waiting for you," he said, motioning for her to hurry. Grabbing her overnight bag, Kathe slowly walked to the front.

"Kathe," Collin's face lit up.

"Collin, you're still here?" Kathe quizzed. "I thought all passengers had already left the plane," she said, leaving with him.

"I asked Jay if I could give you a ride to the apartment," Collin stated. "We're all going to the same building."

"I can take a taxi with the guys," Kathe replied. "I usually ride with Yorg, but he had a meeting with the gendarmes."

"Everybody is riding with Steve," Collin stated. "I have my own car and I wanted to talk to you alone. We've got some catching up to do about a mutual friend."

"Our mutual friend made it clear to me that we made hasty decisions," Kathe confided, changing the subject. "The weather here is finally beginning to look like spring."

"Yes," Collin agreed, stopping at his Mercedes. "But not like at your house in Florida. The weather was perfect."

Leaving the parking garage, Kathe noticed O'Brien and Macaby getting into a white BMW. "Quick! Pull over to the curb for a second," Kathe ordered, pointing to the curb. She grabbed JAKE, snapped a picture of them and the license plate of the car. "Let's go before they see me," Kathe said, holding her purse over her face.

Turning onto the main street Collin asked, "What was that all about?"

"Something to do with my job and the reason I didn't work first-class," Kathe answered, sending the pictures to control. She called Keith, "Keith, I'm sending you a picture of our persons of interest getting into a white BMW at the airport . . . yes, I got the license plate . . . thanks . . . bye." Turning back toward Collin, "What were you saying?"

"You know," Collin said, catching up to Steve's car. "I couldn't help but wonder about you fainting on the plane. Carrie Anne said you've been sick a lot lately."

Kathe stared out the window as he stopped at a red light. He turned her face toward him. Tears were trickling down her cheeks. "I didn't mean to make you cry."

She looked at Collin, "I've been through a lot lately. Maybe I need to go back to the states on another R & R."

"Maybe you just need to talk to Joe," Collin suggested as the light changed.

"No, our professions don't mix," Kathe sighed. "The last time we talked Joe made that perfectly clear."

"Sometimes people need to put their professions aside," Collin stated, giving her hand a gentle squeeze. "I wonder if Joe has the same flu that you have. You two were tight in Florida."

Glancing at him, "Collin, please don't say anything to Joe. It would never work between us. I should have never gotten involved with him. It's funny how our lives are like the lyrics in one of your own songs. We are 'Two Worlds Crashing.'"

"That's not true," Collin objected. "I know Joe loves you. I also know he worries about you. I see him checking the Internet constantly making sure you are not in the news. Whether you like it or not, I believe you've become his business," he said, wiping a tear from her cheek.

He turned into the underground parking garage, parking next to Steve. As Kathe opened the door, Collin gently grabbed her arm, "You two belong together. Everyone in the band knows that, even Payton. I think Joe's been trying to call you, but his pride keeps getting in his way. I've caught him dialing a number, lets it ring, and then hangs up starring into space."

"Collin," Kathe interrupted, "I know Joe's been calling me and hanging up."

"Well, now more than ever you two need to talk," Collin affirmed. "Have you checked to make sure . . ."

"There's nothing to check," Kathe insisted. "Thanks for the ride home," she said, opening the door, and reaching for her bag.

"Let me help you with that bag," Collin offered still insinuating her condition.

"I can carry my own bag thank you," Kathe whispered so the others didn't hear. "Thanks for the ride home."

Steve was showing off the view of his new apartment building as they entered the foyer. They entered the glass elevator and enjoyed the view of Paris as it slowly rose on the outside of the building.

"Tierney, want to go over to Steve's apartment with us?" Jay asked, leaning over to her.

"No, thanks," Kathe declined. "I'm going to lie down and get some rest."

"I'm across the hall if you want to talk," Collin whispered as the elevator stopped on their floor.

Kathe leaned over and kissed his cheek, "Don't worry about me, I'll be fine without Joe. He's much better off without me," she said, reaching for her keys in her purse.

"That's not true and you know it," Collin declared. "Joe is in London. You have his number. Give him a call," he said, waiting for her to open the door.

"Don't leave the apartment," Jay cautioned, stopping with them. "Jack and I are going to hang out with them for a while. Then we will be over."

"I'm not going anywhere, except straight to bed," Kathe stated, opening the door, and handing Jay her key. She closed the door, leaned against it, and thought, "Collin knows now."

Across the hall, Travis and Carrie Anne were having coffee. Suzanne was modeling in Paris for the week. She stopped by the apartment to see Collin before returning to London. Unfortunately, she was working with Shaunda, who insisted on coming along.

As soon as Collin opened the door, Suzanne hurried over him. "Do you mind making me a scotch I need to make a phone call?" Collin asked, kissing her.

"It's a little early in the morning, don't you think?" Suzanne questioned.

"It's four o'clock somewhere," Collin declared, looking at Travis.

"I'll join him in the four o'clock world," Jack added, walking toward the bar.

"Me too," Jay agreed. "We just got off work and need to unwind before bed."

"Do you know where Joe is now?" Collin asked Travis.

"He's at Troy's apartment," Travis replied. "I called him a few minutes ago reminding him to be at the recording studio at 5:00 o'clock."

"I need to talk to him," Collin said as Suzanne handed him a drink. "I'll be back in a minute," he kissed her on the cheek. "I need to make a phone call," he said, reaching for his cell phone as he left the room for privacy.

"Tell him Cara is home in London," Shaunda called to him.

"Shaunda, you promised not to talk about her," Suzanne reminded.

"Sorry, I forgot," Shaunda answered, glaring at Carrie Anne.

"Joe, you need to come to Paris!" Collin exclaimed, closing the bedroom door.

"I have no intention going to Paris," Joe declared. "I plan on having lunch and a movie with my parents. Then, I'm due at the recording studio this afternoon at 5:00."

"Guess who was working the flight from Munich to Paris this morning?" Collin asked.

"I know Kathe was on the flight," Joe admitted. "I talked with Travis a few minutes ago. I don't want to hear a thing about her. Don't even bring it up!"

"Oh, I am going to bring it up!" Collin exploded. "Kathe seemed to be avoiding us on the flight. You know she's always in charge and works first-class. She worked a different section. I had to make Carrie Anne ask her to come and see me. When she finally came, I accidently dropped my snack. When she bent down to pick it up, she fainted hitting her head on an armrest. She didn't come to right away and Yorg was called to help. He had to put smelling salts under her nose to bring her around. When she did come to, she ran to the bathroom and puked."

"Smelling salts are very strong," Joe contested.

"However, Yorg made her sit in front of my seat for Carrie Anne to keep an eye on her," Collin continued. "Carrie Anne started rambling that she heard Kathe has been sick and fainting a lot lately. She went so far as to say that anyone else might think she was PG, except and I quote, "We all know she's too proper for that to happen. Carrie Anne wasn't in Florida with us. We all know the two of you were tight."

"What did Kathe say?" Joe urged.

"She denied it and told me not to tell you," Collin confided. "She said it wouldn't work between the two of you."

"Is she for sure?" Joe questioned. "Put Carrie Anne on the phone."

"Just a minute," Collin said, walking to the other room. "Carrie Anne, can you come with me for a second. Joe wants to ask you a question."

"Sure," Carrie Anne replied, following him to the bedroom.

"How did you find out Kathe has been sick lately?" Joe asked as soon as Carrie Anne took the phone.

"Tierra and CC were talking about it, before we left Newark," Carrie Anne replied.

"Do you think she's pregnant?" Joe quizzed.

"I've known Kathe for years and she doesn't get physical with anybody!" Carrie Anne chuckled. "Not even Yorg . . . No, way!" . . . her eyes widened . . . "I'm proud of you!" She giggled hysterically as he continued . . . "I guess you do need to talk to her. Wait a minute!" she screamed. "She can't be! . . . Oh, my, God! This really complicates her life!"

"This doesn't complicate her life," Joe sighed with relief. "This solves our problem. Now she can be with me. She has to quit!"

"No!" Carrie Anne protested with tears filling her eyes. "You don't understand. She can't quit her job now!"

"Why?" Joe begged.

"Talk about bad timing!" Carrie Anne exclaimed, pacing the room. "I can't tell you! But you just messed her up bad! You just signed her death warrant! Joe what have you done? She can't fight! She can't protect herself! What is she going to do?"

"What are you talking about?" Joe interjected. "What do you mean? Carrie Anne stop rambling! You're not making any sense! Tell me the truth!"

"If you tell anyone that I told you," Carrie Anne confessed and took a deep breath. "I will lose my job over this! Now more than ever you do need to know. Joe this cannot hit the media. Remember that man who held a knife at my throat. He got riled at Kathe for throwing hot coffee on him. We couldn't find the knife, so he got off scot-free. Ramsey is trying to keep the press from finding out. That mad man is killing flight attendants at random to get even with Kathe, before he goes after her. He is insane and toying with her. At the same time, Mario LaBasco Jr. is somehow mixed up with this lunatic. That's why they went to Russia. ...Call her on JAKE...Joe, remember not to tell anyone that I told you this . . . bye." She hurried to Collin in the sitting room, "Joe's calling Kathe right now." Shaunda glared out the window with disgust.

Joe quickly dialed JAKE. "Hello," Kathe answered half-asleep.

"Did I wake you?" Joe asked.

Hearing Joe's voice Kathe sat up, "Joe, is that you?"

"Yes," Joe answered followed by silence.

She held her breath hoping Collin didn't call him, "Why do you keep calling me and hanging up?"

"I don't know what to say to you," Joe sighed.

"I think you made it very clear the last time we talked," Kathe affirmed, holding back tears. "Just erase my number and go on with your life. That's what I'm going to do."

"I . . . can't do that," Joe confided. "I can't get you off my mind," he stopped. "I called to see how you're feeling?"

"Tired, I worked a long flight," she answered, looking up at the ceiling, and rolling her eyes.

"I um . . . I talked with Collin and Carrie Anne this morning," Joe stated.

She squeezed her eyes tightly, hung her head and shook it 'no'.

"He said you fainted on the flight and hit your head," Joe quizzed.

"I'm okay," Kathe insisted. "I just can't seem to shake a flu bug."

"I'd . . . I'd like to see you," Joe said.

"We've already gone over this," Kathe objected, "our two professions don't mix. I can't be on a roller coaster ride with you. One minute you like me, the next you've made a mistake. You've done this twice to me, even after you found out what I do for a living. We both have commitments and contracts to fulfill. It just won't work!"

"I admit I deserved that last statement," Joe stated. "It's just when I see you in a life-threatening situation, I don't know how to protect you."

"That's why we're not together anymore!" Kathe argued. "We live too very different lives. You're all about fame, and I'm all about anonymity. By the way, it's not your job to protect me!"

"I've been a moron more than once," Joe confessed. "I'd be on a plane to Paris right now to tell you this in person, but I must be at the recording session at 5:00, or I will be fined heavily again. Think back to how we first met. It was no accident. We were meant to be together. Now more than ever we belong together. I want to talk face to face with you. I am not taking 'no' for an answer. When and where can I see you?"

"I must be crazy for agreeing to see you again," Kathe confessed. "I'm not making any promises. I don't know my schedule yet. Ramsey may call us all back to the states."

"No!" Joe exclaimed. "Ramsey can't . . . I mean . . . please don't go back to the states before I see you. I'll hop a flight over to Paris as soon as I am done tonight. See if you can check your schedule."

"I'll call control," Kathe agreed as Yorg knocked on her door.

"Call me back before 5:00 or text me," Joe urged.

"Okay, I've got to go someone is at the door," she cleared the line.

"I thought I heard you talking to someone," Yorg said, sitting on the bed beside her. "I thought you would be sound asleep."

"I was talking to Jeannie," Kathe lied.

"How are you feeling?" Yorg asked.

"I feel great," Kathe smiled. "I don't know why you keep asking me."

He stood up and pulled her up to him, "Let's quit this game we seem to be playing. You and I both know you are pregnant. It's time we finally confirm it."

"Please don't say that," Kathe urged. "I feel much better, and the smell of coffee isn't bothering me anymore. Sydney gave me something to help settle my stomach. It was just the flu. I guess I got really run down," she said, looking away.

"Well tomorrow morning at 10:00 I made an appointment with Sir Albert at the London hospital," Yorg informed her. "And I'll be in the room with you. I want to know for sure, especially with a lunatic after you and the airlines. Did you forget about that?"

Kathe pulled away from him, "No, I haven't forgotten about Saíde or Mario Jr. Don't worry about me, I'm still fully functional!"

Yorg got right back in her face, "Well, tomorrow I will see just how functional you are!" He turned to leave her room, "I've been up for hours, and I have got to get some sleep. Jay and Jack are in Jordan's room. I'll take Carrie Anne's room. Wake us up and we'll have dinner when you're hungry."

Chapter 34

Saíde Calling the Shots

Dialing JAKE as Kathe left the room, she called control. Luckily, Keith was still on duty, "What's my schedule like tonight?"

"I'm showing you staying in Paris with Yorg," Keith said, pulling up the schedule.

"I have a friend in London that wants to see me tonight," Kathe replied. "Can you put him on a flight departing about 8:00?"

"Negative," Keith answered, checking the radar. "The weather report for that region list a heavy fog warning for that area. It should start rolling into Heathrow Airport around 5:00 or 6:00 tonight. We have already been told that the entire airport will shut down by 7:00 pm. I'm hoping it will be open in the morning before 9:00 am for your flight to land. Otherwise, your appointment with Sir Albert will have to change. I didn't give Yorg that information. He didn't sound like he was in a good mood. Hold on a minute, I have a call from Ramsey coming in."

Kathe held on wondering how she was going to talk with Joe alone knowing how Yorg felt about him. "Are you still there?" Keith returned.

"Yes," Kathe said, sitting on the couch patiently waiting. "Is Yorg asleep yet?"

"He just laid down a few minutes ago," Kathe answered. "Do you need to talk to him?"

"Yes, but I'll wait," Keith replied, checking Yorg's schedule. "I know he has to be tired. Have him call me when he wakes up."

"Are you sure you don't want me to wake him?" Kathe asked.

"No, he's been up a long time," Keith said. "We just received an anonymous tip that Saíde was sighted in Paris. Ramsey is leaving soon. She wants to be there and help search for him. She is sending an alert to all airports in that vicinity. This cancels any plans you have of meeting a friend. If lover girl is not with you, find her and keep her with you. Ramsey will be landing at Charles de Gaulle at 8:00 pm tonight. She'll coordinate the search with the gendarmes. Anything else I can do for you?"

"Yes," Kathe stated. "You are to cancel my appointment tomorrow with Sir Albert. I'm not going!" she cleared the line.

Taking a deep sigh, Kathe called Carrie Anne, "We've got a problem."

"Oh, no," Carrie Anne denounced. "I have no problems. I'm with Travis. I'm not leaving him for anyone or anything."

"An anonymous tip places Saíde in Paris," Kathe stated. "Keith ordered me to bring you over with us."

"No, way!" Carrie Anne objected. "Brock and RJ are both with us now, so I have protection. I'm having the time of my life with the man of my dreams. There's no way I'm leaving him, even if I have to tell the Ole Girl myself!"

"For once in my life, I don't blame you," Kathe agreed. "Maybe if I stayed with the man of my dreams, I wouldn't be in this mess. Just keep your eyes peeled; you know what he looks like. I'll call you when I have more information," Kathe said and cleared the line. Staring out the window at the Seine River, she wondered what to do now that Ramsey was coming to Paris. JAKE rang again.

"There you are," Jeannie said. "It's been a while since we've talked."

"I'm sorry," Kathe apologized, staring outside at the park. "I have got a lot on my mind lately."

"Does it have anything to do with the lead singer for Light Crimson?" Jeannie eagerly, inquired.

"Yes, and no," Kathe admitted. "I can't get him off my mind. Yet our professions don't mix-big time. It will never work."

"You're not going to work at Alby forever," Jeannie insinuated. "You wouldn't need to work anymore if you married him."

"You're such a romantic," Kathe sighed. "You make it sound so easy. I don't think I'll ever trust another man like that again."

"Sure, you will; not all men are like Peter," Jeannie assured her. "I know you well enough to know that you've fallen in love and that you're scared to death. You need to settle down again."

"It's not that easy," Kathe stated. "I've made enemies in this job. Even Yorg said that I will always have to look over my shoulders. I'll never risk my family's safety," she said, noticing Joe on the other line. "I've got another call. I'll call the kids this afternoon. Bye," she clicked over to Joe, "Hello."

"Did you find out your schedule?" Joe asked.

"I have a couple of short flights staying in Europe," Kathe replied. "Keith reported that there is a heavy fog warning for your area. Heathrow will be closing around 7:00 pm, so you can't make it tonight."

"One of the technicians for the studio lives near Heathrow Airport," Joe confirmed. "He called me earlier and said he is renting a flat near the studio for the night. He doesn't want to drive home in it. I can stay with him instead of driving back to my parent's house. I was afraid they would close the airport."

"Do you have a layover at Heathrow tomorrow?" Joe quizzed. "I'll meet you at the airport."

"Not long enough to see you," Kathe lied. "Do you have any sessions tomorrow?"

"It all depends on how much I get done tonight," Joe discussed. "I'm scheduled to finish two songs. I have another session tomorrow morning and should be done about noon. Then I can hop a flight over and meet you at Steve's. I've already checked with him. The guys have plans, but he'll leave a key with the doorman. Call when you get in from work. If you are going to be late, I will probably take a nap. I haven't had much sleep lately. The studio is calling me. I hope they don't cancel the session. I will call you later this evening."

"I'm going to bed," Kathe sighed. "I'll probably get up around 7:00 pm. Call me when you're done with your session . . . Bye."

Hours later, Kathe finally got up after tossing and turning for hours. She couldn't sleep. She showered and dressed for dinner. She went into the living room to wait for the guys to wake up. Sitting on the couch staring at the Seine River, as dusk turned to darkness Kathe thought how stupid she was for letting her guard down. Ramsey and Yorg were both right. She had no business getting involved with such a famous person. She looked down on the coffee table and there was Joe's picture on the cover of one of the magazines. What was she going to do now that her life had become so complicated? She would have to take a leave of absence, but not until Saíde was captured and Mario's plans stopped. Ramsey wouldn't understand her views on the new life inside her. Yorg would never tolerate Joe and quite frankly, she might not either.

Turning on his computer in his hotel room, Saíde reached for a cigarette, as he went online,

"Where are you?" He whined looking for his wormhole to the back door of Alby's Computer System. As he lit his cigarette, "There you are!" typing a few more words, "I'm in! Now, where are you? YEEEEESSSSSS. You took the bait! Hope you had a nice flight, Boss Lady, while I'm finishing my work with your little friends. I'll keep you busy in Paris. Let me see I need to check into a hotel" Opening a file hidden on his desktop scrolling down a list of names . . . "I'll use this name and credit card, and I need to eat at a restaurant nearby. Let me see what is in that area . . . yes . . . I'll eat here. That should keep you out of my way. Now, where did she stash Tierra? What's that other broad's name? Yes, Wanda. Wanda knows ALLLLL. Now where are you? . . . Ah! The Executive Inn in East Manhattan, 3489 South, Room # 2174 for two. Oh! no!" He dropped the cigarette out of his mouth. Reaching for it his hand brushed the keyboard. "I didn't do anything, did I?" he asked, looking at the monitor. "No, everything's the same . . . good," he said, glancing at the time. "Twelve noon, and there's a note . . . 'Confined to Quarters'. Good you should be home and its broad daylight," he said, glancing out the window. "Sunny day-a little cold and a great day to die!" he exclaimed. He shut down his computer, grabbed his jacket and left.

"Tierra, are you up yet?" CC called through the door.

"Yeah," Tierra answered, glancing at the clock on the nightstand. "Oh, my, gosh, it's already 2:00 in the afternoon. Man did we sleep in or what?" Tierra said, opening her bedroom door and entered the sitting area.

"The movie lasted longer than we thought," CC agreed. "But it sure was good. How about a cup of coffee from Starbuck's and a muffin for brunch?"

"It'll take me a few minutes to get ready," Tierra sighed, reaching for the remote and turning on the TV. "What's the weather like?"

"Take your time," CC suggested. "I'm already dressed. It's just downstairs in the lobby. Keep the door locked. I will be right back."

"Great, I need caffeine to wake up," Tierra answered and sat on the couch.

"Want anything else?" CC asked holding the door open.

"Just coffee, a muffin, and my life back!" Tierra complained. "I'm getting sick of being locked up. At least, Kathe and the others are traveling," she replied as CC closed the door.

Hurrying down the hallway, just as the elevator door opened, CC hurried into the crowded elevator. She bumped into a man getting off. "This is my floor," he said, recognizing her as he brushed past. He walked off quickly as the door closed.

Getting off the elevator on the main floor, CC had a nagging feeling that there was something not right with the man that got off on her floor. Shaking it off as cabin fever, she hurried into the long line glancing at the menu. Reaching in her purse, she realized that she left her wallet in the room.

Hearing the door rustling, Tierra put the TV remote down, "I'll help you with the door CC," she said, getting up to help. "Nooo!" she screamed as Saíde closed and latched the door behind him.

"I have to admit you have one lucky family," Saíde chuckled as he reached for his knife. "My country would have already had that jet, if it wasn't for your father refusing the deal! It took me two tries to kill Nicki. This is the third time for you! I also must admit, you've got one screwed up brother. Why Mario wanted you two dead, I really don't know. Your father is the only one I should have killed. But if I don't finish you off, Mario's coming after me," he admitted as CC inserted the key into the lock.

The latch on the door caught as CC tried to open it. CC instinctively reached for her gun. "CC help!" Tierra screamed and ran toward the bedroom.

Stepping backwards kicking the door shut, Saíde threw his knife hitting Tierra in the back.

Shooting the latch, kicking the door open, CC dropped to the left of the doorway, and peered inside. Saíde dropped to the floor, reached for his gun and shot multiple times at the doorway. "Come on in," he laughed as he reloaded his gun. "You're next; I've already killed Tierra," he bragged, dropping some bullets.

CC took that moment to roll over once in the center of the doorway. She raised her gun and fired, striking Saíde in the left shoulder.

"You shot me!" Saíde screamed, shooting CC in the chest. Hearing a commotion in the hallway, Saíde grabbed his bleeding shoulder, stepped over CC, and headed for the stairwell.

Touching down at Charles De Gaulle Airport, Ramsey had already called Jay and Yorg to meet her at Lt. Jaco's office in an hour. Yorg came out of his room heading to the kitchen to get a drink. He noticed Kathe sitting on the couch staring out the window. "Penny for your thoughts," Yorg said as Jack opened his bedroom door to join them.

"I'm not going to Sir Albert's office tomorrow!" Kathe declared. "I already cancelled the appointment!" she glared at him. "You have no right to ever call Keith or Ramsey and make them schedule me an appointment anywhere! I work for Alby Airlines! They do not own me! I'm not married and the only person I must answer to is myself!"

"Wait a minute, Lady!" Yorg snapped as Jack stepped back in his room and closed the door. "In our business I need you, 100 percent. You're pregnancy changes that now! You can't defend yourself or backup anyone else for that matter! Not to mention your life is at stake! I do care about you and the life within you!"

"In our profession caring isn't an option!" Kathe exclaimed, standing up. "I don't know who I am anymore! I should have never let my guard down, much less let a man into my private life or bed again! How stupid could I be? Now my life is so complicated! I am pregnant! Sydney told me before we left for Paris that his implants work better than he thought! He never imagined hearing a fetal heartbeat! He also said I am still fully functional! And that I must finish this with Saíde and Mario! I am the main target! This isn't going to go away on its own! So now, you know!" she confessed, turning to leave the room. "Keith told me that we have to meet Ramsey in less than an hour!"

Hurrying over to Kathe and turning her around to face him, "Caring is a part of our profession! I was just as bitter as you are when the hand of fate took Mikél! However, after everything we've been through, I knew I had a different path! Sydney's wrong about you being fully functional; you're not!"

"How dare you say I'm not still fully functional!" Kathe declared. "Do you think I just got pregnant last night? I was puking my guts out while we were in Russia! My pregnancy didn't stop you from sending me in to save Ivan or your sister, did it? You suspected it then, didn't you?"

"Let's get one thing straight," Yorg insisted. "You are the one who insisted on going to Russia with me or did you forget? Yes, I did suspect it! But you are the one that insisted you weren't. Did you forget that? Now that I know for sure you are pregnant, I am not taking any more chances with your life or the baby's! You are the prime target and Saíde is not going to go away without a fight! Ramsey just woke me up and told me he has been sited here in Paris! We are going to find him and put him out of his misery!

You're going to stay by my side until this is over and then you choose what path you take!" he declared as his phone rang. "Yes, Ramsey, we'll be there in twenty minutes." He walked over to the other bedroom and knocked, "It's safe to come out now. I'm sure you heard what's going on with Kathe. We are leaving in a few minutes."

Ramsey and Lt. Jaco were searching the security tapes from Charles De Gaulle trying to pinpoint when Saíde entered the country as the team arrived. "Glad you could finally join us," Ramsey snarled, checking the time. "While it took you 45 minutes to get here, we found this," pointing to the computer screen. "An anonymous tip was called into Alby Control yesterday afternoon about 12:00 stating that Saíde was on his way to Paris."

"This is a 30-second clip we got from Charles de Gaulle Airport security cameras," Jaco continued. "Notice the second man entering the shop. Watch for a second, he looks straight at the camera . . . there! That is Saíde! He has already passed through American security, flown to Paris and is through customs. How can the third most wanted man in several countries do that?"

"That's exactly what I want to know," Ramsey interjected. "And the reason I came to help secure him. Kathe is this Saíde?"

"Yes, that is Rhasheéd Saíde," Kathe stated as she studied the film. "But isn't it odd that he's looking directly at the camera?"

"Watch this," Ramey urged. "Here's another 15-second clip of the same man outside the airport this time."

"That's strange too," Kathe continued. "He's looking straight at the camera again."

"Perhaps he's gotten away with so much that he's slipping," Jack laughed.

"He's a professional hitman," Kathe reminded Jack. "He doesn't slip; it was on purpose," Kathe noted as a screen popped up on the desktop.

"Well, I'll be," Ramsey sighed, "look who just checked into the Gay Parí with a credit card."

"Jean-Louie Labelle," Jaco remarked. "I had all the aliases of Saíde profiled for any movement. He's also been at the Loire Restaurant for dinner. It looks like he's alone."

"I've got you now!" Ramsey shouted, reaching for her purse while Lt. Jaco informed his men.

Fifteen minutes later, they entered the Gay Parí, "Ms. Tierney, it's been a long time," Ramoné greeted. "We've missed you and Miss Mobley staying here. How can I help you?"

"It has been a while," Kathe happily replied. "However, I'm here on official business."

Showing his badge, Lt. Jaco took over the conversation as Kathe stepped back. "I need to know in which room Jean-Louie Labelle is staying and is he in now?"

Searching through the computer files, "He is staying in room 2958 . . . that's strange . . . the computer says that he checked in earlier this afternoon. It is showing that he is in his room. However, I've been on duty all afternoon and I don't recall him checking in."

"I have a warrant for his arrest," Lt. Jaco stated, taking it out of his jacket showing Ramoné. "I need a key."

Reaching for a card to key to the room number, "Here's one for you lieutenant," he said, handing it to him.

Yorg joined Kathe as she was opening a text message while everyone headed for the elevator. "You stay here," he ordered. "I don't want you up there with this maniac in your condition."

"What do you mean, her condition?" Ramsey stopped, overhearing them.

"She's pregnant," Yorg stated. "She doesn't need to be up there," he said, glancing back at Kathe.

"You just stepped over the line, Vuslick!" Kathe exclaimed. "You have no right to tell her my personal business!" Kathe snapped as she pushed past him heading for the elevator.

"Tierney!" Ramsey snapped. "Just stop right there! He's right! Keep your fanny down here! I'll deal with you later!" Ramsey promised, storming past Kathe. "Perfect timing, Tierney!"

As soon as the elevator door closed Kathe opened the text message again, "Got in early taking nap door open love u c u soon."

She checked again with Ramoné, "Are you sure you don't remember this man checking in this afternoon?"

"No, Ms. Tierney," Ramoné affirmed. "You know that I always remember my guests, even the first timers. It doesn't make any sense."

"It's beginning to make perfect sense to me," Kathe expressed. "He's not up there and he never has been. Have a nice night," she said and left the lobby. She was thinking as she walked outside, "a man we can't find, suddenly stares directly into two different surveillance cameras, and uses a credit card at a hotel and restaurant. He's sent them on a wild goose chase. He's after Tierra and CC," she thought as she called CC, and then Tierra with no answer. She called control, "Keith, I can't get hold of Tierra or CC. Can you check on them? I've got a bad feeling."

"I'll do it right now," Keith said and cleared the line.

Arriving back at the apartment building, Kathe hurried to Steve's apartment anxious about meeting with Joe. Should she tell him? Should she end it? Everything began racing through her mind; could she ever trust another man, her other children, her job, Saíde, Mario Jr.? Yorg's statement, people like us will always have to look over our shoulders, kept playing repeatedly in her head. Turning the doorknob slowly, she said a quick prayer asking for help as she entered the living room. "Peace Roses, Joe remembered they're my favorite," she fondly thought reaching for the note. "Wake me I'm yours! I'm in the second room on the left." She noticed clothes strewn on the couch and on the floor as she walked down the hallway. Slightly opening the door, she peered in the dark room at Joe. He was asleep. "Be with me Lord," she thought and slipped into the room. She quietly walked to the bed to gently wake him.

"Got you!" Shaunda bragged, lunging out of the bathroom, and taking a picture of Kathe bending over Joe.

"What in the world?" Kathe yelled, pulling her gun at Shaunda. "Don't move!"

"Ahhhhh!" Cara, who was lying next to Joe, screamed as Joe sat up.

Kathe turned on the lamp as Joe noticed Cara next to him. "What are you doing in bed with me?" he screamed, reaching for his jeans next to the bed. "Where are my jeans?" He glanced up at Shaunda, "Did you just take a picture of me?"

"Don't you remember leaving your clothes in the sitting room next to Cara's flowers when you welcomed her?" Shaunda lied.

"You're one, crazy broad!" Joe screamed. "You set this up! Kathe's not falling for this, and neither am I!"

"Give me that camera!" Kathe ordered, walking closer to her.

"My God, she's got a gun!" Cara cried, pulling the sheets over her head. "Joe, help me! Don't let her shoot me!"

"I wouldn't blame Kathe if she did," Joe declared as he searched for his pants.

"I saw a pair of men's jeans in the living room, go get them," Kathe said as he left the room. "What were you two thinking?"

"Shaunda thought you would see me in bed with Joe and leave him forever," Cara cried from under the sheets. "You know he still loves me."

Entering the room, hearing Cara's answer, Joe yelled, "I despise the very sight of you! You and everything the two of you stand for is an abomination to me and my friends."

"Joe, get the camera from Shaunda," Kathe requested as Shaunda held the camera tightly to her chest.

"I'm not giving you anything," Shaunda declared and clutched it tighter. "I'm giving this picture to the BBC News! I'm sure this picture and the headlines will ruin her and her job!"

"I'm going to say it one more time!" Kathe demanded. "Give him the camera!" Kathe ordered, stepping closer, raising the gun at Shaunda's head while Joe walked over to her. "Let's see, breaking and entering, blackmail and extortion. Lady, you are going up for a long time." Looking over at Cara peering over the sheet, "Excuse me, you're an accessory and just as guilty. I can see the headlines now. 'British Top Models' in prison stripes forever!"

"I'm not going to jail!" Shaunda bragged as Joe took the camera. "My father's an ambassador and I've got diplomatic immunity."

"I ran a profile on you," Kathe informed her. "Your father's the ambassador to Portugal. In their language, 'Tu no eres allí, tu eres in Paris.' In case you don't speak the language, I said, you are not there, you are in Paris. I knew you were not done exploiting Joe. Now, I've got you! Daddy's money can't help you get out of this one," she said as Joe stood beside Kathe. "Joe, call the gendarmes. I've got to take this call," Kathe requested as JAKE rang.

"I've got a better idea first," Joe chuckled, holding the camera waiting for Kathe to leave the room. "The old saying, he who laughs last, laughs best is true. I can't wait until the paparazzi get hold of this," Joe grinned, placing a phone call. "Are you close by? . . . Do you know where there's a used car dealership? . . . What about those bodyguards we used here a couple of months ago?" Joe asked, taking pictures of the two models hovering together on the bed. Then, he took the memory stick out of the camera and put it in his pocket. "Can you give him a call? . . . Great, see you in five!"

"Tierney, where are you?" Ramsey demanded. "I told you to stay in the lobby at the Gay Parí!" She turned toward Yorg, "I've got her on the phone. You go ahead with Jaco. I'll meet you at the station," Ramsey said, returning to Kathe. "What's wrong with you? I've got a hitman in town with your name at the top of his list and you're wandering around without backup?"

"I wasn't needed there," Kathe affirmed. "I came back to my apartment."

"Yorg gave me the address," Ramsey said. "I'm already en route, 789 Allée de la Broussalle," Ramsey told the cabby and cleared the line.

Returning to the bedroom, Kathe reached in her purse for zip ties. She handed them to Joe, listening to the two crying women, begging him to let them go. "Tie their hands with these. How long until the gendarmes arrive?"

"I called Steve instead," Joe explained. "He should be here in a second. I know exactly what I want to do with them," he laughed, holding up the camera.

Pulling Joe aside, "I don't know why you called Steve instead of the gendarmes? I must keep this legal. Call the gendarmes or I will."

"Oh, don't worry darling," Joe assured her. "After what these two have done to me, the band, not to mention you, I plan on calling the gendarmes when I'm ready."

"Joe, Kathe, are you here?" Steve interrupted as the group returned to the apartment.

"We're in the second bedroom," Joe answered.

"Are you decent?" Collin grinned, glancing at the clothes strewn all over the floor.

"Sure, come and join the party," Joe sarcastically retorted.

"Did he say party?" Suzanne asked, hurrying to the room.

"Oh, my, God!" Travis exclaimed. "Shaunda, what have you done now?"

Kathe pulled Carrie Anne into the hallway as Joe brought his friends up to speed. "I've got to meet Ramsey across the hall any minute. Are you going to be okay with them?"

"Yes, Brock and RJ are keeping an eye out for Saíde," Carrie Anne answered. "Hey, how did it go at the doctors? Did you find out? Did you tell him?"

Pointing inside the bedroom, "That's how it went," Kathe answered. "I must go. Don't worry about Saíde being in Paris. He's in New York. Ramsey's so mad at me, she won't listen. I've got to get back to the states before he strikes. I know he's heading for Tierra. That's why Saíde staged this whole thing. But first, I need something from Joe." She went back into the room and reached for the camera. "I have to go," Kathe explained. "Ramsey's in Paris and she is waiting for me across the hall. Remember your promise to call the gendarmes on them for breaking and entering. I will get rid of the picture," she said as she kissed him and hurried across the hall.

Kathe barely got inside and grabbed a bottle of water when Ramsey rang the doorbell. "Showtime," Kathe thought as she slowly opened the door. "Ramsey, how did it go at the Gay Parí?"

"No one was checked into that room," Ramsey snarled. "I've got to hand it to Saíde, his profile is right on the money. He is slippery! Yorg and Jaco are checking out the credit card receipt at the restaurant, before going back to look at the security tapes again. I sent Jay and Jack over to the airport to question the customs agents."

"I have a gut feeling that Saíde isn't..." Kathe started to say.

Ramsey interrupted her, "Speaking of your gut; that's why I came here, instead of going to the station. Yorg tells me that you are pregnant. Perfect timing, don't you think? You have known since the time you met Glitter Boy that this maniac is coming for you at the expense of other lives. What were you thinking?" she reached for her cigarettes. "After three kids that you can't even live with, because of the risk that your job creates, you sleep around unprotected! Are you switching places with Carrie Anne? I can't even believe I'm having this conversation with you!"

"I can't believe I'm quoting someone else," Kathe interjected. "I admit I deserve that. I am pregnant. I intend to tie up all loose ends before I must take a leave of absence. Please don't light that cigarette! None of us smoke in this apartment."

"You don't have the luxury of tying up loose ends now!" Ramsey shouted and took a deep breath to calm down. "Yorg's right; you are too vulnerable in your condition. I've got too much invested in that body of yours. Sydney and I are close to being able to sell some of our inventions to the Pentagon. Not all is lost; there is a simple solution to this problem. When we get back to New York, Wanda will give you the name of a physician that has fixed several of my flight attendants careless indiscretions with no questions asked. Remember Shelley Nobles? She's fine and back at work. She's not falling for married pilots anymore. You'll be back to normal in less than a month, just be more careful next time."

"You do have a lot of money invested in this body of mine," Kathe agreed. "However, the brain and skills are mine. Dr. Sydney did not program that part of me. For your information, this is the real world. I'm not a character in a movie. There's no computer program to make this body fight for you! I am what makes these implants work! My brain, my fighting skills, my marksmanship! You have no right to tell me why I don't live with my other children or judge me for it! You also have no right to tell me to fix my careless indiscretion or even call it that," Kathe declared as Ramsey's phone rang.

"Yes, Keith . . . Kathe said what? . . . My, God!" She screamed as she slumped down on the couch. "Are they? . . . Did you call their parents . . . one shot . . . one stabbed . . . no knife found . . . I'll contact Yorg and Jaco . . . Call me if anything changes . . . I'll be there as soon as I finish here . . . Keep me posted!" Ramsey said as she cleared the line and lit a cigarette.

"What now?" Kathe asked, backing away from the smell.

"Keith said you called and told him to check on Tierra and CC," Ramsey stated. "He couldn't get hold of them and sent the police to check on them. They were found in their hotel room a few minutes ago. They're both barely alive."

"Oh, no!" Kathe gasped, moving further away from the smoke. "I was trying to tell you that I have a gut . . ."

"Forget your gut!" Ramsey snapped. "Keith said Tierra had a knife in her back and CC was shot in the chest! They are both in surgery! I switched their hotels several times myself! No one could have found them!" She screamed, gathering her things. "I've got to get to the station and find out what is going on. I want you to get Carrie Anne and stay in this apartment! We'll be back for you!" she snarled, calling Yorg as she stormed out of the apartment.

Reaching for JAKE, Kathe called Charles de Gaulle Airport and found a flight leaving within the hour for the states. "This is crazy," she thought. "This proves I'm right. He's hacking into Wanda and Ramsey's computers. Sydney is so busy working on breaking the code, he still has not found the hacker that made Saíde's pictures disappear. He is toying with all of us! I knew it! He's the one giving the anonymous tips! That's why he had the nerve to look straight into the cameras. The pictures were computer generated. Ramsey and Yorg are so mad at me, they won't listen. I must get to New York. If the girls live through the surgeries, he will go after them again at the hospital. She packed a small suitcase, put the camera inside and left.

Ramsey arrived back at the station minutes behind Yorg and Jaco. "Did Yorg tell you what happened to my two flight attendants?"

"Yes, and that's what is troubling," Jaco explained. "How can Saíde be on two continents at the same time? One of my men questioned Agent Vincent Papalino, who supposedly identified the picture of Saíde, and said his credentials were in order."

"Has Jay checked in with his findings with the other customs agents?" Ramsey asked.

"No," Jaco stated. "My men are with Jay and Jack at the airport now."

"Have your men bring Papalino in for questioning," Ramsey said. "I want to talk with him myself," she requested as he called his men. "Yorg, what did you find at the Loire?"

"Another dead end," Yorg stated. "No one remembered serving him. Have you heard anything more about Tierra and CC?"

"No, Keith said he would call as soon as he heard anything," Ramsey answered.

"How did your talk go with Kathe?" Yorg asked.

"Not well at all; just like I figured," Ramsey affirmed. "She tried to tell me something about her gut feeling and I tore into her about her gut. I told her she could fix her problem when we get back to New York and be more careful next time."

"You really said that to her?" Yorg fumed. "I better give her a call!" Yorg snapped, glaring at Ramsey.

"I meant every word I said!" Ramsey defended. "In case you've forgotten, I've got several dead flight attendants and two in surgery right now because of her."

"Stop blaming Kathe for this mess!" Yorg argued. "Saíde went after Tierra first! Did you forget that? He missed the mark! You and her father moved her to safety! You're the one who put CC with her as a bodyguard and didn't tell anyone who she is!"

"I didn't do it," Ramsey refuted. "You need to calm down. The FBI put her with Tierra. They've been watching the LaBasco Family for a long time. They needed hard evidence to put the old man away for the murder of some senator. However, after everything we've uncovered, I'd say Jr. is trying to frame his father."

"Just stop blaming Kathe for your mess!" Yorg exclaimed, walking away. "Kathe must be really upset with the both of us," Yorg said as he returned a few minutes later. "She didn't answer the phone. I left her a message," he said as he put his phone in its holder.

"Yorg get your head back in this game," Ramsey requested. "Don't worry about Kathe. This isn't the first time she has been upset at both of us and it probably won't be the last. We need to focus," she said as her phone rang.

"Ramsey, you're not going to like this," Jay reported as they were leaving the Customs Office. "Customs Agent Vincent Papalino doesn't exist."

"You've got to be kidding," Ramsey stated. "Meet me at Tierney's apartment. We're heading back to the states," she said as she cleared the line and looked at Jaco. "I need to know the name of your officer that interviewed Customs Agent Papalino. My men tell me he doesn't exist."

"The officer that interviewed him . . ." Jaco said, checking in his PDA. "Here it is. Ricardo Michele said he was covering for Lt. Aleixandre Mineo, who oversees De Gaulle Airport. He said Mineo had to take a leave of absence because of a family emergency," Jaco said as he quickly switched to his computer and pulled up the work roster. "Come to think of it . . . I have never heard of him. I do remember when I was talking to him, I noticed his accent was strange. Let me check with personnel," he said, picking up his phone.

"I bet he doesn't exist, just like Papalino," Ramsey declared.

"Saíde has really played us," Yorg interjected. "Somehow, he is always a few steps ahead of us."

Jaco slammed his phone down and threw his pen across the room, "How could I have been so stupid? I should have checked his story out with Mineo. Ricardo Michele doesn't exist either!"

"It looks like you've got a breach at your airport security," Ramsey noted just as Yorg's phone received a text message.

Yorg reached for his phone thinking it was Kathe. He looked in disbelief at the screen. "Oh, my, God!" he exclaimed, reading aloud, 'XP38 gone-recognize pilots?' Jaco I'm sending some pictures to your computer. Would you pull them up?"

Chapter 35

The Worst Nightmare

"O'Brien, we're almost out of Ukrainian airspace," Mario boasted. "Let's see what this jet can do. It's finally time to change our call names for chit chat; anything on radar in the area?" Mario Jr. asked, glancing at the design of the cockpit.

"I'm showing a neutral," O'Brien smiled. "It is at 120 degrees off our starboard. It's a Ukrainian commercial airliner. What do you have in mind?"

"We're going to pay them a visit, Leprechaun!" Mario laughed.

"Bad Wolf let's go knocking on their door and see who's afraid," Leprechaun laughed. He typed the latitude and longitude of the airliner to lock onto their IFF Codes. O'Brien was shocked that the screen did not pull up the ID and serial number of the airliner. He tried again.

"What say you, Leprechaun?" Bad Wolf grinned. "Let's go knocking on their door and see who's afraid of the Big, Bad Wolf."

"Bad Wolf," Leprechaun said, frantically trying another port to get into their system. "We seem to have a problem."

"What are you talking about?" Bad Wolf inquired.

"It keeps asking for the authentication response codes," Leprechaun stated. "I'm searching the files for them. Raini must have added it without my knowledge."

"Whom are you talking about?" Bad Wolf demanded.

"Karl Raini finished developing the system, before Yetsun killed him," Leprechaun stated, continuing to search the monitor. "Did Yetsun give you the codes?"

"No, Yetsun assured me when I paid him," Bad Wolf growled, "that you are everything I need to use this technology!"

"I do know how to use this technology!" Leprechaun screeched. "Come to think of it, Raini on completion of this project was acting a little funny when he gave Yetsun an envelope, supposedly containing the activation instructions. If Yetsun didn't give them to you, maybe he is planning on stealing this jet back and selling it to the Iranians himself," responded O'Brien trying to get the heat off.

"I'll deal with this when we get on the ground!" Mario snapped as he thought, "my little brother did intercept the codes. Codes that Tierra's friends might have. I need those codes!"

"Oh, my, God, is right!" Ramsey exclaimed as the first picture appeared on the screen. "They've got it!"

"What is O'Brien doing getting into that jet with LaBasco?" Jaco asked as he brought up all the pictures.

"Buying it from the unaware Russian government to sell to the Iranians we think," Yorg declared, pacing the floor. "This is all thanks to the renegade Gen. Yetsun. We have got to get this jet back! Sydney must break that code now! We have just run out of time! That's the only way for sure we'll know what they are going to do with it."

"How do you know O'Brien?" Ramsey asked Jaco looking at the pictures.

"Every law officer in Europe knows this low life," Jaco stated, pulling up the file on O'Brien.

Flipping through the file, Yorg sees a picture and yells in disbelief, "Stop! Go back a few pages. Not there, just a little further-there! That's him! That's why I thought he looked so familiar. That picture was taken about five years ago," Yorg said, turning to Ramsey. "There was another engineer working with Ivan and myself on the prototype for this technology. His name was Karl Raini, and he had a young, cocky apprentice named O'Brien. Ivan and I refused to work with O'Brien and kicked him out of our office. I had forgotten about him. That is why Yetsun killed Raini and Ivan. Kathe said there had to be another pilot. O'Brien is Yetsun's backup, and if anything went wrong, I would have been his insurance policy. Especially, with him holding my sister as ransom."

"You just perfectly described O'Brien," Jaco stated. "He's as slippery as Saíde and now that I think about it," checking computer files on both men. "Yes, I'm right! O'Brien got into a tiff with Scotland Yard recently and guess who the attorney was?"

"Damiano Genero," Ramsey stated, shaking her head.

"Correct, and those two don't have that kind of money to hire him," Jaco stated. "However, Mario LaBasco Jr. does have the money. We still can't prove it though."

"These pictures tie Mario Jr., Saíde, and O'Brien together!" Ramsey noted, sitting straight up tapping her unlit cigarette on the tabletop.

"It ties O'Brien and LaBasco Jr., but not Saíde," Jaco continued. "We still need to prove Mario Jr. is behind him."

"We're close to proving it," Ramsey affirmed. "Tierney was in Munich with Nicki LaBasco when the first attempt on his life was made. She stated that Saíde was driving the limo for the hitmen. Nicki was murdered at Mario's house. According to Tierra and CC, Alonzo doesn't trust him. It's a matter of time before Alonzo figures out what happened."

"Have you talked with Alonzo about Mario's men faking dental records?" Jaco asked.

"I'm not comfortable with that yet," Ramsey confided. "We're talking about the Italian Mafia. I can't accuse the favorite son of murdering his brother."

"I understand," Jaco replied. "From everything I know about Alonzo DiMeglio, it's just a matter of time until he gets to the bottom of this. I hear he is very thorough."

"Why can't you talk with Alonzo about Mario Sr. being set up?" Yorg asked. "You do have more than just suspicions."

"Not enough hard evidence to go to Alonzo," Ramsey confided. "It looks like Jr. wants to make a side deal that his father is against. From everything I've seen in Senior's profile, he's no saint, but he is loyal to free nations. There is no way he is aware of what his son is doing, nor would he approve of it."

"Then, we're wasting our time here," Yorg suggested. "Saíde wasn't here this time."

"Kathe was right," Ramsey agreed. "Kathe noted that he looked straight into both cameras at the airport. He did that on purpose, he's not getting sloppy, he's getting cocky. Yorg get hold of the Freedom Fighters and see if they have any idea where they are taking that jet. I'll call the airport and have my private Leer readied for you. I will take Kathe and the others back to the states with me and deal with Saíde. I will have Sydney check my laptop for intrusions and have Keith and Wanda get theirs checked as well. Saíde's got to be a hacker and a good one at that."

"I'll have my computer checked as well," Jaco agreed. "Saíde must be hacking into our database! I'll call you after I talk to Lt. Mineo and find where my breach is at the airport," Jaco said as they stood up to leave. "Keep me posted."

Leaving the office, Yorg cautioned Ramsey, "I want you to promise me that you'll be easy on Kathe."

"I'm not going to promise you anything," Ramsey advised as they got into the cab. "That problem shouldn't have happened."

"789 Allée de la Broussalle," Yorg told the cabby.

Arriving at the apartment Yorg could not wait to talk with her. "Kathe," he called opening the front door to a dark apartment.

"Is she asleep?" Ramsey asked. "Look on the floor, you know her sleeping habits," she said, helping him check all the rooms as Jay and Jack arrived.

"Have you seen Tierney?" Yorg asked.

"No, I thought you said she was here with Carrie Anne waiting for us," Jack answered.

"Oh, no!" Yorg shouted, reaching for his phone dialing JAKE. "She's still not answering!"

"Calm down," Ramsey said, reaching for her phone. "I'm calling Carrie Anne, maybe she's not answering because she is with Glitter Boy! . . . Mobley where is Tierney? . . . What do you mean? . . . Where? . . . When did she leave? . . . I'm warning you, I'm in no mood for this! Get your bones over here right now! We're leaving in ten minutes!" she glared at Yorg. "It seems that Tierney is already on a plane to the states going after Saíde alone. She told Carrie Anne not to worry about Saíde being in Paris, he's in New York. Evidently, that's why she won't answer JAKE," calling control while Yorg walked away swearing in Russian. "Keith, I need you to locate Tierney and tell me where she is. Sydney didn't have time to find the hacker in our computers before he started working on cracking the code. Check for computer security breaches and have Wanda check as well. Saíde is hacking into our system; that is how he found the girls and sent me on a wild goose chase to Paris."

"Kathe already asked me to do that," Keith admitted. "I've already been looking for intrusions. The only way he could have found them was our own computers! I haven't found anything yet! I cannot use our computers to locate Tierney. With Tierra and CC down, Saíde will go after her next. If I try to locate her, he will know that too!"

"You're right!" Ramsey exclaimed. "Have Sydney take a few minutes to help you look for a backdoor or some other spyware. Maybe he can trace it and find Saíde," Ramsey ordered. "I'm coming back to help. I'll get my own flight, so I can come in unannounced."

"I've already asked Sydney," Keith replied, scrolling through his computer files. "He said he is too close to crack the code to stop now. We will have to wait."

"Let Sydney work," Ramsey approved. "As soon as he cracks the code, have him help you," she said and cleared the line.

Yorg came out of his room with his bags as Carrie Anne and Travis opened the door. "Where's Sherrod?" Yorg yelled.

"He's on his way to the states," Carrie Anne answered.

"With Kathe?" Yorg quizzed.

"No," Travis replied. "When Carrie Anne told him, Kathe was leaving for the states, Joe tried to reach her, but she wouldn't answer. He said he had to go alone and find her. He's not going to lose her again."

"Let's go," Ramsey interrupted them grabbing her bags and laptop. "We've got planes to catch."

"Just one plane to catch," Yorg insisted. "I called Pavel and they tracked the jet until it went supersonic. Then they lost it. I am going with you to the states and find Saíde," Yorg stated as they left the apartment. "What time does our flight leave?"

"Tonight, we have to fly like everyone else," Ramsey admitted. "Kathe already figured out that Saíde is hacking into our computers. She had Keith looking for his entryway. Keith knows if he uses the computers to locate Kathe or book our flight, Saíde will see. You can't go to New York. You can't be that far from the location of the jet. I will help Kathe while you stop that jet! Take my Leer and help the Freedom Fighters. I will have the FBI scramble the files to the computer onboard the Leer on O'Brien and Macaby. Check where they have been seen in that region lately. That may help you find XP38," Ramsey said, taking a moment to sigh. "Yorg, this is bigger than Kathe. She's collateral damage when it comes to stopping the sale of that jet. The Iranians can't have this technology or anybody else in that region. Talk about starting Armageddon!"

"I can't lose her!" Yorg snapped, glaring straight at her as they got into the elevator.

"You won't," Ramsey admitted. "Kathe is a professional, just like Saíde."

"No, she's pregnant!" Yorg snapped, pressing the down button.

"You're right," Ramsey declared. "Kathe is pregnant, but she is not Mikél. Kathe is a trained professional. She knows how to go after Saíde, and she knows how to fight him. Stop comparing the two women. Keith is keeping an eye out for her. He knows she will go to the hospital and see the girls. He has already alerted the guards to let him know the minute Kathe is spotted. The hospital is ten minutes from the airport by helicopter. He'll pick her up himself. Look, before you fell in love with her, you didn't care if I sent her into a burning plane with ten terrorists. Now, your vision is clouded with love, worse than Glitter Boy. Just let Kathe do what she is trained to do," she finished and hailed a cab.

"What did you just say?" Yorg glared at her as the cab stopped.

"I said," Ramsey reiterated. "Before you fell in love with her you didn't care what situation I sent her into. De Gaulle Airport, Terminal D, Alby Airlines, síl vous plaít."

Chapter 36

Tierra's Hospital Bedside

Landing at Newark Airport Kathe took a cab straight to St. Luke's Roosevelt Hospital. She knew Saíde was somewhere in New York and would be checking the status of the girls. At the hospital, she used her ID to pass through tight security. She was escorted to ICU to visit CC first. CC's parents were half-asleep when Kathe startled them. CC's father quickly reached for his gun. "Wait," Kathe said, showing her ID. "I'm Kathe Tierney. I'm a security agent for Alby Airlines. I work with your daughter."

"Yes," he said, holstering his weapon. "CC has mentioned you several times."

"Constance could never decide what she wanted to be when she grew up," her teary-eyed mother sighed, looking at her daughter. "A flight attendant like me or an FBI Agent like her father. Now look at her."

"With the way the world is today neither profession is safe," Kathe admitted, giving her a hug.

"You're right," Mrs. Sims admitted. "Air travel has changed drastically since years ago when I was a flight attendant. I used to think her father had the only dangerous job in our household. I have lived through him being shot several times, but she is different. Constance is my only little girl," her mother wept harder.

"From meeting the both of you, I can see she comes from strong stock," Kathe comforted her. "I know she'll pull through this," Kathe reinforced, checking the time. "I want to visit Tierra before I go to work. I'll check in with you later."

"Thanks, for the encouragement," Mrs. Sims said.

A guard was waiting for Kathe as she left CC's room. Kathe hurried to the nurses' station as he called control-alerting Keith that Kathe was there. Showing her ID to the nurse on duty, "I am Kathe Tierney with Alby Security. I would like to see Tierra LaBasco. What room is she in?"

"She is in four," the RN stated after she checked the roster for Kathe's name and pointed to the left. "She is neither conscious, nor stable, only stay a few minutes."

Kathe took a deep breath as she entered Tierra's room, not noticing that the bathroom door was just closing. She broke into tears as she saw her friend's frail body as the bathroom door reopened slightly.

Pulling the chair closer to the bed, Kathe sat down, dried her eyes, and held Tierra's hand. "Tierra I'm so sorry this happened to you and CC . . ." she took a deep breath to stop crying. "I'm going to get your brother without waiting for the proof you needed to give to your father. If Nicki would have gone to your father and told him what he knew, he would still be alive. The coded document that Nicki intercepted was meant for Mario from Gen. Yetsun. That should have been enough proof for Nicki to go to your father. Yorg and I saw Mario and Giorgio in Moscow with Gen. Yetsun previewing the test flight of an experimental fighter jet, XP38. I can place Saíde at the first attempt on Nicki's life. I saw him driving Nicki's limo. It was Saíde at the boutique in New York that day, when I foiled his second attempt to get you. That's all the proof I need that links all these people together with Mario. If you can hear me squeeze my hand," Kathe requested as Tierra's hand slightly moved. "You can hear me!" Kathe's eyes widened as Tierra tried to open her eyes. "You moved your hand and tried to open your eyes," Kathe smiled, standing up still holding Tierra's hand. "It was Saíde that did this to you, wasn't it?" Kathe asked as Tierra squeezed her hand again. "It was him," Kathe confirmed. "You squeezed my hand again. While you get better, I've got work to do. The way it looks, Mario is a hacker. He is framing your father for the death of a senator, so he can take over the business. Just for the record, I'm going to take Mario and Giorgio down, even though I'm pregnant! There," she sighed, "I finally said it! I'm pregnant! Perfect timing, isn't it?" Kathe confessed. "Ramsey and Yorg are so mad at me they won't listen to me. I wish I knew Alonzo better. I know he suspects Mario is up to something. That's why you overheard Mario and Alonzo arguing at your father's house, before the funeral. Unfortunately, I've got to finish this alone," she said and left the room. She passed Alonzo DiMeglio in the hallway as she hurried to the elevator. The bathroom door widened as a shocked Mario Sr. emerged.

Passing the nurses' station Kathe stopped recognizing someone, "I've never seen you outside of control," she said to Keith. "Ramsey has to still be out of the country. What are you doing here?"

"I promised a very upset Russian that I'd keep an eye out for you, since you've been MIA," Keith confessed. "I've already reassured him that you are at the hospital visiting Tierra and that I'm waiting outside the door. I think you better call him and Ramsey."

"We don't have time for small talk," Kathe said, leading the way to the elevator. "Did you find out how Saíde got into our computers yet?"

"Not yet," Keith stated as they switched elevators and headed for the rooftop. "Wanda and I have looked all day."

"Has Sydney broken the code yet?" Kathe quizzed.

"No, but he said he should have it within the hour and it's not soon enough," Keith reported as they got into the helicopter. "The Freedom Fighters texted a picture to Yorg showing Mario and O'Brien in XP38 about three hours ago."

"Anything awry in that area of the world yet?" Kathe wondered as it lifted off.

"No reports of any unusual problems in that region," Keith declared. "Ramsey is on her way back to help us look for Saíde. Yorg's in her private Leer on his way to help the Freedom Fighters find the jet," he said as the helicopter landed on the rooftop of Alby Security.

Getting off the elevator neither Kathe nor Keith noticed someone hiding behind one of the tall plants as they entered control. "Thank God, Keith found you!" Wanda greeted her. "Have you seen the news today?"

"I was not lost," Kathe clarified. "I knew exactly where I was," Kathe answered, sitting down at Wanda's computer looking at her monitor.

"I take it you didn't see the news," Wanda giggled. "Joe Sherrod's 'ex-wife' made the news and not as the famous model. You must see it!" Wanda raved, reaching around Kathe to pull up BBC Headlines.

"What in the world?" Kathe questioned, hurrying over to her suitcase, pulling out the camera. "I told Joe to call the gendarmes!" Kathe exclaimed, looking for the memory chip. "It's gone! He took it! Et tu Bruté!"

"What did you say?" Wanda asked still chuckling at the news.

"I just learned a valuable lesson," Kathe said as she crossed her heart.

"Which one of the two girls tied to that ugly used car is Sherrod's 'ex?'" Laughed Keith as he read the sign above the windshield. "High maintenance, low mileage, cheap, no warranty, all sales are FINAL!"

"The one on the left," Kathe sighed. "He picked the wrong time to get even with her!"

"What's that supposed to mean?" Keith asked, looking up at her.

"It's a long story," Kathe said. "I'll tell you about it when I'm not in a hurry," she closed the Internet and began opening the system files.

"I have checked the entire system for any anomalies, it's clean," Wanda reported, looking over her shoulder. "By the way, the Ole Girl called and told me to give you the name of a doctor here in New York," she said, holding up a sticky note.

"You can tell the Ole Girl where she can shove it!" Kathe snapped not even looking up.

"Hey, don't shoot the messenger," Wanda said, backing away from her. "Lady, I'm on your side. Is it Sherrod's?"

"Keith while I'm working here," Kathe ordered, ignoring Wanda, "please get me all the information surrounding the recent death of a Sen. Bernard Frank of New York. I also want to know what committees he served on."

"You've got it," Keith said, hurrying to his office.

"Okay," Wanda continued, fiddling with a pen. "If you don't want to tell me, it's your prerogative. It could only be one of two choices, and they're both excellent in my book!"

"I did it!" Dr. Sydney exclaimed, bursting into the room. "It was the hardest code I've ever worked on, but I cracked it!"

"I knew you could do it!" Keith proclaimed, rushing out of his office.

"I have to call Ramsey, and Yorg," Sydney stated. "We've got a major situation at hand. Kathe I'm glad you're here. I want you and Keith to hear this," he said, reaching for his cell phone and conferencing them. "Ramsey, hold on a minute while I connect Yorg . . . Yorg, you are on conference . . . I cracked the code! . . . I must admit; it was one heck of a code! . . . XP38 must be shot down or we must get control of it . . . The codename for the technology on board is Chameleon. Yorg, you were right; it has the capability to mimic IFF codes. Thank God, this document was intercepted! Whoever has that jet, and these codes, will control the world. I do mean the entire world!"

"Are you sure?" Ramsey asked.

"Sydney is right," Yorg agreed. "Chameleon has the technology that can capture the IFF codes on any plane it encounters, read them, and change theirs to match it, so they can't be locked on by a missile. Then, it can change its codes back and shoot down their unsuspecting opponent. They can easily flip back and forth between 'Friend and Foe' at will. That is one of the reasons Ivan and I were taken off the team. We were dragging our feet completing it when Gen. Yetsun suspected it and separated us. We understood the magnitude of power this technology possessed. We felt bad after we started working on it. You know the rest."

"Without these codes Chameleon will not work," Sydney explained. "These codes contain the authentication response codes. They must have these codes when they lock onto a potential target to reverse the IFF."

"Is there any way O'Brien can reprogram the authentication response codes and use them?" Yorg questioned.

"No," Sydney responded. "I have already checked for that possibility. According to this document, Karl Raini, who by the way was a genius, finished the work that you and Ivan started. O'Brien was his assistant, but from what this says, Raini was afraid of him. He also noted that Gen. Yetsun began favoring O'Brien and he didn't trust them. He was worried for his own life. He encrypted these codes, so neither one of them could use the weaponry, if something happened to him."

"I knew Karl Raini and that is just what he would have done," Yorg confirmed. "We worked together on another project. He finished the details, placed them in an envelope, and gave them to a buyer. When the buyer went to use the weapon, he had to contact Raini for the encrypted codes. He said it was our Life Insurance Policy. I'm turning this bird around; Mario and O'Brien cannot do anything but fly the thing. They'll come straight to us when they realize they must have the document that we intercepted. Whatever you do, put them in a safe place. I'll contact Pavel and see you soon!"

As Yorg disconnected the call Sydney glanced down at Wanda's monitor, "What the heck! Did you see that? Kathe, get up! Let me sit there!"

"What's going on?" Ramsey demanded.

"I think I just saw a blip on Wanda's computer," Sydney stated. "It's right here . . . no! . . . yes! Gotcha . . . Oh, yes! I found our leak; we've got a hacker and I see traffic on a backdoor. Keith, bring me your laptop. I need to use it." He continued typing as Keith sat his laptop next to him. Turning quickly to it, Sydney assessed the firewall for the database server and sent in its sniffers to analyze the traffic on all the ports.

"What are you looking for?" Ramsey quizzed. "Who's in my computers?"

"Someone is checking on the status of Tierra and CC," Sydney stated. "It looks like he is trying to find out if they are at the hospital or the morgue," he reported, typing frantically trying to find the IP Address.

"Saíde!" yelled everyone at the same time.

"Can you trace it back to his location?" Kathe asked, watching over his shoulder.

"Hold on, I don't want him to see me," Sydney said as he typed frantically and hit enter.

"Glad you are on our side," Wanda replied nervously looking over his shoulder.

"There," Sydney smiled. "He's in a backdoor from . . . hold on . . . he is using several servers . . .. Paris . . . London . . . Madrid . . .. hold on this guy is cagey . . . I'm losing him . . . no, no, no . . .. Tehran . . . back to Paris . . . Gotcha! He's here in New York City . . . hold on . . . his IP Address is . . . okay, and let me cross reference that to a physical address . . . he's at . . . There you are . . . 1604 Brooks Way, Apartment #23, E. 72nd Street . . . in the Bronx," he said, continuing his search as Kathe bolted out the door. She didn't see the person still hiding behind a plant take the next elevator.

"Come back here!" Keith yelled, chasing after Kathe just missing the last elevator down.

"What is going on now?" Ramsey demanded.

"You're not going to like this, Boss," Wanda cringed. "Tierney just bolted out the door going after Saíde. Keith is trying to stop her."

"Wanda, call her and tell her to wait for backup," Ramsey requested. "If she doesn't answer, text her. My plane is in final descent now. I will be on the ground in twenty minutes," Ramsey said as Keith rejoined them shaking his head.

"I lost her," Keith gasped.

"I told you that you were getting out of shape," Wanda chuckled.

"Keith, get on my computer and change the status from withheld to notification of kin for Tierra and CC," Ramsey ordered.

"No!" Sydney snapped over his shoulder, "keep that status or we will lose him for sure. Just wait, let me keep him surfing the files to buy Tierney some time to get there . . . Oh, no!" Sydney screamed, looking at the second monitor . . . changing to that computer . . . "He has got several ports with encrypted tunneling protocols running . . . I'm going to clone the tunnels on another port so we can monitor him! Wow! Wait a minute! Someone is tracking Saíde . . . and they just found his IP address . . . Now they're also checking Alby's employee rosters and the schedule for . . . hold on . . . he's scrolling . . . Tierra LaBasco . . . scrolling again CC Sims . . . scroll . . . and . . . Kathe Tierney?"

"It has got to be Mario!" Ramsey exclaimed. "I hate it when Yorg is right! Mario must have realized he doesn't have the encrypted codes and he is coming for them!"

"This is a more sophisticated tunnel . . . almost as good as me," Sydney replied, typing feverishly. "I'm sending sniffers in to see if he has other tunnels running and he's . . . he's . . . he's bouncing off different servers also . . . it looks like his base is blanketed . . . let me try another port."

"What does blanketed mean?" Ramsey asked.

"He's very sophisticated!" Sydney admitted. "Wow! One of the old timers in the business! I didn't think there were any of them left. Blanketed is a term for outdated technology. He has found a way to combine them to hide his original server . . . But maybe, if I go here . . . no . . .. here . . . no . . . or . . . I try to open it with . . . Bingo! Found you! His original server is Paris, France . . . IP Address . . . 10.71.34.11 . . . Physical address is at . . . 911 R. de Rivoli . . . screen name . . . Romeo101 . . . oops!" he exclaimed, typing quickly then hitting enter . . . typing . . . enter . . . Changing tunnels . . . erasing his tracks . . . I am Top Dog! . . . Oh, Yeah!" Sydney exclaimed, raising both arms in victory.

"Are you still with us?" Keith asked, admiring his work.

"He almost saw me, but I'm faster than the old man," Sydney gleamed, turning around, and stretching.

"Keith, when the two of you are finished playing on the computer," Ramsey began. "I want you to call Jaco and bring him up to date on everything. Give him the address of the hacker. Ask him to check and get back with you. We are on the tarmac. The guys and I are heading over to help Tierney."

"Do you want me to continue checking on the death of Sen. Frank?" Keith asked.

"Why?" Ramsey inquired as she was deplaning.

"Tierney wanted to know everything about his death," Keith replied.

"Why?" Ramsey asked.

"She didn't say," Keith stated.

"Have Wanda do that while you call Jaco," Ramsey requested. "Sydney, put that document in a safe place!"

Getting out of a police helicopter on the roof of the 54th Street Station in East Manhattan, Kathe thanked the officers for the lift. "I will go with you downstairs," Officer Blake offered as another helicopter landed on the roof of the next building. "Ms. Tierney follow me, and I'll get you through the station onto street level."

"You just saved me a lot of traffic," Kathe said, following him to the front door. "I'm bringing this monster in alone," she thought as she walked out of the building. "Evidently Ramsey hasn't alerted the police . . . she's afraid to spook him." Hailing a cab Kathe quickly got in as she received Wanda's text message that Ramsey was on the ground and heading her way.

"What address madam?" asked the cabby.

"1604 Brooks Way, E. 72nd Street, Bronx," Kathe answered, checking his name on his ID on the visor.

"It's about 30 to 45 minutes away this time of day," he said.

"Miguel Sanchez, if you make it 15 minutes, there will be another one like this," she promised handing him a $100 bill.

"Lady, you just got in the right cab, hang on!" Miguel smiled, reaching for the money, and putting it in his pocket. He pulled into traffic cutting off a BMW as they sped away. Another cab pulled into traffic to follow them. "Got business there?" he asked, making small talk while looking in his rearview mirror at her.

"Miguel, watch the road!" Kathe exclaimed as traffic stopped and he screeched to a halt.

"Get out of my way!" Miguel stuck his head out the window and yelled trying to get around a car. "Sorry ma'am," he complained. "It looks like an accident."

Using JAKE and accessing the Internet she checked for a better route. "That is 66th East," Kathe directed. "Take a right here, get on Lexington to 3rd Street, then right on East 72nd. I am showing no traffic, hurry!"

"Move that hunk of junk!" Miguel shouted, laying on his horn. "If this idiot moves up just a few inches I can make it."

"Get on the sidewalk," Kathe ordered, pointing to the right.

"There are people on the sidewalk," Miguel warned, looking back at her.

"Use your horn, and slowly get over now!" Kathe demanded as Miguel slowly followed her orders. Within a few minutes they were heading down 66th East free from traffic. "I want you to pass the last building slowly. Turn right on East 5th Avenue and go around the block," she requested, using JAKE to check for outside surveillance cameras. "Two on the roof facing both streets, and one on the traffic light angled toward the front of the building," she noted as JAKE continued searching for more. As the cab turned back on East 72nd Street Kathe told Miguel to pull over and stop. She checked the range of the camera facing her. Programming JAKE to video two minutes of the front of the building she gave him another $100. "Thanks for getting me here so quickly. I want you to turn left on 5th Avenue and leave that way."

"Are you sure you don't want me to wait?" Miguel asked with a smile.

"No," Kathe said while programming JAKE to override the frequency of the cameras. She used the new video feed, getting out of the cab.

Hurrying to the entrance, Kathe had JAKE scan for cameras inside and found two. Quickly taking more video feed, overriding his live feed to show hers, she entered the lobby. "Man, this guy is thorough," she thought taking the stairs to the fourth floor. Approaching the landing JAKE noted a panoramic camera facing the stairs and the elevator across from Saíde's room. Blocking that feed, allowing her to enter the floor, she reached for her gun and called Sydney. "I'm outside Saíde's apartment. Can you tell me where he's located?"

"Give me a second to bring up the satellite," Sydney requested. He quickly scanned the apartment for any life-forms. "He is not there. Just a minute," he checked with his infrared cameras to note any explosives. "Do not! I repeat do not open that door! I am showing the door is hot! There is also an unusual number of explosives inside the room. Look out! There is a single person approaching behind you from the stairwell."

"Thanks," Kathe whispered, positioning herself around the corner as the door opened. Saíde walked in carrying a bag of groceries.

"It's Saíde," Kathe whispered.

"Ramsey ordered you to wait for backup," Sydney warned her. "She wants to help you bring him down. She and the guys are minutes away. Lt. John Tanner has alerted Lt. Chris Buchanan of NYPD of Saíde's zest for killing. She doesn't want Saíde spooked, and NYPD is surrounding the area, but holding off. We're worried that if we spook him, he could turn into a suicide bomber and blow the building. I'm patching JAKE to Ramsey's cell," Sydney stated bridging their phones.

"Recognize me?" Kathe glared at Saíde as she held her gun straight at his head. "Do not move! I am not one of the flight attendants you so easily murdered," she ordered as he started to reach for his gun. "Keep your hands where I can see them!"

"You stupid woman!" Saíde yelled. "Where is the big Russian you are always with? Is he off with your big, bad boss looking for me in Paris? Surely you do not plan on bringing me in all alone," he laughed, stepping between her and the elevator. "I think the little FBI agent thought she could protect my target all by herself. She found out differently when I shot her at point blank range."

"By the way you are favoring your left arm," Kathe interrupted, "I think you didn't make out as well as you're telling me. It looks like you have taken another hit. The bandage on your hand is a bullet from me the other day on the rooftop," she smirked as the elevator door suddenly opened with Joe standing there.

"Kathe!" Joe shouted as he realized she had her gun drawn.

Saíde threw his groceries at her grabbing Joe out of the elevator, bringing Joe's arm behind his back, and raising his knife to his throat. "Isn't this how we met?" Saíde laughed, obtaining a better grip. "Where's your coffee pot now? How are you going to stop me from killing this one?" he asked as he pushed the knife just enough to break the skin.

"Ahhhh!" Joe screamed as a trickle of blood dripped down his neck.

Listening to the situation, Ramsey calmly told Kathe, "Use JAKE to stun Joe; with him changing to dead weight, Saíde will drop him, and you can get a shot. Kill that monster!" Ramsey ordered as Saíde touched his Bluetooth device.

As Kathe reached for JAKE, Saíde screamed, "This is your lucky day!" He slung Joe at Kathe and bolted for the stairwell.

Pushing Joe aside, Kathe shot Joe with her Taser, "That's what you deserve for betraying me!" He fell to the floor jerking uncontrollably as she headed down the stairs in pursuit. "Ramsey, scrape Joe up off the floor in front of the elevator and send him with Carrie Anne to my house in Florida. He's been seen with me. He will be safe there."

"You Tasered Glitter Boy!" Ramsey beamed. "It's about time you saw him for what he is!"

Running out of the building, Saíde raced toward 5th Avenue dodging people on the crowded sidewalk and running out into the busy street. He ran right in front of a Mercedes as the driver slammed on her brakes. Kathe ran out of the building, heard the screeching tires, and ran toward the street.

"Get out of the car!" Saíde screamed as the woman froze in shock. He fired randomly into the crowd on the sidewalk to cause more panic, before raising his gun at the woman driver. She opened the door screaming. He reached into the car, shoved her to the ground, side swiping two cars, speeding away. Kathe maneuvered around the panicking crowd fleeing in all directions. Police on foot flooded the area to help with the crowd. Kathe made it to the corner in time to see him speeding away.

"Saíde is getting away!" Kathe screamed as Ramsey neared the scene.

"NYPD is getting choppers up," Ramsey stated as her limo stopped in the traffic jam. "What does the car look like?"

"It's a . . .," Kathe started to say as a cab laid on its horn, making its way over the curb, around the sidewalk, and stopped next to Kathe.

"Lady, I had a feeling you would need me again!" Miguel exclaimed as more police entered several of the buildings. "I knew you were some kind of spy with that technology!"

"Move over, I'm driving!" Kathe ordered as Miguel quickly slid across the seat. She got in the driver's seat, shoved the gear into drive, and sped away in pursuit. "Sydney, can you see a 2008 Black Mercedes and where it's heading," Kathe asked, looking for street signs.

"West on Terrace Drive," Miguel stated.

"That is West on Terrace Drive," Kathe reiterated.

"He is two miles ahead of you and merging to the right on East Drive," Sydney reported. "Wow! He purposely caused a horrific accident involving quite a few cars . . . and he's throwing out small explosives at the cars. Both choppers are staying with that situation," Sydney reported. "Two cars are on fire."

"Ramsey, Saíde thinks he killed Tierra and CC," Kathe realized. "His work here is finished. It appears he rigged the building and is causing havoc on the freeway to show his real identity as a terrorist!"

"Copy that," Ramsey said as Ralph pulled the limo over and parked. They all ran to the building as Ramsey called Lt. Buchanan of NYPD. "Our hunch was right. It appears he's rigged the building to blow!"

"Copy that," Lt. Buchanan replied, ordering his men. "We're evacuating the entire block!"

"He must be heading for the Central Park area," Miguel surmised.

Kathe hit the gas, weaving in and out of the lanes, trying to catch him.

"Great driving!" Miguel complimented, holding on to the handles around him.

"Thanks," Kathe said, maneuvering in between two semis.

"The Mercedes is slowing down on Terrace Drive," Sydney reported. "He turned right on Cherry Hill . . . it seems to be making what looks like circles . . . it's a cul-de-sac . . . he is just circling," Sydney reported as Kathe arrived at the accident site. She flashed her ID and used the emergency lane to maneuver around the scene. "Wow! He just bailed out of the Mercedes as it went into a lake."

"Say again?" Kathe questioned as she finally got back on the road.

"He jumped out of the Mercedes as it went into the Lake," Sydney repeated. "Another car is approaching . . . He got into a black . . . 1969 Shelby Mustang. They're heading East on Terrace Drive. You should have a visual soon. They're coming toward you!"

You got it!" Miguel exclaimed. "Hallelujah! This is my lucky day!"

"How did you end up here?" Ramsey asked Joe as he was coming out of the effects of the Taser.

"Kathe, shot me," Joe sighed still very weak. "She shot me!"

"You're lucky she just used her Taser," Ramsey declared as NYPD, Swat, and the Fire Department evacuated that floor. "How did you get here?"

"Being a rock star has its advantages," Joe revealed as he tried to sit up. "I called a private bodyguard that we have used to help me. He knows someone with access to a helicopter. I followed Kathe to a New York precinct. I saw her get into a cab and we caught them."

"Take Joe to control!" Ramsey ordered Ralph as Jay and Jack helped Joe stand up. "You stupid Glitter Boy!" Ramsey confirmed as Lt. Buchanan joined them.

"Lt. Chris Buchanan," Ramsey stated, showing her ID. "Special agents Towers, and Davies will assist you in evacuating the buildings. That room is rigged to blow. The door is armed and there is a large quantity of explosives inside," she pointed. "We don't know how much time we have. Someone in a black 1969 Shelby Mustang just picked Saíde up and we lost them."

"He's probably going to get close enough to check on the building," Buchanan declared. "Then, he will blow the building when he is far enough away, and enough police are inside."

"That sounds like the scenario," Ramsey agreed. "That could be easily done with a cell phone," she said, glancing at Jay. "When you two are finished meet me at control," Ramsey said, getting in the elevator with Ralph and Joe.

"Kathe is trying to protect you!" Ramsey snapped as they left the building. "You just signed your own death warrant by showing up here! If you love her, you will do as I say!" She looked at Ralph, "Don't worry about me. Yorg and John Tanner will be here any minute. Take Glitter Boy to control and pick up Carrie Anne at the hospital on the way. Make sure Joe does what Wanda says or shoot him yourself!"

"After Joe just caused us to lose Saíde again," Ralph declared. "It will be my pleasure!"

"Sydney," Kathe said, searching for the Shelby. "I don't see the Shelby Mustang. How far is it from me?"

"What the sin!" Sydney screamed as his computer froze. "I lost him!"

"Sydney, I repeat," Kathe reiterated as she was two miles away from the Terrace Drive Exit. She slowed down, "How far is the Shelby from me?"

"Just a minute!" Sydney exclaimed, quickly rebooting his computer.

"Let's see how they like that," Mario laughed as he pulled the Shelby over and stopped. "Saíde help me peel the film off," Mario said as they got out of the Shelby. They pulled a long black film from the front bumper over the roof down to the back bumper. "Now, we're not driving an all-black Shelby," Mario smiled as the wide silver-racing stripe changed the look of the Shelby. "Let's go," he said, throwing it in the trunk.

"What happened?" Ramsey inquired, listening to Sydney and Kathe as she watched Ralph put Joe in the backseat of the limo.

"I lost transmission," Sydney reported, frantically waiting for the computer to pull up the satellite.

"We're blind without the satellite," Kathe declared as she took the next exit and turned around. "The only Shelby we passed had a wide, silver-racing stripe. I just turned around on Terrace Drive and I'm heading back to you. Saíde got a call in the hallway. He said it was Joe's lucky day and slung him at me and took off. My bet is that Mario picked him up."

"That very well could be," Ramsey declared as she lit a cigarette. "Sydney, how did you lose transmission of our satellite?"

"Something jammed it!" Sydney huffed still checking his computer.

"Jammed it!" Ramsey screamed, taking a drag off the cigarette. She acknowledged Yorg and John Tanner joining her. "I thought you were hack proof! How the heck can something jam my satellite!"

"I need a few moments alone," Sydney stated and cleared the line.

Ramsey called Wanda as Yorg and John Tanner listened, "Ralph is bringing Joe Sherrod to control. The idiot showed up here. Saíde saw him, and yes, he just signed his death warrant . . . Carrie Anne went to the hospital to visit Tierra and CC. Ralph is going to pick her up on his way in . . . Ralph is to take them and Sydney with the codes in my Leer to Kathe's house in Florida. They will be safe there."

"But Boss," Wanda protested, "that's not a good idea since . . ."

"Just do it!" Ramsey ordered and switched calls to Kathe. "Tierney," Ramsey continued, "meet us back at control. NYPD is evacuating several blocks anticipating Saíde blowing the entire building. Yorg just arrived with John Tanner. Do you think you can obey this simple order?"

"Saíde has surveillance cameras all over the street as well," Kathe reported. "He's not going to let anyone inside his apartment, much less find his cameras. He must be with Mario right now. They are probably watching you from another computer. I have already turned around. I'll see you at control."

"You're right!" Ramsey added as Yorg pointed the cameras out to her. "I see two cameras from where I'm standing. John, I know you don't have jurisdiction in New York, but it is a matter of time before he blows the building," she said as more Swat and fire departments rushed into the surrounding buildings.

"Buchanan is evacuating the entire area," John said. "Several boroughs have sent personnel to help. I've already sent some of my off-duty officers. We're almost finished. I'll see you back at control," he said and hurried off.

"You're right again my lady," Yorg called Kathe. "I owe you an apology for not listening to you in Paris. I'm the one whose judgment has been clouded by your situation, not you. He's got to be watching from somewhere nearby. From the look of the cameras, they probably contain self-detonators with a two-mile radius or less. From the look of things, NYPD has most of the people out of this building and those around it. They are pushing traffic back for several blocks."

"Welcome home," Kathe smiled. "I'm surprised you are here. I was told you were en route to help Pavel find XP38."

"Mario has it," Yorg admitted. "But he can't do anything without the codes. He will come straight for us."

"Maybe, we should just destroy the codes," Kathe suggested as she took the New Jersey Exit. "That technology in the wrong hands is just too dangerous."

"We can't do that," Yorg stated as he and Ramsey moved further away with the crowd. "But you just gave me one heck of an idea!" he exclaimed, calling Dr. Sydney.

"Use this laptop," Mario said as he reached behind his seat and handed it to Saíde. "Let's see what is going on at your apartment," he ordered, screeching the tires of the Shelby Mustang. He got back onto the Turnpike headed East toward 72nd Street.

"So, you're the man behind the voice and the money all these years," Saíde responded, wondering how Mario found him. He opened the Internet and checked his cameras.

"You do have the apartment ready to seal when the police try to get inside, don't you?" Mario asked. He put the car into sixth gear, weaving in and out of traffic.

"I always seal my places so I can't be traced," Saíde said, glancing over at Mario. "Only this time, I decided to leave a bonus," he said under his breath. The traffic slowed to a crawl as they passed the exit ramp to East 5th Avenue.

"Make sure Tierney and Vuslick are not inside when you blow the place," Mario warned. "I need them alive just a little while longer. They seem to have something I need."

"No one is near my apartment," Saíde stated. "The entire floor is empty," he said as he switched to cameras on other floors. "The entire building is empty," he said, switching to the outside cameras. "I see the cops are evacuating the buildings around it also and they are blocking off streets."

"I guess after your little excursion on the freeway," Mario glared at him, "they figured out you are going to blow your apartment. What is the range of your bombs?" Mario asked and reached to reset the mileage to zero. "I want to be far enough away not to get stopped."

"Two-mile radius," Saíde answered. "I have already measured each direction. Where are we going?"

"Somewhere we can talk alone," Mario stated as he sped up. "I want to head north."

"Exit 221 heads north," Saíde replied. "It's two exits further."

"Blow it now!" Mario exclaimed as he noticed the odometer. "We're two-miles away."

"Just like I planned," Saíde smirked as he quickly typed a few commands and pressed enter. They watched on the screen as they heard the explosion. "Nothing to trace me with anymore," Saíde began laughing while Mario took the right exit on the Turnpike heading north.

"That explosion was more than your apartment and the cameras!" Mario exclaimed, watching the debris fill the sky. "Why did you do that?"

"I wanted to leave my mark on this town," Saíde bragged. "It is time they know who I really am," he declared as he turned around and watched the smoke. "I took out your sister and that FBI agent," Saíde smiled as Mario weaved in and out of traffic. "Now that my job here is done, you can drop me off at the airport and I will disappear. That is unless you need me for anything else. You sound like you want to take Tierney and Vuslick out yourself. However, I do have a certain score to settle with that broad."

"I do have business with them," Mario stated. He took the Palladino Avenue exit in East Harlem and turned left at the light.

"Anything you need me to help you with?" Saíde asked as he noted the obscurity of the area. Mario turned right on East 121st Avenue. He took another right on 1st Avenue and stopped in front of a junkyard underneath several layers of freeway junctions. "This is how we talk alone?" Saíde asked, noticing several cars inside with men getting out.

"Oh, don't mind them," Mario said, rolling down his window as Giorgio opened the gate. "I never travel alone. This is where I thought we could talk."

"I see you found him," Giorgio greeted as they slowly drove through the gate.

"He leaves an easy trail," Mario laughed as he got out of the car.

"We saw the smoke and debris from here," Giorgio stated.

"He wanted to leave his last mark on New York City," Mario replied, glaring at Saíde. "Get out of the car, Mr. I Decided to Leave My Mark!" Mario ordered. "You were told to keep it simple! You were only to blow your apartment and the outside cameras! You took upon yourself to have a reign of terror on the freeway and blow the entire building! Now, you've linked me with that! I have a few other details to clear up with you! For starters, my sister and that FBI agent are still alive!"

"There's no way they could have lived," Saíde said as he frantically checked the hospital records on the laptop. "My knife struck Tierra square in the back, and I shot that agent at close range in the chest using .38 specials with hollow points. Their status has changed to withheld due to the notification of the next of kin-that means they're dead," he refuted as he slowly got out of the car.

"No idiot!" Mario exclaimed. "It means they are on to you! You have botched up every hit I sent you to do! They've even found your tunnels and know all about you! How do you think they found your apartment? How do you think I found you, you stooge?"

Noticing the placement of Mario's men around the yard, Saíde stepped back toward the car and pleaded, "I'll finish the hit. I have finished every mark."

"Yes, you have," Mario agreed as he glared sideways at him. "Yes, indeed you did, but only after you left a trail of dead flight attendants strung all over two continents! I warned you to leave the women alone! You just couldn't do it!" he screamed, looking Saíde straight in the eyes. "I warned you not to endanger my plan! You're the one that got that boss of Tierney's and the Russian poking their noses into my business, trying to find you. And with the help of my little sister, they intercepted something from my dead brother that I need!"

"If it's a coded document, I know who has it," Saíde tried to bargain. "I intercepted an email from Ramsey to a Dr. Sydney. I will get them for you."

"You will get them for me," Mario repeated, shaking his head, glancing toward his men. "Giorgio, he's going to get them for me," mocking Saíde laughing loudly. He reached for the back of Saíde's head and yanked it toward him. "You couldn't get anywhere near the airport now!" Mario screamed in his ear. He shoved Saíde against the car and realized that Tierney was right. "I already know who has it. That's not your problem," Mario declared, taking off his jacket, and handing it to Giorgio. "Looks like Tierney was right by the way you're favoring your left arm. The FBI agent shot you. Now, that is your problem!" he chuckled, pulling a knife out of his boot.

"I don't know what you are talking about," Saíde said, reaching to his belt buckle for his knife. "I'm not quite sure why you are doing this?"

"You're not quite sure why I am doing this?" Mario mocked him again. "Giorgio, he's not sure why I'm doing this," he smirked. He lunged at Saíde as he moved away from the car and out into the open. "This whole mess started when you missed an easy hit on my sister. I even told you where she was. All you had to do was kill her!" Mario snapped as he circled Saíde tossing his knife back and forth in his hands. "Her boss alerted my papa, and he got involved. Next my brother caught on to my plan and I sent you after him. You botched the first attempt so horribly bad, that I had to bring him to my house, and hand him to you; just to make sure it was done!" He lunged toward Saíde. Saíde jumped back barely missing the blade. "Let me see . . . where was I . . . Oh! Next, I sent you back after my sister. You missed her again and were identified by her and that FBI agent. By the way, my papa's men were looking for you. I lost a lot of time trying to run interference to throw Alonzo DiMeglio off; and that's not easy to do! I still must keep looking over my shoulder for him," Mario admitted. Then catching the top of the sleeve of Saíde's left arm, Mario spun him around, slammed him face first into the fence and shoved his knee into Saíde's back.

Clinging to the fence Saíde took a deep breath as he clinched his knife. He turned around quickly and lunged at Mario, who was caught off guard. As Mario took a few steps backwards, Saíde grabbed him by his left arm. Saíde swung Mario around, bringing his left arm behind him, placing his blade under Mario's neck. Giorgio started to help. Mario began laughing, "Is this all you've got?" he motioned for Giorgio to wait. Mario head-butted Saíde. Mario turned around, grabbed Saíde's left arm and placed his thumb on the wound, applying massive pressure. Saíde let out a painful scream, bending straight down, raising his head up into Mario's chin. Mario let him go. As the two separated Mario continued, "Now!" he smirked, shaking his head. "Now you have been caught hacking into the airport computers. Not to mention, they have traced your tunnel back to your address," he said, pointing straight at him. "Tierney was even able to block the feed on your own cameras and caught you off guard at your own front door! I hacked into your cameras and watched the whole thing! Why do you think I called and ordered you to stop what you were doing and come to me?" Mario screamed. "I couldn't take the chance of her taking you in, oh, and get this!" He screamed louder, "She could have brought you in all by herself! Single handedly and pregnant!"

Holding his arm, still in disbelief Saíde pleaded, "Let me finish the hit. I can change my appearance and my accent. That's one of the reasons I have never had a charge stick to me. You can't afford for your sister to live. She knows all about you and your plan. You won't be able to get near her alone. What else do you want?"

"No, the only reason you have never had a charge stick to you," Mario bragged, "is because of my attorney, Damiano Genero! The only thing I want," Mario demanded as he kicked the knife out of Saíde's hand and caught it, "is for you to die!" He screamed as he cut Saíde in the midsection. Saíde fell forward. Mario used Saíde's own knife to slit his throat. Saíde glared at Mario in disbelief. Mario dropped both knives as Saíde slowly fell to his knees, and then face down to the ground.

"Giorgio," Mario said, glancing at his watch without looking back, "We have got another mess from this imbecilic to clean up! I've got a few people to check up on."

"Yes, Boss," Giorgio replied, tossing Saíde's wallet to one of the men. "Wipe off Saíde's knife, put it back in his buckle and throw him in the Harlem River," Giorgio ordered. He opened the limo door for Mario. "I showed the boys where to throw Saíde's body. With the current, he will turn up in a few minutes right across from the NYPD. Now that you took care of him, how are we going to get the codes?"

Lighting a cigar in the backseat, "Giorgio," Mario grinned as he opened his laptop. "You gotta have patience. Mama always said, 'Mario, you gotta have patience. Everything comes to you in time.' Glancing at the news from his laptop, as they turned on I-278, Mario started laughing loudly. "Giorgio, Mama was a genius! I just quoted her and look what just came to me," he laughed and sadly shook his head. He stared out the window. "She was a genius. She figured out what I was doing. It's too bad I had to kill her."

"Boss, what did you say?" Giorgio asked, handing him a drink.

"Look," Mario said, turning the laptop so Giorgio could see the screen. "It looks like there is a side of Kathe Tierney that we didn't know about. Watch today's BBC News," he said as he replayed the news.

"That's Kathe Tierney holding a gun on those two women," Giorgio stated. "Who's the guy in bed?" Giorgio asked as the newscast ended at the used car lot scene.

"Where did we just see that man?" Mario asked, taking a drag off his cigar.

"It can't be! In the elevator a few minutes ago!" Giorgio noted as Mario paused the newscast, split the screen, and pulled up the taped video from earlier. He rewound the film to the elevator doors as they watched.

"Kathe!" Joe called out as Saíde threw his groceries at her and grabbed Joe out of the elevator.

"I knew she was pregnant, but not with Joe Sherrod's kid," Mario laughed loudly.

"Now, that is a surprise!" Giorgio exclaimed as he turned the computer back toward Mario. "I thought it was the Russian's."

"My mama was right," Mario said as he picked up the intercom hailing his chauffeur. "Our plans have just changed. Take the Steinway Street Exit, turn right on 19th Avenue and find a place to park for a second. I need to look for someone."

"Boss, you're always so calm," Giorgio stated as Mario positioned his laptop. "With Alonzo's men all over Newark Airport and that hospital, you boldly fly in undetected. I have been trying to figure out how we could get near Alby Control to get the codes. It's impossible."

"I told you that dame would come in handy," Mario laughed, hacking into the New York Times. "First some finishing touches on my papa," he typed a few seconds and hit send. "Now, I need to find Sherrod. Let me see if he has used his credit card lately . . . yes, he has used it, and today is my lucky day. He's in New Jersey staying at the Courtyard Marriott near Newark Airport." He picked up the intercom to the chauffeur, "Take me to LaGuardia's Heliport."

"Boss, we can't go there," Giorgio warned. "That would be suicide if Alonzo's men see any of us."

"As soon as Ramsey or Tierney see the news, they will figure out what my next move will be," Mario concluded. "We must beat them to Sherrod. If we take the Turnpike, it will take too long. Stop worrying. We will wait here at the hotel and send four of the Jersey men to get them. Alonzo doesn't know them."

Chapter 37

A Change of Plan

"Wanda, what is the status of the girls?" Ramsey asked as she entered Alby Control with Yorg and Kathe.

"No change," Wanda replied without looking up.

"Did you get my Leer off with the packages," Ramsey asked, passing her desk.

"It's in the air as we speak," Wanda replied, glancing up at her.

"Did Sydney get my satellite back up yet?" Ramsey asked Keith as she poked her head in his office doorway.

"Not yet," Keith replied. "He's still working on it. Something jammed it from a mobile station. That's all he said."

"Something mobile with that power would have to be military," Yorg added, holding the door to Ramsey's office open for them.

"Tierney, you need to see this," Wanda called to her as she pulled up an obituary. "Sen. Bernard Frank had an interesting career. His way to the Political Top was a little iffy, with several trips to the Middle East, and contributions that just suddenly appeared in his bank account. He served on several committees, including Appropriations and the Ways and Means."

"That is interesting," Kathe said, sitting next to Wanda. "What else did you find on him?"

"I thought you would never ask," grinning like a Cheshire Cat, Wanda continued. "Watch this," she said, bringing up another news article complete with a picture. "There he is and look who is standing next to him, whispering in his ear?"

"That is one of the Joint Chiefs of Staff, isn't it?" Kathe asked as Ramsey and the others joined them.

"Yes, that is Gen. Robert Thompson in charge of the Air Force," Wanda stated.

"What is this all about?" Ramsey asked, glancing at the article.

"We all know that Mario Sr. is being investigated for possible involvement in the death of Sen. Bernard Frank," Kathe stated.

"Only with everything I have seen," Ramsey shared, "Mario Jr. looks more like he had something to do with it."

"That explains how Mario Jr. has XP38 and not his father," Yorg added.

"You're right," Kathe glanced at him. "With Nicki and Tierra out of the equation, the only person left in his way is his father," Kathe replied as Wanda pulled up another news article of the investigation.

"The old man is not that easy to overthrow," Ramsey declared. "He has a ton of loyal men at his side, headed by his Number One Man, Alonzo DiMeglio. From his profile he is one Tough Mother to deal with."

"Your kind of guy, right Boss?" Wanda laughed, grinning up at her.

"So, the only way to get rid of his father is to frame him for a murder of a major political figure like Sen. Bernard Frank?" Kathe concluded.

"Yes," Ramsey said, pointing to the computer screen. "There is the military connection and reason."

"Mario Jr. would have to kill the senator to cover his tracks," Yorg surmised. "That way Mario Sr. and Alonzo would not find out."

"With his father out of the way, Mario Jr. will take over the business," Kathe said. "And by selling XP38 to the Iranians, it will show the other family bosses his strength to lead them."

Mario needs the authentication response codes to sell the experimental jet to the Iranians," Yorg continued. "Without the codes, it's just another jet. Somehow Mario is able to either hack into military computers or has someone on the inside helping him."

"Since Mario is a hacker like Saíde," Kathe noted. "He now knows we have the codes."

"But he doesn't know Sydney cracked the code," Keith reported. "After the Satellite was jammed, Sydney added something to control's computers to protect them from any more tunnels. He also restricted access."

"Yeah," Wanda added. "He said not even the Pentagon can get in now."

"Mario is desperate for those codes," Ramsey warned. "But I don't think he will risk coming here to control to get them. He will have to have us bring them to him."

"How?" Wanda asked, looking at her.

"I have no idea," Ramsey said, reaching for her cell phone. "We are going to have to be ready for anything. Yes, John . . . positive ID! . . . Are you sure? . . . Yes, Tierney can . . . where did you take him . . . we will be right there," she said and cleared the line. "Well, it looks like I might be wrong. Mohammed might be in the mountain."

"What?" Kathe asked.

"NYPD just pulled a man out of the Harlem River across from East 110th Precinct," Ramsey reported. "His passport says his name is Jual MehrdAd AKA Rhasheéd Saíde! Tierney can positively ID him, let's go."

"This proves that it was Mario that called him away from me earlier," Kathe confirmed. "He just handed Saíde to us."

"Yes, it does," Ramsey agreed. "It seems that I will have to retract my last statement. Mario is brave as sin and still in the area. It might be a long shot, but Wanda, check the flight records here and at LaGuardia to see if a private jet landed recently from Paris. Also, check with Jaco to see who the councilor was that was working with Mario and the gendarmes during the investigation of Maria LaBasco's death."

"I'm on it right now!" Wanda grinned, turning to her computer as Ramsey's cell phone rang.

"Mario is a phenomenal hacker," Sydney confessed as Ramsey put him on speaker. "I have done some digging of my own and found his 'lair' so to speak. He has been hacking into the military recently and that's how he jammed our satellite from a laptop. I also found out that he met Saíde in a chat room in 1999. He called himself 'The Professor101.' He taught Saíde how to hack into computers to locate hits. Mario was one of the best of that time period. He was known for hacking into several computers and framing others to take the fall. Several people went to jail for his deeds."

"Framing people seems to be one of his specialties," Wanda smirked as she continued to work.

"Mario has been feeding the media with information to frame his father," Sydney continued. "He has also been monitoring Saíde all along. He hacked into Saíde's cameras in the Bronx this evening and watched him with Tierney. Mario is the one who called him off. He needs Tierney to get his codes."

"Great," Wanda sank in her chair. "'Big Brother' has been watching us!"

"Is he watching us now?" Ramsey asked.

"No, everything at Alby is now so restricted that nobody from the outside can get in," Sydney reported. "What we have to decide is what to do with the codes. Should we destroy them? The inventors are all dead, except for O'Brien and Yorg, who only worked on one aspect of the project. If we destroyed the codes, it would take years to redesign them. Or should we give it to the Pentagon, which by the way, I am totally against. Look at how corrupt it is."

"Ramsey," Wanda interrupted, "I've got the information on Maria LaBasco's death. The councilor was Jacques dé Laurent."

"That's the councilor that signed the orders letting Saíde walk away from Flight #1014," Kathe interjected.

"Good work, Wanda," Ramsey sighed, "now it's all coming together. Sydney, go on."

"It started out with Mario Sr. wanting to get into our political arena to buy people when he needed them," Sydney continued. "Frank was as dirty as they come. From what I have ascertained, he and the Senator had a falling out about selling this technology to the Middle East. Mario Sr. pulled away from the project."

"Evidently, his son perceived this as a weakness in his father and decided to take over the family business," Ramsey concluded. "Yorg, get in touch with Pavel and see how the search for XP38 is going. It might be just another jet, but it still has technology that our military could use. Sydney, two things: First, find Alonzo's email address, send him the proof you have concerning the media and Jr.'s hacking abilities. Tell him to research the Councilor Jacques dé Laurent. He was working with Mario in the investigation of his mother's death and that we have proof he forged documents for Saíde. Secondly, Yorg explained his idea to me. Have you done it?"

"Yes, it's done," Sydney declared. "I will forward the information to Alonzo," he reported as she cleared the line.

"Yorg, Tierney, let's go," Ramsey said, picking up her purse. "We have a dead body to identify."

"What next?" Wanda screamed. "Kathe, that's a great picture of you! And look at Joe Sherrod!"

"What picture?" Kathe asked, racing back to Wanda's computer.

"Not good!" Kathe said, reading the article.

"How long has this been on the Internet?" Ramsey scoffed.

"It was not there about an hour ago," Wanda assured her.

"Interesting reading for his fans!" Ramsey exclaimed as she glared at the picture. "I told you he was nothing but a Glitter Boy!"

"I can't believe Joe would announce this for a publicity stunt," Kathe sighed. "He knows the importance of my anonymity and I have people after me," she said as she finished reading the article. "Now, he's announcing he's going to be a father."

"Thank God, we got Joe away from here," Ramsey concluded. "I'll bet Mario's men are all over his hotel. Wanda call John Tanner with the hotel information and ask him to send some men over to check for them," she said leaving.

Security was tight entering the morgue. John met them at the front desk along with Lt. Chris Buchanan. "Ramsey, I think we've got him this time," he said, showing her Saíde's open wallet.

"I'm pretty sure you do," Ramsey admitted as they entered the room. "I don't like how we got him.

At least, we have one problem solved in this mess."

"Tierney, are you ready?" Chris asked.

"Yes," Kathe answered as he lifted the sheet on the dead man. Kathe glanced at the body, "That is definitely Rhasheéd Saíde."

Laying the sheet back down Chris happily said, "Finally, we can sleep nights. I will relay this message to all investigative services worldwide. We have the third most wanted man in the world!"

"Not quite the excitement I expected," John stated as he noticed the non-excitement in the room. One of his men whispered something to him.

"John, this man was handed to us," Ramsey replied as she lifted the sheet. "Did your men check the Courtyard Marriott Hotel for Mario LaBasco Jr. yet?" she asked, glancing at Saíde's body.

"Bill just got word that neither Jr., Giorgio, nor any of his known men were seen at the Marriott," John stated.

"Put an APB out on them," Ramsey requested. "But don't pick them up. I need to know where they are," she said, looking up at the examiner. "Did you find any kind of knives on his body?"

"There were no weapons on his body," Dr. Sue Weatheral answered. "All he had was his wallet."

"This man was noted for disappearing knives," Yorg stated. He took a pair of rubber gloves off the table and put them on. "You don't mind if I pat him down myself, do you? He must have a place for hiding them."

Putting on a pair of rubber gloves, Tierney began undoing his belt buckle, "This buckle is a bit larger than most," she concluded, taking it off him.

"It is," Yorg stated as he felt it. "I don't feel anything different about the buckle."

"It has to be here!" Kathe exclaimed as she ran her finger down the squares of the buckle. "He was clever; remember the placement of the cameras outside the apartment."

"Yes, he was very cagy, using several different types to mask their appearances," Ramsey recalled.

"I don't think he will mind if I do this," Kathe said, slamming the buckle on the edge of the steel table. Raising it back up she beamed, "Bingo!" She held the buckle up for all to see. "Look at the top right corner."

Chris pushed in on the corner as the end popped up. Pulling a knife out of the buckle, "Well, look what we have now. A three-inch ceramic knife," he declared, holding it up.

"Undetectable material just like Sydney warned," Ramsey admitted.

"This is what I saw Saíde hold to Carrie Anne's throat," Kathe confirmed. "And the one I identified in Paris that was found next to Nicki LaBasco."

"I'll tag the knife and belt as evidence," Dr. Weatheral told Lt. Buchanan. "By the looks of this blade and the slit on his throat; it appears to be a match. The abdominal wound was by a second knife."

"Not that it will bring back all the flight attendants he murdered," John gloated, "but the monster could not have died a more fitting death."

"This is not over yet," Ramsey reminded him. "Saíde was just a hitman for Mario. We still have to deal with him."

"I'll get the APB out on him on my way back to the office," John confirmed. "Thanks, Chris and Dr. Weatheral."

"Anytime John," Chris replied. "Sue, please send a copy of the report to all of us when you're finished with the autopsy," he said as they left.

Chapter 38

A Conflict of Interest

"Joe Sherrod didn't return to the hotel last night," Giorgio reported as Mario came out of his room in the Crowne Plaza Hotel near LaGuardia. "Maybe they saw the news, and already have him in hiding."

"Giorgio, there you go worrying again," Mario said as Giorgio handed him his coffee and newspaper. "I'll find him. Did you order my breakfast?"

"It's on its way," Giorgio said as room service arrived.

"First things first, after I eat, I'll find Sherrod," Mario stated as he sat down at the table and glanced at the headlines. "Saíde left his mark on New York City," he said, holding it up for Giorgio to see. "It's almost too bad he died before he saw the headlines. He took out the entire five-story building. Two people are still missing. I don't know how she did it, but Tierney knew he was going to blow the entire building. I must hand it to NYPD; they evacuated the two buildings and four blocks in record time. It says eight people are dead on the Turnpike with twenty people in the hospital. Five people are listed as critical."

"If you hadn't pulled Saíde away from Tierney yesterday," Giorgio admitted. "The headlines would have been different."

"Not a chance," Mario stated. "You noticed how Linda Ramsey always kept the killing sprees of Saíde out of the papers. She didn't want bad publicity about the airlines."

"You're right," Giorgio agreed. "Ramsey must have Sherrod stashed somewhere. She knows we'll go after him."

Mario turned on his laptop and took a sip of his coffee. "Have I ever not found someone I have looked for?"

"You've always nailed your opponent," Giorgio said, sipping his coffee.

"Credit cards are the telltale sign of today," Mario said, taking a bite of his toast while typing with one hand. "Who would have thought years ago, how easy it would be to follow someone with their buying power . . . that's odd Sherrod hasn't used his card, since he checked in yesterday at the Marriott," he said, brushing the crumbs from his hands. He quickly checked Joe's credit card history. "Let me see, now that we know he is going to be a father, where could the happy event have taken place . . . Somewhere away from the band . . . somewhere that only Tierney would be with him . . ."

"She's like a fricken ghost!" Giorgio exclaimed. "You've never been able to find anything on her, much less her credit card history."

"I figure she's about two months pregnant," Mario remarked, scrolling Joe's account. "Where was Joe about that time? Got him! Two months ago, remember the newspaper articles about the rock star that got upset and walked out on a contract in California? He turned up in Daytona Beach, Florida. He made front-page news when he decked a man in a restaurant that was bothering a friend. Remember the concert in Orlando for the flood victims? Now the new song he wrote in three days makes sense. What was the name of that song?"

"Yeah, Boss, I remember it hit Number One overnight," Giorgio remarked. "Pieces of Love! That's it! Pieces of Love!"

"That song must be about them meeting," Mario grinned. "It describes falling in love with a security agent, doesn't it?"

"She's driving him crazy," Giorgio laughed. "She can't be seen in public, and his face is plastered over every news media in the world. She must have a home somewhere."

"You're right," Mario chuckled still scrolling Joe's credit card account. "Somewhere to get away from Alby, and Florida is far enough away from work that nobody would recognize her. She usually flies abroad. Now, let me see if I can find a house address. She must have a house or condo down there," he said as he stopped the screen. "This might be it; 9002 South A1A, Ponce Inlet, Florida. He paid for a pizza one night about 9:00," he said, googling the address for a view. "Giorgio, look at that mansion on the beach!"

"Wow! That must be Joe Sherrod's house," Giorgio retorted. "That's not the house of a flight attendant!"

"I don't care who owns it," Mario grinned, closing his computer, and reaching for his cell phone. "I suddenly feel like a vacation to Florida. Get the boys ready."

"Ramsey, glad you're back," Keith called from his office greeting her as he answered the phone.

"Wanda has Ralph checked in today?" Ramsey asked, stopping at her desk.

"He checked in last night about 10:00 pm, and said the house was packed," Wanda replied.

"What do you mean by packed?" Ramsey demanded.

"I tried to tell you that Tierney's family is staying there on spring break," Wanda stated, glancing at Ramsey.

"Do you mean to tell me," Ramsey fumed, "that you let me send people I'm hiding, where Tierney's family is vacationing? They have never gone there! Of all the blame times for them to start now!"

"I tried to tell you, but you just yelled just do it, and hung up on me!" Wanda screamed, back at her.

"Do you always obey me?" Ramsey yelled, trying to call Ralph. "He's not answering this morning. Where is Tierney and Yorg?" Ramsey asked, entering her office, and turning on the lights.

"They stopped at the hospital before coming in," Wanda answered, walking over to the doorway. "And they told me that Mario Sr. was just arrested there. CC's father told them that The New York Times suddenly produced documents that prove Mario Sr. murdered Frank. The motive was to conceal new weaponry that was being sold to the United States. According to the paper, Mario Sr. was going to steal it and sell it to Iran."

"Well, isn't that a good twist of truth!" Ramsey declared, sitting down at her desk, and turning on her computer. "It seems that Jr. is out of time and desperately trying to get his father out of his way. Gather Kathe's team ASAP. I know Mario is heading straight to Florida. Have the Cessna Citation Mustang ready for them! They need something with speed to beat him there!"

"Ramsey," Keith said, hurrying into her office. "We just got a call from Homeland Security. The military picked up a blip on radar about 4:00 this morning near Brunswick, Georgia, and then lost it. We are on Red Alert Status until they locate the vessel."

"Any other details?" Ramsey inquired.

"No, but they have to know more than they are telling us," Keith deduced. "They said for us to have all pilots placed on Red Alert, and report anything out of the ordinary, no matter how trivial it may seem."

"You're right," Ramsey agreed. "I have a friend at the Pentagon. I think it's time I call him," she said, scrolling down her address book. "Close my door behind you," she said as she held her breath and dialed the phone.

"Tom," Ramsey cleared her voice. "Yes, this is . . . it has been a long time."

"Well, if it isn't the notorious, Linda Ramsey," Col. Tom Jenkins grinned, standing in line at the snack bar in the courtyard of the Pentagon. "If my recollection is correct, it has been four years and two months since the last time we talked. You said you would meet me here at this very snack bar and never bothered to show."

"I might be a lot of things," Ramsey admitted as she cringed, "but I am not a homewrecker. How's the wife?" Ramsey asked, leaning back in her chair.

"I lost Pearl to cancer about a year ago," Col. Jenkins sadly said. "She never found out about us. Are you still at Alby?"

"I'm still at Alby Airlines," Ramsey grinned, "I'm Head of Security. I just got back to work and was told we are on Red Alert. Tell me what you know?" she asked as he walked away from the snack bar.

"Ramsey you know that it's classified," Col. Jenkins smiled.

Turning her chair around, Ramsey glanced out her window to watch a 767 takeoff, "If you won't tell me what you know, let me tell you what I know. I was told your people picked up a blip on radar and lost it near Brunswick, Georgia."

"That's what NORAD is circulating, go on," Col. Jenkins urged, sitting down on a bench.

"This is totally off the record," Ramsey offered, watching another jet takeoff, "and between two old friends in different high places, agreed?"

"Agreed," Col. Jenkins confirmed. "Go on."

"About three months ago," Ramsey began. "Alby accidently got pulled into Mario LaBasco Sr.'s family business. This is very complicated. My top security flight attendant, Kathe Tierney, stumbled into this when she foiled a terrorist attack onboard one of our flights."

"I saw that the terrorist was killed last night," Col. Jenkins reported. "Rhasheéd Saíde was the third-most wanted man."

"Yes, after months of looking for Saíde," Ramsey explained, "we finally traced him to an apartment in the Bronx. Just when Tierney had Saíde in her sight, he received a phone call and fled. He turned up dead two hours later. He was practically handed to us."

"Mario LaBasco Sr. just made the news about an hour ago," Col. Jenkins interrupted. "They are indicting him for the murder of Sen. Bernard Frank of New York."

"I've got proof that they are indicting the wrong LaBasco," Ramsey declared. "It seems that Jr. is setting his father up so he can take over the family business."

"That is a matter for the police, not the military," Col. Jenkins refuted.

"True," Ramsey agreed, "but the reason the two LaBasco's got into a tiff, so to speak, is a military reason and a big one."

"I'm still listening . . .," Col. Jenkins said, saluting a soldier passing by him.

"Mario Sr. was working with Sen. Frank and what looks like Gen. Robert Thompson about two years ago," Ramsey began. "They were trying to purchase an experimental fighter jet, XP38, which contains outstanding stealth weapon technology."

"You're piquing my interest," Col. Jenkins smiled as a co-worker passed.

"Frank wanted Mario Sr. to buy the XP38," Ramsey continued. "He also set up a deal for them to sell it to the Iranians, which Sr. would not do. He said it was treason according to my sources. Evidently, Jr. thought his father was showing weakness. He took it upon himself to talk with the senator and buy XP38 that Frank arranged from a renegade Russian general, named Yetsun."

"I have heard that name," Col. Jenkins affirmed. "It's common knowledge Yetsun would sell his own mother for the right price."

"Mario's brother, Nicki, intercepted a coded document on how to use XP38's technology onboard and was killed for it," Ramsey confirmed. "His house was ransacked and his Number One Man, Dider was killed for the document. Their sister Tierra, a flight attendant, who works for me had several threats on her life recently. Each time Mario Jr. said the problem was solved and she came back to work. The last time the FBI assigned Special Agent CC Sims to fly with Tierra. They wanted someone on the inside to help prove Mario Sr. killed Frank. Saíde hacked into our computer and located the hotel where I was holding them. Evidently, Mario sent Saíde to find the document. Tierra was stabbed in the back and CC was shot at close range. I have got the document here and my computer expert recently broke the codes. Jr. needs the codes to sell XP38 to the Iranians. Without these codes, it's just another YAK U38."

"I will tell you," Col. Jenkins smirked. "The Pentagon is not worried that Russia has any technology that would shake us."

"And I tell you differently," Ramsey grinned. "Its codename is Chameleon. It has the capability to read IFF codes, while passing within 200 miles of another jet and change its own codes to mimic theirs."

"What the heck?" Col. Jenkins snapped, standing up. "We didn't know that!"

"It seems that Jr. found out that Kathe Tierney has a famous boyfriend, who we hid at her house in Florida," Ramsey explained. "I had my private pilot, Ralph, take him and two other people there. Now Ralph's not answering his phone, which means one thing. Mario found them. That's why Mario stopped Saíde from fighting Tierney yesterday. She's his insurance policy. The technology won't work without the authentication response codes, which we have in our possession. The blip you saw is probably XP38 coming to pick up Jr. when he gets the codes. He already has a buyer in the Middle East. We found that Frank had visited the Middle East several times and had quite a few contributions from that area. That is why Junior, not Senior, killed Frank. It was to keep his father and his Number One Man, Alonzo DiMeglio from finding out what he was up to."

"Are you sure about all of this?" Col. Jenkins asked, hurrying back to his office.

"Have I ever steered you wrong in business?" Ramsey said as she took a deep breath. "I need a favor."

"Let me make some calls," Col. Jenkins stated. "I need to get some pilots in the air to look for XP38," he said, entering his office, and turning on his computer.

"Negative," Ramsey warned. "Mario Jr. hacked into your computers at the Pentagon and jammed my satellite yesterday evening when we were tracking him."

"How did you know our computers were breached last night?" Col. Jenkins demanded, sitting back in his chair.

"My computer expert found Mario Jr.'s tunnel in our computer system and traced him back to his lair," Ramsey admitted. "He found out how Jr. jammed my satellite from a laptop with a U.S. military satellite. Mario can easily find out where your jets are and pick them off. There is another man working for Mario Jr., named Timothy Paul Patrick O'Brien. O'Brien worked with Raini toward the end of the project. We found out from pictures sent by Freedom Fighters in Russia a couple of days ago, that O'Brien and Mario have XP38."

"Man, Ramsey!" Col. Jenkins affirmed. "How did you find out about O'Brien? We've been tracking him and his girlfriend, Sabrina Aline Macaby, with Homeland Security for months! Only they did not say it was for this reason!"

"I have my ways Tom," Ramsey concurred. "XP38 is coming to us. I want that jet just as bad as you do. I do not want to start Armageddon! That's what that technology would do in the wrong hands. Your pilots are no match for this. I need a two-seater Joint Strike Fighter F-35. Capt. Yorg Vuslick also worked on the project with Raini. It was his job to program the Chameleon Technology into a regular YAK U38. He refused to do it and Yetsun murdered his wife. Then, Yetsun sent Vuslick here to work with Alby Airlines on the pretense of a cooperative International Anti-Terrorists Program to get him away from the project. Dr. David Sydney, my computer expert, who broke the code will be onboard with him. Together they can bring it down. What do you say?"

"You know how the Pentagon works," Col. Jenkins stated as reading though the information on his screen. "It looks like Homeland did suspect this technology exists. They are trying to find it so NORAD can use it. I will go along with you on one condition. We end up with XP38 and the codes."

"Do I have a choice?" Ramsey asked, snapping a pencil in half.

"No, you don't have a choice!" Col. Jenkins gloated. "I say that when this is over, you come back and work for me. You are one heck of a lady! And you always have been."

"Tom, I was vetted and worked closely with you at the Pentagon for years," Ramsey sneered. "How do you think I know how the government works, and how to get around it?"

Four and a half hours later, Yorg approached the small New Smyrna Beach Airport, "This airport is so small this administration laid off the traffic controllers."

"Well, at least we should be able to slip in and out of here easier," Kathe said as the Mustang Citation landed on the runway. "Ramsey said she has a blue SUV waiting for us on the side road by the car lot. It's about five miles from my house," she said as Yorg parked the jet at the end of a taxiway.

Forty-five minutes later Jack parked the SUV on South Peninsula Drive near the Lighthouse.

"This is a good spot," Kathe admitted. "This road goes straight to my house," she said as they approached Kathe's house on foot through the park. They carefully positioned themselves in the middle of the walkway that connects the park with the beach, paralleling the south side of her house.

"There are quite a few lights on," Yorg whispered to Kathe as putting his duffle bag down.

"Mario's definitely here," Kathe whispered. "Look at the tower."

"I see him," Yorg added. "He's armed with an M-16."

"The grounds are crawling with Mario's men," Jay whispered as he and Jack joined them.

"Look in the master bedroom," Kathe said, looking through her binoculars. "Cartoons are on TV, and I see Joey sitting on the bed with Heather and Christy. Pete is lying on the floor. Get down! There is a guard coming out on the balcony lighting a cigarette."

"Jay, Kathe, check the beach side of the house," Yorg whispered as they all crouched down further. "Jack, check the north side of house. I'll check the front. Do not engage and be back here in five minutes,"

Yorg said as they synchronized their watches.

Yorg slipped around toward the front gate, being careful not to attract the attention of the guards in the tower. He made his way through the palm fronds toward the side of the house following along the front fence. He spotted in his peripheral vision someone waving a white handkerchief. Recognizing Alonzo DiMeglio, he followed him to the park.

"Capt. Vuslick," Alonzo reached to shake his hand.

"Alonzo DiMeglio," Yorg said, shaking his hand. "I know who you are, and that you work for Mario LaBasco Sr."

"It seems we have a common enemy," Alonzo stated. "I was sent here to help you," Alonzo continued, motioning for his men to come out.

Yorg looked at his watch and touched his earpiece, "Alonzo DiMeglio is here. Meet us at the park by the bathrooms."

"I have not trusted Mario Jr. since the strange death of his mother," Alonzo admitted as the others joined them. "Ms. Tierney," Alonzo said, shaking her hand. "Mr. LaBasco heard you that night crying at Tierra's bedside. Since then, we started putting things together that happened over the past two years. I had a rather lengthy discussion with the four New Jersey men that Mario hired to try to find Sherrod. I know that Mario used an Iranian by the name of Rhasheéd Saíde to kill Nicki. He sent Saíde to kill Tierra and Ms. Sims at the hotel. Mario did finally kill Saíde after he called him away from you yesterday evening. My men watched Mario takeoff from a private airstrip near La Guardia and followed him here. We anticipated the arrest of his father. Someone emailed me proof that Mario was feeding lies to the media. He also sent us proof that Mario was working with Councilor Jacques dé Laurent covering up the murder of his mother. Mr. LaBasco sent me to help you take Mario and Giorgio down."

"Our boss, Linda Ramsey, had the email sent to you," Kathe confirmed. "I knew it was only a matter of time before you discovered what Mario was doing. He is holding my family hostage inside my house."

"I know," Alonzo acknowledged. "I also know that you are pregnant and the father, Joe Sherrod is inside too. When we arrived, Mario's men had already taken the house. To our surprise, the house was already occupied with people having a barbeque. My men have already checked the perimeter and they have the house locked down tight. We have not found a way to enter without incurring several casualties. Mario is a cold-blooded killer. He will not hesitate to use children to get what he wants."

"Does Mario Sr. know what this really is all about?" Yorg asked.

"Yes, it is about greed, power, and treason," Alonzo admitted. "Something Mr. LaBasco did not want to be a part of. Sen. Frank was alive and mad as heck when he and Gen. Thompson left the house two years ago in Corté de Azuré. Mr. LaBasco refused the deal they set up with Gen. Yetsun, and the Iranians. Mario was upset with his father that day and stormed out of the house. He must have met with Frank and Thompson to renegotiate the deal."

"I can get us inside without being seen, if your men can help ours secure the outside," Kathe affirmed. "Mario has brought a small army from what we've gathered. Dr. Sydney, who works with us, owns the house next door. He is also one of the hostages inside my house. We can use his house as a safe house for my family as we rescue them."

"XP38 has to be somewhere near," Yorg surmised. "Mario already has it in his possession, and he knows we are onto him. He is desperate to get the authentication response codes and head for Iran. Nicki intercepted the codes and that is why Mario killed him. We found them in a secret panic room that Tierra, and Dider only knew about."

"I knew at the meeting after the first attempt on Nicki's life that Mario seemed desperate to get Nicki alone," Alonzo confided. "I tried my hardest to get Mr. LaBasco to bring him into our protection. Mr. LaBasco knew the brothers didn't get along but went with the advice of the other family leaders. I made a promise to him and Giorgio then, that if anything happened to Nicki, they were next."

"You're not going to want to hear this Kathe," Jay advised after he and Jack discussed the situation. "We need to wait until after sundown. You said yourself, Mario brought a small army. They out number us four to one; we need to work in the shadows."

"I agree with them," Alonzo concurred. "Mario won't make a move until nightfall. They know you're on to them and that the military is searching for XP38. They'll have to keep the Russian YAK U38 hid. This beach is packed with witnesses. Not to mention from what my men have surveyed; Ponce Inlet is a maze to have to get out of in a chase. The sun will be down around 6:00 pm. That's when we can make our move."

"I agree with you," Yorg concluded. "We can get into Dr. Sydney's house without being seen. We'll wait for nightfall."

Inside Dr. Sydney's house, Alonzo asked Pauli to send for some food, while Kathe brought Ramsey up to speed. "Alonzo," Ramsey began, "I feel relieved that you are joining my team to take Mario and Giorgio down. I have a great deal of respect for Mr. LaBasco and you. You can imagine how petrified we all felt watching and proving Mario was methodically taking your family members down. I understand this is hard for Mr. LaBasco to find out. I also realized that you had to get hard evidence to take to Mr. LaBasco and the other family leaders. I offer my condolences for the loss of Nicki, and Maria LaBasco. I guess our working together was inevitable since this last situation began with Tierra. I did not want to get into a war with your family."

"I understand your concerns," Alonzo confided. "Mr. LaBasco and I appreciate the care and protection that you have given not only to Tierra, but Nicki as well. It was Ms. Tierney that came to Tierra's bedside the other night and brought this to our attention. It was her speech that pulled Tierra out of the coma. She wasn't supposed to live through the night. I think she knew Mario wouldn't stop until she was dead and gave up. After Kathe left, Mr. LaBasco came out of the bathroom and sat down at Tierra's bedside, she opened her eyes and began to talk. She explained some of the times Kathe risked her own life to save her. Both Tierra and Ms. Sims will make a full recovery. Mr. LaBasco is sickened that the son he trusted the most, would do such a thing. I am to stay with you until this entire situation is finished."

"I saw you as I left Tierra's room," Kathe admitted, glancing at Alonzo. "Tierra and CC had both told me that you didn't trust Mario. I knew it was only a matter of time before you discovered what he was doing. I wanted to tell you what we found, but I didn't know how you would take it."

"I want you to promise that you'll never be afraid to come to me for help," Alonzo offered. "I could never repay you for what you have done for Tierra and her family."

"There's one other thing," Jay added. "I have done some extensive research on Giorgio Pulini. I've found him randomly disappearing to Marseille, France; however, I can't find out where he goes. He doesn't stay in a hotel or eat at any restaurant. Would he have a specific place to go?"

"I wasn't aware that Giorgio ever left Mario's side," Alonzo admitted. "Mr. LaBasco set each son up with his own territory in two separate countries. I will check into it. It is odd that he would go there. That is the main center of Antonio Falcini Sr.'s business. We have been rivals over territory for many years. As a matter of fact, there is a rumor that the Falcini's are trying to take over some of Nicki's territory. A rumor I could never prove. It appears that Mario started the rumor to try and get to Nicki."

"To go there several times a year and never leave a signature," Yorg added, "it would seem he has a specific place to go."

"I agree with you," Alonzo concurred. "Can you email me what you have?"

"I'll do it right now," Jay said as he went to get his iPad.

"That is a concern," Alonzo admitted as the food arrived. "Mario would have to mask Giorgio's leaving from the family. We are supposed to know what each branch is always doing."

"Alonzo, if you'll give me your cell phone number," Ramsey suggested, "I'd like to add you to our communication network. That way, you can converse with us all the time."

"I would appreciate that," Alonzo said, giving her the number.

Hours later, the sun was finally going down. "My men will join yours and secure the perimeter of the house," Alonzo decided as he and Yorg checked the back of Kathe's house from Sydney's upstairs window. "I want Mario and Giorgio! They are mine! I made a promise to them that I will keep!"

"You can come inside the house with us," Yorg agreed.

"Pauli, it's time to clear the perimeter," Alonzo declared.

"Jay, Jack, go with Pauli and his men," Yorg ordered. "You men get in position and give us fifteen minutes to get inside. We need to assess the situation before you begin to clear the perimeter. Take them down quietly so you don't tip our hand."

"Copy that," Jay said as they left the house from the northern side.

Approaching the south front gate, Alonzo and Yorg followed Kathe through the palm trees. She opened a secret door on the last pillar of the gate. They followed her down the steps using JAKE as a flashlight. A long tunnel located under the driveway lead to an area under the front steps. She opened a door that entered a small area, where there were two more tunnels. Yorg whispered pointing to the left, "I'll go to the kitchen and upstairs. Meet you back here in five minutes."

Motioning for Alonzo to follow her, Kathe took the tunnel to the right that led to the family room. Cautioning him to stop, she pushed a button at the end of the hallway. A panel slid open showing a two-way mirror into the family room. There they could see Mario and Giorgio sitting outside by the pool having a drink. Mario was working on his computer. In the family room watching TV were Jordan, Patti, Ben, Peter, Helen, and Joe plus several armed men. Behind them, Kathe reached for another button that opened a door, which led to a circular staircase leading up to the master suite. Again, pressing a button, another two-way mirror opened showing her bedroom. There they saw the kids asleep on her bed and the floor. The guard was dozing.

Yorg met them back under the steps, "I found Ralph, and the other pilot dead in the garage. Six guards are eating in the kitchen. Carrie Anne, Sydney, Jeannie, and Bob are being held in the Asian room with two guards. What did you find?"

After telling him, Alonzo checked his watch, "The outside perimeter is clearing now. We need to clear the Asian room first, then the master bedroom, lastly the kitchen and family room."

"I want to secure the kids and adults out of the house, before we start the kitchen and family room," Kathe finalized. She picked up JAKE to check in and explain the situation to Ramsey. "It's a go, and no word on XP38 yet."

Putting silencers on their guns, Kathe, and Alonzo followed Yorg to the hallway, and peered through the two-way mirror into the Asian room. Motioning for Alonzo to stand back, Yorg signaled for Kathe to take the guard on the left next to the door. He would take the one reading a book in the right corner chair. Kathe acknowledged Yorg as she pushed another button. A hidden doorway in the corner pillar of the room opened. Stepping out into the room, surprising the guards, they shot them both dead.

"What took you so long?" Sydney whispered, grabbing his computer from under the bed.

"Daylight," Yorg quietly chuckled. "I thought you were crazy when you designed these tunnels. But they really are handy."

"I have been racking by brain trying to figure out how to get over to my house," Sydney admitted. "I'll have to rethink my escape plans using these tunnels."

"Kathe!" Jeannie exclaimed, running to her. "That man is crazy. He shot two men right in front of all of us!"

"He is insane!" Carrie Anne cried. "He was bragging about killing Nicki, Tierra, and CC."

"The girls are not dead," Kathe whispered, checking her gun. "They will recover."

"Where are the children?" Bob asked, hugging her.

"They are safe," Kathe stated. "We're going to get them next. We must hurry, follow me." Locking the secret doorway, Kathe led them down the tunnel into the area under the steps. "Wait here and be very quiet," she ordered.

"We've got the first packages," Yorg called Jay. "There is a tunnel from Sydney's kitchen that connects to the tunnel under Kathe's front steps. I will notify you in a few minutes to come and retrieve the adults and children," he said, hanging up his phone. He handed Sydney a Walther PPK, "Just in case something goes wrong."

"Thanks," Sydney said, putting the gun on the safety. "I need to find XP38."

"I saw Mario on his computer," Kathe added. "He has to be communicating with O'Brien."

"Go, save the children," Sydney affirmed. "I'll locate the jet."

Returning to the master bedroom, they watched through the mirror as Giorgio entered the room. The guard was asleep on the chair. They watched as Giorgio hurried over to the guard and slapped him across the face, "Why are you sleeping?"

"Mr. Giorgio," the man stammered, springing to his feet, waking the children. "The kids were all sound asleep, so I must have dozed off."

"You fall asleep again and I will shoot you myself," Giorgio shouted, glancing around the room at the children. "Mr. LaBasco is tired of waiting for your mama to come! The Iranians are threatening to cancel the deal!" He stormed over to the bed and grabbed Heather. "You'll do," he said as Heather screamed.

"Leave my sister alone!" Pete yelled, jumping up from the floor, and reaching for her. Giorgio slapped Pete across his face so hard that he fell to the floor.

"It seems that your knocked up mama isn't coming to get you fast enough!" Giorgio shouted. "We're running out of time! Maybe you can persuade her to hurry with your screams as we torture you!"

"Pete!" Heather cried, reaching out for him as Yorg pressed the button.

The tile on the back wall of the shower separated. Kathe pushed past Yorg, hurrying out first. "They're all in danger because of me," she whispered. "Giorgio!" Kathe called out as she rounded the corner into the room. She raised her Walther PPK with the laser dead center on his forehead. "I'm already here!"

"Don't even think about it!" Yorg warned the guard as his laser tagged him across the chest. Astonishingly, the guard gasped at the red beam. He dropped the gun, putting his hands up. "Slide it over to me with your foot," Yorg ordered.

"Mama!" Heather cried, reaching fiercely for her as Giorgio pulled Heather back.

"Mom?" Pete questioned, holding his cheek. "You've got a gun?"

"Giorgio, let my daughter go!" Tierney ordered as Alonzo came around the corner.

"I think you need to do as the lady asked," Alonzo calmly declared as Giorgio gasped. "What's the matter? You didn't think I was smart enough to figure out what you and Mario were doing? You know," he said, pointing his finger at him. "I warned you and Mario that if anything happened to Nicki that you'd answer to me. I must hand it to you; you must have been planning this before Ms. LaBasco died. An accidental death that never sat right with me. Mr. LaBasco and I both want to know who did it, you or his favorite son."

"You're as dumb as the old man," Giorgio declared, trying to drag Heather toward the door. "We pulled this off right under your noses!"

"Stop!" Tierney ordered. "One more step and I will shoot!"

"Not with me holding your daughter!" Giorgio smirked, shoving Heather to one side, and reaching in his coat.

"Wrong!" Kathe shouted, shooting Giorgio in the hand. Heather fainted. Giorgio dropped her to the floor and grabbed his bloody hand. Alonzo lunged for Giorgio shoving him against the wall.

"Take the kids and leave!" Yorg ordered.

"Help!" Giorgio screamed, knocking Alonzo on the floor in a fierce fight.

"Yorg, carry Heather, I can't," Kathe ordered, taking Yorg's position. "I will be right behind you. Hurry! I hear reinforcements coming up the stairs!"

"Okay," Yorg concurred, picking up Heather. "Come on kids!"

"Christy, hold Joey's hand!" Kathe requested as they followed Yorg. Joey pulled away from Christy and headed back to his mother just as the guard lunged for her.

"Joey, go back!" Kathe screamed, shooting the guard in the chest. The guard fell backwards.

"Mommy!" Joey cried, running to his mother as Mario's men began kicking at the door.

"Joey, come back here," Christy yelled, peering around the corner as the door flung open. Seeing more of Mario's men, Christy panicked and ran back through the secret shower door.

"Joey, go with Christy!" Kathe ordered as she shot the first man entering the room. The second man jumped back, reached around the doorway shooting sporadically. Diving for Joey and rolling with him away from the bullets, Kathe returned fire. She kicked over a nightstand, wedging Joey between it and the wall.

Alonzo knocked Giorgio to the ground, pulled a knife out of his boot, threw it at the gunman's hand and pinned it to the doorframe. The man screamed out in pain, dropping his gun. Giorgio charged Alonzo knocking him down to the floor. "Get out of here!" Alonzo ordered Kathe as she reloaded her gun.

"Not without you!" Kathe argued. "More reinforcements are coming!" she warned as another gunman appeared.

Alonzo pulled Giorgio around, using him as a shield. "I've got unfinished business, get out of here!" Alonzo yelled as Kathe grabbed Joey, fleeing to the bathroom and through the shower as Yorg met her.

"What about Alonzo?" Yorg asked as Kathe closed the doorway and locked it.

"He said to leave him!" Kathe exclaimed. "Quick, reassess the family room," she requested as she carried Joey down to the others.

"Take him," Kathe said as she kissed Joey and handed him to Bob. She knelt beside Heather, who was sitting on the floor, leaning against the wall. Heather was resting her head against her knees, sobbing with Carrie Anne trying to comfort her. "I'm sorry," Kathe said, tearfully moving Heather's bangs out of her eyes. "I'm so sorry that I scared you when I shot Giorgio. I had no other choice. He was reaching for his gun. He would have placed it to your head. I could not take that chance," she explained as Heather hugged her mother tightly.

"Mom, you saved us," Pete cried. He reached around Heather and hugged her tightly. "Where's Grandpa, Dad, and Uncle Jordan?"

"They are holding them in another room," Kathe answered. "We're going to get them next."

"You can't," Carrie Anne cried, jumping to her feet. "They know you're here now."

"How are you going to rescue them?" Jeannie asked, holding Christy tightly in her arms.

"That's not for you to worry about," Kathe answered as she called Jay. "The packages are ready, come and get them," she said, turning to Sydney. "Did you locate XP38?"

"Not yet, and you were right," Sydney explained. "Mario has been communicating with O'Brien. I intercepted some emails between them. O'Brien is to leave Macaby at an airstrip and come pick him up."

Just then Jay and Jack opened another passage, scaring the children, which lead to Sydney's home next door. "It's okay, these men work with me," Kathe reassured her family.

"Where is Yorg?" Jack inquired, holstering his gun.

"He went to reassess the situation in the family room," Kathe answered.

"Kathe," Sydney interrupted. "O'Brien is somewhere offshore with XP38, but I cannot pinpoint it yet. According to the map, it's on an island that doesn't exist."

"Where is Alonzo?" Jay questioned.

"I had to leave Alonzo in my bedroom," Kathe said, hugging her other children as they cried. "I'm so sorry for putting you all in danger. I will never do it again, I promise! Never again!" She glanced over to Jay. "Is the outside secure enough to move them?"

"Let me check with Pauli," Jay answered, reaching for his cell phone. "We found a few stragglers and were securing them when you called."

Chapter 39

No Other Choice

Furious Mario kicked over an end table, spilling the contents all over the floor as he called O'Brien, "We've got a little problem! Have you figured out how to activate the system, yet? . . . I can't believe this! . . . just get here by 9:00 pm . . . yes, I will have it, or I will kill everyone left in this house!" Mario screamed. He glanced at the hostages standing at the end of the stairs and called up to Giorgio. "What's going on up there?"

"I told you she would come for us," Jordan bent over whispering to them.

"Who's here?" Peter listened.

"Kathe's here, she coming to save us," Ben sighed with relief.

"What are you talking about?" Peter whispered. "My ex-wife is nothing but a little . . ."

Helen interrupted, "Wimp and dressed like a slut the last couple of times we saw her." Helen chuckled, sitting up straight on the couch.

Mario turned around, "No talking, shut up!"

Joe leaned over as Mario turned around, "It's obvious, you don't know Kathe anymore. I wouldn't say that to her face," looking Helen straight in the eyes. "You might live to regret it," Joe grinned. He sat up as Giorgio and another man dragged Alonzo down the stairs.

"Well, this party keeps getting better," Mario grinned as he pinched Alonzo's cheek. "Where did you find him?"

"That broad Tierney was with him," Giorgio reported, dropping Alonzo. "She has taken the kids and other adults. Several of our boys are dead. She shot me in the hand, while I was holding her own daughter," he said while tying his handkerchief around his left hand. Peter listened in disbelief.

"Where is that broad?" Mario screamed, kicking Alonzo in the side as he fell over.

"With Puff the Magic Dragon," Alonzo painfully stated.

Mario kicked Alonzo again in the other side. Yorg watched through the two-way mirror by the bar and had to chuckle at the old man's answer. He hurried back to the others.

"We've got to hurry," Yorg reported as he returned to the staging area. "Alonzo's in trouble."

"Thank God, he's still alive," Kathe sighed.

"Yes, he's alive and he's one tough man," Yorg whispered. "Mario was kicking him and asked him where you were. And Alonzo answered, 'with Puff the Magic Dragon.'"

"We've got to hurry," Kathe said, hugging Pete one last time. "Jay, you know where to take these people. Go now. Sydney let me know the moment you find that jet."

Jack come with me," Yorg ordered, heading back upstairs. "Kathe we will wait for you to enter through the mural."

"I will be right there," Kathe agreed.

"Mom, aren't you coming with us?" Pete cried holding onto her tightly.

"No," Kathe answered, gently moving him back. "Jay will take you to safety. I want you to stay with Jeannie and Bob. I want you to always remember," she said, pointing her finger at each child, "just how much I love each one of you. I've got to save your grandpa and the others." She watched them leave through the secret passage. As the door closed and locked safely behind them, she headed to the family room.

Watching through the mirror, Kathe waited a moment to give Yorg and Jack enough time to get into position. Alonzo was badly beaten, and Mario was pulling him up to his knees. "Are you ready?" she whispered to them.

"Affirmative," Jack answered, lying on the balcony floor, peering through his scope.

"Affirmative," Yorg answered. "We can't kill Mario yet. He must call O'Brien to bring in XP38," Yorg said, lying on the floor on the right side of the stairway.

"I'm activating the Hologram now," Kathe said as she listened to Mario from inside the tunnel.

"Wait," Yorg said, listening to the conversation. "Sydney, record this; it might be useful later."

"I'm one step ahead of you," Sydney reported from next door.

"This whole mess is your fault!" Mario screamed as Patti buried her head in Jordan's shoulder. "You and my weak Papa refused a billion-dollar deal!" Mario shouted, pistol-whipping Alonzo again. "I begged him not to turn it down! But you...you kept telling Papa to stop . . . who's the sorry one now?"

"It's treason!" Alonzo answered with blood dripping down his left eye. "What are you thinking? Your Papa wanted no part of that!"

"My Papa used to buy and sell people for what he wanted!" Mario lashed back. "Money is money! There's no difference! Sen. Frank was the mastermind behind this deal! He didn't think it was treason! Because of you and Papa, I couldn't move fast enough! I found out that he was going to offer it to the Falcini's'! After that incompetent Saíde botched the first attempt on Tierra, Frank got scared that I couldn't deliver! Never trust a politician! I killed that sorry imbecile myself!"

"Our family business is a lot of things!" Alonzo admitted. "But selling this type of technology to the Iranians would destroy the free world! The Falcini's would not have accepted the deal either! Only, you are greedy and power hungry enough not to realize that no one in the free world would be safe, including you! That's what your Papa kept trying to make you understand!"

"You are a pathetic, old man!" Mario laughed, sarcastically. "Look at you; the great Alonzo DiMeglio, feared by most families for your ruthlessness! My Papa's Number One Man!" Mario let go of Alonzo and stepped back. "You used to be on top of every move! Lately, you've become as soft as Papa! My own mother figured out what I was planning! I begged Mama to join me and get rid of Papa, but she wouldn't! She laughed at me!" he glanced over at Giorgio. "She called me crazy and threatened to tell Papa!"

"You killed her!" Alonzo exclaimed, spitting in his face.

"You imbecile!" Mario exclaimed, wiping the spit from his cheek with his sleeve. "Yes, I killed my mother! You weren't even smart enough to figure it out! I even manipulated Papa and the other family leaders to send Nicki to my house! That way, that idiot Saíde, who missed him once, could finally kill him! Now, I have you to thank for bringing me Kathe Tierney!" he laughed louder. "I don't know how that broad keeps interfering with my plans! Now," stepping closer, "one more time, where is she?" he placed the gun pointblank on Alonzo's forehead.

"Now," Kathe whispered. She stepped through the Hologram of the Lighthouse Mural on the wall by the bar. "I'm right here," she said, calmly placing the laser site of her Walther PPK on Mario's forehead.

"Kathe!" Joe sighed.

"Don't move!" Yorg shouted, jumping up from the top balcony. He shot one of Mario's men that ran out of the kitchen.

"Drop your weapon!" Jack warned as his laser tagged another man that stepped out from under the balcony, trying to get a shot at Yorg.

"Where did you come from?" Mario demanded. "There's no door there," he snapped as he shoved Alonzo to the floor and pointed his gun at her.

"Like Alonzo said," Kathe answered. "I was with Puff the Magic Dragon."

Giorgio grabbed Peter, placing a gun to his head, as he backed toward the sliding glass doors. "Put your guns down or I'll blow his head off! Vinnie, Antonio, grab a hostage and hold them as shields! We've got three sharpshooters in the room! They can't get all of us!" Vinnie grabbed Jordan and Antonio grabbed Patti.

"Kathe," Sydney interrupted via her implant. "I found XP38. It was on a hidden island just off the coast. It's approaching; ETA ten minutes. I have reconnected Ramsey. She's listening."

"Sorry Ben, for what I'm about to say," Kathe apologized. "Have at it, Giorgio. That's my ex-husband. For what that woman," Kathe moved her head toward Helen on the couch, "did to me and my children and he allowed it! Go ahead, I don't care, shoot him," Kathe laughed as Helen cried out.

Giorgio moved one step back and looked at the floor, "He just wet his pants!"

Peter fainted and dropped to the floor. Giorgio grabbed Helen and held her as his shield. Mario stepped backwards and grabbed Joe off the couch.

"Good one, Kathe," Ramsey chuckled. "I have alerted the military. O'Brien has finally surfaced. I don't want him running, so I'm holding the military off until he gets there."

"Well," Mario announced getting a better hold on Joe. "I do think you would mind if I killed this one! The father of the child you're carrying," Mario smirked, shielding himself with Joe. "I'll tell you what," he snickered again. "I'll trade you! The codes for the daddy! What do you say?"

"No deal," Kathe said, calmly keeping her gun pointing straight at him.

"I don't think you understand!" Mario snapped. "I will drop this idiot right in front of you!" he warned and connected his Bluetooth. Kathe glanced up to Yorg and nodded her head. "We've been breached! It's low tide, bring it!" Mario ordered and disconnected his earpiece.

"You are the one who does not understand," Kathe scolded. "I have been put in a no-win situation. I don't know what to do with Joe either," she said as Joe's eyes widened. "I warned you, that you couldn't be seen with me. You know what I do for a living. I trusted you. And what did I get in return?" she glared straight him. "Just one picture plastered all over the Internet and look what you caused. Not to mention your last announcement, Daddy Glitter Boy!"

"I had nothing to do with it!" Joe pleaded. "I don't know how the picture or announcement got there! I swear!"

"Yes, you do!" Kathe blasted him. "You pulled the memory chip out of the camera when I was in the hallway talking to Carrie Anne! You knew I would take the camera! And you put the announcement of our child on the Internet after I Tasered you for your betrayal yesterday! This mad man found me because of you! This is just the beginning! Do you know how many people I've sent to prison?"

"You are one, cold, beautiful woman!" Mario laughed. "What do they say? Another time, another place, we could have been great together!"

"Stop," Kathe interrupted, trying to buy time. "I just got over morning sickness and you are making me sick again."

"We aren't so different!" Mario snapped, repositioning his grip on Joe. "We could be good together! You have got nothing in common with this idiot!"

"Good, Tierney keep him talking," Ramsey iterated. "ETA is three minutes. Once it lands, we can shoot him."

Yorg whispered to Kathe, "Try moving him away from the couch, so we can get a better shot."

"Let's see," Kathe continued as she tried to move Mario. "I rate you up there with child molesters! You killed your own mother and brother! By the way, your sister and CC are still alive! You are trying to frame your father for the murder of Sen. Frank that you committed! But I should thank you for killing Rhasheéd Saíde! You saved me the trouble," she said as Peter and Helen looked at her in disbelief.

"You're welcome," Mario smiled. "I'm glad you realized I handed him to you. See we are starting to bond."

"I don't think so, I wasn't finished with your traits," Kathe continued. "You are greedy, power hungry, cheating, and treasonous! Did I miss anything?"

"And are you not a murderer?" Mario laughed. "How many people have you killed?"

She shrugged her shoulders.

"See, we aren't all that different," Mario boasted.

"But, unlike you," Kathe affirmed, "I don't kill innocent people. Forget it, you're not my type."

"You're right," Mario laughed, waving his gun up toward Yorg. "You surprised the heck out of me. I thought you and the Russian got it on."

Yorg leaned over the balcony and aimed at Mario.

"What's the matter?" Mario taunted Yorg. "Don't you speak English?"

"Where I'm going to send you," Yorg informed him. "Language is the last thing you'll need to worry about!"

"In this business," Kathe interrupted them, "no one really knows what I'm capable of doing, not even Yorg."

Mario glanced toward the couch and pointed his gun at Ben.

"XP38 is coming in," Jack stated, raising his scope to the lights coming in offshore.

"Yes, right on time," Mario bragged. "There must be someone here you care about. These people were barbequing at your private house with your children. Stand up old man!" Mario ordered as Ben stood up. Mario shoved Joe down and snatched Ben. He placed his revolver at Ben's temples. "Ben, isn't it? She called you by name. You must be the one," he said, grabbing the back of Ben's hair. Ben flinched in pain.

"Stop!" Kathe ordered, watching XP38 hovering over the ocean.

"Well, now I've hit a nerve!" Mario laughed. Kathe glanced up at Yorg and Jack. They both shook their heads-no shot. Mario pulled Ben's hair again, "Give me the codes or I'll kill him on the count of three. One," Mario laughed. "Two," he laughed harder.

"Stop!" Kathe ordered, lowering her gun. "I have the codes! Let him go!"

"Tierney, what are you doing?" Ramsey questioned as she sat straight up in her chair.

"What I have to do," Kathe whispered as sand pelted the house loudly as XP38 landed. "Ramsey you were right. Joe is nothing but trouble."

"What did you say?" Mario asked, glancing around at the noise.

"I said what do you want me to do?" Kathe replied, loudly. "I know how to work Chameleon!"

"No, Kathe!" Ben pleaded. "I'm not going to let you do this! I'm a sick old man! I'm not worth it!" Ben cried out. Kathe stepped over Alonzo's body carefully dropping her gun and JAKE on the floor next to him.

"Tierney, don't do it!" Ramsey ordered as Wanda and Keith joined her.

"This better not be a trick!" Mario warned, holding Ben tighter.

"No trick," Kathe said. "That's the one man that stood by me when Peter" she nodded at him, "took off on me. My life for his. I'll go with you," she said, walking closer to Mario.

Trading Kathe for Ben, Mario backed toward the sliding glass doors. He held his gun to her belly and looked up at Yorg and Jack. "One shot and I'll shoot her in the stomach. She better be right, or I will eject her without a parachute," he said as he called O'Brien. "Can you see in the house? Yes, that's Vuslick...Arm one of your rockets and lock onto this room. I'm coming out with a hostage. If anyone moves, fire the rocket!" he ordered, glaring at Yorg. "Now, who's sending whom somewhere?" he laughed loudly and looked at Giorgio. "When we are up in the air. You know what to do," he backed out of the house. He took his laptop off the patio table and left with Kathe.

"You heard him!" Giorgio stated, holding Helen closer to him. "Nobody moves, or we'll all go up in smoke!"

"Jay," Yorg said, watching Kathe leave. "Have Pauli and his men hold their fire. XP38 has a rocket locked onto this house."

"Copy that," Jay answered, watching from the inside of Dr. Sydney's house.

"Sydney, can you see what's going on?" Yorg asked.

"Yes, we're all watching," Sydney declared.

"Sydney, can you tell if the rocket is really armed?" Ramsey questioned Mario's abilities.

"Yes, he's not kidding," Sydney admitted, checking his laptop. "It is armed and locked onto the house."

"Don't anybody move until I tell you." Ramsey ordered. "Yorg, sit tight. He's got the advantage. I have an F-35 Stealth waiting for you at the Lighthouse as soon as he takes off. You're going to have to take Sydney and fight Mario from the air. If by chance O'Brien gets Chameleon working, you know the ramifications better than any fighter pilot the military has. With Sydney's help, you should be able to take it down."

"You're mine!" Yorg promised, peering through his scope at O'Brien sitting in the cockpit. "I should have killed you in Moscow years ago! This isn't over yet!"

"Kathe, what have you got in mind?" Ramsey asked.

"Kathe, answer us," Yorg pleaded. "What do you have in mind?"

"Ramsey was right all along," Kathe whispered, walking ahead of Mario down the windy walkway. "I have compromised my family for a Glitter Boy, who compromised me. Now, I'm carrying his child and I only wish it was Yorg's child," she quietly admitted.

"Kat, the child will always be mine," Yorg promised with Mario's head dead in his sights. "I promise to get you both out of this. And I always keep my promises to you."

"What are you doing with that woman?" O'Brien asked Mario on his cell watching them walk toward the jet.

"Sydney, can you hear what's going on?" Ramsey asked.

"Yes, but it's windy outside," Sydney answered, trying to minimize the sound of the wind. "It's hard to understand. I just refreshed the link with the satellite, listen."

"She's my insurance policy," Mario boasted, reaching in his pocket for a remote. "Put the weapon system on autopilot and come down and help me with her. She says she knows how to get the system working," Mario said, grabbing Kathe's left shoulder. "Turn around and don't get any ideas. See this remote," he dangled it in front of her. "This was added by O'Brien when I first took over the jet. It controls the original weapons system from my fingertips."

"Did you copy that?" Ramsey asked. "Sydney is that possible?"

Sydney enhanced his infrared cameras, "Stand down, he can do it."

"How could she know how to work this?" O'Brien demanded as he opened the canopy and climbed down.

"Do you remember Raini naming the project Chameleon?" Mario asked.

"Yes, but Raini only let us work on one section of the project," O'Brien admitted. "He was always so secretive. That's why I can't get it to work," he scowled. Mario instantly turned his gun on O'Brien and shot him between the eyes.

"That's not what you told me when I hired you!" Mario exclaimed, clutching Kathe by the shoulder. He pulled her up the ladder to the cockpit as he rambled. He shoved her into the cockpit, "Mama always said, Mario if you want something done right, do it yourself. So, help me after I hired those two incompetent imbeciles, if you are lying to me, I will eject you out of this cockpit without a parachute. And, if you don't believe me, watch the first thing I do when we're in the air."

Changing phones Ramsey immediately called for backup. "Tom, send your vehicles to the house now! Mario's going to blow it! Heads-up everyone! We've got to get you out of the house! He's going to blow it up!" Alonzo slowly activated his earpiece and heard Ramsey. He inched his right arm toward Kathe's gun. "Yorg, as soon as you can get the people out the front door, cars are waiting! Jay, clear Sydney's house now!"

"I'm back online," Alonzo whispered. "Ramsey's right, Mario's going to blow this house up." Yorg and Jack watched Alonzo slowing pulling Kathe's gun and JAKE to him. "Giorgio's mine! The rest are yours. On one, are you ready? One," Alonzo whispered, rolling over several times to clear the couch. "Now!" Alonzo shouted, shooting Giorgio in the side of his head. Yorg and Jack simultaneously took out the other guards.

"Look out!" Jordan yelled, dropping to the floor covering Patti as several more guards ran out of the kitchen. Yorg jumped over the rail on top of a guard and snapped his neck, while Jack and Alonzo took out the rest.

"Everybody, out the front door!" Jack ordered, grabbing Ben by one arm. "He's going to blow the house!"

"Ramsey, I know what to do," Sydney reported, restudying the schematics of the YAK from inside the Hummer. "Kathe, can you hear me?" Sydney asked as Mario climbed into the rear cockpit.

"Yes," Kathe whispered as she cleared her throat.

"I can get you out of this," Sydney continued. "Once your helmet is on, you can't talk. He will hear you, so follow my lead."

"Okay," Kathe agreed quietly as Mario yelled.

"Put your shoulder harness and helmet on!" Mario ordered as he connected his laptop to the onboard computer. He disengaged her controls and lowered the canopies. He then called Giorgio. "I have decided to cut all my losses!" Mario smirked as Alonzo answered Giorgio's phone from inside a Military Hummer.

"Don't worry, Mario," Alonzo answered. "I've already cut the rest of your losses!"

Mario started the engines and turned the thrusters downward. "I guess I should thank you!" Mario chuckled as XP38 rose in the sky, blowing sand and trees.

"What are families for," Alonzo chuckled. "Oh, and by the way, you are next!" Alonzo promised getting out of the Hummer in the Lighthouse parking lot. He watched XP38 circle the house out over the ocean. Then Mario released the missile.

Watching her house explode, tears streamed down Kathe's cheeks, "Did my family make it out?"

"Everyone is safe," Ramsey assured her. "Jay and Jack are escorting Carrie Anne and your family back to control. They're boarding a military jet right now. I have Ylia and a team of counselors already on standby when they land."

"And I'm coming to get you," Yorg said, zipping up his flight suit. "I promise."

"I'm Capt. Hiltree," he introduced as he handed Yorg his helmet. "I was told you know how to pilot an F-35."

"It's not that much different than our YAKs," Yorg answered, climbing the ladder and glancing around the cockpit.

"I heard Mario threatened to eject Ms. Tierney without a parachute," Capt. Hiltree stated. "There is an extra parachute under your seat for her. Any questions?"

"No, thanks for your help," Yorg appreciated as Capt. Hiltree climbed down.

"And I've got your backs," Alonzo added. "Now that the military has joined us, Gen. Thompson will do everything in his power to get his hands on you. Sen. Frank was very specific about how Thompson could make people disappear."

"I will keep you online with us," Ramsey said. "We may need a favor."

"I was hoping you would say that!" Alonzo acknowledged and turned to Pauli. "Get the Leer, we're leaving."

"Ramsey," Sydney explained, "Yorg and I will lure Mario out to sea. You need to find out if there is a ship off the Florida/Georgia coast. We want Jenkins to think he will help rescue Kathe. Alonzo, we need you to arrange a very fast boat to pick her up and hide her. Kathe has GPS, so I'll know exactly where she lands."

"Consider it done!" Alonzo promised, scrolling down his contacts. "I'll be off the coast waiting for your coordinates."

"I'll contact Jenkins and call you right back," Ramsey said, switching phones to call Col. Tom Jenkins on a different secure line.

Chapter 40

The Sacrifice of Love

"Clear the area!" Capt. Hiltree ordered as Yorg, and Dr. Sydney's canopies closed. Hiltree signaled the all-clear. Yorg started the engines of the Stealth Lightning II. Using SLOLV technology, the thrusters turned downward, the jet ascended straight up. It hovered over the Lighthouse, while Sydney connected his laptop with the onboard systems.

"I'm in," Sydney told Yorg. "Give me a second to locate Kathe and bring up the program."

"You don't have to download Chameleon to this computer, do you?" Yorg asked as he changed directions and headed over the ocean northward.

"Negative, I would not download this technology onboard any system," Sydney replied. "I would love to see the look on Professor101's face when he realizes he has been hacked. With my modifications, Chameleon can be run from my laptop."

"That's why we all agreed to destroy it," Yorg reminded them.

"Be careful who hears you say that!" Ramsey warned. "I had to make a few promises to Col. Jenkins. There's no way, I'm going to keep them."

"Mario will play it cool," Yorg added as he followed the coast. "He'll stay under radar no higher than 600 feet using the ocean as cover just like me."

"That YAK is also stealth," Sydney reported, pulling up the satellite imaging on his laptop. "Keep an eye out for Mario until I link with Alby's satellite. Then I can find him."

"Hold on Jenkins is calling," Ramsey cautioned and answered her office line.

"There's Kathe," Sydney smiled as her GPS signal instantly appeared on his screen. "He's following the Florida coast heading north on 3.58 at 480 knots."

"Jenkins is getting nervous," Ramsey returned to the line. "I'm keeping him at bay. I told Jenkins that if they spook Mario, he'll go supersonic. I have an agent onboard."

"Roger that, Mario is still beyond visual range," Yorg replied, changing his airspeed. "I'll increase my speed to 550 knots to catch him."

"We should have visual in four minutes with the increase," Sydney reported. "Watch your afterburners; we want to surprise him."

"Thanks, for the hot tip," Yorg declared. "You know computers. I know jets. Afterburners are not a problem at this speed."

"God is with us," Sydney gleamed as he nonchalantly hacked into Mario's computer. "Mario connected his laptop with the YAK's onboard computer, just like I knew he would. His own laptop just uploaded the changes I made to Raini's work," Sydney laughed. "Man, I'm good!"

"Jenkins wants to listen to our frequency," Ramsey said, putting him on hold. "Jenkins is en route to Brunswick. He wants proof that Gen. Thompson was working with Sen. Frank. He has to be careful, since he could get court-martialed for this."

"Send him the same email that I sent Alonzo," Sydney stated. "But take my address off first. Under no circumstances will I put him on this frequency. There's a reason I work for you and not the government. It's the same reason we are destroying this Chameleon Technology. This administration is full of lying politicians and generals. Where is my ship?"

"I'm sending him the email," Ramsey said, pulling it up. "Jenkins is still working on the ship. He must use caution, not to alert Gen. Thompson," Ramsey chuckled. "I bet Thompson will sweat bullets when this hits the news. He'll be in front of a firing squad. In my opinion, Sen. Frank got off too easy for treason."

Looking over the cockpit, activating his program, Mario typed in the code name Chameleon. The system came alive. "Well, I see you were right," Mario laughed as it asked for the authentication response codes. "I need the codes now. What are they?"

"The authentication response codes," Kathe repeated for Sydney to hear.

"Tell him Raini used his dog's name and birthday," Sydney told her as she repeated to Mario. "He named it after his dog, Bruzier 05 28 04," she repeated as Mario typed.

"Well, I told you we were bonding!" Mario smirked.

"Hold on, Jenkins is calling again," Ramsey said. "Sydney, the SS Biltmore is 100 miles offshore across from Brunswick, Georgia. That's where Mario is heading. Jenkins' men found Sabrina Macaby at an old airport there this evening. The runway showed signs that a large jet landed and took off from there recently."

"We're heading that way now," Alonzo confirmed. "I've got a speedboat already waiting for us to land."

"Copy that," Yorg acknowledged. "We'll meet you there."

"I'll be there on time," Alonzo answered. "I've also arranged for Kathe's quick disappearance."

"Copy that," Yorg stated. "We're thankful you're helping us."

"Our Chameleon is ready when you are Yorg," Sydney affirmed, listening to them.

"Roger that," Yorg replied and noted the changes in his trajectory in the windshield. "Kathe, this is what is going to happen," Yorg began explaining. "Mario will be able to read our IFF codes. He will think he has changed his to mimic ours, so we can't lock on to him. Mario's IFF codes won't change. I'll let him shoot at us a few times, so he'll think it works. I'm going to maneuver XP38 near the SS Biltmore, so the military will think they are getting it. You heard Alonzo. Once Sydney ejects you, he'll take you from there. Then, I will destroy XP38 as we all planned."

"I can't wait to test this out," Mario bragged unaware that Kathe was still in communication with her team. "We will stop and refuel, then test her out over the Atlantic on a passenger jet."

"Why would you test this out on a passenger jet over the Atlantic," Kathe repeated for Sydney to hear.

"I don't trust you!" Mario retorted. "I can't sell something that doesn't work."

"Don't worry, Kathe," Sydney declared as he pulled up Alby's satellite. "He'll never get that far. There is XP38 at our ten o'clock," Sydney reported as it showed up on the satellite.

"I don't see him," Yorg said, checking his radar. Yorg descended breaking to the east to prevent detection. "Kathe's GPS shows her at latitude 45 north longitude 25 east," Sydney reported, looking at the global map on his computer.

"Now, I see him on my radar," Yorg said, sliding in just below him at 400 feet.

"Kathe, we're just below you," Sydney reported, pulling up the stats on the YAK again. "Your seat has a built-in parachute. I know Mario has disabled the controls in your area. However, I will be able to reinstate them when we are ready. There is a hood that is located just over the top of your seat. Pull it down around your neck. That protects you from spinal cord damage. First, I will blow the canopy, then you will pull the lever between your legs, and up you go. I will set the chute to open at 1000 feet, so you will clear the YAK."

"Kathe," Yorg added. "We have skydived lots of times together. This isn't that much different. You're going to have to unbuckle as soon as you hit the water and get out of that seat. Don't get caught in the chute itself," Yorg warned her. "Are you comfortable with this?"

"What's behind door number two?" Kathe questioned, looking out the window only seeing black.

"You're the bright one that got into that jet!" Yorg teased.

Mario realized she was talking, "What did you say?"

"Nothing," Kathe replied. "Where are we heading?"

"Iran after we have a brief stop in Brunswick," Mario admitted. "There is someone that I have to attend to," he beamed. "I can smell the money already, lots and lots of money!"

"You're insane!" Kathe snapped. "Money you will never spend! They'll double-cross you, just as you double-crossed your own men at my house!"

"Kathe," Yorg interrupted. "Are you ready? It's time I come knocking on his door," Yorg warned slowly climbing to 600 feet. "Hey girl, look to your right. I see you," Yorg waved, pulling alongside the YAK.

Mario turned his head slowly, making eye contact with Yorg in utter disbelief. "What the heck? Where did you come from?" Mario screamed, throttling up. Yorg followed him through the clouds. "He's still behind me!" Mario panicked, realizing Yorg was right on his six. Mario banked to the right, heading for more clouds, while his Chameleon read Yorg's codes. "F-35," he laughed. "I'll change this Russian foe to a friendly to match his," he laughed, activating it. "Now, I'm a friendly and you can't lock onto me!"

"Mario thinks he has activated XP38 Chameleon Technology onboard the YAK," Sydney stated, activating the real Chameleon, and changing their codes to match XP38. "He read our IFF codes and changed his to match ours, he thinks," Sydney stated. "I'm the one who changed the codes. We are now flying as a Russian YAK. Let's try to lure him to the SS Biltmore, play along with him and he should follow us."

"Looks like I don't have to wait to test this out," Mario bragged. "Let's see how he likes not being able to lock onto me. Then, I'll change and lock onto him," Mario laughed as he rolled to the right coming around behind Yorg. "I love this thing! Got ya!" Mario laughed and changed his IFF codes back to a YAK. Then he locked onto them and fired a heat-seeking missile.

"Hold on," Yorg warned. "He thinks he's locked onto us." Yorg released flares and rolled to the right four times. Yorg came up behind Mario as the missile simply veered away from them. "Kathe, are you okay?"

"Yes," Kathe whispered, watching the cloud of smoke from the flares. It looked like a large guardian angel behind them.

"Not a bad pilot for non-military," Yorg stated as he took the F-35 vertical. "But let's see how long he can keep up with me."

"How did you do that?" Mario blurted. "You, lucky pilot!" he yelled as he followed. Mario flipped and locked onto Yorg again. Yorg again released flares, pretending to have to roll out of it as the missile veered away and exploded.

"The SS Biltmore is finally showing up on radar," Yorg stated, watching his radar for the YAK.

"Good, even though Kathe knows we're okay, her heart rate is going off the chart," Sydney reported, monitoring her vitals. "We need to get her out of there!"

"Hold on, I am going to 650 knots, let's see if he will follow," Yorg said, speeding toward the SS Biltmore. XP38 followed closely behind them.

"What is the matter?" Mario chuckled, locking a guided missile and firing. "Are you trying to run away from me?"

Kathe smiled as she watched the missile, again veer away from the F-35. "Thank you, Dear God!" she whispered.

"What? How does he do that?" Mario screamed, locking onto them again and releasing another missile. "What's the matter? Are you changing your mind about lovers?" he grinned. "Little too late to change now, don't you think? You better stick with the rock star; this one is about to be toast!"

"You don't know Yorg like I know him," Kathe refuted as Yorg listened. "He promised to come and get me. And he always keeps his promises to me. Him I do trust!" She confessed for all to hear. "That's why I told Joe today that he and I were a mistake. I should have listened to you and Ramsey. I just cannot believe how much I must have hurt you. You were always willing to stand by me, even now that I'm pregnant. The only regret I have, is that I will never be with you. I can't believe how stupid I was. You were right there in front of me all the time."

"Yorg," Sydney tried to get his attention. "Mario's locking on again, play along and drop the chaff so he will follow us," Sydney warned as he noticed Yorg was not responding. Sydney dropped the chaff as Mario locked another missile on them. As the missile blew up, Sydney yelled, "Yorg, get your head back in the game!"

"I know he has two more sidewinders," Yorg reported. "I will keep playing games with him. Are you ready to activate Kathe's controls? Get her out of there!" Yorg ordered, still thinking about what she said.

"I know computers, you know jets remember," Sydney retorted as Mario came around behind them again. Yorg maneuvered away from him. Mario locked on again. Releasing chaff again so XP38 would follow, Yorg banked into the morning sun.

It was just beginning to peek over the horizon, "There's the SS Biltmore, 120 degrees north off our starboard side. Just a little closer," Yorg said as Mario was catching up to him.

Banking right and rolling away, Mario tried to follow to the left in a scissor maneuver to come around at him, using machine guns this time.

"Well, his sidewinders work!" Yorg yelled, rolling away from XP38 in a straight spiral, trying to get as close to the ship as possible. "Sydney," he called as Kathe listened. "Get Kathe ready to fly. Ramsey, do you copy, we need to get Kathe out of there," Yorg announced. He accelerated as fast as he could to get closer to the ship, eluding more machine gun fire. "Mario is so busy trying to get me, he doesn't see the ship."

"Copy that," Ramsey answered. "I just found out that Jenkins is en route to the SS Biltmore. The Biltmore has you both on radar. They will follow you down. Sydney, when you are ready."

"I'm overriding Mario's computer, give me a second," Sydney said, trying to activate Kathe's controls.

"There's no cap to pull down," Kathe whispered as she felt behind her seat.

"No!" Dr. Sydney exclaimed, trying another way. "O'Brien disabled the parachute system! I cannot fix it!"

"Yorg," Kathe whispered as her eyes filled with tears. "I want you to know that I love you," she said, reaching between her legs for the lever. "I'm collateral damage! Blow the canopy and destroy this jet! I do not want to die with this monster!"

"Whom are you talking to?" Mario demanded. "You aren't going loony on me, are you?"

"My team!" Kathe finally admitted. "That's who I am talking to the entire time! I'm wired! Blow this jet out of the sky!"

"Not on my shift!" Sydney blurted. "Yorg, I saw Hiltree hand you a parachute, take it with you. I'll blow your canopy the same time I blow hers as we come around facing XP38. On your way down, cut away from the seat and dive after her. The sun is coming up and you should be able to see and catch her. First, watch your monitors," he chuckled, pressing enter. "I have linked our screens together and prepared a little surprise for Mario. We could all use a good laugh. Then, I'll see you two later."

"Sydney, how are you going to land this vessel?" Yorg asked. "You are not a pilot," Yorg questioned, reaching for the extra parachute.

"Ramsey, hold off the SS Biltmore's rescue planes and boats as long as you can," Sydney requested. "We don't want their rescue teams to pick them up. Make up something, buy us some time," Sydney said, taking over the control of the cockpit with his computer. "Computers can do anything with the right person behind them. I'll program mine to land this jet after I destroy our target."

"What is this?" Mario yelled. He watched an animated tunnel appear on his windshield with a Chameleon coming out of it. It stood up on its hind legs, faced him, and shook its finger at him. 'Bad Boy, you have just been hacked by the best Wizard of them all! GAME OVER HA! HA! HA!' Sydney then blew both canopies, surprising Mario and causing him to lose temporary control of XP38.

Shooting straight up and away from the aircraft, Yorg quickly took off his hood. He checked around for Kathe. Unbuckling from his seat, he spotted her still in her seat, descending toward the water. He rolled off to the left, pulled his arms close to his sides freefalling toward her. She spotted him, unbuckled her seatbelt, and flipped forward away from the seat. She held her arms and legs apart to slow her fall. Mario tried desperately to regain control of XP38.

"Sydney, fire when you are ready!" Ramsey ordered with Alonzo listening.

Dr. Sydney's computer stabilized the F-35. He changed his IFF codes back to being a United States F-35. He linked into Mario's computer for audio.

"Where is that broad?" Mario blurted regaining control of XP38.

"Mr. LaBasco," Alonzo called. "I'm adding you to our secure line, so you can listen."

"I had it all," Mario Jr. rambled. "Until Tierney got into my business. I killed my own mother, brother, and sister, not to mention that sleazy, Sen. Frank. I finally had my father and DiMeglio right where I wanted them-charged with Frank's murder. I would have had the respect of all the other families as leader," Mario admitted as he desperately looked for Kathe. "Until you showed up in my life . . . Where did you go . . .There you are? You're free falling. You are one brave Mother, but I've got you now!" Mario screamed, circling toward her. "I get two for the price of one. How touching, there is your brave Russian almost to you," Mario laughed, watching Yorg opened his arms and legs to slow his descent. "You almost made it! But almost isn't good enough!" he bragged, watching them reach for each other a few times, barely missing. Then, finally they grasped each other by the wrists. Yorg pulled Kathe close to him and pulled the ripcord as Mario locked onto them.

"I don't think so!" Sydney exclaimed, turning his craft toward XP38. He locked two missiles onto it.

Mario's alarm signaled that he had been locked onto. He checked his Chameleon and screamed, "I'm showing you as a friendly. How can you lock onto me?"

"I have to admit Professor101," Sydney admitted as he circled around to face him, "you were ahead of your time."

"Who are you?" Mario demanded as he searched the sky for him.

"Your worst nightmare!" Sydney exclaimed. "A better hacker than you," he confided as he distracted Mario and laser tagged the craft. Sydney placed his finger on the switch. "I do want you to know that Chameleon could be reprogrammed to work from any laptop," he said, firing the missile. Mario watched the missile coming straight toward him. He threw his arms across his face. "I'm destroying this technology! May it burn in hell with you!" The missile obliterated XP38.

Watching debris falling in the sky, Alonzo said to his boss, "Mr. LaBasco, it's over. Before the jet blew, did you hear Mario's confession?"

"Yes, Alonzo," Mr. LaBasco sighed. "The doctor assures me that Tierra and CC will fully recover. The knife was a millimeter from Tierra's spine. We've been blessed. Do what you must do to mop up Mario's mess."

"I will," Alonzo continued. "I have recorded his confession for the other families. I will finish here and see you soon."

"Oh," Kathe sighed and dropped unconscious in Yorg's arms as a piece of scrap metal brushed against the back of her head. Yorg strained, trying to hold her motionless body with one hand and cut his parachute away with his other. He dropped her. Then, desperately cutting the cords watching her fall into the sea. Taking his helmet off, he dove after her seconds after she plummeted in the water. He spotted her sinking to the left of him. Sydney noted the drop in her heart rate as well as her blood pressure and used her implant to wake her up. She pulled off her helmet just as Yorg reached her. Reaching for her face and holding it with both his hands, he leaned to breathe air into her mouth. They rose to the surface.

"Kathe, you're okay," Sydney said, watching her vitals come back up.

"Something knocked me out," Kathe replied. "I fell into the water unconscious. Yorg has me now."

Yorg held her in his arms treading water. Kathe leaned into his lips and kissed him.

"Alonzo, they are at 31.8 north 81.6 west," Sydney relayed.

"Copy that," Alonzo replied as the captain of his boat spotted them. "We've got a visual on them. We're en route to pick them up."

"Roger that, advise us when the package is safe," Sydney requested. He changed Kathe's GPS link solely to Ramsey's laptop. "Ramsey, XP38 is destroyed," Sydney reported with a sigh of relief. "I have emailed you the only link with Kathe's GPS. I rigged my laptop with acid to destroy it after I land on the Biltmore," he said as he programmed the F-35 to land on the deck. "I think you know what has to come next."

"Sadly, I do," Ramsey admitted. She sent Wanda and Keith out of her office.

"You are mine, Lady," Yorg stated. "Whether you knew it or not, and you always have been," he confided and kissed her.

"Yorg," Kathe said, looking in his eyes. "I am sorry . . ."

Pressing his fingers gently against her lips, "You have nothing to be sorry for, no one will ever know. Where do you want our family to live?"

"I don't know," Kathe answered, holding tightly to his neck. "The world is ours."

"I see Alonzo's boat," Yorg stated as the cigarette boat headed toward them.

"I can't believe it," Ramsey said, listening to them. "I am losing my two best operatives. Too many people know you and your skills, including the military. Jenkins' ETA is five minutes. He wants to personally bring all three of you back to the Pentagon for debriefing on XP38 Chameleon Technology."

"That cannot happen Ramsey!" Sydney interrupted as the F-35 touched down catching the hook. He threw the thrusters into reverse stopping the craft.

"Ramsey," Alonzo interrupted as he quickly pressed enter on his laptop. "I just emailed you the favor you needed. Keep me anonymous and forward it to Jenkins. We would not want Gen. Thompson to do this again."

As Ramsey read his email she exclaimed, "You got that right!" She blogged the email and forwarded it to Col. Tom Jenkins.

"I'm running out of time!" Sydney exclaimed as his computer shut off the engines. "The SS Biltmore's crew is approaching me."

"You must destroy your laptop and leave no trace," Ramsey warned. "It's obvious you cannot help the military without your laptop."

"You're right," Sydney agreed. "I just work for you."

"Copy that," Ramsey said as Jenkins' computer alerted him of an urgent email from Ramsey. "Don't worry. I will get you out of this. Hold on, Jenkins is calling."

In flight toward the SS Biltmore, "Where did you get this information?" Col. Jenkins asked.

"From a very reliable source," Ramsey confirmed. "I'll stake my reputation on it!"

"That is good enough for me!" Col. Jenkins exclaimed and forwarded it to the White House.

"Ramsey," Sydney continued after listening to her conversation with Jenkins. "What was that all about?"

"Alonzo sent me the information on Gen. Thompson concerning his dealings with Gen. Yetsun," Ramsey conveyed. "I just forwarded it to Jenkins. Hopefully, that should get him a pretty high promotion and help defuse his anger when he finds out he is not getting Chameleon or the codes."

"Do you think Jenkins will still take me to the Pentagon for questioning?" Sydney asked.

"I'm sure of it," Ramsey affirmed. "When he does, all you have to say is that your computer was destroyed. All your records were destroyed with it since you were using it in the field. He has no proof that XP38 Chameleon Technology ever existed. That's why we gave him Thompson," Ramsey stated, finding the link on her email that Sydney had just sent. "Kathe, I'm monitoring you until you are safe. Alonzo has everything under control."

Kathe while in Yorg's arms, watched the planes leave the SS Biltmore to search for and rescue them. "Ramsey, it's the best for all involved; goodbye old friend. You know what to do with my children."

"It's already been arranged," Ramsey agreed. "Ylia and a team of experts are waiting for their arrival. Carrie Anne hasn't let them out of her sight. This has brought out a side of her I never expected. Don't look back."

As they swam toward Alonzo's boat, "Kathe, it's never goodbye," Sydney promised. "You will hear from us someday." He pressed enter on his laptop one last time watching it melt as his canopy opened. The report of Kathe and Yorg being missing at sea filled the air, as did the arrest of Gen. Robert Thompson.

Breaking News: "This is Robert Morwitz of FNN News. We are covering a covert operation between Alby Airlines Security and the United States Air Force. It seems to be linked to the alleged mobster, Mario LaBasco Jr., the late Sen. Bernard Frank, and Gen. Robert Thompson of the Joint Chiefs of Staff," he reported. The camera switched, showing Gen. Robert Thompson in handcuffs being escorted out of the Pentagon. "We are awaiting Linda Ramsey, Head of Security at Alby Airlines, and Col. Tom Jenkins of the United States Air Force to make a statement momentarily. It is reported that two of Alby Airlines' security team are missing at sea. Mario LaBasco Jr. was also killed today in the skirmish." The camera switched over to the podium with Ramsey and Jenkins approaching as the world watched.